MAKEDONIA

MAKEDONIA

The Gordian Knot Unraveled

(AN HISTORICAL NOVEL)

By

GEORGE A. RADOS

iUniverse

MAKEDONIA
THE GORDIAN KNOT UNRAVELED

iUniverse books may be ordered through booksellers or by contacting:

iUniverse
1663 Liberty Drive
Bloomington, IN 47403
www.iuniverse.com
1-800-Authors (1-800-288-4677)

ISBN: 978-1-4917-8237-8 (sc)
ISBN: 978-1-4917-8238-5 (e)

Library of Congress Control Number: Pending

Print information available on the last page.

iUniverse rev. date: 12/10/2015

CONTENTS

INTRODUCTION

My attempted work on Macedonian history presented as a novel through the millennia, contains fictitious events and characters, closely interwoven with real and proven historical persons and facts, as well as locations and toponyms (names of places). As a Historian, and I have documentation of my status as such, I will avoid being one-sided as many have been eeither because of a belief or because of 'name enhancement' or, because of political affiliations.

What I do attempt here, is to make a casual reader find his/her place alongside the historian and the true Macedonian (this victim of political strife), throughout the centuries. In other words, to tell the truth as much as it is humanly possible, as I came to realize it myself, after years of research, studies and agonizing. This truth, although (at times) is hard to swallow or too simplistic to accept readily, is coming not only from the heart (which can always err) but also from the mind, from the chambers of calculated logic, methodical investigation and source analysis. Whenever documentation of event(s) was impossible, I took the liberty to (re) construct factoid(s) judging from events that followed and from eventual outcome. When factoids from other author(s) truly appealed to me in a sense that something of that sort could have happen, I adopted the idea. Plagiarism not being my cup of tea, I made sure a similar story would be told somewhat differently and I ask to be excused.

This is not the history my teachers taught me at school, for only a minority of them was conscien-tious enough to look into and transmit the facts independently from the dictated political lines of our times. This is not, therefore, a history which modern 'special interests', propaganda and 'educated' lies have saturated our society with. I disregard these, for what they are: political and personal reasons for gains of prestige, land and money.

Throughout this work, historical places-names-events and dates remain unchanged, the most pre-vailing opinion(s) accepted as such. There is only one exception: Phonetically, everything is written consciously closer (as the English language permits it) to its original pronunciation/spelling. If you find you have discovered a 'misspelled' or 'mispronounced' word or name, do not blame the typeset-ter or the proofreader.

Getting my information to create the plot of the chapters, I studied numerous works of others (an-cient and contemporary), interviewed and consulted with even more persons, from all spectrums of view on the subject. I made sure I covered all ethnicities involved and all walks of life. I talked to educators, doctors of sciences, historians, peasants, merchants. They are Albanians, Bulgarians, Hel-lenes, Serbs and Turks. Too numerous to mention them one by one and in fear I will omit any one (unintentionally), I thank them all! They freely gave me their time and opinions, their knowledge, their hopes and aspirations! Many, in private and with the request not to mention their names, admitted errors and expansionistic views of their government(s). Some, had or continue to have wittingly and willingly (or by necessity), become instruments of government policy. I will always be grateful to them and, keeping my word, they remain anonymous!

I traveled the width and length of the geographically recognized Macedonia. I visited places and towns; I climbed its mountains and crossed its rivers. I needed to have a personal knowledge of all possible angles of the place and its people of which I was about to write its history. I needed confirm-ation of what I was told, of what I read through other people's works, of what my conclusions were. I needed to know if (when names were changed to another language) appellations kept the same meaning as in old. I believe my narration of this historical novel will allow you to come tothe same conclusions.

Any wrong doing, is solely 'mea culpa' and I beg forgiveness. I merely hope of becoming a small part of broadening your understanding and compassion on Macedonia and its peoples and I thank you for choosing these books as your companion to my thoughts and convictions and, perhaps, that will allow you to revise your own…

George A. Rados

Instructions: How to easily read my appellations

    As I indicate in my introduction, many of the names, locations and spelling will look totally unfamil-iar to you, because of my effort to write them down as close to original pronunciation as the English language allows. Whenever I was in doubt or there was conflict of grammar, I used the Greek mode. I will give you the alphabets and examples bellow, to make your reading and understanding easier.

English	Greek	Other languages	Pronunciation
A, a	A, a	A, a	Always a -as in alpha
B, b	B, β	B, b	V, v (in Greek), the sound of mp/bu (in Asiatic/barbarian Example: Vouvaris (Greek), Boubar-yioush (Persian)
C, c			There's no c in Greek. As it's in other ancient languages.
Γ, γ			No such a letter in other languages
D, d	Δ, δ	nt/nd	As th (in Greek)-like in:These
E, e	E, ε	E, e	Always e, as in: ever
F, f	Φ, φ	F, f	As f or ph, like in fun/phone
G, g		gh	Any Greek word having a g, the letter is pronounced as γ (like in yes). Example: Gavanis/Γαβανης
H, h	X, χ	ch/kh	As in horse (Greek)
I, I	I, ι	I, I	Always i -as in inn
J, j	J, j		No such letter in Greek. As j or i in other ancient languages.
K, k	K, κ	kou/khu	Always a k (keep) in Greek. As kh in Asiatic languages of the time.
L, l	Λ, λ	lou	
M, m	M, μ	mou	
N, n	N, ν	nou	
O, o	O, o	o	
P, p	Π, π	pouh/phu	
Q, q			No such a letter in Greek

R, r	P, ρ	rho/rhou	
S, s	Σ, σ, ς	sou/shou	
T, t	T, τ	t/tou/thou/touh	
U, u		u/ou	Combination of ou/oo in Greek, for the sound of u/oo/ou
V, v		vou/vouh	See for sound of B (in Greek) above
W, w			No such a letter in Greek
X, x	Ξ, ξ	Hou/ksou	X in Greek is like our H in English. The sound of X in Greek is like our ks. Example: Xenophon/Ksenofon
Y, y	Y, υ		Always i, as in mill (Greek), if in the middle or end of a word. If in the beginning of a word, Y, y sounds as in yes (both Greek and Asiatic)
Z, z	Z, ζ	zouh	as the English sound today.

I use a combination of letters, ae, ks, ps, fs, or ts, to bring the original sounds. Original pronounciat-ion always prevails when allowed by English. Examples: Parmenion/Parmenio, Zefs/Zeus, etc. The same goes for Asiatic names (Dar yush/Darios/Darius). I hope the above will help you pronounce (close to original) all 'misspelled' names. Again, all errors are mine.

BOOK ONE

Dedicated to my progenitors and my wife (for her patience and faith in me) -as well as to my children.

CHAPTER ONE

SECTION ONE

FOLLOWING THE ROOTS
OF THE TRIBE

From Pre-Alphabet Storytellinig to Circa 700 BCE

"It is a terrible thing that we are not only
unable to surpass, (but) even to understand
the deeds of our progenitors!"
Andreas G. Rados, Makedonian Ellinas, freedom fighter W.W. II

The stranger, a short, stocky man in his late—times three—ten years, had come late that wintry after-noon at the small town, looking for shelter to spend the night, for both himself and his pack animals. He was a southerner from the parts of Thessalia, the town of Farsalos in particular. He was hoping to get a good exchange at the market next morning, hearing that the Orestids (Orestians, as others call-ed them) were people who would deal fairly with merchants. Of course, the merchandise had to be of good quality or, lacking that, honestly priced. He knew he could be a fair candidate for that, because he was new in the business, eager to please, thus creating a steady, faithful clientele and income.

Asking the locals for shelter, he was shown to the second decent building he could detect in the whole array of thatched huts. A servant-like old man of untold years, answered his call at the massive door set. The old man directed the merchant to the stables across the yard, the heavy oak doors closing behind with a thunderous bang. He assured the visitor of the good care of his horse, the three loaded mules and the two donkeys, adding that the merchandise would be safe and found intact the next morning. The old man then, showed the Thessalian through the main entrance, to a room where he was offered warm water to wash, as well as dry, clean clothes to use during his stay.

The rather long (for the merchant's stature) hiton/tunic made of wool, felt very nice, as it covered his chilled body. Not offered any sandals, he re-tied his fur-lined leggings, making sure the soles were cleaned properly. As he could see, the floor of this room—although of packed earth—was immaculate.

He suspected the same for the inner chambers. Of the two young adults helping him in the process all this time, none looked in any particular hurry to get him ready, nor did they present him the usual servitude of household slaves (a common sight in the southern kingdoms). Come to think of, neither did the old man, already lost in the depths of the inner house. Were they all freemen? Hired hands? The place didn't look wealthy enough for such extravagance! Yet, as he had observed, everything was in place and clean! From the hiton to the towels, to the floor and the walls. The only small blemish, the upper corners toward the ceiling. There, the untold years of smoke from the torch-lights could be detected, as a darker color covered them.

Being finally ready, he was shown (passing another set of heavy, copper-framed doors) to an inner, larger room. Right across from its entrance and at the far end, there was an elevated area. Against that wall, at its center, a stone-hewn chair, modestly higher than a dozen wooden others, forming a circle facing it, with the house hearth and an altar in-between. A tall, as ancient (but much better kept) man than the first oldie, rose from that stone chair for a formal greeting. Aged, a rough life past him (war mishaps not withstanding), he had a regal presence. He was filling the huge room with an aura, commanding instant respect. Youths occupying the wooden chairs around his, rose in respect also.

The Thessalian merchant introduced himself, raising his right hand in formal greeting, allowing the host to see there were no hidden weapons. "Kloppas from Farsalos, son of Hilon. Hospitality is great-ly appreciated Sir and, as a token of my gratitude, you will have in the morning a first choice present from my merchandise, free of any charge or exchange!" A spark lit the old man's face and cloudy blue eyes. Ah! A shrewd buyer, if it comes to that!

The old man extended his right hand in welcoming, his left pointing in direction of the honorable seating, to the right of his own stone chair. The youth seated in that chair, moved to the direction of another. Kloppas turned his observation to the young ones attending (what?). None looked older than ten plus four years of age. "Please, be seated!" The rasp, but still strong, voice of the host indi-cated politely. They all did. "We have had our supper just a while ago and I am about to teach these young ones our clan's history!" the host apologized. "Please, feel free to join us, add what you think proper from your travel knowledge, while some food and wine comes your way!" he concluded.

Kloppas inquired the youths' average age. "Ah, they are mostly ten, to ten plus two years old.

Spring lambs, but they have to be educated about their clan and tribe rather than spending their time in the mud with their plays. But, you didn't tell me, would you mind listening to us?" "I am sure I can learn more than I ever learned, dear Sir, by listening to you! My schooling was neglected! My parents, enslaved in Ferrae long time ago, managed to become free and free me as well just a year before their death! I was three times ten in age already, rather old and late to learn anything more than keeping account of my wares and my bartering goods. Please, feel free to educate me as well!"

The old man nodded pleasantly, sat on his chair making himself comfortable. At that moment, the two young men who tended Kloppas' cleaning earlier, showed-up. One was bearing a plate full of roasted pork slices, with greens and dark, but freshly baked bread. The other, brought a large wine container, peculiar in looks, indicating local craftsmanship, rather than the Korinthian or Aeginitan art Kloppas was used to see further south. The food plate (also of local earthenware) was placed on a small stool, before Kloppas. The wine bearer served the host, with utmost respect, first. The visitor next and the youth sitting around, came after that. The young ones were served in smaller cups, water freely added on top. Kloppas stood up to offer a spondi/wish. He approached the hearth and the small stone altar before it. The hearth's fire was giving a strong, yet pleasant heat as he approach ed and its dancing flames were giving a variety of shades on the altar. The latter was made from lime stone rock, simple but decent. Kloppas offered first from his wine cup to Dias Ksenios, the father of all gods and mortals, protector of every foreign visitor, every 'xenos/ksenos'! He continued the spon-di, offering next to goddess Estia, goddess of households and, next, to all gods and demons of good in-tend. He repeated his wishes with a portion of his food thrown to the fire. Turning his back to the altar, he offered a few drops of his wine to Plouton, god of the underworld, to his ancestors and the ancestors of his host, letting it drop on the ground, on top of the stain other such offerings were done through time. He turned, facing his host. The old man seemed very pleased by the care and piety the Thessalian xenos showed. He made his own offers, reciprocating in mentioning Kloppas' own ances-tors and they all resumed their seats. Kloppas to eat and listen, the host to clear his thoughts and voice, the youth in anticipation of untold deeds of glory.

There was only one thing bothering Kloppas by its absence. Though formal, the old man had not bother to proclaim his own name. Ancestors mentioned during the spondi, meant little when not con-nected to the name of the offering man. A dark foreboding clouded Kloppas' mind for a second, but he brushed the thought away. Had the old man assumed Kloppas knew the name of his host? No one else had called him by a name thus far! Respect to his presence was obviously given by all, more than normal. Appellation? None! Kloppas made up his mind not to ask. Let's wait and see . . .

"Anyone who comes to this region" the old man's raspy voice resonated, startling the audience, "either born mortal or god-sent, even a stranger, a xenos (a look of apology to the visitor) from lands afar, never failed to fall in love with the beauty of this land! Nor he failed to appreciate the gifts Gea, the Mother Earth, made available to the people, with the consent of all other gods—of course! Tall mountains, green meadows, rivers and lakes full of fish, forests abundant with game! All that makes our lives easier than for what other clans and tribes have on their lands. Even the sea produce is not that far away from us! As snow and ice is available from our high peaks, myself, your fathers and other notables of our clan, always manage to have salt-water fish brought here, as fresh as it comes.

Our living here on and around the Pindos mountains with peaks so high, rivals (and I mean no dis-respect!) the god's own abode, mount Olympos. Our valleys, sheltered from harsh weather, produce just about everything a man needs from Dimitra, the Mother Earth. Artemis has blessed us also with the abundance of game animals! As for the life giving water, lakes and rivers provide it for our fields our livestock and ourselves! The snow-caped peaks are the source of two of our great rivers: the life giving Aliakmon who springs from Vorreas' favored mountain and wanders crossing beautiful val-leys before emptying its waters to the ever moving sea. The other mighty river is Axios. That one is located further than river Lydias, the way the sun rises. Axios springs from the far side of Vorreas, above the Lynkestian lands, then flows straight to the direction of the hot summer winds, emptying its waters in the gulf of Therma, by the lands of the Vottieans and Anthemountians. On its way, it waters all the great plains, with god given abundance! There are a couple more rivers further to the sunrise, beyond our related clans and tribes, toward those of the clans and tribes of Kokyges, Gygo—nes, Vissaltes and other Thrakians. Those are the rivers Strymon and Nestos. The former springs from beyond the Rodopi range, crosses the Orvylos mountains to the plain of Parorvylia and Sindiki, passes through Dysoron and Vrontous mountains, forms lake Kerkinitis and empties in the sea by the lands of the Kristones. The latter, Nestos, Springs from Aemos range and travels by the lands of the Laeii and Sartres, before it flows into the sea across the island of Thasos, by the lands of the Ido-nes. The names of those rivers are taken to honor mighty Kentavri warriors, the ones claimed to be half men half horses! Our

Thessalian guest here, should be very well versed about them, even if he has no proper education. Those Kentavri were all over Thessalia as well." Kloppas nodded in agree-ment and the old man continued.

"To be truthful, not all of these areas belong to our clan the Orestians or Orestids (as others prefer to call us). As we all know, there are other clans and tribes all around us, with their kingdoms and state of affairs. Many of them, like us, belong to the same tribe, the Makedni. Most are close related by blood, to be called cousins. Haones and Molossian Ipirotes are such, as are the Thessalian Perre-vians and Magnites (another look toward Kloppas for confirmation which was met). The Elimiotes, Tymfes, Lynkestes, Eordeans and Imathians are the same as us. Next to them, as the sun Ilios rises, are other cousins of ours, such as Almopes, Mygdones, Vottiaeans and Anthemountians. More dis-tant are the Pelagones, Dassaretes and Derriopes, toward the Vorreas winds and the Pindos peaks. The rest of our neighbors are native Pieres, Rahelians, Krousians, Sythonians, all with mixed blood from old Pelasgians, Danaans and us. Further, there are the hostile tribes of the Illyres (though some have distant blood relation with us, like the Vryges), such as Tavlantes, Dexares, Penesti. Then, there are the dreaded Dardanes, the Peones, Maydi, tribes of their own. Last but not least, are the fore mentioned Thrakes, such as Idones, Vissae, Odomantes and others."

All this time, the accent of the raspy voice changing tones of emphasis in its north Dorian dialect, one not readily understood, made Kloppas realize why other Aeolian speaking merchants were re-luctant in bringing their wares so far north. Why, the dialect wasn't even allowing the naming of the four points of the horizon. To the sunrise side, instead of east, to the direction of the hot winds in-stead of south. Let alone missing vowels from words, when that suited the very local accent rather, than the regional one! No wonder Dorians in general were considered rough speakers and the Make-donians (Makedni in their jargon speech) even more so! As a former slave, to be able to talk a more refined dialect was a blessing, but only among southerners, Kloppas realized. He turned his attention back to his host.

". . . course every now and then, war breaks among us. That's because one clan wishes to rule over another, or over disputes on grazing grounds, water rights and timber or game and things like that. Not too long ago, at the time my great grand mother was barely of birth giving age, the tribe of Peo-nes overtook by force the Axios river plains, up to its gushing mouth by the sea of Therma! They came close to overrunning even us, if it wasn't for our resilience and our own high mountains! They have retreated by now, as you know, after the tribe of Pieres, united with our clan and those of the Eordeans and Imathians, forcing them to go! Under my grand father's leadership, the Peones were pushed back to the plains! They are still strong power though, don't forget that! At times, we still have to listen to their saying!"

So! Was the old man the grand son of Kleodeos then? The legend of the Pindos slopes? Kloppas felt awe, for (if that was the case) this very man, his host, had to be none other but Anaxarhos himself, the one reason Kloppas' parents were sold as slaves! A legend by himself, Anaxarhos was the creator of untold number of raiding, daring and blood-letting. Now Kloppas was provided hospitality at a place who's owner was the cause of his father's enslavement? Kloppas felt awkward and angry. Was he bound to duty of revenge at the person of his host? If so, what the chances of coming out alive? Worst yet, as recently freed man, what were the chances of being resold as a slave? Odds weren't at his side. He bit his lips hard. Ah! The sound came out of his mouth unintentionally. Kloppas looked around. No head had turned his way. Absorbed as they were to the old man's narration, none heard a thing. "Better that way" . . . He'd have time to think, to plan. This and now, were not the place and time.

His parents may have ended-up slaves any way, considering their lot of worthless property back home! He cursed a secret spell to bad luck demons and turned his attention back to the speaker.

". . . to the cold winter's wind direction from us, further up the Pindos range and by the side of the great lakes, Vrygiis (the major and minor ones), is the kingdom of Lynkos or Lynkestis. It is flanked by the lands of Dassaretis and Derriopos above ours, the Pelagones and Almopes on the other sides.

As I told you, they are also Makedni, mixed-up with the original stock of Pelasgians and that of the Danao-Aheans, as the latter immigrated at a time about five times ten generations—maybe more.

These Danao-Aheans moved also beyond Olympos and Ossa, through the river valley of Pinios who waters Thessalia (another look of wanted geographical approval, got Kloppas' reluctant nod. He was still very angry.) but they didn't stop there. They passed the Aeolian lands building their cities and forcing many Lapithes and Magnites to seek new life in the islands. Aheans settled in Larissa, they built powerful kingdoms such as

Iolkos, Ferrae and Farsalos. Moving into Viottia, Orhomenos be-came their center. The Kentavri were forced to consolidate in high places on mount Pilion and in Perrevia. Further, Danao-Aheans moved into the island of Pelops, the Peloponnisos, the one connect-ed to Attiki with only a narrow strip of land, the isthmos of Korinthos. There, they built powerful Mikynae, Tyrins and overtook Argos. At a later date, they even took over the kingdom of Minos, the island of Kriti, by the hot summer wind! They adopted easily a form of records keeping from the Kritans and other islanders, making their own changes of it—as needed. They would put those marks on clay plaques or waxed wood plates and thus, they were able to tell by that what they did or needed done, long time after Memory itself would forget.

By the time (as I have been told) my great-great-great-grand father was of warring age, these power ful kingdoms united under someone named Agamemnon. He brought them to wage war against the kingdom of Tria and, after some ten years of siege on its capital city, Ilion, they took it and burned it. Some of our related clans and tribes, the ones toward the sunrise, participated in that war and (although Tria's people were not of our blood) took the losing side as their cause, to their utter sorrow I must add! The victorious armies of Danao-Ahean power raided their homes on the way back from Tria, taking much loot and slaves.

We, Orestids, stayed out of it. We had our own problems to worry about. You see, Illyrian tribes came down hard on the Haones. These Haones, although closer related to Molossians, are our own cousins also. We had to come to their aid, for we knew—if they would lose against the Illyres—our turn would come next. This event was also the cause for one of very few times Lynkestis came to our side, king Drakon leading their troops. We are all well aware of Lynkestis being of the same blood and tribe with us. We are also well aware that it's their nature and aim to always put their clan first, the tribe second! Of course, when it comes to dealing with Illyres, blood is thicker than greed! In any event, we combined with forces of Lynkos, Haones, Molossians and Elimiotis to manage and send the dreaded Illyrians back to their caves. It took us more than seven years of war to achieve it!

Some long time after these events, another tribe related to us and the Danao-Aheans, the Iones, came this way through, to Thessalia and Viottia below us. Some made home the region beyond Viot-tia, named Attiki. Some moved to the coastal islands, like Skiathos and Evia. They were the

11

descend-ants of Ion, brother of Magnitas and our progenitor, Doros. They did not come by the sword. Most were merchants rather than warriors. They also brought to us some new expression in speaking manners. So, when one meets one of them and none is careful in conversing, there's always a mis-understanding at work.

Even Thessalians, more used to that kind of speech and being the offspring of Thettalos, Magnitas and Aeolos, have trouble when dealing with Aheans, Kritans or Athinians. Our guest here, can easily verify the truth of my words!"

Kloppas took the lead from Anaxarhos' remark, to confirm the differences between dialects, mak-ing sure to point the advantages of the softer, more worldly effects of his dialect over the harsh Ma-kedonian. A small victory, in retaliation of the years in slavery he had to endure. Anaxarhos, as the old man obviously was, picked-up his narration from where it was left, without being disturbed, per-haps unnoticing the verbal jab of his guest.

"The Thessalian Aeolos, after his death, was honored by the gods for his decent life and made king and ruler of the winds. Now, mind you, we all claim common ancestry from years before memory, years before the Great Flood. We all come from Ellinas, from Defkalion and his wife Pyrra, as well their brothers, sisters and kinfolk. Granted, many of us are of mixed stock also, hence the speaking vari-ations. But, even to those who were here from the beginning, the tradition comes down the same, albeit names and dates are a bit confusing. You see, some people didn't keep Mnimosyni, the memo-ry records, faithfully. Some times, the ones who did put their markings on clay, did it according to the need of their tribe or clan and confused us even more! The fact remains that, in spite variations, we all speak the same language, worship the same gods and, we all hate foreign intruders!

Here in our kingdom, where my ancestors have ruled since memory is lost in the mist of Hronos, the all governing Time, the land took its name rather recently. It happened when Orestis, the son of that king Agamemnon, whom I mentioned before, came here to rest. He, Orestis, was given a chase by his own consciousness through the Erynies. He had killed (you see) his own mother, avenging the death of his father Agamemnon, by her lover's hands! Now that's a story worth telling eh? But that's for another time. First, we have to know our own! I only have to tell you this part of it, for it is necessary to connect it with our own traditions, as they were passed down to me from my elders. King Agamemnon had gotten all the Ellenic tribes under his rule, up to Thessalia. As I said before, he sacked Tria becoming supreme among kings and common, only to come back home and be slaughtered in his sleep by his wife's lover. None really blamed young Orestis for taking justice in his hands. Nonethe-less, gods forbid matricide. Orestis wandered a lot, before his consciousness turned from Erynies to Evmenides and allowed him to settle amidst our people. Our ancestors honored him and his followers from Mikynae and Peloponnisian Argos (Diomidis' fate wasn't any better than that of his overlord's, Agamemnon), as Argian kindred had Orestis to lead. We named our land Orestis and they named the new town they built, Argos Orestikon. You all know that Argos Orestikon is the second most im-portant town after our Levaea here. The other Argos we know, the one they came from in Pelopon-nisos, was founded by the hero Perseas himself, even earlier in time!" Needing some liquid to soften his throat, Anaxarhos took his wine goblet and emptied it, nonstop! Kloppas looked, amazed at the quickness of the consumption. All knew of the Makedonian drinking habits, but he never thought he would witness such a fast drinking of undiluted wine, all with no apparent effect! Now, Anaxarhos was clearing his throat, ready to resume.

"Ugh . . . eech! Hmm . . . where was I? Ah, yes! Not long later, my family took over our clan and united it with the Eordeans and Imathians. We warred against the Vryges, Illyrians by blood, but more apt to being civilized. Can't tell which way that war would have gone, if it wasn't for the Dorian tribe. In years long before this event, Makedni had become numerous and many moved past Thessalia, look-ing for lands available. A good number of them lived in an area between Thessalia and Viottia for a long time. Their leader was a man of note, named Doros. The area they settled, was named Doris, in his honor. They multiplied again with the passing of time and became a separate tribe, close related to us, due to common ancestry. Many say that Makednos, one of our own progenitors, was Doros' brother, from another mother. So, when we warred against the Vryges, Dorians came to our aid.

They brought with them weapons of iron and established themselves as an upper class warriors. They helped us throw the Vryges out of our lands. Some of them run to hide further up, beyond mount Skardos, around the lake Lyhnitis and the synonymous mountains.Most of them were pushed toward the rising sun side of the country. Pressed from the other clans and Thrakian tribes, they managed to cross the strait of Elli, the Ellispontos sea and settled in the old Trian plains, filling the void. Because the indigenous clans of that area could not pronounce the sound vee properly, the Vryges were called Fryges and such they remain. Eordeans, Imathians and ourselves, divided the new lands. The Imathians were the lucky ones, as they inherited the gardens of the last Vrygian king, Midas, a lovely area, full of fruit trees and vineyards! Orestis, gained mainly the name of the best clan of the region, along with ample number of Dorians who settled among us. Most of the Dorians (although masters of war with their new arms), did not become our masters. They moved toward the hot summer wind direction again, traversed Thessalia and entered Viottia. Finding resistance, they took Thivae, where the future hero, Iraklis was born soon after. The last descendants of Kadmos and Idipos were ousted and gone. Next, the Dorians took Orhomenos and Iolkos, the latter making the mistake of coming as Orhomenos' allies and both cities were turned to ashes. Orhomenos was later rebuilt. Now, the bulk of Dorians continued its way, by-passing Attiki, on account that the acropolis* fort of Athinae was built on a too steep rock and held a strong resistance. The Dorians moved to the isthmos of Korinthos and in Peloponnisos. Athinae became the city in charge of Attiki since, thanks to the king Thiseas. Many Iones though scared by the Dorians, sailed to the islands and across, to Asia. The place they landed and built their cities, is now called Ionia. Others, thinking of sailing to the island of Sikelia, rounded the capes of Peloponnisos, in an effort to get there. Bad storms sunk their ships and the sea of their demise is now called Ionian.

The Dorians meantime, brought an end to most of the Danao-Ahean kingdoms in Peloponnisos. Gone are Tyrins and Mikynae! Pylos was burned to the ground! Argos, Korinthos and Sparti, were. All cities have had an acropolis, a most fortified high place/hill within the walls. All, except Sparti. overrun, Argos and Sparti becoming purely Dorian. What Aheans saved for themselves, was an area from the lands of the Korinthians, to the Ionian sea. Naturally, it is called Ahaia. The Ionian islands off its coast were never invaded and still have the indigenous peoples of Pelasgians, Danaans, Aheans and, who ever of the Iones managed to save his life when the ships sunk on the way to Sikelia.

Another part of Peloponnisos also remained in its native hands, that of the mountainous and heavily forested Arkadia. Goddess Artemis, protector of animals and forests, had a lot to do with the rescue. Nonetheless, many

Arkadians, fearing for their lives, sailed to the island of Kypros where they built many cities."

The old man cleared his throat once more, took a deep drink from his goblet (which was refilled im-mediately by the attending young man) and seemed lost in his thoughts for a long time. One of his hands held the goblet, the other played with his long, cloud-white beard. Kloppas found time to re-flect. Anaxarhos was (by all accounts) a very old man. Yet, even with his back bending from age, he was towering a full head taller than Kloppas, when they first shook hands. The Thessalian vividly brought that memory back. The handgrip itself, indicated the vigor of a man half the age of such an old Chieftain. Scars were clearly visible on the man's hands and face and, Kloppas was sure, a larger number of them hidden under the long hiton covering the old boddy. He was also sure that none of the scars were on his back. All of them on the front, made during confrontations with the enemy. An-axarhos was still a force to recon with.

Kloppas turned his attention on the youth, sitting around on a circle. They had not lose any of their attention to the μυθος, the narration. A couple of eye contacts, a whispered exchange of a word or two said, in awe of such knowledge. But their thirst for more, always remained intact and obvious.

Anaxarhos drank some more, cleared his throat the customary (by now) way of his and picked-up his story telling. "I got carried away, please excuse me! I am an old man now, you can see that, with much to tell and little time to do it! I have to put my line of thinking in order every now and then. So, yes, we altered our speech and name with the coming of these Dorians up here again. Now we are cal-led Makedonians instead of Makedni, taking this lower Dorian appellation for our tribe. It does not matter actually, since both appellations mean about the same. In old, Makednos meant one who re-sides up on high places, like mountains. In this new version, it also means we're tall <u>and</u> living on high elevation. Both are true. Makedonia is mostly high country, overlooking the coastal plains. Take a look at our guest, who—I hope—won't be offended with my comparison. Most of us in this room, <u>are</u> taller than he, more fair in complexion and blue eyed. Pelasgians, Iones and Magnites, tend to be shorter, with a darker complexion but not like that of the Kritans. On the other hand some of our clans toward the rising sun, mixed at times with Thrakes, have even lighter hair. The Thrakians are totally blond or red haired. The difference is, you can tell a Thrakian from afar, on account of his etching his whole body with that bluish signs on his skin and the gold beats on his hair and beard. Some of us here, mixed in blood to Molossians and Haones of Ipiros, also have red hair and we all know how red these cousins of ours are, both in complexion and spirits—no pun intended. But they have been more mixed with Illyrians than we . . . I guess gods needed some variety when they made us.

Speaking of gods, our religion has not changed much with all these comings and goings. All of us, being of same blood and traditions, continue worshipping the same gods as before Μνημοσυνη, the goddess of memory lets us remember. We have only given more prominence to the power of Zefs, as opposed to Mother Earth Gea. We revere her greatly, for all the fruits Dimitra, Μητερ, offers to us. But, now, Dias Zefs rules undisputed, being the victor against the Titanes and his own father, Kronos—for that I will tell you all about at another time. He rules then, over all gods and mortals, male and female. Accordingly, the ancient Oak Oracle in Dodona, with its Holy Doves roosting on its branches, has been re-dedicated to him, Mother Earth taking the second place. Similar changes occurred in Delfi and the island of Dilos. Delfi got under the protection of Apollon-Ilios, although it had priestess Pythia serving the underground goddess Kyveli before. Now, Pythia is the voice of Apollon. Python, her snake was killed by the god, but she still receives her trance from the depths of Omfalos, the chasm which leads straight to the bowels of the underworld, the mouth of Kyveli. She has to mix that with dafni, the laurel plant, beloved to Apollon, in order to have her prophesies understood by the in-terpreting priests. Dilos, as I said, is also taken by Apollon, although the island is made totally of Pel—asgian population.

There is one thing bothering me though with regards to religion—and I mean no disrespect to any of the gods and goddesses: that of us used to be blessed in a special way by having the Musae, those immortal daughters of the Great king Pieros, that first ruler of Pieria, living on the slopes of Pierian mounts. Since the upheaval with all this tribe moving and of the time the Iones arrived, the Pieres, direct des-cendants of that Great king, allowed Athinians and Thivans to take the Musae away. Now, these pat-rons of the arts and human endeavor, live stranded on the mounts of Kytheron, Ellikon and Parnassos. It was done so that their knowledge of arts would be given to Iones rather than remain with us...

Now the slopes of Pieria, even divine Olympos, remain silent. Thessalian Ossa and the valley of Tempi, undisputedly the most beautiful gift of Pinios river, hear none of their voices and songs. Maybe that is the reason why us Dorians do not have the skills Iones have in poetry, ceramic works and such arts. Further, we have no experts to etch signs on clay tablets and keep our records straight. We only have what Dorians are known best of: war and hunting weapons, horses and javelins, swords and slings. Better, I guess, as those are helping us keep our lands from being taken by the likes of Illyres, Dardanes and Thrakes. On a personal note only, I wouldn't mind confessing that I would like having the Musae still on our side. I hope one day the Pieres will pay for their sin and Makedonia will be the center of knowledge once more!"

Anaxarhos stopped his narration and that brought Kloppas back to reality. He had been so engross-ed by the old man's story telling, he had the impression he was living the events as they were trans mitted through the air to all ears in presence. Anaxarhos looked at him and smiled politely. Kloppas forced himself to reciprocate. He still was angry, not gotten over the fact that Anaxarhos was the main cause of his enslavement in his youth. All right, Makedonians did not have slaves of their own but the fact did not bother them to sell defeated foes to other tribes. Kloppas had a good idea that neither the very old man who opened this place's doors in hospitality, nor any other person here had any remote connection of having or being a slave. The first old man, the serving young ones, all were making their living by their services and in exchange of what they needed, in form of pay or bartering. They were all free Makedonians and that was that . . .

Kloppas drank from his cup and ate some fruit while the young man made sure the consumed wine was replaced almost at once. Kloppas was getting rather tipsy now. Southerners never drank wine undiluted. There was always plenty of water mixed with Dionysos' potent fruit in every occasion. But this was not south, this was Makedonia.

"As you know, Aris, the war god, is our major deity after Zefs and his brothers, Posidonas lord of the seas and Pluton, lord of Adis. That is, perhaps, why Iraklis, the Dorian hero, had so much trouble under his cousin Evrystheas. Ira, being the spouse and equal to Dias, got insulted having a second place in the hero's mind, on top of being jealous as Iraklis was fathered by Zefts. Ira may be residing in Peloponnisian Argos, but Dias, Posidonas, Pluton, Aris and Dionysos with Apollon are the rulers of men's places, all, except Athinae. There, there's no doubt goddess Athina is the one who holds the ropes! The Athinians may be giving lip service to the rest of the gods, but they take all oaths in her name and, they hold the Musae at their disposal. I am afraid that the Pieres will eventually have to pay a big price for getting caught sleeping. Their current king Pieros, times ten plus four since the time of the first Great one, put even personal work building a temple of Dias at the foot of Olympos, by the sea, exactly where the Musae had their shrine standing for untold years before. He now names the location Dion. I don't think the Musae will take the insult lightly, in spite of their reverence to the Father of gods and mortals alike. The Pieres are to pay a hefty price, I am certain and it has nothing to do with my own reverence to Zefs, whom I respect most.

I see that our guest, the merchant from Farsalos and son of Hilon, is getting tired! I take no offence by his sleeping face and, I hope, I give none! I know the trip must have been tiresome, our wine strong, the story telling long and he needs some rest. We will be having the story continued tomorrow evening. Ser, if your business is still holding you here in Levaea, if you find my narration of any interest to you and your bedding tonight good, you're more than welcome to share the same tomorrow."

Kloppas did take offence. He knew, inside, he had drifted a bit. Not a good sign on behalf of a visitor and a prospecting merchant in the house of his host. The fact that he got caught dozing by an old man with rheumatic vision and the fact that the same man was/is the old forgotten but not forgiven foe, made him feel inferior and that offended him. He was shrewd enough not to show it. He had need of business in this forsaken town the next morning and, in reality, he had enjoyed the story, until he dozed off that is. He made his excuses as polite as he could and he was shown to his sleeping quarters, which he had to share (he soon found out) with the old servant he first met. Well! His former status still showing eh? He would teach a trick or two to these rough northerners later. If a chance would be given to him, a chance would be taken!

The next morning he was up with the first light. He got himself ready and, before leaving for the market, he left a nice wine amfora, for his host (a promise was a promise). Hospitality now paid, he had in mind of doing business and then leave before the evening closing of the market.

The day started very slow though, people doing their own chores before looking for bartering his wares with local goods. They were also very good barterers. He started making some profits late in the after mid-day hours. By then, his hunger and curiosity took the best of him. His plans for insult and revenge forgotten, he returned to the house of his last night's host.

Venison was the meal of this evening and it was well prepared. The wine was served strong again, care taken this time to leave a water jug by his side. Later, during the talk by the host, grapes with some goat cheese were placed by him, to escort his thirst. He noticed the same array of servants and the same array of youth attending with the same sitting arrangements. One would think a day had not interrupted last night's talk. Anaxarhos had his mouthful of wine, his customary clearing of throat and he picked-up from where he had stopped. "There's quite some time now since I am not the king of this clan anymore. My son took over, the year I turned eight times ten plus five. That is three springs ago. I cannot mount my horse any longer, nor can I hold pace on a march or in battle, with the rest of our warriors. He's a very smart boy, my son is! Not only does he make a good king in battle, he's also a very thoughtful man in his relations when dealing with other clan kingdoms. I can't say that for myself when I was in charge . . ." "That's for sure!" Kloppas felt like calling out loud. He kept his mind with difficulty, trying to pay attention to the narration. ". . . I was rather impulsive and quick to draw my sword, something which cost us at times." The old man continued. "There are some unpleasant re-sults and memories, I have to admit that. Now that I am in charge of teaching my son's children and their peers, I have to make sure they learn from my mistakes, as well as those of their fathers.

Wisdom comes from knowledge only. Why, a costly war that I started—I have to admit—against the Eordean and Tymfean clans . . ." The old man's words hit Kloppas like a slap on his face. "Is it then, when you raided Perrevia and Ferrae, chasing Tymfeans and my parents got sold as slaves?" He felt his blood boiling with the thought. But realizing that Anaxarhos' reference was about a much more recent event, he felt embarrassed, as a next thought came to him: it was during this, more recent, event that his father, Hilon, found the opportunity to get away (with a dead master's gold on hand) and come to Ferrae to free his wife and son, buying them out from their master. Anaxarhos, after all, had helped Kloppas' family—after he had been the reason of the initial loss of their freedom! Kloppas shook his head to clear it from these thoughts and pay attention to the narration.

". . . My son brought an end to this loss of lives almost at once, promising his first-born daughter to their king's son—if he ever gets one. He, my son, married himself also, to a second wife, an Eordean woman, daughter of the old conniving bastard, Pavmenis himself. Both of the opposing neighboring clans were delighted and made the proper sacrifices for peace. They took oaths to be following us in battle against any others. I would never have thought and done that myself, but I could still see the difference between loss and gain. My son avoided life loss and gained allies! What amazes me the most, is how this second wife of my son gets along with his first one, all in the same house!

Any way, our herdsmen since, can take their cattle, sheep and goats by the mighty Aliakmon on the Tymfean region, or on the gentle slopes of Eordea. We still have problems with our cousins of Lyn-kestis, for they (not only) want the leadership on all of Makedonia, they're also dumb enough not to realize that only united we could be able to stave off the raids of the Illyrians and Dardanians from the lands of the cold Vorreas wind. Fortunately, against the former we have our cousins, the Molos-sians and the Haones. Against the latter, well, one can only hope for help from other clans, related to us by blood.

Now, to more recent events on my son's good mind of ruling. It proved him wiser than I could pos-sibly have been, had I have the need. Not that he didn't consult me either. My opinion, and I can see it now, was much of narrower dimensions than the resolution my son finally adopted, albeit a painful one. As it happened, one of our big landholders and, therefore, a man with some following and some responsibilities as well, the son of Pamenis, Klitos, thinking narrowly (as perhaps I would in this case) and on impulse, permitted one of his dependent families head, Kleonidis, to dam an area by one of Aliakmon's tributary rivers, the Gorgias. That, by itself, is nothing of note. The cattle needed a place with permanently running water, especially during the hotter months of the year. Gorgias is such a river. A well thought decision on behalf of Klitos, as a responsible leader of his people's needs. What was not taken under consideration, was the vicinity of the dam to Elimiote border. The result-ing pond, not only covered the area belonging to them without their knowledge, but, because of four days and nights of constant rain (after the dam was built), the water came up much faster than anticipated. Covering a larger area than thought at the beginning, resulted the ruin of few Elimiote huts. Worst, the flood happening at night, caused the drowning of sheep, goats, few cattle and, the death of four Elimiotes. A herdsman in charge, had his sons as keepers of the herds there. They used the same sleeping accommodations as their charges, causing them to drown also…

Naturally, when the news reached the ears of the Elimiote king, he got very angry and sent word to Klitos, demanding compensation for the loss. Klitos answered back that he was willing to do some-thing about the goats and sheep lost, but not of the humans. It was their folly they had not post watch during the night. Alkamas!" Anaxarhos turned his attention to one of the young boys. "You do not have to put your head down in shame, nor to feel that what I am telling reflects on your family! I know, we all do, you are related to Klitos. As I said a while ago, I would have probably done what he did. Now, that puts me in the same bracket with him, doesn't it? Telling of our misjudgments, makes us reflect and not repeat them! Besides, your uncle proved himself wise in the end. Now let us resume. Where was . . . ah! King Parmenion, the current king of Elimia, argued that the case could not be proved, once all of the boys were dead and couldn't argue on their behalf. Besides, that argument of Klitos was irrelevant, he said, as Klitos should have planned better. Since he didn't, he should pay now—or else!

Klitos of course, asked for support from his neighbors and several other family heads armed their men and came to his aid, ready to put-up a fight. As king Parmenion's men were getting assembled for a show-down, no doubt, Kleonidis and some others raided the Elimiotic camp and inflicted some light casualties, in the hope of scaring them off.

This act brought the opposite result. It raised more protest and threats from Parmenion, who de-cided to lead his men in person now! Again, if you ask me, my first act (on impulse) would have been to rush in support of my clansmen and ask questions later. Not so for my son. Oh, he asked me for my advice before he took any action, that's for sure. He asked the advice of other elders too, like I did when I was leading. Like me, he did not follow the opinion of the majority, deeming it too servile in certain aspects or too rushed and dangerous in some other aspects. He knew that either side was say-ing mostly what they thought it would please his ear. Like me, he rushed into the thick of trouble. Unlike me, he did not carry a sword.

He jumped on his best horse, not bothering to wait for the royal chariot, with only an escort of ten men who were fast enough to keep-up with him. They reached the Elimiotic border overnight. Our king, my son, ordered Klitos to make sure no further action should be taken, unless specific orders would come to him from my son in person, or by a messenger carrying the king's ring as proof of authenticity. That done, he left one man, Ion, the son of Iolas, for good measure with Klitos and, with the rest of thenine men of his escort, crossed into Elimiotis.

They soon ran into the advancing party of king Parmenion. They were coming against us in full battle gear! My son stopped with his escort at a safe distance, gave his men orders to wait but to be ready to rescue him, if rescue needed. He dismounted then and walked up to the Elimiote line, right hand up, in proper peaceful salutation. He went straight toward king Parmenion, who was easily seen among the first in line, riding his royally embellished chariot.

From what I was told later, Parmenion originally had given orders to have my son dispatched as he would come closer. Seeing my son's bravery and admiring it, he changed his heart. He stepped out of his chariot also and told his men to wait. As the two approached each-other, the most important and unbelievable act took place, before all present. Although my son is Parmenion's senior both in age and status, he addressed the Elimiote king first and with respect. Further, as the space between them closed, my son opened his arms and embraced Parmenion, calling him his future (if it ever happens) name, as an in-law and equal! According to later agreement, my (only days old) grand daughter, Yakinthi, will wed Parmenion's son when they both come of age.

Parmenion was taken aback, for good reason and, with not much of an option but to respond in ac-cordance of the situation. The two of them sat down on the ground (another willful indication on e-quality from my son) and heard each-other's grievances. They parted after some time, with the promise to return in two days' time, each escorted by ten men only and by the full array of the two family parties originally involved in the incident, from grand parents to infants. On their parting, my son gave— first agaion—the proper salutation.

I know all these things in detail and as they took place, not only because (out of respect) people are bound to inform me, but because my son (out of more respect) gave me a first-hand full account, a-long with his motives behind his actions!"

Anaxarhos stopped his narration to ask for some more fruits and wine for the company, drank from his golden goblet (Mikynaean remnant, no doubt) and picked-up the story again.

"Two days later the parties returned to the pre-arranged place and on time. My son had with him Kleonidis and his family, Klitos (as the landowner) and his family, along with the ten men for escort. They were all unarmed—except for their personal daggers. Parmenion did the same, bringing along the priestess of goddess Dimitra, since the whole incident was caused (by human intervention) on Mother Earth's landscape. His party consisted of the herdsman Harilaos, who's sons had drowned that fateful night, the remaining one son of his, along with the man's wife and daughters. Parme-nion's escort was also ten men, armed with daggers only.

The priestess asked all of them to take the appropriate life and death oaths, in the name of the mighty goddess, telling them that—no matter what the outcome of the human verdict—Dimitra would receive her due respect and appeasement. In return, the goddess would find a way to reward the pious and innocent, as she would destroy the guilty!

With that said and done, the story of the incident was retold before the priestess, who now was flanked by the families of the immediately concerned and my son with Parmenion. With it, there were accusations and counter-accusations from both parties, tempers rising and falling, for neither party (in spite of oaths taken) would just state the facts and forget personal interests.

Finally, when the going started getting against Kleonidis' cause, he sprung against Harilaos and, producing a dagger hidden in his cloak, delivered a fatal wound. Everybody stood astonished, un-moved on the ground each was holding, except my son. He sprung in his turn and with a special hit (I taught him that in his youth) to Kleonidis' private area, he sent him cold to the ground! While every one was still amazed and dumbfounded by the speed of events, my son nodded to Ion and his men. They drew their daggers and put Kleonidis, his family and Klitos with his in a circle, daggers ready to be put in action at their slightest move! My son raised an arm to prevent Parmenion from taking any further action. He dragged Kleonidis (now just starting to coming back to his senses) before the dying Harilaos and king Parmenion. 'I solemnly say to you all—he said—the goddess' decree, through her priestess, will come to its fulfillment, as it was stated! Before your dying eyes, Harilaos, Kleonidis is going to meet Tartaros and Pluton's dog, Kerveros, by the hand of your only remaining son! Your soul then, can be set free to be guided by the goddess to Haron, who's going to lead you to the Illysian Fields, so you can join in a bliss your other sons and ancestors, in the presence of the mighty gods and heroes. The dagger which will arm your son's hand, will be supplied by king Parmenion's own!'

Parmenion nodded in agreement and gratitude and drew his dagger. Harilaos' son, a youth of ten plus four springs, ashen in the face but steady in hand, did his duty with a clean cut of Kleonidis' throat.

'Hear me out now Makedones!' My son purposely used the whole tribe's name, to have both, Ores-tids and Elimiotes included. 'It is the goddess' will and foretell that justice will be given in full! Kleo-nidis deceived us all and paid with his life! Yet, his debt is not paid all in full. His first born daughter, come here, Kalliopi, is to be given to Harilaos' last son, as his wife or concubine, according to his own wish. She is to give him sons and daughters, regardless of her status before him. That will force her never to take action against her children's father! The rest of Kleonidis' household, as well as his property, are to be transferred to . . . what is your name, son?' 'Antigonos, Sire!' 'Antigonos, then, son of Harilaos, is to inherit Kleonidis' sons, to have them serve for the rest of their lives. Their offspring though, will be free to chose their living, the time they turn of age, free of any further obligation! As for you Klitos, although you did not betray me by raising a hand to protect your investments in Kleo—nidis, you did let me down by not making sure treachery like this one would never take place.

I, therefore, order you to have all of Kleonidis' family males castrated, so they will not be able to produce any more unworthy members! Then, you will supply with dowries all three of Harilaos' daughters out of your own property, adding something extra to what our customs dictate. Thirdly, you being a recent widower, will wed Harilaos' wife and hold her in respect. Your own sons will do that also, like she's their natural mother, until the day you both die! Is that in agreement with your honor, sir?'

Klitos was, obviously, not exactly happy with the prospect of all these arrangements and expenses, especially getting married to a woman who (until few moments ago) had been someone else's wife.

He disliked even more the adaptation of the last son and all Harilaos' daughters. Further, he had just lost one of his family's good servants, not to mention his grief over his own wife's recent death due to fever! No, he wasn't happy at all! He was smart enough to recognize, on the other hand, that Kleoni-dis had acted foolishly in the first place, then in total disregard of explicit orders from the king. He knew also his own duty was to come and investigate the initial incident himself, instead of taking Kleonidis' word. Granted, Kleonidis had proved himself loyal in the past. Loyalty did not mean justice though. Klitos knew where he was standing. He, with unbecoming lack of sense in his overall responsibilities, had put his king into a predicament, shameful—to say the least! He counted his blessings. With a deep sigh, he resigned to accepting the judgment by saying so. 'Good!' my son said. Then, turning to king Parmenion: 'So that no one says that I am not fair, I will replace the stock of sheep, goats and cattle, out of my own stock, head for head and let it be known that, from now-on, nothing is to be done, concerning and affecting our two clans, prior to consulting both of us first!'

Parmenion, obviously moved, accepted my son's judgment and declared, for all to hear: 'From this moment-on, Elimiotis will trust and follow Orestis, in good and hard times alike!' He vowed that, be-fore the goddess' priestess and in the name of all gods dwelling on top of Olympos, as well as the ones in the underworld.

The priestess helped them to administer preliminary oaths and offer libations out of the royal wine flasks. First to Dimitra and her daughter Persefoni, then, to Dias Father of all, down to the last deity and local heroes, with special emphasis on invoking the names of Ellinas and Makedon (as progeni-tors). A special offer was given to war god, Aris, to appease him for not shedding any more blood in a battle among the two clans.

Arrangements were made to have a common celebration with the new face of Selini the moon god-dess, which would also be the starting point of Klitos' new wedlock with Harilaos' widow, Kynnani, thus giving her the time to burry her lost husband and mourn enough, before she'd get her new one!

For that wedding, the groom's party would start from our town, Levaea. The bride's would start from king Parmenion's town, Aeani. Both, would converge to Vokeria, by the way of old Midas' gardens. As my son explained to me, he wanted to get his father-in-law involved and not only as a witness to the two clans' good will and closer ties. My son wanted old Pavmenis to feel equally close and obligated, because of his position and role, as the host of such a deal taking place in his lands. Pavmenis being vain, as I know, was delighted and I certainly could do nothing but agree with my son's plan and thoughts!"

The usual clearing of throat, some more reflection and food taken, escorted by generous portions of wine drinking. Kloppas, like the youth around him, waited with great anticipation for Anaxarhos to resume his story. Kloppas took an investigating, discreet, look at the youth called Alkamas. The young boy did not seem to be offended any more by the telling of his relative's, Klitos, misfortune, nor did the other boys' affection (or lack of it) toward him seemed to have altered. They were all back to their attention paying to the story, as ever before.

The raspy voice took Kloppas away from his observations and back to the story. "As preparations started in earnest, we saw that all sheep, goats and cattle due were sent to Elimiotis, head for head, out of our family's stock. About the same time, we received a herald from the region of Elis, below Ahaia, in that island of Pelops, the Peloponnisos I have mentioned to you. This herald, all dressed in white, with a crown of limber olive branches, holding his decorated with twisted vine staff, was ac-cepted for audience at my son's megaron hall, Kloppas, for you to know, the other house like this one but closer to the market. This herald, like many others from Elis, was sent to traverse the whole area.

The aim was to have athletes (all had to be Ellines by proof of descent) go and compete at the Elian Holy place called Olympia, in honor of Zefs and the immortal hero, Iraklis. This event is taking place every four years, late spring time, just before the ripening of Mother Earth's fruits and their gather-ing from us the mortals. This competition includes running, boxing, javelin throwing, the diskos throw and the stone throw. Accepting the invitation, meant to send the best person in any of these events and not to be at war with any of the kingdoms or cities in Ellas! Nor should any Ellinas do any harm to any competitor or, for that matter, a spectator going or coming from these games. There is always a truce to be held for a whole month prior and a whole month after the competition, so athlet-es and spectators alike can travel unimpeded, to and from!

We found the idea presented an excellent one and my son, with all the heads of the ruling families of Orestis, took the proper oaths. Parmenion and Pavmenis did the same, as did other kings and clans. This contest was scheduled to occur the following spring, counting the day of the herald's visit. We all know the competition is said to have started by none other but Iraklis himself, in honor of his father, Olympian Zefs! I, truly, know better. Iraklis, has left us mortals, way before these games were proposed. He went to lofty Olympos and joined the gods about the time my own father was just a young kid. Iraklis' obligation to his wicked cousin and king of Peloponnisian Argos, Evristheas, ful-filled, he had taken his wife Deianyra away, toward mount Ita, the one adjacent to the Hot Gates' location, the ones named after the healing springs. The hero found his death there, because of Kenta-vros Nessos. Nessos, you see, was one of the few remaining leaders of the Kentavri tribes, a Pelasgian stock. None of them was ever half horse and half man! My grand father told me that, knowing better than many, as he fought for and against them many a time. You remember what I told you of Dorian iron swords? No Pelasgian bronze was ever a match to them! Kentavrian horsemanship and fighting did nothing against Dorian sword and spear. Their ability to live on horseback, only helped a few of them to save their lives, fleeing up on the mountains around the gulfs of Pagassae and Malis. Nessos' clan was among them. When Iraklis came upon the location with his wife Deianyra, seeking a place for himself and away from the machinations of his cousin Evristheas, Nessos managed (with a pre-text) to hand a cloak dipped in poison, to Deianyra. The pretext and her purpose, was that she would thus keep Iraklis with her, for ever. The real purpose: Nessos wanted revenge against the Dorians and, who best but their greatest champion as his victim? Deianyra believed the Kentavros and dress-ed the hero herself, as he was readying to go and chop wood for their hearth. The more Iraklis work-ed and perspired, the more poison shipped, through his pores, into his body! After hours of agony, he finally died going mad and building-up a pyre himself, into which he threw his aching body, setting it ablaze.

Nessos was hunted-down by Iraklis' kinfolk, sons and others. They, after all the hero's deeds, had also suffer from Evristheas' hands. Leaving Peloponnisian Argos, they had gone after Iraklis' trail, unwilling to live in Peloponnisos any longer. Out of Nessos' clan, very few survived as the Iraklides, Iraklis' kinfolk, chased them all over Thessalia . . ."

"One of the reasons you north upstarts started raiding my country?" Kloppas had to bite his tongue from saying that out loud. He, instead, refilled his cup with much watered wine and took a long, de-liberate sip. The old man was a good story-teller, a good host and, Kloppas wanted to receive know-ledge along his profits from this place. "I better keep my mouth shot and my ears and eyes open!" He thought of his initial anger at Anaxarhos. It was still there. Blood doesn't turn to water overnight! But, along with his anger, there was also a growing admiration (and secret jealousy?). If his father's father had such a hold to tradition, such stories to tell, would his clan's resistance take heart and turn defeat to victory? Would he have been a free man all his life? More questions than answers, so, "Pay attention!" reminded himself.

". . . they mixed-up with other Kentavrians and spent their time teaching people in Thessalia and Makedon, as to how to ride and be the best of horse riders. We all know that the best horses and the best riders are Thessalians and Makedones. Some people also say that these Iraklides are slowly head ing now toward our areas. I don't know if that is true. I haven't seen any of them and no stranger, coming through, claimed to belong to their clan—yet.

Any way, back to the point where my talk dragged me into Iraklis' affairs. The people of Elis had nothing to do with the hero himself. Deianyra though, was a woman from their clans and tribe, so now they felt they owed the hero some, long due, respect. Hence the idea about the games in his honor and the rumor of him starting them. I guess, this way, they expect better response and participation. We are getting ready to send our best men there and hope they win!"

Kloppas wondered if heralds had gone by his town, Farsalos, asking for participation in the games. He was sure Farsalos was not left out but he had no immediate knowledge. His work of taking his wares from town to town, never gave him the opportunity to get involved with events, unless he hap-pened to be there when those events were happening.

The narration of the Orestid past with bits of glory and occasions of failure continued well into the night. At the end and with the promise of Anaxarhos to continue again the following evening, Klop-pas informed his host that the present night was his last in Levaea. He had a successful bartering of goods, making a good profit. Time to head for the next town the very next morning. He thanked his host for hospitality given and presented him with another Korinthian made cauldron. Anaxarhos reciprocated by giving Kloppas a mountain lion's pelt and three wolf furs. Kloppas tried to refuse the wolf furs, stating that the hospitality given, with the food and drinks and story telling, was more than a repay for his wares. Anaxarhos looked at him straight and giving him a firm and friendly hand, told him something that made Kloppas shiver. "I wish I could give you your parents back, free as they used to be before my coming to your town!" "You knew? . . ." was what Kloppas could say. "Yes.

You look too much like your mother. She was who convinced me to seek one master for both, her and you! War brings misery to many, even when it comes from necessity! I waged many wars out of need, many out of what I thought was needed. None really out of sheer need to wage war! Let's leave things as they are and look for a better future!" There was nothing else Kloppas could think of saying. He bid his host a good night and headed to his quarters. He departed the next day, earlier than the first crow of the cock, not knowing if and when he would ever set foot in Levaea again . . .

The happy songs and oath exchanging in Klitos' wedding on one hand and the oaths of the three kings for close relations on the other, were given under the best omens, weather and intentions. Guest arrival in Vokeria, not far from lake Vegoritis, took place seven days before the event. King Pavme-nis, puffed-up with the thought of the role he had to play, was more extravagant than a gizzard like him usually cares to pay. The wine was flowing on the street—so to speak—rivaling the extravagance exhibited by the Orestid and Elimiote kings.

Herds were driven to town, to be given as presents to the groom, to the point that Pavmenis had to build a special corral, to keep them in. Many other guests brought gilded weaponry and old artifacts, remnants of the age of the great Mikynean schools of art. From Parmenion's side, came fine robes and linen for the bride's new household, gold and silver, a dowry worthy her troubles and her new status. Everything came loaded and secured in trunks, on the backs of pack animals. Everything, in-cluding the animals, would remain with her, as part of the same dowry.

Pavmenis surprised all the guests with another extravagance: Aside of the lodging arrangements for each guest (according to individual status), he undertook the supplies of food and wine for the dura-tion of the festivities, a whole ten plus four days and nights.

Finally the festivities were over. Anaxarhos was sure that Pavmenis had come to regret such an ex-travagance on his part, as sobriety replaced the mind Dionyssos' liquid fruit had bestowed to all rev-elers. With Klitos taking his new bride to his estates, a meeting of the three kings was held, to decide on the number of persons (according to their merits) to be send to Elis for the games in Olympia. Care was taken to have equal representation from all three clans, with the overall purpose to see any or all Makedonians crowned as winners.

Alas, all of the planning came to nothing. Hordes of Illyrian warriors from the tribes of Vryges, Atintanes, Penestes and Tavlantians (the latter being the leaders), attacked en masse. What was their final aim, was unknown. Usually, they would come in small raiding parties, take what they needed and speed back to their lands, as fast as their individual loads would permit. Not this time!

Messengers from the tribe of the Haones and the clan of Lynkestians, came asking for help, telling that the barbarians were united under the leadership of one, named Gavrantj, Gavrantis in Makedo-nian. Any town taken by them, was garrisoned at its acropolis, not left bypassed as in the past. If the town did not have an acropolis, they razed it to the ground and sent its population in chains to Illyria to its coastal slave markets. Infants, old and weak, were put to death at once! Few animals and fields were left to few survivors, under guards, obviously for future exploitation. This type of an attack, was new and scary. Haones and Lynkestes were not able to stop it by themselves . .

Illos, the Lynkestian king, as any Lynkestian, was a very antagonizing person. Even in cases of such a great danger, he was apt to doing things his own way or nothing at all. Obviously, this attitude brought friction between him and the Haones, who (aside from being outnumbered by the Illyres) had to deal with Illos' whims. The more numerous Illirian tribes were pressing on two fronts. Some, were crossing the fords on Eordaikos river and on to Haonian lands, others were coming from above the lake Lyhnitis and through the mount Varnous passes into Lynkestis. Instead of asking immediate help from Orestis and other Makedonian clans, Illos sent his forces through Dassaretis to help the Haones, but not as an ally who listens. The result was that many lives were lost, Haones had to with-draw back and desperately ask for help from Molossis. Meantime, Illos had to face the invaders all by himself and in Lynkestian grounds.

He took a stand between the twin lake side, by the Major and Minor Vrygiis lakes. Gavrandis prov-ed himself a much better general. Faking frontal attacks, he sent a part of his raiders, including the best of his horse riders, around the Minor Vrygiis and had them fall onto Illos' rear. Any Lynkestian hamlets and towns by-passed for that reason, did not send messages to Illos because they presumed the raiders were coming for them and took off to the heights. The Illyrians fell on Illos' troops from both sides then. His force panicked and an untold number of Lynkestians got killed. Illos made it through with only a few of his best horsemen, now asking in despair for help from anyone and willing to follow Kerveros himself to Adis, as long as that would send the Illyrians away.

An emergency council took place in Levaea as these disturbing news were heard. Runners were dis-patched immediately to neighboring clans, such as Perrevia in Thessalia, Elimiotis, Tymfea and Eor-dea. The Lynkestian messengers were sent back to their king, with assurances that help would be on its way soon. It was suggested to tell him to withdraw his meager forces on high ground and avoid battle but keep harassing the enemy as best as he could. What hamlets and towns were still under him, it was proposed to have them evacuate to strongholds with an acropolis, as to further delay the enemy progress.

Thessalian help from Perrevia's principal town of Olooson responded to the call before anyone else.

They reported to Anaxarhos' son, king Stenor, placing themselves under his command. While pre-parations were underway in earnest and troops from Elimiotis had started to join, other bad news reached the Makedonian camp from the Axios river regions. Pelagonia, Almopia and Amydon were attacked and invaded by the Peones and Maidi, who (apparently) were taking advantage of the Illyr-ian onslaught. Vottiaea and Imathia had mobilize every available body to aid the neighboring clans, for they were sure to be attacked next.

There was no way the Makedonian clans could face the enemy on two fronts at once. Something had to be done, and done fast! The three kings present now in Levaea, Stenor, Parmenion and Pavmenis, advised these messengers to go back to their own kings and tell them they either had to follow the same plan as for the Lynkestians, or to see if they could buy the invaders out, their lands being flatter than Lynkos, with not so much of high mountains to withdraw. Help would come after Lynkos and Haonia were secured.

In a few days, all available horse riders from the leading families and clan heads, plus the contin-gent from Olooson, moved out toward Lynkestis and the desire to face Gavrantis. Any minor clan heads who did not possess adequate number of horses and as many peasants could master some sort of weapons, were ordered to escort women, old folks and children to well fortified locations and acro-polis forts in Levaea, Argos Orestikon and Keletron, the settlement by lake Keletron. They were to wait there until victory over the Illyrians or to continue resistance—in case of defeat.

The combined forces of Orestis, Elimiotis, Eordea and Olooson, rode toward Lynkestis. Another force from Tymfea and Molossis, led by the Molossian king, Tilepolemos, the one who claimed direct descent from the hero of the war against Tria, Ahilleas! They were to move upward to Haonia and seek battle against Gavranis on a second front. Advised from the Oloosonians, the force moving to Lynkestis, had each horseman bring two extra mounts with him. In other words, one horse to ride on, one to load with the battle equipment and the last one free of any weight. These mounts would be rotated on the way, so none would be too tired by the time contact was made with the enemy. The day of the battle the free mount would remain free until the charge, so as to remain fresh. King Ste-nor had his own advise. He asked for the riders to be prepared to attack in three waves. The first was to carry three javelins instead of the usual two and use them effectively, downing as many a foe as possible. The second wave, would follow right after the first with two javelins on hand. That would give the extra impetus needed to secure penetration and panic in the ranks of the enemy. That would leave the third wave of horsemen with almost no javelins, but they would not need them. A retreating enemy in panic, could always be brought down by a sword slice on his back. Meantime, the first two assault squadrons, could retrieve javelins from the dead and continue, or simply follow the third one in the chase, according to battle needs and development. The plan was accepted and the Oloosonian squadron served as scouts on the way, being -as Thessalians- the more experienced horse riders. They would also form the third squadron on the assault.

The first forward enemy units were observed at the outskirts of the town of Keletron, in Orestis proper. They were burning and looting the isolated and scattered farm houses and huts. Looking from above the mount Askios, they could be seen to have burned the town and laying siege to the acropolis of Keletron. Obviously, the message from Stenor to seek safety at the acropolis had come on time. This acropolis of Keletron is located on a hill jotting into the lake and connected with the rest of the land by a very narrow, neck shaped, lower hill. A wall built at the narrowest point of this connection, was giving the defenders a vantage point of defense. Orestid casualties did not appear to be heavy and the main enemy force had camped before the land-neck across from the acropolis.

The Oloosian scouts informed the three kings that the enemy has his own scouts patrolling the small plain by the lake and their own camp, though they had no idea of the Makedonian force on the mountain itself. So, decision was made not to attack at once, but to wait until the next day's early morning hours. This way, every available horse would be fresh and the riders ready, after a good night's sleep.

Guards were placed, to keep an eye on the foe's movements and all preparations were done in silence. Before the sunrise from the peaks of mount Askios, while darkness still covered the narrow plain below, the Makedonians assembled at their starting points of attack. Prior to that, king Parmenion had an excellent idea. Unnecessary clothing was torn to strips and the hooves of the horses were covered and secured. That muffled the sound and let the enemy continue sleeping. Just before the order of attack, seers took omens by casting animal bones, a live sacrifice deemed too dangerous so close to the enemy lines. The indications were favorable. The order of attack was passed down by soft voices. The first assault squadron moved in unison and in silence.

Captured Illyrians told how they felt, after the battle was won. It really had to be very scary when, at the time the difference of colors in the early day's light cannot be told, as all looks either black or gray. How one feels when the woods' edge looks like it moves closer and closer? One realizes that his eyes are tired keeping watch for hours and thinks tricks are played on him. He rubs his eyes and takes a closer look, thinking (perhaps) he shouldn't have that much wine the night before . . . Was that faded light a glow of metal, or the whitish feathers of a predator bird's underside of extended wings, falling at its prey?

The realization that a charging cavalry is upon you, comes only too late! What made it more horrible, was that the senses didn't allow you to believe what the eyes were seeing! You'd think you had fallen asleep, on duty, while standing up and dreaming! Dreaming, for you hear no galloping and you know that dreams are silent. Then, you hear a comrade's scream of pain, his agony in death come early by a javelin piercing his body! You dream-see the next javelin flying toward you and you realize, too late, that death is indeed mostly silent when he comes to get you! You never hear your own cry. Maybe the next guy does . . . Maybe he will have time to parry, perhaps time to draw his sword and warn others . . . But you don't know that, you don't hear it! All you hear, is blood rushing in your head and, what you feel, is how slippery your hands are, as they try to pull the javelin out of your sternum! Perhaps, your last look tells you that the tree line at the woods' edge got lost in the dark again, because your eyes are rolling back in their sockets . . .

Victory was complete! The besieged at the acropolis mounted their own attack, killing or capturing the Illyrians camped by the neck-like land connector. They had put-up a desperate fight around their leader, trying to protect him, in vain. Even the town folks and the peasantry, took heart and came out from behind the wall, armed with pitchforks, axes, clubs and stones, after the few surviving and running for dear life, Illyrians. Whoever surrendered, was corralled and tied, for later exchange of hostages, or for slave markets of the city-states in Thessalia.

Proper burial was given to fallen Makedonians on the site, the common grave dug by the captured Illyrians, after their bones were extracted from the funeral pyre. Thanks offering to the gods follow-ed, with many sacrifices. The dead Illyrians were buried as they were in a common grave, after all items of value were taken off them and distributed among the victors, according to individual valor and place.

The three kings and their army didn't stay long there after that. They pursued the retreating Illyr-ians to the upper parts of Orestis and into Lynkestis proper. The campaign lasted the whole time Selini, the moon goddess, takes to show her face and hide it again, for two times. Along with this vic-tory, came the news of another one, from the Molossians and Tymfeans, led by king Tilepolemos. They met with the second army of Illyres, by the banks of Drilon river, delivering another crushing defeat on the invaders.

Lynkos now restored to king Illos, he begged to be excused from the war to follow against the Peo-nes, his kingdom having the most suffering out of this Illyrian war. That being the truth and seeing the need of repair and peace in Lynkestis, the other kings agreed to continue without him. The Illy-rian threat was something of the past now and the Makedonian kings could breathe easier.

New offerings to the gods were given, as the army departed toward Almopia. The king of the Almo-pes, Amyntas, joined with few of his men who had escaped the wrath of the Peones. The combined forces started liberating the first villages and towns of his kingdom, Evropos by Lydias river, being the first one.

It soon became apparent that garrisons could not be left in every town freed. These towns were easier to be assaulted by small forces, than being defended by even large ones! Makedonian numbers were not as numerous as the Peonian ones and the latter would not come to face battle now. Second reason for not leaving garrisons, was the fact that the Oloosian contingent could not remain in Make-donia much longer. They were needed back home, for the harvest of their estates. Makedonians were closer to home, plus their fighting force was made out of clan heads and land lords, who had a son or a father to look for the harvest by the hired hands of the peasants at their estates.

As it was, they pressed forward, chasing the Peones where ever informers told them where they would be. Peonians kept on moving around, testing the Makedonians to see how long they would stay away from harvest and homes. Four appearances of the full face of Selini came and went. Klitos had joined the force meantime, his obligation as new husband (and a father of near grown-ups) fulfilled. He came to join fuming at the thought that he missed such an engagement against the Illyres. The chasing around continued without conclusive results. The Peones continued coming and going on fast raids, not willing to come to a set battle. The Oloosians returned to Perrevia, with a promise to come back, if help was needed again. The kings, Amyntas, Pavmenis, Stenor and Parmenion, made sure the Thessalians brought enough spoils back home, to make them want to return again, when needed. Even Illos sent from Lynkos some of his spoils.

Fall was approaching and winter could not be far from the doorstep. The Amydonian king, Leo-haris, being pursued by the invaders some time earlier, had taken refuge up on the mountains of the near-by, three-pronged peninsula, beyond the seaport of Therma. Some of his men had joined the combined Makedonian force though—all good and valiant riders. Their leader, Leonidas, was present at the meeting held, to see what could be done that winter. The Imathian king, Menelaos, also had to leave his kingdom and seek now hospitality in the court of Illos, in Lynkestis, because the Imathians could not resist the Peones and Maidi who had taken fodder and produce for their own wintering.

Soon winter came hard upon the region. Snow, ice or mud, covered the ground most of the time. As the people went hungry, many died from lack of provisions. Refugees from all affected areas came to temporary shelters in Eordea and Elimiotis mainly. Every possible preparation was made to accom-modate them and resume the offense in the following spring. Due to these emergencies, no one was prepared to go and compete at the games in Olympia. The Elians got offended and disregarded us as semi-barbarians, who do not bother keeping their oaths. We were warring they said, at a time of truce. We took the insult in stride. We knew we weren't warring against other Ellines, war against barbarians for one's own life shouldn't count.

As spring replaced winter and the melting snow rolled down the mountains in the form of water, the river beds came to overflow and flood covered most of the valleys and plains. We took the time for more preparations against the enemy. Either the gods would favor us or we were lost! To our delight the horsemen from Olooson returned, along with a squadron of retainers, sent by a big land lord from the neighboring city of Larissa, one named Alevas. He claims to be direct descendant of Aeolos, the Lord of the winds, and Thettalos, the Danao-Ahean hero, who ruled Thessalia so many gener-ations ago, no one remembers how many any more.

We prepared two armies, both on horse, as before. One traversed Almopia, the other crossed Vot-tiaea and both converged into Amydon itself. As before, we by-passed hamlets and minor, unprotected towns with no forts or acropolis and headed toward the cold Vorreas winds following Axios river. The Peonians and Maidi, thinking we were heading straight to their principal town of Vargala, came converging from all sides they were dispersed since last summer and tried to block our way. They picked-up a place, on upper Axios, by the location of Stenae. In their rush to do so, they exhausted themselves and their horses, so they could get there first. We had the same plan, riding our horses in relays, as we had done against the Illyrians. We dared our opponents now to coming out of the nar-row pass of Stenae, by faking attacks and swift retreats, wave after wave. That tired their horses even more, as we were forcing them to give us chase, before re-attacking them with each new wave. We finally lured them all out of the pass. Tired as they were, they couldn't keep-up against our vigor and we were even lucky, as their leader was among the first to fall.

A huge number of them was killed and, whoever saved his life, is still running (I hope) further up the Aemos mountains. The spoils we got, were divided among us and all the prisoners were sent to be sold as slaves at Therma, the profits going to the ones who had their homes ruined the summer past.

Having just a few days of rest, the army started on its way back, mopping-up the areas by-passed before. Word was sent to refugees in the three-pronged peninsula, telling them they could return to their homeland. Many Amydonians and Vottiaeans preferred to remain there, as they had find good refuge. Their new home lands were named Mygdonia and Vottiki now. The lands around Amydon and along the flow of Axios, were augmented by volunteers who wanted new estates and renamed to Amfaxitis, as it straddles the river.

Upon completion of the campaign and the mopping-up, the combined Makedonian forces came to rest in Veria, Imathia's principal town. From there, each contingent would travel home. By that time harvest was about to start and the herds were half way down from summer pastures, for the shearing of wool and preparations for fall and winter lodgings.

All these events were told to Anaxarhos in somber tones by his son and, in amazement, by his grand son, Pafsanias, the expedition being his first. Anaxarhos in turn, retold the story many a time to his charges, during cold winter nights by the hearth. But the victory was not a long-living one. The enemy had a new vigorous leader soon and, reorganized and with new courage, Peones attacked the following spring again. Moving toward the direction of the sunrise and the sea, they crossed into Parorvylia, defeated the Orvyles, Visaltes and Kristones and camped at the border of Anthemous and the new Mygdonian lands. The latter clans had no choice but to pay large amounts of stock, produce and fish, so they could be left with their lives and properties. Makedonian clans did not have the stamina to regroup and start a new campaign, nor did they have an accord, since the kings quarreled with one-another for supremacy of the region

> "…ready to accept and assimilate, we recreate! What others get from us, they present it as their own. We accept that too, so we re-create again!"
> Leonidas Faitas, Korkyrean Ellinas

II

"My name is Asteropeos, son of Neagenis, son of Irineos, son of Alkamas, son of Iolas, son of Men-andros, son of Toroneos, who was the great grand son of the first great Toroneos, the builder of this city. Before him, they say, it was Exarhos, son of Fidon, who (in turn) was cousin of Iason from the town of Iolkos from his father's bloodline and related to the Myrmidonian Ahilleas (who's deeds are sung by Omiros), on his mother's side.

My kin and dependants live at the middle peninsula of the land between the rivers Axios and Ehed-oros (toward the sunset), and Strymon on the sunrise direction. I say middle peninsula, because this land between the above mentioned rivers is a bigger, rounded peninsula, with two other (finger-like) protruding ones, on each side of this in the middle. We call ourselves Sythones, on account of the old legendary king Sython. He was the only son of Kyveli, the underworld goddess, and the mortal Perin-theas. At some time he had fallen asleep and, from his sweat Kyveli conceived an only child, Sython.

When Sython grew to manhood, he betrothed the daughter of the local Anax, king of the indigenous Leleges. The newlyweds moved with their household, servants and livestock alike, in this middle pen-insula and that is how it got its name that long ago, in Ahean appellation. The wife of this Sython, a beautiful dame named Akti, fell in love with the charms of Nireas, the wave mover, whenever Posido-nas (the sea god) wishes. Akti,

37

then, followed Nireas one morning, swimming on many of his waves, all the way to the sunrise side, finger-like peninsula. Consumed by the deity, her body was found at the tip of mount Athos, where the sea breaks fall against the land. Since then, that peninsula took her name, Akti.

Now don't take me as a bubbly old man when I tell you all these things. I just want you to know who and where we are, in case you happen to be visiting or you are shipwrecked hereabouts. As I was saying then, Sython got so upset of his loss and his wife's infidelity and folly, he became ill in his mind and started chasing their own daughter Pallini, for she looked so much like her mother! Pallini was terrified by her own father's advances and she run for protection seeking her mother's spirit, as she knew she could ask for favors from her and her lover Nireas. Pallini followed her dead mother's spirit advise and hid herself at the marshes of the hidden gulf by the tip of our Sythonian peninsula, fed by the gulls and the seals Nireas would send every night -as servants to her.

Sython could not rest though! He searched high and low, until one observant servant (full of hope for a generous reward) told him of the place. Sython decided to act at night and kidnap Pallini, as she would be asleep. But the seals were equally good servants of their master and warned her on time! She jumped into the night covered sea and the seals carried her away. In the darkness, Sython thought Pallini had gone to where her mother's body had been found and headed to mount Athos' promontory.

The gods, knowing all mortal desires, let the fool waste his time searching there. Meanwhile, the seals led Pallini to safety, in the other finger-like peninsula, to the sunset of ours. There, she fell sup-pliant at the feet of that first Toroneos I was telling you, who (at that time) was ruling over the clan of the Kanastreans. They were a mix of Minoan sailors from Kriti, stranded there, after Knossos' de-mise, pirates from Ahean Mikynae, as well as indigenous Leleges and Pelasgians, much like my ancestors. Toroneos was so moved by her beauty and her dire need, he pledged himself and his protection of her for life, whether she would like to become his lawful wife, or remain as his esteemed guest. She was taken by his kindness and his stature, she readily agreed to become his queen. The nuptials took place soon and, during the celebrations, Sython and his shipmates arrived there, still in search of her.

When Sython found the reason of such a merriment in the country, he became twice as angry and incensed! He and his men disguised themselves as merchants and managed to get close to the couple.

At a pre-arranged signal, they drew their swords, took beautiful Pallini (in spite her and Toroneos' fight) and run to their ship. God Posidonas saw the sacrilege though and would not allow Aeolos, the god of winds, to send a favorable breeze for casting off. Each time Sython had his men try to row out to the sea, the winds blew waves against the ship and cast it back at the beach anew!

Toroneos and his men, armed now, came down at the beach and a great battle took place. Seeing that he was loosing, Sython cut Pallini's throat, rather than losing her to his foe. Then, asking his mother Kyveli to help him, he managed to pull away to his kingdom, for the gods owed Kyveli a lot and they couldn't refuse her her son's safety for the first time. But Sython would not be granted the same favor again.

After Toroneos buried his beloved Pallini where she had died, he left his kingdom in charge of his cousin Ptolemeos and, with his best, hand-picked men, went after Sython seeking revenge. Kyveli could do nothing for her son this time. Sython was chased and cut to pieces, any of his followers that survived taken slaves. Toroneos kept the land as his and built this town, Toroni. The peninsula, known as Sython's land though, kept its name and now we call it Sythonia and ourselves Sythones.

Ptolemeos, honoring his cousin's grief for a love lost, named the Lelegian peninsula Pallini and that is how it is known to this day.

Through the passing of the years, we saw many changes in our lives and customs, most of them be-ing more than gradual. Men from the 'island' of Pelops, Peloponnisos, as from many other parts, came to us as pirates or traders. Some took what they wanted and left. Others stayed here, still look-ing to find something. Through intermarriage, we developed blood relation with these clans from the south, north, east and west of us. So much from Thraki to our east, as much from Therma and Axios to our west. Our blood, by now, is evenly mixed with the Idones and Visaltes, as it is with the Maked-ni.

We trade our timber for ship-building as far as Korinthos, fish to high places beyond Axios, also smuggling ceramic vessels from Aegina to our south, when the trendy winds of Aeolos allow. Most of our profit comes though from the sea, blessed be Posidonas and Nireas! Especially, since Toroneos dedicated Pallini's hiding marshes (by the hidden gulf) as sanctuary to these gods. By the way, seals come out to the beach every night there, asking for the lost beauty with their crying voices…

Every so often, we also trade with cities from Asia, like Karia, Lydia, and even Finiki and Kypros. They speak, the Kypriotes do, our language, but with lots of idioms of their own, maybe taken from Finiki or from the times the Kypriotes left Arkadia. That, makes it hard for us to understand them, most of the time. The Kypriotes are the ones who tell us they trade with other tribes further south or further east, from places where the hot summer wind never cools or places where great rivers, Axios being a mere brook before them, flow. They tell us of name-places like Egyptos, Assyria, Vavylonia and others we can hardly pronounce. All these trading tribes of those far places are barbaric, their languages very hard to understand but also very strong. I tend to believe the Kypriotes merchants, 'cause I know (from family tradition) that the Kritans were trading with such people, many gener-ations ago. Only, the Kritans did not think of them as barbarians. The Kritans had adopted quite a few useful things from those tribes, especially from Egyptos and Finiki, when Kriti was the center of trade. Nonetheless, I challenged one Kypriot merchant named Theagenis, to bring me proof of his tales.

I got word last night that Theagenis moored his ship just before the harbor closed, bringing copper load, in exchange of leather goods and gold nuggets. We do not mine gold here, for there's none in our peninsula. Our fishermen smuggle a lot of it from the Pangeon mountain area, which belongs to the Idones. After taking care of my household needs early in the morning, I came to the market place by the harbor and I met him making his deals with local merchants. I waited discreetly aside, until he finished. Once we had our customary greetings and pleasantries, I reminded him of his promise in bringing proof of his boasting the last time we had seen one-another. He replied he was glad I remembered, cause he had all the proof I needed, on board of his vessel! Would I be kind enough to honor him with a visit at supper time after the market closed? In my mind, I was reluctant to accept the in-vitation readily, because (though I know him as a good merchant and a steady customer) I know that the difference between a merchant captain of a ship and a pirate, is never too great!

My status not allowing me to show any fear or second thoughts, too much reluctance and use of the ordinary excuse of business which had to be taken care until late, I gave him a polite but tentative re-sponse. I did not like the idea that I could end-up being 'napped' away to spend a life rowing an oar or as a slave in a distant land!

Now Theagenis is not a fool. He has spent time dealing everywhere and with many a people of any kind. I had shown him nothing indicating my inner thoughts, yet he knew at once. He smiled and as-sured me he had the most noble intentions and that a jar of good wine from Kytion (a Kypriot city) was waiting for my taste and in honor of Dionysos. That and my active curiosity won and I made the promise more pronounced this time. I returned to my household late after the mid of the day, clean-ed my self up and left word not to be expected for the night meal. I asked two servants to escort me (armed, just in case) when the market was about to close, to Theagenis' ship. On our way, I pur-chased a nice Aeginitan water-pouring container from Amfilohos the Korinthian, to bring it as a present to my Kypriot host. My day had been thus far a productive one, albeit slow. I dealt a lot of business, passed judgments, agreements were taken under consideration, fines were imposed to the ones of bad faith, as well as other affairs of the state, so that our side would not end-up losing in any shape or form. Now I was on my way to visit Theagenis. The distance was not so great, but it took time to get to his vessel, for I had to stop many a time as I headed toward the moorings. Many, not dealt during the day with, wanted to acknowledge my presence and make themselves noticed. I took my time, greeting and handshaking, followed by words of notice taken, for I wanted my host to have ample time preparing for my reception. In the event, I sent one of my servants ahead with my pres-ent, to Theagenis' broad merchant ship. The other servant was following me with the torches unlit as yet- at the proper respectful distance of two paces behind and to my left.

We arrived at the ship as Theagenis was appearing at the top of its plank tied on the gunwale on one end and resting on the shore at its other, for visitors, crew and merchandise access to and from the ship. I nodded to my second servant a dismiss, to joint the first one now sitting on the rock a ship's line was attached and I walked up the plank. As I came to its top, Theagenis' arms closed around me in a friendly but strong hug, one that almost reeled us over! Regaining balance and calming his ex-citement, he uttered words of excuse and greeted me properly this time, kissing both my chicks, as we held hands at full arm's length, to show no concealed weapons were hidden on either one of us.

After that, he gracefully showed me the way toward the seats prepared under a thatch-covered space, by the helmsman's oars, obviously reserved exclusively for Theagenis' use, judging by arrang-ed personal items. I noticed my present occupying a prime place and well secured. Some of Thea-genis' mates were on the ship and gathering at the prow side, curious of me but not trying to show it. I knew that others must have gone to the taverns around the harbor, to spend their valuables in wine and women and sleep there.

We started with the ordinary few pleasantries and idle talk, mixed with semi-serious comments on market prices and planned schedules ahead. After a while, Theagenis indicated it was time to eat, drink and make good friendship. I agreed as gracefully as my rumbling stomach would permit, fear-ing he would perhaps take offense by its noise produced from my hunger. He either did not notice or preferred to ignore it, as politeness and hospitality demands toward a visitor. He clapped his hands once.

Out of a dark cover amidships by the mast and below from where we were seating, emerged a figure coming to us, bent almost in two. The figure had its hands pointing forward down -but palms up- a sign I took as one indicating a readiness to obey orders. I could not tell if the figure of this person was a man's or a woman's. It approached and I noticed a cover on its head of weaved material of some kind, coming down to shoulder length and, at the dim light of an already set sun, I could see it was wearing a long dress of a very fine material and texture, allowing the body shape to be outlined, but with no further details.

There was no noise made as the figure walked approaching us, so I thought he or she must be bare-footed, or the sandals worn were made out of very soft hide. Theagenis gave a sort of an order in a language I could not understand, one hard to my ears, as there was no apparent and distinct vowel pronunciation in its words -like we all are accustomed of hearing. Yet, the sentence was warm in feel-ing, with a demand of respect in its use and a certain fondness and harmony in its vulgarity. 'It is E-gyptian' Theagenis volunteered, to satisfy my obvious puzzlement.

The person taking the order, straighten-up. A vague suspicion of mine became reality, when the two torches (one on each side of our seats, secured in special receptions on top of the gunwale) were lit.

My surprise wasn't so much that this person obeying Theagenis' order was a woman of a very young age, as much as that I could see now very clearly every detail of her anatomy. That's how transparent her dress was! I felt embarrassment and averted my eyes (with difficulty, it's true), to much of Theagenis' amusement. He informed me that this was the way most Egyptian women were dressed and, after my initial shock, I would get used to seeing her like he did, with no embarrassment at all. I took another look at her. She was standing on the side there, before us, by the torch on the port-side of the vessel, very calm and indifferent of my critical looks at her person.

I did pay attention to her face next. Though she had it covered with all kinds of artificial colors, I could tell that she indeed was a very young person. I estimated no more than ten plus six years old. Her face did not seem to have any lines on it, paint or no paint cover. Her skin being much darker than ours, even when compared to a sunburned one, looked very soft but very firm also. That trans-parent dress of hers was without sleeves and on each of her upper arms were coils of gold bracelets. One ended-up as a kind of a snake, proportionally very flat, almost two-dimensional. The other coil had the image of a bird on an upright position, very stiff looking and equally flat -as the snake. She was much shorter than I originally thought, for now I could see she was wearing a kind of sandals, much elevated. On a more careful inspection, I noticed this elevation was caused by the sandal soles, made out of felt, like the type we use inside our helmets and parts of armor, to protect us from rub-bing against the metal. Still, it was a wonder to me, how silently she walked and kept her balance at the same time!...

Suddenly I became aware that, by my taking the time for my observations, I had neglected my host, a totally impolite thing to do. He accepted my apologies with grace and he stated that my behavior was completely understood. How did I like her? He wanted to know. I pointed that, although her facial features were showing a very young and healthy individual, accented by her smooth skin and overall posture, I had my reservations about the scale of her beauty, for her cheeks under her eyes were rather too high set. Her eyes, despite being large and almond-shaped with long lashes, were los-ing (in my opinion) because of all this paint cover. Her mouth, albeit symmetrical and full, its lips were rather too thick for my taste and too pronounced with that red stuff on them! Actually, I had taken it as blood when I first saw her! She had a definitely good set of teeth, showing pure white as was accented by her dark facial color. Finally, I pointed that (according to our perception of beauty) her buttocks were way too high in proportion, although well rounded, while her breasts relatively small. Was it because she was still too young and undeveloped? And, by the way, looking at her feet now, it seemed to me that her size was very close to a young man's rather than a girl's! As for her hair, there was nothing I could say about, since all was covered by that peculiar cloth, nothing near to our women's peplos/veil. Yet, I had to admit that, somehow, she was very likable, provided one kept oneself open-minded and could overcome the first shock.

Theagenis turned and told her something. She, very graciously I might add, undid her head-cloth cover. Her head fully exposed, I could see -by the torch's light- she was endowed with raven-black hair, very short and curly. Aesthetically speaking and as we understand the term here, the site dis-pleased me, for it made her head look smaller in proportion to the rest of her body. I stated so, but, as I was finishing my statement, I was also changing my mind! Not that my observations were in-correct. But -you see- her overall appearance in spite (or because) of our accepted rules of proportion and her lack of these, made her so much likable, one could say he could find her almost beautiful, the more one looked at her.

We started eating and drinking what a burly sailor (who served as cook) brought to us and Theage-nis nodded his understanding to my opinion and proceeded to explain all about this young girl's story. Her name was rather unpronounceable in our language. Even he, knowing enough Egyptian to go-by in conducting his business, could not call it without a mistake. He had made-up his mind, cal-ling her a (sort-of) nickname, Nessouna, like we sometimes do, with our own, Niko for Nikodimos or Mahi instead of Andromahi and so-on. The girl had readily accepted it and that was that.

Between bites of well prepared mutton with garlic, greens, mouthfuls of red Kypriot wine, served by a one-eyed, old, pirate-looking Thrakian slave, Theagenis picked-up his narration in earnest. He got her against an account owed to him by her Egyptian father, a high official, who had unexpectedly fallen from grace with the local monarch, a person called Farao -or something like that. So, the of-ficial not being able to pay Theagenis any more, had compensated this way. The Farao, meantime, had some more enmity against this high official, her father. He ordered his execution along with all his wives, children and close kin, ordering that poor wretch's friends and associates out of Egyptos for life! The name of this official was deleted from all state and private records the Egyptians have at their disposal, by the way of marking them on stones and walls. He was hailing, the official did, from upper Egyptos, way far beyond a great desert, by the waterfalls of the mighty river Nilos. This Nilos is navigable all the way from the sea, to these waterfalls. Some even claim Nilos is navigable even after the waterfalls, to a place the sun-god, Ilios, burns daily with his heat. Theagenis did not believe that story though. As this Nilos flows through the country of the Ethiopes, it passes through great cities, among which, Thivae, synonymous to the Thivae in Viottia, although not related. This Thivae is almost as big a city as Vavylon, the one by the other mighty river, the Tigris! In this Egyptian Thi-vae is where the Farao resided, absolute Master of all living, adored as equal to the gods! Past that city, the

Nilos continues its flow, turning desert to arable plain, traversing by the tallest monuments on this earth, the Pyramides! Now these Pyramides are nothing else but cone-shaped tombs with four faces, built for each great Farao, when put to rest and his soul travels to meet the other gods. Among these Pyramides there's also another, most unusual structure. It has the head of a man, but the body of a crouching lion, called the Sfynx. It's such an old monument, no one knows if it's been built by humans or the gods themselves. Finally the Nilos comes to empty his waters into the sea, from five big mouths! He needs those for all the water he carries, though not even those are enough at times. Then he floods the arable lands, covering them in water, a kind of blessing after he retreats. These mouths of his form big islands between them, called Deltas -I don't know why, the name coming from the Finikes.

At that, Theagenis shifted his body and produced (from somewhere behind his back) a clay tablet, hard from being baked in fire, with strange marks on it. He said the markings were Vavylonian and were telling his transactions and accounts when he'd made port in Tyros. The Egyptian markings were different, as were the Finikian ones, which recently were adopted by some of our cities by the Asian coast, in Ionia, in order to keep records in our own language. I didn't believe half of what he was saying, but good manners prevented me from saying so.

Next, he turned addressing Nessouna in her language. While he drunk some wine and ate, she re-treated briefly and returned, holding carefully in her hands a cylinder with double wooden handles, one on each side end. She nodded to the one-eyed pirate servant to move some of the food aside, thus making room in front of me. She came close and put the contraption on the emptied space. It was the first time that I was to such a close proximity with her. A very pleasant odor, undetected 'till now, came from her body. Not as strong as the one when we use olive oil to cover our bodies and then scrape it to clean the dirt off, but, as I said, very pleasant. On my inquiry, Theagenis told me it was a lotion made of rose pedals, honey and water. I asked him to tell her that I liked it. Theagenis translat-ed and she flashed her white set of teeth to me in an open smile, flattering her eyelids rapidly. He told me she was very happy to have pleased his guest, even in such a small way. I felt embarrassed again and started paying strict attention to only what her hands were doing. She unfolded the parchment, moving the handles she was holding in opposing direction from each-other. My eyes widened as I saw symbols marked on the material. Some looked like birds, some like human bodies, others zigzagged like snakes, while others had different shapes and directions, many enclosed in a short of a frame all around them, or just by themselves.

Theagenis seeing my amazement, explained that all these were telling a story. In this case, it was an account of the ship's present cargo, named by kind, volume and value. I am afraid I looked very stupid as I asked him how he could tell. He couldn't, but she did. Not only she could tell, she was the one who had these marks made on papyros, for that is what the material she marked the marks was on! I touched it. Though somewhat drier than the fresh leaves of plant, I could tell it was made from one and flexible enough to be rolled, each piece of it connected to the next, somehow, making the whole length and width of the opened cylinder, ending-up on the two handles. I asked if she could tell what was marked. To Theagenis' request, she picked-up this papyros and started telling, in her lan-guage, eyes darting from sign to sign to picture. I couldn't make out if she started from left, right, up or down! I know from legends told, that Mikyneans used to have something like it, reading it from left to right, then right to left and calling it letters and words. That art is lost for many generations now.

Maybe what Theagenis says about Ionians in Asia, is true then. Of this type presented here, I know nothing at all. Paying attention to her sounds, I made sure I marked in my mind some I could retain easily and tried to place their images in their rightful place within the text before me. Then, I asked if she could repeat all over again. When she did, she voiced the exact same sounds I marked in my mind -at least as far as I could tell.

Theagenis told me that, among other things, she was his record-keeper when dealing with his Egypt-ian affairs and, yes, he could trust her. Besides, where would she go? She was given to him for life and, even if she wanted to leave him, she had no kin left nor could she return to Egyptos, on account of the Farao's orders! He treated her like one of his own kin and she was indebted no less. I was shocked to see that a woman was in power to do a job we could trust to males with excellent memories only, after testing their integrity for a long time before making it an official position.

We continued eating and drinking for a while, each in his thoughts. Finishing the meal, fruits were presented to wash the mouth with their freshness. Among these fruits, some small, dark brown ones, very sweet, with double pits at their center. I was told their name: dates. They come from trees which grow in Egyptos and other Asiatic warm countries, sometimes right in the middle of a desert! I won-dered if that was the sweet fruit of the Lotofagi, which caused Odysseas' comrades to forget their mission. Theagenis stated that Omiros was a poet who knew much more than mere mortals like us, but even he had not specify what kind of fruit and cause of forgetfulness and death Odysseas' com-panions tasted. The evening had progressed into late night and, not wanting to be judged as an ad-vantage taker of hospitality, I begged to be excused and I invited my host to visit me at my household the next day, after the market closing. He accepted and promised a second surprise for me.

My walk back to my estate and household was uneventful, being short in distance and having the town well guarded by all entrances and exits of the walls. My way home was also well lit by my two servants holding their torches high, one ahead, the other just behind me.

I had a nice sleep that night, in spite the quantity of the good Kypriot wine consumed. The next day in the morning, after the performances devoted to gods and Estia, the household deity, I poured some oil mixed with wine on the ground by my garden altar, in memory of my ancestors and the under-ground gods. Next, I had some figs, nuts and honey for breakfast, washing it all down with sour goat's milk. I was ready for the day. I got dressed-up with the help of one young servant and went to the Agora for the daily business. There, I met Apellas, the wine merchant from Kyrros, the Vottiaean town by the hills of mount Paikos and by the banks of Lydias river. I know he can get me the best wine of Makedonia, from the lands of the Eordeans or the Imathians, the Vottiaeans, even the Pelag-onians. He agreed to sent to my household some pythos jars, in exchange of my services on a deal with the tanner Leonatos, son of Sosos, the Kristonian. I know Leonatos personally, so I agreed to mediate. As I reached the Agora proper, I met with the heads of prominent families, as we had to dis-cuss the pros and cons of an Athinian delegation, promising us earthenware from Attiki, on better terms than the Korinthians had to offer. We decided to grant them the deal but keep the Korinthian delegation also happy, by ordering bigger quantities of their delicious sun-dried grapes. Both trans-actions would be serviced by ships from the island of Evia, in exchange of leather goods (of which we had a surplus). The day promised to be loaded with events and decisions, for we got word that a mix of delegates from Amydon and Vottiaeans had just arrived on urgent matters. I sent word to my es-tate to expect me late but have everything ready for my bath, cause I had in mind not to miss my din-ner with Theagenis and his associate, no matter what!

Time was precious, the coming of the delegates urgent, so we received them at once. They informed us that their people were in dire need of new homes to settle, on account of a big invasion from Peo-nia and the Maidi. If we could grand them the space to rebuild, they were ready to move-in en masse and become our allies and defenders, in case of any further Peonian pressure toward the peninsula. We did hear what had taken place in early summer at the plain of Amydon and we had our anxieties on this late Peonian attack, as it did not look like the usual raid and go affair. Our bet was to use the time, since fall and winter were not far off and that would (and should) be enough to have us fully prepared, in case nothing else would stop the intruders from marching against us. We had already met with delegations from Pallini, Akti, Krousis and Rahelous, forming a 'do or die' alliance. We felt very sorry for the fate of the Amydonians and Vottiaeans. If we could not accommodate them, the winter would (most definitely) be a hasher foe to them than the Peones and Maidi!

We asked them to retire and be taken care of, until we would discuss the need of a fast and fair solution to the problem ahead. I ordered some of our minor notables to accommodate the delegation and the rest of our clan heads and myself, got to work at once. There was not much of a debate. Their problem would soon be ours, if steps were not taken for its remedy. I sent word to the upper parts of our peninsula, with fast riders, to the clan heads there. They were to receive the refugees with kind-ness. Amydonians were to settle from the foothills of Ypsizon mountain and the lakes Koronia and Volvi by mount Kissos of the Anthemountians, up to the lands of the Kristonians, by the mountains of Vertiskos and Kerdilion. As for the Vottiaeans, they were to settle below the Amydonians, from Ypsizon and Holomon mountains, skirting the Rahelous and Krousis lands to their sunset, all the way to the bay where Strymon river comes to rest at the seashore, as neither we or the people of Akti use these areas extensively. I also sent a word to their king and notables about it, as we have excellent rapport with them, on account of our past connections.

Next, I called the refugee delegates back and informed them of our decision. I have never witnessed in my life (before or after), such a grateful address by anyone! Their new homes was approved to be called Mygdonia and Vottiki, in memory of their old countries. They were given fresh rides and an escort, to rapidly go and inform their kings and compatriots for their impending exodus to their new homes!

By the time we took care of this emergency, the hour had gone late into the day, pass the mid time. I asked to be excused and left our notables to work out the details on any further deliberations, leaving Tyrrimas, son of Kissios, whom I trust, to keep an eye on any other minor affairs. You see, the fact that I am their king, does not mean that I can come and go as I please all the time. That, goes with the Thrakian kings and others. Here in Sythonia, to remain king, means making sure none of the elders and notables are to be displeased. One always must consult them, give them gifts to show their favor is noted and appreciated, ask their permission for some things, lead them bravely into war (when one comes at the doorstep) and always, always come-up with a decision which would be acceptable by the majority, if not by all!

Not that I am disallowed to take action when something needs speedy response, but I better have that action bring the right result! One too many side steps and any of those notables is capable of moving against me, taking the will of the rest by his side. Just counting on my immediate dependents and household relatives and servants for help, I am really nothing much, regardless the faith and tenacity of my men in my person!

One last thing I had to do before I retired to keep my promise to Theagenis, was to propose and assign a leader for the fair allocation and distribution of the promised lands, so no one in our clan would hold grouch and claim injustice. For that job, I proposed Selefkos, son of Androklis, a notable from the town of Siggos. He accepted. Fearing favors granted to him later for a job well done, Alitas, son of Iason, lord of lands with olive trees at the slopes of mount Itamos, also asked to share in parti-cipation of the task. I know the two of them, Selefkos and Alitas, are not the best of friends and there is always friction among them. Yet, I saw the need of playing politics in this case and, to keep things as evenly as possible, I agreed and so did the majority of the notables. The task was a big one and a man could need help. Being busy, could keep them both happy. Especially Alitas, whom I did not trust as a very strong-headed person, but I respected his father. Lastly, at the Agora's public Altar, we had a sacrifice performed by me, honoring all the gods and Posidonas' priest saw the omens being favorable. I then left, heading for my estate and household, to see things for my guest this evening were done properly. By necessity and on a second thought, I made arrangements to invite Alitas' father, Iason, along with a couple of other friends of his, but of a lower rank, so the mixed company would give the appearance I wanted. Elevate Iason in favor before a guest, placate Iason's depend-ents friends, while you oblige them to feel they owe you now a favor or two. Arriving at my house I made sure all accommodations would be as perfect as possible, when my guests arrived.

I was more interested on Theagenis and his friend and associate he brought along (his second sur-prise to me) than the rest of the guests, So, when the dinner finished along with the day's events talk, after a bard sang reciting the heroes deeds from Omiros' Iliad, I begged Theagenis to stay longer and overnight, if need be, so we could have peace and time to talk our kind of affairs. He and his friend accepted. I saw the others to the door as time came for them to leave, with a good word and a present for their honoring my house with their presence and returned to the room, eager to learn more.

I found out that Theagenis' associate was a Vavylonian subject but not of Vavylonian blood. His name, Nataniyel (I had some difficulty catching the exact sound of pronouncing it) ben Yousef. Ben meaning something like: the son of, as with us, when we call someone Yparhos and add the ending idis for his son, hence, calling the youngster Yparhidis. Nataniyel's clan name was Yioudas (as close as I can come to it), while his tribe is called Hibrou and they are under the Assyrians and Vavylon-ians. The reason I had not meet him yesterday, was simply because he had gone to the town of Siggos, on a business pursuit. According to our geographical understanding here and the knowledge on tribal names, he is a Simitis, blood related to Egyptians or Haldeans, but a distant relation as such, lost in time. Nonetheless, theirs is a closer relation than our blood relation with the Illyres, or even the Leleges. Theagenis agreed with my opinion, while this Nataniyel just smiled. He later insisted that we are much less informed about tribes, than we think we are. His manners, I did observe during the dinner, were very polite and correct. Now with the three of us alone, he continued behaving the same way, but I could not help thinking that he had some arrogance hidden behind each statement he was making.

That bothered me a bit but I put it aside, because, as he hails from those parts, he probably knows best about his people and, maybe, those are their manners. He told me he was born in Vavylon city, a wonder of construction and aesthetics, but his line was full-blooded Hibrou, from the land of Israyel.

His parents became Assyrian slaves, as did all other people who were defeated by that tribe from Ni-neveh. He had managed to work for his freedom and buy his rights out. He left Vavylon some years ago, a young boy, looking for better prospects in life and became a merchant. He and Theagenis had met at Sidon, the Finikian city of commerce and became partners. He could speak (as I discovered at once) our own language, although with a heavy Arkado-Kyprian accent (I thought), heavier than Theagenis' who had shed it somewhat, after so many years dealing with us. Nataniyel could also speak fluent Vavylonian and Assyrian, not counting his own tribal language. He was who kept the records of the business in those languages, making things easier in dealing, than Theagenis' meager knowledge would. Their profit had increased since the two met and that was what Nataniyel was in for! He said he did hope to start his own business soon, unless Theagenis would come up with some better incentives for him and their partnership.

As Nataniyel was saying these words, I noticed Theagenis' face saddened and I realized that their ways would soon part. Meantime I was completing my observation on this stranger, as I had start from the moment he had shown at my doorstep. He was rather short and dark-skinned, by our own standards. Darker than a Kritan but lighter than the Egyptian girl of yesterday. Slim in stature, he had a long, curled beard, Assyrian (as Theagenis said) fashion. His long, equally curled hair were dark brown and kept clean. His nose formed a long, sharp curve, being leaner than the Egyptian's. He had rather thin lips, which covered a good set of teeth. The most prominent feature of his, were his eyes. Darker than his dark brown hair (almost black) and clear, would not stay long in one object alone. They would shift, from this to that, judging, pricing. The only time those eyes got dreamy and lost in the steadiness of a faraway picture, was the times he talked about his people's tribulations, his parents and his country. His long fingered hands were soft, indication of a man not used to manually earning a living, nor a warrior. Measured body movements, showed me his closeness to himself and an assurance that he was always right before he'd act or state something. That, with my previous observation of some arrogance in him, bothered me some more. For I know for sure, nobody is right or perfect all the time. Why, even the gods are known to make mistakes some times.

By my saying so on one occasion, he simply smiled his 'I know better' smile. I thought it was as open a contempt, as his guest status would allow! Theagenis remarked about that smile, equally upset as I.

Nataniyel answered that, according to his beliefs on deity, it was natural to smile at our childish con-cepts of God. He emphasized the word god, like there was no (conceivably) other deities but one! He re-enforced his emphasis by saying, straight forward, that our gods were false ones. The Vavylonian, Assyrian, Finikian and Egyptian ones, being as false as the Olympians -he concluded, as a matter of fact!

I really felt offended by that remark but, raised by advocating one should speak one's own mind freely and straight forward, I let it pass by, bringing in mind also that I was the host. I just could not help in raising an eyebrow, to show my displeasure. Theagenis argued in my stead, letting me realize this was not their first time exchanging words on the subject. My interest to see the outcome kept me quiet and attentive.

Nataniyel stated, as a matter of fact, that there is only one God, who's holy name is Yahveh (here came again my feeling of his contempt toward us)! Theagenis refused to give-in, starting a heated debate. I soon came to the conclusion that Nataniyel had to be a true believer of his preaching and a rather fanatic one. It was very interesting to be observant of such passionate debate. I still did not like Nataniyel's high-handed approach. Every one is better than others at one point, so are the gods -in their domains- with one overseer, Dias. How could one god, see everything, be everywhere, hear it all, know it all (all at the same time!), act in all at once, was beyond my understanding, let alone my acceptance! I kept my peace staying out of their debate, as my place required. I intruded only here and there, to calm things down with some offer of sweets and wine, or posting a question. Did his tribe have Oracles like ours in Dodona, Delfi and Dilos? No, that was not Yahveh's need! He could and would speak to special people too, but in a totally different manner! He could present Himself anywhere and his special people were called guides (like our prophets and seers?) and, through them, Yahveh could lead His people through the right path! In the end, Yahveh would send to the land of Israyel and His Hibrou followers a very special guide, the Messayia (?), who would elevate the Israyel Tribe above all tribes and nations! Now that, I thought, is a dream!

Nataniyel proceeded then, telling us a story of one great guide, not the so-called Messayia, named Moshe, who passed all kinds of tests in proving his faith to Yahveh and finally led Nataniyel's ances-tors out of the Egyptian bondage, humbling the mighty Farao single-handedly, performing all kinds of miracles! Moshe, with help and guidance from Yahveh, ridiculed the Farao, bringing pestilence on the Egyptians, parting the sea to let the Hibrou pass through, fed the multitude in the desert and brought Yahveh's commands from the tip of a high mountain! Yahveh called this Moshe to heaven but did not let Israyel unprotected. Another leader, Yeshoua(?) took charge and led the faithful to the promised land of Khanaan(?), after tumbling the high walls of Yiericho(?) with a simple blast of the trumpets mind you!

Now, I had to admit, that was a fascinating story, a rival to any of Aesopos' myths. It took all night telling it, listening and debating it but, as far as I was concerned, it was just that, a very good story. Theagenis stated the same opinion also, adding that Nataniyel's such nonsense was the only cause of their arguments. Nataniyel raised his shoulders in indifference to our opinion and (clearly now) took the posture of one who knows best, one who faces children with no concept of grown-up people's business. I felt the blood rushing to my head but I stop short of giving him a lesson, finding such an act beneath my own station. I did not protest or tried to ridicule Nataniyel. Theagenis did that for both of us.

We broke-up just before sunrise and I did not insist that they should share breakfast with me. To be frank, I was pissed. Not at Theagenis, I had asked of him for proof and proof he brought to me. I was pissed off by the high-handed mannerism of Nataniyel, though (I admit it) I felt admiration on his persistence to his convictions. He should demonstrate that, in a more refined manner though. Of course, him being a barbarian and a liberated slave, manners are something he didn't grow-up with.

I did not meet with Theagenis that day again, nor that evening. I was too busy taking care of my own urgent affairs. The following morning, I found out they had set sail already and a jar of good Kypriot wine was left for me, token of Theagenis' thanks for my hospitality.

I often think of them since, them and the Egyptian girl. My anger about Nataniyel's ill manners is gone. I pray to the gods to keep them all safe and prosperous, whether they believe in all, one, or none. I do hope and expect Theagenis to return soon again, for more trade and stories to tell of strange people..."

"The relocation of the refugees from Amydon took great effort, since they came to us with whatever each one could carry, no tools, no provisions and with the winter fast approaching. We helped them to build new homes in the area by the lakes we now call Mygdonia and their new principal town, which they named Terpylos, on account of its four main wall gates. The ones from Vottiaea were busy building their own between mounts of Kissos and Ypsizon and the bay above Akti. Food was in short supply, although we had excellent harvest. Many of their young, their old or infirm, died through the winter.

My own difficulties were great also. Many of my people felt cheated because they had to share the produce with the newcomers. People started talking behind my back. I made a quick move, remind-ing them that all which took place, did so under the original agreement and consent of theirs, in help-ing relative kin-blood in an hour of need. Would they like, I asked, to be treated badly had they have to cope with such a problem, as refugees themselves? If they had to relocate to a new land, wouldn't they expect any possible help from the grantors of such land?

Many saw reason and supported me. Some others were brought to agreement after promises of good returns were made, during times the new settlers would have to compensate us, as they recover-ed enough and in near future. Yet, there were many who turned against me openly. First and fore-most, Alitas, son of Iason. Aside from their lands by mountain Itamos, they used to have land and serfs where the Vottiaeans now hold and call Vottiki. Although he had agree to the deal and those parcels of his land were allocated to refugees by lot in the presence of all, he reneged and rose to open rebellion! I had to fight, in order to hold my own.

If that was not enough, traders from the island of Evia demanded their share of merchandise ex-change and bartering, not willing to wait until things got better. I sent envoys to them, twice. Both times they rejected my overtures. I had to weather it out as best I could. It was late spring, a year after I last saw Theagenis, the year of all Ellenic games and athletics about to happen in Elis. I was still chasing Alitas around in hope of bringing his revolt to an end, forcing him into a battle, as a last resort. Then I received word that a fleet of war ships came from Halkis, Evia's major city, placing Toroni under siege, as their payment for goods received by us, had not been paid. Technically, they were not fighting us, as a general truce had been declared, on account of the games. But my town was blockaded, its people soon to succumb because of starvation. I had no choice but to abandon my chase of Alitas and come to the town's rescue -if I could accomplish it.

As I approached with my army, I found the surrounding area desolated. Toronians had left their farms for their safety in the town and the Halkidians had taken all there was, for their use, burning what they couldn't take. Turning to Ellanodikes in far-off Elis for justice, was out of question, there was no time! A small consolation of sorts was the destruction of Iason's properties and olive groves by mount Itamos. That meant Alitas would soon be out of funds for his revolt. It also meant less produce the coming season, hence more famine. I hurried to rescue my town, with plenty of anger in my heart.

The Halkidians never expected me to arrive so speedily and they were caught by surprise. We run first to their ships and burned them all, except five, which we rowed to the secret gulf, for our own use. Not having a place to go and now surrounded by us, the Halkidian force came to me for terms of surrender. Not one was killed. Instead, they were all put under arrest, to be sold at the slave markets after the truce was over, or to be exchanged for a hefty price. Such price could eliminate our debt to them, plus, I could now go and finish my job with Alitas, when the truce would come to its end.

But first, I went to meet the Halkidian chief of their expeditionary force, now captive. I discovered, through him, that things could not be so easy after all. He informed me that another fleet from Eret-ria, another major city of Evia, would soon be on its way, after the games were over. Soon, he boast-ed, the captives would turn to captors! For, he was sure, Halkis would also send new force to rescue their compatriots. I felt my spirits reaching a very low point. How could I possibly put-up against three fronts?

Then, I explained to him my difficulties and their cause, because he saw me in such distress, he was moved and felt compelled to ask. He listened without interruption. When I finished, he told me he understood my dilemma, because the whole island of Evia was experiencing hard times. All Halkis and Eretria wanted, was to be compensated, somehow, on what the deal was with our original trade.

After that, they would leave me about my business! If not, they had to come and take by force, or they would face famine and revolts back home too. These words depressed me even more and I did not sleep all night, thinking to find a way to solve this problem.

Early the next morning I offered wine and olive oil to god Posidonas, promising better offer next time, since everything was now so scarce. Then, the idea hit me! I only wished Nataniyel to be here,

For the idea was given to me by god Posidonas to whom I made the offer and goddess Athina who cleared my head! His Yahveh was far and indifferent, not the ever-caring and all-knowing god!

I went to talk with the Halkidian chief. I had him sit next to me, like a guest rather than a captive and I came straight to the point. I recapped the reasons and obvious circumstances which prevented me in keeping our end of the deal for the time being. I emphasized their own grim situation, as well as Eretria's. If they would insist on taking by force what was due to them (I never denied we had to pay our debt), a long war would ensue. That would bring more victims and hardship to all concern-ed. Further, it could probably cost me my kingship and I knew of no other who would be willing to come to an understanding in solving the problem. And a solution I did have, if both Halkis and Eret-ria were willing to listen and act accordingly.

He looked at me in all seriousness and asked to hear what I had to propose. I am certain, he was thinking I may have had second thoughts and I was afraid of their combined strength and I was trying to buy time. I pointed to him that, by holding them in chains, I had the upper hand and the supposed alliance between the two Evian city-states was not as secured a fact, judging from the enmity between in other matters. He understood my motives of offering a solution was not fear then, but a true effort to avoid any further bloodshed, as well as stability for future relations.

I proceeded with my plan, as I realized now that I had all his attention and good will. Halkis and Eretria, I said, had a very big surplus of mouths to feed, while produce was at low ebb, with no ap-parent means of relief. We had similar problems, due to events out of our control. What we had and they didn't, was space. We couldn't pay but we had plenty of open land to be cleared, inhabited and worked-on, for good living. What about this kind of exchange? What if we would provide land to the willing Eretrians and Halkidians? Their surplus numbers were free to come and settle. The debt paid in kind, would ease tensions and bring (I hoped) closer trading, along with numbers to resist further incursions from the barbarians above!

He liked my idea of solving the problem the way I proposed. Upon his promise to act in good faith and with the rest of the prisoners at my disposal, we agreed to have him go as my ambassador of good will and secure the co-operation of Halkis and Eretria. I set one of the captured ships (manned by a crew of my men) to sail, sending him to find the Eretrian fleet. He had to convince the archons of both city-states of my good intentions and return with their answer as soon as possible. That done, I calmed the anxiety of my Elders and clan chiefs, stating the Eretrians were still far away, waiting for the truce of the games to expire, before moving against us. Then, I returned to my task of punish-ing Alitas and his followers.

I did not have to chase and war against them. Being isolated up in the mountains of Ypsizon and Holomon, not supported and sustained by the newly established settlements of Vottiaeans there, he came to me begging for pardon. I turned him to the judgment of the Elders. They found him guilty and he was executed. His followers were sent to start clearing space for the settlers to come, with a promise of being absolved, after proof of good conduct. Meantime I sent word to Pallini and its king Dimitrios, about my deal with the Halkidian chief. Dimitrios being under our leadership since Pto-lemeos' days, agreed readily. All we had to do now, was to wait and see…

As it happened, Timoklis, the Halkidian chief, met the Eretrian fleet ready to sail, the games now finished and the truce at its end. In spite of the two clans' mistrust for each-other, both city-states held common council and accepted my idea. They sent word to me in his person, that both cities were about to send many families to settle in areas we would assign and they would approve. I went to work at once. Having with me king Dimitrios and the second-in-command of the Halkidian prisoners (Timoklis being in charge of returning the others to their city), a man named Irineos son of Diomidis, we started surveying the countryside. Allotments were assigned in the areas above Pallini and Sytho-nia, between Krousis and the new establishments of Vottiki. These areas have plenty of everything! There is game, woods, pastures and access to the sea. Most of all, they are thinly populated by either clans, us and the Pallinians. Irineos was very pleased and in full agreement of these allocations.

I manned another ship and sent him to bring and guide the new arrivals. It was done speedily. By the way, these new families of settlers, call themselves apiki/colonists and their allotments apikies/col-onies. Since most came from the city-state of Halkis, they named their new homeland Halkidiki. A few of them, mostly Eretrians, even got permission to go and, together with Vottiaeans from last year, built the town of Stagiros or Stagira. Even Toroni itself let some settle among us! Another site is Potidea, at the narrow neck of Pallini. Some, claiming lost in a storm, settled in Mendi, across the gulf of Therma, to the annoyance of Pieria and Makedonia."

"Many years have passed since then. I am not the king anymore. My son, Leonnatos reigned in my place, for ten and five years. That is until two years ago, when he got killed in a battle against these very Halkidians we gave land and means to make a living! My grand son, Asteropos is now king of Sythonia and the kingdom confined within the reaches of this middle peninsula. But I am happy, for we are at peace and we mind our own. I realized too late, you see, that my allowance of space to Hal-kidians, Eretrians and, later, Korinthians, brought us waves of new settlers, who never satisfied them-selves with what they were given. If they had united with us, as originally was proposed and agreed, I would have really been happy and our state one of the strongest in Ellas. It worked the other way around. As soon as they saw they could stand on their own, they ignored us and developed their own ties and policies, mostly with our enemies, ignoring their own mother cities as well. But, what is done, is done. Maybe my pride of bringing initial peace, offended the gods… No sense crying now over spilt milk.

As for Theagenis, I heard about his horrible end, from none other but Nessouna. She came to me one day, about seven years after the last time I saw Theagenis and met her. She had paid, she said, her way here, first to a vessel from Alikarnasos, a Dorian city by the south-west tip of Asia we call Near and others call Minor, to the island of Dilos. There, she stayed in service of the sun-god Apollon, for almost a year, earning her next passage to Limnos and Tenedos, on a Rodian ship. Her next stop was at Vyzantion, a Megarian apikia/colony. Once the Rodian ship had to continue toward Kolhis, after crossing the Propontis straits onto Efxinos Pontos, she stayed at Vyzantion until its return, except if she'd find another vessel sailing toward us here. Finally, Haris, an Athinian captain, took pity on her and brought her to Thasos. By then, she had spend another year plus two full moon changes in trans-it. At last, a local fisherman from Thasos, offered to bring her here, stopping first at Neapolis, on the Idonian country.

All this adventure, she claimed, because Theagenis had offended the gods and this is how it happen-ed: 'Nataniyel wanted to leave Theagenis, as soon as we arrived in Kypros.' She started. 'He stayed a little longer, not so much because of Theagenis' entreaties, but because the next stop would be Sidon, the Finikian city-port, close to Nataniyel's ancestral land. He had learn, in Kypros, that many of his tribe had left the bondage of Assyria secretly, returning to ancestral hearths. He now wanted to go and find his roots. Theagenis understood all these -to a point. He wanted Nataniyel to there, but just as a pilgrimage. Like you go to Dodona or Delfi and we, Egyptians, go to the oasis of Ammun, for the Oracle, to learn about our fate. Then, he wanted Nataniyel to return! Of course, Nataniyel would not have any of such a deal! He wanted to go and reside in the city of his ancestors, one called Yierousha-lem (or something to that nature).

Nataniyel was willing to continue business with Theagenis, only through a common mediator in Sidon or Tyros.

When Theagenis, desperate, threatened to alert the Assyrian magistrates, Nataniyel laughed at his face. The Assyrians, he said, had their own trouble against the Vavylonians, who were winning the war. What could they do for a lone fugitive from the tribe of Yioudas, lost in the multitude of tribes?

Theagenis then thought of a plan. He pretended he went along with Nataniyel's wishes and, also, that he started believing at no other god except that Yahveh. To prove it, he even offered a sacrifice in one of the temples Nataniyel's compatriots have in their quarter within the town of Kytion. In spite of that show of faith, Nataniyel was gone in four days after we reached Sidon, taking with him all the wages owed to him. Theagenis got really upset. He spent days looking high and low within and out of the city. He gave-up when he found that it was impossible to learn Nataniyel's where-about. He load-ed the ship with a cargo of spices, with destination the Rodian city of Ialyssos. Making a landing at Kytion again, added copper and iron to his cargo, along with Kypriot wine from Pafos, not heeding to the warning of that one-eyed pirate-mate of his, Mahas, for overloading. In his anger and hurry to set sail, he omitted offerings to Posidonas and the other gods. We made it up to the cape of Patara, by the mouth of river Xanthos, where bad weather caught-up with us. We made offers to the gods then, to no avail. They were angry in the first place for sacrificing to Yahveh, then, leaving Sidon without offering them their due.

Before the ship sank, Theagenis, sensing his end near, made me swear in the name of Isis, Ammun and Dias, that I'd come to you, if I was to live, under your protection. As you see, I have! Through my time of travel to come here, I learned your language better than when with him, so as to petition my case and tell you the story, the way you would understand me best. Besides, it's impossible to goback to Egyptos. I know not if I still have family there and, the Farao's order (either dead or alive) is good for ever! I was sent away from country and kin, never to return.'

That was her story and the fate of my friend Theagenis. I honored his wish and kept her within my household. When my own wife could bear me no more children, Nessouna was good to give me an-other two sons and three daughters. We all know they're bastard children, but they're good, re-spected, respectful and mine! I made sure they've got enough of their own, though none can claim status or high placement in our kingdom. Their children, my grand children, are numerous and well recognized by all. They do have darker skin, dark-brown eyes, a little wider noses and, long, curly hair. All, but one. Young Lampos has everything they do, except two things: he inherited my nose and, more important, my blue eyes in a cloud-white setting! He is the reason you, the visitor, can now read these events of the past, as he learned how to etch on skin, the signs you perhaps can read or have them read to you aloud!..."

> "If modern Ellines believed less the 'sincerity'
> and 'interest' of foreigners but more in their
> own abilities, then, even the ancient ones
> would come back from their graves to admire
> us!"

Yiorgos I. Rados, Peloponnisian Ellinas, freedom fighter, Balkan Wars

III

Damasj was seated on a rock outcrop at the foothills of mountain Mezap (Messapion in Makedoni-an). His herd of cattle was grazing down the slope by the Axios river valley which opens up becom-ing the wide Makedonian plain, further toward the sea. His own herdsmen were keeping a keen eye on the herd and could be seen riding every-so-often, bringing back a stray calf or a bull which dared to linger away, because of play or because a bunch of flies had been too annoying for the animal.

Damasj had taken off away from the others, in need to collect his thoughts and come to a very im-portant decision. Cattlehands not being particularly famous for their intellect, with a main concern on their food, women and wages, he kept an eye on them too, from above. He felt above them by far, not only because he owned the herd and had rights over the men (more so than on the animals) but mainly because of his responsibilities for the welfare of both. He tried to play his flute with a smile at the thought of his present location, above them, coinciding with his feelings for them, but he gave-up. The time was not proper for silly thinking.

Everyone in Vylazora knew that as long as a herder was doing his job properly was one to trust. Damasj was then the man to work for, the herder who took care-of to the very last need. Of course he was not alone in such a respect and status, he knew it. Although the majority of land was harsh and herds-owning clan heads in Vylazora and Shtobi were rather ill tempered, there were a few well placed land holders and cattle owners like him, much more refined than the brutes dwelling above Astivos river in Bargal or and further up, in Shkopi.

These very lords, these land holders had asked him to undertake a very serious and dangerous task. They came and asked him to lead them in rebellion against the upper Peonian lords, the ones dwell-ing in Bargal and Shkopi. This task did not only have hidden and serious implications in case of failure, it was also a subject of moral debate as well. True, all of the conspirators (including Damasj) had common blood with the clans of Pelagones, Orvyles, even Amydonians. But, they also had more common blood with the Peones above, as well as the Maidi and, in lesser degree, with the Dardanes. None of these conspirators could really claim a higher status or stronger ties with any other clan, all being of almost equal influence and power. Yet, they had chosen him to lead them in revolt.

There was something common in all of them, something calling for separation from the brutes and masters from above. But, what kind of separation were they looking for? Separate from whom and from what? As far back as oral tradition could carry, they all had been there, part of the nature, one with the mountains, their well-being coming from the river, the herds, the game and the looting from raids. There were no clear lines to be drawn between the conspirators and the lords of the north. The only clear thing all conspirators knew and felt was that of not really belonging, not really making it in the 'inner circle'. That feeling was because the lords of the north were looking down on them like lesser parts of the whole.

Oh, they were Peones themselves alright! The forests and the valleys were part of their being, the nourishment of their existence, all of them being born, grown and buried in the same fields and slopes of hunting and warring, for generations past and present. Damasj couldn't find any difference of them from the 'north' Peonians. They could easily be compared to the Dardanians, the Laeii, or to Maidi. Fierce in war, free in spirit, ready to pick-up and roam, ready to raid and plunder, able providers of their meager needs, hunters, herders, fishermen…

Yet, again, there were differences. Only the clans dwelling in these parts were willing to have more permanent settlements, domesticate not only the beasts of burden and war but, also, for the pleasure of one having one's own. For not wanting to depend on constant plunder -always being on the run- but with fields to toil at and gather fruits of labor and sweat! Damasj's own dwelling hut in Vylazora, could not compare to any in, say, Atalanti or Therma, but was more of a habitation than any in Bargal, Shkopi or Zaparja! Plunder, just for the sake of it, pillage -just to take things away, rape at the spur of the moment, were the things which did not set well any longer.

To be sure, they had their share of misdeeds a-plenty. Why, only during the last raid south, they fol-lowed Okse Darjag (the Makedonians called him Oxydarkis) in his venture. Granted, they'd done that because his power would not let them have an alternative -you were either on his side or you were dead! Then, once on the campaign, they had to kill or be killed. After the massacre at Stenae where Okse Darjag had been killed, Damasj and most of his neighboring clan-heads left the Amydo-nian territory (loot and all), glad that it was over and came back to their herds and plots. Not so for the north clans. Under the leadership of Lept Darjag (Leptodarkis in Makedonian) Peones and Maidi returned to Amydon and further south for more plunder.

Seeking revenge and looting for they considered the loss at Stenae unjust, they put to sword any-thing that would move! Unlucky Amydones who survived the first assault, had to emigrate further south, their homeland an open waste. On his return and loaded with loot, Lept Darjag punished Damasj and other land holders of Vylazora and Shtobi, for not assisting his cause. Shtobi had all its youth from ten springs and under taken hostages in Bargal and Zaparja, while Vylazora was burned to ashes. Many a notables were killed and Damasj, along with others, had to offer numbers of horses, sheep, goats and cattle, just to be left alive.

Lept Darjag/Leptodarkis, had a few turns of the moon-face left to live. During a drunkard's brawl, he accidentally fell on his own sword and died, the very night of his return to Bargal. The lords of the northern Peonian clans started fighting each-other for the succession, but none of them had enough followers to become the undisputed leader. Vylazora (its Peonian appellation sounding more like Viilaj-zoraj) was left aside, out of the fray. It gave time to have the town rebuilt. That was when the Peonians of its surrounding areas started saying it was time for them to have a leader of their own.

Damasj knew they would turn to blame him, if they were to be defeated and punished -again- by the north lords. So, when he was asked to lead, he asked for time to think first. As long as the lords were fighting each-other in the north, time he did have. As the motion started turning on its own wheels though, a leader would appear sooner or later. Then… then what? He did not have a desire in put-ting a claim on the overall leadership of Peonia as a whole, nor the power to do it. The clans of the area were not numerous enough, which meant he would have to ally with elements he despised -if he made the decision to gain the leadership of all. It meant that he soon would have to treat his kin and neighbors like a Lept Darajg, out of the necessity of self preservation. Leadership of all Peonia was out of question then, because he knew he could not, would not, get that high to find himself so low…

A solution was needed soon, as was the necessary time to implement it. Maybe he could get help from the Pelagones, the Almopes or both? Maybe… He didn't think such an alliance would bring much of a result, for even they had ask for help from clans as far south as Orestis, Eordea, Elimiotis and Thessalia. He certainly could not ask them to help. As for the Amydonians and Vottiaeans, they would be more than happy seeing Peones bleeding, fighting one-another. And who could blame them?

He decided he would go down to where the herd was, take a calf and offer sacrifice to the gods. But which gods? The local Kavyrej of the Parorvyles, seemed good enough, protecting that mountainous clan from every calamity -thus far. The same deities were called Kavyres by the Makedonians and they led them to victories over Peonia… So be it then, the gods Kavyres could be on his side too! He got up, stretched his hands and body, observing the distant Vardarj/Vartharios river merge with the waters of Aksjo/Axios, the sun reflecting its rays on both. He breathed deeply the fresh mountain air. His herders, below, had gather the herd up-close, making ready for the mid-day meal. Damasj started climbing-down like a goat…

The small, dusty, weary, riding band of men, was very happy to see smoke rising at a near distance. They were riding for days now, as other bands like them, bringing an urgent message to towns and to land holders. Oh, they'd stop here and there, in towns and hamlets, delivering the message and have some food and drink given to them, mostly out of fear. Most of the area in these parts seemed to be on the poor side though, hamlets far-apart and mostly burned-out in recent time. No cooking fires in many places, the food consisting of fresh greens, nuts and wild honey. As for drinks, mostly water or a scarce goatskin with some fermented, curdled milk. Whom ever else they encountered, were nomad groups who'd rather hide than risk an uncertain meeting.

The riders were warning the clans they could locate and meet, that the Dardanes were coming en masse and help was needed to oppose them, if Peonia was to remain a power worth its name! Any warring clan had to stop its quarrel with any other and rush to the aid of their lord, Tiraj! The smoke they could see at a distance meant there was someone there, hopefully a hamlet, which, in turn, meant food and drink. They were disappointed to see there was but a herd and its herdsmen were more, in numbers, and well armed. That would require asking, not taken food and hospitality. Whatever the response, it would be freely given, without fear or second thoughts. One rider of the band rode ahead, to see what kind of arrangements could be made.

Damasj held his men at ready, as the on-coming rider approached. Greetings were exchanged and the request for hospitality accepted. On inquiry of the band's presence in the area, a detailed explan-ation was given, with a promise of further explanations on any questions asked, during the meal. Damasj's interest grew immensely as these words were exchanged and promised a good meal and a long rest before departure to their next destination.

As the rider went back to his comrades to inform that food was available, Damasj sent two of his men through the trees and high shrub, to the nearest clan heads, to ask them come at all speed that evening in Vylazora. They were to be told of important news and the decisions to be made, based on these news, at once! In turn, these clan heads were to send speedy riders of their own, inviting other clan heads from further away. Meantime, the riding party of messengers from Tiraj had approached and more formal greetings were exchanged, along with oaths of respect on the given hospitality, as well as on receiving it.

During the meal, information and answers to questions were given on the current events and, as some of the nearest clan heads preferred to come, instead of meeting in Vylazora later, the whole story was repeated several times. In the end, Damasj handed a big flask of sour milk to the riders, stating that (regretfully) there were no accommodations available for the night. He suggested they should return speedily to their lord, Tiraj, for every available warrior was surely needed by him, to repulse or delay the enemy. He, on the other hand, would pass the emergency call to the rest of the clan heads, collecting every available warrior and come to aid Tiraj. They should be going soon, no need for delaying further...

They parted, the band riding northward. Damasj left adequate number of men to lead the herd back, sent one good rider to keep an eye and make sure the band was truly riding north and, taking the clan heads present, he rode in all speed to Vylazora. He sent heralds around town, asking the locals to the meeting, the moment the clan heads located further away, would appear. He, then, wait-ed at his own front door. Soon, his household was filled with people, from the inner court, all the way to the front, by the wall. Looking at their anxiety, he made-up his mind. With a bit of good timing and some luck, things could work-out after all.

He rose and, as quietness fell over, he told the story in favor of the ones who came late and didn't have time to listen to facts, mixed with rumors from active minds who thought they knew it all. When he finished, opinions were given and taken, under oath that nobody would be held responsible of where he stood or on what he said, until decision was made by the majority, as to what action should be taken. Every one, from the important ones before the open fire of the inner yard to the last soul struggling to hear, by the edge of the wall, took the oath. There would be no holding back, no change of heart, under penalty of death, including the whole household of any offender! They had to come to a decision as a whole and that was how it would be kept, excepting none. Conversation with its pros and cons lasted until the late hours of the night.

When a decision was finally made, Damasj stood up. He walked about ten paces away from the circle, toward the dimming fire and made his move. Once he was to lead them, once the whole re-sponsibility would be sitting square on his shoulders, he asked that he, his family and property, would be inviolable from this moment-on, until fortune would lead them to success or demise. Be-coming their leader, was prize enough on his head, as the north would soon find out and post it. He did not need any back-stubbing before the final result. A special oath was to be taken by all present and the ones who would join later. Then, whoever was ready should come and stand by him. Who was not, he had to leave at once, for -by the next day's end- he and his all would be considered as an enemy, to be put to death on sight, property taken over!

All the clan heads stood-up in unison, voicing approval. One by one, according to individual pres-tige and seniority, they started taking the required oath, before Damasj and the old soothsayer of the clan, Griba, the one-handed. Next, when all oaths were taken, as a first step of separating themselves from the north, Damasj told them that henceforth he was to be called and known as Damasias. There were immediate questions as to why. He looked at them for a long time, making them think he would not answer. Then, his answer came soft but with undisputed authority and finalization. He wanted to be known as such, for two reasons. First, in case of failure, the north would think they had to deal with a Makedonian who, somehow, managed to lure this clan into rebellion, therefore go after him only, leaving the rest of his family to survive, if possible. Second, he intended to bring the clan closer to the Makedonian elements in all aspects, when -as he hoped- fortune would crown their efforts of separation from the north. A good-sounding Ellenic name of a leader, should smooth future relations with the intended association with the Makedonian clans. This, he added, was the first and last ex-planation he would give, concerning his plans for their future. Had this idea come from a chief like the late Lept Darajg, would anyone have dared to ask any question? That was all then. They could try to find suitable names of their own, taking his lead. Now they ought to dismiss and start working for the cause. In spite of the late hour, runners were dispatched to the towns of Ashtuva (Astivos in Maked-onian) and Shtobi (Stovi). They were to receive the same oath in his name, from the elders in those towns, as well as any elders and clan heads who wanted to unite under Damasj/Damasias' banner. These clan heads were to prepare at once and come to join…

The next morning, other runners were sent to the mountainous lands of the Parorvylian clans, send-ing the message to be armed and ready, but remain idle for the time being. Damasias was assuring them that, if all went well, he had no intentions of becoming their overlord. Why else would he be asking them to arm? He might need their assistance at one time. If not, all was well. If he would lose, they would be excused by Tiraj, as taking precaution against any possible move against them. Either way, they now knew Damasias' plans and could act wisely. Did they want independence? It was to their advantage then to listen and have a chance of governing themselves free from Tiraj and the North…

Damasias did not stop there. He sent additional runners to the tribes of Aftariates and Laeii, the Thrakians, dwelling on and to the east of the mountains Orvylos and Rodopi, requesting them to give themselves a chance to rid the Peonian rule, by following his instructions. The same runners were to continue north, to the country of the Agrianes, at Zaparia. They were to offer the Agrianian king to ready himself, for advantage could be at arm's length, depending on the result of the Dardano/Peon-ian struggle. That was all he could do for the moment, aside of arming and preparing his own troops for the show-down. He and his clan received the levies from Astivos and Stovi and moved northward, following the Axios river flow, in reverse, slowly.

They arrived at the confluence of river Vardarios (named after the special type of poplars growing only there) and they camped. If the Dardanians were to win the battle against Tiraj and come forth, it was sure the Agrianians would fall into north Peonia for the final kill. That, in turn, would bring them against the Dardanes, who would not sport any share of the spoils. With a little bit of luck, Da-masias could then declare for himself (with support from the Aftariates), as the Parorvyles -he was sure- would come to his side, after his assurances on their freedom. In any event, none of them was fond of Peonian, Dardanian, or Agrianian 'protection'. Their commitment on his side, was more or less assured and, that done, there was no stepping back!

On the other hand, in case Tiraj would be the winner, Damasias hoped he would be too exhausted to go against three, potentially more, opponents. Still, everything was too risky and his calculations could become his death warrant, depending on actions, reactions or lack of, from all other elements in this game. For that exact reason, he ordered his scouts to spy on all directions and instructed them to inform him at once, of any and all observations on developments and troop moves they would detect.

On the third day after Damasias' troops had camped, word came from the scouts that Aftariates and Laeii had gathered on the foothills of mount Dynax but they were not moving further. Their placement looked purely defensive, as they had erected palisades in front of them, their horse on each side of their flanks. That was good news. They had committed themselves. Now Damasias would stand firm in place. An alarm, given in the late after mid-day hours, brought excitement in the camp.

Damasias ordered battle readiness. Everyone mounted his horse and took his hiding place in the near-by woods. There was some time of high anxiety, when a runner came to announce that the contingent coming their way was a friendly one, from the town of Doveros, the home of the Paror-vyles. A deep sigh of relief escaped Damasias' lips and rode to meet the newcomers. Their leading man, a fellow named Arpal, informed that more were coming from other parts of mountain Orvylos.

The clans of the region, he said, committed themselves to the last man, come what it may! Damasias blessed the gods and the Kavyres in his mind. His last offering to them didn't seem to have gone wasted. As more riders from other clans continued coming, they all camped hidden among the woods, waiting to hear from riders sent in secrecy, for the result of the impeding battle between Tiraj and the Dardanians.

The battle took place at Dnakz/Dynax, where the river valley narrows. Tiraj chosen battle ground was a wise location, but the Dardanes were, simply put, too many. In spite of inflicting heavy casu-alties on them, they were able to break through, while the Aftariates and Laeii were observing from the upper slopes, keeping their defensive positions. Tiraj run for his stronghold, Shkopi, through the mountain passes of Dynax and Messapion. The Dardanians followed in hot pursuit on his heels. Shkopi was taken and burned to the ground. Tiraj would have lost everything, if it wasn't for the unexpected help he received from the tribes of Argestei and Penestei. They feared that, if Peonia would become a Dardanian country or a vassal state, their turn was next. They sent their troops then and took the Dardanians by surprise falling on their flanks, as the latter were crossing the ford on Axios, chasing the retreating Tiraj.

United now, they pursued the Dardanians back to their lands and they all stopped, exhausted. A long truce was declared and Tiraj returned to rebuild his stronghold at Shkopi. He was fuming, finding that the southern region declared independence and almost had an apoplexy! He did not have the power for another war so soon. So, he forced some skirmishing against Damasias, with no result. Tiraj could not intimidate any one now. He could only lick his wounds and keep an eye on events which could give him an opportunity later. On the further north, Agrianes were harassing the Dard-anians now, so he was safe from that threat. All balance was brought to a standstill and he had to count his blessings. For now, he remained the undisputed chief of the parts of Peonia remaining under him. He knew, the clans and lords of those areas would soon be calling him a king, for they were even weaker coming out of this war. He started looking forward to adopting a proper appel-lation to his name. Darjag was a proper Peonian title, meaning head of a group. Two leaders before him had that distinction and, although much weaker now than they ever were, he liked it! It was a boost to his vanity…

Jubilation was in order at Vylazora, Astivos and Stovi, as well as at Doveros and the whole region. The mount Orvylos clans officially named their holds Parorvylia and kept the name as indicative of the birth of a new, united tribe. Aftariates and Laeii formed closer ties with the Agrianes and the Peones of Damasias. Tiraj had to lean on the support from Argestes and

Penestei. Enough to sustain his holds, but no threat to any. He decided to let the south chieftains run their affairs as they saw fit.

He hoped their eventual quarrels would bring them back under his fold.

Damasias was officially proclaimed king of the southern Peonia. Not wanting to have any connect-ions with the past, he rejected the Peonian Darjag. No pure Ellenic title was to be adopted either, for fear of insulting Makedonian sensibilities, along with those of the Amydonian former victims of Pe-onian cruelty. He made-up his mind to use the title of βασιλευς, which (although meaning king) did not match the original αναξ/anax. Vasilefs then, and the new name of south Peonia would be, from now-on, pronounced with a more Ellenic appellation, Paeonia! Adopting these mid ways, he had reason to believe his kingdom would get closer to Makedonia and Ellas, without offending old and hard-to-die beliefs and ideas of his clans -now a new tribe. He did not want to cross the lines of hard distinction as yet, if his plans were to succeed. He wanted success, more than he wanted any titles and honors to his person! He wanted Paeonia to become a land equal in progress of any of the southern kingdoms and city-states. Assimilation was the answer, but it had to be a slow progress!

He sent heralds to Amfaxitis, the former Amydonian lands, to Almopia, Eordea and Orestis. He even sent ones to Anthemous and Mygdonia, asking for trade, open roads, promising no further aggression -at least for as long as he was in charge of the South Paeonian clans. He asked that they could send him their commodities, their know-how men of skills, in exchange of leather, silver mined from his lands and free passage of the amber coming from the misty north, but most of all, he asked for recognition of an independent Paeonia and a peaceful co-existence.

Reluctantly, delegations from all these parts and men of trade started arriving in Vylazora, Stovi and Astivos. As relations started warming up, more ventured their passage and luck doing business with the barbarians of yester year. There were quarrels, to be sure. But those were minor incidents which take place anywhere, any time. The newly found room for exchange and profits from both sides, kept all differences easy to control and diffuse. Then, came the problem of accommodating all these newcomers. There was not enough room in those towns and, what there was, could not reach the southern standards by far. The new huts erected for multiple use, helped create greater confuse in all aspects, bringing fear of disease -most of all!

By orders of Damasias, within the next four years Astivos and Vylazora took a new look and shape. From mere small towns or large hamlets, the two became full sized towns, Stovi following close behind. Housing became more sophisticated as it became more numerous. Experts in building such structures from the Ellenic colonies in Anthemous marked wide spaces between structures, creating roads and room for healthier conditions. Timber was not in shortage, nor was stone. When clay was needed for bricks, clay beds in the vicinity provided the necessary material. New methods were intro-duced for brick manufacturing. A mixture of short-cut pieces of straw and clay formed the brick squares, left out in the sun to dry first, then used for wall building. Because of a severe earthquake on the third year since these activities started, a hired mason from Vottiaea and his apprentices, came to teach the skill of baking the bricks before using them, thus making them more durable.

The first permanently located temple, built of stone brought down from the mountain Messapion quarry and was worked on site by combined Paeonian and Anthemoundian masons. It was dedicated to the war god Aris, for without his favor, the Paeonian kingdom would still be living from raid to raid. The Kavyres, favored deities of Damasias were not forgotten. Within the same temple site, a big altar -made out of one single stone- was erected in their honor and decorated on all four sides by a Sythonian stonecutter. The temple itself was particularly pleasing to the eye, its front door having a three-cor-nered extension of a roof, supported by four columns fluted appropriately in Doric style and giving the whole structure an additional grandeur. Of course, it took longer to build by this newly introduced way than the old wood-mud-thatch way they knew. The language difference was another problem, producing equal delays in every-day dealings. Most of the locals used the harsh Peonian dialect, having trouble with Makedonian -let alone with south Ellenic visitors or instructors. Newly arriving merchants from Halkidiki, colonists from places like Eretria, Halkis, Aenia, Marillos and Stagiros/Stagira, increased the confusion.

Damasias knew that these merchants and masters of skills, were looking at his Paeonians with con-tempt and were laughing behind his back. He also knew he needed them, because they were intro-ducing these skills to his people, skills which brought profit and knowledge. He issued strict orders to all who dealt with the newcomers, to be taking no offence on comments made, in hope that the jokes made on his people would wear off -as time went by.

The tenth year of Damasias' elevation as the Paeonian Vasilefs, was marked with games and ban-quets. Invitations were extended all over the south and west. Many kings from the neighboring areas came over and not only for the festivities. Aside their personal participation in the games (king Aste-ropeos won three events himself!), treaties were made for further exchange of goods, military assist-ance -in case of need- and further craft imports. Special ceremonies for oaths of support and assist-ance were taken by Damasias and king Asteropeos of Sythonia, his son and heir Merops, king Kis-sios of Anthemous and king Dimitrios of Pallini. Also oaths were taken by representations of the citizens of Aenia in Rahelous, Spartolos of Krousis and Aloros of Pieria. As from the north, Tiraj was getting too old for trouble, the Dardanians had succession problems and only the Aftariates seemed to be the force one should keep an eye on...

At the end of that same year, Damasias received the happy news of having his first-born son. He had other children, but they were all daughters. Two out of his first wife, a Paeonian of good lineage, one from his second wife, an Amydonian. Now, his third wife, a girl from Anthemous, had finally given him a son! She was the daughter of Androklis, high priest of Therma and brother of king Kissios.

Damasias thought of giving the infant his -long deceased now- father's name at first. But the name would be a constant reminder of the old Peonian dialect and ways, plus, a very difficult one for the Anthemountian mother to pronounce. He loved his father but did not like the past. Damasias made-up his mind to name the infant a Makedonian name: Alketas. In order to appease his father's spirit, he first made offerings, asking forgiveness. Following his broader plan, he employed a couple of set-tlers from Gigonos, a town in Halkidiki, colony from the island of Evia. The wife of this couple was to help Damasias' wife, Gygea, as well as the other wives, in raising his children on a more Ellenic fashion. The husband was charged to teach Damasias' son -in time- a pure Ellenic dialect (Doric or I-onian did not matter) but, mostly, teach the child something called scripture. With that, the Gigonian claimed, young Alketas would grow to be a man further above the others, more than Damasias was or would ever be! For scripture was an invention of the Musae themselves, given to man for added wisdom! Damasias was far from being a fool and knew that wisdom combined with bravery, were the exact means of keeping the kingdom intact and independent. Bravery, he could install the kid with, by himself. Scripture was a totally different matter.

The following year proved that his own wisdom had been adequate, with the established alliances he worked so hard for. Aftariates and Maidi attacked southward, overrunning Parorvylia and raiding Amfaxitis and Paeonia's south-east villages and hamlets. He sent as many a horse lancers as he could muster, later leading these forces in person twice, to no avail. Each time the raiders retreated to high peaks of the mountains Orvylos or Messapion, where it was difficult for his horse to climb and chase. As his horsemen would retreat, the enemy followed down the slopes and raided some more.

Forces coming from Amfaxitis to aid him didn't bring any better results. When winter arrived, the raiders withdrew to their lands with all the loot produce and herds they could carry, leaving Paror-vylia and the south-east of Paeonia desolated. Imported food and livestock improved the living some-what, until the next spring. The raiders returned in greater numbers followed by the Laei, who hop-ed for easy loot, to pay their share of submission to demanding Dardanes.

Damasias asked for help from elsewhere and got response from Sythonia and Pallini, sent by their kings, Merops (he had taken over from his father Asteropeos) and Dimitrios, respectively. They were called oplites and did not come as horsemen -like it was expected. They were heavily armed with solid breast and back plates of bronze, latched together at the shoulders above and sides, under their arms. They were holding on their left hand a shield, big and round, covering most of the body -when crouched. This shield was called their oplon, hence the name oplites. On their right hand they held a spear, longer than the customary javelin and on their side a short sword was hanging from a cord over their left or right shoulder. When they stood or walked in close formation, they presented some-thing like a solid wall, shield on the left protecting the next man's right, as well as the bearer's front.

The spears protruded leveled from the front two lines (they were arrayed eight deep), for attack or defense, the lines behind holding their spears upright. They were not that many. Only twenty, times ten, but they were willing to fight and demonstrate their ability to do so.

They prepared their battle formation and asked Damasias to send his best horsemen in a mock at-tack against them. They stood, eight deep, almost one against the other. The attacking horse would run -each time- on them but the horses would rear, not penetrating, as they met this solid mass of men and arms! Many a rider fell off their rides, men known of their ability to ride even wild horses!

The mock attack was repeated several times, until some riders got seriously injured and the demon-stration came to an end. To Damasias' inquiries, he was told the formation was called falanx and it was introduced to them by colonists from Evia and Korinthos. He was very impressed by the per-formance, but he wanted to know what would happen if horse units would attack from the right side of this falanx or, if the enemy was numerous, could circle from behind. Then, were they surely doom-ed? Or perhaps not?

Their answer to this question was that the falanx could have the Paeonian horse to protect its flank and rear or it could form a perfect square and fight from all sides, until relief could arrive. They considered only one thing as a draw-back. With all that heavy armor, they could not chase the enemy a long distance. For that, they would rely on Paeonian horse but before the ground became rocky and unsuitable for horse.

It was becoming obvious that much co-ordination between these oplites and the Paeonian horse would be needed, if success was to follow the campaign. They all put themselves to task, practicing a number of mock attacks and defenses, while horse regiments were patrolling the borders constantly. These were taxing times for the Paeonians and the refugees from Parorvylia but each did what could for the common good. The patrolling regiments were replaced in equal intervals, so as to have each drill with the oplites as many times possible, before a late spring campaign would get under way. With the leaders of the falanx and scout horse, Damasias surveyed the border areas between the mountains of Orvylos, Messapion and Kerkinion.

Their choice of a suitable place for their plan, was the area by the springs of river Pontos, which traverses from Kerkinion, through the lower hills of Orvylos and empties its waters on Strymon river, across from the town of the Sintikes, Tristl (Tristolos). The falanx gathered and camped by the springs, the mountain flanking its sides. Along them, it had a force of about three times twenty horse, mainly to be used for delaying tactics and for message runners -when in need. The rest of the horse hid in near-by hamlets and cattle corrals, which were used in winter months protecting the animals. From that point on, all they had to do was wait and see.

The enemy spotted the falanx camp, the fifth day after they arrived at the springs. It was a small group, either marauding on their own or scouting for their larger force. Part of the horse and a section of the falanx gave them a deliberately slow chase. First, to show they were there to fight but, mainly, to indicate weakness in concerted action, therefore an easy target. The story repeated itself for the next seven days. Every day, some enemy force showed-up. Every day, there was a slow, not coordinated response of a chase from the falanx. Damasias grew skeptical, feeling he could not have his men and horses sitting idle in hiding for longer time. He ordered to have the horses exercised, ev-ery morning before dawn and every evening after dusk, carefully and after making sure there were no enemy troops in the vicinity. Still, there was plenty of idleness in-between and he didn't like it.

Then, on the wee hours of the eighth day's morning, a runner came with the news that the enemy had come to camp at the foothills of mount Kerkinion the evening past. They were holding the higher ground some distance from the springs and some skirmishing had already occur with their arrival.

By the time Damasias sent the messenger back with orders to hold, by the time he had his force gather and ready to move, another runner came to report that battle was given and in progress, the falanx holding the enemy. Now was the time for the horse to flank the enemy from both sides.

Damasias moved with as much speed as his horse force could master. On the way to flank the enemy they met some units of Aftariates and Maidi, coming to join their comrades. Those they dispatched to the last, taking them piece-meal as they met them. Once the encirclement was completed, they fell on a surprised enemy. The annihilation of Maidi and Aftariates was complete. Very few were captured, much fewer escaped to bring the bad news home! From Damasias' side, five Paeonians were dead, ten wounded. From Amfaxitan allies, two dead and six wounded. As for the falanx, they had only three slightly wounded men. Instead, they lost some of their servants, who were the carriers of the oplitis' armor, before and during the battle. You see, these servants were slaves and, having no protection at all, were easy prey from flying arrows and javelins.

After the battle was over, honorable funerals were given to the Paeonian and Amfaxitans fallen, as a mass grave also, to the servants. Two separate monuments marked the commemoration of their valor. The battle booty was split in three equal parts and the enemy dead were left in the care of the villagers around, for stripping and disposal of the bodies.

The falanx leaders expressed the desire to march into the enemy country and give then a taste of their own medicine. Their notion was supported by the Amfaxitan allies and the Parorvyles, who had lost the most out of this latest invasion. Damasias would not hear of it. He did not want either of the two northern tribes to be wiped out altogether. As he explained, a weak north frontier would bring back either the successor of Tiraj, or worse, the Dardanians! As long as Paeonia would have the support of such good neighbors as them, things should work well. Meantime, he would like to keep in his service any oplitis of the falanx was willing to stay and train Paeonians in the new way of war. He was offering free land for their sustenance, they could have new servants from the captured enemy and, he would personally see, they would be welcomed for as long as they wanted to stay.

Leoharis, the king of Amfaxitis and an old man now, also expressed that he would welcome any of the falanx oplitis in his kingdom, with the same terms. First things first, they all returned to Vylazora for much needed festivities…

All in all, five times ten men from the falanx stayed in Paeonia and about twenty went with king Leoharis to Amfaxitis. The Parorvyles, their homeland mountainous, preferred to keep their old ways of warfare, light and on foot. The rest of the falanx returned to their homes in Pallini and Sy-thonia, with all the war spoils of their share and many additional presents from Damasias and Leo-haris.

In Vylazora now, Damasias called for a council of all the elders and land holders, asking them to give some portion of their lands, suitable enough to accommodate the needs of the oplitis number staying in Paeonia. That done, preparations got under way in earnest and, before the next winter closed-in, all armor and shields were made out of felt and wood, for the training on the new style of warring. Of course, that was not enough. Damasias knew that felt and wood could not win wars! A good number of smiths was also needed, to forge real weapons, according to these new demands! Vylazora, Astivos and Stovi were already over crowded. He placed a call for smiths from neighboring states, to come on very good terms. He split the oplitis numbers in small groups and sent them in land properties close to villages and small towns. He would settle the smiths there also, along with the sons of the local clan heads and land lords, the latter to start training with the wood and felt weapons at hand.

On suggestion from one man from the oplitis falanx named Iakynthos, the most open to invasion areas of Paeonia were to be trained first. Reasoning his proposal, he said he knew the enemy, if had in mind to strike again, would strike at the most open and weak spots to do it. What a surprise, if that spot was found to being not weak (as thought) at all! Damasias liked the idea and ordered the arrangements. But many of his clan heads and land lords started having second thoughts about all this training and the foreigners going to and fro. They feared they would lose not only land given to the oplitis, their horse power would end-up being second to the falanx. Damasias had to assert all his persuasion and even threat the clan heads at the meeting before winter.

Iakynthos was a big help. He asked for (and was given) permission to speak, before the gathering of the elders. His arguments were always well presented and, for any counter-argument, he had a logic-al answer ready, impossible to dispute. Later, when Damasias asked Iakynthos to know how was he so well prepared and by what means he knew the answers to questions put so bluntly forth, he stated that all was due to his education. When pressured further, he told Damasias (with a smile) that, in Sythonia, people learned how to read and write when still young and trained by southerners to work upon their thoughts and express them, debating the pros and cons, alternating positions and views.

Competitors were spending time under the watchful eyes of the teachers, who were also the judges. To Damasias' further inquiries, it was told that these teachers held classes at various land lords' estates, out in the open. Aside from reading, writing and debating, the worthy sons of these land lords were to memorize the Iliad and Odyssey of a poet named Omiros and trained also in athletics.

"What kind?" Damasias wanted to know. "Well, diskos, sfyra and javelin throwing, running, and things like that. This way, the youth is developed, having sound mind and body. In Sparti, a city-state in the south and a peculiarly dual-king running leadership, emphasis was specially given to athletics and rough living, so they could endure more than any in war."

Damasias was more impressed. Until now, he had the Gigonian teacher of his son, a more-or-less secret. From the day of this conversation with Iakynthos on, he made sure all land lords and clan heads were aware of it, one way or another. To their inquiries he variably told them that his hope was his son would become ever-so-much better than their own. When time would come for him to take over and rule, young Alketas would be above all! Of course, this brought-up jealousy and de-mands. Damasias was careful to give-in gradually, after various concessions were made by the land lords, securing the king's hold over them more so.

Naturally, the Gigonian teacher could not handle all the young men coming to attend and learn. Be-sides, some were showing genuine interest, while others were forced by their fathers to come, as to not show less eagerness in making their sons better. A few more teachers had to be lured-in then. Fewer than needed responded, even fewer staying on permanent terms to perform the task. Paeonia, to the southerners, had the connotation of a barbaric country. None the less, Damasias could not be disappointed. He was in his tenth and third year as king, after his affair with Tiraj (and the likes) was done and finished. With a bit of luck, another ten years could go by and Alketas, old enough, would be able to take over, all clan heads bonded under him...

There were but few artisans in Paeonia, as were traders, smiths, builders and, now, teachers. His people were slow in learning and changing their ways from roamers to a stabilized society, Damasias realized, but they were learning. If he could keep his guard up and did not rush, did not become im-patient, the future wasn't looking so gloomy. One problem remained the most serious of them all: language. Generations would pass before this barrier could be lifted. Damasias wanted to give most emphasis to this task, molding the young pupils into one thinking machine, thinking the southern, the Ellenic way! Yet, he did not want them to learn how to quarrel the way the southern city-states did. There was no unity achieved that way. His eyes turned momentarily in the western part of the Make-donian clans. There, Orestis seemed to be in charge of most neighboring clans, but nothing to the ef-fect of, say, a Tiraj. Though Tiraj was nothing more than a brute willing to put everything underfoot for his own, personal benefit, a man of absolute power -but good intents and will- was the solution in avoiding further and often invasions in the general area. He discussed these thoughts with Iakynthos several times. The oplitis-instructor was against such ideas. It would impede the free will and deter-mination of individuals to achieve αρετη/excellence, in venues only to which the individual will could lead.

Damasias argued that the very city-states were but individuals under the rule of a king or a group of strong men. Yet he valued the opinion of this remarkable man with so much knowledge. He fol-lowed that end, toward good relations with the southern city-sates and kingdoms. He gave in-structions to the teachers. They were to encourage the young ones in any way possible, while disci-pline should be strict -no doubt- the punishment should be measured with care and the award should come often and freely, a lesson to be heartily followed.

Next, Damasias adopted a semi-mandatory custom, which was suggested to him by Thestios, a son of king Illos of Lynkestis, when the former paid a short visit, on his way back from Amydon in Amfa-xitis. The prince had taken the road up river Axios and, before following the Erigon, stopped at Stovi. The Lynkestians being of independent nature, he explained to Damasias, had even more independent clan heads and land lords leading them. If the king wanted to have some say in state affairs, he had better have a good leverage on them! One, such leverage, was to have the sons of the clan heads serve the king as pages from age seven, to when one would officially become a man, killing an enemy in battle. The girls would also serve the queen, from seven years old, until their marriage. In the interim both were staying at the court, learning the art of war by the king and for the king! This way none of the lords would decide to argue with the king while his son or daughter, were in court. Prestige and positioning were incentives enough, to have the lords willingly do that. Yet, many a time this custom was followed when and if it suited a strong land lord. But Lynkos was Lynkos and the king did not always have the means of imposing his wish.

Damasias knew that the same arguments would pop-up in his kingdom, had he express the wish to establish the same custom. Regardless the dependency of his clan heads, thanks to measures he took in times of their need, they would never accept such a service. But he could see and appreciate such an idea. In discussing the subject and in search of an optimum solution with Iakynthos, the Sythoni-an came up with an answer!

What if the king (Damasias) would establish this custom as an award in-stead? An excuse could (and should) be the excuse, as well as the criterion. A boy who was good in wrestling, for instance, could be the king's own representative during games. In order, therefore, to have time for better and continuous training, the boy should be invited to spend time by the king's side. Another, good in writing, could become one of the king's own scribes, and so forth and so on. All should be honorary positions, according to individual abilities, with the thought (introduced in their minds) of chances for betterment. Obviously, all would have to stay by the king's side and for the king's use. Later, appointments commensurating their abilities, and grants, would serve as a 'repay' to their devotion toward the king. By the time of their adulthood, they'd be in closer relation and obedience to the royal house, than to their own relatives.

"For this thought" Damasias laughed, "Iakynthos deserves to be named general, in charge of the Paeonian falanx, for life!" "Therefore" Iakynthos countered, "closer to the king and very grateful of the appointment!" They both laughed and, soon, the idea was put to work. Emphasis, was decided, should be given on young men who promised scholastic betterment and the award to each, becoming the king's scribe.

The two men worked out the program. As the young boys come to manhood, they would be appointed in various positions within their own clans, not only as successors of their fathers but as executors of their king's wishes, teachers of the next generation and record keepers of the area and clan! A good base of learning, an example worth mimicking. Before long, the seeds of this new trend would take roots, nourishing production of new seeds…

Kersej was not a clan head. He was not a part of any particular clan either, nor was his Father or any before him, for as long as he knew. There had been no talk of family roots or actual allegiance to any of the clan heads or land lords. As a kid, he remembered, he had to help his mother packing-up whatever she would point-out to him and his two younger brothers and follow the pack animals in the direction his father had taken, be it to war or hunting. Sooner or later they would catch-up with him, set the hearth under an ill prepared wood and thatch hut, cook a meal and be a family of some sort.

In the summer months it did not really matter. When too hot, the protection of the so-called roof was enough, the playing and running to streams with other boys (when company was near) or his brothers, would give a sort of pleasure and carefree times. Winter was another story. No matter how well they would dress the interior of their hut with furs and animal skins, there were always more holes discovered to cover. Snow, ice or rain, would always be a part of constant discomfort and misery. Nowhere to play and nowhere to hide from Father's anger! Many a time they'd share the meager space, cuddled with the animals for added warmth and out of preservation interest for both, humans and beast. When a cave was available at any given location, sometimes things were better, sometimes worse.

Kersej's family came to 'settle' around Vylazora at one time and he grew-up with Damasias, who's family had an overall precedence on the clan heads of the area, therefore, over just everybody and everything. As kids, they used to gang-up (in the summer time) against others, especially protecting Kersej's two younger brothers -always prone to run into trouble.

They used to swim in the same shallows by the river Vardarj/Vardarios, getting their share of trouble or their share of spoils when their fathers returned from war. Before long, Kersej' Father attached a sort of fidelity on Damasias' old man, the dreaded chieftain Gruba. The family became 'accepted' though free to come and go, as Father pleased. As they grew up, Kersej and Damasias parted their ways a lot, but still considered each-other as sort of leader-follower friends. When the split between north and south clans came, his Father took Damasias' side. Out of fear and habit in following his old man, personal acquaintance, combination of all three factors, Kersej did the same. As a grown-up man now, he developed a very independent spirit, especially after Father's death. He'd do what his mind put him doing first, ask for reason or excuse later. Perhaps, if he happened to be at another place on the time of the split, he would have been on the other side of the camp now.

When Father died in one of the skirmishes against Tiraj and things came to settle down, Damasias granted Kersej and his brothers an area, the one they were living out-of now, for good services rent-ed, to hold as their own. There were a few good meadows within this land, enough to raise cattle, a few horses and sheep. There were also plenty of brooks and wooded areas for fish and game. He and his brothers, with their wives and the offspring running between their legs, accepted the present (some blood was shed for it, was not so?) and Kersej was happy roaming around, fishing or hunting. The work needed done, was taken care by his brothers, his wife and theirs and his mother, old, but still useful and active. Being the elder now, they had to bid and obey his wishes.

When some builders came to his place from Eordea, Damasias told him that he and his family had to assist them in building a hamlet, as permanent housing of their own, year-round. Kersej could viv-idly remember the discomfort of his youth, but he was used to any discomfort by now. He did not ob-ject to the idea, knowing he could come and go as he was pleased. He put his brothers to clearing a nice area for the houses and the animal stables and corrals and help the builders. In a few years time, they turned themselves to peasants, southern style. It suited him fine. Every harvest, he'd go with them to Vylazora or Stovi, and they'd get provisions at the market, in exchange of their produce. He, as el-der and head of the family, would get his fair share. With animal pelts from his hunting, he added even more to his own family's wealth. He certainly could not see himself doing what his brothers did.

Permanent housing? Agriculture? Taking care of animals? Ha, ha and ha! Hard as he had it in his youth, outdoors, free roaming and hunting, was the life he loved.

When war broke out with the Aftariates and Maidi, he and his brothers joined Damasias again, riding proudly at his side, on their own free will, the adventure and prospect of loot -as Kersej was seeing it. Deep inside his mind, admired the efficiency and discipline of the falanx, but bold personal bravery and horse charge was still his preference, so his initial enthusiasm got lost soon after. When he found that many hours of constant training were needed to coordinate his actions with others by him, he threw away the armor and shield he had made. His dislike was in getting orders to stay in line with others in battle and support -as well being supported- by the heavy shield. Then, it was the language. Although he could understand and speak decent Makedonian and Halkidian dialects, his speech had that harsh Peonian quality, not easily understood. To the amusement of others, he would revert to pure Peonian, swearing his way through. That, was always a subject of teasing and laughter but, he couldn't take that either. It led to some serious quarrels, causing Damasias' own intervention to calm things down.

After a while, Kersej gave-up the falanx and associations with the troops altogether, returning to his loving pass time of roaming and hunting. If war was to come again, he would ride his horse proudly, like he did before. He would take orders from Damasias, but from no other Paeonian clan heads, certainly not from Sythonians, Makedonians or any other southerner. Not from the ones hiding be-hind a shield and calling themselves men! That, may have brought results, but it wasn't exactly the brave man's fight! Bravery, as he saw it, and lust for freedom, was to him facing the enemy on equal terms. If one was unseated from one's horse, the other was expected to dismount, and then fight!

As it turned out, he gave his shield and armor to his younger brother, Korjed. This young one, took the task of becoming an oplitis much more seriously and, before one knew, he became a first-rate one. Not only that, he became totally Makedonized! He readily adopted the manners and dialect of Makedon as was spoken in those north-eastern parts, insisting to be called by the new name appellat-ion, Korednos. Kersej was much amused, as one suited perfectly to his proper Peonian name. He made lots of teasing remarks, laughing at his brother, remarks he wouldn't take kindly from others on himself. Eventually he gave-up, especially seeing the middle brother of theirs, Aliaksej, turn his name to Makedonian Alexandros…

Later, a point of dispute was raised between Kersej and Damasias. The compulsory, yearly donation of one tenth of all produce and variable income of each family, to the king's treasury. Kersej could see some reason behind the obligation. He, as head of his family, was receiving from his brothers a better return of all valuables for barter or exchange than they. The king, as head of the whole tribe, had the same rights. But Kersej could see the point only partially. To him, such a measure was need-ed in case of war, natural disasters, or other emergencies. On a yearly basis, regardless of aboun-dance (or lack) of income, the measure was something he could not understand. He figured that he was given the land and animals as a reward for services rented, an exchange like bartering. The land and its animals, along with the people in it, belonged to him in its entirety. If they were to be return-ing parts of an exchange each time a king was asking for it, what was the sense of it being given in the first place?

It took a lot of patience and effort, but, finally, Damasias was able to explain and be understood of the needs a royal treasury had and its ability to function in times of peace, as in times of war. None-theless, Kersej did not look more favorably at this added obligation. He simply accepted it as a necessary evil, one which nobody could force him to like! He took of to hunting more and, there, he felt totally free and at peace. Let the brothers of his care for family obligations to him and to king, let the wife run after the needs of the household and his two growing sons. They were the ones who had to change.

During one of these hunting spells of Kersej, Damasias came to pay a sudden visit. Kersej was sought and found, to his utter disappointment, having to give-up hunting some good deer. The king asked for hospitality, as Paeonian custom required. As Paeonian custom obliged, it was freely extended by the host. Damasias brought with him expensive gifts for the three brothers and their families, something for each one, according to status within the household structure. Kersej felt obligated to do his best in accommodating the king and the underlings he had along. Thank the gods, they weren't that many!

They all sat down, like in the old good days, on even level, under the shade of a near-by plane tree. A wild boar killed the day before was roasted; Kersej's wife worked the fire. It would be stored in their stomachs -Kersej joked. While the wives did the cooking, the kids of the three brothers brought jugs of strong, local wine and placed them in the brook's running cold water, to have it chilled.

Before long, the tongues turned loose and childhood memories were revived and re-told, the young brood often reminded of their duties, as they listened intensely, forgetting hospitality manners. At the end of their meal, the king asked Kersej and his brothers if they would take a stroll with him, away from the others, so they could have some serious talk. As they started their walking by the brook, up-stream toward the meadow, Damasias started explaining the reason of his visiting them…

The land holders and clan heads, he said, were sending their firstborn sons and daughters to his household, to be better trained at anything their nature compelled them to follow. He, as an old friend, knew that Kersej' s family was not equal to a clan head's and, as land owners, they were new and rather small holders. On the other hand, he knew of their devotion to his person and the services all had given at war, as in peace. He figured, he said, their firstborn sons and daughters ought to have the same opportunities as the sons and daughters of more prominent families. He had in mind to promote the offspring of several trusted followers in the future, taking (naturally) under consider-ation their eagerness to better themselves and their proof of capabilities to that extend. So, being such old friends, he would start with this family…

They had walked way past the clearance of the house complex and into the woods, following the path the animals and Kersej (in his hunting spells) had opened-up, going two by two, for it was really nar-row. Kersej was listening intensely and thinking hard. Stolen looks back at his following brothers, were telling him they were ready to accept this proposition happily. Not so, as he was concerned. He was feeling discomfort, the idea of separating from his firstborn, totally alien. Didn't he follow his Father everywhere as a kid? Didn't Damasias follow his? What if he wanted his son to follow him in hunting or in war? Shouldn't that be his, only his own, choice and decision? Was this a king's new way of taking more from each family? Wasn't a tenth of all property income enough? The king now wanted to take their firstborns in his service. Not for a day, not for a week or for a month either! This seemed to be a permanent, long term demand and there was no deal! As a host, an old friend, as a free, spirited man, one who served with faith and distinction, could and would speak his mind to the king.

He went for it, stating that the king was asking too much. Besides, hands were needed for the work still to be done at the estate, husbandry for the animals, for the yearly harvest, for fishing and game so the tenth could be given. If the king were to take those hands away, what next? The presents he brought to them, albeit magnificent, could not cover the price of his asking as return. Ample hos-pitality was already given. When necessity called, blood was given too! And, if the king didn't like it, he could take the presents and the estate back and be gone. The family could go back on its old ways and owe nothing, to anyone! One thing the king should remember, he had become king on account of people like Kersej, his Father and brothers, who had given freely and had taken only what was due.

Damasias' temper rose quite high hearing all this and he had to put a great effort in keeping himself calm. He knew well of Kersej's roving spirit, with no real worries as to what tomorrow may bring. Still, he hoped that even Kersej would not be so narrow-minded. Then, again, those words were said with such a passion, made him think again, reconsidering. Maybe that was what his people really wanted. Maybe, independent and better managed future was not of their interest at all! Maybe he should let them be the barbaric, semi-nomadic followers, not the leaders! Perhaps, his own ambition had taken them all too far. Deep inside him though, a voice was telling him loud and clear that he was right. Paeonia's future would rest on his ability to bring people like Kersej out of their cocoons, to a more open, more productive society. There was only one way to have that happen, his way! He carefully and politely asked for extension of the hospitality, for night quarters.

Kersej had not much of an option. According to custom, he freely had offered hospitality in the first place, to both, the king and his party. The offer had to remain open, for as long as the visitors made their stay. He was mad though, for what he conceived the king was taking advantage of! He smiled inward, as a thought occurred to him. Extension of hospitality was freely given. There was little room to share the night though. Would the king mind if, reminiscence of the past, he was to share quarters with the host at the stables?

Damasias' face reddened at the hidden insult. But he didn't want to use force. He had not come here to pick a fight. He had to use persuasion and common sense, not make things worse. His host had not refuse hospitality, he offered sharing the same accommodations, albeit at a much lower status. If the host thought he was cunning, Damasias had hidden tricks of his own. Maybe, there was still a way to avoid an open confrontation. He accepted as graciously as his anger permitted. On their way back to the hamlet, no one uttered a word. The sun was setting and they all walked ostensibly lost in their in-ner thoughts.

They were now approaching the houses and were just around the hill, before the furthest sheep corral, when they heard the commotion. Sheep were bleating and the roar of a mountain lion could be clearly heard above all. They all ran toward the corral, swords on hand. Kersej knew for some time now, that the sheep and some cattle were victims of some mountain lion(s) lately, but had not been able to track the beast(s) down or find the den. They arrived at the corral and could see at once how serious the situation was. The enclosure, made of thorn bushes, stone and wood, was torn at one place. One of the king's attendants was laying on the ground, dying from claw and bite wounds, one lion taking pieces of flesh as the man was breathing his last. Obviously, there were one or more lions inside the covered section of the corral also, having a field day, as sheep could be seen by its entrance, running like crazy onto one-another but not seeing the opening for their escape. The other men of the king's escort were just coming from the houses, having secured the women and children first, but still at a distance. Kersej, his brothers and the king rushed all as one, on the lion above the dead man.

With multiple sword thrusts, they brought the beast to its death. The other lion(s) laid, aware now of the human presence, inside the thatched enclosure of the corral, in the darkness. The structure being low, the men had to crouch in order to get through its sole entrance/exit. It was a difficult moment as they entered, one after the other. Alexandros stayed by it, to fend off any lion trying to escape. Damasias, Kersej and Korednos pushed in, searching in the very dim light, listening for any noise which would direct them against the beast(s). The sheep had gathered at one end, still bleating, still restless but undecided as to what route to take. One lion (a female as it proved to be) was spotted at once, her eyes giving her away, shining in the dim light. The three men jumped on her with cries of sorrow, mixed with triumph, their swords hacking and thrusting. No sooner had they killed her, when her mate came out of the dark, onto Kersej's back. He felt the pain of claws digging, by his shoulder blades and the beast's foul breath on his neck. The impact sent him sprawling down and the pain clouded his mind. Next, came a horrible roar and death throes. Clearing his eyes, Kersej saw the king pulling his sword out of the beast's heart and pushing its dead weight away from him. Kersej knew then, he had lost his game of will and wits and his king had won. For Damasias, having saved his life, there was not a thing Kersej could now refuse him! He passed out...

Damasias knew it too, but his first concern was to see that Kersej would recover. Thankfully, the wounds were not life threatening, though they occurred in a sheep corral full of dirt, so he needed care. Damasias had Kersej moved into his house and sent for Olganos, the physician from Almopia. This Olganos was reputed t have inherited the family tradition of physicians, going all the way back to generations, when the first of his family was a pupil of Asklipios himself! Now, Olganos was in Damasias' service, always at the king's disposal. He came, as fast as the horse he rode on would bring him. He cleaned the wounds and placed an ointment of his own, then dressed them with strips of clean cloth. He then, asked for hot water and an empty wine cup. When it was brought to him, he opened his travel bag and took out a pixis, a medicine container. He opened it, measured a portion into the wine cup and added hot water. He stirred for some time and took a small taste of it. Nodding his satisfaction, he held the head of the coming-to Kersej and had him drink it all. He ordered everybody out of the room, suggesting that Kersej should be left to have a good night's sleep. He would see him again, by first morning's light.

Everybody exited the room as asked. The king inquired next about his sleeping quarters at the stab-les. To the protest of Korednos and Alexandros (feeling much more obligated -the king saving their brother's life), he insisted they had to obey the host's wishes. Both brothers showed their king to the stables and the whole retinue slept the night in the mangers, where the cattle and horses would feed and sleep during winter…

The next day, Kersej insisted on getting up and attending his business with the king, in spite of Ol-ganos' objections. Kersej stayed in the room long enough for the changing of the dressing on his wound and, walking as steadily as his own power and pride allowed him, went to meet his king. He found Damasias and the others sitting together in silence, eating fruits and drinking goat milk.

Expressing his gratitude and debt to his king for saving his life as best as he could, got Damasias' response that he would have done that for any good old friend, as he would expect the same from any and all good old friends do for him, adding that Kersej was surely the first among those.

This exchange of words sealed the deal. Kersej's honor (or rather his personal concept of it) would never allow him to dispute anything Damasias would say or ask in the future. Yet, the king's tact gave him the room to decide for himself and, that face-saving, was much appreciated…

By the fourth hour after that morning's sunrise and after the proper offerings to gods and ancestors were made, the king and his party departed, followed by the firstborn sons of Kersej, Alexandros and Korednos, as well the firstborn daughter of the latter...

> "The pride Greeks take in insulting the insults
> of their own discord, is their ancient and
> present permanent cause of their misery, as
> well as their creativity and triumph!"
> Giovanni Ziorlini, Italian, raised in Greece.

IV

The young maid was looking out, toward the orchards, as they were descending in unison with the gentle slopes of mountain Vermion, some of them still covered with the early morning mist of a promising bright day. Her face had the serious look of a person deeply concerned about important, beyond the, supposed, care free times of her years. She was resting herself against a Dorian style column of the peristylion, the colonnade on the sunny side on the far end of the palace. Nothing elab-orate, as far as structure goes, Pentelic or Naxian marble being too expensive an item to be brought in Imathia. The columns were made here of local porous stone, a bit crude, compared to any south-ern city-state's ones. But they were made with care and love, as anything else her parents, king Menelaos and queen Kleopatra, had ordered made in their small kingdom.

The girl's hair was let loose in the early morning breeze, the color of honey. A light cape covered her shoulders, embroidered with the red and black of the Imathian royal colors, hand-made by her own mother. Looking at the natural beauty extending below, Pelagia, a natural beauty herself, felt a pang in her heart and her dark blue eyes let some of their own mist to be mixed with the one in the air.

She was born and raised an Imathian, here in the town of Veria, place of happy childhood dreams and years. Now, at the age of four plus ten, her childhood had been shuttered. Her father had made the announcement last night at a banquet, that she was betrothed to the son of king Illos, Temvros of Lynkos. Not that she had anything against marriage. Her two parents were a perfect example of marital bliss and parenthood. She knew her time would come sooner or later and judging by her par-ents' example, seemed to her that this was the thing to do, when coming of age. She only did not like the idea of marrying Temvros! She first met him six years ago, when her family asked for safety at the court of king Illos, because of the unstoppable Peonian move into Imathian lands. She would have rather had her father ask for the hospitality of Elimiotis or Orestis, even of Pieria! Lynkestis was a real backwater kingdom and, with a (time-wise) recent Illyrian invasion just resolved, life was to be even more miserable. Making things worst, Temvros, two years older than her, was there to torment her! His older brother, Thestios, was killed during one of the many Illyrian raids on Lynkos. Old king Illos had turn soft on his last offspring, something which Temvros fully knew and took advan-tage of!

The memory of her encounters with Temvros, made her shudder and a fresh spring of mist from her eyes rolled down her cheeks. She never met in her entire life, a person more boasting, more ego-centric! Temvros would take her toys away and smash them, just to see her cry and beg, repeating, as he asked, that he was her great benefactor, without whom all her family would have been sold to slavery by the dreaded Peones! He would find any excuse to down Imathian values and custom, just to make her feel inferior. On her protest, he exulted the Lynkestian hospitality, as something much greater a princess of peasants and earth-tillers could ever hope for. She was lucky already, he wasn't throwing her to his hound dogs! She would then run to her parents, tears running uncontrollably, asking them to leave, to go back home. The aggravation was greater when her father and king Illos were away at war, trying to free Lynkos and her homeland from the cursed Illyres and Peones. Then, Temvros, the heir to the Lynkestian throne of a proud and ever-lenient father, could really be out of control!

She could not go and tell her parents back then, of all the insults she suffered from Temvros. In spite of her youth, she understood that Father and Mother needed king Illos' hospitality and help, as much as he needed their presence and support. Besides, sooner or later, they'd all go back home. But most of all, she knew exactly who she was. She was the daughter of a king, descendant of Makedon, from his great grand mother Veria, their own capital town taking her name -when built.

Lynkestian kings claimed ancestry from Makedon and Iraklis also, but, judging on Temvros' character, she would agree to it using a lot of salt on it (for preservation) for later, further analysis...

Two long years passed for her, before they returned home to Imathia. Now, goddess Tyhi, her luck and destiny, were sending her back there, to Lynkos, its harsh people and climate, to Temvros. She had gone to her Father once more, this time telling him everything. Menelaos seemed to be most con-cerned and sympathetic to her plea, but, as he explained, he had given his word to Illos already and, through that, her hand to Temvros. There was no way Imathia's king going back on his word. The implications could be very severe, in more ways than one refusal to an agreed wedding! She should have come to him and tell her sufferings, as soon as they returned home, four years ago!

Besides, he reasoned, that was a child's behavior back then! Now Temvros was a young man of six plus ten years old, old enough to have acquired some wisdom and manners! Additionally, the wed-ding was set in two years' time and time was the cause of many changes. She should be preparing, but not panic! Lynkos' life was harsh, but no flesh and blood of this household ever proved in being a weakling. They all could and would face life's harshness with proper dignity and resolve, especially when Imathia's interest was of paramount importance.

As to Lynkestis' aspirations of becoming the master power of all Makedonia including Imathia, well. Her future king and husband might be thinking so but she was to become his wife and queen! With her upbringing, bloodline and wit, she could elevate the interests of Imathia alongside. Now she should be the good girl she always has been, go back to her loom, for no Imathian was ever called idle when needed to prepare for the future. He, her own Father, would see she'd get what was best.

She left her Father in bitterness. Not that she didn't understand his position, not that she lost love and respect for him and his wishes, nor that she thought he didn't love her and wanted the best for her either! Nonetheless, she was disappointed and expected something different, something more! She went to meet with Mother. Understanding between women was more apt to finding common ground. She was right, as far as understanding went, but the result was just the same...

As her six plus tenth year approached, readiness for the upcoming wedding put everything else aside. Pelagia even found herself immersed in the fever of preparations and anticipation! Well, not all, but most of the time. Nature herself seemed to being in a very festive mood. Guests were invited from all Imathia and the neighboring kingdoms, their kings declaring a truce to all and any hostility (Elimiotis, Tymfea and Eordea were at war against Orestis), so the travelers invited at the wedding, would be able to go unimpeded to and return from. The presents from the neighboring kings, started arriving a month ahead of the designated day of the nuptials.

General dispensation was issued from king Menelaos' treasury, so each Imathian would have more than adequate reason -and means- to partake in the celebration, no matter how poor the person was!

The town of Veria surpassed all other town and villages in Imathia, decorating its market place and the temple of goddess Estia, the household deity. Only one sore point. The refusal to participate at the festivities, from Orestis. Imathia had always been a good ally of the Orestians for many gener-ations. But, now, the prospect of closer ties between Menelaos and Illos, was taken as a blow to the Orestid supremacy claim on Makedonian affairs. Adding the well known aims of Lynkos, this blow was more than any Orestian king could take! Good judgment averted any further unpleasantness, threats of war, or counter measures. There was also the agreement of respect for the travelers who would want to cross Orestis, on their way to and from the wedding, avoiding other round-about ways. But, a participation? Well! That was really asking too much!

King Illos being an old arch-rival of Orestian power, could not resist the given opportunity this truce was presenting him with. He had a choice of his route to Imathia. He either could go through Eordea, by Kellae and Vokeria to Veria, or through Orestis, by Keletron, to Argos Orestikon, to low-er Eordea and on to Veria. He chose the latter. He made sure his retinue included a detachment of his best horsemen, the crests of the riders' helmets equipped with brand new, long horsetail hair, their breastplates shining like mirrors, wearing gilt edged greaves and the fanciest trimmings for their horses.

Passing by the towns of Keletron, Argos Orestikon and Levaea, they caused quite a sensation! Reaching at each one of these major towns, Illos made sure he would ride on his royal chariot, guilt-ed with gold, ivory and silver. Temvros was riding on a specially well-trimmed horse, to the right of his father, dressed in a ceremonial bronze-on-ox hide breastplate, shiny bronze greaves, trimmed with gold and silver in meandering designs, his shield dressed in bronze, with a coiled body of a viper emblazoned on it -the royal sign of Lynkos. His cloak, covering his back, was dyed -along its edges- with the purple of Finikian dye.

The Orestian king, Merops, could do nothing but get at the gate of Levaea in as much splendor, greeting them and offering the customary hospitality to travelers under truce. The offer was politely declined (to his relief) and the Lynkestians continued their road to Imathia, camping during the night out in the open, rather than ask for shelter at any Orestian hamlet. They passed on to Eordea trough the Vermion and Askion mountain passes, down to Mieza, the legendary gardens of the Vry-gian king Midas and, finally, into Veria itself.

They found the festivities started and, as the retinue proceeded through the main street, Imathians and guests were cheering and throwing flowers on the path before them. They arrived at Menelaos' palace with difficulty, as the crown was thronging in the vicinity, to better see and enjoy the specta-cle. They were shown to their quarters and a formal reception followed, during which Menelaos and Illos made the official announcement on their intention to unite their children under the bonds of the imeneos/marriage. The process was ritualized by the priestess of Estia, the hearth and household goddess, Menelaos presiding, as befitting the Makedonian customs. The actual wedding would follow in seven days' time, the groom leading a mock attack at the bride's house, 'abducting' her from her 'despairing' parents. But first, the young maid and her future husband had to be 'introduced'. After this 'introduction' they would not be allowed to see each-other until the final moments of the wed-ding ceremony, for the bride's face would be veiled over from beginning to end, when the groom would lift it for the customary kiss of acceptance and protection.

Pelagia was brought before her Father, her Father-to-be and her future husband, by her Mother and her maid-friends of the court. She was wearing a long, sleeveless imation dress, at the hem of which, one could barely see the front end of her sandals -as she walked. It had a light blue hue, like the bright, clear sky of that spring day. Her waist was accented by a golden belt, resting rather loosely on her hips, held by an ivory buckle. The dress was gracefully kept on her shoulders by golden porpes/clasps, embroidered on its edges and hem with gold. On her head, she was wearing a fine golden crown, in the image of two, connected almont-tree branches, their leaves and flowers life-like! She gave the groom-to-be a short look, then, she cast her eyes down, her face blushing.

Looking at Temvros, one could easily see he was pleased and taken by her beauty. He approached her with the formality demanded by the ritual and, after a long look at her downward face he leaned and said the words to be heard by her only: "Sorry for our past time together! I was wrong! I am here to make sure your life hereafter, will be a happy one with me at your side! I swear it, in the name of Estia and all gods! I know it is difficult for you to believe me, but I don't take oaths lightly and I recognize, now, how wrong I was then!" He kept his eyes on her for a moment or two longer, to make sure she heard and understood. Then, with his own face blushed, he returned to his father's side, nodding his satisfaction to her parents.

Pelagia followed all these movements of his with her eyes, sneaking looks, as her head stayed down-cast, wondering if she heard the words he whispered to her, or it was a figment of her imagination. A gentle pinch on her arm, by her Mother (standing beside her) reminded her, her duties. She walked to the two elderly kings, followed by her Mother and maids, and she paid her silent respects, touch-ing with her lips the extended right hand of each one. Then, the women withdrew to their quarters, leaving the men for feasting and drinking bouts in the courtyard.

This, men only, festivity would last (with some relief breaks in-between), until the day of 'abduct-ion' and beyond! Bards, dancers and magicians, would add to the entertainment. The women had their own celebrations at their own, private quarters. That, included (along their merriment) last minute love stories, husbandry and other obligations in need to be reminded to the future bride.

Strangely, Pelagia felt much more relaxed. Her new encounter with (obviously grown-up) Temvros, had a big role to play on her comfort. Not only had he grown to being a handsome young man, he al-so looked much wiser than the brat she used to know and fear. Maybe, her Father was right after all.

She didn't like her necessary relocation though. She did not like the dreary climate of Lynkestis, its wild people, its -even wilder- winters. She hoped that, in time, she could get used to that also…

The 'abduction' of the bride from her household, met all the formalities of the call. There were some minor injuries on both parties, as men from both families (lost in their stupor of drinking all those days) were eager to 'take' or 'protect' from, but that added color and desire for more mer-riment in its aftermath. The groom and his bride got the blessing during a long Ymenean/wedding ceremony, at the temple and Altis enclosure of goddess Estia. Then, followed by the bride's dower and their escort, the couple took the road back to Lynkestis (this time, through Almopia). Banquets and meetings with the two elderly kings and their guests in Veria continued for another fortnight!

The young couple arrived in Lynkos (many a stop made on the way, to see and be seen by celebrat-ing subjects) after many days of journeying. One added reason for their slow process was that Tem-vros did not want Pelagia get over tired by the trek. As she came to know him again and, little by lit-tle, he proved of being exactly the opposite of what she feared of him and she became thankful to the gods and her parents for such a nuptial choice. Before she really knew it, she fell, head-over-heels in love with her husband! The result of their union soon became obvious to all and the boy they brought to the world, looked very healthy and extremely active. Temvros was proudly stating that, with a son like this one, they would never be idle and bored parents. They named the kid Pafsanias…

Temvros, as the only remaining child of Illos and Efrosyni, had his childhood years spoiled by both his parents, his peers (sons and daughters of clan heads) living at the royal household and common people, alike. Many of them did it out of love, others out of necessity or fear of Illos, as others to gain the favors of the king. Only his parents had given him everything unconditionally, asking nothing in return. When he met Pelagia for the first time and his spoiled demands for constant attention were met with her impassable wall of silent dignity, he was surprised and angered. He did whatever he could think of, to make her exist at his Father's house as the refugee she was, constantly reminding her of her (and her parent's) dependence on the good will of Lynkos! Existential hospitality to any and all Imathians seeking the protection of Lynkestis against the roving Peonian hordes, had to be brought before her in every occasion! He was conveniently forgetting of Lynkos having, at the same time, the Illyrians roving in Lynkos and, that Imathians were there to co-defend the land along with his Father's troops.

The fact that Father bowed, by necessity and despair, swallowing his pride and asking for help from Orestis against the same marauding Illyrians, never crossed his mind. His love and care was entirely devoted to himself, his parents and to the glory of Lynkos, in that order. Any other human concerns, feelings, needs, were of no importance to him what-so-ever! He knew he was hurting her, that she was running to her parents asking protection and departure from her tormentor, as he knew her pride and dignity would not allow her tell what exactly was bothering her. He also knew king Mene-laos being aware of his Father's pathological love toward the last son of his loins and the need of no friction in the relation of the two kings. So, he pushed, having no real concept of damage done in particular, knowing only his intuition of him being safe by doing what he was and his self-centered ego compelled him to push to the limit!

He realized his error after she left, although not consciously -to begin with. The turning point of his realization, that his self-importance was not the center of the world, happened to be a hunting acci-dent which occurred four years after her departure. He got his manhood status when he was five plus ten years old, by sneaking out one early morning and going after a mountain lion, armed with his bow and arrows and two javelins. He was lucky (he knew it well now) that he spotted the animal first and the wind was carrying his scent away from it. He had the time for good aim and his arrow pierc-ed the beast's heart, sending it to sprawl dead, down the slope. He had it skinned and brought the pelt home, to everyone's admiration. Only his parents had turned ashen faced for a long moment but, embarrassed, embraced him and praised his bravery, as soon as their sock passed. He learned not a thing from that, though it was the beginning. One year later, the accident to change his character, oc-cured.

There was a group of them, five young men in all, who went hunting, before the coming of winter would close in and bears would be hibernating. They went up on the peaks of Varnous. They were able to locate and track one bear rather easily and put it to run. The chase lasted most of the day and things were getting out of hand, for everyone was tired and prone to mistakes. When asked to give-up he refused, for he didn't want to come back empty-handed, ordering the group to continue the chase.

As the shadows of dusk started to fall long on the mountain slop, they managed to corner the animal and moved in for the kill. The trapped beast decided to reverse the roles and attacked them! Being tired from the long chase, they were slow to react and careless in their defense. One of the compan-ions was instantly killed from a sweep of the bear's forearm, which broke his neck. Temvros being next to him, received the end result of the same blow, for (being younger and faster) he had the speed to jump backward, the blow missing half its mark. Nonetheless, the bear's claws tore his breastplate, tearing his flesh and causing a terrible pain. His blood gushing out, he fainted thinking this was his end…

The other three men had, by this time, recover some of their courage and their javelins and swords put an end to the beast's life, but not before one of them, Kinos, son of Apellas (a strong Lynkestian clan head), fell seriously wounded. His brother, Perseas and the other man, Filippos, son of Fidon, being the older ones in that small group, fell in despair. With one dead and two wounded from their group, Filippos was dispatched to go and seek for help.

The night passed in total discomfort. Not so much for Temvros who was drifting between conscious-ness and deep coma-like sleep, as much as for Kinos, who's screams of pain were muffled by sheer will power and, Perseas, who didn't know who to look-after first. One was his brother, flesh and blood of his own, the other being the king's son and his personal protégé! As dawn broke, Perseas remained at the side of the wounded, offering what help he could. Being in war before and realizing Temvros' wounds were not life threatening and, aside from lost blood, no imminent danger, turned his attention to his brother. Kinos' case was much worse. Despite the protests from the future king of Lynkos, Perseas didn't bother much except of making sure to clean and dress Temvros' wounds. He used strips from Temvros' own mantle for that, an expensive item in Lynkos. The tearing raised more protest from Temvros. Perseas was told by him that when he would feel strong enough again, Perseas would live to regret such a waste! Perseas retorted that, if Temvros was so strong as to cuss and threaten, he should get up and go fetch some water, for it was badly needed for use, in taking care of Kinos' wounds.

Temvros stopped then his threats and protestations, but he didn't move to help. He told himself, he would have Perseas' head on a platter for such an insult and insubordination! He could not, would not, allow a subordinate to ignore his needs, so much so, as allowing orders directed to his royalty on top. "Just wait until Filippos returns with help!"-he thought...

It so happened, that the gods had other plans for him. As it was late fall, one of the freak storms (so common in the high parts of Lynkos) developed on Pindos and dropped its white shroud on Varnous and Temvros' small, stranded party. By the time Perseas was gone to the nearest creek for water and came back, everything had turned to white.

Perseas cleaned his brother's wounds and dressed them again, using strips from the same mantle, ostensibly oblivious to Temvros' further protest, moans and groans. Next he brought in some more water, cleaned Temvros forcibly and occupied himself skinning the bear. By the time he finished, the snow had everything covered well enough, to have the area completely altered. Perseas ordered, yes, ordered(!) Temvros to give him a hand in covering both, himself and Kinos with the bear's fury skin, to keep warm. With that, he took off in search of shelter. He found one small for the three of them cave, but it would have to do and the royal brat would have to be happy and cooperate -like it or not!

Actually, Perseas knew, the young prince was scared more from the close call, than hurt. Living in the palace guard, he also knew how spoiled the future king had been all his life. Perseas would have to face a difficult future -if any at all- in case something really wrong would happen. He returned to the injured, after he built a fire by the cave's entrance, to keep animals out (and the dampness off the cave). He had difficulty finding his brother and the prince, because the snow had them completely covered already. He had Temvros stand up, cut some bear meat and placed on the fur skin. Then, picking-up his brother over his shoulders, the way he learned in training, and holding him with one hand, ordered (for a second time!) Temvros to help him pool the bear's fur skin, loaded now with the meat he cut. Their horses were long gone, taking off right after the encounter.

Temvros was shaking, because of the cold, his injuries and, mainly, his anger. "Let the dog-darn son of a peasant carry me too!" he thought. "After all, I am his future king!" Surviving this, he would have to make sure all his subjects would serve him first, and foremost! Besides, he was also wounded!

Perseas had every intent on helping the prince, knowing he was wounded and him being the one who cleaned the wounds. Having his own brother in much worst condition than Temvros, did not leave him with any choice but to look after the more serious of the two. Seeing the stubbornness of the spoiled prince, he started walking toward the cave, holding his brother over his shoulders with one hand, the other pulling the fur skin with the cut of the bear's meat on it. It was a difficult tusk but he didn't turn to see if the prince followed. Temvros, on the other hand, stood there looking in disbelief of the 'audacity' of his 'subject'! Soon, he became aware that the snow, falling as hard as it did, started covering the trail the loaded man had left behind.

Temvros felt, for the first time ever, scared. What if Perseas would not return for him? He was ex-posed to the elements, feeling weak from loss of blood through his encounter and with the spectrum of being left alone to his fate! He bit his lips. He wasn't dead yet and, treachery would be surely pun-ished upon his eventual return home. He got up, unsteady, taking a few hesitant steps. He felt dizzy but he headed toward the direction Perseas had taken. He became more confident, as he noticed he could follow the fading tracks with not as much difficulty as he originally suspected.

He found the cave and Perseas attending the fire at its entrance. Kinos was placed at the innermost, sheltered and wrapped in the fur skin, the bear meat placed on a natural rock shelf across. Temvros went by the laying, unconscious man, not even looking at Perseas. Kinos was well covered up to his head. Temvros noted perspiration on the wounded man's forehead, partly because of the heat from the fur and the fire near-by, partly because he was running a high fever now.

Temvros now noticed that Perseas acknowledged his arrival with only a momentary look toward him. A look that (although quick, to avoid any encouragement -other than it happened- of protest) showed some emotion. It was obviously some sort of concern (relief or gladness?) but, at the moment, Temvros didn't care to investigate its reason or aim. In any event (he thought) he would find out, sooner or later. He placed himself next to the wounded man, sharing the cover of the fury skin. He was cold, weak and hungry, more so than angered. His anger could wait until rescue. He wouldn't forget it!

Now, Kinos started talking, then mumbling, then crying, in deep sleep and always feverish. Help had better come soon, but Temvros wasn't sure about that anymore. He could see the snow covering everything outside and kept on falling at a rate he never witnessed in his life before! He ventured the question to Perseas, since the man was a few years older. Perseas' muttered answer was that he had not seen such a storm before, either. He then stated that he would go to retrieve as much of the bear's meat as he could, before wolves would get to it, digging it out of the snow. But, first, he would bring in some more wood for the fire.

Temvros made a face at the prospect of eating bear meat and voiced his displeasure. Perseas, like a father would do to his ignorant and self-centered child, answered that all game (by now) had taken refuge to their hiding places. Unless help and provisions were to arrive soon, provided Filippos could manage to find them, they would have nothing to eat -maybe for days! So, he'd go and bring some more meat from the killed bear and Temvros was to rest assured that -when hunger settled in- bear meat could taste like the food of the gods! Meantime, while he was going out, Temvros should get some snow and place it on Kinos' forehead, thus keeping the fever down. Doing that, should help him recover some of his spirit, instead of sitting idle and brooding. He should also melt some snow to have water, instead of venturing out to find a brook later. Before Temvros could come up with an answer to Perseas' audacity in giving him orders, the man had turn around and left, disappearing behind nature's white curtain…

Anger, got hold of Temvros again. He was not about to obey orders from any of his inferiors. He pulled the fury hide away from Kinos' body and placed it across, at the other corner of the small cave, making sure there were no stones or dead branches under, so as to have a smooth rest. He lay down on it and covered himself. Before he realized it, he fell asleep. He dreamed he was back-home, rescued, with Perseas punished for his treachery and insubordination. He dreamed of young Pelagia crying at his feet, for he had her toy bear gutted, leaving nothing to play with. Her crying was very annoying to him and he was thinking of how to invent a new punishment, to show her how much more dependent she was on his good will, by letting her being alive, instead of taking care of her like he did her toy bear. Her cry turned to a wail and that woke him up. It was dark and the fire was nearly gone! Perseas was nowhere to be seen and Kinos looked dead, exposed to the cold wind and snow, which entered that side of the cave. Few steps further out, the entrance to the cave was almost closed by the snowdrift.

Temvros felt the panic taking a grip on him. Was he left alone to die like Kinos? Had Perseas come to find him asleep, his brother Kinos dead and decided to take off on his own, leaving Temvros to his fate? Temvros could not tell, except that he suspected that. He felt hard to breath, the cave being full of smoke, since the fire smoldered (for some time now) unattended and the snow drift would not let much of fresh air come through the entrance. He got up and worked frantically, to push the snow drift out of the entrance way. He felt weak and the piled snow weakened him even more. He soon dis-covered that the snow outside the cave had reached up to his waist in depth. The good news was that he started breathing easier, as fresh air came to replace the smoke and it was snowing no more.

He cleaned an up-hill like path, shoving snow on the sides, while stepping and packing what was under his feet. He could see the day coming to its end, as the light was dimming. There were low clouds, creating a fog which would not let him see far. A sudden groan from inside the cave made him jump. He went back and found Kinos trying to turn on his side facing him and uttering some-thing. Well! Kinos was not dead yet! Maybe, it was the gods' will not to let him die, but live and pay for his brother's desertion. Ha! That would be a twist!…

Temvros approached the wounded young man and guessed right; Kinos was asking to have some water. Temvros, took couple fistfuls of snow, packed it hard between his palms and let drops fall onto the mouth of Kinos. The wounded man leaked the melted snow, a look of pure gratitude in his eyes covering Temvros' face. Temvros let some more melted snow drop into the opened mouth and let the rest of the snowball in the hand of Kinos. Turning around, Temvros picked the fur and re-covered the young man, telling him to lay still and not try any talking, not yet. Looking around, he managed to collect a hip of dry wood Perseas had stacked earlier and some dry pine leaves, brought in by wind and animals through the years. He placed them carefully in the almost dead fire and, blowing hard at its embers, he gave a new life to it. He added some more dry wood and turned his attention in improving the cave's entrance opening.

By the time he finished, he was both exhausted and famished. "Damn you Perseas! You will certain-ly pay dearly when all turns back to normal!" Temvros promised in his mind. The night had come though and nothing more could be done until the next morning. He spent that night attending the thirst of Kinos, his own, the fire and sharing the comfort of the dead bear's fur. Wolves' howling made any sleep impossible, but no animals ever came close, obviously because of the fire.

The next morning's dawn found Temvros taking care of Kinos, as best he could, first, finding an added strange pleasure in doing so. Hunger was something permanent in his mind now and, he guessed, in Kinos' also. There was no more fever burning the wounded young man, who spent most of the time sleeping, waking-up only when having a bad dream or when in need of water. Temvros put the last of the dry wood on the fire and, turning, told Kinos he would return shortly. He took his bow and quiver and went out. The snow, covering everything, made his progress in walking very difficult. As far as he could see -the morning fog still low- there was no movement except his own, an eerie silence dominating. Snow drifts were sometimes chest deep, sometimes knee high. The slope being uneven, there were cavities difficult to detect, all covered by snow. He fell in many of them, causing a tiny avalanche (at times) from the surrounding snow piles. He feared he could break his neck. Panic was fought, by his anger and determination to show that he would overcome any treachery and that the guilty would have to pay in the end. He could detect no animal tracks and wandered where the last night's wolves might be hiding.

He continued his difficult walk toward where he thought the dead bear might lay. He'd stop every-so-often, trying to catch his breath, still weak and his hunger more demanding than ever. Sweat was pouring down his body, making him feel the icy air more so, under the gusty wind. He continued his plowing through the snow.

He suddenly came upon a clearing of the woods, with a majestic oak tree in the middle of it. He was ready to continue, wondering why a tree (not unusual by itself) ever caught his attention and forcing him to a second, closer look. On one of its lower branches, there was secured a large chunk of meat, resting a safe distance from any non-tree climbing animal. The snow covered the area around this oak tree and had a darker hue at a spot almost directly under that branch, not caused by any shade.

Was this the place the bear had been killed? He did not think so, for (he could remember well) the rocks surrounding the spot where the kill took place. This was an entirely different location, much closer to the cave. Taking him such a long time getting here, was only due to the snow and his weak (at this time) body. In any event, it didn't matter. He was lucky to find a good chunk of meat hang-ing on this tree, unspoiled. He'd take it back to the cave and throw that damned bear meat away. The only concern now, if he'd be able to reach it. So he thanked the gods and asked for their help.

With renewed determination, he came under the oak. He saw right away that he could not reach the branch, let alone retrieve the meat. He tried to jump-up but the snow was impeding his movements.

There was no way for him to climb, the tree trunk being too wide and straight for his arms to hug and climb. He was ready to lose control in his despair, when a thought came into his mind. He took his dagger belt off, knotted it around an arrow, placed the arrow to his bow and let it fly, aiming at the hanging chunk of meat. He did not pull the bow-string much, for he didn't want the arrow to be embedded to the tree -after piercing the meat. It worked! Now, the belt hanging down from the ar-row, could possibly be within his reach. He was utterly disappointed to find that, when he jumped, he still couldn't reach it. He backed off, catching his breath, collecting all the remaining strength he could muster. Gave a wild yell jumping up but his fingertips could only touch the belt, without grasp-ing it! The snow, packed hard here, softer there, did not give him a sure footing and was the real cause of his failure.

He decided to rest first, then, clear the area for better footing and free jump. There was no way he would abandon such a god-sent gift, even if it would take all his strength away. When he felt he had recovered most of his power back, he started cleaning. Stopping only to rub his freezing hands and have the blood flow again, he noticed that the darker color he first detected here under the hanging meat, turned from that of a rusted metal color to pure blood-like red. Then, an involuntary cry came out of his mouth, as his fingers reached and uncovered part of a human torso. Frantic now, he worked until he uncovered the face of a dead Perseas. The dead man's eyes were wide open, looking in horror beyond, mouth muscles in a set determined grinning of defiance, in spite of the knowledge of the outcome.

Temvros sagged onto his knees, trembling uncontrollably and, this time, the cold and hunger had nothing to do with it. He cried, like he had never done before, immune to cold, hunger and time. When he was able to collect some semblance of calm, he dug the rest of the body out. He wanted to know who or what caused Perseas' death. He soon found out the answer and realized why the dead man's eyes were showing such a horror. He had been eaten alive so-to-speak! Marks of sharp teeth were visible on the chunks of meat missing from his body. Claw marks were also visible all over his uncovered legs and hands, one leg completely gone! The stomach and chest cavities were torn open, the entrails all gone. His body (what remained of it) and his blood was the reason of the snow covering him being of darker hue.

On Perseas' side lay a half-drawn, sword and a broken javelin, its iron tip missing. The deadly attack on him had apparently come unexpectedly, until the last moment! But, if so, how was the meat chunk hanging from the tree branch? Did Perseas know his death was imminent and threw it up there? If the animal(s) was/were after that meat, why didn't he let go and save himself by running back to the cave? Had he placed the meat up the tree first for safe-keeping before he met his fate? Those, were questions which Temvros could not answer for himself, nor could he ask Perseas, for dead men weren't apt to talking, or so Temvros thought…

He retrieved the broken javelin and started picking-up the half-seethed sword, for he had to bring them back with him. Kinos was entitled to them, as he had to know about his brother's death. But, when Temvros lifted the sword, he noticed the weapon was not half-drawn but half-seethed. He also noticed blood marks on the sword. Placed, and found, by the right side of the dead man and close to his head, it could not mean the blood was his. No Makedonian would sheath his sword blooded, not cleaning it first, regardless of his abilities as a dying man. He'd rather leave it unsheathed than risk the possibility of having the weapon stained and rusted before being found and delivered to the next of kin.

Temvros pulled the sword out of its scabbard. In-between the hilt and the tip of the blade, there seemed to be deliberate markings. Temvros recognized them as letters! So! Perseas could write? Much of it was smeared but Temvros eyes could make out this: "W....s. Kil..d some. No m..e run...o man....ope kin....nds.e.t.ves.yb...ther". This was written by the dying man, in hope that it would be found? In his own blood or that of the animal(s)? Temvros thought about the message itself. What did it mean? Some words were easy to recognize and understand. He'd have to work on the rest and try to get the meaning. Not right now though.

He placed the sword back in its scabbard, ever so careful as not to have the blood letters smear more and mess them further, then securing it around his waist, using the dead man's belt. Next, he picked-up the broken javelin and, using its pointed metal butt, he reached for his own belt, still hanging from the arrow, attached to the chunk of meat on the tree branch. Weaving it around the belt and jerking it downward in sudden, strong pulls, he finally managed to bring the whole thing down. He covered the dead man with snow again, having no way (or strength enough) to dig a grave, since he did not want to use the sword and ruin what was written in blood and his own dagger was unsuitable on the frozen ground. He made sure to pack the snow as tightly as he could, in hope of discouraging the return of wolves or other predators to return and finish the job. With the will of the gods, rescue would come soon and a proper burial would take place. There was one more question in his mind: Why didn't the predator(s) finish eating the corpse? He had no answer.

He started plodding his way back, using the wake and tracks he had made coming. It saved some energy he badly needed, for the weight of the meat he had to carry and his sudden weakness. The real-ization of such misfortune -in such a short time- had a great impact on his mind and body!

Temvros reached the cave well past the mid-day's mark. The weather didn't look promising, but no more snowfall -for the time being. He found Kinos sleeping deep and soundless. He touched lightly on his forehead. No fever. Better let him sleep until thought was collected properly, until the message on the sword could be deciphered and until food was prepared. Bad news is always better taken with a full stomach...

Temvros secured the meat close to the chunk of the bear meat, now thinking that adequate provi-sion should be kept in store. He went out again and returned shortly after dragging a long branch of a tree he noticed and which had not fall on the ground but stood suspended where it broke from the trunk and it was not too wet. He placed part of it over the fire and cut a small piece of the meat he brought. He, then, held that meat with his dagger over the fire, letting it cook. With his other hand, he drew Perseas' sword -ever so carefully- and started reading the message. The first word certainly meant to say wolves. Then, it said: killed some. So, Perseas had killed some of the attacking wolves, with (perhaps) enough time to place the cut portion of meat on the tree branch? No more run, the message said next, rather easy to read. Obviously then, Perseas had run away from his pursuers, until, loaded as he was, he got tired (impeded by the snow?) and couldn't run any more. The rest of the message was very hard to decipher and understand. Temvros had to think of a reason why Perseas did not drop the meat and run to the cave, saving himself?! As he obviously had killed some wolves, the pack had probably stopped to eat their dead kin -one would think. Dropping the meat he carried, would also have given him additional time and freedom to reach safety behind the fire and the small cave entrance. Unless... Unless Perseas had already lost his one leg (or part of it) and that was the reason he could not run any more, that was the reason he did save the meat for them, knowing he had no other choice but to stand and fight to the end? Perhaps, that was when the final, deadly bites from the wolf pack were delivered, when Perseas was securing Temvros' own survival, instead of trying to save his own life? These thoughts reversed Temvros' feelings toward Perseas, instantly! Poor Perseas! What a horrible death! Temvros cried in remorse for a long time...

He eventually turned his attention back to the sword. The next 'words' were: ..ope kin....nds.e.t.ves.yb...ther. Now, this was a challenge! It looked like having something to do with the king(?), maybe. But, if so, the king was days away, at the palace, perhaps still unaware of their predicament. There was no way Filippos could have arrived there so soon to pass the news. Was there a possibility that Perseas was referring to Temvros himself as his (future) king? Or, perhaps, it had nothing to do with a king at all? In the whole undecipherable part, there were just three letters together: kin. It could mean just that, kinfolk. But, putting this under scrutiny, it did not make any sense at all! On the other hand, if Temvros' inclination to believe that Perseas was referring to him as his future king, things would have to be re-evaluated and past sentiments to be placed under a completely different perspective.

Some noise made by Kinos, forced Temvros to turn and look toward Perseas' brother. The thought came to him, that the last word on the sword had to be brother. Before that, by letter y, was it an m? My? My brother? Did the dead man mean Kinos? The rest was even more difficult to decipher, pro-vided that, what was thought as right -for the moment- proved to be right; period!

Temvros decided to let things be as they were for a while and checked the meat cooking. It was done on its one side, so he turned the dagger it was held by, the other way. The smell of the meat, cooking, made his hunger ever so greater. He resisted the desire to eat it half cooked. No other sickness was needed here. He suspected this meat was also part of the killed bear and wanted to cook it well. It would be his first time ever (hopefully his last also!) having to eat bear meat. He did not want to take any chances. The odor apparently woke Kinos up and he was making some weak noise. Temvros went close and assured him that both of them were about to have some food soon.

Night was approaching again and the first howling -followed by many other- not too distant, chilled their blood. Kinos' weak voice called for his brother. Temvros lied that Perseas had gone to see if any help could be found and that he was to return shortly. He figured there was plenty of time to tell the bleak truth, later. Right now, what Kinos needed was rest, peace of mind, and food!

Temvros turned to attend the fire again and the cooking piece of meat. If help would not arrive by the next day, guided from the smoke which could be seen from distance (he was sure of that), he was to go out and seek some more wood. The wolves' howling told him such wood gathering would not be an easy task and thanked the gods for this day's missed encounter with them. He was very concerned about Perseas' 'buried' body. Had he repacked plenty of snow on top, enough to block the scent? He thought he did. Still, he was surprised they had not finish eating Perseas' body altogether! Why would they leave it half eaten? The only logical explanation he could think-of, was based of tales he heard through the years. Wolves had to have a pack leader. If their leader would get old or died, a younger one (or ones) would challenge the old (if still alive) until one would defeat the other, thus be-coming the leader of the pack. If the old leader died unexpectedly, the younger ones would fight each-other, until one would prevail, suspending any other action in-between. Therefore, any prior victim, serving as food, would not be touched by the pack, until the new leader would permit it, having the first share of it. But those were tales. Had something like that happened in this case? It seemed ir-relevant at this point. Temvros could only hope the remains of the body would be left there untouch-ed, until such time a proper burial could take place...

Having in mind all these thoughts and hypothetical solutions to the problems, Temvros checked the meat. It was finally cooked well! He took Kinos' dagger and, with help from his own, cut a good por-tion, which he cut again and again in small pieces. He put it on a peel of bark from the tree trunk by the fire, brought it to Kinos and started feeding him. This act of his caught him by surprise and al-most missed the wounded man's mouth, as the thought occurred to him. This was his first time (ever) Temvros truly cared for another human being -aside from himself! Further, he was discovering a new-found pleasure in doing so and, reflecting on it, he almost forgot about his own hunger.

Finishing later his own food (by the way, bear meat is certainly edible when one is hungry enough), he went by the fire at the cave's entrance. Several pairs of shining eyes could be seen in the near dis-tance, moving to and fro. Low growls, half barks, made sure they accentuated the wolves' ominous presence. Angered and saddened at the same time, Temvros turned to the cave. He picked up his bow and some arrows and returned at the entrance. He placed an arrow and bent the bow, carefully ob-serving the movements. The burning fire played tricks with the light, so he stepped beyond it, placing it behind him, but not far. He waited some, so his eyes could adjust. Then, he followed the pair of eyes closer, the ones which seemed to belong to the boldest of the beasts. He hoped this was the leader. He aimed carefully and let the arrow fly.

A piercing cry of pain was heard, then growls and the noise of cracking bones followed. Then, sets of eyes were seen traveling back and forth, now appearing, now gone. Temvros noticed after a while that the noise and the eyes were going further and further away in the darkness of the cold night, until they got lost. He prayed there would be a quiet night ahead. He returned inside the cave, pushed the big branch further onto the fire, judging it would last the whole night and settled down. Across him, Kinos had fallen asleep again. Good! He needed the recovery and, sleep was one among the best medicines!...

Temvros woke-up at first light. No night's sounds bothered their sleep and he was thankful. He looked around. Kinos was still sleeping and the fire was going well, though more wood would be in need, soon. For now, he cut some more meat and skewered it on a long twig, over the fire. He saw the need to change Kinos' dressing of the wounds. He woke the man up and took the old strips of cloak off the wounds. He placed plenty of snow on the cavity side of a large piece of tree bark, set it by the fire to have the snow melt and cut some more strips from his cloak. When the snow in the bark had turn to water, he washed Kinos' wounds and re-dressed them with newly cut strips, throwing the old ones into the fire. He shared some water with Kinos and, the meat done, he fed him again.

Kinos was recovering very speedily and he started asking more and persistent questions. Temvros helped adjusting Kinos in a seating position, his back leaned against the cave's wall. He tried to avoid answers, making light conversation as to Kinos' condition and his own admiration on how well the wounds started healing. Suddenly, Kinos' face grew dark, his eyes locked across the cave on his brother's sword and broken javelin. Out of his mouth, the question popped forcibly, with no room for evasion. "Where is my brother?" Temvros cursed his carelessness for leaving these items out in the open. Now he had no other choice but to give the sad news as gently as he could. He praised the dead man and, while doing so, he found added satisfaction from his praise, which concerned another individual, not himself. This realization of his tremendous maturity within few days, made him ex-press his silent thanks to the gods and Perseas' spirit.

Kinos took the sad news with courage, a great deal for a man just recovering from such an ordeal as his own. After Temvros felt that Kinos relaxed a bit from his anguish, he told him that he was going out for some more wood and left the man in his privacy, free to think and mourn his brother's loss.

Temvros was lucky to locate a fallen tree, not far from the cave and started chopping off the branch-es which were not buried in the snow, so they would be the drier ones. He made a sizable bundle of cut branches and started carrying them toward the cave when, from the top of the hill, cries of joy rang in his ears. The rescue party led by Filippos, had seen the smoke from the fire and came to the cave. Now everything (or almost everything) would be right again...

The rescue party brought provisions, horses and clothes. Temvros dressed himself with clean, warm clothes and helped the others with Kinos' cleaning and dressing, which amazed (and amused) Filip-pos. He led

Filippos to the location of Perseas' body remains. They cleaned them and placed them respectfully on a litter, with orders to have the man buried with full honors of a hero, upon return at home. Then, to his insistence, he cooked some more of the bear meat still in the cave and, after offering to gods, they all had a good portion of it. Finishing their meal, Temvros ordered to have the cave cleaned -come spring time- and sanctified and dedicated to goddess Tyhi and the Fates. They all camped in and outside the cave that night, their last night there. Wolf howlings were heard again, but very distant this time and Temvros dreamed of a smiling Pelagia with sky blue eyes. The next morning they started their return home, with Kinos on a litter following the one of his dead brother, with Temvros riding by his side while Filippos was leading the group...

Since the days of that event, Temvros' character changed drastically. The egocentric, spoiled indi-vidual, became a young man of compassion and concern, not only for members of his immediate family, but for every Lynkestian. Traces of the old cockiness, were channeled to Lynkestian image projection only, a trade which was impossible to abandon. When he talked to his Father about start-ing a family of his own, he begged the king to intercede for the hand of Pelagia. His father and king, embraced proudly his son, giving him the blessing.

From the wedding day-on, Temvros' love affairs were his wife, his son, the parents and other family members and Lynkestis -in that order! For himself, he would graciously receive what was freely given and nothing more!...

> "...coordinated political front on foreign affairs
> in Ellas (Greece), is worst than the domestic one.
> It is like the perfect woman of one's dreams, an
> elusive fiction, a poor judgment on reality!..."
> Leonidas Faitas, Korkyrean Ellinas

V

"We are not, not all of us, native sons and daughters on this parcel of land we call Vottiaea. All through the years and since antiquity, many tribes and clans came and went, always leaving their marks behind. Thrakian

Visaltes, Amydones, Vryges, Peones, all passed through, because our land is rich and mostly flat and open. One can easily come down to our flat land from the heights of the up-per mountainous slopes of sunset direction, as easily as from the cold Voreas wind and the sunrise, Thrakian side. From the direction of the hot summer winds, there's the gulf of Therma (or Thermi, if you pre-fer), an Anthemountian town, open to the sea, therefore to pirates. So, we have had many 'visitors'! Whoever stayed here for good, no matter his origin, adopted our land like it adopted him in a total way, only lovers can witness and understand, like the line my own family came from.

We did come from the sea, refugees from the island of Kriti, descendants of Minos, the gods' ap-pointed judge of the dead, when, the great disaster stroke the island. The volcanic island of Thyra had an eruption, which sent most of it at the bottom of the sea and created such earth movements and tidal waves that brought total disorder and created havoc to our state of affairs and well being! Its force covered tremendous stretch of areas, as far as Egyptos and Assyria! For seasons on end, the sky would rain nothing but tefra, the volcanic ash and the sun was covered for many moon changes (we couldn't see those either), causing total crop failure.

The Aheans on the main land took advantage of this loss of order and came to conquer what was left. So, some of us took on to the ships and sailed here. I know about all these events, because of the tradition in my family on carrying through generations, the story of our clan. When the Danao-Ahe-ans warred against Tria, we -from our new country- supported king Priamos. Although not related, we had excellent commercial and cultural ties with them from the old days of king Minos, which continued after our arrival in this land. Beside that, the loss of our original place in Kriti by those same Danao-Aheans, was giving us the opportunity to extract our revenge. Our double axes sent many of them to Adis, but we ended-up on the losing side again…

On their way to return to their kingdoms, they raided the shore areas of Vottiaea, coming all the way to the end of the shallow waters of the Pella lagoon, due to their easy access from the sea. Since, most of our major towns are built further inland, like Kyrros and Ihnae, the only connection to the sea being the village of Pella, close to the mouth of river Lydias. As the years went by, we all became one with the local clans, called by the Great Bard (and all the rest after him) Vottiaean Makedonians.

The latest disaster, befallen on our small parcel of land, was the Peonian invasion a few years back, which forced many to migrate to the land called

Vottiki now, by the three-pronged peninsula. Now, we are under the 'protection' of other Makedonian kingdoms, according to each one's strength or weakness, clans like the Orestids, the Elimiotes or the Imathians, are the 'allies'. When we arrived from Kriti, Imathians, Eordeans and Almopes used to be totally independent. Now, like us, their kings owe allegiance to the king of Orestis, or Lynkos, or Elimiotis, depending who has the upper hand at any particular time.

Because of the rivalry between those royal houses, we, Vottiaeans, have been left to our own devices -more or less. Our governing houses, are equally divided between the house of Kyrros which claims ancestry from Magnitas, the brother of Makedon and our own town of Ihnae, which -of course- claims ancestry from Minoan Kriti.

My name is Idomenefs (they like to call me Idomeneas or Meneas here), a reminder of the Danao-Ahean chief, who first ruled Kriti after its conquest by the Athinian king Thisefs/ Thiseas. I come from a long, traditional line of priests, worshiping the mighty power of Posidonas, the ruler of the seas and earth-shaker. It is a very old tradition in my family to succeed from father to son, gener-ation after generation. It is something, one doesn't find happening in most clans, neither around here nor in any of the kingdoms and states below Olympos, unless, one goes to Kriti. There, it remains a tradition, as it is here with my family in our clan.

With the same tradition in mind, another custom has been also kept, the husbandry of cattle. Our bulls, Posidonas' favorites, are the best all around. The god also blessed us with the raising of excel-lent horses, another animal species he favors. Nonetheless, this area is also the provider of the best fruits and cereals, as the climate is more moderate than that of the inland kingdoms. We are so bles-sed, we rival Imathia, with its inherited famous gardens of Midas, so abounding in fruits and cereals.

Because of all these reasons, most of us have turned to agriculture, animal husbandry and products, which we exchange for other needs from our neighbors. Merchants arrive from places like Athinae, Korinthos, Aegina, Hios and Efessos, provided the pirates get caught sleeping or, with good luck, are avoided. Halkidians and Eretrians from the island of Evia started coming also, bringing earthenware products and Finikian-colored linen.

From above Peonia and Dardania ways, whenever the area is without invasion and wars, amber, gold and silver comes to us for exchange in our markets. As from the mountain kingdoms, the plentiful forests of Orestis, Elimiotis and Lynkestis provide the timber in exchange of hides, horses, cattle and the fruits of our earth.

Naturally, all these activities brought more influence in all aspects of our lives. One can say the Vot-tiaea remains weak as a state, yet strong, exactly because of all its importance and interest to and from the neighboring kingdoms and states through commerce and good, productive soil. I have to admit, this is a very precarious balance of internal and external powers, pulling and shifting now here, now there. Even in customs and beliefs, the influence of various external elements is strong and introduction of the Thrakian cult of Dionysos and the Kaviri has been adopted many generations ago-after changes which suited our mentality and state of character. Obviously, Zefs and the rest of the Olympians are worshipped also here, as it is proper in Ellas.

The creation -in recent years- of a lower Peonian kingdom named -more to approach us better- as Paeonia, became another polarization center among local powers, Vylazora being its main town. If it gets strong enough and remains within more civilized conduct -as its king declares- it will serve as a buffer to the incursions from Dardanes and other barbarians. We have sent to Paeonia many of our masters of trade, as well as other teachers of various disciplines, which improved our relation with them and, I hope, secured our independence and importance a bit more. We also keep prime interest on the three-pronged peninsula, to the sunrise, named now Halkidiki, on account of its many settlers from the city-state of Halkis.

Our hope is that this balance of power remains as is, although rumors have it that a storm is, per-haps, under way, coming from the sunset mountain states and, namely, Orestis. For all of us who have access to the king's court, this rumor became the talk of the day for some time now. There is some anxiety for events to come, potentially bad for us, and it is a fact that several changes occurred in those upper Makedonian kingdoms. Naturally, all rumors -as well as facts- have to be taken with some serious consideration on future gain or loss, but, as we say in our parts, where there is some smoke, there has to be a fire burning!

To make it clear, the rumor has it that the kingdom of Orestis has employed three brothers and their kinfolk, who arrived recently from Thessalia and stayed with their relatives first, in the region of Makedonis, between the mountains of Tymfea, Kamvounia, Olympos and river Aliakmon. This area was the small kingdom of Karanos first, then of his son Kinos, now succeeded by Tyrimmas. They all were and are Dorian clans and descendants from Iraklis, since the first move of the tribe, many generations ago. Now, these three brothers employed by king Antiohos of Orestis, are the sons of king Timenos, from Argos in Peloponnisos, a kingdom far to the hot summer wind direction. They are kinsmen of Tyrimmas and his clan, because Timenos is the brother of Karanos, therefore of same descent. The names of these three newcomers are Gavanis, Aeropos and Perdikkas. They are good oplites warriors and excellent horsemen, perhaps because they spent time in Thessalia.

As I mentioned, they came to Makedonis and stayed with their kin, Tyrimmas, who's under the pro-tection of Orestis and Antiohos. The latter, happening to be at war against Tymfea, Elimiotis and Paravaea, called for their assistance. Thanks to them and their fighting ability, Antiohos won the war and now, he is the undisputed leader in that part of Makedonia, his appetite far more increased. The kingdoms of Lynkestis, Eordea, Dassaretis and Imathia are not too happy with this development, but being rather weak now because of recent invasions from the barbarians, could do nothing but protest.

It may be that all of us are soon to become Orestid subjects. I was asked by our king to be looking at the omens given by our daily sacrifices and, so far, I have seen nothing good. Omens do not seem to favor our wish for the customary balanced power among the neighboring states. We should, perhaps, keep a close observation on the moves of these Timenides or Argeathes brothers…

I have to go now and report the latest from the omens from today's sacrifice, to our king. In actual-ity, there is nothing new since yesterday, or the day before. The same unfavorable results! May god Posidonas help us, for our king is an old man and his heir to the throne still a young pup of two plus ten springs! I think I will have to invent some mild lies of no consequence on my way for the audience and that, falls among my duties…"

"Somewhere, somehow, something went wrong!
We are more concerned of what others may
think of us or of what they say or do to us, but
not of what is *right for us to do!*"
Andreas G. Rados, Makedonian Ellinas, freedom-fighter WW II

VI

Pelegon knew his family was indigenous from time immemorial in this land of Pelagonia. He also knew they were never anything more than simple people, with a small plot of land and an equally small herd of goats, sheep and just two cows. These two cows especially, were the beasts of burden, the team which helped tilling the small plot and the wagon pullers, when produce could be brought to the market for exchange of other needs. He needed a bull badly. A beast like that could be used to fertilize these and other cows, bringing some extra bartering room for the meager family income.

But life was never easy. Yet, it was the life the family knew. During especially heavy winters, the dried-out cow dung proved to be the best fire-starter for the hearth, not to mention its insulating properties when it was applied on walls of the family's huts and white-washed after it dried. Milk from the cows, the sheep and goats, served as bartering power, making sure some would stay for family consumption in food supplement, either in its form as a drink, or in the form of cheese.

Shearing the sheep wool provided countless months of work for the women folk, preparing rough garments to clothe the whole family. On good years, it was an added blessing, as the excess wool could be sold in the market. As for meat, it was meant to be spared for exceptional, feast days.

The biggest trouble was the land plot. The soil wasn't what one could call rich. A few anemic fruit trees here and there, some grazing space and the rest full of boulders, remnants of the old rock the ice from Pindos range had sent down untold years ago. Why did the family keep it? Pelegon didn't really know, except that it was part of the family's 'fortune' and that was that.

He was a strong man, Pelegon was, the strength stemming from years of wrestling with the earth, the elements and living. During his youth, he had to be the tallest man around, with the broadest shoulders. His palm could easily cover the head of a grown man and his arms could lift the heaviest load. Even now, after all these years of hardship and misfortunes, stooped and past his prime, he could easily match the height of a good-sized southerner. He met with many ups and downs in his life, mostly downs. Many a time -as a young boy- he had to follow his parents, running for dear life up on the Pindos range, when the enemy raided the region. As an adult and with a family of his own, things had not changed. Dardanians, Penestes and Peones kept on coming as they were pleased, burning, looting and killing. Nine out of ten times the family would return to the plot and hamlet, finding nothing left, only to build-up again on the same spot and with the same meager means, until the next raid.

Once, he happened to own a horse and, during one of the usual barbarian raids, he was called by the local big land holder to enlist in the cavalry, chasing the intruders. He proudly obeyed, given a spare sword and a javelin. Thank the gods for that horse. He made it back home in one -more or less- piece, for the campaign was a total disaster! As a matter of fact, that horse died from exhaustion, a few stadia before reaching back at the hamlet. He did not own a horse since, nor did he go to war again. He'd just take the family and run.

The main family income came from the two cows, which served as a milk source, as a team pulling the plough and as transportation, pulling the wagon to the nearest town market. He would have them impregnated every so often as to have another cow or bull produced. The new cow would serve the same way, the bull for rent to others who wanted their cows to reproduce. As the aged ones would fulfill their mission, they served to supply meat for the house or the market. Disease and raids never let him have more than two for long. As for his goats and sheep, he had the same type of luck in their numbers. When there was a good year, sheared wool from the sheep would lighten the burden a bit.

As for the plot, aside some anemic fruit trees, the cereals produced there were just enough for the household needs. The most recent Dardano-Illyrian raid almost brought him to his grave. You see, Pelegon's Tyhi blessed him to have four daughters and two sons. With a poor plot like his, the main income coming from the few animals he owned, his daughters were an added burden. Oh, not that they were not of any help or incapable. No! But, who -in his right mind- would ever allow women (the ones of age) to take the animals grazing at the slopes with marauding barbarians raiding at will?

His daughters were good in helping Mother at housekeeping, milking, cheese-making, garment sewing. But those things were not bringing any added income or bartering for needed goods. They were helping in consumption of severely restricted food availability only. As of his two sons, one was only two plus ten, the other just over eight springs old, not much of a help from those quarters either, eh?

Now what happened and almost caused Pelegon to meet his ancestors, was this last raid of combined Vryges, Penestes and Dardanes. His elder son had asked to go hunting, to supplement the food at the table, taking with him the younger one also. Pelegon, feeling that -sooner or later- the junior had to learn the skills, gave permission for the boys to hunt together, provided they'd stay near the plot. He took the rest of his family to Keramiae, to the market. The wife with the two youngest daughters got on the wagon, guiding the cows. He, the two elder daughters and the dog, led the small herd of sheep to the shearing place.

The bad news found him there, at the market. People started running, dropping everything on their way, just to make their run faster. The barbarians were coming back! He picked-up his family and started for home, to see what could be saved there, forgetting sheep and cows. Approaching the tiny hamlet of theirs they met with a neighbor, Klitos, son of Polyperhon. He had started heading to Keramiae looking for them. The enemy had passed already their hamlet, on his way to Lynkestis. They pillaged and burned what they couldn't carry, killing whom ever was unlucky to be on their way. Klitos witnessed the killing of Pelegon's younger son. The older had sustained a very bad head wound, trying to protect his sibling and run toward the mountain. He was surely dead by now! Klitos himself was not in any better condition, as he received several arrows in his chest and back, none of them fatal though. They had left, thinking he was dead. Later as he found Pelegon, he took him and sought medical attention by anyone who knew how to dress wounds…

Upon hearing these devastating news when he came-to, Pelegon turned his eyes toward his womenfolk and after an indescribable, painful look, he collapsed, his hair turning white instantly! He remained unable to move, even talk, for many months after; when he finally recovered somewhat, he was much less of the man he had been. Oh, he'd do what was expected of him in order to sustain the family, but he did it in a trance-like fashion, eyes mostly vacant. The only time there'd be a spark in them was the time a story of revenge was told -taken against the barbarians. But, before long, even stories like that ceased to bring a lapse toward his old self. The body of his older son was never found, a victim of the wolves and carrion birds -no doubt.

Within the next few months, his wife died -who knows from what pain and what unfulfilled dreams. The property, bad as it was to begin with, became worthless, unattended. The half burned house never repaired, was more like an uninhabited ruin than shelter for the remnants of his family. One after the other, the cows died and the sheep and goat herd sold or slaughtered for some food. The oldest of his daughters, Terpsinomi, had the good fortune (and looks) to get married to a merchant from the town of Antania and she was gone. The second in age, Adea (favoring

Pelegon's physique), had to play the role of mother, sister and wife to the few remaining in the 'household'. Relatives and friends tried to help by offering various tasks to Pelegon, in exchange for needed food and clothes. He was never a person with any status in their hamlet, but he was well known as a dependable and hard working man. They had to push him to do something now and he was doing it half -hearted, prefer-ring to take long walks instead. As months and years went by, people supported him less and less. He became the pariah of the hamlet and shied away.

He continued taking his long walks, stooped, white haired before his time. People were curious as to why he was doing it and many followed him from a distance, for many weeks. Seeing the walks were just walks, they lost interest and gave up. There was another rumor that Adea was selling herself to any passing-by stranger, in order to feed her young sisters and her strange father. As she looked more like a man, she wasn't making exactly a fortune on that. Her two young siblings, eight and five years of age now, weren't even called by their names anymore. Everyone was referring to them as 'Them', two ragtag young girls always hungry, always dirty, always left to themselves…

Then, there came another rumor making its rounds in the small hamlet. Some of the people, the ones who helped the family in the past, or were still trying to do so, started finding valuables, hidden (but hidden in order to be found) in their houses, stables, land-plots and such. They were finding a silver cup here, some furs there for bartering at the market (or used for domestic needs) or an added goat or sheep to one's herd. Not one person was missing anything from his household, nobody found something belonging to him into someone else's plot! Things were appearing out of nowhere, added to one's possessions. The folks also noticed that Adea was benefiting even more having these 'gifts' found in and around the dilapi-dated 'house' of Pelegon, as she went to sell most of them for food and clothing herself and 'Them'. Neighbors renewed their interest on Pelegon's affairs but, since they were unable to discover anything more than his usual long strolls and unable to find who the donor(s) of such valuables was/were, they soon gave-up again.

Their only concern became a fear of retaliation, for (most of) these 'donations' were found to have come from previous Dardanian or Illyrian ownership. These 'gifts' worried them most and for the longest time. Since no retaliation appeared from Dardanes or Illyrians, they soon became accustomed and expected the 'gifts' to continue.

Some long time went-by and Adea seemed to be making a true profit because of these 'presents'. 'Them', the two young sisters of her, improved in appearance, better dressed and fed. 'Them' even got their names back -after some effort to remember. The older of the two had the name Dorothea (meaning god's gift), the other's name remembered as being Evridiki (meaning good judgment). Adea, herself, stopped her 'profession' and had the hut fixed to look more like a house again! In two more years' time, she found a man with whom to get married, the same one who fixed her house. Attalos, of course, was not a choice-prize, but he was a good husband, a conscious provider, a shoulder she could lean-on and a second father to the young ones. Within a short time after their nuptials, they had their own two brats to raise, two fair-looking (considering the looks of the parents) boys.

Her wedding to Attalos, coincided with the stopping of 'gifts' found, at the houses and plots of the ones who used to help her. As for Pelegon, he continued his coming and going, unnoticing and (for the most time) unnoticed, living in his own strange world. It was Adea's duty to catch-up with her Father (when he'd show-up) and mend his rags or give him a forced bath and a general clean-up from lice. He withstood all treatment with the same indifference and absent-mindedness, as with all else in his so-called life after the loss of his two sons and his wife.

As Adea's well-being improved and no need for a helping hand seemed to be in need, the 'presents' to her also diminished, with only an occasional 'gift' on certain dates marking the younger ones' birth anniversaries -for both of her sisters and her sons. This brought a little discontent among the neighbors, relatives and friends and roused (once more) their curiosity overall. All came to nothing again, as every attempt to investigate and find the source of the 'gifts' brought no result. The only topic for discussion, now, would be the Dardanian or Illyrian raids.

It became apparent -and strange- that through the years and since Pelegon's great misfortune, no raiding parties had come back again, until, the spring ten years past that tragedy, the event reoccur-ed with a great force. A strong army of Argestes attacked the region, sending everyone who was fast on foot or horse, up on the Pindos range again. There, they heard (for the first time ever) of a small band of Pelagonian braves, giving a good retaliatory lesson on the invaders. The news came to them from a traveling Thessalian merchant, a very old man named Kloppas, who, played dead and 'never mind of losing the merchandize which can be replaced'. He survived and 'walked-in' to tell them the story.

"There were the raiders" he said, "plucking off from the dead whatever they could, when, from the woods' end, came upon them this whirling wind (blessed be the gods) of brave Pelagonians, and gave a taste of their own 'medicine' to the surprised invaders. These braves were led by a very tall leader (even when judged by Makedonian standards) with so horrible a face, no wonder his presence -only- spread terror among the invaders!" The merchant said he was equally terrified by the sight but his curiosity and his happy feeling of seeing the enemy getting a good measure (of what had given) back, kept him looking when he could. He still had to play 'dead' and lay among the other victims of those dreaded and hated Argestes. He was amazed, he said, seeing that monstrous-looking warrior spear two of his opponents at once -so great appeared to be his strength! When asked to describe the looks of that warrior, he said that the left side of that horrific face was almost missing, leaving a horrible grim -like the very underworld's own smile- permanently facing friend and foe alike.

"The raiders gave a last effort, concentrating all they had, on this one warrior" the merchant re-sumed his narration "They attacked him in numbers, forcing him away from his band of supporters.

Even then, his power almost overcame their desperate and vigorous drive. He killed more than half of his attackers, their own leader among the first. But, their numbers were overwhelmingly uneven. Attacked from behind, as well as from the front, he sustained several mortal wounds, which would have finished any other person much sooner. Finally, with a great yell, he dispatched one last opponent and fell on the ground." Kloppas covered his face at this point, his old, bonny shoulders shaking as he sobbed. "I have never in my life seen such a brave man!" he said, recovering some. "His small band took to their heels after that, being outnumbered by far and without his leadership. The enemy also, their leader lost, withdrew, not bothering with spoils or the dead and dying. Mean-time, I was able to seek and find a better hiding place between some bushes, praying to the gods above and below to spare my life. Suddenly, a tall but stooped figure of a -more than middle aged- man, came running up the slope and behind some boulders, yelling at and shooing the raiders as one would to a herd of animals. This was a rather comic sight and I could have laugh along the amused Argestes, chasing and playing with him, if it wasn't for my fear of being discovered. The raiders also lost their interest soon and one of them gave a thrust of his sword into the man's belly, sending him to roll on the ground. As if that was the signal for their departure, they moved-on. The only living left in the area -to which I can lead you to and show you- were myself (still shaking of fear and excite-ment) the dying old man and the yipes, these high-mountain dwelling feathered vultures, who are quick to respond to the dying smell. I rose on my feet, ready to leave the place. My interest and admiration toward the brave, as well as the pity on the dying old man, made me go and see if there was something I could do.

I got to the old man first. I saw at once that nothing could be done to save him, but I could offer some last minute comfort. I lifted his head and made a small pack of the soft earth underneath, plac-ing his head back again, at an angle now, for some relief. He seemed oblivious of any knowledge as to what was or happening around him, nor did he seem to recognize the human services provided him. In any event, I went looking for some water to offer him. Doing so, I passed by the body of that fallen giant man, with the horrible face. To my horror, I noticed his one eye (his left was missing along with that part of his face) was following my moves! The man was still alive! Fear and panic demanded my run-ning away. My admiration of his deeds and strength brought my steps closer to him. I bent over the warrior and (trembling from fear) I asked if there was anything I could do to comfort him.

He opened his ruined lips uttering words which drowned in a gush of thick blood, along with the odor of a man soon to die. I turned to flee. To my horror, a still strong hand grabbed my leg, stop-ping me dead in my tracks. Fearing I would faint at any moment, I forced myself to sit down by him, warm urine flowing freely between my legs -I am not ashamed to admit. The 'mouth' of that horrible face moved again and I forced myself to lean over and put my ear close to it. More blood bubbles sprayed my face, as did more foul odor. Yet, there was a distinct whisper. My heart ready to fail me I asked him to repeat. 'Bring…me…old man!' He begged. I looked at him incredulously. You want me to bring you over to the old man's side? I asked stupidly. How can I lift you there? His single eye turned hard and cold like death impersonated, yet begging. Oh, I get it! I said. You want me to bring the old man to you! Yes, my heroic chief! Yes, my life saver! I said. I will gladly do it, if you only let my ankle go, I will do it at once! He did let go of me. Happy, I staggered toward the old man, think-ing to keep-on going, for I was at my wit's end. The pity I felt for a dying hero and an old man, made me obey the request. I went and gently lifted the mortally wounded old man and brought him by the warrior's side, almost facing each-other. Exhausted, I sank next to them, unable to even think of tak-ing off, living the moments like in a dream.

With an almost superhuman effort, the giant warrior placed his left hand on the old man's right shoulder, turning him close toward his own face. More blood bubbles came out of his grotesque mouth, forming words I could not hear. I had not the stamina and courage to lean closer and try to make them out. Yet, I could clearly see and witness a deed, nothing short of a miracle. The almost lifeless eyes of the old man, shone instantly full of life and recognition! His right hand gripped the warrior's left one in an effort to bring them closer. I sat there, numb, able only to observe. A trium-phant smile covered both their faces. One old (turning almost youthful again), the other (one of an unspeakable ugliness) full of tender love and respect! I continued sitting there, barely breathing and it was a long time past, when I realized both men were already dead…"

The people of the hamlet followed the Thessalian to the battleground and found Pelegon's body tightly embraced with the horribly looking giant warrior. They tried to separate them. Finding that impossible, they dug a single grave for both and buried them together. Only Adea knew exact-ly who the warrior was but she kept it to herself. Adea and her husband went (a few nights later) and exhumed the embraced bodies. They took them to the small, worthless plot and reburied them under the only tree worthy of any mention, the oak next to the trickle of a brook which marked the bound-ary. Father and missing son were finally reunited and rested in peace…

The plot of land was never sold, or used for any reason. To this day, the sons and daughters of Adea's sons and the children of her sisters' children, hold a yearly gathering under the oak tree by the brook. It's been noticed by the hamlet's people that, during those gatherings, the weather clears-up, regardless of having been bad -or predicted to be such by the best of the foretellers…

SECTION TWO

THE STRUGGLE FOR UNIFICATION

From Circa 700 BCE to 5th Century BCE

"Liberty, is not only in need of daring and blood shed
to be sustained! She mostly needs virtue, reason and
knowledge, so she can be a possession, so she can
become one's permanent mistress!"
Konstantinos Rados, Dr. -Greek Royal Navy/Author, Ipirote Ellinas

I

"Perdikkas was not happy with his treatment by king Antiohos. He
and his brothers had come from the Peloponnisian Argos, seeking
hospitality and refuge -in exchange for services- following the trek of their
great uncle, Karanos and under his protection and employment. Karanos
had come up to these parts years ago, in search of his own father's band of
Iraklides. They, in turn, had left Peloponnisos, on account of the hostility
shown to them by king Evrystheas. His hostility started when Iraklis was
under that king's service, performing all those deeds which made him
famous. This caused Evrystheas to become jealous and hostile against the
hero and all his descendants. So, Kara-nos, arriving here in Makedon,
sought and received employment by the ruling power of the Orestids,
who allotted Karanos the small region of Makedonis as payment for those
services.

Meantime back in Peloponnisos, Evrystheas continued oppressing the
Iraklides remaining there. At last, the old jealous king died, leaving no
heir to his throne. Mighty Zefs had seen to it, as a just punishment to an
ungrateful mortal. With Evrustheas' death, some strife followed in Argos,
lasting some years. The throne finally came to the hands of Perdikkas' own
Father, king Timenos. The people were happy for the assumed peace and
prosperity returned to them. Everything worked fine at the beginning,
Perdikkas grew-up a happy little kid, alongside his two brothers, Gavanis
(the elder) and Aeropos (second-born).

Disaster hit the royal household some years later, when Perdikkas'
mother died unexpectedly and Gavanis got hit on his head by a stone, while
playing rough games with other kids of his age. He did not die though. He
lived and functioned as nothing had ever happened. The ones who really
knew him saw that his behavior in general had changed and his mind had
become feeble. He could not be trusted in anything serious. Time after
time, when under pressure, he always chose to run his mind to utterly

irrelevant subjects, disregarding the task and needs of the present. Aeropos, loving Gavanis the most (after their mother's death), felt responsible for his brother's well being and asked to be Gavanis' sole caretaker, not minding the throne succession in the future.

Succession to the throne of Argos then, in case of Timenos' death, became evident. Perdikkas would be the heir. Perdikkas was happy to accept, until Timenos made the decision to re-marry. Within a year from the wedding day, the new queen gave birth to a new prince. Realizing her son would not have any chance of becoming a king in Argos, she worked out a very wicked plan. First, she started accusing Perdikkas of disrespect. When that did not work because he was very careful, especially before the king and other people, she went with another plan.

She developed a relation with Gavanis, seeing that his mind was not working and he was an easy person to manipulate. At the same time, she tried to offer her charms to Aeropos, who refused and told Perdikkas to be careful of her. She found then an excuse and accused Aeropos to Gavanis, who -in his state of mind- believed and quarreled with his brothers. Then truth was established and the queen found herself against all three brothers. Finding herself against a wall and fearing their wrath, she approached the king, accusing all three of trying to offend her honor and that of their Father!

This accusation brought a greater quarrel, especially between the king and Perdikkas, who came very strongly to the defense of both his brothers. Soon, there was an impasse. Instead of drawing his sword against his Father and king, Perdikkas persuaded his two brothers and their friends and followers, to self-exile. They waited for some time, in the vicinity of Argos, in case their Father would see the truth and reason. Since it didn't happen, they marched out of Peloponnisos.

They heard of their great uncle Karanos' deeds in Thessalia against the tribe of Kentavri and head-ed that way. When they finally arrived and searched the region for the Iraklides, they did not find them there, because Karanos had taken them already and settled in Makedonis, his son Kinos having secured that area, after Karanos' death. But Kinos died young, during a battle of Makedonians against Illyrians and his son, Tyrimmas, succeeded him, with the blessing of king Merops of Orestis -as the overlord. Some years after, king Merops died also and his son, a very young and high-minded Antiohos, became the king of Orestis.

When Perdikkas, his brothers and their followers came to Makedonis, Tyrimmas, being old already and without a male heir to succeed, was happy to see the newcomers from his bloodline, re-enforcing his band of Iraklides. He mediated to young king Antiohos (only five years older than Perdikkas) and the group was accepted and placed immediately in the service of Antiohos. In a matter of a couple of years later, Tyrimmas also died. Some people say his death was caused by a snake's bite. Some others are in favor of him being poisoned. The advocates of the latter are split into two factions. One half like to accuse Antiohos, the other half accuse Perdikkas and his brothers. The simple fact is that none of them ever had any real material reason for such an act. Tyrimmas was content with the current arrangement and so was Antiohos. The two of them had a good working agreement, one using the other, in exchange for employment and military support, with no apparent friction between them. The three brothers were new in the area and much obliged to Tyrimmas, who was blood related and loved by his Iraklides.

In any event, with Tyrimmas gone, a new leader had to be named and approved. The Iraklides and newcomers from Argos, did some shuffling and thinking. Tyrimmas left no heir. Among the elders in the original band of warriors, there was none too strong or close to the deceased leader. On the other hand, the three brothers had followers and were close related to Tyrimmas. Because Gavanis was out of any contest, on account of his condition and because Aeropos was devoted to the welfare of Gavanis and indifferent, the lot fell onto Perdikkas' lap and he was elected by acclamation. This ad-ded to the name of Iraklides the one of Argiades (as he came from Argos). Antiohos made a point of being present and confirmed this appointment himself.

For a time, this confirmation by Antiohos seemed to be the right choice and the relation (military or otherwise) a happy one. Perdikkas showed his ability to lead his oplite warriors, in the service of the Orestian king. When war broke between Orestis against Tymfea, Elimiotis and Eordea, the leading abilities of Perdikkas proved the Argiades to be the force Orestis needed on her side. In spite of the pressure and threats (which turned into action) from Lynkestis and Imathia, Perdikkas brought the war to a very successful end for his employer.

The truce which was called on account of the nuptials between the Lynkestian prince Temvros and the Imathian princess Pelagia, helped bring a more permanent peace, which (as it was worked and agreed upon) gave even greater prestige to the Orestian king and his kingdom.

The following year and when everybody thought that harvest and trade would take their course in peace, raiding Dardanian parties, augmented with hordes from the Argestes and Penestes, moved into Pelagonia, Lynkestis and Orestis. These raiders had the silent support of the Vryges and Dexa-res, as they were allowed to pass through those parts in secrecy. Perdikkas was summoned by Anti-ohos at once and, during a decisive battle by mountain Voion, the invaders were repulsed with heavy casualties. The Orestid casualties were also heavy. Perdikkas lost only a few among his falanx and horse. Many of the Orestian peasants on the country side by the mountain slopes, most of them not properly equipped, were killed either during the battle itself, or during the enemy retreat, as they tried to chase him unorganized.

Antiohos was very upset for the loss of so many of his countrymen and he (unwisely) accused Per-dikkas of not taking proper care of the overall offense. At Perdikkas' arrival in Levaea to work things out, Antiohos publicly refused to recognize the Argiades services. Hence, the unhappiness of Perdikkas, who (justly) felt wronged. He asked for an audience a second time but was refused. The king's herald brought him the message that, instead of asking recognition and payment of services ill performed, Perdikkas should be happy he was holding the ground and estates the king's Father so graciously gave to Perdikkas' kin long ago, when true services took place. Perdikkas should also be grateful for the very ground he was standing on, that very moment! This was too much for Perdikkas to swallow! He took off at once and, having his falanx and horse intact yet, he led them back to storm Antiohos' abode.

The Orestian king was totally surprised and unprepared for such a show of force. After a brief fight Antiohos surrendered. He was spared his life and, Perdikkas feeling magnanimous because of past conduct and not wanting to over offend Orestian pride, allowed Antiohos the rule of the country above Levaea, toward Orestis proper. Levaea and the region of Makedonis, given as gift to Karanos so long ago, now became sole property won by the sword, for Perdikkas and his Iraklides.

Antiohos did not learn his lesson. He tried taking his lands back. He had his best chance when he made a deal with Eordea, Elimiotis and Imathia. These clan kings were persuaded by Antiohos that Perdikkas had become too strong and was looking for their kingdoms. The Iraklidis/ Argiadis/Time-nidis king of Makedonis, proved more cunning and capable than Antiohos once more. He attacked the Orestian clan first, forcing

Antiohos to sue for peace. Then, as the armies of Imathia and Elimi-otis were gathering to move, he fell upon them by the small town of Tyrissa and soundly defeated them. King Menelaos, of Imathia, was among the casualties.

Perdikkas, did not put Orestis under his immediate control, nor Elimiotis, for both were too much for his force to hold. He annexed Imathia though, taking under his protection the heir of Menelaos and first cousin of Pelagia, Antigonos. He also secured leadership on Elimiotis, letting its king who was also named Antigonos, rule. Now Antiohos was isolated and the danger averted. Most of the other clans stood-by mostly indifferent during these developments. Imathia accepted Perdikkas' leadership, not because the people did not like their past king Menelaos, nor because their pride was not bruised. The event itself and the time it took for its accomplishment were totally unexpected by all. By the time the clan heads and land lords realized what happened and gathered around Antig-onos, Perdikkas was in full charge.

He was credited for not following the trend of displacing populations and imposing heavy payments on them. Nor did he take the captured to sale the at the slave markets. Contrary to expectations, he let them return to their families and land, after a customary (but token) ransom was paid. The only thing he insisted upon, was an oath taking by the defeated, to obey his summons when he needed them. To his captains and common oplites, he gave what valuables were taken from the battle field and the lands of only those who fell, without leaving an heir. Although Eordea and Elimiotis re-mained nominally independent, he made sure to let them know that he was now the Vasilefs they had to obey!

There were several parties which did not receive this kind of settlement of affairs as kindly! Most of all, Orestis and Lynkos. Pelagia was uncontrollably grieving the loss of her Father, Temvros, being worried of the new power and -obviously- hurt by his wife's sorrow, looked for an approach with An-tiohos. Temvros and Pelagia, both received her aged mother in Lynkos, accommodating the old queen the best they could, during her last days. Queen Kleopatra did not last long. Within a few moon turns, her broken heart gave way.

Her death brought not only more hard feelings toward Perdikkas from Pelagia, her mourning and curses disturbed and, at the same time, had a profound and permanent influence on young Pafsanias' character. At such a young age, he could not fully understand and rationalize an event like that, since reason and effect had not yet developed in his mind. The loss of his grand parents and the wailing of his Mother, seemed to him so distorted and he resolved never to rest in peace, until this monster, Per-dikkas, paid a full account of his misdeeds!

Temvros, on his part, could not (under any circumstances) see Lynkos' dream for supremacy over all Makedonia being put on hold -or ruined! Further, because of this upstart, his beloved wife and son were suffering, the boy being attached to his mother (more than the usual boy-mother relation) and Temvros was much too sensitive in matters of country and family to be sitting idle and let things take their course, while he was biting his nails!

He knew he was not strong enough to go alone against the Timenidis and he tried his best to form alliances. He had positive results with Almopia and Pelagonia, but not with Orestis. To Antiohos, the enmity between the two for supremacy over Makedonia, was going back too long, to let him think (let alone actually do) working with Lynkestis against a new (to him) danger. He allied himself in secrecy with Tymfea, the Ipirotan Molossia and with the Pieres, in an effort to circle his opponent. Each of these two kings and their coalitions, took their separate ways...

Before either coalition could make a move against him, Perdikkas attacked again. It was the second spring since he was, undisputed, in charge of his kingdom. He brought to the battle something of a novice, not done before nor repeated after, for many years. Aside his falanx and horse, he armed many men with bows and slings only. Those, he drafted from the serf and poor small land holders, with the promise that his share of royal battle spoils, would go directly to them! The only thing he wanted for himself, was their courage and fighting spirit when and if they would be called to join the horse and the falanx.

Perdikkas dealt with Antiohos and his Tymfean allies first. The battle took place by the town of Aeani, in Elimiotis. Perdikkas had his opponents believe that a garrison, left on purpose in this town, was his whole army and that they were ready to surrender. When Antiohos got there and there was no surrender, he had no choice but to set up a siege, in hope he could subdue the town in a short time.

Perdikkas approached undetected, in three columns. He was leading the horse, Aeropos the falanx, while Gavanis was given the archers and slingers, with strict orders (which he understood) to move only when signaled by Perdikkas himself. Gavanis and his light troops were placed on the hills before the town and the river Aliakmon, hidden among the woods of the slopes. Perdikkas and Aeropos came in full view of the enemy, in the open, pretending they were to cross the river in support of the garrison in town. Each time they came close to the river and Antiohos rushed to face them, they with-drew, fainting fear of his troops. On the fourth faint attempt of crossing, Antiohos lost patience and had his troops cross instead as his falanx and horse were fording the river, Aeropos attacked, at the signal given by Perdikkas, with his falanx, making sure to gradually move to his right, following the bend of the river and supported by Perdikkas' cavalry, which was holding back, fainting inability to penetrate. Antiohos sent his cavalry to encircle Aeropos' left, thus splitting his force leaving the right of his falanx unprotected. The minute Perdikkas saw the gap open enough, he signaled Gavanis. He, now charged with his light troops, the archers and slingers sending clouds of arrows and stones on the back of Antiohos' horse and at the unprotected right side of his falanx. At the same time, Perdik-kas charged with his horse and with Aeropos' falanx headlong. The Orestians and Tymfeans panic-ed, turned to face the onslaught from both sides, only to find out that the garrison from the town made a sortie, hurling javelins and dispatching with their swords, the ones who broke off and tried to save themselves on the town-side of the river banks!

Any of the Orestians and Tymfeans who survived because they surrendered, were taken prisoners and were released only when they got ransomed. Antiohos was among them. Perdikkas faithful to his promise, kept nothing for himself out of the spoils. All was equally divided among his troops, even the ransom part, when arrived from Orestis and Tymfea. Antiohos returned to Orestis, a very sub-dued man. Perdikkas honored the few dead his army sustained during this battle. One, sad casualty among them, was his brother, Gavanis. Perdikkas also returned the Tymfean and Orestian dead to their kin, not asking any ransom from them.

Having that side of his kingdom secured and knowing that the Lynkestians with their allies would think well before coming against him now, he turned to face the Pierians. The latter had entered Imathia, from the side of Aliakmon's mouth to the sea, as an easier way, instead of climbing through the passes of mount Olympos into Makedonis. They attacked the town of Veria taking it by storm, selling its citizens at the slave markets, although the Imathians did not offer any resistance, other than that of the few troops Perdikkas had in town.

Perdikkas acted rapidly. He promised his captains and land holders, all the lands of the Pierians. Because, as he said, no Argiadis or Iraklidis ever did any harm to Pieria before, yet, the Pierians had allied with his enemy and put to waste friendly lands and people. By saying so, he hit the right nail. Not only his army liked the idea of more (as sweetened by the recent victory), the Imathians turned all on his side! They were viewing Perdikkas as their avenger now, their liberator!

The two sides met in battle at the plain below Veria, between mountain Vermion and river Aliak-mon. It was hard fought battle, undecided, until the Pierian king, Ellanikos, fell mortally wounded, (as some say) by the hand of Perdikkas. His death started the rout of the Pierians and, the combined forces of Argiades-Iraklides and Imathiotes (who took whatever arms they could find) joining the battle now, giving no quarter to the vanquished. The slaughter lasted until there was hardly anyone left alive…

Within a very short time Perdikkas' forces moved into Pieria proper. Wherever they met resistance, they killed and burned. The news reached every corner of Makedonia very fast. Perdikkas and his Argeades were unstoppable! Most of the Pieres who had the time to flee, got their families and what else they could muster and took off by sea, seeking refuge in any place they could find compas-sion offered to them. Most of them came to find settlements in the lands of the Idones, a clan mixed with old Thrakian Kokkyges, some of the Vryges who -on their way to Asia, ages ago- were left be-hind and Vissaltes. The refugees congregated in that region of Idonia which is between the waters of river Strymon and the bay of Neapolis, by the south slopes of Pangaeon. The lands of the Pierian lords were given (as promised) to the men of Perdikkas who were -until then- without a plot of their own. The Imathians were left to govern themselves, as they agreed they would support Perdikkas' role and policies in the region.

About this time, a devastated Antiohos had an apoplexy. The Orestians sent a delegation to Perdik-kas, with terms of peace. Elimiotis and Tymfea did the same. Antiohos was left to rule Orestis and he did so, bedridden until his death. Temvros found himself left alone to face Perdikkas, who named his now extended kingdom Makedonia. Perdikkas was encompassing in his mind (and pronouncing his vision to all) to eventually master the whole region!

Temvros, being in despair and as passionate as ever about Lynkos' glory and leadership, made a mistake he later came to regret greatly. This mistake helped Perdikkas to establish his hold and prominence as the most legitimate leader and protector of Makedonia. Temvros unwittingly helped the Timenidis line of succession, to an extended future Makedonian state, under that line's rule. Having nowhere to turn for more military support against Perdikkas, Temvros courted the aid of the Illyrian tribe of Tavlantes and their allies, the Skirtones, Enghileis and Vryges. The Illyrian leader was the feared and deceiving brute, Lepti-Varag. Makedonian victims of his, called him Leptivaros, later known as Kleptivaros, deriving from the words kleptis (thief) and varos (weight).

Lepti-Varag gladly jumped in. An opportunity like this was like a god-sent gift to him. He gathered his allies and invaded Dassaretis, forcing its king to follow his lead. He entered Lynkestis next, osten-sibly to aid Temvros against Perdikkas. His hordes of plunderers and blood-thirsty men were not there to behave and serve Temvros' plans. As soon as they entered Lynkestis, people got up in arms.

Their 'allies' had come to plunder. If what they wanted was not given at once, the 'allies' were sure to put the unlucky Lynkestians under the sword! Many instances were reported back to Temvros of such 'allied' bands moving into the hamlets and villages, raping the women and killing the men, always taking with them what could be carried and burning what couldn't!

When Temvros sent heralds to Lepti-Varag asking for restrain and just reparation, his heralds were killed outright! Instead of fighting Perdikkas then, Temvros had to fight against his own 'ally'!

Word of this outrage traveled through Makedonia and Temvros was branded as a traitor and an in-viter of barbarians! These epithets did great damage to his personality and the Lynkestian honor. It was only with great difficulty and with help from Almopia, Pelagonia and Dassaretis itself, that he was able to send Lepti-Varag back. The damage was done by then. Lynkestian reputation was at its lowest for the rest of Temvros' years of rule. He died with the misery of his failure and bad choice, a broken man of high dreams but poor judgment. Needless to say that all these increased Pafsanias' own hatred toward Orestis (Antiohos did not come to aid) and Perdikkas, because Temvros' son con-sidered the Timenid the reason and cause of such a disaster…

As for Perdikkas, he could not have wished for more luck on his personal endeavors! Elimiotis, Eor-dea, Imathia and conquered Pieria, were solely and solidly his to command! Reverence and homage were paid to him from Tymfea and Vottiaea, while delegates from Amfaxitis,

Pallini, Al-mopia and Anthemous, paid respect and recognition to this new Makedonian power and its King, the Vasilefs! He even received heralds from the Thessalian regions and from as far as Paeonia, Vottiki, Sythonia, Viottian Thivae and Halkis, from the island of Evia!

He received all these delegates with grace, disregarding their motives of approach. He knew some came because of good will, while some came with calculated ulterior motives. Meantime, he did not idle himself. He moved toward Pieria, because of a dispute between his new land holders, here, to assure new-found subjects, further, to avert a brooding quarrel which could lead to grave results -if not solved.

The town of Levaea did not, could not suit him any longer as his seat of power, on account of its re-mote location and difficult access to and from most locations of his expanded realm. He was in need of a more centrally located seat to govern his kingdom. The site was sought and found at the north parts of Makedonis, by the border of conquered Pieria, on the north lower slopes of Olympos and overlooking the valley and flow of Aliakmon. Rumor has it that the discovery was purely accidental.

They say that a billy goat, pet of Perdikkas' late uncle Karanos, led Perdikkas as it took-off one day and no one could stop it and bring it back. Perdikkas hearing of it, and curious, followed the billy goat's trek. The animal finally stopped to rest on this particular location. Perdikkas, upon inspection, liked the location and decided to build his town there! He sent for omens from the oracle of Dodona and, receiving favorable response, he named it Aegae, on account of that billy goat! Personally, I don't be-lieve this rumor. First, because I don't think goats can live that long, second, because I think Perdikkas is much more than one who would take a goat's lead in placing his seat of government! But, I am only a merchant from Therma and I only report what I am told.

To continue, I report the context of the Oracle's answer. The auspices were favorable for building a town on that location, if Perdikkas wanted the Timenid line to become renowned! As long as Timen-ides would be buried there, when they died, his House (the Oracle continued) would be the one the whole Ellas would come to know well! Perdikkas -they say- obeyed the Oracle at once. He brought-in builders from every corner and, soon, a decent sized town, with a palace and its acropolis, replaced the scattered hamlets of the area. Being with some revenue in his coffer from the recent success, he took example from Halkis and issued coinage, with Iraklis' club depicted on one side, a laying-down goat on the other!

He figured, good ancestry and good rumor topped with good humor, could never hurt!

Aside from expelling the Pierians and allocating their lands to his troops and trusted (allied to him) Imathiotes, Perdikkas allowed the Elimiotis king, Kleovoulos, to expand his kingdom at the expense of Orestis and let him rule his lands unimpeded. This brought trust and (false) security, but more dependence on Timenid/Makedonian power. Additionally, Perdikkas married several women, one from Eordea, one from Imathia and a third from Elimiotis. He produced three sons and several daughters. His first-born, Argeos, was the heir apparent. Merops and Fidon, his second and third sons, were married (in later years) to daughters of prominent clan heads of the mixed-up, by now, clans in his domain. His first-born daughter was given to Kleovoulos' son Epimahos, when they turned of age. He did the same with the rest of his female offspring, building-up ties with the most useful (to him) neighboring kingdoms.

At the same time, he still remained married to his first wife (before his breaking-away from Antio-hos), the daughter of a past Orestian king, Agis, thus being able to claim the Orestian throne also! I know this first-hand, from my friend and benefactor Alketas, son of Agis and cousin to king Antiohos of Orestis. This story started at the time Karanos was still alive and leader of his Iraklides and under the employment of the Orestian kings…"

"Alketas was sitting on the grass and pine needles, his back against an old pine tree, one of those so commonly grown out of nowhere, planting their roots where forbidding rocks do not allow any other kind of tree to prosper. He was playing an old, worn-out avlos, the hollowed wooden pipe, inherited from his great grand father, Merops. Every-so-often, the gentle spring breeze would whisper its own tones in Alketas' ears, coming from the far and deep end of the ravine ahead, bringing with it the noise of the running river crossing it.

This, latter noise was mixed with bleats and bell sounds from Alketas' herd of goats, along with an occasional bark from the dogs guarding the herd. The animals were semi-scattered within the con-fines of this ravine, nibbling on small bushes and grassy patches of earth. The young shepherd of three plus ten years all-in-all since the day of his birth, was on his way to summer pastures, up on the high Pindos peaks. There was a rich and protected pasture area, known also to his clan but for the exclusive use of his family's herds -by rights. It was located close to the markers delineating the borders of Orestis and Molossia. It belonged to his family by his mother's rights, handed-down before the time of his great, great, grand father settled in the area as part of the Orestian Makedni clan. During the long, winter nights, Alketas heard these stories many a time, sitting by the warmth of the house hearth and listening to his grand mother telling them. He would listen to her talk, while the heavy drapes of Ypnos, the night governing Sleep, was closing his green-blue eyes ready to dream of those old days over and over -as his grandmother's voice was droning and fading- to become one of the multiple ancestors long gone...

By age judgment alone, Alketas was not supposed to be leading this herd of five times ten plus six goats, all by himself. He considered himself lucky, having his family's trust. Alketas became an offi-cially grown man very recently, just last winter. He single-handedly killed the leader of a wolf pack, which was raiding the family's sheepfold. Agis, his Father and king of the Orestian clan was very weak at that time, fighting high fever caused by a poisoned arrow which cost him the loss of his right leg. That happened last fall, during a late-season Illyrian raid, which was unexpected due to the late of the season. Now this past winter when the wolves got into the sheepfold, Agis could only summon kin and neighbors using his battle cry, as he tried to hobble behind his young son. That very cry made the wolves hesitate for a moment. It was more than enough for Alketas to thrust his javelin in the pack leader's chest. As the wolves took off to choose a new one, enough neighbors were at hand to send the lot of them away with heavy losses.

There was a special feast the following day, as Agis -carried on a makeshift litter- led Alketas to the town's shrine. There, by the altar and in the presence of the sage and the clan heads, an unblemished yearling billy goat was sacrificed to the Olympian gods. Father Zefs was foremost in mind of all, as was Panikos and his shadowy Fovos, the helper of the flute-playing, goat-legged god of forests and wild, who could have easily turn Alketas' heart and covered with the cold blanket of terror and cow-ardice, costing the sheep herd and, possibly, his Father's and his own life!

After the ritual of the sacrifice, Alketas was invited for the first time ever, to seat himself among the adult clan heads and share the food, along with plenty (watered-down) wine. He could guess easily the other boys' jealousy, many of them more than two years older, as they sat separated, around the tables set for minors, except his own cousin Antiohos. Although

Antiohos was three full years older than Alketas, he received his manhood rights only the past fall, killing many Illyrians and, pre-sumably, the one who lamed Agis. Obviously Antiohos, being now a recognized man, was seated among men but away from the 'youth'. Still, Alketas could tell of his cousin's jealous mood. Merops, Antiohos' Father and paternal uncle to Alketas, presented him with a gilded leather belt, while Agis handed his son a well crafted sword with a gold nugget on the tip of its hand-grip. Antiohos took his own quiver made by a Peonian master craftsman and handed it to Alketas with words of praise, though his green eyes told a somewhat different story. Alketas accepted the present gracefully, with some words of praise for his cousin's own bravery.

During the same feast, Merops was appointed to take over Agis as king of the clans in Orestis. Agis could not lead in war any more, one legged and Alketas, although officially a man now, was too young yet to succeed his Father. This appointment by acclamation of all present, gave a sudden edge to Antiohos, ostensibly the heir apparent -unless something unforeseen was to happen. Alketas saw the change of his cousin's mood, though Antiohos was quick to cover his triumphant smile with his hand.

Now with Agis confined in town to care for the domestic needs his amputated leg would allow, Alke-tas was the logical choice in taking care of their livestock. He was not feeling bitter from his Father's misfortune, nor for the family's and own demotion. His up-bringing had always been Orestian inter-ests always come first! He was more than happy to still have his Father around, one-legged, with or without the leadership of the clans! Nor was Alketas unhappy with his uncle's elevation to the dignity of the rank. Alketas simply did not think of Antiohos being capable of holding Orestis at the fore-front of Makedonian affairs, when and if his time came to rule. This was Alketas' own private thought and, as a very young adult-member in the clan's affairs, he knew better than voicing his op-inion on the subject.

Besides, occurrences like this one had taken place before. With the grace of gods, Orestis would pre-vail in the future, as in the past. Like when his own grand father had to take extreme measures, even hiring this contingent of Dorian warriors and their families, arriving here from Peloponnisos, under the name of Iraklides, traveling first through Thessalia. Grand father allotted them the lands in Makedonis and Orestian prestige was re-enforced by their help. These Argiades were not exactly new-comers. They were old relatives of Makedonian blood, from the time of the first Dorian descent.

Under the late Karanos, they helped expel the large hordes of Illyrians roving the country side. When Karanos died, his son Kinos took over and under the same arrangements but he got killed fighting for Orestian glory and leadership. He was succeeded by Tyrimas, the current leader of these Dorian Iraklides, in the pay of Agis (first) and now of uncle Merops. Alketas recalled of Tyrimas being present at his confirmation as an adult that day and had presented him with an ivory-handled dagger, with a gold-gilded blade. It was a true work of art and Alketas was very fond of that present. He presently smiled at the memory and touched the dagger secured on his belt.

So now, there he was, leading the herd up the mountains to the summer pastures. He was carrying his weapons, just in case. Two javelins, a sword, the bow and arrows and his dagger. He also had a small shield, in the concave of which he loaded all these weapons and his shoulder bag of provisions, pulling the shield with an attached rope, when the slopes were smooth. The rest of the times he was shouldering them or had them attached to his belt. Leaving home, the only person who saw his de-parture with misgiving, was his Mother Iakynthi.

Mother's status within Father's household, Alketas thought, would have been rather low if it wasn't that she gave him his only male child. She became the fourth wife to Agis, hailing from an Ipirotic line of seers, servants of Mother Gea and, later, of Dias the Thunderer, at the Oracle of Dodona. She did not become a priestess, that position was fulfilled by her older sister. Alketas had no trouble with his Father's multiple wives, since it was the custom for kings to do so, arranging alliances and ties with their neighbors that way. As a matter of fact, Alketas was happy, having the attention of those other wives and his half sisters (two from each of Father's wives!). There was a special bond between him and one of his half sisters, Fivi. Only one year younger, she had already grown and being a very re-sponsible young maid, one who returned his affection without any reservation and a real beauty -in addition to her premature wisdom.

Many a young Orestians were caught strolling up and down before the house, when Agis wasn't present. Alketas, with some help from the servants, was always chasing them away. Her beauty's fame though, kept on driving them boldly back at the doorstep!

With Agis' loss of a leg, Alketas took on the responsibility, among all other things, of guarding Fivi's honor. Even when she had to go to the spring for water or to the river for wash, she never did that alone.

Aside from the rest of women folk of the household, either Alketas or a designated by him servant kept an eye always on her. As for herself, she always kept her eyes downcast when walking the streets, minding her own business.

Nonetheless, Alketas made sure word was out that, since he became man, anyone thinking to offend his sister in any shape, form and way, would have to deal with him personally! Going away for a spell to have the herd up at the grazing summer grounds, he issued strict orders to the household women and servants for extra awareness. He was not too worried though, as he also knew the people's respect to tradition, family values and the special respect his family commanded. But, there was always a chance of on-coming raiders...

The disk of the flaming chariot of Ilios, the sun god Apollon, brought the shade of the pine tree di-rectly under its needle-loaded branches. It was the middle of the day. Alketas placed down his avlos, took a sweeping look to make sure his dogs were keeping the goats together, and stood up. He walked and stretched a little, letting his blood circulate, then took his shoulder bag off the lowest tree branch where it was hanging. He put one hand in and produced a piece of goat cheese. Repeating the move, he got a chunk of bread and a flask of watered-down wine. He ate, slowly and sparingly, for he knew he had still a long way to go. Of course, there was plenty of game in the area and he could always get some, using his bow and arrows. Being spring time, many newborn animals would need their parents to survive; Alketas had no wish to deprive them from that.

He finished his meal and he put his left-overs back in his bag. There was a cave behind the next two peaks, for night shelter. It was used many a time before and he decided to start moving, if he was to make it before nightfall. While shouldering his equipment, he whistled his special tone to his dogs in the ravine. Before he got down there, every goat was already herded together by the well trained dogs. The youngest of them, Argos, three years old and named after the trustworthy dog of the hero king from the war in Tria fame, was barking orders to the other dogs -as was its custom. Argos was the established leader of the rest of the shepherd dogs. While he and his father, Vasiliskos, would be at the tail end of the herd, the rest of them would keep the goats on order, not letting any one lag behind or wander off. Alketas would be leading, the rest would be following behind. Alketas knew of no other dogs as good as Argos and Vasiliskos.

Actually, Vasiliskos was the oldest (fast approaching his two times ten years of hard life) dog being so active and so reliable.

They all arrived at the cave, just at the time when the chariot of Ilios-Apollon was diving behind the Pindos peaks, on its way to the nightly visit with Esperides, those nymphs of twilight, beyond the Ionian sea. New vines had sprung-up along the old ones by the cave's entrance, mixing the spring green with the, half-decayed, ash-brown of old. The combination made the low and narrow cave entrance harder to detect, which in turn made Alketas happy. He knew the cave was safe and empty. He whistled at his dogs again to keep the herd in check and moved to inspect the cave.

First, he created an opening large enough for the herd to be led inside and he did it first, by crowl-ing. The light was very dim but he could still see there had been no other animal or human occupa-tion since last year. He gave a sigh of relief. He did not need an encounter with a mountain lion or any other wild beast. The cave itself was rather big after the entrance part. It could easily house the whole herd plus at least ten, to five plus ten humans. Its ceiling was about the height of two grown-up men, one on to of the other, giving plenty of air (although there was some dampness in there. A good fire should fix that. Alketas whistled at his dogs again and they started pushing the goats through the opening. He counted them as they were entering, mindful of his grand father's advice in making sure he always had things right.

There was always need of such advice in Orestis, for the dangers were many and -mostly- great! The property, even one's own life, could be lost in a matter of moments, on account of false security or be-cause of measures not taken a while ago. Double and triple checking had to develop like one's second nature. Alketas placed his dogs by the entrance -after the goats were in and counted. Some of the dogs were left inside, some out. He went out and found a broken tree branch full of leaves and erased every track he and his herd made coming in, for some distance from the cave's entrance. Finishing that, he picked-up on his return, many other fallen branches and twigs. He re-entered the cave, calling all the dogs inside. Taking a last look outside and nodding to himself in satisfaction, he pulled the vines back, concealing the entrance as best as it was possible. He let the dogs guarding it from inside, hoping no animal or human curiosity would accidentally discover it.

Alketas arranged the dry wood he picked and started a small fire. Thinking of it, he exited the cave again and noted, with satisfaction, that neither the fire nor its smoke were detectable. He made sure to erase again his footprints as he re-entered. Now, taking a container from his bag, he approached one of the goats, one which had recently given birth at the spring's start and, pushing aside her new-born, milked her, filling the container. He retrieved from his bag two earthenware bowls. He filled the bigger one with milk and placed it next to his dogs, observing the animals taking their share in order. Argos (as the leader) was first and Vasiliskos was the last one to drink. Meantime, Alketas placed the first container by the fire, letting the milk in it come to a boil. Sitting down near it, he took out of his bag the left-over from his mid-day's meal and started eating slowly, waiting now for the milk to cool down.

Before he drank any, he made an offer to the gods and his ancestors, pouring some on the cave's floor. Finishing, he took his avlos and, very softly, played some tones of his own arrangement. Vasiliskos followed the tones with his own distinct low yelp, each time Alketas would play some mu-sic. Alketas loved it and always laughed at the sound of the dog trying to 'sing'. The other dogs just raised their ears now and then, some toward the music, some toward the night sounds from outside the cave, none showing any sign of discomfort. Finishing his tones, Alketas laid down using his bag as a head-rest and turned to sleep.

The time when the daylight has not penetrated the retreating night yet but (somehow) its presence is there contributing to Mother Nature's artistic majesty of black on gray canvas, the same time one makes only the outline of the landscape against a distant, blurred horizon, it was the time that Alke-tas woke-up. The goats were still, settled at the far end of the cave. The suckling noises and an occasional bleating from the newborn ones milking their mothers were the only sounds. By the entrance though, the dogs looked restless. Even old Vasiliskos was pacing to and fro, now looking up to his master, now looking toward the cave's entrance, waiting for the order to go. Alketas knew they were hungry and thirsty.

He decided he should let them go for the next hour or so, to satisfy their nature. If he and they were lucky, they would find food and water early, retuning back to him soon. If not, he would have to wait and gain lost time by not stopping during the next day at all. The pasture lands were two days' dist-ance from this point and the master herder, Agathon, with his family and dependents were waiting for Alketas' arrival. If he'd get hungry, he could eat while walking…

Agathon's father had been appointed in charge of the pasture area by Alketas' grand father (on his Mother's side) Olganos. These caretakers were staying there year-round, making sure the place re-mained in Orestid hands and they tended the coming herds during the summer months. A small hamlet had sprung-up on a naturally fortified location and, for the last ten times five years, no one had been able to take away or damage the property.

Alketas opened the cave's entrance a little and let the dogs out. As they did, a darker shadow among the existing ones by the woods' edge moved in alarm. The dogs took off immediately after it, in the silenced manner of the hunter chasing the pray. Argos (as usual) was in the lead, Vasiliskos trailing. Alketas smiled at the sight of a young stag running for life. He exited, being himself excited, to see the dogs chasing it. If Artemis (the goddess of forests and hunting) wanted, the dogs would have their meal within the hour...

He went back in the cave, taking again every precaution in eliminating any tell-tale signs of foot prints and closed the entrance by adding few of the logs he'd collected, from inside. Now that the dogs were out, he did not want any goat venturing at the entrance to be able to get out. He went to milk one or two of them, preparing for his breakfast. There would be no general milking on his way to summer pastures. First, there were plenty of new-born ones, second, it would take him too much time (being alone for the task), lastly, he had no beast of burden with him, nor any canisters to fill them with milk.

Finishing milking a couple of goats, he placed the milk by the fire like the night before. His break-fast had the added luxury of some olives along side the bread and cheese. At the end he drank his milk and waited for the dogs to return.....

Mid morning and the dogs had not yet returned! Alketas debated whether he should let the herd out for grazing, even having the risk of them getting scattered, because they were becoming too restless inside the cave. He decided to take a look first, searching the vicinity and whistled for his dogs to return. He exited the cave, making sure the arrangement of keeping the herd in was not disturbed.

He, then, moved toward the direction the dogs were gone when they chased the stag.

Alketas whistled now and then, waiting to hear (after each whistle) the happy return barking. He was getting no answer. He really started to worry. This was definitely not his dogs' behavior! He returned to the cave, picking-up extra small branches and dead wood on the way. He arrived there, at the nick of time. A few goats (especially some of the yearlings) had come out, as they discovered the exit unguarded, pushing aside some of his blocking brush. He guided them back in a hurry, be-fore other ones would do the same. He picked-up his two javelins, his bow and arrows, the small shield and a flask of watered wine and went out. This time, he made sure the entrance/exit of the cave was well sealed with added brush and wood, even at the risk of that being obvious to any occasional passer-by. Once more, he erased his footprints as he was leaving, to the edge of the woods.

Now, he went after his dogs in earnest. He took the same direction as before and started searching, all senses alerted. He discovered the first dead dog, Fidon, about a stadion paces before an open space, close to six stadia away from the cave. Ahead, in the open, he could see two smooth slopes. The dog had expired facing toward the direction of the cave. On its way back, for a warning? As the dog lay, on the ground, Alketas could not tell what killed it. He could only see plenty of thickened blood on the grass and the dog was quite stiff. Both indicated the killing occurred some time ago. He looked around for clues but everything seemed to be in order. Birds were singing again up on the trees and in the bushes, no more disturbed by his presence. His attention went back to the dog. He turned the dead animal over and saw a small, but deep puncture in its chest. If, whatever had pierced the dog's chest, did not reach its heart, it probably had a major artery severed. Did the stag's antlers do it? Alketas could not detect any other wounds, except this one puncture. No stag did that then! Besides, there was no sign of any disturbance like fighting between animals. If by an arrow, where was it then? Who would retrieve his arrow and why? Were the other dogs dead? He examined the wound closer. The puncture was a straight, round one, no flesh torn as if from an arrow! If a new type of arrow was used, was it retrieved then for fear of recognition or for repeated use? These were questions he could not answer. As for the other dogs, he feared the worst had happened…

He took his time looking around, not moving. Nothing seemed to be within the clear area ahead, un-til the forest started again two slopes down. The grass between these two slopes, seemed disturbed at places. Did the dogs do it chasing the stag, or the dogs' killer(s)? He knew now, all his dogs were dead! This was never a behavior of Argos or Vasiliskos…

Alketas surveyed the area again. One of the grass disturbances lay almost on a straight line bet-ween the dead dog he found and…and what?

Another dead dog? He spent some more time scanning, restricting his movements to an absolute minimum. If there were eyes looking from the other side, he wanted to be as undetected as possible. There was absolutely no movement around him, with the exception of an occasional flight of a bird or the hurried crossing of squirrels, from a bush to a tree. What made him be sure that there was some other presence besides him, hiding, was the fact that he could not detect any birds or beasts of prey, no vultures like yipes and no other cadaver eaters! Those were never absent or far away from such opportunities, unless, there were humans around, scaring them! His own, lonely presence, if that was the case, would not have been much of a menace to them, at least not for the yipes. They would be circling abovehead, away from any danger, until he was gone. There had to be something more causing that kind of absence.

He made-up his mind to find out about his dogs' fate, come what may! He started crawling on the grass slowly, stopping here and there with irregular stops, looking and listening. Nothing! He reach-ed the first slope's crest and he found the next dead dog. It was Lefki, the white colored bitch who had given him the latest litter of sheep dogs, last spring. She met her death exactly the same way Fidon had! Because of her snow-white wooly skin (which caused her naming) he could clearly see several fatal wounds on her, caused by the same type of weapon. Alketas swallowed, in order to clear the lump in his throat. Whoever did that would have to pay dearly! He made a silent promise and a petition to the gods, for swift justice…

He stayed there still for some time more, recovering and re-enforcing his resolution to find and pun-ish the guilty. He resumed moving slower, more careful not to show any disturbance on the tall grass.

In the deep, between the two slopes, he met with the carcasses of six more of his dogs. They lay wide, facing in different directions, meaning that death had come to them from various points. They showed the same type of wounds but giving him no clue as to who or what did it. Ah, but now, he knew the agents of death had to be humans -and many of them. The question though of why all this slaughter, remained unanswered.

Alketas raised his head above the grass, so he could see. There were some more parallel trails lead-ing or coming from the next crest, up to the end of the clearance at the woods' edge. He noticed that these trails were crisscrossing at some places. They had to be made by Argos and Vasiliskos! These were his two dogs still unaccounted for. He scanned around again, taking another careful look. The paths looked like the dogs were turning back, but not really doing it. With a deep (trembling by sor-row and anger) sigh, Alketas moved forward again.

Behind the woods' edge and high-up on the trees, hidden by the green shadows, several pairs of eyes were watching in amusement his slow and painful progress. Alketas finally reached the crest, follow-ing one of the two dog trails. The sun disk had come to its high point now, indicating his progress had taken the best of six hours -if not more. He regretted not taking along just water in his flask, instead of watered-down wine. Although he drank often on his way here, his thirst was stronger than antici-pated. His lips were dry, the shock and effort tiring him more and the heat of this spring day was felt.

He tried to wet his lips with his tongue. No use, for that was dry too!

Alketas did not move again for some time, gathering strength. He crossed this last crest and, his heart leaped! He stayed motionless again, breathing hard. After a while, he raised his head above the grass, for another look. The two dog trails were getting closer, until they met, just before the woods' edge. From his vantage point, Alketas could see the two immobile bodies of his dogs, both in one heap! Argos underneath, Vasiliskos on top, like trying to protect! Alketas could not hold his anguish and anger back, any longer. Without thinking of his own safety, he jumped to his feet and ran to-ward his beloved dogs with as mighty a cry, as his lungs would allow him!

He arrived at where the dogs lay, when a strange whistling sound filled the air. Alketas had no time to identify it. An excruciating pain (on his chest and his back) came in split interval from the one to the other, while his hands were forcibly pulled and immobilized on his sides, a tiding-them-down force almost breaking them-up!

A tremendous light of a sunburst, its spikes extended in space, filled his head and vision and, just before passing-out, one definition came to his mind: two-stoned sinew-rope! The pure white of his sunburst vision became golden, then, deep red and he fell, losing consciousness, on top of his dogs. By the time he finished his fall, the deep red of his vision became one with the dark rusty color of their dried blood...

Alketas felt like he was swimming submerged in a lake or sea, water engulfing his body. First it would feel icy-cold, the next moment unbearably hot. He was trying to surface, longing for air. Every so often, he could detect light from above. He would swim-up for air and, each time, every single gulp of it would send him back into the depths of the abyss! There was extreme pain in his lungs each time, as well as his back and arms. Was it the cause of so many efforts to surface? The pain would travel up his body and mind, bringing him now to cold and, then, to hot waters! He wanted to swim faster, to reach shore, to leave these waters of Aheron, because he knew that -any moment now- the boat of Haros would show-up to take his soul to Adis! And he didn't have the fare to pay his way to the Ilyssian Fields!

He thought he heard voices. He tried to open his eyes. Another sunburst of light hurt him, as much as his efforts to breathe and he closed them fast! That sunburst felt like something familiar. Had he seen it before? He tried to breath once more and a moaning sound escaped his mouth. Everything was hurting him! Through this pain, he tried (one last time) to open his eyes, to see where the water's sur-face was. The same sunburst covered his vision, a dark shape of a bearded face to one side. Posidon? The pain following, made everything extremely hot again! He passed-out one more time…

The lead man, followed by some thirty riders, came through town in a hasty pace, covered by clouds of dust. People milling in the main (actually the only one) street, made -as best as they could- an even hastier retreat, out of the horses' way. Many a fist was raised and some choice epithets were directed toward the horsemen. There was no attention paid and the riders continued, until they came to a halt in front of Merops' house. As the sentry's alarmed inquiries were called, the king emerged from his house, some of his guards rushing behind him, swords and javelins on hand, ready to strike on the intruders. Undisturbed, the horsemen's leader handed the rains of his horse to a fellow next to him and, taking his Argive style helmet off his head, saluted the king with respect. Recognition was ap-parent at once, for the king stopped his guards from rushing-on with his left, while raising his right hand in response to the rider's own greeting.

The leader of the riders was Tyrimmas, escorted by some of his Iraklides. Their obvious state of haste, dusty appearance and foaming horses, was certainly a no good news bearer, but Merops did not want to look anxious before the crowd gathered. He beckoned Tyrimmas in and his suspicion became certainty, as he heard Tyrimmas' hasty report as both headed into the house through the courtyard, while the rest of the riders dismounted and were taken to some rest and refreshments. Merops and

Tyrimmas entered the audience hall (the place had not changed much, since the days of Anaxarhos) and the full report was given by the latter, without any preliminary talk.

Antiohos (as heir apparent) and the nearest land holders and clan heads were summoned at once. As they all came in and took their seats, Tyrimmas told his story again, leaving no details out. The defeated Illyrians of last summer were thought to have returned back to their far-off mountains and country. Apparently, this was not the case! They had, most likely, waited in hiding and let the winter pass, now pillaging, burning and killing people in small hamlets and villages. Their numbers did not seem to be so great, the winter being harsh to supporting numbers in hiding. The ferocity though of these small numbers had doubled, in an apparent effort to extract revenge from Orestis, for their last defeat.

The faces of all of Tyrimmas' audience dropped down, as most voiced the realization of inadequate manpower for the hunt and expulsion of the foe. Most of the eligible men had taken off with their herds to summer pastures, or to forests for wood-cutting, leaving the area more vulnerable to such a raiding party. The enemy could overcome the small armed groups of Orestians stationed in few and far strongholds in the country. Especially when most were unaware of such a danger! The only possible solution seemed to be Tyrimmas' Iraklides, who -because they preferred being warriors- had entrusted their lands and herds to local small lot holders, themselves being free to campaign.

At the height of the discussion as to how the Iraklides could be better utilized, Agis limped in the hall, supported and escorted by his foreman at his summer pastures, Agathon, in turn trailed by two of his sons, Andronas and Damon. Agis' ashen colored face, brought new concerns in the council. They soon found about Alketas' disappearance, the discovery of which, was the work of Agathon and his sons.

After a two day's waiting past the time Alketas was supposed to have reached the pasture land, Agathon took some of his sons and helpers, looking for him. They found the dead and partly decom-posed dogs, as well as the goats in the cave -starved half to death. Agathon sent the herd to the pas-ture land under strong escort, with orders of doubled vigilance. He and his sons then, traced Alketas and his captors' tracks for a while, just making sure of the direction and final destination of the group. After that, they left one to keep an eye on the events there, while the three of them came to town as fast as they could, bringing the bad news to Agis, who was now asking for help. Although a prince was abducted, the need to rid the country of the raiders was greater than the need to save one!

King Merops asked to be excused for a while and walked out of the room, thinking of what he could do. He was immediately summoned back, as a new rider arrived with news as to the where-about of the raiders. It was soon discovered that the abductors and the raiders had to be the same band of Illyrian marauders. Merops made his decision fast and started giving orders. The land holders and clan heads present at this meeting were to go to their estates and arm all available persons. After leaving enough guard in their estates and charging someone to warn other neighbors, they were to return here with all the speed they could muster! Agis and Agathon would stay in town to organize all that was necessary for the defense of the city, having Antiohos as their regent. He, Merops, would follow the trek, as soon as the land lords would return, aided by Tyrimmas and his Iraklides, Damon serving as the guide. Andronas was to pick a few men and start ahead the next morning (being too late now for a start), to see what -if anything- could be done meantime. The decision taken, he sent the clan heads and land lords do his bidding, while asking Agis, Agathon, Tyrimmas and his men, to share dinner with him.

During the dinner time, Tyrimmas introduced to king Merops and the rest in the company, his kin and assistant, a young handsome man, by the name Perdikkas, son of Timenos. Tyrimmas explained that Perdikkas and his brothers Gavanis and Aeropos, with a good number of followers, just arrived from Thessalia and were asking for acceptance and homes in his region. Tyrimmas would be happy to have them. Would the king agree also?

Merops had the need of warriors and he could afford the lands he gave to Tyrimmas. If the latter wanted to offer parcels to his kin from his own, that was well and good! Besides, Merops was happy with Tyrimmas and his Iraklides band's performance. A few more of that kind was a real blessing! He asked the young prince to sit next to him and inquired about his state of mind, about his followers and his past where-abouts, all to be told in detail.

Perdikkas was honest with Merops. He explained their misfortunes back in Peloponnisos, their trav-ails through Viottia and Thessalia, that his brothers and the followers were (at this time) friends and guests of Tymfea, under king Sossos' protection. But, Tymfea was a poor country, often at war against Orestis. Perdikkas did not want to have a fight against his kin under Tyrimmas and king Merops, neither did he want to over tax Tymfea's hospitality.

Merops was convinced of Perdikkas' good intentions and delighted with the prospect of increasing his fighting capability against Orestis' enemies. He promised he would secure space and lands for Perdikkas and his brothers and men in the near future, as things would surely improve, if Tyrimmas would provide for his kin with all necessities meantime. It was agreed upon these terms then, to fully support one-another and a herald was to go at once, informing the Argeades Iraklides about this new deal.

Antiohos listening and sitting by other side of his Father did not like the idea at all but knew better than to contradict his Father's wish and decree. Perdikkas thanked the king meantime, promising a speedy arrival of his troops, which were led by his brothers. He then pledged himself to Merops…

The feeling of being wet and cold, brought Alketas back to his senses. Someone was truly talking. Was he still in the lake or ocean? Was the person talking to him god Posidonas himself? Perhaps! He opened his eyes with an effort, painful, reluctant. No sunburst this time, but his vision still unclear. Well, no one can see as clearly underwater as out in the open air! He noticed he was holding his breath, add-ing to his discomfort and pain. He tried a shallow breath, fearing the water would fill his lungs, but having no choice. The pain when breathing was still there but bearable this time! Most pleasantly, he could fill his lungs with precious air! But, only fish could breath in the water.

A shadow came over his face, taking the vague form of a heavily bearded face, locks of hair and parts of the beard decorated with nuggets of gold. Well, Posidonas or Triton, gold beard or not, Alke-tas would find out soon enough. For the moment, he was happy to be breathing!

The face opened its mouth, sounding words Alketas could not understand. Only seers and trained priests could understand what the gods were saying! A second face appeared next to the bearded one, younger and with only sparse shades of beard, indicative of someone not fully grown-up yet.

This, second face, was answering to the first one, in a disagreeable tone. Alketas thought he recog-nized his Father's name in that conversation, but was not sure. What did Agis have to do with Posid-onas or Triton? The closest his Father had ever come to a body of water, would be the distance of his feet to it, as he would (occasionally) cross a river ford, on his horse! And, Agis always crossed at the shal-lowest of river fords.

A pair of hands, belonging to the younger face and holding a container, came over his head. The container tipped and cold water covered Alketas' face. Not a lake, nor ocean then! The younger face's mouth spoke in broken Makedonian dialect, addressing Alketas. He was telling him to keep as still as possible and breathe shallow breaths. Alketas realized now that these faces belonged to Illyr-ian clan men from Parth! He was their victim on an ambush, as they found his tracks or knew his trek -he didn't know which. Had possibly captured and tortured peasants talked?

Alketas was told by the younger Parth that fewer than three times ten-times ten of them survived the winter up in these mountains. Now they would extract their revenge on Agis' victory last summer and Alketas was part of their plan to get to his Father! He was to serve as their hostage. Yes, it was they who killed his dogs using the two-stone sinew rope, only they had attached iron balls on the ones used for the dogs. Bringing him down, they used the stone, not wanting to kill him right away! He would serve their plan better, alive -at least for a while!

Alketas thought of the two-stone rope. The rope itself was made out of animal sinews, braided to-gether, to a desired length by its user. On each end, good sized stones (preferably from river beds, smooth and rounded) would be attached. Then, the user would spin this rope above his head in the air, finally releasing it toward the animal (or person) it was aimed at. The stones (or metal) attached at the ends, would keep the rope stretched full length, until it would find its target. Finding resist-ance, its two ends (still under its velocity) would come to a sudden stop, causing them to fold and hit with tremendous force against what held them (the intended target)! It could be a devastating blow when metal was used at the rope's ends, as it was with his dogs. Even when having the ends loaded with stone, the blow could be fatal. Had they aimed toward his neck or head, he knew he would not have survived. The younger of his two captors let him know that they feared they used more power than they should and also killed him and that was their argument at the time he was coming to his senses.

Alketas felt his anger rising with every word coming out of the Parthinian's mouth. He wanted to jump-up and dispatch both of them with his bare hands! At the same time, he knew too well that he was too weak to even move, let alone attack them! He decided to take his time to recover. He was to be kept alive, obviously, in order to lure his Father into the trap. He prayed that his father would either not buy whatever they were preparing, or, rescue would come to him some how. If he was to die, he would do his best to take many of these beasts with him!

Meantime he started studying his environs, making sure his captors would think he was in much worse shape than he really was. He let a weak sigh come out of his mouth (breathing was still too painful) and closed his eyes, pretending to fall asleep from exhaustion. To his disappointment, his Legs and hands were tied down immediately by these ruffians. He didn't offer resistance. No use in his condition. His body, actually his upper arms, chest and back were still hurting a lot and he could see, as he was propped against the wall of a cave he was brought in, the marks of black and blue made by the weapon. He concluded that the best way for speedy recovery was to get some real sleep.

He woke-up some time, later. How much later, he did not know. There still was some light coming from the cave's huge entrance, but not much. Was it early in the morning or was the sun setting? He would soon find out, but he still did not know if it was the next day or the same one. The pain was still there but dulled somewhat. He tried to stretch his tied-up extremities. There had been hours without free circulation of his blood and they had become numb. There was no familiarity with this huge cavern and he did not know its location. He started studying his surroundings.

There were a few of his captors by the cavern's entrance (presumably the entrance, because he could not see it, but there was more light coming from there). They were talking, eating and drink-ing. At the same time, they did not seem to be relaxed, for their weapons were kept by their sides. To the right of these men there were some ten or so horses, kept in place by having their front legs tied with rope.

There was some fodder thrown before them and, some were eating. Alketas managed to lift himself up a bit more, now commanding a better view. Further in the cavern, there were about two times ten Parthines laying on the floor, some stretching and yawning but most of them sleeping. Closeby but distinctly separate from that group, he noticed the two of his captors he had seen first, talking to each other softly. Were they the leaders? One of them (as he had seen) was rather young to be a leader but who knows? More light was coming from the entrance now. Dawn then, of the next day? He was not so sure. He felt very thirsty and hungry and dry-coughed, in order to draw their attention. At least a dozen of them jumped-up, weapons on hand. They were alert and edgy all right!

Strangely, Alketas found satisfaction with their reaction. In spite of the pain his dry-coughing generated, he had to smile. If, even a tied-down Makedonian youth could make them jump like that, they should wait and see when they'd get some taste of his wrath! And wrath had returned to him, for he could see—as 'Posidonas' stood now—that he had 'confiscated' and was wearing Alketas' sword, the treasured present from Agis. 'Triton' had gotten the quiver and bow, both strapped over his shoulders. They approached him and 'Triton' inquired what Alketas' needs were. He held his anger concealed and asked for water and food.

It was brought to him, after several repeated barks of orders from 'Posidonas'. Good! Alketas was happy to see that orders were not taken easily. Was there some dissent in the group then? Alketas did hope so. 'Triton' asked in his broken Makedonian if the bread, cheese and milk they brought, was enough. Alketas nodded positively while eating and the Parthinian, feeling talkative, proceeded. His name was Ketro and he had seen his father planting an arrow on king Agis last summer, only to have his life taken by a young Makedonian nestling, the one with a snake marked on his shield.

Now, Ketro was in hope that the party which was about to come in search of Alketas, would have in its numbers that very nestling! Ketro would then have the satisfaction of severing his head from its shoulders, avenging his own father's death! Alketas understood that Ketro was talking about cousin Antiohos. The Parthinian continued by saying that Dorr ('Posidonas') was the leader of this group, part of what remained from last summer's great army of king Skotro. Part of king Skotro's revenge plan, was to hit on isolated Orestians like Alketas or small and unprotected hamlets and towns, lure parties of Orestians sent out in chase and, ambushing them, killing as many as they could! The only reason Alketas was being kept alive now, was just in case proof was needed about his abduction. In that case, parts of his body would be sent to Agis, confirming the fact and forcing Orestians to come for the rescue! Feeling happy and excited by his 'rhetoric' abilities, Ketro proceeded in naming the parts of Alketas they were contemplating of sending to Agis in a few days. An arm, holding his nice dagger—for recognition? An eye? Who knew? They had time to make-up their minds, Ketro was proud to announce.

Alketas felt his anger cloud his mind and tried his bonded hands. The rope was too tight. He, next, tried to kick with his legs, rolling his body against the Parthinian but he missed. Ketro laughed and offered his last information. It was six days since they had captured Alketas and, spies informed the group that Orestians were active in Levaea and its environs. He hoped they'd soon be on their way.

They would need about four more days in finding and following the tracks leading to the ambush. If there was any delay, things could be speeded-up by sending Alketas' parts and planting them on the way. Ketro kicked Alketas and turned away, toward smiling Dorr . . .

Pain, anger and anguish overcame and engulfed Alketas. He had to find a way of escape. Not so much because he worried about his own life, but because king Merops had to know and not fall into the trap. He tried his bonds again. The rope wouldn't give way. He had to take some time to work on it and time was of essence. Alketas cursed his weakness and the fact that, six days had passed since his capture. Was he out for that long? Ketro had no reason to lie about that. Noting that Ketro and Dorr were looking at him, he pretended devastation on the hearing of his fate and, complained about the injustice in life, cowered in his place. They both laughed and turned to their business, leaving Alketas to his thinking and plotting an escape . . .

Unknown to the Illyrians and thanks to Andronas' capability, the scouts and the party of following king Merops (led by Damon), knew the exact direction they had to go, as soon as they departed from Levaea. Starting early the very next day after the news brought in to him, king Merops avoided the detection of Parthinian spies, who, seeing the commotion within the town itself later, they thought the Orestians were still preparing and they so reported to their king Skotro. Satisfied, he took his troops from Keletron and went to meet the band hiding in the cavern, holding Alketas hostage.

When the Orestian force camped on their first night out, Perdikkas proposed to join Andronas in scouting ahead, having with them extra horses, so relays of information could be going back and forth, keeping the king alert of any and all possible changes of events. Merops and Tyrimmas agreed and Perdikkas joined Andronas and four others, scouting ahead, after a few hours' rest.

They moved fast and parallel to the track Alketas had taken, arriving at the open meadow without being detected. They found a secluded area to hide and tie-down their horses leaving one Orestian to guard them and sending another to inform king Merops of their progress. The four of them left, cros-sing the open ground after nightfall. A quarter-moon light made their task following Alketas' track easier, though Andronas had some trouble, on account of the dark and the Illyrians, who made a good job erasing most of the tale-telling. The cadavers of the dogs were found—cleaned by the birds and carnivores. As they approached the edge of the woods again, tracks were easier to be seen, because of multiple coming and going from the abductors and their horses, despite the effort made by the Illyrians to erase everything. Andronas was proving his fame as the best of trackers. He prov-ed himself of being better than a hound dog as he was a very silent stalker. Now, the four of them were moving much slower and careful of possible outposts placed by the enemy.

It took them a good portion of the night to reach cover under the trees at the edge of the forest. By the early morning hours, they located the cavern and all the Illyrian outposts. Their questions now, were: is Alketas held by this group? Is he still alive or killed at some other, undetected location? They had to wait and find a better opportunity to investigate. Daylight would help them better, as the day was promising to be a bright one and they looked around for good vantage points to hide them-selves. They did not worry about the scout left with the horses, he knew how to keep them quiet and he had been instructed to wait in ready. Either they would return, or king Merops would find him, guided by Damon.

They agreed that Andronas and Perdikkas would climb and hide in the thick cover of leaves on the majestic oak tree before them, observing from its height. The other two scouts, Mahon and Filon, were to hide in near-by thickets, between them and the trail to the horses. They were to cover a retreat—if successful—running away with Alketas. Otherwise, they were to intervene only if a diversion was deemed necessary. Andronas and Perdikkas took off their breast-plates and covered them—with their shields—under some bushes near the tree, lest the on coming sunlight would shine on them and give the party's location away to the enemy. Next, they helped each-other climb up and stayed still, their backs against the oak's thick trunk, seeing and listening. They had with them their swords and bows with arrows.

The enemy camp came to life soon after their taking cover. First, a couple of riders came out of the cavern heading in the direction of Vattina (on the other side of mountain Voion) toward Dassaretis' borders. Some others took several horses to graze or exercise, passing almost under the oak where Perdikkas and Andronas were hiding. Few more went to the near-by creek for water and, few others (judg-ing by their weapons and purposeful strides) directed themselves toward posts, to replace their night guards. Andronas whispered to Perdikkas they should consider themselves lucky, they had not fallen onto one of those during their approach at night. Perdikkas readily agreed.

There was a sudden commotion coming from behind and under them, the tree trunk being in their way of vision. They cautiously looked around it. An outpost guard, hidden in the bushes just to their left, was caught sleeping, by his replacement! Well! That was a really close call! The man had been very well concealed, for Andronas not to have seen him! Thanked be the gods he was soundly sleep-ing when they came! Now, the unlucky guard was taken toward the cavern and they soon saw him paying with his life for his weakness to fall asleep during guard!

To that end, another commotion turned their attention at the cavern's entrance. They saw Alketas coming out of it, escorted by two other Illyrians. One had the air of a leader and mid aged; the other, younger and agitated. Andronas could understand some Parth dialect and, because of the loudness of the younger Illyrian, he realized that Alketas had insisted on being taken outside, for his bodily needs. Apparently, that was a thing the younger Illyrian did not consider to be a necessity. He was pointing to the older one that body needs could have taken place in the cavern, especially since they were not to stay there for too long a time. Their horses were doing that in there and, what difference would it make if their captive would go meet his ancestors soiled?

Alketas was walking rather unsteadily and with obvious difficulty, the sign of his legs being tied recently. This was obvious by the marks and dried blood at his ankles. His hands were still tied by the wrists, placed together in front of him. There were black and blue marks on his upper hands and his naked chest and back. He and his captors took an animal trail, leading to the left from where Andronas and Perdikkas were hiding in the oak tree. They soon disappeared in the green lush of the forest.

Perdikkas looked at Andronas and they both nodded to each-other in agreement. First the one, then the other, came down descending slowly and with care not to make any noise. Undetected, they reached the ground and, using the existing bush and tree cover, followed the same trail Alketas and his two guards had taken. It was not a difficult job, because, neither Alketas nor his captors were taking any precaution in moving silently, Alketas having no reason to and the Illyrians, because they felt secure in such proximity to their camp and comrades.

Finally they stopped by a secluded place and Alketas asked if he could be left alone for his bodily needs. The younger Illyrian translated the request and they both laughed. Then, the 'leader' nodded his consent. They both checked the area for a possible escape route or any other misdeed by their hostage. Perdikkas thought (for a long moment) that he'd been discovered, as the elder Illyrian's eyes scanned long and persistently in his direction.

Satisfied, the two Illyrians withdrew about twenty paces, under the protests of the younger one. Al-ketas, making sure he could not be seen by them, knelt before a stone with rough edges and started rubbing his ropes against it, frantically. Andronas looked at Perdikkas, making some silent motions. Perdikkas nodded his understanding and, moving stealthily, he loaded his bow with an arrow. And-ronas, silent as Haron personified, moved to the other side of the two Illyrians, now taking a piss in plain view of each-other, joking and kidding about the size of their genitals. Andronas made a noise. The Illyrians, not bothering to cover themselves, moved to investigate. One moved toward the noise and Andronas, the other toward Alketas' location.

Andronas jumped on the back of the elder and, pulling his head back by the long hair, sliced the Il-lyrian's throat. Dorr fell on the ground not knowing what happened. At the same time, a 'thunk' on a tree trunk indicated that Mahon, seeing the whole scene from his hiding and eager to help, had miss-ed his target, the advancing Ketro. Realizing he had become a target, Ketro let out a warrior's yell and speedily drew his sword running toward Alketas who'd raised himself up holding the stone. Meantime Perdikkas, letting a soft curse out, followed the Illyrian's path of death, trying to aim while running. He reached the place finding Alketas turning and blocking Ketro's attempt, hands still tied, paring the blow of the sword with the stone he held. The force of the blow and speed of the attacker carried both of them down on the ground, forcing them to tumble a few times over.

Alketas still weak and tied, was slow in getting-up and thought he was about to die—for sure—this time, for Ketro was already up on his feet and attacking, his eyes red and wild with hate. Alketas felt and heard the air whistle by an arrow flying past his ear, as he still was getting up to face a certain death. His surprise was equal to Ketro's who, receiving Perdikkas' arrow in his heart, had his last step half-taken, one foot up in the air. The other foot, gave way and his body collapsed awkwardly on the ground.

Alketas recognized the make of his saviors' helmets, but could not see who they were.

Andronas with Mahon (who looked at Perdikkas apologetically) and Filon (now out of his hiding) approached. Perdikkas cut Alketas' rope from his hands, nodding all of them to follow in retreat.

The surprise of the unexpected rescue passed, Alketas wanted to know who his rescuers were and thank them. Perdikkas raised his hand for silence and Mahon made the point that 'thank yous' should wait, once it was sure the yell from Ketro had, by now, created an alarm among the Illyrians in the cavern and out in the woods. They'd better get going now, while the surprise lasted! Alketas agreed but picked-up his sword, dagger and belt from Dorr and his quiver and bow from Ketro, before moving. Supported now by Perdikkas and Filon, Alketas followed Andronas' lead to the waiting horses and escape. Mahon was covering their retreat a few steps behind.

They had not reached the edge of woods and the meadow yet, when they heard the sound of Illyrian horns sounding the alarm. By the time they were in the clearance, arrows started flying in their di-rection. Thankfully, those were not escorted by the whistle of the two-stone ropes, nor were they of any accuracy. They reached the place Perdikkas and the others had their breast-plates and shields hidden and, while half of them put them on, the others were providing cover, sending arrows at the oncoming Parthines. Alketas stood in awe, noticing the sign on Perdikkas' shield. The sunburst of his vision/dream, while wounded and captured, was on it! Alketas had to know who the man really was!

Then, suddenly, a new much more welcomed noise delighted the small group (their situation being rather bleak at that moment). The Orestian paean, the war song, resonated through the hills and the force led by Damon came out of the forest. King Merops being in the forefront of his troops, fell upon the (surprised and caught in the open) Parthines. The Illyrians put up a staunch resistance. They fought hard for their lives, but in vain. Tyrimmas and his Iraklides fell upon them from behind, having surmounted the hill from the other side. The battle was short in duration but a bloody one. From the Parthines none escaped. They were all put to sword. The cavern was explored in case any one was hiding in it and all the looted valuables were recovered.

Alketas was sent back to Levaea on a litter and with strong escort, against his protests and wish to follow the troops. King Merops with Tyrimmas and the bulk of the troops, headed toward the town of Vattina.

Word had been received that Skotro and his raiders found strong resistance there and were detained in besieging the town. The same news had reach Antiohos in Levaea. Having received some re-enforcements from clan heads outside the town, he left Agis with Agathon in charge there and he headed toward Vattina leading these new levies. He was itching to get into action. The two Orestian armies fell upon Skotro and his Parthines from two sides, like it was prearranged but—actually—out of pure coincidence. Within the following two weeks, all Orestis was free of the in-truders.

Orestians suffered a serious blow themselves. King Merops, being of high spirits after their victory, went after a mountain lion they happened to run onto, on their return to Levaea. He went after the beast unprotected, not waiting for right equipment or escort. As some from his personal guard tried to follow hurriedly, he galloped after the animal. At one point, the lion turned to defend itself. King Merops' horse got scared and, stopping suddenly on its tracks, forced the king over. Merops lost his hold and, flying overhead, fell upon a rock, crashing his back. The few of his guards, who managed to follow close, chased the lion away and prepared a litter for their injured king. As they were trans-fering the king to meet the rest of the troop and have him looked by a doctor, he breathed his last.

Antiohos was acclaimed the new king on the spot, by all clan heads present. They continued their return to Levaea, for king Merops' funeral rites. Upon their arrival in Levaea, Merops' body was washed and dressed in proper, kingly attire. A pyre stage was prepared in the middle of the agora of the town and, under the seer's guidance and prayers Antiohos placed the customary gold piece for the king's passage to the underworld, on his Father's dead body. He scaled down and, in unison with Agis, Alketas and Tyrimas, set the pyre stage on fire. When the king's body was consumed by the fire and all was burned, the seers and their helpers picked-up his bones and washed them. A funeral pro—cession with all the king's ceremonial armor and family gifts were brought to the royal grave site and Merops was interned. During the funeral banquet that evening, a second disaster occurred. Tyrim-mas fell suddenly ill and, within the night, he also died. The doctor attending him suspected poison-ing. Having no proof—as everyone at the banquet ate and drunk from common vessels—the case re-mained a mystery.

The next day and after Tyrimmas' own funeral and banquet, Perdikkas was the chosen new leader of the Iraklides, his own followers led by his brothers having arrived from Elimiotis already. At the ceremony for

Perdikkas' accession, Antiohos pledged continuous support—as his deceased Father would want—confirming Makedonis region for the Iraklides and Perdikkas took an oath of subordi-nation to the Orestian king, as Tyrimmas had done for Merops. Alketas, thankful as he felt toward Perdikkas, talked to his Father and both asked permission (and got it) from Antiohos to attach their services (and the services of those under them) to the Iraklides, moving the family from Levaea to some estate they had close to Makedonis, by the Elimiotian borders. Thus, they would also serve as liaison between Antiohos and Perdikkas.

Antiohos' aim by agreeing to this, was to have Alketas away from any influence in Levaea, feeling more secure on his throne, though he knew that Alketas had no desire to be of any hindrance to his plans and thinking of ruling. Agis was the one who could be of nuisance, as senior and ex-king. The idea of having both out of Levaea was a god-sent solution for Antiohos.

The following years brought the well known wars of Orestis against the neighboring kingdoms and the succeeding invasions from the barbarians, resulting on the animosity between Antiohos and Per-dikkas. Alketas and Agis being the main proponents in rewarding Perdikkas for the support he pro-vided, Antiohos seized and imprisoned Agis. Alketas managed to take the rest of the family to Per-dikkas in Makedonis, afraid the same fate would come to them. When this happened, Antiohos put Agis to death and placed a reward for Alketas' capture.

It was during the relocation of Agis' house that Perdikkas met Fivi and they fell in love. He asked for her hand and the rest is history—as they say. Alketas was now connected with Perdikkas by blood and, with his personal pledge of support, their relationship took a new, closer meaning. In Alketas' mind there was still the subject of the shield with the sunburst on, which needed an explanation. De-termined to have a fully deciphered answer of his vision in connection with Perdikkas' shield, Alketas went to the Oracle of Dodona. He traveled there by-passing Orestis, through Elimiotis and Tymfea, disguised as a peasant.

As we know, Dodona is located in Ipiros, under joined Molossian and Haonian pledges of protect-ion. The Oracle and its precinct are dedicated to Zefs, the Father of gods and mankind and Dioni, one of his beloved mortals. It was established as such from immemorial time, a shrine to Mother Earth. On the branches of its ancient and holy oak tree, votives of copper, silver and gold were hang-ing, donations from untold numbers of petitioners, rich and poor alike. When a wind blows—as it al-most always does—the chiming sound of those votives gives a sense of awe. The holy doves nesting on it, witnesses of the eternal love of Dias to Dioni, are used to the sound and they remain perched or continue pecking on the food the visitors are so generous of providing them with.

Every petitioner coming to Dodona asking for the Oracle, has to bring an unblemished animal, ac-cording to one's own wealth or lack of it, for sacrifice on the altar. If the omens are favorable, the pe-titioner is approached by a priestess who's escorted by two acolytes (also women), each holding a narrow-necked earthenware pot. This narrow neck allows only one hand of the priestess to enter through it. If she brings out of the pot from her right-hand standing acolyte a bronze-made oak leaf, the petitioner's request to place a question is granted. If the priestess' hand comes out holding a flat stone (exactly the shape and size of the bronze leaf), the petitioner has to go through a ritual of puri-fication, sacrifice another unblemished animal and petition again. After a favorable outcome, the petitioner whispers the question to this priestess. She then reaches for the acolyte's pot on her left. If she brings out a silver acorn, the answer is positive, the petition will be fulfilled. If her hand comes up holding a stone the size of the silver acorn, then the petitioner's request is deemed impossible, as de-nied by the god. At the end of either verdict, a male priest (the one who slaughters the sacrificial ani-mals on the altar) strikes at a bronze shield hanging from one of the lower branches of the holy oak. When its echo dies, the next petitioner can approach and the procedure is repeated from sunrise to sunset.

Alketas brought an unblemished ram, emblem of his family's recognition back home. It was sacrificed and the omens were favorable. The priestess, her face wrinkled and her body frail from untold years in the service of the god, came to him flanked by her two young acolytes. Her left hand moved toward the pot on her right. It entered through its narrow neck and came out holding the bronze. A sigh of relief came out of Alketas' mouth. Alketas now had to bend low, to whisper his request, the old woman being so short. He told her he wanted to know why he had seen the sunburst, a star of six plus ten pointed rays, exactly the same as the one on Perdikkas' shield, especially when he did not even know the man existed! He was also curious to find out if his family would come to be the leading one in Orestis and Makedonia again.

The old priestess looked up at him for a very long time, contemplating. Then, made a face he could not tell was a gesture of mocking or just smiling, she said that his question being two-fold, she would give him a two-fold answer too! Turning somewhat toward the other acolyte, her right hand moved to the pot on her left. Before she had time to reach it, a fluttering sound made all of them to look up. A fine specimen of a 'golden' eagle—this majestic bird favored by mighty Zefs—descended from the clear sky! The doves perched on the oak tree, scattered in all directions looking for safety. The bird of prey paid no attention to them. The eagle dove straight at the altar and its talons closed on the sev-ered head of the sacrificed ram Alketas brought. With an ease and purposeful slowness, the bird ex-tended the full span of its wings and moved, carrying the ram's head to the sky! The priestess' hand stood still above the pot as her eyes followed the bird. It headed toward the few puffy fair weather clouds which blocked the sun at the moment. The clouds parted like if they were ordered to part and the sun shone, its golden rays forming six plus ten spokes piercing through the parted clouds. The light hurt the eyes and the eagle disappeared from view, becoming one with the sunburst . . .

Everybody let an involuntary cry of awe! The noise of the two earthenware pots falling from the hands of the acolytes and shattering brought them back. Had the god given a special answer? The old priestess held Alketas' hand, shaking. Without a word, she pulled him to follow, the acolytes falling one step behind and obviously aloof with their thoughts. They all moved toward the Altis, the wooded sacred hill beyond the altar and the temple. Alketas kept his head down, perplexed by the event and with deep fear in his heart.

They reached the middle of the Altis and, against the slope of the hill, there was a dark entrance. The two acolytes picked-up a torch each, left by the entrance from a previous use. The torches were lit from a cauldron full of burning herbs and spice woods, the smell of which was too strong for Alke-tas. One of the acolytes led into the entrance, the other trailing this strange party of four. Down they went, on a narrow and slippery path, followed by a winding set of steps in a tunnel. If it wasn't for the torches and their flickering light, Alketas knew they would all have fallen, breaking some bones! At the bottom of the steps, they entered a roomier place where moist and darkness made breathing harder. Alketas looked around but couldn't see much.

The odor of decay and dampness in this place, the trembling flames of the torches playing tricks with light and shadows, forced an involuntary shivering on Alketas. A husky voice calling his name from somewhere to his left, made him jump. One of the shadows moved closer turning to a shape of a human (if one could call the crone which approached him such). If the old priestess seemed to him old when he first show her, this one was time personified!

The priestess and her two acolytes fell on their knees, pulling Alketas to do the same. His heart beat faster! There was utter silence for a while, then, the crone spoke again. She (she was a woman after all!) told him that the god had spoken to him in person, not through the usual words from the priestess' mouth. Because he was unfamiliar with the god's tongue, she was here to interpret. The answer to his two-fold question was this: The house of Agis, being the ram's head emblazoned in every male member's shield, would be carried high by the favor of Dias—as the eagle showed them. But it would be surpassed by the house of Timenos and forced to serve the sign of the sunburst, its house and its descendants, those six plus ten spokes of sunrays!

A long silence fell between them. Alketas got lost in his thoughts, contemplating the significance of the crone's words. The only thing he could hear was her breath wheezing in and out, losing volume, until there was complete silence. He raised his eyes. She was nowhere to be seen. He felt the weight of a hand on his shoulder, prodding him to turn. He did and the priestess with her acolytes led him back to the world. The audience ended, the verdict was pronounced. Alketas and the house of Agis were to serve and follow the shield with the sunburst, wherever it would lead . . .

This is a true story, as I heard it from Alketas' own mouth! Lord Alketas is my friend and benefac-tor and we spent many a day and night together, next to a warm hearth or out in the nature's ele-ments. Trust among us was built through years of shared good and bad alike!"

"Historical theory without archaeological
proof is still a theory and it should be
treated as such!"
Marcus A. Templar, American

II

Perdikkas was not blessed with any children from Fivi. Nonetheless, the two of them were always in love with each-other and she helped raise his children from other wives he married. Fivi died before her husband, in a last attempt of having a child with him. Long before this misfortune, Perdikkas had bestowed to Alketas the area around Levaea. Upon Alketas' death years after Perdikkas' own, his two sons, Agis and Parmenion, remained the lords and land holders of the same estates, serving Perdikkas first, then his son and heir Argeos. They showed the same devotion their Father had shown to both kings. It became a tradition the Agis house being the 'right hand' of the House of Timenos, as the Ram was destined to serve the Sunburst!

Argeos, succeeding Perdikkas, worked very hard consolidating and expanding the inherited king-dom. When king Kleovoulos of Elimiotis was pressured by Thessalians from Farsalos (in alliance) with the Athamanes, Argeos came to his aid, bringing Elimiotis (temporarily) closer to Timenid de-pendence. About the same time, Argeos extended his kingdom securing Vottiaea. Now, the Argead/ Timenid/ Iraklides kingdom included Makedonis, Pieria, Imathia, and Vottiaea, having control on Eordea and Elimiotis! His further attempts in expanding his kingdom on Almopia were stopped by the combined forces from Orestis, Tymfea, Elimiotis (which turned against him), Dassaretis and Lynkestis! Before the new power of the Timenos House, even Lynkos and Orestis were joining hands. During his six plus times three ten years of rule (only four years short of his Father's rule), Argeos had the misfortune of seeing settlers from southern city-states come and establish new city-states just on the line of his expansion dreams in Makedonia. Being preoccupied with the machinations of the kings from Elimiotis, Orestis and Lynkos, he was unable to halt this creation and establishment of new city-states by the coastal areas he considered his.

Kypselos of Korinthos first, then his successor Periandros, placed a great pressure against Makedo-nia with help from the Aeginitans and the Athinians. With their combined naval superiority and power through their commodities exports, they managed to bring Argeos in an economic dependence—according to their monopoly whims. The newly established city-states on the shoreline were (by na-ture of their settlers) either Korinthian, Aeginitan, Athinian or Halkidian allies, supported by their mother cities. Halkidian influence and pressure in the Halkidiki peninsula was a great factor, since Halkidian silver coins became the standard, trusted for its true value and becoming the exchange way of almost every deal and transaction. Aegina and Athinae competition created emporia-stations which—in turn—were fast becoming city-states of their own, adding

161

a choke-holder on the promotion and free bartering of Makedonian products.

The only outlet in the dealings with the southerners and source of revenue for the royal treasure was the fact that Makedonian exchange power of goods rested solely in the discretion of the king. That measure was established with the land holders and clan heads' sanctions on 'spear won' lands, since the early days of Perdikkas. It specified that all land and its fruits, was under direct royal control, enabling the Timenid House to have some dearly needed independence in the overall dealings on import and export. The Timenid House—recognized now by all as the Makedonian king-dom—when it came to dealing with the city-states and being naturally resourceful, could (at times) dictate its own policy on trade. Lack of sea power made this policy a difficult task though.

Internally and for the rest of Makedonia as a tribal unit, things continued to evolve the same ways as before. Antiohos was succeeded by his son Ypalkmos. The relation of Orestis with the Timenid/Ar-gead Makedonia remained hostile. In Lynkestis, Pafsanias succeeded his father. Temvros—a disap-pointed and heartbroken (after the misfired effort in gaining control with Illyrian help) man—passed his kingship to his son. Both Temvros and Pafsanias still nursed a hope of prestige recovery, their dream remaining as such. Pelagonia and Paeonia remained the closest allies to them. The Pelagonian king, Fidon, gave his daughter Ellaniki to Pafsanias and his son, Kynetas, married Damasias' niece Verinno. Damasias' own son, Alketas, died shortly after the start of his own reign, warring against the Dardanes and north Peonians. He was succeeded by his first cousin, Python. The Anthemountian kingdom had its own problems, first receiving the brunt of the settlers in Halkidiki, then a fight for succession between the two grand sons of king Kissios, Antilohos and Mahaon. Mahaon won in the end, actively helped by the Potidaeans, Korinthian settlers having their city-state in the narrow con-necting land by Pallini. Amfaxitis was a bit more stable as king Podarilos was holding his own—for the time being. Kristonia, Mygdonia and Vissaltia, forming a lose alliance, were straggling to stave-off either Thrakian or Halkidian domination, while Sintiki, Idonia and Odomantiki were now independent now under Thrakian rule. Akti was very much under Stagiros and Akanthos, two very powerful city-states, settled by Halkidians from Evia and from the island of Andros. Thasos island was trying its muscles pressuring Idonia and settling towns on the Pangaeon area, as well as by the mouth of Strymon. Lastly, we from Krousis, being even a smaller state than Anthemous and located just above Potidaea and Olynthos, came by necessity closer to Vottiki, Ramelous and Sythonia.

In all fairness, Sythonia was the only remaining true kingdom of old, not allowing much of new settlers within its current borders. Its king, Asteropeos (the second one) died recently, leaving the kingdom to his nephew Ptolemeos. Ptolemeos not only resisted further outside influence and settlers, he also became the reason, we from Krousis along with Ramelous and Vottiki, have some free lands and policy of our own!

Next, Ptolemeos formed an alliance with Filippos son of Argeos, grand son of Perdikkas, placing the coastal city-states between our states, thus controlling the interior. Ratifying this alliance, Filippos' young son Aeropos (only two plus ten years of age) is to be betrothed, soon, to princess Iakynthi of Sythonia, a direct relative (in spite of what some say—she is of Egyptian blood) of Ptolemeos. For this alliance (or rather because of it) I am sure there will be a lot of pressure applied on Sythonia and on Filippos, from Korinthos, Aegina, Halkis and Athinae. My own opinion is that Makedonia and its allies cannot present a common front against external influence and penetration in its politics and commerce. My reasoning is that too many clan kings have their own ambitions and ideas, none being in position or willing to make any kind of policy acceptable by others, nor compromise anything for the common good!

The only consolation for leaders like Filippos and few people like me in Makedonia is the fact that these city-states and the barbarians on the other side all have conflicting interests concerning our space and state of affairs. This fact always gives us a respite. Some of us do see the need of a solid and common front. Most of us are too stubborn and divided to remedy this 'illness'. It would take a very strong and cunning king to unite the whole area. I am neither strong, nor cunning and Filippos does not have the resources—not yet. My own bet is with the Timenides though. It seems to me that the family has a unique interest in Makedonian welfare—regardless that theTimenides are newcomers (relatively speaking).

As it is, even I—a faithful supporter of a unity—cannot openly declare my preference. I am only a small clan head, a medium size land holder, in the small state of Krousis. All my properties and inter-ests lie within this confinement, greatly exposed to the power of the city-states, because of their settlers and fleet. I believe that, if Timenid Makedonia had a good harbor in possession, if it could train good sailors, things could be different.

But there's nothing much on the west side of the gulf, except Pella and that is blocked by Aloros, Methoni and Pydna, across the shallow lagoon. Besides, it would take many generations to transform mountaineers to sailors, even without any external inter-ferences!

I know that Filippos (for one) wants to unite all other kingdoms, even if he does not rule them. He fears both the barbarians and the city-states, wanting us (as Makedonians) to be able to turn those two forces against each-other rather than have them turning against us! We hold a very close re-lationship the King and I. And, I say King, because he is the one! All the others are petty kings, en-tangled in their narrow, petty affairs, opportunistic and vain within their imaginary glories . . .

Filippos and I met for the first time, in one of those rare occasions when Makedonians co-operated with one-another, during the great Thrakian penetration in our lands, eight years ago. Then, by all indications, the Odrysses seemed to be unstoppable. Their drive was so great, it scared even the coastal city-states, as their mother states were forced to send hundreds of oplites to help hold the in-vader. As I hope you understand, Korinthos, Potidaea, Thasos and (in lesser degree) Aegina and A-thinae, have their appetite wetted with the chunks of Makedonian and Thrakian lands they got on the coast. Any Thrakian (Odryssian or otherwise) supremacy, would have turned their dreams into nightmares! In any event, Filippos united all of us—albeit temporarily—and we sent the Odryssians back to their country, after great loss of life, livestock and produce.

Filippos is is one of the very few, Filippos is, well educated people I happen to know. Although he has his scribes for the royal correspondence dealing his business with the city-states and us, he can read and write on his own, such as when the two of us correspond. He keeps this ability secret, so he can always check if a scribe puts on the wax tablet exactly what the King dictates or not. I know, first-hand, him sending away one of his Evian scribes last year, because he caught that scribe having written a com-pletely different text from what the King had ordered! Knowing Filippos, I am sure he would have liked to make a good example out of that Evian. But he didn't want his secret out, nor he could really afford a show-down with Halkis -the Arhons (Archons) of which had recommended that scribe to him. Instead, he thanked the scribe for services rendered, excusing the dismissal on account of financial reasons. The King gave that scribe a nice severance pay and presents and sent him pack-ing!

I don't know if any of his remaining scribes are smart enough to have gotten the message. I do know (and the King does too) that, somehow, many of them find ways to inform their states of origin about the King's intentions. He has one or two Makedonians doing some of this job, but it is difficult to have more of them educated and ask them to accept a position they all consider inferior.

Just between us, I think it would be easier for him to make his countrymen sailors. You see, because of all the uncertainty (invasions and all), most Makedonians are on the move so-to-speak. Even the land holders and clan heads have their winter and summer places for the safety of their families and herds. This mode of a transhumance comings and goings is caused by the hard times and invasions from every side. People can hardly keep-up with their sowing and harvesting, building and re-building after each invasion or local war! They have no time thinking of education.

Unless the boundaries are secured, there will be no luxury of real education, no city building like in the southern city-states! The existing scattered townships are the ones which are (mostly by nature) well protected from assaults. Even then, there's always a chance of having the town overrun. Look at Levaea! Since the town was burned down in the early years of Argeos' rule, it never got to be rebuilt again! It was found too risky and very approachable to sudden raids from the enemy, any enemy! So, people didn't feel secure returning to towns like it. Now, aside from a shrine in honor of Iraklis, one can find nothing else telling where Levaea was.

In order to secure the borders, co-operation is needed by all. That is the one thing no one is willing to do. As I mentioned before, each king looks after his petty interests. Filippos' state is in a far better condition than the rest, but not in such a degree as to dictate acceptance by the others, peacefully or by force. Yet, Filippos is trying to unify us all! Knowing him the way I do, I am certain he would even agree to stepping-down (if there was ever a chance to convince the rest to unify).

On this subject, I guess we are no better than our southern kin, with its city-state quarrels and wars each summer time. The difference is that they have only themselves to worry about, whereas we have them and the barbarians knocking at our doors!...

Word came to me recently that, in Attiki, the Athinians are experimenting with yet another form of governing themselves. Having the ancient custom of kingship abolished many years ago, they have been governed by a number of big land holders and clan heads, collectively. Now, there's one of them there, Solon is his name (though I am not so sure about it yet) and he has been appointed to refab-ricate their government and their social structure. He is rearranging the clans, severing old ties and obligations to strongmen. I do not know of any details yet, but he's supposed to be a very capable man.

Filippos (and I agree) would wish to have the luxury of time for experiments like this one in Athi-nae. You see, regardless the constant bickering and fighting among themselves, the southern city-states do have time on their hands. They war for a few weeks, then, they call a truce and gather their harvest and settle internal affairs. By the time that's finished, they have either found a solution to their fight or they forgot all about it and all is well.

Up here in our lands, every spring and summer there is an invasion of sorts from the north or the east, followed by pressure for more settlers and colonists from the city-states, who are keen in send-ing away their undesirables to start new colonies in our soil! Then, we have the wars among petty kings. By the time each one of these problems is faced off and everybody is sent back home, the harvest is mostly ruined and reconstruction and recuperation gets us well into winter, while preparations are under way, as to how we can avert another invasion the following spring.

Meantime, reports from Korinthos have it that Periandros (their Archon-in-charge) is in trouble but keeps on holding the helm of the state, sending away in exile his detractors. They -of course- will come to establish new colonies here. From across the Aegean sea in Asian shores, the established (for many generations ago) colonies of Aeolian, Ionian and Dorian settlements -many of them large cities of their own merit- are more stable in affairs. When their population increases beyond control or there are opposing parties to their government, they send colonists in the coastal areas of Propontis, Vosporos, or Efxinos Pontos. Some even venture toward Sikelia. In the interior of the Asian coast across from the Aegean, the Lydians have established a powerful state and they are the nominal overlords. But, aside of some token contributions in coin or in kind, they let those city-states govern their own and do as they please. There's a persistent rumor that their Lydian king, Kryssos, is the wealthiest man alive. There are other reports also (mainly from Rodian and Kypriot sailors) that, further inland, the kingdom of the Assyrians is in war with the one from Vavylon and subjects of both are in unrest, revolting against their masters.

Although these events (if true) take place far away, there is fear among the Kypriots that, because of the upheaval, there could be interruption of commerce on spices, copper, wine and other commodi-ties. It is reported that the Finikian purple-died textiles are already out of reach, just because of such a rumor! Meantime, Egyptos is not the powerful kingdom it used to be, most of the trade from there gone the byways, taken over by Finikian pirates and nomads of the desert.

As if all these bad news were not enough, we may have increased troubles stemming from the north and east of river Istros, beyond Thraki! There is another, new and numerous tribe, called Skythes. These Skythes are constantly on the move, living in wagons and raiding vast areas. Thrakian Trivalli and Odrysses have come to know these Skythes already and their experience out of these newcomers' ferocity has taken large proportions. Skythian warriors fight while riding on horses, with bows and arrows, which they discharge from a distance and are very good in doing it! If and when they are forced to fight on foot (rarely), they use long swords and have no protection of their bodies -like shields or cuirasses. They fight naked, not caring of death or wounds and have their bodies painted! I was informed of that by my new Thrakian servant who met these barbarians once and he still has nightmares in his sleep! He told me that even the Skythian women follow their men into battle some times, fighting equally hard! I guess the legend of Amazones has some truth hidden in the mist of time.

I hope, and suppose, we will not have to come to blows with these Skythes, ourselves. As it is report-ed to me (and I have no reason to doubt my Thrakian servant's words) Skythes prefer to live in open space -as they are in constant move. Thankfully, there are no large and open spaces in our mountain and sea confined lands. The Skythes do not seem to be interested in wealth either -my Thrakian tells me. They fight because they like it and are indifferent to property. Oh, they like silver and gold, they have many crafted (made or stolen) trinkets hung on their bodies and their horses' bridles, but that is just it, decoration! I am tempted to think that this tribe is a blessing in disguise to us, as it keeps our barbarian immediate neighbors in a state of anxiety, allowing them no time to make plans to raid us!

On the other hand, I don't see us trying to take advantage of the information we receive, nor of the opportunities given to us by such discord and preoccupation. Nor our southern kin seems to have any interest on these events, aside of promoting their immediate concerns of profit and expansion as city-states. They just keep on sending settlers and try to monopolize everything in trade, so they can fat-ten their purses...

I wish, now that we have closer relationship with Sythonia and, because of the imminent relation with King Filippos, we could (somehow) get under his banner of the sunburst. I see such approach as the only solution to our external dictation in policy, as well as to our internal strife for recognition and supremacy! But, as I stated earlier, I am just a small clan head and my word and thoughts don't carry the weight of decisions -as needed. As a matter of fact I know many of my fellow citizens con-sider me as a person likely to become a turncoat and they are ready to accuse me, if it wasn't for my bravery in battle. This has been demonstrated in several occasions and my personal smartness (no bragging here!) of having the composure in facing them down at each general assembly!

My personal correspondence with King Filippos is carried by the most trusted members of my clan and some servants. They know nothing about the contents of any letter to and from the King. It is easy to do this, since most of the carriers are illiterate. The diptychs or triptychs (depending on how long the letters are) are usually hidden within the goods I transport overland or ship by sea to his kingdom. His answers come to me, stuffed in a royal present of a goose or a deer, as he often hunts.

Naturally, neither one of us employs any scribes to write our correspondence. After I read each of the King's messages, the wax covering the diptych or triptych is melted down and replaced anew, so there is no trace of what was written -in case one falls into the wrong hands.

I have to write to him on a new subject I hear of lately. Athinae started having real trouble with its near-by island of Aegina. Aegina has a more powerful fleet and has taken some commerce away from the Athinian hands. What keeps them from warring is the personal connection of one Athinian strong-man named Drakon. He deals with many of the Aeginitan councilmen, elders and merchants. I am sure they will come to blows sometime, be it sooner or later. If so, there might be one headache less for Makedonia and Filippos!

Evian interests from the cities of Halkis and Eretria remain very highly active, as also is from the city of Megara, located after Athinae, on the road to Peloponnisos. Megarians settled some emporia on Thrakian and Makedonian coastal areas recently, some times just by themselves, other times being helped by other cities too. This activity means one thing: The emporia and market places of theirs will soon become full-sized colonies -the time any conceivable excuse or opportunity arrives! Megara, has already secured such places by the straights beyond Ellispontos sea, at the so-called Pass of the Cattle -the Vosporos.

I hear of all these things (which I verify when possible) because of my dealings with many, especially merchants. I send reports (without failure) to King Filippos the way I mentioned before and, I am sorry to say, there is not much he can do -most of the time. Every now and then, through my services and contacts, he is able to induce Thrakian tribes in attacking the new settlers -instead of attacking us. Unfortunately, this is always a very costly proposition which (many a time) backfires. Thrakians cannot always find the loot they are after from the settlers. They may capture as many as they can for ransom but, let us not forget, these settlers are mostly unwanted in their city of origin. The citi-zens who exiled them, are not too keen in paying ransom to free them! They can be sold, next, at a slave market but that doesn't bring enough. Slave markets are full of prisoners of war and those captured by pirates. The settlers also come as armed oplites, remaining as such until their settlements are walled and protected. The Thrakians do not want to waste time and manpower on those! Then, they turn on us, for revenge. Other times the bribes from the colonies and city-states are received more favorably by the Thrakian chieftains. Adding the constant threat from Illyrians and Dardanes, King Filippos' hands are always busy parrying blows from left and right!...

Ah! Here comes my trusted (that's because I can loosen his tongue with some strong Makedonian wine) friend, Polydoros. He's the son of Timoklis, the Samian. They have excellent wine in Samos too! Polydoros looks all business as he approaches, which tells me he has important news to talk about. After the customary greetings and his usual jokes about my thick Makedonian accent, opposite to his 'refined' Ionian one, I offer him my usual invitation to a cup of the great Dionyssos' gift to mankind. He refuses (politely but firmly) the offer, claiming work pressure and time limits on his visit at my place. By saying that, I understand that he has important news to sell but he won't be ready until he deems the price is adequate. I do not insist on my offer, claiming I am also too busy. His eyes betray a confirmation as to the importance of his knowledge. I continue playing the fool's part. I will have Pefkestas, my first-born son, shadow him when he goes and I will find out what all this is about, in a cheaper way -perhaps. Polydoros and I make our business deal, offer libations in order to seal it and I let him go. I call on Pefkestas and one of our serf hands and send them after Po-lydoros…

Four hours (according to my sand-clock) later, Pefkestas returned with his report. Polydoros had gone, apparently making new deals, to a couple of local wine merchants and, then, he spent too much time with Andromahos, the Korinthian pottery dealer. Whether on business or otherwise, my son could not tell. Both of them had gone into the house Andromahos keeps at the back side of his shop, leaving out front his trusted slave, Adamas from Allikarnassos, for business transactions. Pefkestas also informed me that Polydoros is in constant company with the Aeginitan Kleodotos (another mer-chant), sipping wine and frolicking with Erodikea, the reputed etaera from Korinthos, at Leonidas' tavern. My son also told me that he left our serf hand across Andromahos' shop keeping tabs, in case Polydoros decided to move to another place.

Before my son had finished his report to me, our serf hand arrived to tell me that Polydoros and Andromahos had gone to the tavern, where they met with Kleodotos. He left them there (making sure they intended to stay and drink) and came to let me know. I thought this would be a good time to join them. I was sure their tongues would be loose enough by the time I arrived and it would not cost me as much to learn what I had to. Sure enough, I found them there, drinking and already loud.

My serf hand had also followed for possible need of protection and I gave him a secret look, letting him know that he could stay around, unobserved. He understood and pretended walking about with purpose, while I joined the trio.

Erodikea was at half point on reciting a love poem written by Sapfo, while half of her revealed her ample endowments to any and all in Leonidas' tavern. In spite of their obvious interest on Erodikea's 'treasures' (so much more than for her reciting ability), they all greeted me with enthusiasm, owed to my social status and the credit I carry wherever I go. Leonidas himself came to serve me with a new-ly filled container of wine (the best of Samos -he said) and refused to accept payment from my purse, although I insisted on treating the whole company of his customers present. I asked him, then, for a private room and I gathered Polydoros, Andromahos and Kleodotos in there, asking Erodikea to come along and continue to entertain us.

After a small offering to Dionysos and the ancestors, we all started drinking again, Erodikea picking up from where she had stopped. I made sure to proportionally water my wine, every time my cup was refilled by a girl servant Leonidas had assigned. Erodikea finished her recital and received a very warm reception from all of us at her closing lines. Appreciating that, she let some more of her beauty to be seen raising an even warmer reception by the thunderstruck Polydoros! We all got involved with the usual small talk after that, on business, families and trade connections with other states. As I discreetly prodded Polydoros for news of political interest, I noticed he was taking great efforts in keeping himself 'buttoned-up'. I realized I had to move slow, with patience, for the twinkle in his eyes was telling me the old gizzard had knowledge of some really important news, about which he either was unwilling to reveal before company, or, he was fishing for exceptional profit before he would 'spill the beans'. Either way, I had to take my time and pretend only casual curiosity, mixed with mild indifference.

Erodikea came to assist me, unknowingly, when she decided to inquire on the upcoming nuptials of prince Aeropos of the Argiades and princess Iakynthi of the Sythones. The face of Polydoros turned immediately to stone and his hurried gestures of dismissal -followed by words of denial of any know-ledge and development- made my mind to try another method of approach to find out what he really knew. I secretly motioned to Erodikea, pointing (at the same time) at my purse so she would under-stand that ample compensation was to come her way, to get into the trouble of finding more on the subject. I saw she understood and I changed the subject. After a while I got up and prepared to leave. I convinced Kleodotos and Andromahos to follow me, presenting them the excuse of an important deal I had lined-up, one which would profit both of them. They wanted to stay but the prospect of a good profit made them agree -grudgingly. We left Polydoros in the capable hands of (already ad-vancing) Erodikea…

Once we got out of the tavern, I briefly went over some details of a very good deal I had worked some time ago, of exchanging a fine Makedonian wine quantity with Korinthian pottery and Thraki-an animal pelts. Then, using the pretext that it had become later in the evening than I realized, I dis-missed Andromahos and Kleodotos, promising them to take care of the final deal first-thing the next morning. I knew I could do it without any hindrance, having in mind to assign it to my son, while I would have a free hand doing what I had to.

I went home and asked from the household help to bring Erodikea to my reception room, no matter the hour of her arrival. I went in there myself, calling for a cup of wine mixed with honeyed water.

My wife walked-in soon after, to greet me. She asked me if I was to have something to eat, though the hour was past supper time. I thanked her but I declined any food. Knowing me, she said she un-derstood and she asked if the -soon to come- guest would need any food and/or sleeping quarters. I answered that the visitor would come in secrecy, exchange some vital information and leave at once. To be on the safe side (you know what wives can think of and do!), I told her who the secret visitor would be and who was the source of information, but left it at that. I knew she wouldn't ask for more details. She just gave me the look so well known to me, meaning: "I trust you, but be careful and be quick in your dealing with her!" She then gave me a good-night kiss and withdrew to her chambers.

Erodikea was very late in coming to me. I had almost given up any hope and I was ready to retire, when she was announced. First thing I asked her was if she was sure she had not been followed. She assured me in the name of all gods that, escorted by her Thrakian guard, a deaf-mute giant watch- dog, would be enough threat to any one wishing to know her where-abouts and scare him away!

I offered her some wine and a seat. I started counting the customary amount of silver (when deal-ing with her for information). She stopped me. To my puzzled look, she informed me that what she learned and was ready to divulge, was something worth a special price! I should decide what was due to her, after I heard the whole story. Sleep and fatigue left my body at once. I refilled her cup with wine and pushed the bowl full of fruits and nuts, encouraging her to try. I picked-up my cup and a handful from the bowl and sat across from her, the hearth giving us nice warmth, comforting the chill in the air brought by the late of the night.

As she leaned over, excited of what she had to tell me, the upper part of her fine-weaved dress part-ed, revealing a set of the most beautiful breasts I have ever seen! I pulled back surprised by this un-expected display, holding my breath and feeling my face redden (though there's been a long time since I belonged to the innocent youth). She smiled at me and straightened herself, in silent apology. This was what I heard from her and reported it to King Filippos in a letter written at once -after her departure (and a very generous amount of silver out of my purse):

"Haridimos of Krousis to King Filippos of Makedon, greetings.

Sire, I hope my letter finds you and your family blessed and preserved in good health by the gods! I wish to inform you that I and my family have their blessing also and we are looking to be of service to their will -as well as yours.

Unfortunately, my earthly news concerning your policy in state issues are bad. I heard (from a very reliable source) that Sythonia has been attacked by the Thrakian Kilaetes and Vistones, supported by Halkidian and Aeginitan ships -which ferried the attackers.

The town of Siggos has already fallen, because their attack was a total surprise. King Ptolemeos was killed, as he rushed to repulse the invaders, in an ambush! In addition, an Eretrian squadron of war ships has anchored before Toroni and put this town under siege, all enemy forces merged.

Princess Iakynthi and the rest of the royal family members are within the town and safe -for now. But the heir to the Sythonian throne (being just an infant) is incapable of rallying the citizens and the morale is very low, for obvious reasons.

I do not expect the siege to last more than a week. If there is a way for us here to get into action to preserve what we may, do not forget that I am always ready to serve you. I am waiting for your in-structions.

May the gods preserve you and your family and guide you to a right decision. Remaining your faithful servant, I bid you fare well.

Haridimos son of Pelegon, from Krousis."

When I finished, I rushed to wake-up my son Pefkestas. I gave him the instruction to be ready for departure before the sand emptied from the hour-glass' upper half. Then, I alerted three of my most trusted servants to ready eight of my best horses, arm themselves and prepare to escort my son! I re-turned to the reception room and I composed three more letters, one for each of my close associates in Anthemous, Amfaxitis and Vottiaea, asking them to provide my son and his escort with anything needed for their safe arrival in King Filippos' realm.

By the time I finished with those, my son was ready and reported to me. I gave him my instructions regarding the contacts and impressed upon him that speed and safe delivery of the message to the King, were most important -as the lives of royal members were at stake! I walked him to the gate of my estate and saw him leave in a dust, as the first rays of Apollon's chariot in the sky were coloring the cheeks of Eos, the nymph of daybreak. I slowly returned to my hearth and made an offering to the Olympian gods for my son's safety and Makedonia's future. Then, I ascended to my sleeping quarters and into the waiting arms of my wife...

I did not sleep at all though. Kleodotos and Andromahos being eager to make a profit (as it was promised to them the night before) were at my door within the next hour. Since I had just sent my son on his mission to King Filippos, I had to get up and conduct business with them, aided by my Thrakian servant Kessos, of whom I made a mention before. They got much more than a good deal out of me, as I was eager to get rid of them in a hurry. Since there was no way at this hour to go back to my bed, I took off heading for the market. News of the attack on Sythonia had reached the ears of our citizens and merchants alike, thanks to an early arrival of an Efessian vessel. Its captain tried to dock first in Toroni, only to find it under siege by the Thrakians and the Halkidian, Aeginitan and Eretrian sailors. He wisely (and timely) changed direction, coming here instead. Now the market was naturally buzzing with the news and various degrees of anxiety and concerns.

I sought to meet the captain of this Efessian vessel. Its mooring was pointed to me by Hilon, the town's loiterer -you know, the one with the 'feeble' mind who prefers to get hand-outs instead of doing what he's actually capable of. I did not give-in seeing his open palm but I offered a good day's work, if he was interested in making his wages. He swore behind my back and took off flying, when I turned around in a pretended anger.

I walked briskly and found the vessel's captain, Xenofon -I was told was his name. The guard on duty by the ship's plank, rudely told me that the captain was too busy deciding what to do with his merchandise, now that Toroni was out of reach, to have idle talks with curious visitors. An Athinian silver four-ovol coin (miraculously produced by me) placed in his hand, made his mind and manners change in no time. He asked to be excused and, calling someone else to cover his station, went up the plank. Within a short time, captain Xenofon appeared and personally invited me to come aboard.

We sat by the prow, next to a wooden statue of Posidonas. One of the sailors brought us wine and dried figs and a bowl of honey to dip them in. Xenofon told me the wine was coming from Nemea in Peloponnisos, the figs from Gythion and the honey from Athinae, from the Ymitos beehives, widely known for its quality. I freely admitted that, after I had my first fig dipped-in and tasted it. I asked him then, what kind of cargo his ship was carrying, my interest in it being that he was talking to the best merchant dealer in town. He said -with a smirk on his face- that we were drinking and eating of it. I made a few offers and received an equal amount of counter-offers until we closed a deal of me buying the whole cargo, much to his relief.

I changed the subject and asked him of what he was making out of the recent events in Toroni. He told me that -in his opinion- this was a joined venture of Aegina, Korinthos and Eretria. Aegina provided the bulk of the fleet, Korinthos the money and Eretria with Halkis were providing the colo-nists armed in oplites armor. All had a hand in bringing the Thrakian Kilaetes and Vistones, with a promise of plentiful looting and slaves. This, he said, he knew as a fact, having a lengthy discussion with another captain (not as lucky), who was caught and forced to sell his cargo at a loss, to the be-siegers. To prove the truth of his words, he pointed the particular ship moored some distance to our right, toward the mouth of the small river emptying in the bay.

Reasoning, he said, Sythonia was the last area in Halkidiki resisting the settlement of more colonies from the city-states, adding the fact that preparation was made for a closer relation with King Filip-pos (which would allow Makedonia some added power against them), the city-states were taking a predominate step to block such a relation and acting in a cunning manner. I professed my sincere amazement regarding the cunning minds of those leaders and asked the captain how long he thought the town of Toroni could hold against such odds. According to his calculation and, consider-ing the size of the attack, he guessed two weeks -at most. Especially, he said, as the Sythonians got caught unprepared. I expressed my amazement once more, offered the customary libations for a deal done and I excused myself, to go and tend to my other businesses.

Once back at home, I composed several letters to associates of mine, in town and in Therma, Gigo-nos and, Aloros across the gulf. I asked those associates to find and send me within the next five days, a total of five times ten hired hands, armed in Halkidian armor, regardless the cost. I sent these messages using the illiterate runners in my employ. That done, I returned to the harbor looking for two Thasian brothers (and ship captains) Selefkos and Athamas, sons of Kriton. These two brothers were the best known smugglers of the north Aegean. Their ships were the fastest available and always at a right price.

I was able to locate one of the two, Athamas. I hired him (vessel and crew included) for the follow-ing twenty days, promising a whole year's wages plus any available loot, if no questions were asked about the mission I needed them for. They were all happy to accept and, the deal done, I returned home waiting for my son's return, hopefully with Filippos' instructions for action taking. Pefkestas and his escort returned the fourth day after I dealt the ship hiring, the sixth after they had gone to see the King. Pefkestas brought to me the King's letter which read:

"King Filippos of Makedon son of Argeos, to Haridimos of Krousis.

My good friend, I send you greetings and hope the gods bless you and your kin! I received your letter with the distressing news which was brought by your loyal and brave son. Makedonia's security and future alongside my personal honor suffered great insult, dictating now some immediate action to be taken! Unfortunately, there's not much I can do in such a short time, nor can something be done openly. Available means for armed action are severely restricted, since I cannot match the combined fleet of the aggressors nor their land forces. For Ptolemeos himself, all is to be considered lost. Many a good Sythonian will have to pay the price with enslavement and disgrace -to my sorrow- as they fall victims of such a treacherous act! You know how painful that is to me.

We must act though and with all possible speed, ensuring that we will do what we can to save as many as possible, including royal family members still alive. For this reason I send you -in care of your son- the sum of ten times five Halkidian silver talents. Makedonian coinage cannot be used, since we don't want any one to know we are behind this venture.

See that you put this silver to any use you deem necessary, to secure the lives and freedom of as many individuals, the royal family having first preference. I also ask you to see that false information reaches the ears of our enemies, concerning the fate of Ptolemeos' family, at least until we bring them here, under my protection. Additionally, I am sending you ten times ten of my best men in small groups, to meet you and support your efforts. They will be equipped with Korinthian armor and pose as mercenaries, in search of fortune. They will be following your orders -as if I give them!

In hope to have the grace of the gods on your side, I expect to hear from you soon. Until then, fare-well!

Filippos son of Argeos, king of Makedon."

"An afterthought: If there is need of additional silver or if you have spent already out of your own for this cause, please consider your loss a profit. I intend to pay you back, twice the amount!"

The dyptihon letter was sealed with the royal signet of Filippos' ring, so I would verify its authen-ticity, although it was my son who brought it to me. I read the letter a second time, making sure I understood everything the King was wishing me to do. Finished, I melted its wax leaving no trace of it for any (possibly) improper eyes. I was happy knowing that the King and I were thinking along the same ways. I made a silent promise not to let him down and I got to work at once.

The armed men I asked my associates to send me from Therma, Aloros and Gigonos, had already arrive in secrecy and my Thrakian servant Kessos had them lodged in one of my estates, out of the town. I went to meet them leaving instructions to my son to lead the King's men (as they would come) using different ways, to the same estate and as inconspicuously as he could, so we would avoid any detection and undue questions from any elements in town -friendly or otherwise.

Everyone arrived there by the time of the evening meal. To be in charge of the whole troop, mine and the King's, I placed a familiar face, the son of Krateos, Derdas. Derdas was not only trusted by the King, he and his father had gained my own unlimited trust from past ventures, with excellent results! My trusted Tharkian servant Kessos, was assigned to Derdas as my representative and information source, since neither my son nor I could participate -both being very well known and traceable. I handed the silver King Filippos sent me, to Derdas. He was to see the Thasian captain Athamas and his crew compensated very amply at the end of the venture, plus what other payments and bribes he would find necessary -not forgetting his troop's own expenses. I told them they would have to pose as soldiers of fortune, pirates who heard of possible easy loot and rape in Toroni. They were to place themselves under the attackers' employment, making sure they would be the first to enter the city and reach the royal quarters, placing claim on the persons of the royal family and its depend-ants. They were to let the enemy believe the 'captured' were to be sold in slave markets, later. If any one was to give them any trouble, he was either to be persuaded to forget the humans and go after the palace's treasures, or to be dispatched on the spot, making it look like a spoils quarrel turned in bloody squabble.

The 'prisoners' were to be brought immediately to the ship, which was to sail as soon as possible -without raising any undue suspicion among the besiegers. At that point, Athamas interrupted me, to make a very sound statement. If we were to save as many as we could, he said, one ship would not be sufficient, considering the troops and its crew members. He was willing to place a second ship in our service, leaving the additional expenses and payment to my own good sense for services rentered. We had several past deals, he said, to both parties satisfaction. Trust was mutual after all!

I saw his point and readily agreed, continuing my instructions. They should sail back here to my estate, secluded as it is, by the cape of Mega Emvolon. Then, I would board one of the ships and lead everyone across, at a secretly pre-arranged place in King Filippos' realm.

The operation was crowned with success! Derdas and Kessos gave me all its details once they picked me up, on their return trip and on the way to King Filippos. They arrived at Toroni, they informed me, barely three days -before the town fell under the final assault. Derdas was very convincing pos-ing as a leader of soldiers of fortune. He could speak the southern dialect without any Makedonian accent -when he wished- on account of being held hostage at Farsalos for years, in his youth. The rest of his 'comrades' in arms and the ships' crew, kept to themselves out of fear of recognition. The ex-cuse presented to the besiegers was that they trusted no one but their leaders and themselves.

There were many a Thrakian complains of newcomers risking nothing by coming late and only for the loot. Fearing rejection, Derdas offered his troops to have the most difficult assignments of the siege and be the first to attack on the final assault, sustaining the highest (possibly) injuries among the attackers. That offer kept complaints to a minimum and a general acceptance. I might add here that the presence of Kessos -as a runaway Thrakian slave- made things looking more convincing and legitimate in the eyes of the enemy.

For the following two days, our troops took over the most dangerous assignments before the walls, with an eagerness which prompted the Athinian mastermind and chief general-behind-the-scenes, a certain Ermolaos son of Kallinoos, to commend their bravery. Naturally, this kind of performance cost the lives of many a defender, as well as some of our own, since we lost ten good men (I promised a generous compensation to their families). It was a necessity though, a risk well taken, in order to achieve our final goal.

On the third day, the one of the final assault, Derdas placed our men (as promised) at the very front and most dangerous point. The final battle was fierce -as always happens to be. We lost another nine men during that.

Most of the rest from our troops sustained wounds, some serious ones, some not so, before and after breaking into the town. Our men let the Thrakians and Aeginitan oplites and sailors go after pillage and rape, while they dashed straight to the royal quarters, at the top of the small acropolis, the town's last defense place.

They found hardly any resistance there, since most of its guard had placed themselves at the walls-and had fallen fighting there. The royal family some servants and a few defenders found hiding and were taken by our men (after brief explanations). They were tied like trophies, in keeping-up with the pretence, further apologies left for later time. To some of Athamas' sailors who followed our troops into town (looting promise had to be kept and shared with the ones staying by the ships on the ready), assured that fewer attackers would be around the harbor at the final hour of escaping, by encouraging other sailors to abandon ships and go to town for loot, pillage and rape! Soon the harbor was almost empty of all attackers.

Athamas' sailors took what they could from the vicinity to the harbor of the town and kept the way open for our escape. They did that, as a disciplined team and I paid them my respect (and some more silver) for that. When the 'prisoners' escorted by our troops arrived, they boarded the ships with no lingering around at all! Athamas was determined to sail while confusion still rained in the area. As itwas, a few from his crew still did not make it on time and he was forced to leave them behind. He did not worry though for he had told everybody (knowing they'd show-up sooner or later -unless killed-from nowhere and with no inquiries as to what held them back). The missing rowers were replaced by Derdas' men. They left Toroni burning and, undetected, got on their way to come and pick me up, arriving at Mega Emvolon in the early hours of the morning. I boarded the ship with the royal family in it and we took off, this story and proper apologies said and given to all rescued while sailing to the prearranged landing place across the gulf and at the shores of Pieria.

We reached the shore without any further incident and, as soon the 'cargo' was put to shore escorted by Derdas and his good men, I returned to the ships with Athamas and Kessos (who sustained a rather superficial wound on his neck in Toroni) for our return trip to my estate…

When we arrived, I paid a grateful Athamas the agreed sum of silver, plus a generous bonus. This money was actually King Filippos' own. Derdas handed the silver I had given him back to me, on our way to Pieria. I did refuse to take it at first but Derdas had his King's orders to obey. Since Derdas had spent very little of it, his instructions from the King were to hand it over and have me cover for the expenses, plus the King's promise of double pay! Hence the bonus to Athamas!

As far as I was concerned, I was happy to have served, saved the members of the royal family and had my expenses paid for. Some silver left over, was given as a bonus to my associates in Aloros, Therma and Gygonos and their crew of men, as well as to Kessos -for his family still in Vistonian Thraki. For the curious neighbors of mine, my coming and going was translated as chasing Kessos, when he run away from me. His neck wound was ample proof of my saying. Athamas and his crew had lots of 'salt' added to my story, on their own.

About ten days later, I received a letter from the King, stating the following:

"Filippos of Argeos, king of Makedon, to Haridimos of Krousis.

My friend, greetings! There will never be adequate ways or means which will pay your good service to Makedonia and me! Nonetheless, I want you to know that I will be at your side as and when you ever need me to!

For reasons I am sure you understand, I cannot pursue the former plans I had in connecting my House with that of Sythonia's Ptolemeos. For all intent and purpose, Sythonia is out of any plans for closer relations -for now. The kingdom cannot be recovered without placing the whole of Makedonia in danger with, possibly, dire consequences. The royal family of the Sythones perished -as I am sure you have heard- somewhere in a slave market, as we learned that its abductors put them for sale and, as far as anyone is concerned, we lost track of them.

As for the… presents you were so kind delivering to my shore, I can tell you this: They are all grac-ing with their presence various estates of mine, along with the estates of other distinguished Maked-onian noble houses, like the house of Agis or Kleovoulos or that of Klitos. The 'major' present which lost its pair before you 'purchased' for me, remains -as a 'masterpiece'- in my estate near the town of Veria. Complimenting it, the 'minor' one is also there, since they don't seem to look as nice when 'separated'. In time, I may see that the 'minor' gets connected with a house like Agis or Klitos, for a better, perhaps, use in the future.

Your 'Egyptian' present is scheduled now to join the house of Parmenion son of Pallas from Evro-pos, the next harvest time. I hope you can arrange your business in a way allowing you to be present when that takes place. A 'sponsor' is needed at the time of the 'dedication'!

Meantime, I hope that you and your kin and dependants are in good health and have the blessing of the Olympians, as the gods can offer you favors more openly than I!

Farewell then, my friend, until we meet again!

Filippos son of Argeos, king of Makedon."

This is the only one of the King's letters I never destroyed! I kept it in my study and read it every-so-often! It makes me feel good, for all my 'presents' have found a fitting place in the King's Maked-onia. I continue my services to him, because I truly believe his kingdom is the answer to all external interference and danger, as long as our people of same descent and beliefs remain divided and 'an-chored' in stagnant waters of isolated seas of self indulgence. As for Kessos, he's a free man but he prefers to stay in my service for the rest of his life...

> "I was Marshal Tito's ambassador in the Middle East. You can easily check that. I know the 'Makedonian' language was ordered by him! I will not admit it in public though, for I still have family to care for, even now being in the U.S.!"
> Stevan.....(name withheld as promised)- Croatian

III

Iraklonas had just returned to his estates in Astivos after long talks and negotiations with other Paeonian notables, who were supposed to help in raising troops for king Python. It was in the early days of the month Daesios and the mountains were still covered by the last snows of a long winter. The northern Peonians fully under Dardanian influence by now were getting bolder with their raids south of river Vardarios and the Messapion Mountains.

Since the deaths of Damasias and his son Alketas, Python was made a king but was unable to keep-up with progressive programs set from the previous two. Lords and clan heads (although attached to the king by habit or necessity) started drifting apart in many ways, especially in cooperation with the vigorous training Damasias had established -not such a long time ago!

The result was very little cohesiveness within the structure of an army, when one was needed. In fact, there was no army to count-on at all! That was a fact which invited the raiders, not slow to realize that old days were here again, causing the abandonment of small towns and hamlets, for the safety of fortified towns such as Astivos, Vylazora and Stovi. Many a people reverted to transhumant life finding it safer to wander in small groups, than trapped-in in undefended towns!

First to go were the teachers and artisans Damasias had such hard time to lure from the south into Paeonia. Administration of state affairs came next, turning to its old and dysfunctional point of only three generations ago! Iraklonas knew that Python was not the only one to be blamed. As Python was (by nature) an easy-going person, land holders and clan heads had taken advantage, thinking of their personal gains only. Now, each one would like very much to try his own luck on a bid for the throne.

What kept them in check were two simple facts. No one was strong and bright enough to form a magnet of attraction for the others and, the Dardanes were always ready to deliver the same courtesy in Paeonia -as in other weak states. Under the banner of Python, they all looked as if one could count on their power or fear it. In any case, one thing was absolutely sure: From the biggest land holder to the last serf, nobody wanted a central strong government any more than being under Dardanian rule. Neither of the situations was of any help, and the Dardanians weren't exactly stupid. Prodding and probing had already started…

So, there was this 'truce' between the king and his subjects in Paeonia, procrastinating the moment of the inevitable do or die. Iraklonas knew also that only the king and the fools wanting to replace him could not see it. Iraklonas started the early spring trips and meetings, trying to arrange all kinds of deals with other land holders and clan heads. He had no wish in becoming a king himself nor did he want any fighting between Python and any other lord. Foremost, he did not like the reverse of fortunes and Dardanian dominance! He really believed in Damasias' dream and he was willing to see his compatriots (any one of them but -preferably all together) stand firm in preserving Paeonian in-dependence. Just for that reason he was willing to bend-over and kiss the feet of all clan heads and Python alike. He was very disappointed in discovering that his wish was almost an impossible one. His tries in negotiating seemed to be inadequate. He,

Paeonia did, was in need of a strong hand to support independence and progress. Once there was none coming from within, solution had to come from an outside source...

Southern city-states were out of question in his mind, on account of their tendencies and policy to rule their 'allies' as underlings, as unequal semi barbarous servants of their 'higher' political status.

Besides, it was well known that city-states would not easily venture in supporting a kingdom where their ships could not bring re-enforcements or help a necessary evacuation -when one was needed.

Additionally, the city-states were not fond of a steady government, changing their own every-so-often creating political turmoil with their now oligarchic, now democratic, or tyrannical form of handling the state affairs. In-between all these changes, hundreds of their citizens were taking their fortunes in exile, creating new city-states in someone else's lands, usually by force. Paeonia had enough of her own problems; no need to invite new ones. News of what was happening in Sythonia and other coast-al areas was a great factor in discouraging any remote thoughts in taking any such initiative!

Meantime here at home, Paeonian silver mines (which could buy help during Damasias' times) had been closed-down for lack of needed expert hands, to properly do the work. No one was willing to take the risks involved and do mining. Peasants in those areas were unprotected from bandits and raiders from the north -the mines being close to the borders. Slaves were a rarity, for most would be captured barbarians, therefore a great risk and liability each time an invasion took place—and those were many and often. The silver veins close to the surface, easy to operate 'on the move' fashion, were not rich enough to buy adequate means of outside or local protection.

The economy of the state turned—first among other things—to the nomadic ways of old. Coins were rare and hardly used. Bartering became once again the main way of exchange. Iraklonas had to think hard in finding a true, trustworthy ally and that needed to be done fast! He made a survey in his mind, considering all the neighboring states and their affairs, once more. To the east, Parorvylia was too busy fending-off Thrakian incursions, changing alliances as suited the local interests, by be-friending Amfaxitis or Kristonia or Sintiki, practically all weak states themselves. To the west, Pela-gonia, Derriopia and Lynkestis could barely make it, holding their own against the Illyres and the Dardanes, as well as—at times—against Orestis or the Makedonian state of the Timenos house.

The bad name of Lynkos inviting Illyres was not yet forgotten despite all the efforts of its kings to put that disgrace out of mind. Almopia was under Timenid influence and the states in Halkidiki pen-insula had the aforementioned problems with the city-states of the south.

Iraklonas had no means of knowing what the Timenid King had in mind on Makedonian affairs nor could he just go ahead and ask. Forces (dividing ones) were working against people with thoughts like his, egos taking precedence over a general welfare of the tribe. Iraklonas had to find and asso-ciate with people who had the following prerequisites: First, love for their country as a whole, not just clan petty squabbles. Second: Integrity and a broad mind—along with a will to take calculated risks. Third, equally important, enough following from the general public for added support in hard times.

He knew he could steer Python (if and when necessary) to the direction best suited for Paeonia in particular and the area as a whole. What Iraklonas did not know (he dared not seek) was what most of the thick-headed Paeonian lords would do, if he—Iraklonas—were to be left alone, without any exter-nal (in combination with his internal) ability to show muscle! Not that he was afraid to go down for his belief. He just could not see any excuse (any good enough excuse) to have Paeonian blood shed, so others could take advantage.

He returned back to his estate worn out mentally and physically. He found all kinds of people wait-ing for him, with all kinds of transactions and deals to be made. He sent messages through his serv-ants, telling politely to the people he was to see the petitioners the following day. He went to his private baths and, after a long time of cleaning, contemplating and (finally) relaxing, he asked to be announced at his Father's quarters. He found Korednos old and paralyzed from an old battle 'gift' waiting for him, propped-up in his bed. Iraklonas greeted and hugged his Father, a wised by trials and the weight of age Korednos, then, sat by the bed-side and the two conversed in hushed voices . . .

Three days later and after settling all his personal affairs, Iraklonas sent to all his trusted friends and dependents an invitation to gather at his estate. When they all came, they had their customary niceties of small talk and gossip first. That done, Iraklonas called for the meeting, offering first to the gods. It took place in the estate's big audience room, with food and drinks like any social gathering would; only the discussions were of very serious matters.

Rumors had circulated recently of a person, a clan head from Krousis by the name Haridimos, who—according to these rumors—had been the instrument King Filippos used in saving some important Sythonians when Toroni fell. Some were claiming that the saved persons were none other but the royal family! Iraklonas wanted to find out, he said, if those rumors had any foundation, so he needed all the knowledge or advice his gathered friends had on this subject. To show how important he con-sidered any information on this, Iraklonas ordered to have old Korednos brought-in. He was carried by the servants and propped on a couch, at the head of the table set for the affair, so the old clan head could participate in the conversations and decisions to be made.

They spent hours of discussion, some hardly touching the food and wine (a phenomenon) and all a-nalyzing and comparing rumors. They came to the conclusion that further investigation was needed, since, neither King Filippos, or Haridimos were advertising any connection between them. Also the where abouts of the Sythonian royal family was untraceable, their destiny a big mystery. Did they survive? Unknown. Were they sold in a slave market? No answer.

The gathering ended finally late in the night, with the understanding that any further information on the subject had to be verified and passed on to Iraklonas, immediately! To some questions as to how he got so interested in the fate of that family and the relation—if any—between Filippos and Ha-ridimos, Iraklonas gave a vague excuse of old personal ties between his Father and the late king Pto-lemeos.

When the guests departed, Iraklonas and Korednos had again their own private talk, on the need (or lack of it) to pursue with the investigation. It was agreed between them, that if Iraklonas wanted to have as a complete picture of the affair as needed, he would have to do some first-hand in-vestigation of his own. They also agreed that no open approach was possible or advisable. To obtain the friendship and assistance to Paeonian needs, a man like Haridimos could not be exposed (provid-ed there was such a thing) any more than Iraklonas or the King himself! Korednos suggested that Iraklonas had to approach Haridimos under a pretext, probe him and—according to judgment— either present the Paeonian plea for help or return home in search of an alternative. During this try, corre-spondence should be constant, in case the former had any news to report—from the investigation of their other friends.

Iraklonas and his Father went to sleep very late that night and this private conversation between them continued for days, implemented by news of further rumors and reports from their associates. At last, it was clear to both that Iraklonas had to start on his own, from the very place where this whole story started, Toroni. On a pretext that the needs of the household demanded at least one slave (and what better place to find a good one than Toroni?), Iraklonas headed for Sythonia.

He knew his cover was a thin one, for it was well known Paeones did not have much of a slave trend for various reasons, one being they did not dare (could not) to trust any slaves left in charge of their households when masters were on the go, facing or avoiding constant intruders from all sides. Iraklo-nas could not come with a better excuse though, finding that this one had to do the trick. So, he got ready to go on his own. He gave instructions to his sons Damasias (in honor of the dead king) and Ko-rednos (in honor of the old patriarch), to take care of their Grand-father and the estate, accommo-dating the petitioners and dependants in his place. He then went to his late wife's grave. Adea was killed a few years ago during a raid, while trying to protect their children and old Korednos. Iraklo-nas had his private conversation with the dead, poured a libation at the grave, mounted his horse and, having a couple of mules and a donkey tied behind, left looking for answers.

He made sure his pace of traveling was not putting pressure on his mount, while he spent his nights in well chosen and concealed locations in the open country or in small hamlets. He did not want any undue recognition. It took him a full fortnight to arrive in Toroni, by which time he joined a caravan of merchants. They were bringing furs, skins and timber to the colonists already occupying the site. Their merchandise would probably be worked and (perhaps) resold to them as finished products from cheap slave labor. He had joined the caravan to observe and learn how to deal and hoped his entrance in Toroni would be somewhat unnoticed.

While traveling with this caravan he developed a friendly relationship with Damoklidas son of Pro-xenos, a second generation Eretrian whose family had established presence in Halkidiki since the last days of Asteropeos' kingship in Sythonia. Damoklidas had a warm feeling for the Sythonians and suffered with their misfortunes. But, as a merchant, as a person who's background and interests were mainly on the side of the south city-states colonization, he was a pragmatist ready to turn to his advantage any given opportunity on the fortune or misfortune of others.

The fact that the new Halkidian settlers had already half-rebuilt the town and a new, improved defense wall was almost ready, the fact that the leaders of the colonists (with Halkidian, Eretrian and Athinian money) were ready to open trade thus having the profit flow almost uninterrupted, made the situation more than suitable for Damoklidas. Sure, he felt sympathy for all the Toroneans who got killed and their families sold to slavery! But that was something which he, personally, could not correct—let alone that he could profit under the right opportunities!

Iraklonas presented himself to Damoklidas as a moderately wealthy man from the north, one who would like to give a try dealing with the slave market. He claimed he was looking for a well educated Sythonian, to school his two young sons in southern ways of life. Damoklidas told him that it was a bit late to look for good Sythonian slaves, the town being sacked some time ago. One never knew what the gods had in mind though. Maybe there were still some good specimens left, provided Iraklonas was ready to spend the right amount of money.

He, Damoklidas said, would do Iraklonas the first (and only) time favor by giving him some inside knowledge for the right moves and procedure. The Paeonian accepted the advice, with obvious grati-tude and it was agreed to share lodging at Timotheos' inn, the first business in operation after the burning and looting of Toroni. Timotheos, a Halkidian, had rushed to fill in the void and his business was returning him huge profits already. Sharing a room there, the money saved by Damoklidas could serve as payment for Iraklonas' receiving good tips for his intended purchase. So, they did share a room at the inn. The structure was located close to the harbor gate and it did not take an expert to know it was re-built in a hurry and out of left-overs from many a burned or demolished building from the sacking of the town. The only truly new materials applied (physical or animated) were the roof tiles and the current proprietor.

Timotheos came to receive his two guests in person, while assigning the reception of other guests to his helpers, hired ones or slaves. Damoklidas basked in the honor of recognition of his importance by the innkeeper. After settling-down in their room which Iraklonas found of being confining and rather expensive—but clean—they both went to the inn's courtyard, seeking a seat under the grape vine's awning, to have refreshment and to 'scope the situation'—as Damoklidas put it.

It was late after the mid-day hour when Iraklonas and Damoklidas picked their spot, being among the first to come to the inn. Soon the yard was covered with the later coming clientele, some calling on friends seen, others walking among the crowd, finding a vantage place to seat—all of which was very amusing to Iraklonas. He discovered soon that their seats in this yard (although seemingly—at first—a rather remote corner) allowed them to have an overall view of any body and every body coming or going.

Timotheos and his motley crew were pushing and rushing in and out, carrying the orders, bringing an extra seat-bench, calming quarrelsome customers with a false promise of speedy service with a smile or a threat of a clenched fist. Iraklonas and Damoklidas were served a semi-sweet red wine from Nemea, a town of the Argolid region, in Peloponnisos. The Paeonian clan head made sure he amply watered-down his cup. He came here to loosen other people's tongues, not his own—he thought. Iraklonas paid the cost of the wine, to Damoklidas' delight, poured a libation on the ground and took a sip. The wine tasted very good and he figured that with some luck, someone would be feeling happy enough to forget precautions and start singing! He ordered a second jug of the same and paid the young, clumsy girl who came to serve, generously. Was she a recently enslaved Toron-ian?

Iraklonas' attention was soon trained toward a party of four loud speaking and (definitely) rowdy sailors, seated next to him but at another table. They had the distinct Thrako-Thasian accent in their speech. One of them, a burly giant with the reddest hair and beard one could ever imagine, with hands almost lost in gold bracelets and fingers loaded with rings and blue designs etched on every exposed part of his body, seemed being the foursome's leader. Was he their captain maybe?

Iraklonas looked at Damoklidas, eyes questioning. Damoklidas nodded back knowingly and, rais-ing his cup and voice (to be heard above the clatter) and called the sailors. Would the best known contraband captain Athamas, the Thasian, and his mates like to join them? Here was a Paeonian gentleman who would like to take a risk on his luck, purchasing a slave or two and southern exported commodities! Here was plenty of good wine to be shared, during negotiations. The sailors accepted the offer readily. Before long, new jars full of Nemean wine were brought and consumed. Tongues were loosened and comfortable thoughts of mind were expressed, warmed by the new comrade-ship. Iraklonas tried to keep his head leveled and clear, watering his cup when the others weren't looking. He discovered that, regardless of doing it, he also was getting under the wine's influence.

He also discovered that the giant red-haired man was not captain Athamas but his first mate, Pank-ratos. The captain was the least of a person anyone would think him of being in charge! Small in stature, he was a puny guy with dark skin and his eyes which could not rest in one place long. Not long enough (any way) to allow someone to detect their true color! Yet, his handshake at introduction was a steady one, warm but not sweaty, indicative of a person true to his dealings—once an agree-ment was reached.

Pankratos got his name from his youth boxing at the Olympic competitions. No one knew his real one and he'd forgotten it too! The other two sailors in that party of four were cousins from Leros but gave no names. After a few jars of wine were consumed, one of the cousins let it be known that he had made a fortune for himself, from the loot and slave trade when Toroni fell and because of that, his was the last trip taken under captain Athamas. He was to go back to his island of Leros and buy himself a house and land.

Iraklonas showed more interest than he intended when he heard that and asked for details. The sailor looked equally eager to boast some more, when captain Athamas (in a 'drunken' gesture of carelessness) smashed his wine cup on the sailor's head, sending him to reel on the ground uncon-scious. Was it a real drunken gesture, an accident? Iraklonas thought rather not, as he caught the look of Pankratos to the other cousin-sailor. The second cousin was fast to pick-up his mate and lead him out of the inn's yard, uttering lame excuses.

The incident sobered Iraklonas at once and he did not pursue any further questions. They parted much later like new-found friends, with promises to hook-up the next day for possible deals. Iraklo-nas did not sleep that night, thinking for a more subtle way in approaching the captain again next morning. The more he thought, the more he was convinced that the captain never got drunk! His rending the sailor unconscious was not a drunkard's deed! The sailor was about to talk on a subject the captain needed no one to know and Athamas silenced his talkative sailor as discreetly as the circumstances allowed, demonstrating a quickness of thought and cleverness.

In the early hours of the next morning Iraklonas had decided. Captain and crew had something to hide from general knowledge, he could feel it! If the sailor's talk was just a general boasting of any pirate's pride after the sacking of Toroni, his captain shouldn't (wouldn't) have any objection of such talk, especially when discussed before a landlocked individual from the 'semi-barbarous' north who would certainly be awed and believe any tale! Iraklonas was sure it had to be some-thing much more serious behind the 'drunken accident'—something not supposed to have reached the ears of anyone. Could it be that it had to do with the rumor on the fate of the Sythonian royal family, the involve-ment of King Filippos and Haridimos of Krousis?

Iraklonas suspected such an involvement but could not be sure or come to a conclusive end without knowing more. He got up from his bed and silently, so as not to disturb a snoring Damoklidas, he got dressed and left the room. He crossed the inn's yard having in mind to seek-out captain Athamas, be-fore the morning hours' clamor of the day's business dealings. The inn itself was already busy in cleaning and preparing for the day. Iraklonas sat at a table by the entrance and ordered a breakfast of cereals and honeyed milk. While eating, he considered his options of approaching Athamas.

He opted to tell the truth and see what kind of a result that would bring. If he was wrong, two things could happen: Athamas would laugh and dismiss him with a good excuse of yesterday's 'acci-dent' or, he could try capturing him and sell (or kill?) him at a slave market to silence any further rumors. Either way, Iraklonas knew Athamas would appreciate honesty. Either way, Iraklonas was prepared, especially in case of slavery, to give a good fight! He had his long sword hidden under his cloak, intending to use it—if the need arose . . .

As things developed, he never had a chance. He had hardly crossed the inn's gate for the road after his breakfast, when he heard a faint noise behind him. He turned, sword in hand. There was a sharp pain on his head which sent him rolling on the ground. His last thought before passing out was a sense of failure. Darkness covered him, before he had a chance to even see his assailant(s) . . .

He came to, much uncomfortable and in severe pain. His arms and legs were tied-up leaving no room for movement, although he felt the motion of being in a moving cart. His mouth was also covered tightly, allowing no sound. His breathing was very difficult, allowed only through his flaring nostrils. He guessed there was a big lump (a very actively throbbing one) on his head, where he had been hit, causing this headache now. He opened his eyes with an effort, for even doing that hurt him a lot! When the streams of black, red and other color hues were finally gone and his vision became somewhat clear, he saw that the cart (or wagon) he was in was covered and, in the dim light under the canvas, he could see a number of various jars, coffins and other containers laden with—who knows what. Those were all around him, making his presence almost invisible, even without a cover canvas.

He tried to yell something, anything. No sound could come out of his well covered mouth. He tried to move. Nothing! Impossible! He was well tied-up and wedged among the jars, sacks and coffins. This effort to move or yell, multiplied the throbbing of his head to an almost unbearable pain! Was that his end then? He didn't think so, for he was still alive! He only had to wait and see…

Now the road noise started to pick-up. Various voices could be heard and carts, horses or other quadrepeds mixed with humans appeared to be coming and going. Salutations were heard and, when apparently addressed to the driver(s) of the cart he was in, were met with a discouraging grunt or a total silence. After some time, there were no other attempts of talk by the road travelers, either be-cause they had gaven-up or because they started minding their own. Iraklonas was feeling very thirsty. He thought of trying to make his presence felt but the memory of the pain when he first tried, convinced him to wait. At any rate, he was alive! Whoever took him needed him alive and with life there are always chances of changing one's own fortune or misfortune.

Presently there were more frequent stops of the cart or wagon he was in. Short timed one at first, taking longer—as time went by—and with shorter intervals of moving. He realized they had to be coming closer to some sort of a check-point, perhaps they were coming close to a town. If so, this was giving him a slight hope. There was a chance he would be discovered and— hopefully—freed! Perhaps, freedom wasn't far away. The cart/wagon came to a jolting stop, after an initial move of a few turns of its wheels. Silence, then the harsh voice of a sentry, asking about the contents of this wagon and its destination. Someone from the driver's seat—Iraklonas guessed—gave a soft spoken answer, which he could not clearly hear and make-out. The sentry gave a very respectful answer, begging a difference his job was such that he had to stop and check all cargoes going into the town of Mekyverna.

The man driving the wagon replied something, again using a soft voice. Whatever it was, it did not deter the sentry from doing his job, for the cover of the wagon was lifted from one side and Iraklonas could see the sentry's helmet crest, as he was trying to take a look at the cargo. Realizing his chance, Iraklonas tried to move violently and make some noise. A sudden commotion from behind the wagon, on the road, muffled his effort. The helmet crest turned to the direction of the commotion and disap-peared. Apparently (though Iraklonas could not be certain for he couldn't see) the cart which was behind the one he was in, did move forward, in an attempt to skip inspection or because its driver got tired of waiting for his turn.

Iraklonas heard the sentry give a yell. The cover on the wagon came back down and an order to proceed was barked. He heard people (sentries?) mounting on horses and going after the runaway(s). His captors, Iraklonas was now sure there were more than one of them on the wagon, let a hearty laugh (was the other cart incident a staged one?) and prodded the pulling animals to start forward again.

Iraklonas had no other option but to wait and see what his future held. Every bone of his body was aching and he realized it would take him a long time to have the full feeling of his extremities again. There were no more stops for a long time. The noise of a bustling town was now evident but the wagon continued through until the town was left behind and only the occasional pass of other travelers was again the sole interruption of the monotonous squeak from one of the wagon's wheels.

It started to get late in the day, as—even under the cover—the light was getting dimmer. Iraklonas had a very hard time in trying to stay alert, fighting for any hint of his where-abouts. He was hurting, he was thirsty, hungry and, mostly, angry. The ambiguity of his future was another thing to ponder. He had no idea who his captors were or why he was captured and transferred. To . . . where? All these things were driving him mad.

Suddenly the wagon came to a full stop once again. The sound of a gate opening reached his ears as did the muffled conversation between his captors and people from the gate. There was some more forward movement of the wagon and then stopping one more time. Now the cover got pulled off. Above, the stars had started their appearance in the evening sky and on the left—as he was laid down—Iraklonas could detect a distant torch light. A dark shape of a giant climbed inside the wagon. Athamas' mate? The shape moved some of the cargo to make more room and bent over Iraklonas.

The man's size, silhouetting against an already dim contrast of the departing daylight, was enough to discourage any attempt of entertaining an effort of escape or resistance. This giant seemed to have come out of the misty times of yore, when giants were at war against the gods of Olympos! He picked Iraklonas like one would pick-up a small rag doll, placing him over his enormous shoulder.

Any grunts of protest and pain didn't seem to register at all. Another pair of hands, from a side blind to Iraklonas' vision, brought a cover over his head, making Iraklonas' ability to breathe even harder. They did not want him to see what? Next, the giant stepped off the wagon with an ease un-expected from a man (even a giant) carrying such a weight (Iraklonas being an exceptionally good-sized man himself).

The giant started walking on an, apparently, evenly paved area, toward the torch lights. In spite of having his head covered, he could still 'see' the difference between darkness and light. A door opened and the giant had to stoop to get through it with his cargo on the shoulder. Three steps forward, then they started descending. Five steps down, Iraklonas counted, then five more forward with another door opening and closing behind them as they passed through. Seven more steps down. A turn to the right followed by four more steps and another door opening and closing. Now, the air was definitely heavier, smelling like in a wine cellar. Four plus ten more steps forward so-to-speak, as the first three were to the right (following the giant's movements and heading), five to the left and the last six steps straight ahead. Iraklonas kept-up with the step counting. He thought that, measuring his own stride against the giant's, the total distance had to be over fifty steps. With or without the blindfold on his head, Iraklonas knew he would a have hard time retracing those steps, if and when an opportunity was given, due to enormous stride of the giant. Was the giant taking the steps one at the time or, skipping some—because of his height— during their descent? The light coming through the blindfold was at times brighter and flickering, indicating passage by lit torches. Was his blindfold to eventually come off? Were the lit torches to be left lit? Questions came and went through Iraklonas' mind, unan-swered. One thing seemed being steady, the smell of wine. Ten more steps followed to the right of his carrier and the giant put Iraklonas gently down, on a packed-earth floor.

Next, Iraklonas was turned, face down on the floor. The rope tying his feet and hands was cut fast and efficiently. Blood rushed free at last, first numbing his extremities more and giving him needle-like pain punctured innumerable times, all at once! He passed out, not knowing that his blindfold was removed and his mouth gag taken off but he was, once again, tied down by chain attached to the wall . . .

He came back to his senses, probably because of moisture upon his chapped lips. He opened his eyes. A girl, slave or hired (he couldn't tell) was sponging his face. His body was still hurting a lot but now he found he could move his limbs. Doing so, he produced a rattle. He saw he was shackled, one end of his chains secured to the wall, the other—dressed with leather—wrapped around his wrists. Yet, he felt more comfortable than ever (since his capture), as he had been propped-up against the wall, seated on a thick layer of hay.

The girl was observing him with polite—as well as distant—interest. He asked for some more water and, while he was getting it, he observed his surroundings. His chains were embedded on the wall on either side of him but there were enough links to let him have some space and free movement. He saw he could stand, take a few steps in any direction, lie down or—as he was now—sit against the wall.

As far as he could see under the dim light of a three-wick oil lamp at the far end of this room and by its heavy, closed door, the place was an actual wine cellar, serving also as a prison. Big, earthenware containers were stacked neatly in rows, amidst the unmistakable odor. They were too far to be reach-ed. The girl poured some more water for him, seeing he had finished what she'd given him before. He put the cup on the floor and uttered his question, knowing well he wasn't about to get an answer. The words formed and came out of his mouth on their own. Where was he? Why was he held?

It was like he had talked to the wall. The girl's face remained unemotional. Not even one of her face muscles moved as she looked at him. He knew she wasn't deaf, for she responded when he asked her for water before. He guessed she had instructions to remain silent or she simply chose to. He put his hand onto one of hers and pulled gently, forcing her to look at him and repeated his questions. Softly but firmly, she pulled her hand away. She turned around picking a dish up from the floor. He saw it contained some bread, a chunk of poultry and vegetables, all stewed. She handed him the dish, moved a jar of water closer to him and, getting-up, she headed for the door.

Ignoring all his protests, she got to the door, knocked on it and when it opened by someone from the outside she passed through and disappeared. The door closed again with a heavy thud. Iraklonas let a sigh out of his mouth and drank some more water from the cup. He tried to get up and did so with some difficulty. His whole body was still aching. He touched the back of his head, where he was hit (was it yesterday?) and let a soft cry come out of his mouth. A big bump was still there with some dried-up blood. He had been whacked a good whack!

Iraklonas paced to and fro for some time, to have his circulation restored close to normal. Finished, he sat down and picked-up his dish full of food and started eating. He discovered two things. First, he was famished and second, this food was exceptionally well prepared. He checked the piece of poultry on the dish. It tasted very good but he was unfamiliar of this type of fowl. Then, a thought occurred in his mind. He had knowledge of a domesticated fowl species introduced a few decades ago, but never seen in Paeonia yet. The species had come from the parts of Asia and it was called by the Ion-ians Alector (for the male which was in the habit of crowing repeatedly every dawn). Kota was its fe-male counterpart, laying eggs and clucking constantly. The famous bard had mentioned this species in his poems, but it was not broadly known or used yet. Too bad Paeonians were slow in accepting anything new and different, because the bird was very tasty when cooked.

Iraklonas was enjoying his meal immensely and he forced himself to eat slowly, to enjoy it more. He was not given a knife, so he ate pulling it apart with his fingers and with the help of the bread. He smiled at the thought; his jailers knew their job and didn't leave anything which could serve as a weapon or an agent to set him free. They wanted no surprises.

Eventually he finished his meal, feeling his strength returning to him. He washed his fingers off, using some of the water left in the jug and made himself comfortable leaning against the wall to which he was chained. He observed the room again, to familiarize himself with his surroundings. His location was almost directly across from the heavy wooden door, some five plus ten paces away—if one kept it a straight line. On both sides of the door was a clear space, making the entrance clear and open to what might be brought in or taken out.

Then, there were the rows of large earthenware containers of Korinthian, Aeginitan or Athinian or-igin, full of wine—for sure. These containers were neatly stocked in rows, with corridors between them, wide enough to bring or take more, close enough for reaching either side row—if one walked in the middle of each aisle. There were some close-by but his chain was just short to reach. Well! His captors didn't want him getting drunk either!

He continued observing. The stone walls were expertly laid by masons who knew their trade well, with fine cuts and perfect fit of each stone to its next. To the right of the door and almost touching the ceiling was a dark opening—a rectangular one. Judging by the scant light from the oil lamp on the other side, to the left of the same door, Iraklonas figured this opening was about three arms in length and two arms wide and, looking carefully, it was barred. A vent? Probably. The air in the room al-though heavy with wine odor, was well circulating and there was no other venue for such a circulat-ion—besides this opening. Finding nothing else worth of study and deeming what he saw of no partic-ular importance, he concluded that nothing could be used to set him free or to defend himself with. He relaxed against the wall and, before he realized it, he fell asleep.

Iraklonas woke-up at the sound of the door opening. The same giant who brought him in here, he guessed, entered the room. A hood with openings for the eyes and the mouth covered his head. His voice, matching his impressive stature, asked Iraklonas if there was a need for taking care of nature.

Iraklonas answered in the positive. He needed to go bad and that was not the only reason. Iraklonas wanted to see and judge his surroundings outside of this room. He was disappointed to find that the giant produced another hood with only one opening, that for a mouth. Whoever his captor(s) was (were), obviously did not care if he'd make any noise but did not want him to see anything! He was abducted to a place under the abductor's total control. He did not know if the giant's hood and his own blindfolding meant anything good. Was he to be led for his execution and nature's call was the excuse? I am still alive, he thought. And that was most important.

Iraklonas saw he had no choice. He let the giant place the hood over his head, unresisting. His hands were unshackled, only to be tied with a leather strip again and with great efficiency. With the giant's guidance and assistance (not one word exchanged) they went through the door and up the stairs. Leaving the wine odors behind, Iraklonas could soon smell the fresh air of open space. Although covered with the hood, he could tell the day was a bright and warm one. He could feel the rays of Ilios and its light penetrated through the hood's fabric. They walked exactly four times ten paces and he heard another door opening before them. More steps ahead, four of them, then straight ahead. Iraklonas could feel brushing against bushes at times now, one of them definitely a rose bush. He felt soft earth under his feet and patches of grass, short and tall. They were probably out in the fields . . .

Haridimos had received an urgent message from Athamas, telling him the captain ran onto a Paeo-nian who, posing as a well to do merchant, had asked strange questions under the pretext of looking for easy gains through slave marketing after Toroni's fall. One of his sailors (the message continued) had more to drink than he could handle and said some things he shouldn't have. The sailor was taken care-of promptly though and Haridimos was not to worry about further leaks. Now, Athamas was holding that Paeonian captive, in care of Haridimos' own servants plus some of his own and on the way out of Toroni. Did Haridimos want to question the prisoner or should Athamas dispatch the 'merchant' as he did the sailor?

Haridimos asked the messenger where the Paeonian was held. When he was told they had him tied in a wagon, gagged and that the wagon could easily 'fall' in a ravine on its way to nowhere—if that was what should be done—he gave instructions as to what Athamas should do and follow those to the letter. Now, in the early morning of a promising late-spring day, Haridimos was at his estate, outside the boundary of his home town, watching from its peristylion (the colonnaded walk-way) the tied-up and blindfolded Paeonian led outside the wall of the house complex. The captive did not look like a merchant, this was certain.

Haridimos was not sure why he did not order the man's death. His guess was it was his curiosity of finding-out why the Paeonian would pose as such and ask questions about the affair in Toroni. Depending on the outcome of his interrogation, the man then could live or die.

Haridimos walked into the room he used for audiences with his farmers, local clan heads and other clients, as was his right. He asked Kessos (always being two steps behind of his 'master' and always ready to serve) to assist by seeing that someone would bring wine and bowls of fruits and honeyed nuts for breakfast. He would start the interrogation by sweetening-up the Paeonian. It was better to befriend and get the answers out of trust, than through threats and torture. He considered the latter as an evil thing, resorting to it only when all other venues were exhausted and absolute necessity was the paramount factor.

A steward came into the room bringing the drinks and the fruits, setting them where Haridimos in-dicated and moved to the side, ready to assist at first call. Kessos returned holding a hood and helped his 'master' put it on. All precaution had to be taken, as one never knew the will of the gods. As that was done, Iraklonas was led into the hall, still blindfolded, his hands tied in front of his torso, wrists together. With a nod from Haridimos toward the giant, Iraklonas was seated and the blindfold was taken off his head. The giant remained by his side, ready to act—in case of any trouble.

Iraklonas blinked his eyes a couple of times and looked around, surveying. He felt satisfied of his surroundings. At least, as things were, there was a good chance of talk and negotiations. In accord with the questions asked, he would do his best to extract himself from danger while learning of his captor's aims.

He looked at the obvious man-in-charge and asked politely that—since they apparently were to have breakfast—he needed to wash his hands and face before having any. Haridimos liked the observant nature of his captive and was rather impressed by the unexpected Paeonian civilized manners. He nodded to the servant standing by. A bassinette with scented water was promptly brought in and Iraklonas washed his hands and face, the leather rope tying his hands undone. Next, the 'host' had the steward pour wine into the cups. Both 'host' and 'guest' stood-up and made the customary offerings to gods and ancestors. Iraklonas to Dias, the Kavyres and his ancestors, Haridimos to Dias, Estia and his ancestors. They both did it by going to the small altar in the middle of the room, pouring some of their wine into a shallow receptacle which had a chiseled-out channel leading onto the earthen floor, already stained by previous offerings. Iraklonas' wrists were re-tied.

They returned to their couches and their cups were re-filled. They toasted each-other's health, like two good friends getting together after long time, like the perfect guest-host relationship. They had their first sip and a mouthful of honeyed nuts and Haridimos came straight to the point. Iraklonas had to use both hands to hold his cup and/or eat some nuts, while Haridimos said he was going to be honest—as his special interests with certain affairs of his in Toroni could allow him. He needed the same from his 'guest'—if some understanding on Iraklonas' actions and curiosity was expected. He (Haridimos was careful not to mention his name) would then judge and act according to greater interest on both parties.

Iraklonas suspected the hooded man seated by him was none other than Haridimos, regardless that the 'host' kept his identity a secret. The man had to be Haridimos of Krousis! Judging from the length of the trip since his capture, Iraklonas deducted that his captivity's place and location was within Krousis. Provided he was right, he had found what he was looking for! He had in mind to tell the truth about his inquiries, anyway. Honesty was his best venue. In case he was wrong, the worst thing it could happen to him would be to be sold in a slave market. In that case, there was always hope of escape. If they would put him to death, well, he was sorry and regretted his failure.

He told his story and reason for his search, leaving nothing out. His 'host' listened intensely, without any interruption until Iraklonas finished. There was some lengthy silence. Finally, the 'host' made a sign to the guarding giant. Iraklonas felt the powerful hands lift him up from the couch and thought his end had come. Instead, he was put to standing and his wrists were untied, the giant mut-tering excuses and asking for pardon for any and all harsh treatment he caused. Meantime, the 'host' removed his hood off from his head. Now Iraklonas could see the face of his captor. Salty colored hair, rather wavy, eyes deep blue and set apart, under a heavy set of eyebrows, large forehead but not because of receding hairline. He had a quite crooked nose leaning to the left of his face, probably the result of a powerful blow, some time past. There was a moustache and beard (well trimmed) covering most of that face, giving it an even more dignified authority. The 'host' stood-up in turn and slightly bowed his head in recognition and new respect of his 'captive'.

Haridimos asked, very humbly, for forgiveness for all and any mistreatment. He explained the need of making sure that a person making all the inquiries Iraklonas did, had to either be a truly trusted one and be included in the knowledge of the secrets, or to be disposed leaving no trace. With his honest account of reasons and aims, Iraklonas matched the information Haridimos had collected for him, so the trust was gained and all possible assistance would be given, by answering questions or in any other way. Meanwhile, Iraklonas should consider himself being a true guest, to be treated with as perfect hospitality as possible by means afforded by Haridimos and his dependents.

Iraklonas was sure now, but still wanted to hear it from his host. He sent a questioning look at Hari-dimos, who, understanding the meaning, smiled and formally introduced himself. Yes, he was Hari-dimos of Krousis and he did play a role during and after the taking of Toroni. Details would follow in time, after finishing their breakfast and during exercise and bathing time. Iraklonas curiosity and re-quests would be met in the best possible way, along with true hospitality. But first, one small matter had to be taken care of!

Haridimos turned to Kessos and asked for a dyptihon and stylos to write with. These two items provided, he wrote to captain Athamas:

"Haridimos of Krousis, to Athamas of Thasos, greetings!

I have to thank you my friend, for the efficiency with which you dealt on matters concerning our understandings and agreed deals. You do need to tighten-up on the reliability of your crew members though! I am sure you already took steps to that effect. I suspect the sailor who boasted before our Paeonian guest, was the one who spread the rumor about our Toroni affair. Who knows how many ears this rumor has already reached. That cannot be repeated nor tolerated! Use what it takes to pre—sent the whole story as a drunkard's tall tale. If any financial need arises let me know at once!

Farewell and take care of all business stemming from this incident."

The dyptihon wax tablet was sealed and was given to the waiting giant who happened to be—as Iraklonas had suspected—none other than captain Athamas' shipmate, Pankratos. Pankratos asked once more for forgiveness for any unintended harm done, to which Iraklonas assured that he would have done perhaps even more, had he been the one protecting such a secret and that there was no animosity on his part. Pankratos gave a studied look at Iraklonas, judging that the man was capable of doing what he said and, nodding satisfaction, wished them all farewell and left.

Iraklonas stayed for ten full days at Haridimos' estate and the two men opened-up their concerns to each-other, forming a bond and a friendship which lasted their life time! In keeping-up with pretence of the purported business in Toroni, Iraklonas sent a message to Theotimos' inn and to Damoklidas that, finding that early morning captain Athamas, he was able to purchase a few slaves through the services of the Thasian captain. Due to unstable conditions in his country, Iraklonas was forced to leave suddenly and he was sorry. The message was accompanied by few silver Halkidian coins, pay-ment for Iraklonas' stay at the inn.

Covering all aspects they could think to keep-up with the pretence, Haridimos gave Iraklonas an escort of three of his own household young men, sons of farmers from his estate, to pose as slaves purchased in Toroni.

All three were well educated and could be used as needed. Upon arrival back in Astivos, Iraklonas registered them as his property. He assigned a plot and a household task to each, asking for one tenth of the gains produced from their labor. That should be enough in fencing off any possible curiosity and questions from neighbors.

Within a few years, the enterprising spirits of these three young men was more than obvious to the benefit of Iraklonas' household. He found an excuse to declare them freed, had them purchase the plots he had assigned at a nominal fee, so as to avoid any possible questioning of their association with him and they lived as his free clients-assistants having their own plots and families.

Iraklonas' correspondence with Haridimos was kept at a regular basis under the pretext of com-mercial ties, along with exchanges of ideas benefiting both men's goal for a better future of their states. King Filippos was informed (of course) by Haridimos and a strong basis for close relationship between the Timenid House and Paeonia was set to build upon, Filippos making an alliance move and king Python (guided by Iraklonas) accepting it . . .

Unfortunate circumstances brought a setback to the three men's dream for a bigger and stronger Makedonia. King Filippos' son Aeropos was to have been betrothed—as we know—to princess Iakynthi of Sythonia, forming a solid alliance between the two states, each across the other on both sides of the gulf of Therma. The aim of such alliance was to check any further expansion of south city-states colonies in what was considered Makedonian sphere of influence.

Makedonia and Sythonia could have thus stopped—through their 'partnership'—the pressure and interference from Korinthos, Eretria, Halkis Aegina and Athinae or, at least, be able to impose their own pressure on those colonies from a financial point of view. Now, with Toroni and Sythonia falling in the hands of Eretria, this dream was not feasible. These southern colonists were heavily armed oplites. Makedonian land lords and clan heads were not keen to dismount their horses and train the oplitis way. Even Paeonia, after the initial success of Damasias' experiment, had returned to its old ways of warfare.

Filippos knew very well that his power was strong only for repelling invaders fighting on horseback. Easy in, easy out—so to speak—in engagements. His finances could not support a steady oplites troop under his personal authority and needs, his clan heads and lords disinclined to obey such a request.

A strong man in the city-state system had more power upon citizens and clan heads, albeit a tempo-rary one, than the King of Makedon in his state. The reason was simple. In a city-state, because of its development, there were no strong clan heads as such in Makedonia. Instead there were classes, groups of citizens, vying with each-other for supremacy and control of state affairs. Depending which class came on top it had the final say—for a while. In Makedonia, Filippos was the undisputed leader with a say on general issues but always under the 'blessing' of his land holders and clan heads.

Any Makedonian could come to his court and demand from the King this or that, talking as his equal. The class separation could not permit such a thing in a city-state. Any difference was solved there by a stasis, a revolt of some kind, resulting in exiling the heads of the defeat-ed party, by creating colonies elsewhere. Oh, there were classes in Makedonia too but the King had to have the support of his clan heads and land lords, as they had the support of their dependents. Constant threat from all fronts did not allow Filippos the luxury of pressing his clan heads into a more cohesive subjection under his rule. In spite of the monopoly of natural resources from the state by its King, the royal treasury did not have the revenue needed to 'buy' internal and external influence. Transhumant life—as it was still the ways in Makedon—was making the task even more dif-ficult.

He, therefore, decided that Aeropos was to get married to someone else. A local Makedonian bond between houses was of more value now. But which house? Filippos thought of the house of Agis. Well established in his kingdom and with old Orestian interests. Of Alketas' two sons' offspring, there was a young girl named Hariklia. She was the daughter of Attalos and Evryklia. Filippos thought of this as a good match for his son. Re-enforce the ties between the two strong houses and have a claim on Orestis' throne—albeit a distant one. Besides, Orestis was a much closer to his kingdom state and part of what was known as upper Makedonia. It was facing a constant Illyrian pressure from tribes who could not forget their past role in pre-eminence, as did Orestis itself . . .

Three years had passed since Toroni's fall and Filippos judged it as time to have the unification of House Timenos with house Agis. The tie with the old house from Levaea and Argos Orestikon should become a finished deed. Filippos examined and sought support on his decision from trusted clan heads within his kingdom and external supporters such as Haridimos and Iraklonas. Finding he had what was needed, he sought the consent from Attalos himself. Since Attalos' desire coincided with his own, the deal was made public.

Unfortunately neither, the King nor his clan head, bothered to consult with their offspring. Hariklia did not have much of a choice as the obedient daughter of her parents. Attalos and Evryklia were the kind of 'proper' Makedonians who had instilled their concept of values and responsibilities on their children, Hariklia and Adeos. On the other hand, the antipathy between Aeropos and the young girl was a well known fact—since the days of their infancy. There had been times a special watch was held on them, as to not harm one-another, Adeos taking the side of his sister—naturally. With the passing of the years, the children learned to avoid each-other's presence, being chillingly polite when there was no other way. But, if Hariklia's upbringing and status dictated obedience, Aeropos was another matter.

He, by the Makedonian standards, had become a man two years ago, killing a mountain lion single-handedly, having—by tradition—his own saying on matters concerning him alone. Prior to this, he had lost his Mother some years ago, to fever (hardly being a lad of seven years then) and brought up by several nurses and paedagogues. Now, on his five plus tenth year, he thought he was loosing his own Father too! In all fairness to everyone's concern, Aeropos had lost the proper guidance by a strong father, since his birth. Filippos had been a very busy person with the affairs of the state, to look after the needs of a growing son.

Not that Aeropos was left unattended through all these years. But he lacked the one most important thing any young person gets: True family love and care, through which discipline and appreciation of values derives. Certainly, Filippos loved his son more than he could ever show! But that was a cause of their rift. Not showing his interest to his son's needs, brought no response from Aeropos. Any such lack of response let the King look for easy ways out. Aeropos grew not knowing his Father's love and never cared to find out why. To Aeropos, there was more than enough of understanding his needs from servants. They well understood that no complaint should ever come out of the child's mouth to the King's ears.

This conclusion affected Aeropos' discipline to the effect that it was nonexistent. Naturally Aeropos as heir apparent had a free hand in (almost) everything. His ego boosted by that, he turned to being a brat who thought there was nothing he could do wrong, nothing he approved or rejected which would not be so. Only in the presence of his Father and King was Aeropos somewhat attentive and mindful. Not that he had the needed respect toward the wishes and wisdom of his Father, no! It was just the animalistic instinct of a minor before someone major and the observation of the behavior of others in the King's presence, plus Filippos' own demeanor and regal stature which kept Aeropos' lack of respect undetected—until it was too late!

Aeropos' hate for Hariklia and his notion that his Father was wronging him, first wanting to engage him to royalty then canceling that and asking him to take a bride he hated—and from a minor house mind you—turned Aeropos a rebel, though not one who would go about it openly. Had he ever, Filip-pos would have, perhaps, a better end and Makedonia would not have to go through adventures which cost many lives, territories and Timenid House prestige!

As it was, Aeropos felt very offended by the 'demotion' of his wedding planned for him. He was knowledgeable enough in politics to realize that a union between the House of Timenos and that of Agis' Argeades would greatly displease the Orestid king. Pelegon son of Arraveos was the king of Orestis at the time, related to Agis' Orestid house from Argos Orestikon— remember, coming from the line of Antiohos' first cousin, through his sister Arsinoi. Holding a part of old Orestis belonging to Filippos' Makedonia and managed by the descendants of Agis, didn't sit well into Pelegon's mind.

Setting aside all old quarrels he formed an alliance with Lynkestis' king Lampos and the aspiring king of Elimiotis, Sossos. Neither one, separate or combined, could measure up to Filippos but they could make him think twice when dealing against their interests. Still, they were cautious, looking for dissent from within Filippos' realm.

The overture then made by Aeropos through Sossos (who in essence was under Filippos' overlord-ship), came as a godsend bonus to Pelegon! Couriers between him and Sossos kept a secret corre-spondence going and, through their contriving, they filled the mind of Aeropos with promises not intended to be kept. They, his 'friends' promised to do everything and anything for their 'future King', but they needed all the cooperation and information he could provide them with, until such a time would come they'd feel capable in reversing Aeropos' 'misfortune'!

Aeropos fell for it. It was suggested he should befriend certain people (for his own protection)—as it was clearly stated in one of Sossos' messages—and, when action was about to be taken, Aeropos would be timely notified to remain at Aegae, for his country would be in need of a guiding hand at once! At the same time his 'friends' needed to know the King's daily itinerary, his habits, of all closest friends, everything in every possible detail—if they were to be of any help to Aeropos. He obliged not realizing the meaning of those promises, or didn't care to.

Haridimos and Iraklonas got their information about all these moves when it was too late, after the dreadful events took place and, as they could not afford demonstration of their relationship with the King (other than as accidental or business related one) they had to go along with the 'official' pre-sentation, keeping their knowledge to themselves.

It all happened with the first stretch of good weather after a long and harsh winter, the ones which hit so hard when they come in Makedonia and spring was welcomed with relief at Filippos' court. As Iraklonas and Haridimos recalled, it was the same year the Athinian law-giver Solon, took to self-exile at the Lydian king Kryssos' court and Drakon became the strong-man of Athinae.

King Filippos (as so many others in Makedonia) was itching for the outdoors. He organized a huge mountain lion hunt, to make good of so many months of inactivity—as he put it. The upcoming nup-tials of his son and Hariklia later in the spring, gave him the opportunity to invite early many of his personal friends. Among those invited were Haridimos of Krousis and Iraklonas of Paeonia (both coming under the pretext of negotiating mercantile rights). When Sossos found out about these invitations (he was also a recipient—as client king), he secretly advised Aeropos to drink a potion pre-pared and delivered to him, which would make him feel ill, just a few days prior to the hunt's com-mencement, excusing him from participation.

Aeropos followed this advice—probably thinking it as a prelude to repetition of such 'illness' and final cancellation of the wedding. When King Filippos expressed concern, he was reassured by Sossos that the prince would be in good hands if he and his personal physician (who happened to be present and 'very knowledgeable in treating such illnesses) would be permitted to stay. Sossos could join the King at many a future hunts! Meantime the King could entertain his guests and be constantly in-formed on the progress of his son's recovery—a matter of few days!

So, the hunting party left from Aegae for the heights of the Pierian Mountains. It was the official report which stated that the King's death was caused by a huge mountain lion. Iraklonas and Haridimos knew better—to their sorrow and despair. Their disadvantage in coming out and telling the truth, was that they both were 'simple' foreign dignitaries, they did not have any true connection and backing from clan heads and land lords present, nor could they bring the assassins (even if it could be proven who they were and what part they had in the conspiracy) before the new King, for both Iraklonas and Haridimos were suspecting anyone and everyone.

All the two friends could do was to pay their 'respects' to the new King at Aegae, 'finish' their deals on 'business' and depart, not even staying to attend the royal funeral! Only when they reached safety after the cross of the Vottiaean borders and the 'escort' of the new King was left behind, only then they let grief become apparent as they discussed and reviewed the 'accident' in its details.

Filippos was among his friends for most of the hunt and everything seemed to be going fine. Few lions, bears and wild boars had been killed already and there were occasions the King had allowed the last thrust of a javelin or a sword to be performed by a special guest, at a particular beast. The Athinian Fidipidis (he was negotiating timber exports) was one of them, as was Iraklonas. Then, it was reported that an extraordinary big and mean lion was seen in the vicinity and a few peasants were brought to ask the King to rid them the menace of a man-eater. The hour being late, it was de-cided to resume the hunt next morning. Sossos' own cousin Sirras, reported the next morning that some of his men had located the tracks of this lion, followed the beast and had it, more or less, trap-ped! Would the King be doing service to his country men, killing the lion in person? Filippos was all happy to perform the task. He nodded to a few of his personal companion-guards to stay with his guests and, taking only three of them as his escort, followed Sirras with a gallop.

Attalos was concerned by the King's order to remain with the guests, as he was in charge of Filip-pos' personal guard and he voiced that concern. Haridimos and Iraklonas happened to be near and heard but there was nothing anyone could do, the King had given his order. They remained in camp, waiting for the King while getting their own gears ready for decamping—upon his return.

It was almost the mid of the day when news of the King being attacked and killed by the lion reach-ed the camp. The King's body was brought-in soon after, escorted by Sirras and his men who also brought-in the bodies of the three companion-guards of Filippos. Some of Sirras' men looked like they had to fight for their lives, as they came with torn clothes and multiple wounds. Despair and confusion reigned in the camp, soon bringing accusations as to who was to be blamed. Sirras was quick to accuse Attalos for not disobeying the King's wish to go with only three of his personal escort.

Attalos countered that Sirras had more than enough of his men. He should be protecting the King and his three escorts! The two men came close to drawing swords against each-other, blood prevent-ed from being spilled by cooler heads.

Everybody now gathered around the dead King, trying to pay a last respect, trying to have a look at the torn body of their leader friend or, for some, secret enemy. Iraklonas had done that already. While Attalos and Sirras were accusing each-other, the Paeonian had gone to see Filippos' body lay-ing among his three companions. They all had claw wounds, like the animal had done a truly thorough job on all. Too thorough, Iraklonas thought. He bent closer and took a careful look on the bodies. The wounds appeared to be made of claws from the animal but many of them too deep to correspond to any size lion, regardless how big! Also, there were no mouth bites! A lion, having done such a job on its victims, was bound to have bite marks left on them also! Pretending he was paying a lasting farewell to the King, his Paeonian eyes (with years of hunting experience around Messapion) caught a shining metal piece embedded on the King's neck. Letting his grief show momentarily (at the risk of being asked questions he didn't want to rise), he covered the King's body with his own, his hand secretly and frantically digging to extract that piece of metal. He managed, as other mourners (their surprise by this act gone) pulled him away, uttering words of hidden contempt—as much as angry reaction—at such a display of woman-like emotion. The King was not known as a person who'd cultivate such close relationship with any man, let alone a semi-barbarian from Paeonia!

His task completed, Iraklonas weakly protested and excused his behavior, holding in his palm the metal piece and nodding secretly to Haridimos. The latter jumped-in with apologies, explaining Paeo-nian 'customs' and extracted Iraklonas from the group. The two arranged to be among the first to return to Aegae. They spoke very little on their way back, fearing eavesdropping from the escort they did not trust. While traveling back to Aegae, their only conversation exchanges were to express their shock on the King's untimely death.

Upon their arrival, they asked for an audience and presented their sympathy and sorrow for the great loss, before the new King. Aeropos looked as if in sock himself but indifferent to their presence and the two had a sigh of relief, as soon as they came out leaving the royal hall. They contacted their 'business' associates closing some deals (to present that all was in order) as fast as they could and made ready to leave town. Meantime Attalos was formally accused of negligence and sentenced to a life exile from the kingdom, that very same day.

[He reportedly got into an accident on his way to Anthemous, where he planned to retire. Obvious-ly, no wedding took place and the house of Agis fell gradually to a second tier of importance and in-fluence during Aeropos' kingship. As for Hariklia, she married (years later) to a distant cousin, keep-ing the house of Agis intact and on its own.]

Haridimos and Iraklonas got worried—as they prepared to leave— when Sirras appeared at their lodging escorted by a detachment of armed horse riders. Soon they realized that his only concern was to have them out of the kingdom, fast. The riders with him were a so-called escort, in the name of King Aeropos, to see them safely to the border! The two friends did not need any persuasion.

They finally stopped at the Vottiaean village of Kyrros, leaving Timenid Makedonia and its 'escort' at its border, when Iraklonas and Haridimos decided to talk extensively while having supper at the sole inn in town. Iraklonas produced the metal object he had extracted from the King's neck. It had the shape of a hook, which could pose as a claw. Attached to something like an extension, a wooden handle, could have done a lot of damage on anything. If there were other hooks/claws like it hitting the King, then a murderous act had taken place, making it look like a large lion did the deed! Certainly, this hook/claw did not belong to the King's armor or weapons! Was that observation of any value, any proof? Probably not, not by itself, not without any eye-witness willing to support such theory! And what of the animal itself? No reports of it being killed were ever given. Did it escape? Or was there was no lion at all, just the excuse to isolate the King and have him killed?

Haridimos and Iraklonas came to the conclusion that nothing further could be done by them. They continued their trip the next morning, arriving at the village of Pella by late mid-day. The following morning they were to take separate roads. Iraklonas would ride to Evropos and from there he would cross into Paeonia, while Haridimos would board his ship moored at Pella's wharf cross the lagoon and the gulf of Therma, to his estate in Krousis. They promised each-other secrecy, life-long friend-ship and to continue keeping in touch with one-another.

> "...This Government (U.S.A.) considers the talk of 'Macedonian Nation', 'Macedonian Fatherland' or 'Macedonian National Consciousness' to be <u>unjustified demagoguery,</u> representing NO ethnic or political reality, seeing in its present revival a cloak for aggressive intentions against Greece."
> E. Stetinius, Secretary of State-American.

IV

Evriklia was a young girl of six plus ten springs old, as young as her age showed by most standards, except her wisdom. In wisdom she was very advanced, far beyond her age. It was not because she had spent time under guidance of wise men or women, nor because she had been taught by family exam-ple and tradition. She had been orphaned at the tender age of six, losing her mother during the great Dardanian raid ten springs ago. The following spring and during a minor raid, her father was taken hostage. Finding out that he was not a clan head or a land lord (therefore no ransom), his ab-ductors sold him at the slave market of Methoni, never to be found or heard-of again.

Evriklia was left to fend for herself, as she was 'side-stepped' by the raiders, both times. She would have surely died if it wasn't for the swine herder Dimitrios and his wife, Terpsino. They were among the few survivors of their hamlet, escaping death or slavery by a miracle! Not that Dimitrios and Ter-psino went out of their way in raising Evriklia either. The couple was not blessed with any children of their own, though both Dimitrios and his wife had gone to the Asklipion in Samothraki, several times—while still young.

Finding the child wandering and semi-starved, eased Terpsino's pain for children of her own, but-Evriklia being a female—this finding meant one more mouth to be fed, without much of return in wages earned, plus a dowry of some sort, when Evriklia would become of age to marry. These things considered, did not induce any special care or love from Dimitrios toward the child. He loved his wife though and, taking under consideration his own status, he knew he should count his blessings for having a wife at all.

Terpsino's desires and wishes were Dimitrios' own through-out the years of their union. He always did his utmost to provide. He would go and solicit his availability to herd and care of swine to vari-ous land lords and neighbors alike and they knew they could trust him. For over three times ten years now, he had not lose, miscount or misplace one hog, one little offspring! From his neighbors and peasants, he was taking his wages in kind. From land lords and clan heads in coin—if available.

Pelagonia was never a rich canton and its 'protection' from Lynkestis not particularly effective for most of the times. Pelagonia's king, his nobles and peasant rubble were dependant on the ability of Lynkos to protect and the 'good will' of raiders not to bother raiding! So, life in general, was not an easy task—but Dimitrios managed a living.

He had a sixth sense in times of danger and that was what saved him (and Terpsino) during raids.

Dimitrios would disappear (only the gods knew where) herd and all, until the raid was over. He then put his—most of the times—ruined hut back in order, deliver the swine herd piece-by-piece to the rightful owners (the ones still alive) and ask for his wages. If there were any swine left to his keep because the owner was killed or sold to slavery, Dimitrios would sell to the higher bidder for things needed in his household. Terpsino was happy in following and helping her husband and was a rather caring surrogate mother, while Evriklia was really a child.

During the past three years Terpsino's attitude towards Evriklia came to change a lot. The child was a child no more. Evriklia had become a woman, a beautiful woman, despite the rough life and nonexistent amenities to keep one with proper hygiene and care. Almopian women were famous in all Makedonia for their beauty and, everybody knew Evriklia's mother was from Almopia! Aside from that, Evriklia's beauty was getting to be something exceptional! And, what was making things worst, this 'child' seemed to have more brains than all the land lords and clan heads of Pelagonia put together!

Terpsino was not exactly a dummy herself. When Dimitrios would return home bringing news and orders from the authorities for the clan members, or wage promises for the care of the swine herd, innocent remarks and observations by Evriklia were making more sense than the idle talk and fat promises. So, Terpsino aging and (now) scared of losing her security and what little comfort her husband's occupation could provide, started being very jealous of Evriklia.

In actuality, Evriklia was a young woman full of respect and gratitude toward her foster parents. As for Dimitrios, his love for Terpsino did not leave any room for other thoughts, considering his self esteem and the fact that she was a very capable woman, making ends meet at the most difficult times. Nonetheless, the idea had registered in Terpsino's mind and there was no way she could or would see things any different, ever!

She needed not fear of Dimitrios. What didn't happen with him, happened with his half-brother Aratos. The man had his eyes on Evriklia for some time now, but he managed to keep his intentions to himself. He found his chance one day when the young woman was left at home alone, taking care of the day's meal and tending some hogs in their pen. Dimitrios with Terpsino had gone to the market in Antania the nearest town to their hamlet, to trade. They came back that evening to find Evriklia half-conscious in the hogs' pen, her clothes torn, covered with mud and animal food and ex-cerment! It was a miracle the hogs didn't do anything to her, as she had spent so much time laying unconscious among them!

It took a long time for Terpsino to clean Evriklia up, bandage her scrapes on hands, knees and face.

It took much longer time to get the young woman out of her shock, as she wouldn't let anything and no one touch her, regardless of the effort and soothing she received from both, Terpsino and Dimitri-os. It was weeks later when the couple was able to put the story together and that, after a lot of prod-ding, promises and threats. During those weeks, nobody could sleep at night. Terpsino and Dimitrios perplexed and trying to find a way to remedy this insult and Evriklia—still in shock—not understand-ing how 'uncle' Aratos could do such a thing, so suddenly and unprovoked, so brutally!

When all detail about the horrible deed finally emerged, Dimitrios and his wife came to making two decisions: First, they would sever the already distant relationship with Aratos. Once more, as Dimit-rios put it, bastards proved of being an unreliable lot of bad luck. Second, they had to take care of Evriklia's immediate future, for they couldn't afford any more mishaps either because she would be found pregnant or, bad mouthing from neighbors (misfortune always finds a way to be known) and employers. Evriklia was confined to her draped-up corner of their common room (not that the poor girl had in mind of going someplace), while Terpsino was force-feeding her with some cheese, olives, bread and sour milk.

The couple spent lots of time discussing Evriklia's future, amidst her sobbing in sleep, hog squeal-ing, rain, snow and mud (the hut was again in need of major repairs). They both agreed that Aratos' deed could not be brought before the clan head for justice, because the stigma on the family would be beyond repair, for talking to the clan head meant the case would go public. On the other hand, Ara-tos had to be found and be forced (if needed) to compensate. Would he marry Evriklia? Dimitrios did not think so. The coward was nowhere to be seen since the day he shamed them all! To try and marry the girl to someone else now was out of question. Her lost virginity made that proposition obsolete!

Keeping her home was equally out of question, in case she had conceived. Then there was nothing to hide and the shame on the family would crash every hope of survival. To move elsewhere was also out of question. Where a hog herder could go this late in life with a wife and a pregnant 'daughter'?

They concluded their only option would be to sell her! Lending her could be easier, stating economic hardship (not a lie) but her possible birth-giving to a child would be their ruin. Selling her was more difficult a task since Makedonian shyness on slave dependence existed, but more pragmatic. Besides, the buyer did not have to be a Makedonian and, if she was with child, well . . . better to have it take place out of any Pelagonian territory and in the hands of some stranger from the south! They had a use of slaves there, money to buy them and, that money would be of tremendous help to their house-hold!

The truth is that they arrived at such a decision after long arguments. Dimitrios was concerned on the morality of it, both on family honor and as adoptive parents, Terpsino (her jealousy gone) on grounds of misgivings and (being a woman) as an indirectly injured party. They were decent people, albeit rough on the edges. And, because of that, it occurred to none of them to check on Evriklia during those arguments. They had gotten used to seeing her sitting on her straw mat silent, rocking back and forth while holding her hands crossed against her breasts. They simply did not think of her!

Evriklia had started feeling claustrophobic and paranoiac as she was now left alone for long times and, in many an occasion she would go to the hogs' pen, rain or shine, standing there looking but not seeing, then run back in and collapse sobbing uncontrollably. When Dimitrios and Terpsino were discussing her future (and theirs), she'd sit rocking and saying nothing, with neither of her 'parents' knowing if she could hear or understand their predicament. She heard their arguments, she was a-ware of their final decision and, she discovered she did not care . . .

Two months later, the three of them got onto Dimitrios' cart and headed for the market in Pissaeon, the main town in Derriopos and known as a slave trading center. In spite of its proximity to Illyrian kingdoms, southern slave traders were in numbers, looking for good buys. Arriving there, Terpsino took Evriklia to purchase provisions and load them on the cart, while Dimitrios strolled the market trying to locate foreign merchants he thought they were side-dealing on slaves. He talked with many of them to no avail. They either weren't interested outright, or they were dirty cheap with their offers. It was getting late in the day and Dimitrios was thinking he was wasting time, when he run onto a merchant from Megara who had sailed north to Pella and then, trekked to Pissaeon. His name was Epimenidis son of Epimenis and he was willing to (at least) take a look at the 'merchandise' and then name his price.

Epimenidis had come to sell Korinthian sun-dried grapes, in exchange for cash, timber and pelts. His own slave had died while disembarking in Pella and if this girl, Dimitrios was talking about, was of real good Makedonian stock and used to carrying all kinds of loads (and cook!) she would do as a replacement.

They sought and found the two women by the grain depot. Evriklia was in the process of carrying two bags full of grain on her back, Terpsino being on the cart, ready to stock them. Terpsino saw Epimenidis' eyeing Evriklia, his mouth dropped wide open, and—contrary to her past shyness—she told him outright that whatever price he and Dimitrios had agreed upon, had been doubled by her! She could see at once—as a woman—the money they would receive had to be worth Evriklia's true value.

Epimenidis being a true, seasoned merchant, recovered his composure and purposely counter-offered two thirds of what Dimitrios had originally mention. It took them quite some time of arguing and hard negotiations to finally come to an agreement of mutual satisfaction. Evriklia observed the whole process like they were dealing for something else, something which had nothing to do with her.

When the hand-clasp of the two men sealed the deal, she became Epimenidis' property without saying a word . . .

Epimenidis spent that night sleepless, trying to figure how and when Evriklia would be ready to re-turn his investment—with plenty of interest. The young lady (with proper training) could be made to a first class material. Smooth, honey-colored skin, excellent set of teeth, deep-sea blue eyes and a golden crown of fine, long hair, she was a specimen one would pay ten-fold to have (after he was done with her)! Her hands were the tale-telling of her harsh life, as were her sandal-less feet. But, in time, those would soften-up too!

He had taken the time (after closing the deal with Dimitrios) to ask him and Terpsino all kinds of questions. Every time, they seemed reluctant to provide answers. He had to remind them several times of the sum of their agreement (coin and kind), to have them talk. He understood that Makedon-ians were much more private people than others, especially on matters concerning their family's af-fairs, but he also knew that every detail about Evriklia's life was of utmost importance to him—if he was to develop her the way he had in mind. While prodding, the young lady was standing by their side, seemingly indifferent, lost in her own thoughts, her own world. Any questions addressed to her had to be emphasized repeatedly, to bring her out of her state of mind she was in and respond. Her eventual responses showed her cleverness but also indicated—beyond any doubt— she was totally in-different of her future.

Epimenidis smiled inward as he studied his new investment. Give her time and proper company and training, he thought, and she would be a whole new person, worth a fortune! With expert probing and prodding, he found out what exactly happened to her and understood completely her behavior.

He paid the cost of her purchase in coin, Dimitrios and Terpsino being flabbergasted by the number and weight of so much silver on their hands! It was their first (and last) time of feeling somewhat im-portant and capable of doing something to improve their status. Terpsino was especially emotional as she saw her 'daughter' being taken away and under these dire circumstances but the money received was undeniably a plus, a security for their old age. They would move now to a bigger, protected town-away from their misery of suffering and bad memories . . .

Epimenidis led Evriklia to his tents, set on the fringe of the town and showed her her sleeping quart-er, located in his own tent—a hastily put drape separating his travel bed from her own. Her beauty and intelligence shown—regardless of her current state of appearance—gave him the desire to act like a man, any real man, would to a slave like her. He wanted to feel her breasts in his hands, have her legs around his waist and taste the fruits of Eros until exhaustion, right there and then! But Epimeni-dis was a good investor, a merchant who had full knowledge of his purchases. He knew not to make a move, not now, not until the time was ripe. Time (again) and proper guidance would bring him more than this moment's want!

He lay down on his mat, thinking in the silence of the progressing evening of her, of his interest in her. He did not have any supper nor did she. He was too elated with his investment; she was too une-motional with her destiny. He turned, facing at the drape separating them. No movement could be detected in the dim light of a single oil lamp and there was utter silence. Somehow, he knew she wasn't sleeping either nor thinking his thoughts. He didn't mind. He could think and dream of the day (or, rather night) by himself—for now. Sleep came to visit him finally, just before dawn.

Two days later his business in town were finished. He ordered the tents to be folded, his merchand-ise to be loaded on the pack animals and they headed for the village of Pella. He spent the whole day there (after a three day trek through Almopia), arranging his local dealings and getting his ship ready for his return trip to Megara. They departed the next morning, 'hugging' the coast, due to opposite winds out in the open sea. They docked at Pagassae in Magnisia, one of the best protected ports of all Thessalia. It took them four days to get there. He picked-up his profits made there by his associates, replenished the ship's water and food supplies and sailed toward Halkis.

It took them another two days in getting near, only to spend half of the day waiting for the strong sea current of the strait to change direction, so they could beach. They made one more stop at the bay of Faliron, the main Athinian post, late the next day. Epimenidis ordered to stay the night so he could deal with his Athinian colleagues the following day. Two and a half days later, they arrived at Mega-ra, after a scary hide-and-run they had to play with Aeginitan ships in the Saronikos gulf. Aegina and Athinae were at war—as usual—and every ship coming from the direction of Faliron bay was (more than likely) to be considered as a war prize.

Epimenidis walked in his house, followed by a passive Evriklia and a dozen servants and hired hands, carrying his collection of goods for storage. By the time he finished ordering, arranging, cata-logueing and receiving anxious clients, the time was getting late. Every one seeing Evriklia standing by him, wanted to know about her. Epimenidis answered to the ones he considered most important but, soon, he figured he would never have anything done on time—if this continued. He called for his aged housekeeper Arsinoi and sent Evriklia with her, instructions given to have the girl cleaned, fed and settled in the household, until he'd have the time to discuss future arrangements, later.

It took him much longer to finish with all his business, than he ever thought it would. In actuality he had but forgotten all about Evriklia when, long past dinner time, he entered the house proper, look-ing for something light to eat and relax taking a warm bath. He was really taken by the beauty of the young, clean and nicely dressed woman he saw, sitting next to his housekeeper—by the hearth. Both women stood as he entered the room and Arsinoi asked him of his wishes.

There was some time past when he realized he was standing there gaping and the question asked was addressed to him! He came back to reality with difficulty and asked for a bowl of soup and his bath to be ready when he would finish his meal. Arsinoi answered with a respect of a hired hand, but her head also shook in disparagement, like a mother to her son who's about to do (or have done) something not exactly fitting the guidelines of his upbringing.

As she left the room to see about his orders, Epimenidis let a big sigh come out of his mouth. He was again now the master in his household, his business and this slave. He started talking to Evriklia, the tone of his voice that of the investor, one looking after one's interests in a new venture and nothing more. He asked Evriklia to give him (again) a full detail of her life as she best could, assuring her that all this repetition and knowing about her would lead to nothing less than her best interest!

They conversed while Arsinoi came with a servant bringing Epimenidis' soup and he ate between narration-followed-by questions-answers, Evriklia's voice reluctant and breaking from unpleasant memories forced to be recounted. Arsinoi sat next to the girl soothing when needed, prodding when the master was out of words at a given moment. Overall, Evriklia remained composed and coherent, a fact which didn't escape the notice of both master and his old servant. At the end, Epimenidis told Arsinoi to take Evriklia to her chamber and come meet him at his bath for further discussion. The two women left and he walked to his bathroom. He met Diogenis, a trusted Kritan slave who was waiting to serve. He had at his side two other younger slaves, ready to bring steaming water for their master's bath as well as helping him clean and relax. Epimenidis ordered a partition and a stool placed on its other side, for Arsinoi to sit and talk— when the old maid would come.

He was bathed and Diogenis' young assistants were massaging him when Arsinoi came to the baths.

He started talking to her behind the partition. He had his long term plans he said, so she better pay mind to what he was asking of her. Arsinoi and Evriklia were to depart soon for Korinthos. They would find lodging and Epimenidis had a letter to write, a letter of introduction, which Arsinoi would give in person to the famous Korinthian etera, Lais. Evriklia was to be trained by Lais and the latter could name her price! Evriklia was to learn all the secrets of Lais' trade, leaving nothing to chance! The art of pleasing one's lover, the know how of stimulating dying conversation at a banquet, in poli-tics and arts, such as poetry and music. He was willing to invest not only his money but also on the time needed for Evriklia to become an etera equal—if not better—to Lais herself!

To Arsinoi's inquiries as to why he had to do that, once Evriklia could be kept at home and pay back his already large investment in her by cooking or do other house works, Epimenidis firmly re-mined his old housekeeper that this was his desire and Arsinoi had only to obey, as that was her business! All arrangements should be done fast and the two women were to depart for Korinthos no later than seven days—counting this one. Arsinoi should not worry about the housekeeping here, as her assistant, Myrsini of Lesvos, served under Arsinoi's guidance long enough and now would be the time to prove her worth, or he could sell Myrsini and find someone else.

They continued talking for some time longer and, during that, Epimenidis charged Diogenis with the task of escorting and providing protection for the two women, by staying with them in Korinthos.

Actually, Epimenidis concluded, both Arsinoi and Diogenis were excused and relieved from their present duties right that moment, so they would have only their new task to take care of, as he would have one less thing to be thinking about and look after the business!

By the time all was said and finalized, the hour had past the middle-of-the-night mark. Epimenidis was not tired at all—even that late—being all excited with his planning. Getting to his sleeping quart-ers, he spent another hour of revising and improving his picture of future prospects. He fell asleep without realizing it and woke-up late the following day—but he didn't care. He was happy with the arrangements and knew that both Diogenis and Arsinoi could be trusted to do what was needed of them! He got up, washed, ate a few pieces of fruit for breakfast, then he went to the house's altar to make his offering and walked out to the yard, ordering to have the front doors opened for the day's business . . .

Three more years passed until Epimenidis saw Evriklia again. If his first impression of her was one of admiration toward a nice-looking young girl, this time he was awed before her beauty! Lais had more than kept her part of the deal! She returned to him a lady refined, fit to be among the immortals in beauty, composure, intellect and political knowledge and understanding. Epimenidis found that Evriklia had been trained to perfection in voice control for poetry, as in playing the lyra and the flute. All the silver he paid for her seemed worth spending and he dreamed of the huge returns he would profit in a very short time. He arranged to have one more present of a thank-you token, sent to the aging etera of Korinthos. Lais' time was over, Epimenidis thought. Evriklia was now the rising star!

Epimenidis' first reward for the risk and expenses taken, was an unforgettable month of love mak-ing, testing (and approving) all assets, including conversation, intellectuality, politics, reciting and music. So much so, that one morning after her return from Korinthos and a month of bliss, Evriklia woke-up to find her master dead by her side, smiling the smile only a completely satisfied person has when time calls for the eternal reunion with the ancestors . . .

Poor Epimenidis did not have any relatives who could claim his fortune and inherit his vast proper-ty. The ruling class of Megara's elders deliberated for a long time, before coming to a logical (and profitable) conclusion that the city-state should shoulder the responsibility of managing this fortune.

The apple of contention and (to many) discontent in the process, none other than Evriklia! All elders wished (naturally) to have control of Evriklia, each one for himself! Each of the elders was unwilling to consent to her being the property of anyone else and, all of them (or at least the married ones) were in fear of their Megarian women.

There were endless debates when old Kallimahos' sense of civic duty prevailed. Like everything else, she should be put to use in the same manner! She should serve the special interests of the city-state as a whole and never mind the needs of the few leading archons! He convincingly indicated they could all profit from her services, with their proper guidance—naturally. They all knew, he attested, her capabilities. News of her excellent performances (and a first-hand experience by most of the elders invited in Epimenidis' symposia—while still alive) had become established facts, her fame traveling already beyond the Megara borders. The city could use its etera like Korinthos had used Lais. Evriklia should become (as state property) the courtesan who would guide with her charms statesmen of other city-states visiting Megara, in a most beneficial way for Megarian interests!

In order for the elders to protect their interests, she should have a retinue of servants trusted by them and which retinue would complement her status as a well trained, well known and well-to-do etera, ambassador of Megara's 'gifts' to any weak leader(s) of another state. She would become the holder of special fortunes, for the benefit of all Megarians but, mainly, this fair city's Fathers and Archons!

They all found his idea an excellent way to profit both in prestige and money, provided she would meet their expectations. Then, the elders divided into two groups. One, with Kallimahos in charge, to provide Evriklia with the 'proper' clientele, the second group (under the leadership of cunning Proklidis) to see that Evriklia and her small retinue would accept and perform such a delicate task, with maximum of efficiency! Obviously, Evriklia was to profit for herself along the lines, as Lais had in the past, serving herself and Korinthos. Proklidis was the right man to oversee her acceptance, being a veteran of great renown in wheeling and dealing himself!

They all discovered that Evriklia's beauty and training was accompanied by a truly sharp mind, something naturally given to her by the grace of the gods and, with her years in Korinthos under Lais, that something had become a powerful weapon! The city Fathers were ill prepared in negotiat-ing that, to their financial sorrow. She agreed to 'work' for the city, provided she would keep her trusted persons as a retinue, under guidance and commission from the elders for five years. At that time, she and her retinue would become free, with their option to continue 'working' for the city open to Evri-klia's discretion! She told them she was aware of her value, with enough reputation and clout already—in case they had ill thoughts in mind—and she could buy her freedom in a short time, as enough interest on her future was shown by her teacher and mentor Lais (Megara and Korinthos having common borders), who raised money to pay for Evriklia's freedom already. So, it had to be her way, or no way at all!

Proklidis had found his match, if not his better. Within a few days of intense negotiations and to show the elders' good faith in her, she was declared a free person. She could use and live in Epimeni—dis' house, for as long her services to Megara would keep her in the city; they agreed upon five years. She also could have the servants of Epimenidis as her own. Evriklia would profit a tenth of the city's income through her services, plus negotiated bonus—each time results went beyond expectations!

The first test (a triumphant result for Megarian interests through Evriklia) was soon to come. Because of the city's geographical position, Megara was pressured for closer ties, an alliance, from both Athinae and Korinthos. Both sides needed and wanted Megara as an ally or satellite state in their struggle for supremacy in the area. Korinthos was ahead in the competition at the time, as a city straddling the isthmus connecting the main land body of Ellas to Peloponnisos, having easy access on both sides of it, the Aegean to the east, the Ionian to the west.

Athinae sent a delegation to Megara offering presents alongside threats. Athinians being keen orators, covered their threats under pretext of dangers lurking on account of Korinthian plans to ex-tend its sphere of influence but the wise city elders understood well that 'alliance' with Attiki would bring the city under the strong 'protection' of Athinae, eliminating their freedom of choice, literally!

The Korinthians responded by sending their delegation—while Megarians were deliberating the Athi-nian proposals. Not being as 'refined', they came up-front with threats of blockading Megara with their naval forces and possible open hostilities, unless Megara was prepared to turn the Athinians down!

Megarian elders were divided as to whom the city would mostly benefit from; Athinae or Korinthos and the fierce speeches of pro and con were tiring the delegations of the other two city-states, who now openly started threatening with war!

Kallimahos thought it was time to find if Megara's trust in Evriklia was something they could count on, especially during such difficult times. She accepted the challenge. She organized and held two separate symposia at her house (formerly Epimenidis'). For the first, she invited one representative of each fraction between the elders. During the symposion she clearly demonstrated to both that no matter whom Megara would decide to attach itself with alliance, the terms of it would have to clearly state that Megara would be an equal and full partner of such alliance. That resolved and ratified, it did not matter if it was with Korinthos or Athinae. Both fraction leaders saw Evriklia's points of logic, appreciating her sound counter-proposition and enjoying her hospitality, beauty and artistic extravagance she offered them during their meet and symposion.

Next, she invited the leaders of the Athinian and Korinthian delegations and repeated her achieve-ment, by proving and convincing both, that Megarian cooperation given in equal measures to the two neighboring states, would be immensely more profitable to all. Megara could be the commercial hub on land—as well as by sea—between the two rivals, with open market for both. She presented the dan-gers of a conflict suggestively, between recitals of poetry, dance and flute music. Could Athinae real-ly afford an open war against Korinthos and Megara while already at war with Aegina? Would the Korinthians throw Megara to the Athinian bosom with a blockade which could easily be rendered useless? Provisions and armed help could come from Athinae to Megara by land, especially when the two states were so bordering. Then, how would Korinthos anticipate and null a combined Megarian and Athinian fleet at the entrance of her approaches to the gulf of Saronikos? Allying to Aegina? She was sure Aeginitans would be really demanding concessions of Korinthos in the Aegean markets, to join in a more adventurous war!

The most satisfaction taken by her was that she achieved her goal by having all parties feel they alone had come-out as the winner of these negotiations! Naturally, knowing her place as a woman in the society of Megara and through her training with Lais, she had not come out openly with her sug-gestions to these much puffed-up delegates and elders. She saw to it, they rather thought of her ideas as their own.

At the closing of the deal, she invited all the delegates and the elders to one more symposion, for an unforgettable evening of beauty, charm, hospitality and a feeling of accomplishment and common di-rection, one would think that the goal of these three city-states had always been under the same guide lines of a united, common policy, since time immemorial!

There, during this last closing-of-the-deal symposion, some news arrived (brought-in by Kallima-hos) from the distant, 'semi-barbaric' region of Makedonia. They all knew Evriklia was hailing from that region and the gossip was in hushed tones. Her hearing being as sharp as her mind, she heard most of what was said. Finding the right moment to engage in that conversation, she commented in such a studious manner, they all admired her perception of political, as well as commercial implicat-ions, one more time. From there-on, conversation flowed freely and opinions were given and taken, everyone participating and presenting views and solutions.

Now it was time for Evriklia to keep quiet and hear as much as she could, of the latest news in her country and of what the southern city-states Archons and politicians made of it. They all soon got in their politicking and even forgot about their host. The Timenid King Filippos of Makedonia was pro-bably assassinated, although official reports had him killed during a hunting accident—and good rid-ance! Filippos had become a thorn on the side of many a south city-state and a big unknown factor on the well being of their colonies in and around Makedonia! With his planned wedding between his son Aeropos to the Sythonian princess a little while ago, he could have 'closed' the gulf of Therma and perhaps the one of Toroni. The Athenian delegates were congratulated by both the Megarian Archons and the Korinthians, for the assistance they provided to Eretria and the Thrakian plunder-ers, by sending them a true general and a score of settlers. They returned the accolades to the Korin-thians for their assistance on the venture and wished them good luck on their next planned venture in the island of Korkyra. Evriklia wanting to hear more about Makedonian affairs, discreetly turned the conversation back to original theme, pouring wine in the cup of Proklidis and whispering her question in his ear.

The heir of Filippos, Aeropos, was not even close to the will, power and political dexterity of his father. Understanding—too late—the reason of the Elimiotian Sossos' 'friendship' attacked, but was soundly defeated by the combined forces of Orestis, Elimiotis and Tymfea! Whatever lands Aeropos had inherited from Perdikkas, Argeos and Filippos from Orestis were gone! Next, Lynkestis annexed Pelagonia and Almopia, king Lampos of Lynkos placing none other than Sossos as king of Almopia. The Orestian king Pelegon was all too happy to consent such a move, as he annexed Eordea. Elimio-tis followed their example, putting Tymfea under its 'protection' and 'guidance' and enlisting itself as the Thessalian Perrevea's ally.

There was nothing else left for the Timenid House but to sue for peace. All Aeropos got under his rule, was Makedonis, Pieria (with Aloros and

Methoni being independent colonies) and Imathia (as a client kingdom). Ambassadors from Lynkestis, Dassaretis, Derriopia (they too wanted a piece of the action), Pelagonia, Almopia and Tymfea, were meeting the representatives of Aeropos in Aeani, the Elimiotian king Sirras (first cousin of Sossos) being the host and directed by Sossos. Arbitrators from Ferrae and Farsalos were called in, Aeropos vouching on grounds of their long time friendship and assistance to all Makedonia. The city-state of Potidaea had been elected as the presiding force, being of a neutral nature and located in Halkidiki.

When that was mentioned, the Korinthian delegation picked-up the lead of conversation, all agree-ing to inform their Archon back home and send word to Potidaean delegates to see that House Time-nos would not lose too much. A very weak Makedonia was as bad as a very strong one! The rest of the party agreed with that statement. Their talk continued (Evriklia listening but pretending she was just there to entertain), all parties consenting that Aeropos had no choice but to ratify anything the arbitrators were gracious enough in granting him. There was some laughing when it was reported that Aeropos' peace delegates in Aeani were none others than the sons of Kinos and Ariston, both an off-spring of the exiled Orestian house of Agis, Klitos and Agis 'the younger'! They figured Aeropos was running out of supporters.

Most among the guests of the symposion foresaw there would be more fighting in Makedonia and, for the good of their purses, prosperous days of bargaining for timber and slaves were ahead. The slave trade words were said rather loudly by the Athinian delegate Polymahos and anxious heads turned at the direction of Evriklia, while an uneasy silence fell among the participants of that con-versation. They needed not to worry. Evriklia seemed preoccupied sharing a joke with Kallimahos and the Korinthians Proxenos and Theoharis and was not listening . . .

Four days later an agreement was officially ratified and the Korinthian and Athinian delegations returned to their city-states happy. The following morning Evriklia was visited by the Megarian elders. They bestowed upon her the highest honors their city offered for 'epikourous', the non Me-garian residents of the city-state. Megara, they said, was in love with her and not just because of her beauty! Kallimahos then stood-up and informed her, the elders' decision to authorize for a trip to her native region, to Makedonia! She was to see that the persons in charge of the Timenid House in Aegae, even the King, were to become her friends, therefore Megara proponents in commercial and political advantages over any other city-state!

Instructions as per special interests and demands of Megara to Makedon would be arriving to her by curriers, carrying specific instructions and information to her, as Megarian needs and policy would demand each time. In order to ease her acceptance at the court of Aegae, she should program and start a tour of many states, heading north until she would arrive at Aegae. Kallimahos put emphasis in the elders' trust in her abilities noting she had passed her test with excellence just a few days ago! Now she could show them if she could do better, away from Megara and on her own, escorted—obviously—by her trusted retinue of servants and some guards (for road protection). Money to start with would be given to her by the state's treasury in a generous sum, according to her status and her fame.

She asked for a moon's change time, to think and consult with her assistants. The elders agreed and she had several discussions with Arsinoi, Diogenis and Myrsini. At the end of the moon's turn, she sent word to the elders and Archons that she agreed.

Pantoleon was a scion of a respected but (lately) fading Megarian house. His great-grand-father was the last of the house's leading Archons of the city, to the day he died. Pantoleon's father, Antimahidis (son of Antimahos), was a careless soul who managed to spend the family's fortune and prestige in ventures so promising, they never got 'off the ground'. His last venture was a colony up in cursed Makedonia—one which never was built, thanks to that King Filippos, may his soul rot in Tartaros!

Antimahidis was forced to withdraw, taking his followers to Toroni and leaving his bones there. His wife, Kypseli, did everything she could (during Antimahidis' ventures and adventures) to educate and place Pantoleon in the prominent position the family ought to have, but with the little support-if any—from the side of her blood family (they gave-up on her fast!), she was forced to seek another husband, through the council of the elders and many debates between them.

Pantoleon never liked the idea of having his mother wedded to another man. He was used to being free. Last thing he needed was to obey the orders of a stranger! Pantoleon rebelled to the point that Ippalkimos, Kypseli's new husband and a direct descendant of the last line of Megarian royalty, was forced to abandon any hope. Ippalkimos sent the young man away, to some property he owned in the country side, in care of his local foreman Epistrofos. Pantoleon's rebellion continued even there and the result was that he eventually took-off seeking his own ways. He joined a band of pirates from the island of Skopelos.

The whole affair could have ended then and there with Pantoleon written-off as lost, if it wasn't for an incident which took place about the time of Epimenidis' death. The pirate ship in which Pantoleon was a member, attacked a Megarian merchant ship, belonging to Ippalkimos and, worst, Pantoleon got wounded and taken prisoner.

The young man was brought before the city elders and was duly condemned to death by stoning—as the custom was—at the city's outskirts. It was the exact day Evriklia and her retinue had started their trek with their eventual arrival in Makedonia. The guards and stone casters with the condemned man met Evriklia and her company. In charge of the execution was Plexarhos, son of Aristandros, a minor in the cast of Megarian elders, but one with great ambitions. He had not a good relation with Epimenidis while the latter was alive, nor did Plexarhos like Kallimahos or Ippalkimos. All those elders and Archons he considered as blocking stones before the 'gate' he wanted to open for himself, the 'gate' to the power of handling Megara's fortunes by one man—himself!

Plexarhos was a scheming man, thinking of ways to rid himself (and Megara) of the influence from the elders and knowing before hand Evriklia's mission and route she was taking, had worked a way of having the needed opportunity to rise above all, by using her and the man he was about to 'exe-cute'. The paid stone casters had been chosen carefully by him, men who were in his debt, ready to do what he'd ask without question. 'Preparing' Pantoleon for 'execution', he revealed his plan to the intended 'victim'. Knowing the character of the young man, he simply asked him if it wouldn't be to Pantoleon's justification for revenge—and to their mutual advantage—having Pantoleon's life spared? Then, both of them could see the downfall of their common enemies. Obviously Pantoleon would do what was asked of him, to save his skin, then profit—while having his own revenge against his mother and Ippalkimos. He accepted Plexarhos' deal. All he had to do was to have Evriklia admit him in her group and see that her mission would fail (preferably with the greatest possible exposure) while in Makedonia. After that, Plexarhos would see that Pantoleon would return to Megara all pardoned, to inherit what was rightfully his!

It did not take much of an effort from Plexarhos to convince Pantoleon. It was agreed that he was to be stoned in a way which would leave the scars of his sentence, but in good enough shape to 'miraculously' escape death and seek asylum in Evriklia's retinue. Pantoleon and Plexarhos spent some time putting the pieces together. The most sensitive moment would be to have Evriklia believe in Pantoleon's story. Once accepted (and that had to be his un-failed aim) all he had to do was to gain her trust (plenty of available time for that) and strike at the appropriate time! If, by the way, he could do more damage to the Timenid House at the same time, well! That was a bonus Plexarhos was throwing onto Pantoleon's lap! For wasn't Makedonia the cause of his father's demise? Meantime, Plexarhos would be working to achieve the fall of all the elders, those same ones who had cast their vote for Pantoleon's death, first among which, Ippalkimos!

Evriklia started her trip in a very good mood. She was feeling free in most aspects, among friends she could trust and who trusted her, on their way to Athinae, passing by the city of Elefsis, renowned for the Great Mysteries of the goddess Dimitra and her kori, the daughter Persefoni. The day was a beautiful one, mid part of the month Mounihion (by the reckoning of Attiki), the month Artemisios by the Makedonian calendar. A spring day full of flowery odors, butterflies and swallows. The storks were preparing and repairing their nests in the open fields or on the roofs of country houses, giving away their presence with their peculiar standing on one leg and their staccato callings.

Evriklia's company was slowly moving on the road, some of the girls running on the fields and coming back with crowns on their heads, made-out of red poppies mixed with green offshoots from pine trees and their cones, or throwing these crowns on Evriklia's lap. She was sitting comfortably on the seat of a cart drawn by two pair of oxen, across from Arsinoi and Myrsini who had the task of shooing flies and other insects buzzing around them. Above head, there was a nice canopy, made by Myrsini and placed by Diogenis, to keep the strong spring sunrays away from her soft skin. Diogenis was riding next to them, sometimes joking, sometimes joining in their songs. There was a little dust raised by the party, mainly because most of the burden was carried by other carts some distance behind them. They also had a small armed escort (bandits were a rather common sight for any un-escorted travelers), a cook and some hired hands, in case they liked to pitch a tent out in the open, during a route break.

A few of the girls had gone ahead again, chasing butterflies on the road and in the fields. Myrsini had picked-up a popular song satirizing Megara's ruling class (none of them was around to hear it, so, why not have some fun?) and they were all laughing at her articulate manners of mimicking while singing, when two of the girls ahead came back screaming. The small caravan came to a halt. Dioge-nis calmed the two girls (so they could tell what the problem was) and the armed escort formed a protective cordon around the carts, ready for action—if one was needed.

The girls now started making sense of their scare and told Evriklia what their screaming was all about: Just around the bend of the road where the cluster of cypress trees could be seen, they found a badly wounded and almost dead young man laying down in the middle of the road. The two of them returned to ask for help, while the others stayed there (at a distance), keeping an eye at the scene. Diogenis asked five of the escort's men to follow and he galloped ahead to see for himself.

They returned soon afterwards, carrying a seemingly badly wounded youth, unconscious and cover-ed with dried blood. Evriklia ordered to have the man cleaned and have his wounds dressed-up in hope he would recover and tell them how and why misfortune had come to meet him. Diogenis agre-ed, provided that would be done while they continued moving, all girls would remain in the carts and a few men from their escort would ride ahead, in case bandits were on the lose and lurking around. They all obeyed his prudent suggestion and they took the wounded man in one of the carts to take care and, hopefully, ask questions and get answers when the time was right.

About two hours later, Diogenis came to Evriklia's cart and told her that they were going to stop at the next cluster of pine trees down the road, for the mid-day meal. He had the area scouted and all was in order for their stop. They would have some protection under the trees from the strong sun and the area was clean of any obstructions, so they could see the road and the surroundings—just in case. He was still concerned about any possible bandits and he wanted to have a private talk with her, con-cerning the wounded man, while they had their meal.

They arrived at the pine tree cluster shortly and Diogenis arranged having their carts in a circle, saying this would be the best for a defense—if one was needed. Waiting for their cook to prepare the meal, Diogenis brought the young wounded man before Evriklia. She started protesting Diogenis' harsh treatment, as two of their escort guards had the wounded man tied-up and were treating him roughly on the way before her. Diogenis stopped her protests by saying that he recognized the man—now that he had been cleaned and treated. He was, Diogenis said, the one who was condemned to death by stoning, the orders coming from the Archons of Megara. In Diogenis' own opinion, the man should be sent back to Megara and let the Archons decide what to do with him. The man was a known pirate and he could not be trusted or become a part of their caravan. If the archons from Megara had him for death, it was their responsibility to send him back to Megara!

The apparently semi-conscious young man came to life and, with cries of mercy, pleaded for his deliverance from wrong doing. He was falsely accused, he said, because he had been abducted by pirates and forced to fight, for fear of losing his own life! When captured, he was unable to prove that (no pirate in his right mind would appear to testify on his behalf) and that was the reason for his condemnation! Did the lady want to have his murder hang on her soul? Now that the gods spared his life, going against their merciful will? Why, he was willing to serve her for the rest of his life, asking for nothing more than his chance to live, as was already granted by the Olympians. She was begged to let him be of any future assistance to her, offering her perhaps more than what was expected of him and he knew he could count on her equal to the gods' charity.

Evriklia was in good spirits from the start of the day and had first-hand experience of what Tyhi, that divine controller of human fate could weave in a person's life. Against Diogenis' protest, she ordered provision of shelter for the young petitioner. She privately agreed with Diogenis later, in keeping an eye on the refugee, until his devotion to them was proven. Pantoleon became part of the small caravan.

They arrived in Elefsis, a town within the Attiki region of the city-state of Athinae and stayed there for almost two moon-face changes. Their reception in town was something Evriklia never thought could happen to her in her lifetime. People were lined on the street (her escort hadtaken the time to preannounce her arrival) hailing her and her escort like they would a savior of their city. Evriklia was given free staying quarters courtesy of Dimos, the citizen's assembly in Elefsis. Evriklia spent the time there giving receptions and parties for the citizens and what foreign delegations the city had visiting. In return, she was given rich presents in jewelry and in coin (mostly silver Athinian and/or Halkidian obols).

One evening after a reception, Myrsini observed that they all could buy their freedom sooner, if things continued that way and presents were piling-up. Evriklia and Arsinoi were laughing at the remark and Diogenis with (an almost fully recovered) Pantoleon were moving a piece of furniture, when Pantoleon 'lost' his grip. The furniture fell missing Diogenis' foot by a hair, bruising his thigh.

Diogenis let a curse out of his mouth and Pantoleon's face turned red. He said, right afterwards, it was because of his embarrassment for his clumsiness and apologized. Diogenis did not believe, but Evriklia jumped-in and praised the young man for his concern and shyness for an accidental event which caused no real trouble, any way! Diogenis also forgot all about it, later.

It took them only two days to reach Athinae from Elefsis, considering that their caravan had grown to six plus ten carts (from the original five). Most of their first day in Athinae was unpacking gifts given and placing them in display at the house Diogenis had gone ahead and rented for them. It was located on the thoroughfare leading from Keramikos cemetery beyond the city walls, to the Athinian acropolis, past the hill of Pnyx. To get there they followed the Iera Odos, where the Pan-Athinian festival was held every four years. Looking at the acropolis, seat of goddess Athina's temple and last stronghold of defense—if the city ever fell—Evriklia was not impressed, in spite of Athinian boasting.

From what she could see from below, there was a stone rampart on top of a sheer rock, the rooftop of the temple scarcely detected beyond the battlements. She guessed the view from there to be of some reason Athinians were so proud of their rock. Megara's acropolis had much more to show—she thought. The host house Diogenis had rented was on the north-west side of the acropolis rock, enjoying its shade for most of the morning sun but exposed to the mid-day and later hour's heat. It was very spacious though and suited for great receptions, plus it was in an upper class neighborhood.

It had an equally spacious inner garden, framed on all four sides by gracious Ionic style colonnades, their marble taken from the local famous mount of Penteli (that was proudly stated by the agent who rented the house to her). She compared the work to the Korinthian houses and columns. The marble did look to be of better quality but Athinae still lagged behind Korinthian splendor.

The 'Megarian' etera and her group spent double time in Athinae, than what they had in Elefsis. She entertained friends and associates of the Megarian elders and their proxenos ambassador in the city,

Polimahos—with various results. Some of them were open proponents of peace and facilitation of good relations with Megara (and Korinthos in a byway), others equally open in their hostility to the idea. There was some headway in gaining few of the opponents initially, but this came to an abrupt end, one morning at the Agora, the market place. Evriklia with Polimahos at her side and Myrsini, Diogenis and Pantoleon following, were making their rounds looking for imports to be used at Evrik-lia's customary symposia parties. Suddenly, a clearly hostile crowd of Athinians approached them, throwing insults. Evriklia tried to answer lightly and with humor, making smart and funny remarks on the right of free citizens to express an opinion openly. Instead of calming the crowd (obviously coached by its leaders), her remarks backfired and the mob moved menacingly, suddenly producing and wielding clubs!

Before anyone knew, a melee ensued and Evriklia could have been hurt badly—if it wasn't for the speed of Pantoleon. He covered the blow of a club with his right arm (which was badly fractured and took weeks to heal), giving time to Diogenis and Myrsini to pull Evriklia to a hasty retreat. Polimahos and his small escort of servants covered for them, until they all reached back at the house, locking the entrance behind them!

The group was moved after that and with continuous profound apologies from Polimahos and his associates, to a country side estate, by cape Sounion, smuggled out of the city in the middle of the night! After a few days of investigation, the leaders of such a demonstration were apprehended and put to work in the mines. The true instigators of the affair was found to being too important and, staying away from the actual attack, could not be accused of any wrong doing but now kept a low profile. One week after this event, Evriklia and her retinue were inconspicuously embarked to a ship from Faliron bay, with lots of additional presents and apologies, bound for Eretria.

Evriklia was now very fond of and grateful to Pantoleon, something Diogenis did not like but could ill afford to be against. He had the support of Arsinoi in his opinion on Pantoleon and the two agreed to continue a discreet surveillance on him. As for Myrsini, it was more than obvious—even to a blind person—the girl was madly in love with her mistress' savior!

Their trip to Eretria was uneventful but long, due to the cargo ship they were in. Their stay in that city was also a pleasant one and during that, they had a visit from Proklidis who traveled by land and had to cross only the narrow strait from Attiki to Evia. The visit sent Pantoleon into hiding and he begged to be left unmentioned—as he was still in fear of losing his life (as he put it). To inquiries of Proklidis about the incident in Athinae which almost cost Evriklia's life, she gave a vague answer about an unknown savior who got lost in the crowd. Arsinoi and Diogenis were forced to remain silent. Proklidis did not insist on gaining more details. He lived in his own world and was boosted (along his party's elders) by the success of having Evriklia as Megara's ambassador in other states. He concluded his negotiations with the Eretrians on behalf of Megarian interests and with Evriklia by his side and left.

Some days after his departure, Evriklia and her party (Pantoleon reappearing) left from Eretria to Halkis. They traveled overland, the distance being short. They had a very good reception in Halkis with the only Halkidian complain of Evriklia visiting Eretria first, instead of skipping that city alto-gether!

Although Evriklia's previous visit in Halkis was a very short one and she was just an unknown slave in the service of a rich Megarian master, she couldn't help but remember it with mixed feelings. After all, she was now a famous person, a renowned etera, thanks to that same Megarian master!

Looking at the Evrippos strait with its strong tides holding the ships ashore until the tide would change, she made a promise to the dead man. She would help Megara gain renown to honor him, but up to where she felt she had done her duty to his memory and no more!

During their stay in Halkis, merchants brought the bad news that the city of Smyrni in Ionia and the Asian shores by the Aegean was taken and burned by the Lydians, who established a strong kingdom there. On a more local news interest, Athinae had ended its war against Aegina and gained the alliance of the island of Salamis, which, simply meant Salamis was now under Athinian influence and dependence. There was also news from further away, in the depths of Asia. The powerful—until now—kingdom of Assyria was losing the war against Vavylonians and Mides. But those were far away events with as yet to be predicted interruptions on trade.

It was about the month of Gorpaeos by Makedonian reckoning, Metagitnion by the Athinian. The seas were starting to be choppy by the prevailing winds and there was some debate among Evriklia and Diogenis on the feasibility of sailing to the city of Pagasae, located north of Evia and in the safety of the gulf by the same name. Arsinoi was getting rather old for frequent moving from town to town and Diogenis was too conservative and concerned to want a late summer departure, with so unpre-dictable winds.

But Evriklia was getting anxious and she wanted to move. Makedonia was not that far from Paga-sae and they could take the land roads to Aegae, before the winter snows closed them. She had Pan-toleon on her side pushing for a departure and taunting Diogenis for being overcautious for such a short sail of only half a day (with the winds helping). It was two against two. Evriklia asked for the opinion of Myrsini, not realizing the girl was so in love with Pantoleon, she would agree to go to Adis—had he asked for.

It was three against two. The decision made, they prepared for departure. Evriklia hired a vessel from Skiathos, its captain willing to take the risk of a late departure, thinking of spending the winter in his island and with his family, after dropping his passengers and cargo at their destination. They had to wait for an extra four days for favorable winds and tide, which brought their casting-off in the late hours of this fourth day.

Their sail from Halkis to the town of Orei at the north tip of Evia was a pleasant one, as the vessel 'hugged' the island coast overnight. They beached there for water and other provisions in the early morning and, after a while, they cast-off to cross the strait to Pteleos and enter the gulf of Pagasae. But sudden gale winds coming down the strait from a north-east to south west direction, forced them to turn around and seek protection back at Orei. The cargo vessel, in spite the efforts of its captain and crew, missed the harbor and wrecked on the rocks quite some distance from the town or any set-tlement. All was lost to the sea, except their lives! They found a shelter in a near-by cave where they were beached and captain Agathoklis sent few crewmen for help from the town.

His men had hardly gone around the beach toward the road to town when, suddenly, cries of pain and triumph were heard from the direction they had gone. Before anyone could even think to react, the beach was surrounded by armed men, spears, swords and arrows aimed at the small group of passengers and sailors. These armed men were pirates from the island of Skopelos. Their vessel was hidden beyond a small inlet near-by, waiting for a imprudent captain to sail his ship within striking distance or, as in this case, a wreck because of the weather. These pirates watched happily the futile efforts of captain Agathoklis and now they had everybody tied-down. Questions were asked by the leader of these pirates, a certain Gorgias, in order to evaluate each one of his new 'property'. Some of his pirate crew started 'combing' the beach for additional gains, searching the shipwreck and looking at the sea to bring ashore anything they could salvage and of value . . .

The pirate ship arrived in Skopelos three days later. The prisoners were placed in the slave's prison, each chained on stalls with just enough room to take two steps or lay down. Most of captain Agatho-klis' crew were immediately sent to man the oars of other pirate ships. The rest of the prisoners were to provide ransom for their freedom or, lacking that, to be sold at the market in due time. Some of these fearsome and (most of times) fearless pirates were ordered by Gorgias to sail for Skiathos and Megara, asking for ransom for Agathoklis and Evriklia and her group. Meantime Evriklia did as she best could, to ease the conditions of their stay in the pirates' prison, 'entertaining' Gorgias and try-ing to talk him out. She was sent back to join the others each time, conditions remaining about the same. Gorgias was a shrewd man wanting the pie and eating it too!

Captain Agathoklis' ransom came in first, his family well-to-do in Skiathos and wanting him back at all cost! The pirate 'delegation' sent to Megara returned after the winter was gone, empty handed.

Megara, after countless debates, had cast its ballot against any ransom deal. Proklidis lost his life and property defending the prisoners' cause and Kallimahos was exiled, with his property confiscat-ed! The new strongman in Megara now was none other than Plexarhos and he found the ransom beyond Megara's power and interests. He would not take the trouble of negotiating with pirates at all! Let the prisoners be sold or their lives disposed, as it would please Gorgias and his ruffians.

The news about Megara deciding against their ransom was devastating for Evriklia's small group!

More so with Pantoleon, who just now understood who his real friends were and where his actual in-terest was. While Gorgias and his lot were figuring how much which market would give them more for the new slaves, Pantoleon confessed to Evriklia and the rest of fellow prisoners the whole story and the deal he had made with Plexarhos, tears of remorse running down his eyes.

Diogenis could have torn him apart, had he been able to reach from the place he was confined with chains. He would still try that, on first opportunity given! Evriklia felt sorry for all of her friends and servants. She asked from everyone to forget what happened and concentrate at what was in their future, how they could possibly be set free. She had to specifically order Diogenis to let go of Pantole-on past and mistakes, as she asked Pantoleon to really prove his regret of the past, by his future acts!

It took her some time convincing Diogenis but her insistence finally prevailed. It was time now for all to think of a way out of this predicament.

Evriklia sought and had a new audience with Gorgias. During their talks, she presented the pirate with a simple choice. What was the total worth of the whole group to him? Was it three talents? She would pay him four! He could keep most of her group as hostages, until she would come with the full amount, provided she would return with it within acceptable (to both) time limit. The prisoners would have to be found in the same—if not better—condition and he would, perhaps, have an extra bonus coming his way! Of course, he could try to sell them one by one on different markets, but she knew there was no guarantee he would be able to raise half of the amount he was asking and she was willing to pay. Could they have a deal then? Evriklia would have to be send to the mainland with one of her two men in her retinue and old Arsinoi, who was in need of better conditions the pirates could or would offer. The rest of her party, girls and men, servants or slaves, would remain in Gorgias' keep, until her return with the four talents of silver, plus a bonus.

Gorgias was a shrewd man and knew his limits of profit. A seasoned pirate like him could smell an occasion—when it presented itself. Four talents of silver was the kind of money one would not neglect taking it under serious consideration, as well as the extra bonus! He could tell Evriklia was honest with her offer, as he could see she would be capable to raise the money—and fast!

The deal agreed, he sent Evriklia with Arsinoi and Pantoleon on a small boat to the land of the Magnites and Thessalians, close (but not so close as to endanger his boat and crew) to the town of Pagasae. Evriklia and her servants were left at the outer shores of the 'bent arm' peninsula, the one protecting the gulf from the open Aegean. All Evriklia and her party had to do, was to climb mount Pilion, Pagasae being located on its other, inner side. Climb with Arsinoi in tow? Out of question! Evriklia did not want to lose her aged friend on their way to buying their freedom. The woman needed to be sheltered and taken care of, regardless of weather or road conditions! Her captivity, although Gorgias had treated them better than others would, had done enough damage to her already.

When the boat of the pirates left them, Pantoleon built-up a sort of a shelter and he took-off on the steep slope of the east shore, seeking for a village or hamlet and some help. He came back many hours later, escorted by about half a dozen of local shepherds, carrying some refreshments and makeshift litters, to bring Arsinoi and Evriklia to their hamlet. They stayed there for a few days, to recover and, deciding that Arsinoi would have to be spared from any further hardship, she was left at the care of the hamlet's residents, with a promise of great rewards upon Evriklia's return. She and Pantoleon departed for their short journey to Pagasae, on top of borrowed donkeys.

Evriklia remembered, on their way to Pagasae, the name of a good associate of Epimenidis whom she met briefly on her way to Megara— so many (yet so few) years ago. She asked Pantoleon to present himself upon their arrival at Pagasae, at the house of Theoklimenos, the dealer on Finikian-died textiles, and ask for an audience with her.

Theoklimenos had a sharp mind and never forgot the beauty his late friend Epimenidis was so lucky to have and so proud of. He agreed to see her at once. Evriklia was admitted at his house and told her story and adventures, holding nothing back. Theoklimenos was moved by the misfortunes of Evriklia and friends, promising help. He assigned quarters for Evriklia and Pantoleon to stay and clean, send-ing a girl-slave of his to the market to purchase some more befitting outfit for her. He then called upon his friends and associates for dinner and discussion that very evening.

They were all thrilled with Evriklia's company that night and undertook the raising of money need-ed for her companions' ransom. Theoklimenos had already dispatched men to bring Arsinoi and give the promised rewards to the hamlet's families. During the stay at Theoklimenos' house, it was point-ed to Evriklia that, although Pagasae was very pleased in having her among its citizens, was not the town from which she could make the money to pay back the silver sent to the pirates. Although there were plenty of merchants' traffic in town, it was the type of transitional business, with no bigwigs residing there, or spending sufficient time in Pagasae so she could build a clientele. It was recom-mended that she should take her group (after their return from Skopelos) and seek residence in Lar-issa, the main inland city of Thessalia, with many a prospect and not far from the passes to Makedon.

Theoklimenos undertook to write an introductory letter to the leading Larissan family of Alevades, taking full responsibility for Evriklia's reception there, as he was guaranteeing Evriklia's trustworth-iness to them. Meantime Pantoleon was given a ship and an armed contingent of trusted Pagasaeans, `to bring the ransom for the rest of Evriklia's group to Gorgias and free them. Evriklia was given a modest house at the outskirts of Pagasae, to stay with Arsinoi and wait for the return of her freed retinue. They had the pleasant company of Theoklimenos and his friends, as often as they could spare the time to visit and had some relaxing time, rewarded by Evriklia with her charms, her poetry and exchanging news from the rest of Ellas and the known world.

Evriklia heard of Megara's continued grip of power by Plexarhos, who now was appointed Archon for life, of King Aeropos being still under Orestian and Elimiotian pressure and of Derriopis being the open gate to raids along with Pelagonia. Thessalia as a whole was rather quiet, but other city-states were getting ready for war, each vying for which one would be the 'protector' of the Oracle in Delfi . . .

By the time the hostages were freed and returned to Pagasae, it was the end of Apellaeos or, in Athi-nian, the month of Maemaktirion and the winter cold had already settled, promising a rather harsh time ahead. Due to this fact, it was arranged for Evriklia's group to stay in that same modest house just outside Pagasae, making do until next spring. At the same time, Theoklimenos and his friends would provide, in exchange of the good time and entertainment the wintry weather would permit.

The following winter months went by very slowly. There were a few good times in the company of the Pagasaean friends but, mostly, there were times of boredom and want of more space and comfort.

Xandikos was especially the month of oppression, as a late winter-early spring snow storm came down from mount Pilion, covering everything in white, ruining most of the almond trees (as they had their flower buds opened, fooled by the rather warm spell of Dystros, the previous month). Slowly, Xandikos (Elafivolion in Athinae) was finally gone and the first fortnight of Artemisios was occupied with the vigor of preparations and the air of spring.

A messenger was sent to the Alevades family in advance, returning from Larissa with the good news of Evriklia's acceptance there and extended hospitality for as long as she and her party wanted to stay. A final symposion was given to Theoklimenos and his friends and Evriklia went out of her way to show (with her girls) proper gratitude to their Pagasaean friends and benefactors. She was except-ionally moved when Theoklimenos told her that he and his friends—in gratitude of what she and her girls offered them—had the fair idea of granting her one full silver talent out of the four she had to re-pay them in due time, aside of the personal presents they were giving now as a token of good luck! Evriklia reciprocated by inviting each Pagasaean for a personal session in her private chamber. The-oklimenos was the very last and most time-spending visitor.

The very first day of Daesios, Evriklia and her party took the north-west road to Larissa . . .

Aeropos was not in a good mood. In fact, he had not been in a good mood since he took over the Makedonian throne. All his so-called friends proved to be his and Makedonia's worst enemies!

His old silent "I don't know what I don't see" passive participation on the events leading to Father's death, was enthroned heavily in his mind and heart and, regardless of many offerings at the altar, the dead was visiting Aeropos' dreams on a nightly basis, questioning.

Morale was low in his kingdom, in spite of the stability he managed to secure at his frontier (thanks to unblemished and steady support from land lords and clan heads of some prominent houses like A-gathon's, Olganos' and Agis'. They were the heart and body of Makedonian resistance when all seemed to have been lost. They were his delegates when peace was finally ratified! And yet, he knew he had done them wrong too.

Because of external support to his opponents from Korinthos, Potidaea, Megara and Athinae, his state was now more like a puppet state than an independent kingdom! The colonies established by Eretria and Halkis by the mouth of Aliakmon, controlling the approaches of the Pella lagoon and the gulf of Therma since the time of Perdikkas, were the dictators of his policies—as was seen fit with the ones from the southern city-states. Neither Perdikkas, Argeos nor Filippos were able to oust or put under their control these colonies of Pydna and Methoni, nor were the Anthemountians, Krousians and Sythones strong enough to resist colonies across the gulf and on their lands.

Macedonia's surplus in timber, meat and cereals was heading south at almost no profit for the royal treasury and causing the peasants to hide what they could, preferring their own secret bartering for goods of their need. All these difficulties were rendering him unable to pursue the interests of his state in a steady manner. Land lords had to support the keeping of troops out of their own, while asking the same peasants to tend the fields and herds, all at the same time. This way of running the state, was making the clan heads more independent than he would have liked them to be. Yet, he had no other choice.

He was obliged to marry (forced was a more accurate term) a couple of neighboring princesses, an act which tied his hands even more, as he found himself aligned to the whims of the kings from Tym-fea and Elimiotis. Aegae turned back in time before Perdikkas, becoming again a hamlet rather than the principal town of the kingdom. Most of Aeropos' subjects had return to transhumant pastoral-ism, making more difficult the collection of levies in produce or manpower.

Being only too well aware of all these difficulties, the rumor that a well known etera was on her way from Larissa, soon to arrive with her retinue at Aegae, was more than a puzzle to Aeropos. Was she sent by new agents wanting his utter demise and Macedonia's obliteration? What would a famous etera find in a backwater town like his? He inquired and learned she was from Pelagonia/Almopian roots, therefore Makedonian; she had learned her trade in Korinthos and Megara though. There was more fame and riches to be made in the south city-states than could even imagined up here in the stagnant Makedonian courts. She was also caught by pirates and freed thanks to Pagasaean generos-ity and Alevadian support for years in Larissa. Would she stay in Makedonia or this was just a stop on her way to . . . where? There was no answer to most of his questions . . .

She and her party arrived at Aegae without much of a fanfare. As a matter of fact, the only thing announcing her arrival was the occupation of the one property (aside the Royal quarters) which could stand to be called a house among the very modest dwellings of Aegae. The house had been purchased four years ago by the Larissan merchant Amfipator, used only during his rare visits there.

Aeropos felt great curiosity about the coming of such an etera but, as the King, he couldn't and wouldn't approach her, he could not see anyone of her escort either—for the same reason. He could ask one of his clan heads to do so and report back to him, but he considered even that beneath him. What brought a meeting between the King and the etera was the arrival of three delegations. One was from the city-state of Megara the other two were from the colonies of Methoni and Pydna. The Megarian delegation came to tell him that their state had claims of ownership on Evriklia and her whole retinue. The city wanted them back and the King ought to oust them from Makedonia. To his asking of details and reason behind their 'request', he got vague answers about ownership and state interests but nothing solid which would help him form an opinion. The other two delegations told him that they came in support of the Megarians, hinting severe blockade of the commerce, in case the King would decide against the Megarian 'request'.

Aeropos could smell a 'rotten fish' type of a deal between the delegations. Just because of their con-tact, he felt like denying them their 'request', yet—as the kingdom was in need of trade and they were holding the ports—he was in a very difficult position. Makedonia was not really interested in the affairs of an etera (regardless how famous) and the city-state of Megara. But to have the two-city col-onies threatening a blockade of commerce, that was a slap in his face! Aeropos was insulted and he knew he had to give-in, if for economic reasons only. He asked for a few days, to decide what to do, in hope of finding a way to save face and—most importantly—avert future threats or enactments of such blockades.

A message sent to him from Amfipator saved his pride and caused his meeting with Evriklia. He received Amfipator's messenger Melanippos, a well known and honest associate between the House of Timenos and the Thessalian house of Alevades. The man (after the customary niceties addressed to a King) came right down to business. He was sent by Amfipator with a letter to the King, explaining the reasons why Evriklia was asked to be returned to Megara and, in order to help prevent this in-justice, he was to deliver the sum of one hundred talents worth in silver and gold, so the King would be able to arm and threaten the two colonies by a siege from land. The King should not give-in to the Megarian demands or to threats from Pydna and Methoni. On the other hand—and just as a show of good intent—the King should feel free to decide what was best for Makedonia, keeping the brought wealth as a present sent by a true friend. He, Melanippos, along with Amfipator and the Alevades' family had served Thessalian and Makedonian interests faithfully for many years. The King did not need any proof for his trust in them now! All he had to do was to read the letter and decide! Melanip-pos would remain in court and assist when needed, for as long as the King saw it was necessary.

Aeropos read the letter and saw the whole story unfolding. He understood the implications if he would give-in, as well as if he would not. He spent a great deal of time conferring with Melanippos and, when they finished, Aeropos sent for Peridas from the house of Agis and Alexandros, from the house of Olganos. When they presented themselves before the King, he gave them his instructions. One was to visit the delegates from Methoni, the other those from Pydna, each independently and un-detected by the Megarians. They were to convince these delegates to accept the King's decision as it would be announced and depart for their cities the very following day. To help them make their obe-dience easy, Peridas and Alexandros would offer on behalf of the King half a silver talent to each member, one whole silver talent to the leader of each delegation. Time was of essence and Alexandros with Peridas were to report back before the evening's royal banquet for the delegations.

The festivities of the symposion/banquet started in a very good mood. The delegations appeared to be sure of the outcome on the negotiations and the King was more pleasant than ever with his comments. Aeropos had good reason for that. His newfound power with the silver and gold, had bought him the support of Pydna and Methoni, as seen by Peridas and Alexandros. Food and drinks were provided with abundance, a very pleasant surprise to all foreigners, who were expecting much less. The topics of conversation varied, the King relishing his time, the guests showing their due respect and waiting for his announcement for Evriklia's fate. They talked about Solon, returning to Athinae from his exile as its premier Archon and the rumors of a new power in Asia, the Mides.

It was about the time of conversation on these Mides, when the Megarian chief delegate, a relative of the great Tyranos archon Theagenis (who lived at the time of Argeos), made his blunder. Androk-lis, the son of Theognidis and grand nephew of Theagenis, boasted that Megara was not much con—cerned of the aggression and moves in Asia by kings, whether they were called Mides, Egyptians, or any other name! Megara with its assembly of intellects, its Archon, the vigor of mercantile innovation and its strong fleet carrying oplites ready to fight anywhere, could outwit and outmatch any nation under the bridle of a king.

The name of Aeropos may have not been mentioned by Androklis, but everyone knew that the Mak-edonian King was the sole leader in charge of his kingdom with powers far exceeding those of a Meg-arian Archon or a group of them. The insult, for that was exactly the term of Androklis' words, and the attempt of the Megarian to publicly degrade the Makedonian King to the barbarian level of Asia-tics, brought silence in the room. Intimidation could be privately pressed forward from a delegation leader, perhaps, but never before an audience and at a banquet.

Aeropos stopped his private conversation he had with Melanippos at his left by the head of the hall and turned to Androklis (seated at the King's right with the head delegates of Methoni and Pydna—as honored guests) with a smile. One, who knew Aeropos best, knew this smile was deadlier than a bite of an adder and there were many who held their breath. Aeropos rose from his couch and asked for the attention of all guests. He said that all serious conversation had to end, for this night and sympo-sion was dedicated to god Dionyssos and entertainment! As such, he had seen to inviting none other than the famous etera who recently had come to grace Aegae with her beauty and spirit, Evriklia!

She entered the hall, the Megarian delegates half-arisen from their couches in total bewilderment. Her presence was like one of a goddess in all her beauty and simplicity of attire. Evriklia walked in, escorted by Arsinoi and Myrsini, as her attendants. She greeted with utmost respect and grace, the King first, then Melanippos, the delegates from Pydna and Methoni, leaving the Megarians for last.

The King asked (some later said he ordered) the Megarians to move to couches further down the hall, to make room for the famous etera to sit next to him. The insult (open enough) was taken by Androklis with a hardly veiled discomfort and he voiced his displeasure. The King stopped Andro-klis' protest with a move of his hand and said that he had just come to the decision of hearing her side of the story the following morning, before passing a judgment. It was only fair, he continued, as an Ellinas King, to grand equal time to both parties in hearing their request. He called upon Andro-klis' own words on the difference between barbarian Mides ruled by an oppressing ruler and Ellenic custom of hearing before passing judgment. Of course, as free delegates of a sovereign and esteemed city-state, Aeropos concluded, the Megarian delegation could reject his fairness and depart the next morning, escorted in safety up to the kingdom's borders.

At this point, both chief delegates from Methoni and Pydna rose and asked for permission to talk. That granted, they stated that they appreciated the King's fairness and his sense of justice. They believed, they said, that his judgment would be respected by their city-states and they needed no further assurances, no matter what the outcome. They concluded by saying that urgent state matters would force them to depart the next day, not waiting for the verdict upon the Megarian request. Their trust was with the King! Aeropos accepted and thanked them, a smile of satisfaction painted on his face.

This was a strike too many for Androklis, the mouths of his co-delegates open in shock from his next move. Forgetting his place as ambassador and in open contempt, he fully rose from his couch and threatened severe punishment to Makedonia, in case the King's decree was unfavorable to Megarian interests! The affront was more than obvious and a deadly silence fell into the hall. Many Makedon-ian lords rose, ready to strike. Aeropos looked at Androklis sternly and, to the surprise of all the guests, politely excused him from the King's presence. The rest of the Megarian delegates through Theagnos—as their senior now—addressed the King, humbly begging his excuse of them from their colleague's inappropriate behavior. Aeropos extended his pleasure for their continuous presence at the symposion and, before long, things looked like coming back to normal, mainly thanks to the ani-mated presence of Evriklia, with the aid of Myrsini.

Pantoleon heard of the confrontation between the King and the Megarian, as Peridas reported soon after, while in the anteroom of the great hall with Diogenis and other (escorting the guests) servants.

As things returned to normal, he found an excuse to slip-out unobserved and headed for Androklis' lodgings . . .

The next morning Androklis was found dead in his bed, his throat sliced open. The King summoned all the delegates immediately in the audience hall and proclaimed his regret for the untimely demise of the Megarian, insisting that had Androklis keep his wits and depart under escort—as the rest of them did at the symposion's end—such a regretful deed would not have taken place by the hands of an apparent brigand who, somehow, managed to enter Androklis' room! The King proclaimed that the guilty party would be found and brought to justice soon, offering his sympathy to the remaining Megarian delegation. Each one of them (in turn) went out of his way in assuring the King their un-derstanding of his outrage at the killer of an official ambassador and that they gratefully accepted his lavish presents on behalf of the victim's family. They would carry Androklis' body back home, for a proper burial, as soon as the King would provide them his judgment on Megara's request.

Aeropos informed the delegations that Evriklia was to stay in Makedonia as long as she wished, his judgment being a final one. The Pydneans and Methonians thanked the King for his hospitality and his generosity, renewing their faith in his judgments. The Megarians apologized again for their chief delegate's misbehavior, taking his body back home. Megara was (for the time being) now isolated and could take its pride, like a punished dog does its tail. Aeropos, then, ordered a numerous armed escort for the three city-state delegations (he could afford such extravagance now with the Thessal-ian aid). One escort brought the Megarians to the port by Aloros, the other two escorted the Pydnean and Methonian delegations up to their city gates, as a reminder that, along with the payment gift, there was power to be remembered and respected.

The King had many more meetings with Evriklia after that event. Megara never ceased looking for a chance of revenge, succeeding in the eventual blockage of all ports and all Makedonian entrances at the Olympian and Pythian competitions, for many years.

By the time of Aeropos' death (close to twenty years after this event), his relationship with Evriklia grew to a mutual respect and friendship (at first), followed by deep love and dependence on each-other's company. It would not be a lie if one stated that Aeropos recovered in many a way the respect of all his subjects (and foes alike), thanks to the influence of Evriklia, her contacts with other city-state men of importance and, for a good part, the money she could raise (almost at will) for Makedo-nia, during frequent visits in Thessalia and elsewhere.

Aeropos had several offspring in his life. A son from his first wife and heir to the throne named Al-ketas, two daughters from his second wife, married to princes from Elimiotis and Eordea and, three sons from Evriklia. The latter grew-up to become heads of their own clan and land lords of the realm. The eldest was Ptolemeos-Filippos, then, was Dimitrios (in memory of Evriklia's adopted father) and the third son was Apellas. The King's kingdom re-established its prestige among others, although its borders remained vulnerable and confined. There was a firm hold of Pieria and Imathia, improved relations with Elimiotis and Tymfea and friendship with the Thessalian Larissa and Far-salos. These two Thessalian powers could now turn their attention to stopping any further Thivaean attempts to enlarge its influence from Viottia to Thessalia and received Aeropos' cavalry support.

From the day of Ptolemeos-Filippos' birth on and until his last day of Aeropos as King, the late King Filippos' spirit ceased its visits in his son's dreams. The day Aeropos died—the last one in the Makedonian month of Apellaeos (Maemaktirion in Athinae)—Alketas had turned his first plus two times tenth birth date and capable of taking the kingdom under his control. Evriklia outlived her King for almost one more month. She died happy, in the house of her youngest son, surrounded by her family and friends. Pantoleon was wedded to Myrsini and given a good plot of earth while Aero-pos still alive, near the village of Dolihi, by the Elimiotis/ Thessalia borders. Diogenis had moved with his own family to an estate by the sea, becoming a rather successful merchant. Old Arsinoi was (by then) gone and buried in a simple grave at the banks of Aliakmon, according to her wish. As for Plex-arhos, the Archon-for-life of Megara, no record has ever been found in that city-state about his exist-ance, either as Archon or as a common citizen . . .

Alketas was (thankfully) more than ready to take over his Father's realm and duties as the Makedo-nian King. Although his literacy was rather neglected, his other education as an heir to the throne was perfect! His best friends and supporters were Kleanthis son of Peridas, Ilaos son of Alexandros, Evryopos son of Pantoleon and Nestor, son of Diogenis. Next were the scions of houses like Klitos', Perseas son of Nikanor and, from house of Agathon, Antilohos. His own half-brothers were like a twin shadow wherever he went. Ptolemeos-Filippos and Dimitrios were Alketas' younger by four and by seven years, while Kleanthis was three and Ilaos two years older. They all had spent many a day and night forming this inner circle, sitting close to their fathers and 'uncles' and listening to stories of long and short campaigns by the house hearth, or, during their own hunts and their own campaigns, when old enough to do so. Their favored stories from youth were the ones told by Peridas, Alexan-dros and Pantoleon, which took place in Egyptos—as the three had gone there with many others from all Ellas, paid as hired oplites in the armies of king Psamitihos, Farao-king of all Egyptos.

The younger brood imitated actual and imaginary battles fought in the great desert, dreamed of the Mysterious Sfinx, thought of carving their own names on Egyptian monuments like their Fathers and 'uncles' did and, saw before the eyes of their imagination the armies of Navouhodonosor (the grown-ups pronounced that king's name differently) taking the tribe of Yesrael (Israil?) to distant Vavylo-na, as their slaves.

Alketas and his intimate friends came to fight their own, actual battles, against the resurgent power of Peonia—until it run out of steam before Anthimous and Vottiki—and against Megarian and Athin-ian expeditions on Aloros and Dion.

Alketas was married already before his Father's death, to a princess from Lynkos, the great-grand-niece of king Pafsanias—and she gave him a son. The new heir to the Makedonian throne was named Amyntas. He grew, like his Father, forming his own circle of friends and favorites, the sons of Ptolemeos-Filippos Kleodeos and Amyntas (also called Amyntas Mirakios or Mirakion—the lesser), Aeropos and Karanos sons of Dimitrios, Perdikkas and Aristodamas sons of Apellas, Ifanor, Lampos and Kinos from the house of Pallas, Leonidas, Alketas the Short and Attalos from the house of Agis, Parmenion and Attalos the Lean sons of Evryopos and, Nikanor son of Nestor.

The future of the Makedonian kingdom, although far from being a secured one, seemed to be in ca-pable and steady hands, hands of men who had only one thought in mind: Makedonian power recog-nition from all other states and due respect by them to its King! But the southern city-states, the Illy-rians, Peonians, Thrakians and even the Asiatic High Kings, had other intentions, far from being suitable to Makedonia, or to any other city-state for that matter!

> "Any modern Nation which could spring out of the ancient
> Greeks (Ellines) would automatically be unfortunate!
> Unless, it could forget past history of disunity altogether or
> surpass old glories by far! Modern Greeks have done none
> of the two, hence their inability to thrive!..."
> Adan Gregoresku - Romanian

V

It was a very early-spring day. The cold from the high Pindos range could penetrate the double lay-er of furs the man had on top of a coarse homespun sheep-wool undershirt and he knew that even if he had more layers of clothing, the cold dampness would still make him feel the harsh weather, espe-cially when the wind blew in sudden gusts.

Light snow had fallen the night before, a night he had to spend on the move, getting to the pass where he hoped he would find a shelter and some game. Deer, wild goats and fowl seemed to favor and congre-gate at that pass, probably because Eordaikos (Ordak in the Dexarian -as well as Der-riopian and Dassaretian lingo) ceased running its water fast, making a smooth and wide turn to the south-west. The turn of the river and the unusually wide space between the mountain slopes on both sides, creat-ed room for the water in a combination of river/lake proportion and ample space for high grass, reeds and then, trees. The animals liked going there, able to find food and shelter, protected some-what by the rocky slopes of Petrion, before both river and mountain rolled down toward lake Lyh-nitis to the flow's right.

Toward the south, the forested peaks of the Pindos range lead to the slopes of Voion, the one which resembles the outline of a cow -when looked through the distant haze. That is a disputed area among the tribes and clans of Haonia, Dassaretis, Derriopia, and, of course, his own tribe the Dexares. He had no mind in approaching that area.

There had been a very long war, almost nine consecutive summers, between Ipirotes Haones and Makedones, Dassaretians as well as Derriopes and Dexares. Raids from Parthines, Atintanes, Vryges and other Illyrian tribes (not excluding even the Dardanes), added to the confusion and conflict in the region. Old feuds did nothing but add to the fire for need of land, food and living space. The man, Attal, knew all about these, having first-hand experience -on top of the traditional 'schooling' by the family and tribal horror stories.

The trouble with his tribe was that their blood was all mixed-up! They were feeling as much Dexa-res as Dassaretians, Makedonians or Derriopes or Vryges! His own name was a prime example. Which was its right root? What of its original pronunciation? In Vrygian was Ottal, accent given on the o, the sound of l being long. In Derriopian, being closer to Haonian-Ipirotic his name was pro-nounced Attal, its accent falling on the last a. In Makedono-Dassaretian, they added an ending in s and brought the name's accent on its first a, making it Attalos!

What was more confusing, the linguistic differences on the root of the name were zero, compared to and against blood ties and pressures to lead or follow the ebb of military fortunes during lean years, supplemented by extra hard winters and relentless heat during summers.

The gods, seemed to have forgotten to look with any measure of favor at this corner of the land. Arable land parcels were rare and the snows and rain were seldom coming in such a time as to favor the produce. The migration of animals, according to weather patterns, made hunting painful -if not totally unsuccessful. When bears, wolves, lynxes and mountain lions were added, a human hunter had more than a burden in gaining the upper hand...

This past winter, Attal remembered, was exceptionally harsh. Famine had settled for its most part, bringing sickness and death. It was not only because the passes and possible hunting grounds were closed by the snow. But the summer preceding last winter was the driest a memory could recall! Even the fast running Eordaikos had turned to a dry bed with scant pools of dirty water. Lack of water brought lack of fresh shoots of plants, which brought lack of herbivores, which left the carnivores in an almost total starvation!

Because of that, humans were the ones to experience harder times. Many died during that winter and the number of human losses increased toward the end of the season. With warmer weather, snows melted fast, creating flood zones in many areas. That brought illness from stagnant waters and less arable land, less game, more loss of domestic animals to starving predators and humans alike. The tribe was decimated.

Many elders convinced the chiefs to ask for an accelerated rate of births from the clans but, that meant more mouths in need of being fed, from an area depleted of most of its resources. When death would not balance the loss with birth, when competition for food would turn the odds against the tribe, when war would decimate even more and weather threatened the remaining few, the salvation seemed to be only the stealing away from the more fortunate, from neighbors or distant tribes and make a run...

Attal prayed for this spring to be a mild one, with no more sudden floods. One which could bring the green into the few valleys, the animals back and keep the northern tribes content in their areas or, lacking that, direct them to the east or west of his tribe. He also prayed that Makedonian kings were not geared after revenge because of last year's raid.

There were so many questions to be answered, so many tasks to be fulfilled and much pain ahead for a tribe with great needs but no resources! His head was spinning at times like this one, immersed as he was in his concern about his tribe's future. He stopped his walk ahead of his horse, which he had dismounted a short while ago and looked around. He was better than half way into the pass and he thought the hour was getting late. He may have to spend the night looking forward to the next day, in order to find some game to bring back. There were no footprints of any animal on the fresh snow -as far as he could see. The thought disturbed him. Would this be another day with no meat to feed the children and the old ones?

Attal saw the stag emerging from the high wild-rose bushes which formed a barrier of some length before the forest ahead and to his right. The deer jumped over them and stood still, scenting the air. He hastily placed, aimed and threw an arrow, the moment the stag had picked-up his scent and ran like the wind around some boulders ahead. The arrow missed and, striking one of the boulders, broke in two. Attal let a curse out of his mouth. He'd better concentrate on hunting instead of day-dreaming the 'ifs' of life! He had four wives and nine kids to feed, none older than seven springs old!

And it wasn't his immediate family that was his sole concern. There were the elders and other young ones at the village, there were the other adults who went out hunting. It would be a great shame to return empty handed. Such an unthinkable event would give rise to suspicion and rumors of his inability to provide -therefore to lead! There were a considerable number of 'young bloods' waiting for any op-portunity to challenge him and try to grab the lead of his tribe.

Attal was not an old man (by any means) himself. He barely made two times ten plus four years in his eventful life, not all completed yet -until the end of the next moon. With such hard life conditions though, any man aged three times ten was a lucky old-timer, one whom death had passed unnoticed and left him to taste more hardship. He let a deep sigh escape his mouth, forming a small cloud of moisture in the cold air. He noticed the move of his breath's vapors. The light wind had changed its direction, bringing the vapors behind him. The breathing of his horse following him, gave a better perspective of this change. Good! His scent would not be picked by any game ahead.

He took the two bundles tied with rope and hanging on each side of his horse's neck. One, a flask made out of reversed sheep-skin, had fermented goat milk. The other, weaved sheep-wool, contained his meager meals for the duration of his hunt. He drunk thirstily from the first and took a mouthful from the second. Attal hung the two bundles back on his horse's neck and pulled the quiver over his shoulder. He had six good arrows left and five used ones and retrieved, but unfit for another try be-fore repair. He resumed his march forward.

This time he spotted his game first, as it was coming out of a cluster of chestnut trees at the top of the next slope. Attal stood motionless, forcing his horse to do the same. Vapor coming out of his mouth assured him the wind was in his favor. The enormous stag stood at the crest of the slope be-fore the trees checking in all directions, scenting the air. Detecting no danger it started coming down, toward the river. Slowly, a second deer appeared and followed, then, several more. Attal counted several female (some ready to give birth, any day now) and three more younger stags. The deer con-tinued their descent cautiously, toward the river. Attal stood still, waiting for the right moment. It soon presented itself. As the deer approached the river bank, he got obscured from their vision by a number of big rocks between them and where he was standing. He acted with great speed. Let his horse with a soothing motion of his hand for it to stand and he ran behind the biggest rock, an arrow placed on the bow and another held by his teeth.

Attal took a cautious look from his hiding. The lead stag was standing guard looking around for any danger. The other deer were drinking water. Attal waited until the stag turned his attention the opposite way. He jumped from behind his rock and his arrow pierced the animal's heart. By the time the other deer raised their heads up, a second arrow had left to find its target in the body of a second stag. It stood motionless in mid-step for a long moment, wondering perhaps what caused the dimness of light in its eyes (do stags wonder?-Attal thought), before dropping its dead weight on the ground. The other deer scattered in an instant, some jumping into the river and letting the current carry them off.

Attal drew a long knife from his belt and worked fast, slicing-up his victims' bellies and taking their entrails out, food for the carrion eaters. He then retrieved his arrows (economy comes as a second nature to the ones with hardship) and dragged his trophies to his horse. The day was saved. He would return to the village with enough food to feed his family for a few days and the second stag would be his present to the rest of the village. He sat down and started the process of skinning and cutting the animals. He would load them on his horse and return to his people before nightfall. He wished the other hunters had also good luck, hunting as teams or alone.

The others, namely the team of Gerak and numbering ten men total, had lay in ambush for a wild boar hunt. Most of them, after making a wide semi-circle were bush-beaters and noise-makers, to drive the animal (if a wild boar was hiding in the area) toward the four of them waiting at prear-ranged spots, near animal paths, paths which their bush-beaters would force the boar (or any other game) to follow. Gerak and three of the best available javelin-throwers and archers were crouched behind rocks or perched on trees, waiting.

The voices and noise of those driving the game to the ambush points, could be heard in the distance, getting louder -as they were coming closer. Soon, everyone got busy throwing javelins and arrows at their victims. Very few animals were lucky or fast enough to escape. The slaughter stopped as abruptly as it started. A clean-up followed, fast and efficient. The cut meat loaded and the group started their journey back to the village. Gerak was particularly happy with their harvest. Perhaps he could challenge Attal's ability to provide, although the latter had the excuse of hunting alone. Unless, Attal would come home empty handed…

Around nightfall they were approaching the village when they first smelled the smoke (distinguish-ing it later as a darker shade rising in an almost dark sky), among glimpses of rising and decreasing light coming obviously from a fire source. In spite their load of dead animals, they all picked-up their pace to almost a run. Passing the last edge of a hill before the village, the full disaster hit Gerak and his men like a bolt of lightning, forcing them to stop dead on their tracks.

All the makeshift huts of the village were spewing the last whiffs of thick smoke, the last flames ready to extinguish themselves for lack of more material to burn. One lone figure was seeing running like crazy among the fires, trying to put them out, among strewn bodies of people, domestic animals, all laying down with an occasional arrow or javelin protruding from their bodies, pinned on earth, an earth with newly acquired dark colors from bloodied and burned objects!

Gerak and his team came to their senses and, dropping down the hard-won game, ran to help the lone figure with his task. Attal was all covered with dried blood and soot, his tunic burned and torn and trying to find who had possibly escaped death. Every-so-often a sob and a sound of utter agony came out from the depths of his chest, without slowing him down in his search for survivors. Gerak, with help from his team, was finally able to force Attal to stop. There was nothing he could do alone.

They would take over and see what could be done, what could be found, collectively. For now, they all stood there, cloudy eyes looking but not seeing, minds registering but unable to fathom! One by one and, some, in twos or threes, other hunting parties started returning. With faces bewildered, men bereft from loved ones, gathered together, unable to understand, not ready yet to accept and lament!

New snow started falling on the ground, as if nature wanted to cover every transgression. Very few survivors were found by the returning hunters and these were taken care of as best as possible. Then, they gathered in small groups, destined to spend the night together commiserating with each-other's loss.

Attal agreed with Gerak's suggestion (no thoughts now for leadership fight in mind) that 'things' would mainly have to wait until the next morning. In his search among the victims, Attal recognized the burned bodies of three of his wives, while the fourth was missing -along with the kids. There was some remote hope that they perhaps had escaped, but a very slim one. Tracks were not found of them and the night with the new snow falling, would not allow any further research.

The gathered groups lit small fires with debris from the burned village and ate mechanically some of the game they brought, because nature is stronger than grief. The fresh snow was not enough to cover completely the carnage. Instead, it got dirty from the soot and the blood, increasing the smell of devastation, the ugly facts of loss and death slowly registering in the minds of the survivors, reenforc-ed by the whimper and groan of the wounded. Dawn found them all as they had huddled together, like none had made a move.

The morning rays of a weak sun rising from the eastern peaks, stirred some life in the burned vil-lage and they took care of some more of the wounded asking questions but getting few answers. They cleaned-up some space and piled-up some wood for the killed and the half-burned bodies. No clue was found as to who the enemy was. Some of the 'lucky' wounded ones talked, of a strong force of warriors coming and going in and out of the village like the wind of the furies, but no distinct armor was detected to tell a tale.

When all was set for the pyre, the last invocation to the underworld gods was offered by Attal, as-sisted (as he went) by Gerak and the other surviving clan heads. They all numbered now a total of eight times ten plus three, out of a good-sized village of seven times ten plus times ten that, of male adults only and not counting the elders or the women and children. When the invocation ended, Attal threw a lit torch on the pile of wood under the dead bodies, followed by the torches of the other survivors. The flames soon rose toward the sky, emitting a whitish smoke and sweet odor, indicative of a favor-able acceptance of the victims by the gods of the dark...

While the pyre was still burning, a limping figure of a man came out of the south side of the forest beyond the village, approaching. The first to notice this man was Gerak. Not knowing who that was, he drew his sword and charged toward the limping man, giving a warning shout to his comrades. Everybody followed, grabbing their javelins, swords or bows, ready to support Gerak. They soon dis-covered that the limping man was none other than old Dimash, a veteran of many wars and raids and the oldest living -but still full of strength (by their life's standards)- member of this village. He was badly wounded on his left thigh and a broken arrow could be seen at the base of his neck, by his right shoulder. Blood had clotted almost solid on that wound, letting a trickle of fresh blood come out each time he turned his head to answer questions addressed to him from all directions and all at once.

As they all knew, he was left in charge of some other semi-active elders and untrained youth, keep-ing order and safety for their village. He held his left hand up (with difficulty) to make all of them stop asking questions which could not be answered in one word. Attal and Gerak growled an order to that effect and the crowd calmed-down somewhat, waiting for the old man's report.

He took several painful breaths himself, before Dimash started his narration. The enemy, Makedo-nians from Lynkos with aid and guidance of Pelagones, attacked the village about mid morning the day before. They had arrived undetected from quarters no one would expect and too early in the year for such a scale of attack! He fought them until he saw there was no hope left. Most of the vil-lagers were already dead and the place up in flames! He was twice wounded and pretended to be dead. When the enemy was done with the village and moved out, he headed for the woods in hope of finding a hunting party to bring the sorrowful news. Having lots of blood lost, he passed out for a long time. Thus, he was unable to find anyone. As he came back to his senses a while ago, he noticed the smoke from the pyre. Realizing his countrymen were giving a funeral to the victims, he came out of the forest and so, there he was!

Telling his story, tears ran down his face and his voice would crack several times. At one point, out of pain for the loss and weakness from his wounds, he couldn't hold and fell on the ground before anyone was fast enough to give him support. He was ashamed to still be alive but relieved that at least some had escaped by luck and they all grieved now together.

Answering further questions Dimash told them that Gerak's family was all lost, burned in their hut. Attal's fourth wife was seen taking off into the forest on a north-west direction, presumably toward the lake Lyhnitis region and followed by his children. It soon became apparent that the old man was badly in need of immediate care. His words started slurring coming out of his mouth and his thigh and neck wounds reopened and started bleeding again. They took him aside and started cleaning his wounds.

Enmity against Lynkestis and Pelagonia ran high among the survivors. Knowing that nothing could be done against them for the time being, Attal ordered care to be given to all wounded survivors while he, Gerak and three or four other leaders from the hunting parties went by the side to hold a council.

A decision was made that small groups, thus hard to be detected by the enemy, were to run or ride to other villages and camps, see what -if any- damage was done to them and warn the ones who knew nothing about the Lynkestian raid. The same groups were to call on the leaders of those safe camps to speedily mobilize and, leaving a leader of proven experience and valor to guard each camp, con-verge at this village for a general meeting for action to be taken.

The search for his remaining family was given by Attal to three of the youngest in the group, known for their speed and stamina. He, in charge of another small group, rode in search of the last known location of the nearest camp. All available others were assigned to go in different directions as two leaders were ordered to remain with their men and clean the village from the debris while keeping in readiness -in case more survivors would return or the enemy would reappear.

Transhuman ecology due to life's necessities and conditions had the tribal clans living in small camps rather than villages like the one where Attal lived. That made the task of the searching groups harder, for it was well known that any such camp could fold and move in no time, depending on game availability and weather conditions in its area, solely decided by its clan head and camp leader.

Obviously under these conditions, the searching parties for camps and possible survivors had mixed results. Attal found the next camp in about the same condition as his village. Others found out that some camps and villages had received ample warning and moved -unknown where. Many other camps to the north and north-east were completely annihilated!

Contact with the Vryges, indicated that the Lynkestians were heading back to their kingdom, as were their Pelagonian guides.

Attal had to wait for people to calm down first and then seek him instead. On a more personal basis, he was happy to hear that his fourth wife was found with all his children alive, albeit hungry and scared. They were on their way back to the village. He put all his effort in rebuilding, thinking of the coming gathering of chieftains and the storm which would follow.

His anguish and anger continued unabated, for he had made a treaty in person with the Lynkestian king Lampos, only five years past. The last big raid of his tribe against Lynkos had taken place a year prior to that treaty, because there was no other way. Tavlantes, Vryges and Atintanes had unit-ed under the Tavlantian banner and raided Dassaretis, Derriopis and Lynkestis, through the lands of his tribe. For Attal and his Dexares, that time was: join the raid or suffer the consequences. The king understood such obligation, Lampos being a veteran of raids and campaigns himself, agreed to a treaty after things had returned to 'normal'. But Lampos was dead and his son Mahaon was now king of Lynkos for the last three years. Mahaon was against the treaty from the very beginning, refusing to head the delegation -as his father's ambassador- by sending one of his juniors to do the job (he could not totally disregard his Father and king's request).

Now Mahaon was taking revenge for a few small raids which Attal had specifically directed in Pela-gonian lands, because of absolute necessity and with care to have human loss at a lowest possible rate. The king of Lynkos had eyes on gaining Makedonian recognition -now that the Timenid state was somewhat unstable- and control Pelagonia and Almopia, thus considering the loss of some sheep, cattle and goats this past fall as a major offence to his majesty, one in need of revenge in the most severe way! Well! If war was what Mahaon was after, Attal thought, war would be given now to the Lynkestians!

The tribe chiefs' gathering was very animated, as Attal had foreseen. He was accused by many of lack of foresight and direction. They had forgotten how happy they were driving Pelagonian cattle to their homes at the time of famine last fall. To some extent, Attal could not blame them. His tribe had taken a severe blow, from which recovery was to be a very slow process -if any. On the other hand, he was sure that any of his chiefs and clan heads would not have fared any better. They were simply looking for a scapegoat and to take the lead of his people away from him.

He found unexpected support from Gerak, old Dimash and, through them, from few other chiefs. After a long debate, it was decided that Attal should remain the Chief, given one more chance to avenge the loss and mend the tribe.

Attal worked a plan of attack against Lynkos and Pelagonia. He concluded that he would go in person and ask for help from the Tavlant, Penesht, the Vrygs, even from the Dardan tribes! What loot they could carry from Lynkestis and Pelagonia could be all theirs, as long as his tribe would come to inherit the lands conquered. Obviously, they would have to attack through Dassaretis or Derriopia (or both). But, again, Lynkestes and Pelagones did the same, as they came to kill his people! He was sure that, with enough pressure, both Derriopis and Dassaretis would possibly join in. If not, well, they could also become victims of his combined alliance.

As for support to Lynkestis and Pelagonia from other upper Makedonia kingdoms, Attal was well aware of Orestian animosity toward Lynkos on account of supremacy disputes on Eordea and Al-mopia. Makedonia, meaning the Timenid state, was rather weak yet because of earlier losses due to Aeropos' folly, which meant Aeropos' son Alketas (the Makedonian King now) would remain an observer, ready to gain when all was said and done -unless Elimiotis and Tymfea would have other thoughts. The Makedonian tribe being fragmented in so many rival kingdoms should be an easy target to hit.

Attal was sure his plan would succeed -once put in motion. The war needed preparation and they all decided to start at once. Special envoys were sent to the chiefs of several Illyrian tribes, asking for help, starting the hostilities at the end of summer, when Lynkestis would expect that all was secured and having enough time to do the damage before winter would set-in. Attal's logic behind such late schedule was the element of surprise and the reasoning that -if Lynkos could attack them so early in the spring- they could return the favor and attack late in the summer.

A merchant from the city-state of Mytilini on the island of Lesvos had just arrived at Aegae. He stopped at the obligatory port of Methoni first, to pay his passage into the lagoon of Pella and then, load a number of barges up the Aliakmon. He unloaded his wares and reloaded on mules and donkeys next, for the short trip from the river to Aegae. This was going to be his last trip before the fall winds' change, making his return almost impossible.

Selling his wares, he had to hand to Methonian authorities three Halkidian silver staters -for every ten he would profit. He spent almost a whole day at the gates of the city, as customs officers super-vised their clerks counting and evaluating his merchandise. The procedure would be repeated when he would be ready to leave. Methoni was tightening a noose around his neck!

When he finally arrived at Aegae, he sought and received audience with the King. He complained to Alketas that such extravagant demands from a free trader were the cause of the reluctance by most merchants to take the trouble to come to Makedonia! The King ought to apply pressure on the Me-thonian authorities and tell those greedy bastards to let go some of their demands!

Alketas was well aware of the taxes the colony and city-state of Methoni was demanding for passage from every trader coming by the sea. But Methoni could support the demands with blockade of the lagoon, thanks to a powerful fleet and help from its 'parent' city-states of Halkis and Eretria. Added to that, the King was also well aware of the defenses of Methoni. Aside the city walls, there was its acropolis fortress and Makedonia had no siege army or equipment. Even if he were to isolate the city by land, the sea was always open to the fleets from Eretria and Halkis. His treasury was almost at the point of being empty, since exports to the south were taxed when by sea and mostly lost to bandits when by land through the passes to Thessalia and beyond. He promised the merchant he would try to negotiate more favorable terms with Methoni (no sense to try fooling the Mytilinian who knew the Makedonian weakness in arms too well).

Efstratos, the Mytilinian merchant, thanked the King for his interest and concern on the subject, expressing hope for a near future 'righting the wrongs' done to free enterprise and presented him with a gift of two triptyha, the thrice folded wooden contraption, on which wax was applied for writing what one wanted to have another read. In this case, the two triptyha were containing poems written by two new Lesvian poets who were rapidly becoming famous for the power of their compos-itions. The King thanked Efstratos for his kindness and returned the favor by inviting him at the court for dinner and a reading of these poems by the court's bard that same evening. He also prom-ised to Efstratos a most welcomed reception at the market, so his profit would exceed the taxation demands of Methoni by far.

Instead of reading poems that night, a war council was called by the King. All available land lords and clan heads were summoned at the audience hall. A messenger with a small escort had arrived from Lynkestis, asking for help! A strong invading body of Illyrians had invaded and put to waste most of Pelagonia, now advancing into Lynkestis! It consisted of Tavlantes, Penestes, Dexares and Vryges. The Tavlantians were the most numerous but the leadership was in the hands of the Dexa-rian Chief, Attalos.

The messenger gave the whole story as it occurred. Last spring, king Mahaon -with aid from Pela-gonia- raided the Dexares in retaliation of some previous Dexarian incursions resulting in loss of livestock and produce. His retaliation being successful, Mahaon thought the lesson was taught and, a quiet summer with exceptional good harvest seemed to be what he expected. This late in the season invasion from the Illyrian tribes got everyone by surprise! Not only Lynkos and Pelagonia had been relaxed and unprepared, they were losing human life and provisions badly needed to pass the com-ing winter with a relative ease. The House of Timenos through its Makedonian King was now asked to help. Would that happen? The messenger wanted to know. He also informed that another mes-senger was sent to Orestis and Elimiotis but there was not much hope either would help. Lynkos de-pended on House Timenos, recognizing its preeminence in whole Makedonia!

King Alketas did not promise anything after he listened to this messenger's plea. Instead, he asked a few questions of his own. Were this messenger and his escort empowered by king Mahaon to negoti-ate a formal treaty? Were the other messengers and their escort to Orestis and Elimiotis also empow-ered to agree a formal treaty with those kings? If the answer to the first question or to both was yes, were they ready to do so? What kind of actual recognition was king Mahaon willing to offer in ex-change?

The messenger was obviously in a bind. He admitted he had no power to negotiate any treaty, nor did anyone of his escort. They were just messengers, asking for help, counting on Makedonian sol-idarity and support! Personally, he was just a minor clan head sent to beg for assistance. All major land holders and clan heads were with the king on the front line, with all resources available to countermand the invaders. Wouldn't Makedon be magnanimous and lend a helping hand?

Alketas excused the messenger, to discuss the issue with his land lords and clan heads. He called for the messenger not long after and his answer to king Mahaon was rather harsh. Deep in his heart, Al-ketas was suffering and he was feeling for the loss of other Makedonians. He thought he had to teach a painful lesson to Lynkestis and Mahaon though, for all the past enmity and disrespect Lynkos had shown to House Timenos. Keeping a cool profile, he responded to the Lynkestian messenger saying that Timenid Makedonia could not afford being called the Makedon from minor kings only when they were in dire need, then being ignored and disrespected, even attacked openly -when such danger is gone.

Alketas was referring to the role Lynkestis had played at the early days of his father, Aeropos, as King, as well as on his Grand Father's death. He instructed the messenger to go back with his escort and, either empower themselves with authority to negotiate or, king Mahaon should come in person and ask for help! Obviously, Mahaon had the option to deal with the invaders on his own, or hope to get Orestis and Elimiotis on his side.

The messenger, Lahon son of Pefkias, let his head drop in shame and anger. He was a very strong believer of Lynkestian preeminence in Makedonian affairs and this mission was a thorn in his heart. But he had his orders to obey, Lynkos was in dire need of help and, he could see the King's reasons to be cool. Lahon was a page attached to Lynkestian notables and saw the death of Filippos. He knew of the scheming from Elimiotis and the Lynkestian involvement. What hurt him most was the fact that he was, at the moment, powerless to do anything at all. He asked for night quarters to rest his men and horses. They would leave at dawn for Lynkos. Alketas offered the traditional Makedonian hospitality and the meeting was ended.

As the messenger withdrew to the given quarters, Alketas asked his land lords present to see that a discreet guard would be placed outside the Lynkestian delegation's quarters at once. He did not have in mind running a risk of being assassinated in the middle of the night. The following morning, he said, armed escort should be given until the Lynkestians crossed the border and were gone. Mean-time, he and all available land lords and clan heads would convene to work and see how they could have troops in readiness and, eventually, cross through Eordea and Almopia and from there into Lynkestis. He had in mind to aid Mahaon, after teaching him a lesson, albeit a verbal one.

The next morning upon the departure of the Lynkestians, the land lords reconvened at the audience hall, the King presiding. Timenid Makedonia had its own problems facing an insecure future, due to pressure from the southern city-states and their colonies, as well as from Orestis and Elimiotis -the Lynkestian kingdom and Illyrian raiders not counting, as being a permanent worry. During this council, it was agreed that the houses of Agis and Olganos would use half of their men under the ex-perienced guidance of Peridas, to see the recruiting of available clan heads of the country-side and head toward Lynkos. Ptolemeos-Filippos with all his men would become the nucleus of the home force, in case reinforcements would be needed.

The force under Peridas should gather at the estates house Olganos had by the Eordean border, until secured passage was arranged. Alketas would send a messenger to Orestis for that reason. As the Orestians were probably going to refuse because of their competition against House Timenos and Lynkos, the excuse for crossing would be of a different pretext. Alketas was open to suggestions. Ap-ellas came with an idea. He suggested the excuse should be a pretense of going to Paeonia for a new bride for the King. Peonia was friendly enough to go along with the scheme. As to why so many troops for the 'royal proxy' escort, the fact that Pelagonia and Lynkos were not far-off kingdoms under the Illyrian attack, should be good enough. It was a so-so excuse but, for lack of anything better, Apellas' suggestion was accepted.

Alketas indicated he would stay at Aegae, amassing troops from his land lords and clan heads from Pieria and Vottiaea, which would take more time in coming. Besides, he mouthed, the King of Make-donia was not necessarily needed to throw a few barbarians out of one or two minor kingdoms! He arranged so, that messengers would constantly be going back and forth, to keep him and everybody updated and in accord during all phases of the campaign. When a successful end would come near, Peridas should notify him, so he could march and be in person at any treaties ready to be dealt with friend and foe alike.

As it happened, events developed very much like Alketas thought they would, much to his satisfact-ion. First, Orestis accepted the 'excuse' of troop movement. When they found out what the real aim was, it was too late for any protest. Then Mahaon sent a full-powered delegation at the border of Almopia, agreeing that, regardless of the result, Lynkestis, Pelagonia, Eordea and Almopia were henceforth to recognize the Timenid Kings as their overlords, support them in times of danger, work together as if under one leadership (that of House Timenos) in all matters of external policy. In return, Alketas had to agree to the independence of the kings in those cantons, to rule their internal affairs as before. These terms of a treaty were witnessed by all plenipotentiaries from Lynkos, Pelagonia, Eordea and Almo-pia on one side and Peridas with the main land lords and clan heads of his army, on behalf of the King of Makedonia, as Alketas ordered, fully informed of developments -as were unfolded. An offi-cial treaty, he decreed, would follow later, after the campaign was over.

On the battleground, there were no major battles fought. Peridas took over the leadership of the combined Makedonian forces, Mahaon staying out of major involvements, in charge of the defense of his capital city, Iraklia. The shame of Lynkos becoming a 'beggar' to House Timenos, did not fit well Mahaon's pride but necessity dictated he had to bent his back before Alketas. Peridas had now the upper hand over invaders and 'allies'. He divided his forces in strong enough contingents and gained several victories against a foe that now was looking for a way out! As winter approached and cam-paigning became a problem for both parties, most of the Illyrian invaders withdrew back to their ter-ritories. Heralds were sent from Attal and a meeting was arranged for a general armistice.

Alketas sent word to Mahaon. The meeting would take place at Iraklia, the Lynkestian capital city.

To give the impression of solidarity between Makedonian kingdoms to the barbarians, equal place-ments of seating would be provided to both, Alketas and Mahaon. Upon conclusion of the peace and according to terms of Makedonian interests, another meeting was to follow, this time only among the Makedonian kings. Mahaon understood the magnanimity in the suggestion of Alketas, a first sign by a Lynkestian to admit Timenid eminence.

Alketas impressed everyone during these negotiations for peace with his sense of justice. He let 'enough rope' for everybody as to make them think and feel important and independent. Yet, using the same rope, he made sure they were all tied-up behind his chariot! Learning first-hand what led the Dexarians to this war, he imposed to all conferring Makedonian kingdoms (including his own) the obligation to share the expenses for rebuilding, arranged relief for the small landholders of Dexarian territories, as well as of Pelagonian and Lynkestian ones. Lynkos and Pelagonia were not to raid any Dexarian lands in the future, nor were any Dexarian clans or the tribe to invade Makedon-ian lands ever again! In times of famine or pressure from Illyrian tribes or Dardanian attacks, Dexares, Lynkestes and Pelagones were to aid one another, asking for Timenid help during the most difficult times.

Any dispute should be presented to him for judgment and Timenid Makedonia would provide fair and equal share to all. The treaty for lasting peace was witnessed by Attal and Gerak as Dexarian delegates. Mahaon, Antypas, Forvas and Faedon signed for Lynkos and king Plevrias, Nikanor and Sostratos were the witnesses for Pelagonia. For Timenid Makedonia, King Alketas with Ptolemeos-Filippos, Peridas of house Agis, Ilaos of house Olganos and Alexandros of house Klitos were the main guarantors of overseeing that the peace would last.

Attal with Gerak and their escort left for their country the day after the treaty was sealed. Immedi-ately Alketas called for a Makedonian conference and agreement to his dictation of a treaty among the kingdoms. Mahaon was to keep his influence and military help in Pelagonia but he was to return Almopia to the Timenid kingdom. Both Lynkos and Pelagonia were to aid Alketas in any and all wars, as they were to share surplus produce with the Dexares. Orestis and Elimiotis were to be left on their own, with no future contact of any type of alliance between them and Lynkestis. To give a stronger sense of unification between Lynkos, Pelagonia and Timenid Makedonia, Alketas proposed a com-mon type of currency, its initial value power to derive from the war loot from the Illyrian armor and silver captured during the war. The money he proposed would be an imitation (but of distinctly different value) of the Halkidian or Korinthian currency. Having less revenue than those city-states, Makedonia would mint copper and iron coins. Any silver quantities existing or gained in the future, would be saved in the Timenid treasury at Aegae, melted and stored for internal and external use -as need would dictate. One tenth of yearly Lynkestian and Pelagonian assets would be deposited into this treasury. As to local governing of the clans, the individual kingdoms would continue to rule as before. Lynkos was also to assert its influence on Derriopia and Dassaretis. Future cooperation between them and Makedonia as a whole was Alketas' target.

Lynkestis and Pelagonia had no other option. They witnessed the new treaty with oaths and athletic events. Alketas returned to Aegae, leaving his half brother Dimitrios in Iraklia and sending Apellas to Antania in Pelagonia. They were to be his eyes and ears in the courts of Lynkos and Pelagonia. At Aegae, a pleasant surprise was awaiting for Alketas. He found a delegation from Eordea expressing their desire to recognize Timenid overlodship. He felt justified and accepted their petition by sending Peridas with a strong contingent to secure Orestian or Elimiotian neutrality. Let Orestis with Tymfea and Elimiotis 'boil in their isolation!' he quipped.

The Orestian king Efkrator decided to send petition to the colonial city-states of Methoni, Aloros and Pydna, promising a free hand in Makedonian trade. Their reply was a very disappointing one for Efkrator. Tutored by their mother cities to keep House Timenos quiet and contented with his recent success, they sent to Alketas their good wishes and a reduction on trade taxation.

There was celebration at Aegae and offerings to the Olympian gods. But Alketas was nobody's fool. He knew too well that -given a first opportunity- all his new 'friends', 'allies' and subordinates would turn against him. He did not want to press his good luck any further. Tyhi was on his side for now. One step at a time was more secure than a win/lose-it-all adventure. He made a point to involve and educate his son Amyntas, in all aspects of politics and armed power.

Having the taxes eased from Methoni, Aloros and Pydna, he sent a substantial gift to the Oracle in Delfi. He also asked god Apollon for a good future. It was the same year the city-state of Sykion's dedication of its finished treasury temple to the same god. The Delfic answer to his question came back as one not promising at all. The Oracle of Pythia let the King know her prediction of his future would be marked with a great loss and sorrow! Disturbed, he sent another present to the Oracle of Dodona in Ipiros. The Father of gods and men, almighty Zefs, had no comforting words for the King either! Although more gently put, the answer coming back to Alketas was the same: Future pain and loss!

Alketas put all his effort in securing what was gained thus far. In the following years of his Kingship he enforced his good relations with the neighboring kingdoms, keeping Elimiotis and Orestis isolated.

He had Amyntas marry a Lynkestian princess and Dimitrios and Apellas to a Derriopian and Pelago-nian one respectively. Peridas'son Kleanthis, was given the hand of Gerak's daughter Anta (Antigoni in Makedonian), bringing a closer relation with the Dexares. From his son Amyntas, Alketas had the happiness of getting a grand son shortly. They named him Alexandros.

Some four plus ten years passed since and Alketas saw that clan heads and land lords were in good terms with each-other and faithful to his House. Alketas and Amyntas were proud to have an early start, educating Alexandros in kingship and politics, having in mind the glory of Makedonia and House Timenos before all else!

Alketas ruled his Timenid Makedonian kingdom for a total of eight plus twenty years. At the age of six plus forty, he saw the need to retire and enjoy his grand children. Amyntas had been trained and educated to run the state affairs as he represented his Father in numerous occasions, either political or military. He took over his Father's throne at the age of one plus twenty amidst joyful acclamation by all clan heads and land lords. The coronation took place at Aegae with all houses present and dignitaries such as (old by now) Mahaon, Plevrias of Pelagonia and from the houses of Eordea Imathia and Almopia, Alexarhos (house Pavmenis), Arhelaos (house Menelaos) and Kottyfos (house Amyntas of Almopia). Also, from Thessalian Farsalos and Larissa embassies came to express their well wishing.

The coronation took place the same year that Sparti defeated Argos (the ancestral cradle of the Ti-menid royal House), resulting in undisputed Lakedaemonian supremacy in the whole of Peloponnisos and Spartan recognition as having the only undefeated oplites army in Ellas. At the same year, Pisist-ratos returned to Athinae for a second time as Archon of the Attiki city-state. The actual month of Amyntas' coronation was that of Panimos and the late spring-early summer days of celebration transfer-ring the Makedonian scepter to a new King were sunny, warm and without any clouds descending from the mighty abode of the Olympian gods above Aegae. The omens of the sacrificed animals were excellent and Alketas forgot all about his worries of the state and the Oracle warnings. Present among those many guests, a youth of only five springs old. Alexandros son of Amyntas, prince of Makedonia was toying around with his wooden sword and shield, clanging the former against the latter, imitating the men of the Makedonian Assembly. Alketas, a loving Grand Father of the young-ster, was hoping he would live enough to see Alexandros become a capable man and a strong King!

By the true beginning of summer, Makedonia had to stress its power to its limit. Invasion from Peo-nia worked its way through Paeonia and Parorvylia, into Almopia, Amfaxitis and Vottiaea. The Peones were aided by their allies the Penestes and the Argestei. Meantime, Lynkestian and Pelagones Makedones were having their own troubles repulsing a new Tavlantian invasion, aided by (according to the lasting treaty) the Dexares, Derriopes and Dassaretes. The coming winter found the Timenid state exhausted. Peonians ruled Paeonia, Parorvylia and Amfaxitis, with incursions in Almopia and Vottiaea. Pelagonia and Lynkos with Dassaretis and Derriopia stood barely against the Tavlantes, with the Dexares totally losing their independence to them. While Amyntas defended the eastern front, Alketas had to come out of retirement and campaign on the north-west.

The winter brought all activities to a stop, a much needed breathing space! News from the east brought by merchants and travelers, were equally disturbing. A new great power in Asia, called Per-sians or Perses, revolted against their overlords the Mides and subdued them. Led by a strong leader named Kyros (Kurush in their barbaric language), they built a vast empire! This past summer they crossed the Kilikian Gates in Asia-by-the-Aegean and attacked the strong Lydian kingdom of king Kryssos, taking his capital city of Sardis and him in captivity (although well treated)! That implied a total submission of all city-states of Ellas in Asia-by-the-Aegean to this Persian king.

Now, the messengers said, Kyros is sending heralds to Thrakian kingdoms and colonized city-states at Thraki's coast. Asking of earth and water offerings, as indication of recognition of him as ruler on earth, both in Asia and Evropi! Thrakian tribes such as Odomantes, Vistones, Satrae, even Idones Kilaetes and the city-states of the Thrakian coast like Avdira, Vyzantion, Iraeon, Kalhidon and all Propontis obliged after the Persian demand! Whoever resisted was totally ruined and the population was put to slavery! States that declared submission were left to pay tribute and with a Persian leader in charge, called Satrap (Satrapis in Ellenic terms). This new Persian threat was something Makedo-nia could do without!

A war council was held, during which a decision was made (once this new danger was somewhat still distant) to receive the so-called High King's heralds with dignity and avoid any particular of-fense, pretending submission. The idea was to buy time while preserving Makedonian unity. But, as time passed and no Persian envoys appeared, spirits calmed and great effort was put to get things in order, after the combined invasion and loss of ground to Peones and Illyrians.

Almost two years later and during the spring month of Daesios (Thargilion for the Athinian calen-dar), runners from Vottiaean Kyrros arrived to tell Amyntas that the Persian envoys were only ten days away from Aegae! Heralds were sent immediately to all clan heads and land lords, as well as to Lynkestis and Pelagonia. A new war council convened at

Aegae in record time, Amyntas presiding and Alketas advising. From house Olganos was Alexandros and his son Illos. From house Agis were Leonidas, Alketas 'the Short' and Attalos. From the old Imathian royal house came Arraveos son of Ifanor, with his first cousins Mahaon and Klitos 'the Green-eyed', sons of Antigonos, related to the house by marriage. The Lynkestians sent Perseas son of Illos the second, grand son of Pafsanias. A pleasant surprise was the participation from the Dexares (still under Tavlantian control), by the sons of Gerak (house Ierax in Makedonian) Anthrias and Nestor (Andri and Nister in Dexarian). Natural-ly the houses of Ptolemeos, Kleodeos and Amyntas 'the Lesser' were present with all their adult members, living in or around Aegae. From the lesser clans none failed to send someone representing the particular houses but their names were too numerous to mention them all.

Presented before this council, the runners from Kyrros retold their message. The Persian envoys were coming (only three days away by now!) escorted by large numbers of armed men, numbering over ten times one hundred on horse and twice as many on foot! Adding the slaves and servants (the latter also lightly armed as archers), the number far exceeding what Timenid Makedonia could field at such short time. Worst, these 'envoys' were traveling fast for their number, spending with no second thought any amount of silver and gold to have fresh horses and teams of burden animals for their trek. Local clan heads and land lords caught by surprise could not resist both the numbers and the prospect of easy profit and gave whatever was asked of them.

Other Persian forces had attacked the Peones who -originally- tried to resist (feeling strong after their recent success) and now it was reported that Peonia and Paeonia with Amfaxitis had been defeated and turned into a Persian occupied territory. The same was expected to happen with all of Halkidiki and its surrounding kingdoms and city-states. The odds seemed to be overwhelmingly against Makedonia. Aegae was surely not enough of a town to host such a horde. Nor was it adequately fortified a city to resist any siege (if there seemed to be no other option but resistance). The country side was even more vulnerable. The recent strain of wars against Illyrians and Peones had taken its toll.

After long deliberation, the council concluded that a split had to be forced discreetly on this Persian delegation, so as not to raise any suspicion and cause retaliation. Anthrias and Nestor were charged with the task of presenting an invitation to the Persians for a 'visit in a friendly environment' send-ing a message of Persian power to Tavlantians and other Illyrian tribes, thus extending the High King's influence. Alketas thought the 'bait' was a strong invitation to Persian ego. They would not refuse. Anthrias and Nestor were to keep Amyntas informed at all times if the scheme would work or, the Persians were not lured to it. From there on, Makedonia would see what could or couldn't be done. Nestor and Anthrias left at once to meet the Persians, for they were only two days away now...

Nestor came back to report the very next day. Anthrias had convinced the chief of the Persian dele-gation a man of stature and relative of the High King to head with half the 'embassy' through Eordea and Lynkestis to the Dexarian land, in a show of Persian power and might. This Persian chief was named Vouvaris (Buhvahrau in Persian -or something similar to that) had a very good know-ledge of the Ellenic language, being the governor/satrapis in a vast area of Ionian territory in Asia-by-the-Aegean. This Vouvaris was already on his way with Anthrias, leaving his second in command to visit Aegae.

One day later Aegae had a view, never before seen in or near the Makedonian King's court! The splendor of the envoys and their armed retinue could make more than the total revenue in the royal treasury of Makedon. Their horses alone (double the size of the best ones in Makedonia or Thessalia) had trimmings rivaling the splendor of their masters' robes! Hearing the languages of the multitude, one could have his ears hurt and there was no comparing those with even the harsher Ellenic dialect. How could one accept them as descendants of the hero Perseas in that distant past?

The bulk of the armed escort camped at some distance from Aegae, covering the hillside toward the river with multicolored tents of tremendous value, one better than the other. It was like a feast day, seeing the barbarians directing their slaves on the location of each tent, according to one's own status. The people gathered observing in amazement and there was talk for days on end about that display of riches.

The most prominent of the ambassadors had their slaves pitch their tents just outside the town, the tallest of them easily reaching in height the rooftop of the royal palace (if not exceeding it)! As for its width and length, well! The palace looked like a small house in comparison. In front of it, a very tall post was placed and on its top, a huge fabric of greenish color and heavy embroidery depicting a Per-sian face (they said it was the likeness of the High King) amidst two stretched open wings of some bird of pray, was barely moving with the breeze.

With even greater amazement, the people observed the setting of all those tents and emblems being done in record time and a new city sprung next to Aegae in a matter of hours. Then, an armed escort with a herald leading the way, entered Aegae and headed toward the palace, like they knew where they were going, their plumes and long dresses laden with gold and silver embroidery, giving an extra spectacle of grandeur! The two armed royal guards by the palace gate in their polished armor and shields looked like ragtag dolls, discarded by a bored child. They instinctively stayed at attention.

The herald entered alone and was admitted at the audience hall. He was an Ionian in the service of the High King. Although speaking with relative respect, he addressed King Amyntas with an air of superiority and announced that the ambassadors of the High King demanded an audience at once! He suggested that the king should receive them first with the start of the next day's audience, after he would have someone clean the hall and place seats worthy the rank of the High King's ambassadors. The herald would see that there was no offense taken by the delay. Amyntas thought of kicking this bogus Ionian sold to barbaric splendor, out of his court and town. But a look toward Alketas stopped him from ordering so. He held his temper and sent the herald back to his masters with a promise to do what he could to accommodate the High King's representatives. Meantime, he instructed that small parties of the Persian retinue could come to the town's market for their masters' provisions -if any were needed- until sundown. He excused his decision for small parties by saying he did not want the people to get overexcited with the appearance of large groups in such riches and splendor within the town. With the herald taking his leave, Alketas and Amyntas had a serious and lengthy conversa-tion, while workers milled around starting preparations for the next day's reception.

The next morning, as the gates of the town walls opened, a fanfare of a whole contingent of barbar-ians entered the town, heading for the palace. The main ambassadors of the High King were carried in on litters of immense richness, following the Ionian herald and flanked by armed archers and javeliners in long trousers and heavy robes. King Amyntas met them at the palace gates, escorted by his Father and all present clan heads and land lords in their finest clothes, proud and not moved (at least not showing it) by the Persian show of power and splendor.

The King admitted the ambassadors in his audience hall and, after the obligatory exchange of gifts (there was a horrendous difference in value in that exchange), the ambassadors (through the Ionian herald) came straight to the point. The High King was asking for (demanded was the right word) a token of Makedonian willingness to enlist among his loyal subjects, by offering earth and water to them, his ever loyal ambassadors. Amyntas felt small and inadequate before this splendor and show of power by his 'guests' and their armed escort of thousands. He saw -in the eyes of his Father and all other present- the same feeling and sense of awe and his heart sank. What Makedonia could do against (or for) such people? Even with all Makedonian kingdoms united, his army could not be more than eight times bigger than this 'mere escort' of some ambassadors. The Ionian herald under this Persian yoke did not let him entertain any thought of refusal either.

Amyntas looked at his Father and land lords. Same faces of inability, of desperation, of awe! He sadly realized that -if every delegation from this High King was as numerous- no wonder all the Thrakian kingdoms and the city-states of Ellas to Macedonia's east were so quick to offer their sub-mission. He gave his answer. Yes, Makedonia would be on the side of the High King, ready to assist in any way asked. Maybe this would get the pressure from the north and south off! Maybe Persian alliance would bring some years of peace and deter any further invasions and colonization. He told his 'guests' he would make the offer of earth and water on the morrow, during the official sacrifices. Meantime, they were invited to lodging within the town and at the royal banquet this evening. The High King's ambassadors dismissed off hand any lodging. They rudely pointed to him that their tents were by far more luxurious than his 'palace' but, they would accept his invitation to the banquet, curious to see what sort of entertainment Makedonia had in store for the High King's emissaries.

Amyntas felt his anger rising again by the Persians' high handed manners. Alketas' hand fell heavy on his son's shoulder as they both stood to indicate the end of the royal audience. That was enough to bring Amyntas back to his 'diplomatic coolness'. Walking the 'guests' to the palace door he took a look over the town's defense walls, toward the new 'city' of tents and the clamor coming from it. This look convinced him that Aegae were really and truly surrounded by an army. No sense to antagonize.

Let them take some earth and water and let them be gone!

Meantime, he had to feed and entertain them. Good thinking to have Anthrias take half of them toward the Illyrian territories! Aegae could not have enough provisions for all that host. It was hard to accommodate as it was and Amyntas gave orders to all land lords to speedily gather and bring in town all available provisions. He also told them to come to the royal banquet dressed in their best, presenting all possible splendor afforded by Makedonian means in hope of giving a good but somber impression to their 'guests'.

Amyntas asked for Alketas' advice and decided to visit the Persian 'city'. He wanted to have a talk with the leading ambassadors alone, in hope that he could approach them better and have them un-derstand and cooperate rather than impose. He took the old King and his son Alexandros along. The boy was not of age to voice an opinion, but was old enough to get to know how negotiations work-ed.The same Ionian herald announced the King's entrance to the 'city' and Amyntas was gladly admitted. Time the Persian High King (through His ambassadors) to let the poor chieftain take a good look at the showcase of the Haxamanish/Ahaemenis House splendor and might!

Amyntas entered the largest and most decorated tent he had ever seen in his life. The three senior Persian ambassadors made an effort to rise in welcoming but Amyntas asked them to remain seated. The Makedonian King was accustomed to addressing all people as equals. The Persian envoys look-ed at each-other bemused but said nothing. The most senior of the three Persians reintroduced him-self and the other two, knowing the difficulty all 'Yiunis' (Ionians) had of pronouncing Persian names. He was Artavasda (Artavazos the Ionian interpreter said). The one on his right and second in seniority was Farnavakhca (Farnavazos) and, the one at his left, Avi-shareh (Avisaris), third in command. The overall commander Buhvahrau (Vouvaris) was leading a part of their 'delegation' to upper Makedonia at the time he said. Vouvaris was the closest kin to the High King, who now was Kambujyia (Kamvysis), the first-born of the Great Kurush (Kyros) and fighting the Egyptians, ad-ding glory and subjects to His House. But they were all the High King's kin -Artavasda said- thus trusted and empowered to subject all nations and bring them into the fold.

This extended kinship -Amyntas found out- of the royal Persian House was due to the fact that the High King had by custom many wives (their fathers thus becoming kin) and concubines. Through match-making, the High King's sons, daughters, brothers and other close relatives helped spread this extension and all became related. Obviously, the closer a relation to the High King the better!

It was about mid-day when the three Makedonians (Amyntas, Alketas and Alexandros) entered the Persian tent and the hosts offered a meal and refreshments; the negotiations between them and the Makedonian King could be dealt while eating. With a hand's wave, Artavazos had a small army of slaves bringing all kinds of dishes arriving before the flabbergasted Makedonians. Everything was in gold or silver. A great variety of game, sweets, vegetables and fowl, were paraded before the visitors.

Amyntas and Alketas contented themselves with few samples. Alexandros was encouraged to try most of the dishes and report, later, his opinion.

During this meal, negotiations started in earnest. Amyntas trying to ease any and all obligations on behalf of Makedonia, the ambassadors ordering and demanding. Alexandros observed and learned, asking discreetly his Grand Father a question now and then. He frowned at the Persian demands, as he could clearly see Makedonia becoming a client state to a far-off High King but also understanding that this might be a much needed respite and the start of some peaceful years ahead, provided the presence and support promised by a power such as Persia would discourage any invasions from ages old foes!

The final agreement was that Makedonia would provide the High King with all necessities, such as troops and provisions when asked. If war would be conducted in the vicinity, Makedonia would also provide lodging for the Persian troops, as for the few stationed 'security' troops they were to remain in order to secure the Persian presence and remind Macedonia's foes of the High King's presence in the region. It was agreed that the stationed troops would not exceed the present number of the escort camped outside Aegae at the moment, divided in five smaller units and lodged in various sensitive locations, easy to assemble -in cases of need. This would afford easy provisioning and lodging, in ex-change of the High King's protection and appointment of Amyntas as His sole overseer of Persian interests in the region. Also, Makedonia was to send one tenth of its gross revenue in gold or in kind, each time the High King would deem such provision necessary.

Amyntas could see no alternative. Wanting to see most of the Persians gone but enough to remain for added Makedonian security and use against the enemies, he agreed in all demands. Maybe there would come time his kingdom would recover through Persian 'peace' and become a military power of its own right, truly independent and secured!

The banquet that very night started in good terms and with openness, the shadow of the armed am-bassadorian escort camped outside the walls all but forgotten. These troops had been allotted extra local wine and a presence (a very discreet one) of Makedonian militia (they posed as curious visitors and co-celebrants) among them (in case of misbehavior) promised an easy night.

On the left side of the King, all major and minor Makedonian land lords and clan heads that could make it from their estates were present, having among them and sharing the recliners with the minor Persian nobles of the delegation. On Amyntas' right and in the place of honor, were the three major Persians in order of seniority of their rank and kinship to the High King, namely Artavazos, Farnav-azos and Avisaris, followed by the rank order of the royal Makedonian family, Alketas being closer.

Alexandros, as a youth, did not have the right to sit with the adults at a royal banquet but, under the special circumstances, Alketas pointed to Amyntas that the young prince would get an experience not easily repeated in the future and this would be some learning for a future King of Makedon. It was then decided that Alexandros should participate (up to a certain time) but not taking part of any grown-up conversations. He had to keep his eyes and ears open and observe manners and etiquette. So, he was placed at the same recliner with his Grand Father, offered much watered wine and, for the most part, kept to himself except when he felt he needed an explanation or a definition -in order to follow the process.

Trouble brewed somewhere in the middle of the banquet though, as it was found (too late for any remedies) that the Persians were not able to hold the strong Makedonian undiluted wine served to all adults. As time passed and the Persians drunk, they became more insolent and free with remarks totally improper to Makedonian ears. Tempers started to rise on the Makedonian side and hidden (at the beginning) insults were exchanged. Several Ionian interpreters helping the main one were at a loss, not knowing how to translate without adding to the offenses. One of them, a certain Lykaon from Teos, gave a full report of the events at the Athinian citizen assembly years later, at a time when there was some doubt expressed on Alexandros' account and telling.

The incident which topped all insults on Makedonian sensitivity, were strong remarks made by Avisaris as to how there were no women entertaining at this so-called royal banquet, to serve the all- important guests' needs! Illos son of Perseas and grand nephew of king Pafsanias from

Lynkestis rose from his recliner ready to pick-up a fight. Alketas was quick to nod him an order to sit down and Amyntas took over as calmly as he could, explaining to the 'guests' that Makedonian and Elle-nic customs in general prohibited the participation of decent women in men's banquets. Only when an etera was available with her retinue of entertaining girls this could happen and, only if she wanted to participate! As it was, there were no eteres present at the Makedonian court, the last one being Evriklia, long time ago, before she gave her trade up.

Avisaris demanded to know why. Amyntas looked at his Father who, again, nodded secretly patience and lifted his shoulders like saying: Well, what do you expect? He's a barbarian, he wants to know, tell him -it doesn't matter. He won't remember by tomorrow and he'll be gone! Amyntas proceeded to explain that eteres were costing a lot and, the Makedonian treasury could not afford having one or more permanently there or inviting an etera from the more affluent southern city-states. He asked the indulgence of his 'guests' for such an omission. If the court could know the High King's representatives' preference before hand, Makedonia would have take steps to accommodate! Farnavazos laughed and questioned the King if eunuchs were costing the same as eteres or, looking at the direction of young Alexandros, boys could come in this backward country easier to purchase for such high guests' pleasures.

This was too much, even with the strong intentions of Amyntas to keep things under control and a civilized atmosphere! He stood up, ready to tear the offender apart. Alketas, in spite his age, jumped from his reclining seat and placed a strong restraining hand on the King's shoulder. The Makedoni-ans present were all standing, silent in their rage and ready to attack. Alketas motioned to all to resume their seating and, turning to Artavazos -as being the leading Persian- spoke slowly, clearly and with a determination, his face drained from blood but very measured in his manner. The Ionian interpreter had lost all his wits and had to be brought almost violently back to his duty of translating.

Now Alketas tried to explain in stern voice the dos and don'ts of Ellenic customs and especially those of Makedonia, standing almost on top of the Persian who, for the time being, seemed to have come back to sobriety. While Alketas was talking to the 'guests', Alexandros pulled his Father and whispered in Amyntas' ear for some extensive time. When the prince finished, the King waited deep in thought until his Father finished explaining to their 'honored guests'. He then stood up and said that in the interest of the good relation among Makedonians and the High King, the request of the 'honored guests' would be answered. They only had to wait while the young prince would retire to his quarters -as being yet too young- and in lieu of eteres or other entertainment, the royal females would be ordered to appear and entertain as best as they could.

All Makedonians let their mouths drop open, including Alketas! Such a display of meekness in order to please some barbarians was never expected from a Makedonian King! Amyntas took the time of looking at each one of his Makedonians straight in the eyes, letting them know that he had full control of his intention to do what was proper, appearance meaning nothing. He asked all of them to resume their seats and turned his attention to his Father and Artavazos. The Persian envoys seemed now relaxed, pleased they had forced the 'backwater' hosts to do their bidding.

Some time passed and the young prince had already withdrawn, when a servant announced the entrance of the royal females. As was promised, the Queen and her female escort of the royal house-hold walked-in. They came dressed according to Makedonian rules of decency, wearing long dresses and a peplos (long shawl-like, over the head and shoulders fabric), made out of local wool span.

The eyes of the 'honored guests' showed their displeasure as they faced the unsophisticated attires and the aloofness of the ladies. They accepted them (their request being answered) and continued their drinking and eating, conversing through the interpreters as nothing had gone out of order. Be-fore long, some of them started getting bolder and were attempting to touch the women, ostensibly being interested in such a raw way of clothing and describing in foul (to Makedonian ears) terms, their own women's preferences in finer and more revealing garments.

Meantime, outside the royal House, the agora was teaming with youth who had left their houses by orders of their prince, offering extra potent wine to the stationed Persian troops. The same was happening beyond the town's walls, in the Persian 'tent city' and all in the name of 'newfound friendship and alliance between Persia and Makedon'. Doors on houses within the town were knocked on and, to the answering tenants whispered instructions were given to be passed-on to the ones inside. As time passed and the night was well into its late hours, most -if not all- of this armed throngs of Per-sian escort had passed-out, drunk! The slaughter of them always an easy job for the coming out of the shadows Makedonians, young Alexandros leading the way!

Inside the royal House of Timenos in the banquet hall, King Amyntas asked to be excused, because pressing matters of the state would have him go at first light. His 'guests' were free to continue their reverie, in the company of the old King Alketas and the elder clan heads. He commented on the noise coming from outside, saying that their escort seemed to be having equally good time at the agora and beyond the town walls! As for the ladies present, their King's wish was to have them please the 'guests' to the highest! They needed to be excused for a while, for they were in need of putting on something more to the liking of the Persian taste and have some freshen-up before returning for more…company.

The Persian delegation was delighted at the prospect of some more freedom of action with the women. Who knows? Maybe 'backwater' country women could be of more excitement! Artavazos, Farnavazos, Avisaris and the rest of their closest 'noble' friends and officers present, were soon rol-ling out of their anaklindra/recliners, either totally out of their senses or very nearly so! The younger of the Makedonian clan heads and land lords left with their King, leaving the elders and old King Alketas to 'keep' the Persians company.

In short time after the King's departure, the double door of the banquet hall opened, letting the ladies reenter one by one. They were dressed this time in short hitones-like dresses, thighs, legs and arms all exposed but keeping their peploses on their heads. Was that their last bastion of modesty? Their hands were kept behind their backs waists bent a bit (surely a sign of resignation?), in a posture of construed total submission!

Avisaris was the first to rise from his anaklindron, swinging in his stupor, hands wide open in readi-ness to embrace. Unsteady and falling forward, his hands grasped the dress bringing it down. Farna-vazos and Artavazos stood in half motion at the revealed sight. The young woman was a young man! His hands came from behind his back, armed with a sharp Makedonian style mahera, the short curv-ed sword of cavalry. There was no time for any thoughts or understanding. The 'women' fell upon the offenders and each one of them had a mercifully quick death!

The Ionian interpreters were cornered and were asked if they were willing (like Ellines) to cooper-ate. Most of them agreed, with a sigh of hope and relief. Few who did not, were all put to death. Gen-eral cleaning took place right after that, the bodies of the slain taken away and buried with the troops of the tent city, far out of town. The court Seers were asked in next, purifying the hall before a new meeting could take place, to come with a solution on the new emergency...

The other half of the Persian embassy was still in upper Makedonia but everybody knew that they would return soon. Actually, they were expected to approach Aegae within the following fortnight. A decision had to be made; an explanation (a very good one) was needed for the disappearance of the other half stationed at Aegae. What kind of explanation though? Would that lead to a war against the High King? Would it be the end of Makedonia? First and foremost, measures had to be taken -in case of extreme developments and consequences most surely to result after what happened.

All youth, wives, mothers, fathers of true old age, incapable ones of carrying arms, were escorted by some of the men, up at the highest slopes of Olympos and in the wooded peaks of Pieria, just as they were, leaving everything behind. They were trusted under the divine protection of the gods and the nymfes. The remaining, all men of age to carry arms, reinforced the walls of Aegae as best as they could and sent word for help from the more distant clan heads and land lords, including the kings of Orestis, Tymfea and Elimiotis. It was thus managed by Amyntas to have around him about five times a hundred cavalry and as many oplites in full armor as each land lord was capable of producing. These would be his shock troops, led by him in person. The rest of his available force would be under Alketas, manning the walls as archers, javeliners and slingers, being the older and most numerous. All these were recruited town people, surrounding peasantry and herders. Amyntas knew the latter were good stone throwers, either with slings or just by bare hands. He could count on their forceful and accurate aim. In numbers now, they were a match to Vouvaris' Persian escort and that should suffice -for the time being.

By the time all necessary measures were taken, the Persians were reported to have departed from Derriopis securing the good will (fear rather) of the neighboring Illyrian tribes and received a dele-gation from Dardania, which also promised 'quiet coexistence' under Persian tutelage. Now the Per-sians were on their way to cross Lynkestis and Eordea, returning to the Timenid Makedonia, having received earth and water from all places.

There was much anxiety in the Makedonian camp of King Amyntas. Everybody knew that even if this Persian host was to be eliminated too, there were many more 'embassies' from the High King all over the north-east with equal (if not greater) numbers of armed men! Sooner rather than later, word would get to them about the disappearance of these 'delegations'. For one, all messengers, dele-gates and heralds were -by universal custom- persons with special privileges. They were to pass through unmolested and return to sender with answers about their mission(s). Any intent to have a messenger killed or molested in any way was considered a great offense before men and gods alike! If circumstances (as it happened) forced an act against any delegates, the consequences were unpredict-able, as well as regrettable, by all concerned and (in this case) dire fear of heavy retributions existed.

According to well founded reports, Karia, Lydia, the Ellenic city-states of Ionia and Aeolis in Asia-by-the-Aegean, the Thrakian kingdoms of Propontis facing the entrance to Efxinos Pontos and the Skythian steppes beyond, the Kikkones, Idones, Vissae, Odrysses, the Ellenic colonies and city-states of Tharkian coast up to the very doorstep of Makedonia, all had offered alliance or met with devas-tating results caused by the same Persians under Vouvaris. The most recent example were the Peones who were the menace just a year ago and now reduced to meekness and blind obedience to the same Vouvaris now approaching. What if the High King, angered, would send his full armed force?

Amyntas could tell many of his clan heads and land lords had second thoughts already. The 'treat-ment' offered to these -insolent for sure- (but) powerful delegates, brought fear beyond reason! If Makedonia had hard times repulsing known and tested neighboring barbarians, what could be done against a kingdom mustering most (if not all) Asia? Amyntas came to the conclusion that he had but one choice only. The choice of facing Vouvaris and being truthful, trying to explain and excuse the events as they unfolded, the insults given to Makedonian customs, sense of decency and dignity and, hope for the best. He prepared to present himself as the sole responsible person of the whole affair, ready to be put to death or taken hostage, just to make sure his kingdom and people would not suffer any further.

He made his intentions (to meet Vouvaris alone and ask for clemency) known to all clan heads and land lords. He would leave his Father as regent and guardian of the throne and of young Alexandros, while he would go and face what the gods had in store for him! They all voiced their support for the heir to the throne in case Amyntas would perish (a matter taken for granted) and only three volun-teers (from the house of Agis) stepped forward and insisted on going with him to the Persians. Leon-idas, Alketas 'the Short' and Attalos were blessed by their Father and Alketas and these faithful to their promise that house of Agis would always serve House Timenos, set along with Amyntas and destiny.

The small group took with them an Ionian interpreter, a certain Ermolaos son of Yparhidis from Magnisia by the river Meandros. They gave him the staff of a herald, ensuring his safety from any harm and headed for the border of the Timenid kingdom. Their waiting wasn't a long one. The Per-sians approached sooner than expected. Vouvaris accepted them pleased to see the Makedonian King coming to him but perplexed by this very act and the small, unarmed escort and with no Persian rep-resentation. The request of such a King to have a parley at the border of his kingdom, increased Vou-varis' foreboding. Where were his Persian ambassadors? He purposely increased his armed guard about his person and asked King Amyntas in his tent.

Ermolaos presented Amyntas with the request of the Makedonian King asking for audience from the High King's most trusted and closest kin, with him (Ermolaos) translating the parley. Amyntas was truthful about the whole incident and asked for no mercy for himself. He told Vouvaris that, in spite of the grave insults given to Makedonia by the other Persian ambassadors, heralds were invio-lable and his act in putting them to death had to be judged accordingly. As King of Makedon, he held the sole responsibility of the action taken.

Vouvaris listened without any interruption. His face turned grave and blood seemed to have drain-ed off on several occasions, while his hands grasped tight on the arms of his throne-like chair. And, when the King finished, he called his guard to place all five (including the Ionian) under confinement. He needed to be alone and think.

The tent of their confinement was anything but a jail. A luxurious tent, such as never seen in Make-donia before! They were given food and drinks and there were several comfortable couches for them and many more (if there would be any) to recline and rest. Guards were placed at its entrance and it was obvious that other guards were pacing around it. No escape (if one was thought of) would be pos-sible. Leonidas ventured once close to the entrance, just to see what the guards' reaction would be. Their lances were immediately crossed to block any further step ahead, while some archers appeared as if by magic, aiming their arrows straight at him! None uttered a word, yet their move was more than explicit!

Amyntas recommended patience and calm. They would wait for the verdict and take action only when and where circumstances would dictate. First and foremost, Makedonia was in need of no more trouble. If they had to pay with their lives but save the rest of the tribe from any hardship, well, so be it! Meantime they would have to sit tight, wait and see…

It was long after the sun had set behind the mountains of Askion and Vermion and beyond the Pindos range when Vouvaris sent for them. They were escorted to his tent and found him sitting at the same throne-like chair, but dressed in even more impressive garments, surrounded by his high consuls and officers of his army. They were sitting in rich but lower throne-like chairs, each much more valuable than the plain Makedonian throne at Aegae. Ermolaos was to serve as interpreter again. The prisoners were asked to sit on the available chairs across the Persians. Vouvaris clapped his hands once and a small troop of servants walked in this splendid tent of his, carrying all kinds of cooked (but cold) game meat, sliced into small even pieces. They brought also jars of wine, golden cups to drink from and other jars with water to wash before the meal. Seeing his prisoners being hesitant and not knowing what their role would be, Vouvaris smiled and gently indicated that they were expected to join the Persians in eating and drinking. After partaking of the meal, he then would pronounce his decision as it was in the interest of his High King.

They washed-up and Vouvaris asked them what was -if any- the Makedonian custom in performing any sacred rites before, during or after a meal. Through Ermolaos, Amyntas told the satrap that all Ellines with minor variations kept the same customs, like the Ionians of Asia-by-the-Aegean, as the satrap himself was familiar with. Vouvaris replied that he sort of observed that while in Lynkos and Derriopis, but, not having really the time there to compare, he would like to see it now. So, if the King of Makedon had a ritual to perform, he should feel free in doing so!

Amyntas looked at a brazier placed about the middle of the satrap's tent and asked if that served to make offers to the gods, as it would in a royal Makedonian tent during any campaign. Did it repre-sent the presence of the gods within the encampment? Was it lit in their honor?

Vouvaris smiled at the questions and confirmed that yes, although Persians did not believe in many gods -as Ellines did. The Persians had only one god, the Mighty Ahura-Masda, god of creation and truth! "I want you to know that we Persians truly appreciate the truth and we strive to prove our-selves as truthful as we can be during our lives!" Vouvaris said in almost perfect Ellenic, really sur-prising all the Makedonian detainees, even Ermolaos! Amyntas tilted his head lightly, in recognition and appreciation of the Persian's ability to speak Ellenic. He was impressed and happy that he chose to tell the truth from the very beginning. He was sure now that Vouvaris kept record of all convers-ation between the Makedonians and the Ionian interpreter, leaving nothing to chance.

He rose and asked the satrap if he could use this brazier to offer honors then to all gods, including this Ahura-Masda. Permission granted, he chose several fat pieces of meat from his dish and, invok-ing Zefs, Athina, Iraklis and all the rest Olympian gods (not forgetting to include the Persian deity) he tossed the pieces into the brazier. Ermolaos kept explaining in Persian all invocations, for the be-nefit of the other notables observing. Amyntas picked-up his wine cup next and invoked the favors of the underworld gods, Adis, the Maid Persefoni and her Mother, his own House ancestors, including Timenos, the ancestors (not by name since he didn't know them) of the High King and the common ancestor of both races, the legendary hero Perseas, all in the name of Makedonia. Finishing his recitation, he poured the libation out of his cup and went back to his seat.

All the High King's representatives wanted now to know why all these recitations were given in the name and for favor of Makedonia, instead of in favor of the detainees' own fate. Didn't Vouvaris say he would pronounce his verdict at the end of their meal? To that, Amyntas (standing up again) retorted that the lives of four Makedonians did not matter in any way, as long as Makedonia itself was to be left to prosper! Wasn't he counting -as the Makedonian King- his life worth of living it? He was asked by a high ranking Persian seated next to Vouvaris. Wasn't his life more important than the lives of his fellow prisoners as being his underlings?

It was Amyntas' time to smile as he answered that above any King's Law, in Makedonia -as in all Ellas- there's the Law of Gods and Country, which always has precedence over everything else. That Law looked upon all Makedonian lives and fate indiscriminately and equally. No King above the commoner, no peasant worst than a land lord. All Makedonians were of equal value to their country!

Now, when there was concern of one individual's life only, or, even the lives of few alone, the welfare of the country as a whole and the lives of all but these few concerned, had precedence and were of much more value according to the Gods and the King's Law.

Vouvaris looked thoughtful for a long time; his eyebrows almost connected and a deep crease formed on his forehead between them. He turned to his fellow Persians nodding to Ermolaos not to translate and he conversed with them animatedly for some time, each one obviously trying to prove his point of opinion. He then turned to Ermolaos, including him in their Persian conversation. Amyn-tas observed all this and he could not but understand that the Persians were impressed with some-thing, something they were not ready to accept as a given fact or as a basic axiom.

At long last, Vouvaris turned his attention back to Amyntas and addressed the Makedonian King by asking to be excused for his apparently rude manners but, he explained, he and his fellow ambas-sadors had the need to absolutely understand the meaning of Amyntas' words and intentions during the recitations and the explanation Amyntas gave answering their questions. Ermolaos was quite ex-plicit -the Persian satrap stated- in giving them to understand the Makedonian King's attitude concerning his and his companions' fate. It had taken them a while to accept that explanation but, knowing Ermolaos of being a man of honor and true to his word, the High King's representatives were finally convinced by what seemed to be hard to believe if it was said under other circumstances and coming from the mouth of someone else.

Now, taking the words of the Makedonian King at 'face value' -as well as seeing Amyntas' small and youthful escort eagerly supporting their leader's mind- Vouvaris said that he and his fellow Per-sian dignitaries had come to a decision which would serve best the interest of the High King! He told Amyntas that -although he understood the offense to Makedonian dignity and customs by Artavasda and company was uncalled for- the punishment executed by the Makedonians was equally offensive to the High King. That had to be amended the best possible way or Vouvaris and his subordinates would have to answer before the High King with -possibly-their own lives if their judgment proved to be incorrect. As a start, Amyntas and his escort would have to stay at this Persian camp under close escort, except that one of the brothers (Vouvaris didn't care who) should speed to Aegae and summon the royal family and all clan heads and land lords (no exception allowed!) to be gathered at the palace and be ready to receive the High King's judgment. The messenger and the Makedonians had five days to comply with this order -or else!

Since none of the three brothers seemed willing to leave his King (even for such short time and with so much at stake) in his hour of need and confinement, Ermolaos proposed to act as messenger him-self. Permission was given and Amyntas handed him the royal ring, a sign for Alketas that Ermolaos was acting obeying orders from the King. The Ionian interpreter left for Aegae the next morning.

Two days after Ermolaos' departure, the Persian camp was dismantled and Vouvaris with his arm-ed retinue of thousands and Amyntas with the three brothers from Agis house guarded in the middle took to travel in a very leisurely way toward Aegae. They arrived on the fifth day, toward the mid-day time. The Persian army camped outside the town, erecting a palisade around it this time and placing guards. Vouvaris escorted by his subordinates and a numerous heavily armed guard of arch-ers and javeliners entered the town and went directly to the palace. Along were Amyntas, Leonidas, Alketas 'the Short' and Attalos, also guarded by heavy-armed Persians. The armed Persian guard entered first, placing themselves around the audience hall by its walls and by the throne, leaving a strong contingent at its door, facing both in and out. Then, Vouvaris with his captains entered, having Amyntas and the three brothers between them. At the head of the audience hall and on the left side of the throne, Alketas was standing. On the right of the throne was Alexandros, as heir ap-parent. The Makedonian land lords and clan heads were arrayed before them, in order of seniority and importance.

Used to taking the initiative, Amyntas headed for the throne itself only to be stopped by the Persian escort's javelins. Vouvaris stepped ahead and mounted the throne himself, amidst the rising clamor of the astounded Makedonians who -not expecting anything like that- were just starting to react. Vouvaris sighted and summoned Ermolaos and, through him, addressed the Makedonian assembly in Persian. He did not mean to add offense to Makedonia and her King (Ermolaos translated). Nonetheless, he had to show the High King's might, as Makedonians had to prove themselves as true friends and al-lies of that same High King of all nations, through their present and future behavior! Everything had to start from the beginning, before old (as well as new) privileges were renegotiated and recognized by him, the High King's highest and closest kin and representative!

There was the disquieting metal sound of many daggers pulled from their scabbards by many a hot-headed Makedonians, followed by the sounds of Persians placing their arrows on their bows and the swish of suddenly leveled javelins aiming at Amyntas and the assembly. Alketas exchanged a look with his son and they both jumped in the midst, hands raised and voices commanding a stop to any show of provocation! Next, Amyntas addressed his men thanking them for their eagerness to defend the kingdom's honor, noting that the insult offered by the (dead now) Persians had run its course and it was time now for reconciliation. Makedonia had greater needs!

He turned facing Vouvaris and offered his apologies, emphasizing the good will of Makedonia to-ward the High King and his interests. He added that he as the King of Makedon was more than will-ing to observe any and all demands, as long as Macedonia's sense of honor was preserved by Vouva-ris and all the present and future envoys from the High King!

Vouvaris listened carefully Amyntas and the Ionian translator, making sure he understood exactly what was said. After some uncomfortable silence and pacing about, he answered with the following words, nodding his approval to Ermolaos' translation: "The High King would be best served if there is amicable cooperation between the two kingdoms. All Makedonia had to do was to show actively true interest in preserving this alliance without any further rush and impulsive reactions, whether under honorable dictations or any other pretext or excuses! What had happened was something of the past; it was regrettable but it was done! He, in the name of the High King, would order that all the Persian delegations in the future, respect and show such respect to any and all Makedonian customs. On the other hand, Makedonians (including the King!) would have to ask him for any jus-tice henceforth -without taking matters in their own hands. A crime answered by another would never be the High King's way of administering justice. Further, the slain Persians were (regardless of their uncalled-for behavior) the same High King's own kin members and their demise was a direct affront to His person which had to answered to His satisfaction."

Vouvaris added that he was willing to personally intervene and see no further harm would come to anyone, provided the Makedonian King and his clan heads and land lords would agree and submit to the following demands: The first-born son of each clan head and land lord should be sent to him at his Satrapy district in Thraki and Thrakian Asia-by-the-Aegean, assigned to him by the High King. These first-borns would remain at his court as personal guests, until such time deemed necessary or by Makedonian proof of loyalty to Persia beyond doubt! This demand included the heir to the Make-donian throne and Amyntas' kingdom. They were to follow the High King's policy in every way, shape and manner, supply raw materials and persons when asked, to where and when His will dictated! A representative chosen personally by Vouvaris son of Magabuxsha/ Megavazos, therefore kin to the High King at the highest relation, would remain close to the court and some guards would be placed in strategic locations. In return, all previous transgressions from both sides would be erased and forgotten, peace and security at the Makedonian borders would be achieved, commerce and fair exchange would be guaranteed! The answer had to be given to him here and now! Were all these terms acceptable? A positive answer would benefit both kingdoms while a negative one would bring Macedonia's end!

Dead silence fell in the audience hall and one could see that most Makedonian faces were drained of all blood! First to recover was Alketas who sought an eye contact with his son. Amyntas felt the weight of his father's look and raised his head. Father and son looked at each other for a very long moment and, finally, Amyntas nodded his understanding. He addressed Vouvaris asking to be allow-ed to talk to his land lords and clan heads. Vouvaris, observing the last minute detail of the whole assembly's numbness and sense of insecurity, consented. He said in his almost perfect Ellenic accent that the King of Makedon had every right to address his countrymen, provided this would happen right then and there, in his presence.

Amyntas then turned facing his clan heads and land lords and spoke to them, emphasizing the need of Makedon for time of peace. A foe like the Persian Kingdom would surpass many times the danger lurking from Illyrian or Dardanian tribes, or any other local danger as they knew it, to the sorrow of all! On the other hand, an ally like this same Persian Kingdom with such a power would allow the much needed time for peace and prosperity, letting Makedonia govern itself. Once their honor was obviously about to be officially restored by Vouvaris' own admission and dictation to all Persians (and his word had to be kept) as close kin and representative of the High King, it was to Macedonia's advantage to become and remain a friend and ally of Persia. The Makedonian firstborns, their sons, had nothing to fear as guests in the hands of an outstanding and willing to negotiate Satrap. To show further trust in Vouvaris' words and his personal appreciation of all clan heads' consent to these terms, Amyntas would take one step further by offering his own daughter Gygea as lawful wife of Vouvaris, should he accept such offer. House Timenos would undertake this added obligation in good faith to both the clan heads and the Persian delegation!

There was protracted silence from the land lords and much weight shifting from leg to leg as they were all standing, judging, thinking, but there was no dissent or any comment offered either. For some, because they saw reason by their King's words, while some others felt intimidated by the indisputably strong Persian presence and, for the rest of them, because no one else voiced any objection or came-up with a better solution. Amyntas seeing there was at least no objection, addressed Vouvaris again, accepting in the name of all present and as the Makedonian King all Persian terms.

The Satrap looked carefully at all Makedonian faces and lastly rested his eyes on Amyntas, facing him straight and square. Amyntas met the gaze erect, with dignity but also resignation to the (in his judgment) inevitable result. Vouvaris smiled seemingly satisfied and informed Amyntas that he accepted the offering of Gygea's hand, as well the assurances of Macedonia's good will and alliance with Persia. To seal the agreement, he extended his right hand. Amyntas took it and an audible sigh from all present filled the hall.

The next few days passed working out the deal with the help of Ionian scribes and sealing it placing the signets of all participants by their names, while preparations for the wedding were in full gear. The nuptials took place a week after the official ceremony of the new alliance and Persian extrava-gance during its festivities became the talk of all for years. Lynkestis, Dassaretis, Derriopis, Pelago-nia and Paeonia all had their kings and delegates attending. Elimiotis, Orestis and Tymfea also sent delegates (none wanted to offend the Persian bridegroom), as were from Anthemous, Krousis, Myg-donia and the colonies/city-states of Pydna, Aloros and Methoni.

All Persians departed two weeks later, although some garrisons remained (as was the deal) in Ae-gae, in Iraklia Lynkestis, at Vottiaean Kyrros and Paeonian Astivos. Vouvaris' second in command also remained at Aegae, as overseer of the High King's interests and coordinator of all common aims.

There were some discontented Makedonian clan heads and delegates from Olynthos, Pydna and Me-thoni after the departure of the Persians. They were all telling Amyntas he should not have come to terms with the barbarians.

Amyntas had a hard time bringing back his land lords and clan heads in line. Who did Makedonia have as an ally other than the High King? He wanted them to tell him. The Dardanes and Illyres? The Peones and Thrakian tribes? Or, perhaps, the southern city-states with their colonization on Makedonian shores? They had all known nothing but raiding for plunder from the former and imposition of coast blockades from the latter, every time each fancied additional easy revenue for their treasury. Would his clan heads and land lords settle having Orestis and Elimiotis as allies and dictators of Makedonian policy? Each one (and all of them -according to interests) was looking for a complete take-over of nothing else but this very kingdom, the one each and every clan head and land lord present was claiming to have as homeland of honored ancestors who fought through the ages for its independence. Or perhaps they were thinking they were more Makedonians than their own King, sole protectors of the interests of the state? Amyntas told them he was ready to challenge that sort of claim any time one would come out to face him before the whole Makedonian Assembly. All the High King was asking, he said again, was cooperation in case of need, leaving them to look after their own affairs without any take-over, plunder or colonization. One tenth of produce, livestock or timber -if and when asked- was driving anyone into poverty beyond salvation? About the garrisons? Well, all those were a good deterrent for the ones thinking of attacking, as they would aid Makedonia in case of danger from any foe. Further, their Makedonian kin being guests at the court of Vouvaris, includ-ing Amyntas' own son and daughter (as the satrap's wife) should be the best advocates and ambas-sadors of Makedonian interest in the midst of the barbarians and next to the High King's ears.

The land lords and clan heads were thus persuaded. As for the city-state and colonial ambassadors, Amyntas did not bother to offer any explanation of his actions, let alone try to persuade them. Some left his court in anger but unable to realize their threats (Persian presence being obvious to even the blind). Some remained in court because their monetary gains and interests were higher than their proclaimed 'patriotism'. Amyntas never had faith in either, anyway. Weren't those the same ones calling Makedonia barbaric when it suited them and not bothering to distinguish kin-blood from strangers? Weren't they the ones who would like to tear apart his kingdom? The same critics, the same advocates -depending which way the wind blew- imposers of blockades on Macedonia's im-ports and exports when chance was given, had time and again forced Makedonia to an unwilled com-promise and deal. He would very much like to see them try to impose anything on him now! He was itching to see how they would prevent merchants sent from the High King's dominion coming to trade in Makedonia. Only if they had the power to do such a thing, only then would he accept any criticism of his actions!

Amyntas did not live long enough after that to see any real progress in general Makedonian affairs. He died out of a strange illness, not one of his physicians being able to explain or what caused it. His Kingship ended on the third plus twentieth day in the month of Gorpaeos, just a few days shy from his fifth full year as King. Vouvaris came in person to attend the funeral ceremony, bringing back Alexandros and all the rest of Makedonian first-born 'guests' in his care. After the funeral pyre and the King's burial, he made the announcement that Gygea was expecting their first child and, if a boy, he would name the newborn Amyntas! Shortly after, the whole Makedonian Assembly was invited and they proclaimed Alexandros as their new King.

Due to his still young age (he was hardly past his seventh plus ten years since birth) and his role in the slaying of the Persian envoys, Vouvaris strongly recommended Alketas to act as regent -until further notice. Alexandros first, followed by the Assembly, agreed and Alketas accepted. Oaths were exchanged and the deal was sealed by witnessing notables from both sides. A parade of the Makedo-nian army in full battle gear followed, between the sacrificed halves of a male dog while a goat (a re-minder of the one leading Perdikkas to Aegae) led them through inspection.

As events unfolded, Alketas served as regent more years than Alexandros' 'coming of age' warranted. Alketas -in fact- was the ruler of Makedonia for a second time, having full consent of his grand son and the Makedonian Assembly. Gygea gave birth first to a daughter but when she produced a son at her next pregnancy, Alketas left Alexandros to govern, so he could go and witness the naming of a newborn Amyntas...

> "Ellines are told in times of need that they are the ones who gave the light of Knowledge, Democracy and Free-dom to the world and are asked to repeat the feat again and again! So much so, that they don't notice they have been blindfolded and march in the dark now!..."
> D. Th. Delfinopoulos, Makedonian Ellinas Freedom fighter-W.W. II and Teacher.

VI

Alketas took the trip to Thraki and to Asia-by-the-Aegean despite his old age, in order to visit his grand daughter, for Gygea had given birth to a son now, Alketas' first great-grand son! The old King wanted to be present at the boy's name-giving day! His second obligation during the visit was to in-still a further cooperation and support of Persia to Makedonia, as reports of restlessness beyond Peo-nia and Dardania were a daily concern at the Makedonian court. He left Alexandros to rule the state alone, confident that the young King had by now all the wisdom and training required to do so effi-ciently. Both agreed that a stronger Persian presence would be the deterrent the kingdom needed but not having more Persians stationed in Makedonia proper. It was a very subtle, a delicate proposition to present to Vouvaris. "We need your presence, but don't come too close!" Alexandros was sure his Grand Father would (some how) be able to manage a deal.

Alketas stayed at Vouvaris' court for over a year. He enjoyed the company of Gygea, her daughter (now a three year chubby girl with ebony dark hair and sky-blue eyes, a feast to everybody's eyes!) and his great-grand son, the newborn Amyntas! The old King was amazed by the information Vou-varis had on Makedonian affairs. Apparently, the rumored spy system in the High King's service was a fact and truly a well oiled one. The Persian Satrap informed the old King that it was well un-derstood that Makedonia was a client kingdom, not a Persian Satrapy. As an ally and because of strong Persian interest in the region, the High King would increase the Persian presence, but within the western-most area of His domain, namely in Thraki. New troops would be stationed in the lands of the Vissae, Sintikes and Laei, within striking distance from Dardania and outside the Makedonian sphere of interest.

Now Alketas became anxious to return home. Alexandros was keeping him informed with constant messengers, but the old man had grown homesick. He prepared his return. From his own escort, Le-onidas from the house of Agis was the one who asked to be left behind, in order to oversee the young Amyntas' proper education. Actually, Leonidas demanded his staying in the Persian court. His argu-ment was the infant Amyntas needed a proper paedagogue, as was due to a Timenid prince. Obvious-ly, the kid was half Persian and Vouvaris' station in hierarchy would give the best for Amyntas' edu-cation -but that was a Persian one, a barbarian's! A Makedonian (even if only half Makedonian) had to have an Ellenic upbringing. Besides, Leonidas argued, his Father back home had two more sons capable of looking after the family's -as well as Macedonia's- interests! He won the argument and stayed...

Upon his return at Aegae, Alketas was received with honors due to an active King by Alexandros and the residing Persian envoy. The clan heads and land lords present (now named the King's com-panions), as well as the common people, proved to be an added welcome sight for the old man.

Alketas found the affairs between Makedonia and the Persians stationed there since the original deal with Vouvaris much smoother than when he left. This, he found, was due to Alexandros, the returned firstborn 'guests' at the Persian court and because the resident Persian envoy (a man named Armoyiessos/ Armogh Yioush in Persian), son of Ayiapos/Ayupa Osh, was a very capable negotiator and administrator. This Armoyiessos was not a true Persian by blood. His family hailed from a region close to Kafkasos mountains and ancient Kolhis, named Armenia. His whole family was in very high esteem before the High King's own eyes and had received many honors. Armoyiessos was proved to be a man able to reason and find the fine points of negotiating arguments and agreements, when Alexandros' youthful intentions and the clan heads' short-sighted demands were of problematic and ambiguous quality. Thus, Alketas returned to a peaceful kingdom.

As soon as the old King was informed of all important events and plans concerning the governing of the state, Alexandros sought to be left alone with his Grand Father. There was one subject he wanted to discuss, of both state and personal importance. The two sat by the hearth with some fruits and wine served and Alexandros came straight to the point. He was excited and -at the same time- dis-turbed (he said) because he applied for participation at the upcoming Pan-Ellenic competition in the third plus fiftieth Olympiad. The pride and bitterness mixed in his voice announcing that to Alketas, was more than obvious. The old King understood at once that his grand son met with some sort of re-jection from the Ellanodikes, the judges in Elis region where Olympia is located and the competition takes place. He asked for details. Well, Alexandros quipped, the southern Ellines were more eager to prove him a barbarian rather than one of their own. They asked his proxies (and they provided all information) for proof of the Timenid family tree, all the way back to Karanos and Timenos! Korin-thians, Eretrians, Halkidians and Megarians made everything possible under their influence to dis-credit him. The Spartans were more like spectators during the debate, the Athinians were offering lip service to both sides and, if it wasn't for the Argives, the Sikyonians and the majority of the Elian Ellanodikes, he wouldn't have been admitted to enter the race of diavlos.

Alketas took a long sip from his wine cup and remained motionless in his thoughts for some time. A-lexandros thought for a moment that his Grand Father was disturbed with his intention to partici-pate and he inquired timidly if that was the case. Alketas dismissed the question with a move of his hand and emphasized that with a following move of his head. He took some more wine, let a deep sigh come out and spoke his mind.

The southern city-states had to be taught a subtle lesson -he said. He understood and knew their reasoning of their argument. It was all political pressure and holier-than-thou attitude, because they had lost their upper-hand dictation to Makedonian policy since the kingdom's alliance with Persia. He knew that behind the scene, the propaganda would rage and names would be called, mostly out of inability to dictate like they used to. Did they bring any objections to Thessalian or Viottian Thivae participation of athletes? He knew the answer was no! Why? He knew the answer to that too! Thes-salia had willingly agreed to Persian alliance, as did the Viottian Thivans, although no Persian envoys had gone to ask for earth and water from them. The High King accepted their submission but saw no need to send troops there, for obvious reasons. Now, on the other hand, that left these regions free to 'act' as nothing had changed -politically speaking. Although everybody knew it, Thivae could pro-claim affiliation with the city-states, as there was no visible Persian presence in their territory. So could Thessalia and they were both 'accommodating' southern city-state vanities since the need for such was a lot minor compared to what Makedonia could accommodate with for the needs of those states. There was no need for Korinthos or Eretria and Halkis to colonize Thessalian inland, for they were holding the island approaches to its shores. Thivae was just another city-state hardly holding its own influence over Viottia with little gains to offer to the commerce-hungry Halkis and Megara. As for Athinae and Sparti, the former was not (yet) as strong, with competing Aegina at its doorstep and the latter had no interest outside Peloponnisos. Now, as far as Makedonia was concerned, the econo-mic power had shifted from city-state dictation to Persian support. Colonization and sea blockades had to be curtailed -at least for now. Cereals and timber along with animal hides had to be purchased on better terms, for fear they would end-up sold to Persia and extortion with Illyrian or Thrakian threat of invasion had come to end, because of Persian presence. These were the reasons behind all the 'investigating' of Alexandros' Ellenic roots and a subtle form of pressure and 'indignation' by the city-states, amounting to nothing more but jealousy and bitterness for losing some -if not most- of their power in Makedonia. What Alexandros now had to do, was to make sure he would train with vigor to ensure his right to participate in the competition. Better yet, to win the crown of victory! That should be the Makedonian answer to converted insults. Did Alexandros understand all these?

The young King did and promised he would do his best. When something concerned him person-ally, he was very attentive and prone to achieve his goal(s). Makedonian dignity and Ellenic identity was such a concern. His Ellenic pride was hurt though, realizing he got support for his participation based on the fear of a foreign power rather than his blood kinship.

As it happened, Alexandros did not win the diavlos race at that Olympiad. His failure to receive the olive branch crown increased his appetite to try again the next time around. Meantime, the develop-ment of events in the broad Ellenic world were mixed. News arrived that disaster hit the colony in the island of Korsiki, thanks to combined armies of Karhidonians and Etrurians. They took and burned Alalia, forcing its inhabitants to move across to the Italian peninsula, leaving the island in the hands of their enemies. In the islands of the Aegean, Samos received a new strong man, a Tyranos, while Persia was watching from across indifferently. This man named Polykratis followed a naval policy, bringing most of the neighboring islands under Samos' leadership, via its now powerful fleet and piratical (when necessary) pressure on the commerce of others. The Vavylonian kingdom ceased to exist, as Persian armies conquered the city. The news came to Aegae as Athinian merchants came to intro-duce in the market their new decorative style of wares, having red as their prime color motif. For reason of time consumption, not all the news were actually news taken place recently but were 'news' nonetheless.

On Makedonian affairs, the young King (under active guidance from Alketas) worked hard in order to achieve permanent recognition of governing directly the regions of Almopia, Amfaxitis and Anthe-mous. Vouvaris sent the message next that the High King had died, succeeded by a new one, named Kamvysis (Kambujiya -or close to that- in Persian) who was preparing for the conquest of Egyptos now. Alexandros sent a message of Makedonian sympathy for the loss of such a great King but its pleasure of the rightful succession by another, equally great one. In that message Alexandros was pledging Makedonian support to the new High King and subtly recommended the annexation of Lynkestis, Derriopis and Pelagonia, to 'secure' every future support and 'permanently' expand the Persian sphere of influence in those areas. The answer came back partly negative. As Vouvaris ex-planed to his in-laws, Persia was interested in expansion which was not already hers. The mentioned regions had accepted the High King's rule with earth and water a few years back. House Timenos was recognized as the House of Makedon but Lynkos, Derriopis and Pelagonia were to remain semi-independent kingdoms -at least for now! Obviously, Persia did not want a Timenid Makedonia to be the strongest player of policy in the region. Alketas advised Alexandros to accept and let time work on their side.

A southern city-state protest had reached the High King's ears, as Timenid rule over the shores of Anthemous and Amfaxitis obviously was spoiling their designs for more colonization and market securing posts. The High King was warring against Egyptos and did not want any distraction. Soon, the news of his victory over the last Farao/king of Egyptos was known, proving the invincibility of the Persians. A temporary uprising from Illyrian marauders was easily repelled by combined Makedo-nian forces of House Timenos and Lynkos with Pelagonia, ensuring the latter's status as semi-inde-pendent kingdoms. Persia saw them as true allies, helping in time of need and holding past agree-ments. The new High King put down another insurrection, this time from Vavylona, as the ancient city had not easily forgotten its past power, but did not live long to achieve further. He died because of an infection from a wound. Some said it happened because Kamvysis did not respect the Egyptian god Apis, killing the sacred bull. Others said it was because the wound of the King had not been cleaned properly, which caused putrefaction and eventual death! He was succeeded by a close relative of the royal family, a man named Darios (Darayava).

About the same time and during the fourth plus fiftieth Olympiad, Alexandros achieved his goal of being crowned Olympionikis! The name of Makedonia and House Timenos was etched in the memo-ry of Ellas for ever now! With the start of Persia's new High King, Sparti got involved somehow in politics outside Peloponnisos, by invitation of Samians who disliked the rule of Polykratis in their island. Spartan contingents helped in ousting the tyranos/tyrant, but their upper-handed treatment of their Samian allies, forced them out of the island shortly after and back to Sparti.

Some Thrakian tribes then revolted against the High King and Alexandros, keeping his agreements, led Makedonian cavalry to aid the

Persians under Armoyiessos and Vouvaris bring that revolt to a fast end. Persia re-established her dominion in Parorvilia, Odomantiki, Idonia, the lands of the Satrae and the Vissae. Because of that, Mygdonia and Kristonia were also attached to the House of Timenos kingdom. Alexandros let the local kings and notables rule as before, with the understanding that they would follow his lead in all matters of serious nature.

Soon the royal treasury started having more revenue, thanks to those acquisitions and Persian subsidy, via Vouvaris services and the High King's recognition of Makedonian alliance. Within a few months' time a new Vavylonian revolt was put under control, the High King campaigning in person and, with troops from Vouvaris' own Satrapy by his side. Now the High King saw only one solution to bringing peace by stopping the revolts from any subjugated nation and tribe. That was through common economy and common justice within the realm. For that, he issued high quality standard coins of pure gold and allowed captured tribes by the Vavylonians to return to their ancestral lands.

His coin issue became so trusted and well known (even outside His realm), it surpassed everything else in commercial use. These coins took after His name and were called Dariki! The only (partial at that) competition against his currency were the silver staters of Halkis! Makedonia now having some better commerce and more revenue, issued coinage (admittedly far bellow Darikos' quality) with the body of a resting goat (commemorating the billy-goat which was the cause of Perdikkas' building of Aegae so many years past).

In Ellenic politics and city-state influence, Sparti established her hegemony over most of Pelopon-nisos, as she subjugated Messinia and forced Korinthos, Ahaia and other smaller city-states to follow her lead on a do-it-or-else dictation. Only Elis remained out of such lead because of her status as the Olympic state and Argolis, though Argos now was cast much below its former glory.

Athinian wares had by now surpassed the Korinthian and Aeginitan ones in general commerce, though there was some stagnation following the year after the latest Makedonian acquisitions, on account of events in Athinae and Attiki in general. A pair of lovers by the names Armodios and Aris-togiton got in a heated competition with the Athinian strong man Pisistratos. Their quarrelling led to Pisistratos' murder and he was succeeded by his brother Ippias. Ippias obviously wanting to avenge Pisistratos oppressed the two lovers' supporters and that led to a revolt which forced him to leave the city-state and seek refuge at Aegae. Athinians elevated Armodios and Aristogiton to the pedestal of heroes and, finding offensive that Ippias was granted a stay at the Makedonian court, refused to honor prior commerce commitments through Alketas, a fact which cost the Makedonian economy a lot.

Alexandros was forced to go in person and re-negotiate terms with Athinian commerce, thus send-ing Ippias away from Aegae, to the Persian court, seeking the protection and favors of the High King.

Because Alexandros was pressed to negotiate a new treaty (on better terms for Athinae) on timber exports and earthenware on imports, the Athinian Dimos (public) -for now Athinae turned to an all public form of government called Dimokratia- named him in return their Proxenos or Ambassador, able to represent any and all Athinian interests in Makedonia. Obviously a nominal title for the King but, once the Persian naval power was far from the Aegean and Athinae had the means of blockading any or all trade coming from the south, this was a title which empowered Alexandros with partial negotiating ability in matters of interest to both states. Besides, Alexandros following the wise advice of his Grand Father did not want to antagonize any Ellenic state to the point that would lead him to total dependence on Persia. The Asiatic power was good to guard Makedonia from north and east. All other affairs with the south had to remain entre-nous, as strictly Ellenic as possible.

About the same time, the High King Darios perceived to incorporate all Thraki and Skythia beyond the river Istros under His command, according to His plan for universal union under one High King.

He prepared a huge army and crossed from Asia to Evropi through the narrow channel of water named Ellispontos which connects the Aegean with Efxinos Pontos via Propontis and Vosporos. In order to do the crossing he put his engineers to build a bridge made of ships tied together. His army put the rest of Thrakian tribes under His rule and then, He crossed Istros, attacking the Skythians. They had their own war tactics though, which frustrated the plans of the High King. They refused to give battle. They harassed His army instead by using bowmen on horse to attack the Persians and then retreating in their vast open country. Soon the Persian army was exhausted and far from its supply lines. Hunger and loss of life from the harassing enemy brought the moral of the troops to a very low point. The High King was forced to a retreat, placing Istros as the frontier of his vast realm.

Darios returned to his capital city of Soussa, leaving behind a great number of troops stationed in Thraki and looking after His possessions.

By this time Alketas was a very old man and retired from most activities. The majority of his Eteri friends from the clan heads and houses were dead. Alexandros was now the King of Makedon, all Persian restrictions withdrawn. Peace and relevant prosperity of the kingdom had been achieved.

This prosperity lasted longer with the foreign power of Persia than with the Ellenic city-state of Athinae. Another change in Athinian politics brought to power Klisthenis and Makedonia had to re-start negotiations for commerce and open sea routes with the south. Sending proxies and with added personal attention, Alexandros managed a new treaty -after having a real hard time doing so.

A new revolt in Egyptos involved Athinae and helped the agreement. The Attic state sent an expe-ditionary force to Egyptos against the Persians and did not want any side distractions. The High King did not waste any time putting the Egyptian revolt down and the Athinian force returned to Attiki defeated. Just before the closing of this conflict, another revolt started with much bigger impact in Ellenic and Persian affairs. The Ionian city-states of Asia-by-the-Aegean formed an alliance and rebelled. They had some success at the beginning, freeing the coastal areas and burning the city of Sardis. As the Persians freed themselves from the Egyptian campaign and their troops came upon the Ionians, they recovered much of the lost ground. At that, the Ionians asked for help from the other Ellenic city-states. The ones answering the call were Athinae and Eretria, sending naval squadrons and a number of oplites. Sparti -when asked- demanded too much from the Ionians, so she 'preferred' to stay in Lakonia and in charge of Peloponnisos. As Athinian and Eretrian ships were sailing for Ionia, Alketas embarked in a different ship on his way to meet his ancestors and at the ripe age of nine plus seventy years…

Athinian and Eretrian support of the Ionian revolt brought some respite initially but the Persians had the upper hand in numbers and provisions and, within few years time, both expeditionary forces of Eretria and Athinae had to abandon the Ionians to their fate. The High King re-established His rule and (with very few exceptions) allowed the Ionian Ellines to pick-up with their lives, as long as their policy now was to remain aligned to the one of Persia! He was not happy at all with Athinae and

Eretria though. He decided the Ellenic city-states had to come under His rule in their entirety. He sent hundreds of heralds and delegations (with armed escorts -just in case) to all subjected and allied tribes for aid and to all Ellenic city-states for earth-and-water tokens of submission. He got what was asked from most of them.

Sparti's answer was to throw the delegates into a chasm, killing them. Because of that, the rest of Peloponnisos refused the Persian demand. Eretria and Athinae were not even asked, as being the prime offenders and the main target. In later years, Athinian ego boasted they had given the same treatment to the High King's delegates as had Sparti, but that was and is just Athinian 'spice' to their side of the story.

Alexandros was strongly advised by Vouvaris (an aged Satrap by now) to aid the High King with provisions and troops. Makedonia, he reasoned, would be in the main route of the Persian armies' march and could not afford to do otherwise. Alexandros had no other choice. Ignoring the High King would create a very serious danger for his kingdom. Even if the Persians were to be stopped by some miracle, their agents could and would create unrest within his not yet consolidated new regions, plus the barbarian tribes of the north would be given a free hand to renew invasions. On the other hand, Ellenic traditions and blood kinship were hard to ignore! Alketas had advised tight relations with the city-states, at (almost) all cost! Having received but prosperity and aid from the Persians all these years, an infant son (named Perdikkas) and no time for adventures beyond the means of his kingdom's realities, Alexandros wished the old King was still alive. He decided to accommodate both camps -if he could, as best as he could.

Tyhi, the goddess of luck, made-up her mind to be on Alexandros' side for the time being and thank Dias the Father of all for that. Athinae changed its leadership one more time. The rising star of the new administration of Dimokrates (fosters of Democracy) this time a man called Themistoklis. This new man of power in Attiki, had in mind a much broader Athinian role in the sphere of politics and prestige among the city-states, as well as demonstrating a wise foresight of things to come on account of the A-thinian politically antagonistic relations with Persia.

In order to secure Athinae's major role in the Aegean sphere of influence and make Attiki a leading state, he needed (Athinae needed) the vast expanse and resources of the open seas. To achieve his goal numerous merchant fleets and war ships were a must! Why the sea? For one, both

Sparti (on the city-state competition) and Persia (with her Asiatic vast resources) were too strong on land. The two disastrous attempts with the Egyptian and Ionian revolts against Persia had amply proved that Athinae was far from being a major power. If, on the other hand, Sparti seemed reluctant to make a move out of Peloponnisos, Persia had no qualm of flexing her muscles against far-off places. She was preparing to advance and there was no secret that the High King was vexed! His advance with the huge army he was capable of producing, would need a large support fleet, transporting supplies. A fleet like that was in the making, as Persia had secured the cooperation of the Finikian city-states of Sidon and Tyros with free access to timber from the Livanos range and was about to subdue the whole of Kypros island, adding that fleet to Persian naval forces. If one was a pragmatist, one could easily see that the reconquered Ionians would also have to support the High King's armadas with their own crews and war ships.

Themistoklis could picture the Persian advantage in full and wanted to bring it down to size. What the steppes meant to Persian armies during the Skythian campaign a few years ago, the Aegean under Athinian mastery could play its counterpart role now, for Athinian hegemony of the seas and, eventually, of the mainland city-states! He envisioned a powerful Athinian fleet of triremes (τριηρεις) capable of producing a great price to be paid by the High King in his venture against Ellas and be-come the decisive factor of Athinian survival first, then predominance of the seas and, ergo, of Ellas.

But Athinae and Attiki did not have the necessary timber for such a fleet, nor was it readily avail-able within a short distance. The solution would be to import timber from other city-states or king-doms. Sikelia was too far to consider. Asia-by-the-Aegean and Halkidiki were virtually under Persia. Peloponnisos was poor of shipping timber along with Sparti's reluctance to aid Athinae. Only Make-donia could provide, as in the past, albeit under Persian influence yet an independent ally.

This kingdom, Themistoklis reasoned, has the approaches which (more or less) Athinae and her al-lies controled and timber which was accessible and easy to transport distances from the mountains to the gulf of Therma, via the lagoon of Pella. We already are dealing with the Makedonian kingdom on various commodities and under the tolerant eye of the Persian Ambassador at Aegae, Armoyiessos. Dressing-up a bone of a more relaxed commerce on tolls from the colonies of Methoni, Pydna and Aloros would convince Alexandros to look for an expanded commerce with Attiki. A negotiated amount of silver -as a last ditch offer from Athinae- and the deal for extra timber for ship-building should come relatively easy.

But there was no extra silver nor enough cargo ships at the moment to transport Makedonian timber. Would Alexandros' obsession for anything Ellenic (the 'kid' had gone to great length in proving his family roots for the Olympic competition) be a string to pull and get credit for future payments? Themistoklis had to try this venue and Athinian 'good will' emissaries started flooding the Makedonian court.

The King was given to understand that Athinae realized the need of Makedonia to allow Persian influence, even support the Persians in many ways because of that very need. Why! Athinae would have done the same -if Athinae had to 'wear Makedonian boots'! But the previous Athinian admin-istration had blundered badly and now there was no chance of changing course without 'losing face' and the credibility of an aspiring leader among the city-states of Ellas. The emissaries made sure to point out that this Athinian aspiration for leadership was having the same odds of success as a miracle would of a ship adrift amidst the worst storm, but miracles are known to happen and Makedonia would greatly benefit in that case. What was obvious was that the storm was on its way to hit and hit hard! What was needed was the source of the expected miracle and, the Athinians emphasized, Themi-stoklis knew the source was none other than Makedonia!

While this flattery was in full use at the Makedonian court, a true miracle happened and gave basis and substance to Themistoklis' dreams. A new rich vain of silver was suddenly discovered in Attiki, by the already active mines at Lavrion! Now Themistoklis could afford backing-up his words with actual buying power. First he convinced the Athinian citizens of the need of a strong fleet, ostensibly against their perennial foe, the Aeginitans. Being a seasoned politician, one only Athinae could produce and develop, he continued his efforts on two fronts. On one hand he pursued his plan in Ma-kedonia with Alexandros, on the other secured friends at the home front against his rival, Aristidis. Once he gathered enough support and the approval of his fellow citizens, he put his plan to work. He introduced the method of ostrakismos (ostracism) in Athinian politics. With his ability to orate, he managed to have Aristidis ostracized and sent to Thraki, at his personal property near an Athinian outpost and away from the city politics. Meantime, he promoted a new found ally named Miltiadis and now Themistoklis was truly in charge, free to materialize his dream!

Athinae now needed time to materialize Themistoklis' dream but time was a commodity which was in short order. Persia was known to be on the move and the war against Aegina was not developing in favor of Athinian wishes yet! Goddess Tyhi favored the daring soul of Themistoklis once more! This time news, verified news, came from Asia that Darios died from a stroke at a time when his per-sonal servant was reminding him of his oath to destroy Athinae for her audacity to aid the Ionians few years back. Time became available to Athinae as Persia procrastinated. The legitimate succession being of utmost importance set other Persian plans and goals aside. Xerxis (Khshayarsha) now be-came the new High King and he was the one who needed time to establish his hold in his kingdom first, before venturing elsewhere.

The silver mines of Lavrion were producing funds in abundance now. The citizens were well fed and not keen to ask too many questions of public funds for Makedonian timber. Recruiting sailors was also an easy thing to do, as an offer of higher payment was at hand. Many pariki (the free, registered immigrants from the Aegean islands) were easy and eager targets for hire as instructors training Athinian youth in navigation and oarsmanship. Now the time to get ready was bought and ships could be built, crews could be trained, all because of a timely discovery and an unexpected death.

Goddess Tyhi (Fortune) truly looked upon Themistoklis with favor.

Negotiations were sped-up and silver found its way fast to Makedonia, as did the latter's timber in reaching Attiki. Great titles were bestowed to Alexandros, a way which Themistoklis favored the most. Titles cost nothing to Athinae and titles increased Alexandros' Ellenic sense of importance! The Makedonian King was not only reinstated as Proxenos, he was triumphantly proclaimed Phil-Ellinas, this title meaning he was the only one concerned with and active about the well being of Ellas as a whole and this title was installed in all prominent Agora locations in Attiki and Athinae itself! The-mistoklis knew well that all these (if victory came to crown Athinae) could remain as were or revised according to Athinian needs of the time. In case of defeat, well, would it really matter?

The war against Aegina finally came to an end, Athinae being victorious. Aegina had to declare an everlasting support toward her former foe and be happy Themistoklis did not impose the customary severities. They had not yet understood his cleverness. One, who knew him well, could detect a per-manent hidden smile and air about his presence. What made him even happier was the fact that Per-sia had 'bought' the Athinian build-up as a local war against Aegina only and stayed out as a distant observer. With Persia neutralized and Makedonian timber for her fleet at hand, Athinae stood ready for her shot to glory! Themistoklis now turned his attention to Sparti and other city-states for addit-ional support...

"Inside the soul of each Ellinas one can find
the characters of Odysseas, Filippos, Alexandros
and Hadjiavatis, the hyperboles of cunning,
diplomacy, mindless bravery and
miseric whimpering in coexistence and all
combined in one! The trouble is that we do
not know how to use each one as needed!"
Andreas G. Rados, Makedonian Ellinas, freedom fighter W.W. II

VII

The young man was sitting on a rocky outcrop, high-up on one of Pindos' peaks overlooking Lake Lyhnitis. His brows were forming an almost straight line above his eyes, a deep crease on the upper part of his crooked nose being the only thing separating them. He was sitting there for a long time, completely motionless, excepting an occasional sharp move of a hand swatting away a persistent fly which (unwisely) would land on some part of his face.

Obviously preoccupied with deeply concerning thoughts, he looked more aged than his actual two times ten and nine years. Standing up he would measure close to nine stretched-open palms of an average man and his well toned, wiry body, would make him look more exceptional than anyone else in his tribe. Dark blue eyes turning fiery at the least of provocations and long reddish hair falling free on his shoulders added to his leonine appearance.

The young man was the heir apparent to his father's kingship, the chosen one among ten plus two other brothers. The Old Man was a very productive chieftain, taking under account that there were also eight more females born to his hearth -between the already mentioned males. But the Old Man was really old now and crippled. The untold years of raiding, running away and hiding in intervals between plunders and chases, all had taken their toll. His health deteriorated recently even more because of wide spread hunger among the tribe.

Hunger was their number one enemy in recent years. A constant reminder of a life not really worth living with the exception of few times of good plunder or the (even more rare) natural abundance of produce or game within the mostly uncultivated and heavily forested area called home grounds. Yes, there were times when game was plentiful from spring to fall but, mostly, greater famine in times of winter! The god-forsaken Makedonians to the tribe's south and east and the Ipirotes to south and west had left nothing worthy of cultivation to his tribe of Vryges, except few narrow valleys and the dense forests of unapproachable mountains. All the Vrygian power and glory and abundance of old seemed to have gone for ever!

The times when the Vryges were masters of upper Makedonia and most of Ipiros were lost in the mist of a sleepy memory of youngsters, as the tales were told at night time before the heat and dense smoke of a hearth's crackling noise in its vain attempt to keep the gusty winter out of impoverished huts. These were stories of times told by old crones with raspy voices and equally misty eyes to toddlers with unrestricted dreams…

But there were true times of old when the Vryges were ruling as far south as the Viottian Thivae, times before cursed Kadmos and Idipos brought Ahean and Danaan Ellenic power. Times before the Dorian expansion and permanent loss of all that was dear and glorious! The Vryges were pushed to upper Pindos then, caged between the Illyrian tribes and becoming one with them. The few 'lucky' ones, who managed to move through Thraki and across the sea to settle in the east, became the Asiatic Fryges. But even they (according to prevailing accounts) didn't remain free and prosperous for long.

Hittites first, the Lydes and now Mides and Perses became their masters. King Midas had to have truly been cursed by the gods! In spite his riches and fame (or just because of that) his glory and power did not last!

Back in those years there used to be kinship between the Vryges and Makedon. The Ipirotes were not too distant cousins even now. Yet, hardship and years of depravations, years of isolation among various nations, eventually created a total separation between the three tribes. Now, alongside the Il-lyrian pressure and forced blood mixture with Dexares, Tavlantians and, especially, Parthines, the balance had turned and the Vryges became one blood with the Illyrians.

The young man called in Vrygian by the name Eidjik (in Makedonian and Ipirotic his name was known as Evdikos) knew the difficulties and dangers in raiding and moving against Makedon or even Ipiros now. The Ipirotes had just receive new colonists and reinforcements from Kerkyrian and Kor-inthian settlers, all well equipped in oplitis' armor, while the Makedonians had been proved of being a tough nut to crack, especially with Persian support in recent years.

There was much pressure though from further north. The Dardanes had taken the leadership away from the Parthines, Dexares and Tavlantians and, by extension, his own tribe. The last few years had been very hard as natural recourses were inadequate due to heavy winters and dry, hot summers. The perennial hunger was forcing tribes to move against others. In addition, Athinian agents had recently approached the Dardanian chief with promises of large loot and silver.

They did want to keep the Persians preoccupied and weakened along with their potential or existing allies. Makedonia was already a Persian ally, they reasoned, one who was getting rich and stronger because of that. Was it not also in the interest of Dardania to eliminate such a competitor and recover past fame and glory?

The Dardanian chief, king Brugha, was not so naïve and the recent demonstration of Persian might was still in his memory. Besides, he reasoned, was not Makedonia an Athinian supplier of all natural recourses plus timber? Yes, the answer was, but Athinae was about ready with a mighty naval force which could come and blockade the sea access of Makedonia, plus support the land invasion of Dardania and her allies. Wouldn't that be a tremendous source of riches and military advantage to all? End of hunger for years to come, renewed prestige and power and, who knows? It could result in a permanent expulsion of the Persians from the area and Makedonia a subject people to Dardania! As for Athinae, a free hand in all commercial traffic would repay the cost of the silver given now.

Brugha was eventually convinced by the Athinian 'incentives' and now he was preparing to move against Makedonia with the aid of his subject tribes of Tavlantes, Dexares and Parthines. News of Darios' death made things somewhat easier. Perhaps the Persians would be too preoccupied with succession struggles, perhaps the new High King would be content with his vast kingdom as it was and let the affairs in remote (for him) areas develop as they might…

The pressure on the Vryges now became almost a no option. Either they would have to join Brugha and his allies or become his first victims on his drive against an enemy who was nonetheless a combined force of a vast empire and its (strong for the time being) allies. And what had Athinae promised she would do with her fleet, Eidjik was not so sure. But his father's -as well as his own- concern was hunger! The tribe had the very uncertain future of either starving to death, joining the invaders and suffering (perhaps) unforeseen loss of life and failure (in case Persia and Makedonia would react with force and unity), or be victimized for certain from the wrath of Brugha.

Perhaps, Eidjik thought, this was the time to revive old times of prosperity and glory. Perhaps there would be some territorial gains in Derriopis, Dassaretis or Lynkestis. There might be some more space to move, cultivate and hunt. It would be nice indeed! Under Dardanian leadership though? What good would it be to have Brugha rule (even temporarily with no actual occupation of the homeland)? As things were, one thing had remained somewhat secure: The Makedonians and Ipirotes were not moving northward to expand. They were only counter raiding after being attacked or provoked in any other ways. For that, there was always the safety of retreating up on the highest Pindos peaks, until the danger was gone. Cursed be the heavy winters and the scorched summers of late years! Deaths had reached the high-est levels in recent memory and no births were planned (who needed another starving mouth to feed -and with what?).

The hard decision whether to be led by the Dardanes remained. These were not Illyrians by blood, nor were they a distant kin like Ipirotes and Makedonians. They were a tribe of their own, their roots lost in the depth of time, before the large migrations. Ah, but they now had the power! They were leading, followed voluntarily by Parthines, Dexares and Tavlantes, who were Illyrians -therefore kin. What kind of choice did Eidjik's tribe have?

Eidjik stood-up and stretched his limbs to let his blood circulate after all this motionless time. The wind now started blowing stronger, making his unkempt reddish hair cover his face. His eyes became relaxed and the crease between his eyebrows all but disappeared, bringing the latter a bit further apart and giving his face a new look, close to being handsome. The decision was made.

He stood there for some time inhaling deeply the fresh pine scent, looking at the fragile wild flowers sprouting between the most precarious and unthinkable crevices of the rock formation and smiled. If the gods had made life thrive out of nowhere, then there was a chance for his tribe to continue living regardless the outcome of this new venture.

Eidjik started sliding downslope. There would be an elders' meeting this evening, a lot of fermented sour milk to be given to young warriors and preparations the next morning to join the oncoming hordes of armed Dardanians. There was no other way. He arrived at the sample of a village the tribe had as its focal point of all gatherings and called on his men to sound the horns...

The High King Darios had started amassing his troops for the expedition against Athinae and Eret-ria just a few years back. The coming of Ippias at his court had invigorated Darios' will to punish the 'sinners'. The exiled Athinian did everything in his power to convince the High King of its necessity and (of course) the need to replace Themistoklis and enlist Attiki as Persia's ally under Ippias' rule.

Death came to him before his dream of revenge was achieved and Ippias aimed to convince the new ruler of all nations. Darios' son Xerxis had some troubles of his own at the beginning of his reign in Egyptos, thus delayed the expedition.

Finally the time came for its start. With the aid of Finikian ships of war from Tyros and Sidon and transports from Kypros and the Ionian cities (under Persia again), the troops departed sailing on the Aegean. In charge of this expedition were two satraps of renown Datis (Datyish) and Artafernis (Ar-taferna). They were having Ippias as their guide and representing some unsatisfied Athinians who could hardly wait for the end of this 'Dimokratia' in their city-state. After a victory, Ippias would reign and they would benefit again from the fruits of the few ruling the many (as it was some years back) as friends and allies of the High King, or step over the dead bodies of a ruined city!

The Persian/Finikian fleet moved north by north/west, subduing or burning several island cities on its way, arriving at Dilos, the holy island of the sun-god Apollon. They turned it to ruin. Next stop was Eretria. After a short siege, the city fell with out any help from Evian or (worst yet) Athinian al-lied forces. All its spared citizens were sold to slavery or sent to

Sousa as living proof of their defeat and for the entertainment of the new High King. Athinae was now the next victim in line…

The miracle of a battle on the location of Marathon, a small swampy plain of Attiki to the north/east of Athinae -perfect for landing massive numbers of troops- was what drowned the dreams of Xerxis and Ippias alike. Thousands of Persians lay dead in that small plain, slaughtered as they retreated in terror toward their ships. With the sole help from a small Plataean contingent of oplites, Themistok-lis' protégé, Miltiadis led the Athinians and rose as a shining star in his strategic triumph of the few against the multitude! The aid sought by Themistoklis from Peloponnisos and in particular from Sparti arrived two days later, too late for any share of glory. The only thing the Spartans did was to inspect the battle field and admire the deed. Their excuse for their late arrival was a religious fest-ival they had to attend before going to war…

Amidst this newfound glory, Athinian politics did not forget Makedonia. Under the pretext of acting against Persian interests, the Athinian fleet blockaded the access of Therma and the Pella lagoon (keeping their promise to Brugha). When Alexandros protested to Athinian merchant/envoys, Them-istoklis withdrew the name 'benefactor' of the Makedonian King's honorific titles and 'forgot' to pay the last two installments for the timber purchased. Alexandros did nothing about it. His hands were full. He had to repulse the invading armies of Dardanes and their Illyrian allies, plus an increased presence of Persian troops in Thraki and Makedonia proper. Vouvaris was sending demanding messages on behalf of the High King for more Makedonian cooperation, as a new and more powerful Persian fleet transporting new armies sailed from Asiatic ports. This time a very close relative and equally capable man was in charge. Mardonios (Mardahna or Mardanyioush), cousin of Xerxis himself!…

Meantime, the Dardanian invasion had its first victims as Derriopia tasted its onslaught first. Soon, upper Makedonian chieftains started joining the invaders one by one, eager to save what they could at the expense of others. The nominal king of the area, Mahetas, didn't even bother for a show of resistance. He flew to Alexandros' court at Aegae leaving behind him his wives, an infant son and all his daughters. Lynkestis was a different case. Numerous battles took place at the passes of Varnous and at the narrows between the lakes of Major and Minor Vrygiis. King Arraveos did what he could to stall the invaders until help from Alexandros and other Makedonian subordinate kings could arrive, hopefully with Persian aid also! He managed (with great difficulty) to stop the enemy at the foothills of Vernon, before his fortified town of Alalkomenae.

Alexandros could not count on Persian help now, as things were. He gathered what he could out of his own clan heads and from Imathia, Vottiaea and Eordea and entered Lynkos in support of Arra-veos. There was a setback to his effort as Elimiotis moved to annex the kingdom of Tymfea and Orestis formed a separate alliance with Dassaretis and the Ipirotes of Haonia. They amassed their troops at their borders and stood-by, uneasy observers of an uncertain outcome.

Alexandros initiated a battle at the valley of Erigon, between the slopes of Varnous and Voras where the river was easily fordable and, with help from Arraveos (who moved in with speed from Alalkomenae) defeated the combined armies of Dardanes, Vryges and Tavlantes. The Dexares and Par-thines were delayed because of their looting of areas in Lynkestis and did not join their allies in bat-tle. In spite of his solid victory, Alexandros did not have the power to chase the invaders out and saw to a negotiated truce. The invaders were to hold on to what they had taken up to this time. That meant the loss of Derriopia as a buffer kingdom and almost over a third of Lynkos, along with plenty of livestock and slaves. In return, the invaders handed to him all the Derriopian chieftains who had joined the invasion in hope of saving their skin and easy loot. Alexandros put them all to death and threw Mahetas in prison. Derriopis was left under Vrygian occupation and in a very sorry state.

Not having the resources and unwilling to open another front, Alexandros was also forced to recog-nize the annexation of Tymfea by Elimiotis and 'turn a blind eye' on the Orestian alliance with Hao-nia and Dassaretis. He hoped that time and Persian help (when ready to be given) would be his advantage in turning the tables and restoring his prestige and lost ground. In keeping an 'open line' with the southern city-states. He also requested through the unofficial venues of visiting merchants support in the form of oplites' trainers as volunteers for his Makedonian army, in exchange for any natural resources Makedonia could offer.

Thessalia had its own affairs to worry about, as they had declared open support and alliance to Persia and so did Thivae, who was afraid of Athinian invasion of her lands. Sparti was too far by Lakonian views and didn't bother to answer. As for Attiki, Themistoklis' answer was a virtual no! Athinae was readying for a life or death struggle. Every citizen was needed for the show-down against Persia. In a con-ciliatory but also preemptive move, Themistoklis (covering all possible angles) named Makedonia a friend of Athinae but also of Persia. If the High King could not protect his friends, then Makedonia ought to change policy altogether! Athinae would help in good faith and with a loan of silver, if Alexandros would openly come on the Athinian side. The loan could be used by the Makedonian King as he saw fit in repelling his kingdom's invaders and could be redeemed by way of additional timber shipments. No word was said of his back-stabbing with the Dardanian invasion or his 'forgotten' payments of timber already furnished for the Athinian naval power.

This message was duly noted by Alexandros. Vouvaris had sent a message of his own at the same time, stating now that timber given to Athinae for building-up her fleet was against the wishes of the High King and Alexandros would have to do better. This message was escorted for emphasis by additional Persian units entering and reinforcing the garrisons stationed on the fringes of Makedon.

The Timenid King did not have much of a choice. He sent a message to Themistoklis thanking him for offering a loan of silver (Alexandros wanted open options too!) but Makedonia was in need of armed oplites, not money. He warned that further shipments of timber would have to be under the pretense of being used by another city-state, provisioned in irregular secrecy and in cash. Persia had increased her presence in his kingdom and all Makedonian hands were also needed for the country's defense.

Themistoklis couldn't care less at this point! Athinian need for timber was met by now and crews were in constant training with the newly built ships. Sparti and her Peloponnisian allies had prom-ised timely help when and if Persia would strike again. The Aeginitans agreed on stopping any hostilities and her fleet of warships would stand by the Athinian fleet in case of emergency. Makedon now was in the Athinian minds as distant as Persia and, obviously, far weaker to consider. Alexandros' title as Phil-Ellinas was not removed but the relation was distinctly cooled-off as Athinian aims shift-ed again.

On the other side, Alexandros clearly saw that no consideration to Makedonian needs would be paid as long as his kingdom did not subject itself to Athinian demands and policies in leading. As for Persia, Makedonia was an 'open road' from the east. Thraki was teeming with Persian troops and many of the Thrakian kings were eager to come and take part in the spoils, if the High King would decide that Makedon was following too independent lines. What Athinian back-stabbing almost did with the latest invasion, Persia could achieve with 'a blink of an eye'!

Alexandros knew he was doing what was best for his people. Let the Persians be placated. Let the Elimiote and Orestian kings have high hope for Makedonian leadership. Let Lynkestis suffer for a while, it will show them how dependent they were on Timenid good will and all for the better when liberation from the Vryges and Dardanes would come. The same with Derriopis. They would better appreciate the even-handed rule of House Timenos. Finally, let Themistoklis and Miltiadis put him on a side show. There would come time he would prove to them that blood ought to be first in concern of relations than pure politics! Meantime Alexandros was taught a valuable lesson: trust no one, outmaneuver everybody -if you can- and always speak from the pedestal of the stronger or the one who's dearly needed…

Mardonios'(Mardahna) fleet had crossed from Asia to Evropi and was stationed by the colonial city-state of Avdira. Provisions were demanded to be readied as his fleet would stop at several places for replenishment. The same demand was presented to Thasos, Idonia and the Halkidiki city-states. Persian armies from Thraki had already moved into Mygdonia and Anthemous, marching toward Amfaxitis and Vottiaea. Alexandros saw no way out and gave the orders to his clan heads accord-ingly.

Lady Tyhi and god Posidonas threw their lot on the side of the Athinians and Sparti once more. As Mardonios' fleet circumnavigated cape Athos at the southernmost tip of Akti peninsula, it was met with one of the frequent storms in the north Aegean. The storm was so powerful, it forced about one third of the fleet to crash on the rocks of this promontory. The other ships were scattered and thrown away from their course, falling piecemeal at the hands of lurking pirates and Athinian ships. Only a few ships, with Mardonios in one of them, managed to limp back to Asiatic ports. They were badly damaged and in disrepair. Their crews were in dire need of morale boost. Marching from Thraki, the Persian army being without naval support for provisions and flank protection, was forced to partial-ly withdraw.

But Persia was Persia. The High King Xerxis felt mightier than gods, goddesses, nymphs and all of the demons! Ahura Mazda, the one true god of His Kingdom, was willing to teach a lesson to Zefs or any other inferior god of these cursed Ellines! Xerxis swore an oath not to ever give-up and started building an new fleet, calling more troops for His army. This time it would be different! This time He would lead His forces, in person. Vouvaris sent a new message to Alexandros. Makedonia had to gather even more provisions, for an army from all Asia was soon to come. The High King was not fooling around any longer with token forces and inept generals!...

Eidjik/Evdikos was none too happy with the arrangements made after the recent war on Makedo-nia. Granted, there was plenty of food and fodder for now. Granted, looting and pillaging brought some riches to the tribe. But for how long? The Dardanian overlords were getting the lion's share in everything and with good reason. They had the most numerous and better equipped army than the rest of their 'allies'! They had no wives, children and old folks following them. Dardania proper was some distance away and all of their noncombatants had stayed home, awaiting for -and receiving- any and all of the not locally consumed items by the army. Everything was loaded and forwarded to Shkoup (Skoupi in Makedonian dialect) and other Dardanian towns.

Vryges, Parthines, Dexares and Tavlantes were another case altogether. Because of old and prevail-ing customs, because the distance to their homes was comparatively closer, they had all kinds of fol-lowers. Wives, whores, infants and old folks and infirmed, were carried by relatives and friends or simply followed through the campaign. Much needed nutrition for the warriors would go to these folks and, most of it wasted. They were under the impression that Lynkestes and Derriopes Makedonians were born to serve them, with no thought that (unless a Makedonian was treated fairly) they would be looking for a time -soon- to throw the invaders out of their homes! Blood ties were always stronger than obedience to an invader. Depravation and hate would not win the day for the Illyrians or Dardanes. A taste of the same treatment (or worse) from the other side was sure to come, if things would not change. He brought his concerns at the chiefs' meetings, to no avail. As a matter of fact, he was getting the questioning looks, like he was one not to be trusted, even from his own people.

The Athinian fleet presence in the gulf of Therma proved of no actual help to the cause. Makedonia stood firm, albeit weakened. The Persian allies of House Timenos were coming back and in force of untold numbers. Athinae had withdrawn her fleet to the narrow neck of Peloponnisos, arguing with the rest of the Ellenic city-states on the location of their resistance -if it would come to that! It was a blessing that Orestians and their allies, along with the Elimiotes, were not in good terms with Alex-andros!

Eidjik had little if no power at all to make adjustments and correct what he saw wrong. He was the king of the smallest tribe in this war. The Dardanes and Parthines were looting, burning and raping at will, followed by the others, in plain view! His own Vryges were taking the lead from them and they were hard to control. He talked to his father in private and invited some of the most powerful chiefs of his tribe to discuss enforcing restraint. They all agreed the situation was not exactly what it should have been. If their plan from the beginning of this war was to seriously stake a claim on bettering the tribe's fortunes by occupying lots of Derriopis and Lynkos, they needed the cooperation of the locals who were not to be sold to slavery, but remain to till their lands. They were not to have their livestock taken away, but to be encouraged to multiply it for common use. That could happen only if the locals were content with their new lords. Time and mixing of the blood would then stabilize the process and, possibly, this land could become once more the land of the Vryges. With all that which was going on now, such a dream would remain just that.

As much as the chiefs tried, the common Vrygian warrior pressured by the needs of his followers and folks and badly influenced by the rest of the invading tribes, did not respond to the call of restrain. When Eidjik/ Evdikos or some chief were in the presence of a group of warriors, things were rather calm (or seemed to be such). But Eidjik could not be everywhere and at all times. Local peasants then started coming to him lodging their complaints. Soon the cases started diminishing (not because there was no provocation) but, simply, because satisfaction was hard to be given and local patience had come to an end. After a while these locals got organized and started setting ambushes to isolated small bands of marauding Vryges and other invaders.

The other tribes could perhaps afford losses like these. Evdikos had no stomach for such a bloody luxury. Makedonians knew Makedonia better than him or any other of his chiefs and common folks.

They would strike, kill and disappear undetected! When raids in various villages were taking place to locate the guilty parties, the villagers would come up to him with blank, staring eyes. "You lost men in an ambush? None of us has any weapons! None has gone to hiding, for none of us has raised a hand to you or your brutes! You came uninvited, you took what you wanted! Now if some of you had enough and left or got lost or got to quarrels with your own or, perhaps, with your 'allies' and got killed, who's to be blamed? Us? You are known to fight among yourselves for a bit of loot! Search as you wish! We 've got nothing to hide and, further, we have nothing more to lose!"

Reprisals would do no good, he knew that. But frustration was the guiding hand after a while. Some villages were torched for almost no reason at all. The loss of life grew. Resistance hardened and putting them all under the sword was no solution -nor could be done. Vryges had become accustom-ed, through centuries of rough living, to a moving tribe. It would take centuries again to learn to settle and till the land. And this land needed settlers, earth husbandry, more than an opportunistic food gathering and game hunting. Betterment meant to sweat through your work in order to receive its fruits! To have that happen, the locals were needed as guides and to re-instruct the art of husbandry. It was not happening!

Evdikos/Eidjik imposed stricter rules on his people. If and when a local dared come to complain, his word against any Vrygian started having greater weigh in his judgment. This put him in another predicament. This time animosity was developed against him by his own people! Many accused him as a Makedonian lover, a man whose greed guided him in depriving his own folk from getting what was rightfully theirs as victors. That he was in favor of Alexandros, having in mind to receive more riches. Some of his chieftains were forced by peer pressure from their clans to disobey his direct orders. Some, with knowledge of greater power than others in their hands, did it openly. Others did it in secrecy, inventing all kinds of excuses. They all defended their own clans and he was getting isolated. Very few chieftains were openly on his side and he could sense the time was coming when he would have to defend his rights by fighting any and all successors from among his people.

Almost two years had passed since the invasion and occupation of these lands. The few trusted scout and spies sent among the locals, reported back to Eidjik disturbing news. Alexandros and Arraveos were preparing another offense. The Makedonian King had come to deal with Derdas from Elimiotis who promised to assist in expelling the invaders. Derdas was now in ready to secure what he had gained at the beginning of the war. For that reason and because the Persian allies of Alexandros were now numbering a few thousand strong in Makedonia proper, Derdas needed to become an 'ally' of the apparently strongest camp. Alexandros knew of this maneuver but he preferred to fight against Illyres and Dardanes rather than his own kin. He agreed to terms and now he was ready to advance. Eidjik also had knowledge of the pending attack, as he knew that the Dardanes and Parthines, even Dexares and Tavlantes could withdraw in relative safety back to their mountains, in their far-off homelands. His Vryges were the only 'next door' neighbors of Lynkestis and Derriopia. Wouldn't the wrath of Makedon with assistance and encouragement from Persia fall onto his tribe unchecked and with potentially disastrous results? Eidjik was more than sure about that.

He made the first move. He decided to send trusted, secret envoys to both Alexandros and Arraveos. Would it be possible that they 'd work a deal? If Makedon was about to advance in recovering lost areas, Eidjik was ready to withdraw and return to Vrygian lands, provided the King would respond with clemency. Further, while Eidjik was in charge and alive, looted goods and slaves would be safely returned. Anything beyond recovery and restoration, would be compensated by Vrygian services until such a time as deemed adequate return of loss and with the promise of no future Vrygian offense. Provided, again, that House Timenos would come to Vrygian aid if and when pressure and famine would appear becoming the factors for renewed hostilities. On his part, Eidjik was also to secure Vrygian armed support of the King's wars, for as long as his house was ruling the Vrygian tribe.

Arraveos thought this overture was nothing but a Vrygian trick and he strongly advised Alexandros to ignore it. Let the barbarians have constant fear of our next move. Let 'em keep-on looking over their shoulder. That will get 'em demoralized sooner and that was to Macedonia's advantage. Alexandros also had second thoughts but he was willing to try Eidjik's sincerity in order to possibly save lives. Testing the waters (as it is said), he sent a small expeditionary force of his own, convincing Arraveos and demanding from Derdas (as proof of keeping their agreement) the augmentation of this force by sending some of their own troops. A good size combination army then was prepared. It moved across Erigon and attacked the first enemy encampment on its way. The location was near the foothills of Vernon, close to the battle location a little over two years ago. At that point the river bent from north/west to north/east, making a big loop-like turn.

During the battle, the Makedonian general in charge of this attack, Areas from house Apellas, no-ticed the absence of any Vrygian fighters among the enemy. Interrogating some of the prisoners he was told that the Vryges posted in their sector had been called to ostensibly cover another post, for other needs. This meant nothing and Areas continued his advance with caution. On a charge against a second enemy outpost, he personally observed the Vryges running away as soon as the Makedonian force appeared. Was it true that Evdikos was keeping-up with his word?

Alexandros upon receiving the news decided he had to try again. He asked Areas to proceed keep-ing constant guard. Opportunity to find out for the third time was not late in coming. Some villagers informed Areas of a strong enemy presence close to the Pelagonian border. The Pelagones being allied to Argestei, Peones and Laei (and under Persian protection after the defeat of Peonia few years ago), had not been attacked by the Dardanian alliance as they were too strong for such venture.

The enemy, the villagers informed, was located north/east of Varnous Mountains. Areas did not know if the Pelagonian king Ierax was aware of that or if he knew what kind of reaction he should expect in case he had to chase the enemy into Pelagonia. He consulted Alexandros and Arraveos via a trusted messenger. Correspondence delayed Areas a full day. When the plans were finalized and he received assurance that no move from Pelagonia would be made, Areas took his troops overnight through the border and attacked the next morning from quarters that the enemy did not expect to have any danger coming from. This surprise worked to perfection. The enemy was annihilated and no move was made from the Pelagonian side. After the battle Areas sent a new message to Alexandros saying that, while many Vrygian warriors took-off the minute he attacked, many others stayed and fought as vigorously as any of the barbarians. Did the King have any future instructions?

Alexandros became skeptical again. What was truly in the Vrygian king's mind? The need to know for sure before the actual campaign against the barbarians was under way became a must -if lives were to be spared. Alexandros could not allow the Vrygian to set any traps. For the sake of Maked-onian lives, he decided to send a trusted emissary to Evdikos.

When the announcement was made, Alexandros had many volunteers asking to undertake the task. He was compelled to draw a name by lot. The emissary would be Korragos from the house of Dar-ron, an old house originating from Paeonia which had migrated to Makedonis first (at the time of Filippos) and then received lands from Alketas in Eordea by the Lynkestian territory. Korragos grew up among Derriopian migrant workers at the estate of his family and his knowledge of Derriopian dialect would help him pass through unnoticed.

Korragos was instructed by Alexandros to approach the Vrygian king with caution. He was to min-gle with local peasants first, observe what Evdikos and his chiefs were up-to and, after being sure about his personal safety, he was to approach the Vrygian king alone and identify his mission. The question Alexandros was placing square before the Vrygian was: "Do you intend to honor your word? If yes, why is it that many of your warriors continue to fight us? What exactly are your plans to accommodate us when Makedon is ready to strike?"

Korragos was to insist on a plain and speedy response, not allowing Evdikos time to consult with his chiefs or ask for time to further search for an answer. Korragos would have time to accomplish his mission until the new turn of Selini's hiding cycle and return to a full face. Meantime Alexandros should be ready for an all-out assault. Vouvaris was on his way to Makedon, preparing arrangements for the High King's armies. Alexandros would ask for permission to secure once more the High King's northern borders from any future distraction, which would be a good excuse to have also Per-sian troops campaign against the invaders. It would also bring Makedonia to a higher level of esteem, as Xerxis would see that Alexandros cared about the security of His overall domain.

Derdas would again have to keep his aspirations of supremacy over all Makedonia in check, as he would be asked again to honor the agreement and serve under Alexandros and the watchful eye of Vouvaris and his troops. Elimiotis would have to put forth the best of behavior. Dardanes and Illyres had to be checked first though if the agreed current submission of Lynkos and Derriopis was to continue. Both areas needed to know that Makedonia (in other words Alexandros and House Time-nos) meant to keep the pledge of protecting (and ruling) all of Makedonia.

The next morning found Alexandros dispatching messages to Derdas and Vouvaris and Korragos dressed in wool garments and having packed fur covers on his donkey's wooden saddle, departing for his mission. Summer in Aegae did not necessarily translate to summer up in Derriopis…

Grabsh was an able and faithful chieftain to his clan first, then to his king, since the times of hunger and bending one's back to the beck and call of any stronger king of any other tribe, times even before Krush's (Eidjik's father) reign. Grabsh was also very ambitious. He became chief at a very early age on account of his own father's untimely death. By clan rights, his uncle was supposed to become the clan's chief. But uncle Rhub didn't have any children of his own and Rhub was already very old to be producing children at that time. Grabsh then became the chief at the 'prime' age of five springs. Rhub just took care of him and the clan's business until he died when Grabsh was about ten plus one. The family or rather its line was strictly Vrygian up to the time of Grabsh's father's father time when it mixed with Tavlantian blood by marriage. His father followed the trend by marrying a girl from the tribe of Penestei (Penesht in their language) and Grabsh, taking the lead, had two wives; one from the Dexares and the other from the Parthines. His sons carried their mixed blood with the same pride as if it was still pure Vrygian. Grabsh followed each and every campaign, run each and every forest and mountain, crossed rivers and lakes as he was chasing or being chased, present any-where the tribe's fortunes (or misfortunes) led. He had to. Young or old, a clan's chief was there to be the living example to all members. As long as he had his uncle alive, he would listen to Rhub's advice. Later, it was the king. Grabsh became officially an adult chieftain on his tenth -plus four year. That year, a tribal ceremony proclaimed him (among many others) a man capable to lead on his own and be led by his betters according to status. By that time he knew he was experienced enough, like any other (perhaps more than any other) seasoned warrior!

He remained faithful, always vying for recognition, ready to prove that his share of loot was right-fully his, as was his share of misfortune -in times of failure. But lately the tables had turned. He dis-covered he could no longer obey the king's orders! His pride as a Vrygian was hurt. His share of danger was found to be greater than his share of loot, which he had to yet share with his clan. Dardanes were getting the best and most, followed by Tavlantes, Parthines and Dexares. Vryges were left to pick-up the crumbs!

At the beginning the clan's bellies (and his) were full from the Makedonian produce and livestock. Now the local villagers were hiding away most of their products and, worst of all, they had start-ed killing isolated members of his clan. He went to see the king and Eidjik advised him to restrain his warriors from oppressing the peasants further, to treat them like their own and, until an understand-ing of fellowship would develop, to have his men remain in camp or travel in large groups. Were they the victors or the victims of this war? Further, land gained had not been allocated with the locals to work it and serve the victor's needs as they should. The spoils, the early war spoils were already con-sumed and the king wouldn't allow any more locals to be sold as slaves nor villages to be looted. No further advance was in sight as the Dardanes were content (for now) and Makedonian resistance had stiffened. The most frustrating recent orders from the king were not to resist Makedonian advances but run and let them regain what was taken with the blood and suffering of many years.

Eidjik, in the eyes of Grabsh, had become indifferent of his people's welfare! Eidjik was no longer the leader who would lead a raid and distribute the spoils! Eidjik had allowed Dardanian leadership to begin with and, now, he was entreating Aleigzand (Alexandros, in Vrygian/Tavlantian appellation) for an all out Vrygian capitulation. Oh, Eidjik had explained his reasoning for all that, for caution and wisdom. What Grabsh was mostly disgusted with, was what he detected as Eidjik's cowardly be-havior. His Vrygian king had turned colors. He wanted to placate Aleigzand, forgetting that Make-don had been the cause of Vrygian decline generations ago. If it wasn't for the cursed Orests and Lynkos, the bastard Pridik (Perdikkas the first) and the like, Vryges could still be the power to recon with, equal ally or foe to Persia and ruler of these cursed places, all the way to Tessalgha and even Vyiotta (Thessalia and Viottia)! That was the true order of things in those years of yore and it could have been the order now too!

Gravos (Grabsh' name in that cursed language with symbols marking the sound of words) was ready to move against his king and was not alone either. Many of the strongest chiefs were on his side. He had been chosen to strike when the time was deemed proper and that time was very near! He would enter into alliance with these cockroaches of greed, the Attanash (Athinians) and have them stall Persian interference (or perish) until his goal would become a realization. Then he could let them be or teach them a lesson (what kind of people were those Yunes [Iones] any way -turning against their own blood?) of Vrygian justice and rule! Grabsh would then lead all the Vrygians to their former glory and beyond!...

Korragos spent his first few days in a small hamlet in Derriopia, bordering the lands of Pelagonia. He arranged to get a job as an apprentice to a smith. He kept his eyes and ears open, as he absorbed every detail of Vrygian activities and behavior. He soon discovered what the problem was. A man of concern about his tribe, the Vrygian king, wanted to secure their future but had few supporters of his policy. His noble but misunderstood dreams were a difficult (if not impossible) task. What was the Vrygian past was just that, a past! This king seemed to have second thoughts about past glories and turned his attention at the present, more pragmatic situation. That, Korragos thought, was the ele-ment this Vrygian king had to pay his full attention to. Korragos completely understood Eidjik's di-lemma, only because his own beloved Makedonia was facing the same problems over and over. It always takes a very strong king to guide a state surrounded by hostile tribes and constantly pressured and stalled on its progress. But alongside a strong king, an equally minded array of notables and clan heads is needed to implement the king's program and wishes. Korragos was confident of the home support Alexandros was receiving -that element was not missing (at least for now) from the Timenid kingdom. He could now detect that in Eidjik/Evdikos' case, such element was almost non existent! He considered that he had seen and heard enough. It was time to find this king and bring his mission to a conclusion.

Excusing himself to the smith he was working for as a man who could not stay at the same place for more than a few days -as being of uneasy nature- Korragos received his wages, loaded his donkey and headed toward the direction he last heard the Vrygian king was camping. He traversed the distance, taking care to stay out of the invaders' traffic. It was well known that any of their marauding bands could kill a lonely peasant just for the pleasure of seeing blood running and people begging for dear life! It took Korragos four days to locate the king's camp. Now, he decided, was his time to go in the open and ask for hire. A smithy's apprentice was always in need. A king's court, being barbarian or civilized one, made no difference. There was always ironwork which needed hands and knowledge to bring it to use.

His knowledge of Derriopian dialect and his attire played their role and he got a job. He was hired to help make arrowheads for the king's bodyguards. The smithy in charge of Korragos was but an-other apprentice of the Master Smith. The orders were coming through the king's chief of bodyguards, a man called Grabsh, Gravos in Ellenic terms. This Gravos stroke Korragos' fancy as a very suspicious person and an egomaniac, the terror of all who had to deal with him, whether free or enslaved. Gravos seemed to be getting the 'obligatory' type of respect from many chieftains while others could hardly wait for him to turn his back and mock him (very discreetly), especially the ones who seemed to be closer to the king. These were more distant and always on guard in their dealings with Gravos and his 'friends'. Korragos was fast in seeing the reason. Two different camps on state matters and Gravos was the designated 'leader' of the 'anti' camp, as well as the 'sacrificial bull' -in case his 'leadership' wouldn't work. Korragos thought he had to make the chief his 'friend'.

One day while working on ordered arrowheads, he manufactured few especially for the chief of the king's bodyguard. When he was finished, he asked to be brought before the Master Smith and he presented his 'gift' to be given as his personal gift. Korragos was brought before Gravos in a very rude way. He was forced to kneel before the flaming face of an angry chief who, through an inter-preter, asked why a Derriopian slave would waste the king's time on making 'personal' gifts to his chief of body guards. Korragos, careful to keep his eyes low and pretending he was horrified, answer-ed that he noticed the respect all other chiefs were showing to Gravos, an (obviously) great chieftain and he, Korragos, thought a gift like that out of his personal work would only be appropriate. And why there were Makedonian, the same ones on each arrowhead, signs etched? Again, Korragos hum-bly answered that the name of the owner of such arrowheads, the great Gravos, ought to be known to his future victims of war. Was it, then, Gravos' name on each arrowhead? The soft and 'respectful' answer to this was: "Yes! Survivors of the Chief's wrath would be more afraid of him as they would come to know his name."

Gravos made a sound of disgust and indifference to a slave's present and promptly kicked Korra-gos on the chest, sending him on his back to the ground. He ordered the guards to take the 'appren-tice' back to his work, warning him that nothing should be done unless there were specific orders given by him in person. Korragos was pushed and kicked back to work amidst the laughter of his guards.

The chief of the royal guards was pleased by this present though. His ego took another boost and he started treating his newfound protégé on a more humane basis. Korragos never lost an opportunity in fuelling the man's ego. His Derriopian dialect helped him to get a grip of Vrygian fast and soon he found himself listening to a much more relaxed and confident Gravos' talks about the chief's ambition to recreate the Vrygian former glory and how the king was neglecting the need of his people of that past. The rumbling complaints gave Korragos reason to believe he had to speed-up the process, for the time was running short. Gravos was to strike soon and that would spell disaster!

Korragos knew he had to use all caution possible regardless of his anxiety, fearing he would make a mistake and ruin everything. During his 'free' time and pretending he was listening Gravos' rage, he used his imagination in creating all kinds of excuses, ways and means to approach the king without raising Gravos' suspicion and/or wrath. Time was getting short. King Alexandros had trusted him with this mission and Korragos was determined not to fail his King's trust. He had a thought one night leaning against the 'wall' of the common sleeping quarters (a rectangle of upright tree trunks thrust in the ground and covered with thatches over few cross beams for a roof) which might work.

The next day he started working on a javelin, anxious of Gravos' reaction when he'd find out. He managed to avoid the chief's inspections of him for two days. On the third, Gravos approached undetected and, seeing the metal leaf of a javelin's head being worked on, he demanded in his usual brusque manner to know who had given the order to this 'Derriopian slave' and diverted the pro-duction of arrowheads to this? Korragos' heart leaped, thinking this might be his end. He held his anxiety back and humbly told his excuse.

What if the brave chief of the king's guards would take this fine javelin head -when finished- as a personal present to his king? What if, during his presentation, Gravos wished aloud the king to pursue further glory by using this present by his trusted bodyguard against the Makedonians? Wouldn't that bring Gravos higher in the king's esteem and -at the same time- let Gravos see and hear first-hand what the king's plans were regarding the Vrygian future glory? Without waiting for an answer, Korragos proposed to etch the king's name on one side of the javelin's head and Gravos' on the other. This way the Vrygian king would never forget who offered him such a fine present of a weapon.

Gravos' hand rested all this time on the hilt of his sword, knuckles white because of the pressure he applied, ready to strike the slave with such a free and enterprising mind. Although Korragos' heart had almost stopped beating, the young man raised his eyes and looked at the brute with such an ear-nest look of total devotion to his 'master' that made the Vrygian think. A sudden smile appeared on Gravos' face lighting it up on the prospect of his king's appreciation (or the king's condemnation -as the event would unfold). Perhaps this present would elevate him above all close friends the king still had. Perhaps it would give him total access to the king, without any one else's presence and at any time. That would then be his time to strike! He praised the 'slave' for his idea but scolded him and cautioned him not to be taking any further initiatives like this, unless he would inform and get his master's approval first. As a warning on the seriousness of his command, Gravos send his foot flying on Korragos' sternum.

Korragos swore a silent promise while trying to ease the pain and get some air in his lungs. "Father Zefs let me witness this animal's death and I will offer a bull on your altar back home." Gravos had turned around meantime, walking away and semi-satisfied. This 'present' might become his advan-tage against Eidjik, but such 'slaves' ought to be executed at the earliest convenient time. This one, Gravos thought, had been useful thus far but he was reaching his point of no return rapidly…

The javelin head was ready by next early afternoon and shined by late evening -to perfection. Gra-vos picked it up with a hardly covered admiration. The 'slave' had really done a superb job! He awarded Korragos this time with an extra portion of cereals for the upcoming supper and left. Kor-ragos took his time picking-up his tools and cleaned the furnace area before going in line for the evening meal. He was served with envy by the slave 'cook' for his fortune of a double portion and he went to sit against his hut's timber to eat. He did not have time to finish, as two burly guards from the direction of the king's hut came ordering him to follow. His heart leaped again, hoping his plan had started working but fearing this could be his end.

They entered the 'royal' hut and Korragos was forced to kneel before Eidjik/Evdikos' makeshift throne. The king looked at him intensely and for a long time. Then, to Korragos' surprise, Evdikos addressed him directly in a broken but legible Makedonian dialect. Korragos almost lost his cool. Had he been discovered? Why would the Vrygian king address him in Makedonian? He bit his ton-gue to an almost unbearable pain, to recover. His face remained blank, showing little -if any- under-standing of the king's words. He looked at Gravos who also looked back puzzled. Ok, it wasn't the bodyguard who had a notion of who Korragos really was. He turned his attention back to the king.

Evdikos looked at him with a playful eye but his face remained unchanged. He repeated his question in the Derriopian dialect. The 'slave' had an excellent technique -the king said again. Would Korra-gos be interested to work some war arms exclusively for the king's use? If so, he could consider him-self a free man -within reason. If not, he would continue working under Gravos and as a slave, up to such a time the chief of bodyguards saw fit. Either way, his future would rest on Vrygian fortune.

Korragos was happy to see his chance of approaching the king freely but held his position as a hum-ble and simple smith, facing a fortune he never thought of coming his way. He looked at Gravos, then back at the king. It would be his honor, he said, to work for the king. But, wasn't that exactly what he was doing under the king's brave chief bodyguard? It would then be a double honor to serve the king's personal needs and, at the same time, remain in the service of Gravos.

Korragos hoped his little trick would work. Easy access to the king, but constant surveillance of all Gravos' business. The brute could still be of use. Both Evdikos and Gravos looked pleased with the answer. The young Makedonian did not fail to notice a smirk (well hidden from the king) on the chief of the bodyguards face. This one -Korragos thought- needs more attention paid than I have done thus far. He remained kneeling until he was told by the king to take leave. He returned to his 'living' quarters, working in his mind many possibilities of success and failure. He had a very uneasy sleep that night.

Very early the next morning Korragos was awakened by a kick to his ribs from Gravos. He jumped to his feet, eyes low. What the 'master' wanted from his and the king's 'slave'? Gravos went through a long and stern pep talk of growls to let the 'slave' know that he still was and always would be the 'master', the king being as significant as Gravos' own like or dislike of the 'Derriopian' lasted! Kor-ragos asked for permission to speak and, that given, assured his 'master' that Gravos' will and needs would always have priority. Hadn't he stated this yesterday and before Gravos, the king and all wit-nesses? Korragos made sure he had another Derriopian who spoke fluent Vrygian awaken, to trans-late exactly what he was saying to Gravos, so the vain chief would get the proper understanding of his words.

Gravos seemed more relaxed now and said that Korragos would receive his due award when his services to his 'master' were truly proven to be of extra value. Now, he added, the king wanted Korragos to appear for instructions for a new breast plate and in good time Korragos would prove his knowledge as a good smith and armor maker, worth Gravos' and the king's pleasure.

The young Makedonian was escorted back to the king's hut and was instructed by Evdikos how he wanted his breastplate to look. Korragos thought his chances were lost as he realized he was not the experienced smith the king had in mind and this kind of work required. His face clouded. Evdi-kos observing that, looked intensively at him and, abruptly, excused all others from his hut, posting in front of its 'door' the two burly guards he always seemed to have half a step ahead of him. The king now addressed the 'smithy' directly, with his accented but rather proper Makedonian dialect. He knew, he said, that Korragos was not a true smith but rather Alexandros' agent sent to communicate with him. He was familiar with Makedonian workmanship of armor and arms and the javelin head presented to him the day before, was superior to any Illyrian work but inferior of a true Makedonian smith. That had increased the king's suspicion that Korragos was something other than a Derriopian smith, plus the fact that Korragos did not exactly hide his fear when Evdikos spoke in Makedonian the day before. "You see, I am more observant than I let others know!" he concluded. Now Evdikos asked the young Makedonian to tell him truthfully what his exact mission was and what his message was from King Alexandros.

Korragos let a deep sigh of relief come out of his mouth slowly. This king was a much smarter fel-low than any other barbarian he had come across and, certainly much smarter than the boisterous and callus 'master' Gravos! He explained simply and precisely his mission adding his suspected animosity of Gravos against Evdikos. The Vrygian king smiled, impressed by the young man's com-prehension of this 'covered' division among Vrygians and particular aims of Gravos' vanity and am-bitions.

He assured the Makedonian his messages to King Alexandros were honest and would be honored to the letter. He only needed to know when Makedonia would strike, so he could move in a timely fashion and with the least possible loss of life, both Vrygian and Makedonian. Korragos felt admir-ation for the keen perceptions of Evdikos and thought that an ally like him would serve Alexandros more than expected. He told Evdikos that his mission had to come to an end by the moon's turn, three days from this one. Makedonia would attack shortly afterwards and King Alexandros needed to know of Evdikos' decision before that. The Vrygian king recalled his two guards inside his hut. He instructed them to escort Korragos back at his confinement but not leave him alone at any time, nor allow any contact with anyone, especially Gravos. The same night and when all camp was asleep, they were to assist his escape to Makedonian outposts and remain under his protection there until peace had been worked out. They were to obey his orders giving their lives -if there was need for it! Late that same night Korragos and his two Vrygian guards made their way out of the camp. In two days' time they reached Makedonian held ground and Korragos met his King and king Arraveos at Alalkomenae.

The morning of Korragos' 'escape' discovery, Eidjik called a general assembly of his Vrygian war-riors and people. Surrounded by his most trusted supporters, he openly accused Grabsh and his as-sistants of dissention and treason. He had discovered, he said, the 'smith' was a Makedonian agent working all this time under the protection and knowledge of the king's 'trusted' chief of the guards, aiming to act against his life. He had ordered the Macedonian's detainment yesterday, so he could properly collect all evidence and bring him before them for punishment. He had trusted the two guards who were none other than hand-picked men by Grabsh for this duty, but they assisted the 'slave' to escape. Who else was responsible for such an act of treason but the chief of the royal guard and his supporters? The Vrygian king was demanding justice before his people. Grabsh protested, declaring his innocence.

Many of his supporters though (aiming to save their lives and scared by the turn of events) willingly admitted his treacherous aims. Eidjik seized the opportunity. He could not trust the ones who were ready to change sides the moment any difficulty presented itself any more than the ones who openly planned his murder! Could the king, he asked the assembly, trust such hypocrites? Surely not! They would be paid for their treason by losing their lives! Grabsh and his supporters were instantly taken by the mob and stoned to death…

With Selini, the moon's change to a curved sliver up in the sky, Alexandros attacked the strongest encampment of the barbarians. Victory came swift. Many of the Dardanian chieftains perished un-der the sword. Tavlantians and Parthines turned to flight as did the Dexares. The Vrygians had slipped away undetected by their 'allies' earlier during the night. Few other encampments unaware of the slaughter which took place at the first one, met the same fate as they got caught by surprise. The word traveled fast and soon panic overtook all the invaders, now running for dear life back to their territories. Persian riders equipped with bows and provided for assistance by Vouvaris' own expedition force had a field day in targeting the retreating enemy wherever the grounds were accom-modating their cavalry.

Within a short period of time all invaders were out of Makedonian lands. Lynkestis and Derriopis were restored to their people, as many enslaved ones were liberated and refugees were able to return to their homes and fields. Livestock taken by the Vryges was returned and, during an important ceremony Evdikos swore allegiance to Alexandros, who (wisely) declared he represented the High King before attending Persian leaders of the expedition. Alexandros on his part agreed to subsidize Vrygian needs in livestock, fodder and cereals, especially during heavy winters. Peace being restored, Alexandros returned to Aegae. There, Korragos was promoted to serve with the King's body guard and more lands were bestowed to house Darron.

Alexandros did not forget Derdas the Elimiote king. In spite of the latter's word of support and initial compliance, Derdas refrained from sending the promised troops during the final campaign. Orestis and Dassaretis had closed-in and were allied with Elimiotis now, the power of Derdas convincing them to do so. Alexandros pretended though he had not notice the move. He did not want any more Makedonian blood shed right after the latest campaign against the barbarian tribes of the north, nor did he want extension of Vouvaris' 'support' with more Persian troops. There was no need for further Persian dependence because of (what Alexandros considered internal) Makedonian affairs. Besides, his place in the High King's esteem had risen with the security of the north/west frontier and the High King was on the move, approaching. Derdas would have to behave and Alexandros could afford to bide his time. Besides, he could use now Vrygian armed bands when they were needed, without spilling any Makedonian blood...

Eidjik/Evdikos was not exuberant with the peace arrangements. He recognized his huge mistake in tying Vrygian fortunes with Dardanian greed. He also recognized the intentions of the Makedonian King to take full advantage of the peace terms. A hard lesson was taught to him with the blood of his people, a lesson he intended to never forget. He swore to pass it down to his son and from there, to generations in the future: If there is no chance achieving your aims because you are either weak or ill prepared to face the odds, do not depend on others to help you solve your problems! Near disaster had fallen upon his people with the disaffection and dissention of Grabsh and his supporters. The tribe had to turn back to the poor tribal lands without any loot to exchange for life's needs or livestock taken from temporary conquest. Long term vision was amiss back then and he put the blame square on his shoulders.

Thankfully he realized his mistake in time to reverse somewhat his tribe's fortunes, coming to an understanding with Alexandros. With the aid of that young Makedonian Korragos, he secured the flow of livestock, fodder and cereals coming from Makedon in exchange for peace and armed sup-port when it was needed. Time now to lick the wounds and recover! When Alexandros would call, he would provide troops. He had no other choice, until such time when his own power (his people's power) would suffice by itself to promote independent course of action -if he was lucky to see that in his lifetime!

Three winters passed, two of them very severe. The peace held as both parties kept their treaty intact. Vryges did not raid and Makedon saw that plenty of food for both humans and animals was sent before the passes closed. With the snow thawed on the fourth spring and the passes opened, a visitor came to Gjyr, Eidjik's village (there was no real town or city in the impoverished Vrygia).

Korragos was welcomed by Eidjik like a long lost friend, a brother. In any case, the Makedonian was responsible in many ways of Eidjik still being the king of his tribe.

After the customary niceties and exchange of gifts, indefinite hospitality was offered (a very strong custom of the Vrygians to their visitors). Korragos accepted, because it was equally strong a custom to receive what was freely given, but set his limitations. He had again a mission to accomplish and, as soon as that would be achieved, he had to return to his King.

The rumors, Korragos came straight to the point of his task, finally had become a fact. The High King was coming! Actually he was only two plus twenty days from Makedonia proper, stationed at the moment by the lands of the Vissaltes! Xerxis was leading his whole army, the number of which was un-numbered. Only his vanguard was so numerous, it had dried the river Ehedoros by watering men and beasts. Now Xerxis wanted to know if king Eidjik was still His friend and subordinate, as the treaty with Alexandros indicated. In that case the High King was asking for a thousand riders for his campaign against the Athinians and Spartans -and those allied to them city-states of the south. It was now time for king Eidjik to keep his end of the bargain. What would the answer be?

Eidjik kept his secret thoughts well to himself. Was it, perhaps, the time for some compensation? Had the time come for some Vrygian expansion and better life ahead? Would Vryges rule Thessalia again? He feared Alexandros would use him as an expendable force, to meet the ends of his own ambitions and those of the High King! The Persians had arrived in untold numbers! Eidjik did not doubt Korragos' words. If he refused the help he was asked to provide, he and his tribe could be in a dire position. But, sacrifice (because he knew that exactly was the case!) a thousand warriors? Better than losing the whole tribe.

He smiled to his guest and agreed in the number. But there were not enough horses to provide his riders. Korragos promised horses from Makedonian stock provided the Vrygians would come on time to exercise riding them. They would have to be ready as the High King's vanguard would be crossing into Thessalia. Eidjik agreed to that. He stated he had to stay in Vrygia for the needs of his people. Korragos asked for the king's son and heir then, Bardjil, to be in charge of the Vry-gian force. Time for the youth to become a man! Eidjik studied the Makedonian's face. Korragos was serious with his demand. Eidjik had to obey. Bardjil (Vardilis in Dorian-Makedonian dialect) had to be the 'honorary' hostage/leader. There was one more thing. The young Vrygian heir would have a Makedonian general as liaison to King Alexandros and the High King, the old foe Areas. The Lyn-kestian Areas of house Apellas, Makedonian hero during the last war, would be giving assignments to Bardjil and his riders, making sure they carried them. That spelled no independent action, no chance to take advantages. The High King was the Master and Alexandros was His right hand! Eidjik had to agree to that too. The two men closed the deal with offerings to their gods…

"Deep, dark night, deliverer of sleep
to suffering mortals,
You arrive from the Underworld
flying on your fast wings.
You are the one who found the
way to Agamemnon's room!
For with the pain, as with misfortune,
through You we are infested…"
Evripidis (Euripides), Athinian tragedian -died (a honored guest) in
Makedonia.

VIII

It was a mind boggling phenomenon seeing all the Asiatic hordes parading in their entire splendor! Mides, Perses, Irkanians, Parthians,

Egyptians, Araves, Kappadokes, Syrians, Fryges, Vaktres and Indi, the whole of Asian nations! Augmented and supported by the navies of Iones, Finikes, Kypriotes and Kares and the auxiliaries of Thrakian Vistones, Odrysses, Vissae and Laei the Make-donian cavalry with a Vrygian contingent from Evropi's side, ready to be multiplied by the troops from Thessalia and Thivae -once they crossed the passes from Pieria and Olympos.

Tribes unheard-of previously, from lands so far apart no one knew where they were located were following one after the other in several parallel routes. Most of the contingents were dressed in splendid garments, weapons trimmed in gold and precious stones, all in their tribal dresses and with their accustomed weapons, indicative of Persia's contribution to wealth, via its evenhanded guidance and freedom of exchange and commerce within its boundaries. This entire multitude left its mark behind its passage. They dried rivers and lakes in their wake and left behind whole regions without any provisions at all. Remembering Mardonios' disaster by Cape Athos, Xerxis ordered the cutting of a channel at the narrowest point of the Akti peninsula. Engineers and drafted locals worked for months to do it! The multitude of transport ships and galleys of war passed without one of them lost.

Alexandros was glad he had been promptly warned by Vouvaris and had the time to prepare. Provi-sions were stocked and kept in safe key places within the Timenid kingdom, which helped keeping the occasional friction between the High King's multitude and the locals to a minimum. Nonetheless, Alexandros knew his stock wouldn't last long and his subjects would tire from Persian demands, even if the High King's supply agents were willing to compensate and he was anxious to see the Asi-atics cross his kingdom fast. He opened roads as far away from towns and villages as possible, keep-ing regular patrols on them providing the most expedient way for the hordes to pass through.

Keeping in mind the occasional 'misunderstandings' he assigned scouts for every large contingent, so the passes toward the south would remain open and he entertained the most important Satraps (Satrapes) as lavishly as he could afford, so they would keep a favorable impression of him and his people. He did not dare to invite the High King, seeing and understanding that Makedonian ways and means would rather offend than placate Xerxis, as he was used to dealing with such luxury, the Makedonian King would not (could not) be able to provide. He was invited to Xerxis' royal tent a few times though, as the High King was fond of demonstrating his wealth and might to his 'subject' people.

Finally, the High King and his armies moved past mount Olympos toward the Thessalian plains through the valley of Tempi. Xerxis' agents had informed the High King of a first resistance line from the city-states at that location. They had seen congregation of Athinian, Thespian, Plataean and other allied city-states there. The Spartans were reported to be observing again the Karnia religious holiday, but they were to join these oplites troops soon.

Alexandros was at a loss. This location chosen by the city-states coalition could be by-passed easily and Ellines would be outmaneuvered by the enemy numbers in no time! The river (Pinios) being navigable, could also bring Persian troops which could and would come to the rear of the defenders, blocking their effort to withdraw and attacking them on more than one front! He secretly sent an urgent message to the Athinians, asking them to either retreat to a more defensive location or give-up altogether! Apparently (though he received no answer of acknowledgment) they took his message seriously, because they withdrew. Xerxis actually did come up river and inspected the abandoned narrows only a couple of days after the allied city-states' withdrawal from that location.

Immediately after that event, a direct order from the High King made Alexandros suspect that Xerxis might have had some information (but no proof) of the warning the Timenid King had send, for Xerxis demanded that from there-on Alexandros had to join the Persian expeditionary armies in person and with his whole army (cavalry actually -for Makedonia did not have oplites units of true value).

Alexandros had no other choice. He gathered his less trusted (so he could keep an eye on them) land lords, the Lynkestian and Derriopian contingents and (happy to have call them on time) the Vrygian cavalry of Vardilis, under Areas. Alexandros then could use them -instead of his Makedonians- in the event Xerxis ordered a confrontation against the Ellenic coalition with the troops of Alexandros. The Vryges dressed in Makedonian armor, riding his horses and being under Areas, would not let the Persian King know the difference. He arranged (with some clever excuses) to have his whole expeditionary force camp each time a little further than the main Asiatic camps and would not even let Vouvaris come close to that particular unit. He asked and got permission to use 'his units' as scouts ahead of the main body of troops. Questioned by Xerxis, he told the High King that caution was needed in case the city-states would make a stand in a different narrow place and Alexandros didn't want the King of

Kings to lose any troops because of treachery. Xerxis seemed very pleased with Alexandros' concern and gave his permission.

In reality, Alexandros wanted to use mostly (if not only) the Vrygian portion of his cavalry for many reasons. First, he didn't want any accidental detection from the Persian side that some of his 'Make-donians' were actually Vryges. Second, using them as scouts and having to fight against any city-state oplites, the killing would be between Ellines and Vryges, not Ellines against Ellines! At the time he proposed his idea to Xerxis, Thessalian dignitaries were present as free-willed allies of the Persians and they backed his words, for they also feared reprisals from the Spartans and Athinians in case the tables of fortune would be turned. Not knowing that Alexandros would use Vrygians for scouting, they thought that Makedonians risking skirmishes against any or all Ellenic troops gathered at any point of defense, was better than perhaps needing Thessalian cavalry doing the scouting.

Now Thessalia was 'flooded' with Asiatic armies! Xerxis spent quite some time awaiting a possible change of mind from Athinae and Sparti a sign of their capitulation before his might. So, his progress through Thessalia was slow. Before arriving in Viottia, delegates from Thivae came to greet him and confirm Thivan alliance and support. This event boosted Xerxis' confidence of an eventual 'walk' down the Ellenic peninsula. Within few days after the reception of the Thivan delegation though, news that a strong composite army led by the Spartan King Leonidas and his bodyguards had taken hostages from Thivae, forcing the city to change sides and they were fortifying the narrow passage of Thermopylae, the place having numerous hot springs and literally meaning the Hot Gates.

That infuriated Xerxis and he started to move his army toward the narrow passage, as his fleet followed -after some delay- in support. At the same time, the combined Ellenic fleet with the Athinians contributing the greatest part of it but with a Spartan admiral (Themistoklis did not mind ruling from behind the scenes -as he had the power of numbers on his side), came to anchor on the north tip of Evia, blocking the route of support to Xerxis' footmen and cavalry by the Persian fleet.

Xerxis ordered his vassal Makedonian King to send the scout cavalry ahead and ordered the annih-ilation of the 'meager' Ellenic forces that dared to even think of blocking his way! Alexandros order-ed his Vrygian squadrons (iles) to proceed according to the High King's plan. His private orders were not to engage though, unless the Ellenic forces of the south would initiate such a move. As was anticipated by Alexandros, the cavalry returned informing that their advance met 'superior' forces stationed behind a very well defended wall at the narrowest point of the pass, very unsuitable for a frontal attack by cavalry.

The reported allied city-state army was about ten thousand oplites, under the direct command of the Spartan King Leonidas and his three hundred body-guards. Sparti had to observe yet another religious festival and its second King (Sparti had two Kings ruling at the same time as was the tra-dition) was preparing the whole Spartan army to move after the festivities were over. King Leonidas prepared his defenses taking advantage of all available means. On his left he had the steep sides and sheer rocks of mount Kallidromon. Before his main body of oplites there was the old Fokian wall, now re-enforced and, on his right, the sea with the Ellenic fleet of about three hundred triiris (triremes), mostly Athinian.

If these allied Ellenic forces chose to stand their ground, no Persian force would be able to pass the narrows! Xerxis was intrigued by the audacity of these Yunis (as the Persians were accustomed of calling all Ellines -from their appellation of the Iones in Asia) and camped his armies just before the pass, undecided. He sent another message to the Spartan King asking for surrender. Spartan fame was not built-up on retreating or surrendering! Instead, it was reported to him that they were sitting by the wall cleaning and bathing like there was no imminent danger and King Leonidas' answer to Xerxis' demand to lay down their weapons was: 'Dare to come get them!'(Μολλων, λαβε!).

The High King was furious! Xerxis wanted to know if these men were truly crazy. He called for a general assembly of all his Satraps. His admirals advised to wait for two more days, as the fleet was still under way, while an exiled ex king of Sparti, Dimaratos, explained that such a behavior was typical of Spartans preparing for battle. Xerxis was not amused. He ordered a general advance of his land forces and the fleet -as it was. He expected, no, he demanded the clearance of the road and the strait to be opened so he could get to Athinae in triumph within the next two days.

His armies attacked the very next morning, just as the sun was coming up from the depths of the Aegean, red like the blood which was about to be shed, hot like the heat only a battle can generate as is anticipated, as it is fought and, finally, as it is concluded. The lightly -compared to an oplitis' armor- armed forces Xerxis sent against the Ellenic forces was easily pushed back with heavy casual-ties, the Spartans leading and the rest of the oplites following their example. The High King was forced to call his troops back for the day.

The next day the same experiment was tried again with the addition of the naval action and the same result on land, while at sea the Persian fleet was unable to break through the Ellenic and both withdrew at the end to their perspective anchorages. Persians and their allied fleets from Finiki, Kypros and the Ionian cities on the side of the west approaches to the mainland and across the nar-rows of cape Artemision of Evia's north end, the Ellenic fleet on the lee side of the same cape, at Evia's shores. Xerxis' ire was severe and he called for a general meeting with his generals and admirals. They agreed on a new plan. Some strong squadrons were ordered to sail during the night in order to navigate around Evia and attack the Ellenic fleet on both sides, while the frontal attack on land would keep Leonidas and his force preoccupied. Upon the destruction of the Ellenic navy, Pers-ian forces would land to do the same to the defenders of Thermopylae.

Posidonas and Athina had other things in mind though. The two gods who (tradition has it) fought against each-other for the Athinian favor as city protectors, protected the Ellenic fleet by raising a storm rarely seen in those waters in such a time of the year. The squadrons sent to circumnavigate were lost in the rough seas during the night and the rest sustained great damage as they were anchor-ed across the open sea.

Themistoklis and the Ellenic fleet did come out the next morning seeking engagement and it was this time that the Persian navy barely held its ground with heavy loss. On the land, the new armies thrown against Leonidas had again the same fate of those the day before, in spite of Xerxis' threats and engagement of his ten thousand 'Immortal' guards! The miracle of Marathon some ten years before seemed to be repeating itself.

The High King was now ready to kill with his own hands the first man who would bring him any bad news! His kinsman Mardonios brought him (finally) a ray of hope to light the gloom of Xerxis' mood. A local shepherd called Efialtis was willing (under good pay) to lead Persian troops through a secret mountain pass, behind the enemy lines. The order was given. Alexandros' heart skipped a few beats hearing the news. He sent -in secrecy- Areas to inform Leonidas and Themistoklis. The two leaders decided to hold. Themistoklis returned to the fleet and Leonidas dispatched his Fokian allies who (as locals) knew the mountain well to guard the path, while preparing the rest for an all-out defense or, in case of defeat, a speedy retreat for future resistance at the isthmus of Korinthos. He and his Spartan body-guards would remain to the very end, giving time for the rest of the army to withdraw. Themistoklis was to 'keep an eye' on the result and act accordingly with the fleet.

That night the 'Immortal' guards of the High King were led by Efialtis on the secret path. Early the following morning, the Fokian dispatch seeing the Persians coming, took the higher ground, thinking they would defend the location easier. The 'Immortals' hardly bothered with them. They just dispatched a small detachment to keep the defenders busy, while the main body continued its march toward the rear of Thermopylae. King Leonidas learned of the event about mid-morning. Holding the pass was unattainable now! He ordered the allies to withdraw and unite with the main body of Spartans who were (by now) ready to leave Lakonia marching north. Themistoklis was informed also by a small fast boat which kept communications open between the two leaders. The allied fleet was to remain only as long as Leonidas and his Spartans could hold! Only then they could leave to fight another day at another location.

All Ellenic land forces withdrew, except for the about five hundred Thivans who were ordered to re-main (as suspected Μηδίζοντες -Persian lovers) and one thousand Thespians who refused to with-draw, preferring to share the Spartan glory in honorable death. Leonidas now readied himself for the final onslaught. He would die with his compatriots, fighting to the very end, giving more time to the retreating allies. No Spartan, let alone a Spartan King, ever retreats before any enemy and faces death with a smile. He sent a message to Themistoklis and a thank you to Alexandros. Themistoklis withdrew the fleet and Alexandros kept that message for future use.

By late afternoon all Thivans, Thespians and Spartans were dead. Xerxis gave orders to clean the pass of all Persian dead. He did not want his armies demoralized as they would pass by so many dead Asians. Instead, he left all Ellines unburied to be fed to the vultures and placed the head of Leonidas on a long post, so his troops would take heart from the miserable end of a 'stupid' enemy who dared face the might of the Ruler of all Nations! All Nations had to see what the High King's wrath could bring...

Alexandros was ordered to send his scouts ahead again, on the open road to Athinae. The city was reached at leisurely pace (that gave time to Themistoklis to evacuate the citizens to Salamis, Trizina and Aegina -now a staunch ally before the national danger). The few remaining defenders on the city's acropolis were an easy 'meal' and the city was put to fire. All holy places were destroyed and the statues of the local heroes against tyranny (Armodios and Aristogiton) were packed and sent to Sousa while the Athinian fleet -supported by squadrons from Korinthos, Aegina, Megara and other city-states from Peloponnisos- were looking at the smoke rising from their beloved city, unable to inter-vene, at anchorage by Salamis island…

Xerxis now had to wait for his fleet to approach, before the final onslaught against (informants had it that the 'Yunis' were divided now and ready to fall apart) an enemy with low moral and lesser hope for deliverance.

Petitioning the Delfic Oracle, Athinians and Ellines allies received their answer from the Archer god Apollon, the god of sunlight and music: 'Divine Salamis! You will be the ruin of many a mother's sons!' Apollon's Pythia priestess proclaimed. Peloponnisian allies and the Spartans thought this mes-sage was clear. "If we stay at Salamis, our mothers and kinfolk are to mourn many victims! Better to withdraw by the Korinthian isthmus where land forces build a wall as we speak and where they can support us -as we them- by that narrow neck of land! Look how we held at Thermopylae!"

Themistoklis was of a total different opinion though and had facts to back his word. "Remember the naval battles at Artemision by Thermopylae? What saved us was our stand there and the fact that the gods did not allow the Persians to circumnavigate the island. If I have learned something is the fact that we held them in the narrow sea, causing heavy casualties to them. We held the pass like Leonidas held Thermopylae! Narrow place with no room for them to deploy their numbers. Look at the narrows here, between Megara and Salamis! If we depart, who can deprive them from landing at any place in Peloponnisos? They will need no other Efialtis to show them the way through the open sea. In Salamis we ought to stay and give them battle."

To persuade the Spartans and the Peloponnisian allies he extended his 'dependency' under a Spar-tan admiral of a dubious quality as a seaman. He even threatened a complete withdrawal of all Athi-nian ships! "We then better load all families and seek another land to build again our homes! Let the shame be on you, as deserting the only city which alone fought at Marathonas, which alone suffered a complete destruction under our very eyes (here he conveniently did not mention the fate of Eretria ten years ago -as she was also left alone and especially deserted by Athinae), with all that is sacred toEllas set on fire!" Persian spies were sure to report back to Xerxis the 'quarrels' of these idiots, the Yiunis, and the High King was equally sure to inform his subordinates and instill in them the belief that final victory was near. Meantime, what with quarrels what with persuasion, the fleet was staying anchored around Salamis while the Persian fleet was gathering across at the entrance of the straits.

Athinian propaganda (after all was done and over with) had Themistoklis sending to Xerxis a trust-ed servant by the name Sikinos, giving that same report to assure the High King that the Yiunis were indeed quarreling, as well as proposing a Perso-Athinian understanding and cooperation in exchange of a full pardon and rebuilding Athinae, under Persian rule over Ellas. According to this verse, Xerxis believed the 'intention' of Themistoklis and ordered parts of his fleet to circumnavigate Sala-mis, in order to surround the Ellenic navy and destroy it all at once. Whether that stood true or not, Alexandros was not able to find out for sure. Perhaps the High King wanted to repeat the Thermo-pylae move (the mountain path there, the rounding of the island here). Xerxis could also remember his al-most successful move around Evia -if it wasn't for the cursed storm. Here, he thought, were different waters. There was no open sea, nothing but calm channel waters within a gulf stretching from the tip of Attiki to Peloponnisos. The third time trying the same trick could be the charm!

Regardless of who's this idea was the plan was put into action. The Athinian exile Aristidis (the so-called Just) barely made it through the blockade to report the Persian movements. The allied Ellenic fleet panicked. Most were calling for a speedy withdrawal to the isthmus before the Persian maneu-ver closed its pinchers and kept them in the shallows and narrow channel. The Spartan admiral was debating the order when Themistoklis convinced him to stay and fight, saying his famous words: "Πάταξον μεν, ακουσον δε!" (You can hit me, but you have to listen to me!)

As Egyptian squadrons were rounding the island to engulf the Ellenic navy, the Athinians made their move. Ostensibly sailing to join the Persians coming for battle, they fell upon them and then retreated, bringing the enemy against the prows of the waiting Ellenic triiris/triremes. This caused confusion and great loss of Persian ships during the initial engagement. If that was not enough, the usual southern afternoon wind picked-up, causing further chaos among the Persian lines. Meantime, the Korinthian squadron guarding the rear of the Ellenic navy and seeing that no Egyptian ships were on sight (the same wind prevented them from rounding the island on time) turned and fell upon the enemy with added force on the attack against the Persians.

Xerxis ordered the immediate execution of his admiral and left his throne on top of mount Aegaleo (he had the best possible view from that post, anticipating a total victory), fuming in anger and shame! He had no heart left to fight against these cursed Yiunis any longer, although He was the High King and his pride wouldn't let him retreat outright. His kinsman Mardonios was the one who gave Xerxis the excuse. Mardonios promised on his life that the High King should let men below Him do the 'dirty laundry'. If Xerxis would leave Mardonios in charge with selected troops, Mardonios would deliver the rest of Ellas by the end of the following year. Meantime the High King could return to Sousa in peace, knowing that He had accomplished His goal to inflict pain on the Athinians.

Xerxis' ego was soothed. He did punish the Athinians by burning their city, like it was done with Eretria ten years ago. He let Mardonios choose the troops he wanted to keep in Ellas and he took off to Sardis and hence to Sousa.

Alexandros suggested the wintering of Persian troops in Viottia and Thessalia as the most appropri-ate locations due to their proximity to southern city-states. In reality, he simply did not want to have Mardonios' hordes roaming in Makedonia and causing undue trouble. He had not forgotten the hard times of the first Persian visit and Vouvaris was getting older for active protection of his brother-in-law. He offered to escort the High King well into the Thrakian satrapies and, that being accepted, he took the opportunity to further enlarge his kingdom and its prestige. On the way to Thraki he annex-ed the rest of Amfaxitis, Almopia and Kristonia. He was prudent to allow the local kings continue their ruling, excusing his actions before Xerxis as a preemptive and cautionary move, one that secured further the High King's interests in the area. Also, seeing that Persian presence remained too strong and very close to his dominion, he promised full support to Mardonios for the following spring and the new campaign season.

Returning to Aegae, Alexandros sent his Vryges back to their region making sure they had plenty of compensation from the campaign. He had to, in case he would need them again next spring.

For that he received their formal promise and, in good faith, he let them take home all the mounts they used as scouts. He added livestock and cereals so the people could get easily through the Illyrian heavy winter and knew that both Vardilis and Evdikos were very happy and the kingdom's north-west frontiers would be peaceful...

Alexandros took care of his state affairs all winter long. The land lords he had left in charge of his kingdom, the houses of Agis, Olganos, Ptolemeos and Ifanor had all worked in keeping law and order. Royal rights had been collected the people felt secure, summer crops were stored and avail-able when in need. The High King gone, Mardonios camped in Viottia with food coming to him from Thessalia and Alexandros felt rather secure.

Secret envoys from Athinae came to him on behalf of Themistoklis, who was already in a deadly struggle against Aristidis 'the Just' on Athinian political power, in spite of the ever-present danger of Persian armies at Attiki's doorstep. Alexandros and his land lords looked upon that struggle with contempt, not understanding how the Athinian political system allowed personal pathos above urgent country needs.

The message from Themistoklis was full of praise for Alexandros' warning when the Ellenic alliance had camped at Pinios' Tempi valley, as well as purported Spartan gratitude when king Leonidas was informed of the treachery from Efialtis. Alexandros' status as benefactor of the city-states had been fully recognized -the envoys were emphasizing. Alexandros accepted their gratitude graciously and braced himself for the punch-line. Athinians were not known to Makedon of giving praises without a price/request/demand (depending on circumstances) attached to such proclamations.

He did not have to wait. Anaxandridis, the head envoy came right to the point. Athinae was asking for large amounts of timber. Would the benefactor of all Ellas see to its delivery? Alexandros saw the 'request' as it truly was. Themistoklis' Athinae needed to repair damaged ships from the naval battle at Salamis. Themistoklis' Athinae was freely giving accolades in hope of a 'freebee' or -at least- cheap accommodation, in the name of 'boosted patriotism'. More important, Themistoklis' Athinae needed such accomplishment to overshadow Aristidis' Athinae! Themistoklis' ambition was well known to all. Since Marathon, he was known to declare: 'Ουκ εα με καθευδειν το του Μιλτιαδου τροπαιον!' –the trophy (glory) of Miltiadis will never let me sleep in comfort! He wanted to be well above any one else's personality!

Alexandros could care less about Athinian personal goals for added fame, nor for who the next Athinian strong-man would be. What he cared about was the still strong presence of Persia just south of his kingdom, the inability to yet form a permanently strong army of Makedonians (the newly ac-quired and tentatively friendly kingdoms of other Makedonian clans needed time to assimilate and truly connect), the true recognition by the city-states of his right to govern his country without any outside interference. He and his Makedonians had plenty of patriotism. They did not need any bar-barian patronage any more than Athinae or Sparti. Yet, as these city-states wanted their indepen-dent recognition as major Ellenic powers, so did Makedon -so did he! Circumstances would not yet allow such policy though.

The Makedonian King made-up his mind. He would help Athinae but at a cost and his help would have to be very discreet. It was agreed that the needed timber would get to Athinae via Halkidiki. The peninsula was somewhat lucky in serving as a by-way to Persian interests, therefore had more freedom in the dealing with Ellines and Persians alike. Now that his kingdom's borders were expand-ed to neighboring Vottiki, Alexandros came to an understanding with king Evmenis of Mygdonia (the latter being a recent subordinate), king Lyppeas of Vottiki and Sythonia (the former kingdom now being transformed to a loose confederation of city-states and colonies), to have timber transfer-red ostensibly for Sythonia's needs to docked Athinian ships bound for Faliron bay in Attiki. The agreed sum was the equivalent of two hundred Darics in silver, which Alexandros split with Evmenis, Lyppeas and the Sythonian confederation, to keep everyone happy and the deal secret from Persian ears. Athinae paid the price because Themistoklis had no other option. He never forgot nor did he forgive the charge of the cost -when he really expected a 'donation' from Makedon. Aristidis and his party did not forget or forgive either. Athinae, regardless who was in charge, never forgot or forgave 'injustice' against her immediate interests...

With spring approaching and war preparations well under way now, Alexandros was ordered to send again his scouts in support of Mardonios' army. He, in turn, asked Evdikos to comply and the Vrygian kept his word once more. Alexandros met the Persian army just south of Thivae. Soon the Persians were on the move looting and burning what was left from the previous year's campaign.

Faithful to his concern about Ellenic loss of life, Alexandros was sure to inform beforehand the cities and townships of pending attacks, preventing loss of life as the inhabitants would leave their dwellings and take off to the mountains. Homes -he was telling them- could be easily rebuilt after the enemy was gone or peace would prevail. Makedonia had plenty of experience in those matters. He was happy to see they mostly took his advice seriously.

Athinae had to be re-evacuated and was burned again to the ground. The southern city-states again under Spartan leadership (Pafsanias campaigned as regent because Leonidas' son was still an infant and Spartan law dictated one of its two kings to remain in the city), were mobilized amassing -for the first time ever- thousands of troops to face the invader once and for all! They were assembling at the Korinthian isthmus, having in mind to resist there, in spite of Athinian requests to move into Attiki.

Mardonios' spies kept him informed of every allied move. He tried to have the Ellines split or -at least- show difference of fighting valor. He sent envoys (Alexandros had to serve as a go-between) to the Athinians, offering alliance, rebuilding of the city in a more glorious way and a promise of hegemony over the rest of Ellas -obviously under Persian supervision and tutelage. He had strong arguments in his effort to persuade, as the Spartans and Peloponnisians were reluctant of moving north of the Korinthian isthmus.

The Athinians -to their honor- turned down Mardonios but not after real threats to Sparti and the allies of complete abandonment of this alliance were placed at the Ellenic council. Pafsanias seeing the absolute need of Athinian naval and land support, decided to move northward into Megaris and, from there, into Viottia and/or Attiki, to meet Mardonios.

The Ellenic alliance numbering about four times a myriad (40,000) of oplites and auxiliary troops, took positions on the north slopes of Kithaeron, careful not to expose its flanks down toward the plain where Persian cavalry could easily outflank them. Mardonios on the other hand, camped north of the Asopos river, controlling the plain and all routes of supplies, in charge of a slightly larger army. He built a fortified camp further north of the town of Plataea and Asopos became the line separating the two camps.

The opponents faced each-other for sometime, undecided. Delegations sent from both sides to the Oracle of Delfi, were similarly advised not to make the first move crossing the river against the other side. Skirmishes did take place, giving the upper hand to Persian cavalry archers, as they would come and volley at oplites who were trying to take water from the river.

Mardonios was trying to provoke the descent of the oplites from the ridge to the open ground, while Pafsanias was keen of keeping the positions in hope of forcing a Persian attack uphill against his bet-ter equipped soldiers, guarding his flanks free of Persian cavalry charge. Mardonios did what he could to force Pafsanias' move. He sent strong contingents to outflank and interrupt the Ellenic lines of supplies of both food and water, thus forcing them to either withdraw for good or out into the plain, preferably the latter. Yet something went completely wrong with his plan, despite his well calculated effort and partial success of depriving the Ellines of a large food supply and poisoning of water sources.

The agent of this failure was none other than Alexandros himself. The Makedonian King made sure he informed Pafsanias of almost every Persian move and the Spartan regent was able to counteract most of Mardonios' moves.

"I bet the following thought has crossed your mind, dear listener, not only once: how come this man knows all these details about the coming and going of King Alexandros, about the Persian and Ellenic scheming behind the scenes and the actions taken or failing to? I bet you are thinking that I make sure to add plenty of salt on the 'food' which I am serving you! Now, don't try to be polite before an old man! I know what you are thinking, it's all over your face and that doesn't offend me, honestly!

Before you try to defend yourself with another polite excuse, let me tell you exactly how I know all which transpired in such detail: as you know, I am Stasanor son of Agerros, descendant of Tyrimmas on my mother's side, who also was direct descendant -by her father- from the house of Agis. With such lineage, I was one of the most trusted members of our King's bodyguard and, his own private secretary! Although I have not kept written records of all the King's dealings unless I was asked to or it pertained to official correspondence, I was always well aware and cognizant of all his affairs. Being always at his side whether at war or at council, I heard and understood every word he uttered, every move he made and his reasoning behind all that!

Now I am passing this knowledge of mine to you (as I have done with my grand son and namesake) for posterity. My reasoning for doing so -instead of writing it down- is a simple process. Like I said, I saw and participated in all events, what my King did for all Ellas as a whole and for Makedonia in particular. My duty was to write what was asked of me as official records or correspondence. The rest I committed to memory which you can easily verify if you ask anyone decent enough to tell the truth as it is. The easiest task is to know for sure that I was the King's secretary and companion.

As such, I can judge how the Athinians and the Spartans elevated him when they needed him the most and also how they ignored him and degraded Makedonia when they thought any useful to their interests cooperation had run its course! For that reason I detest the policy of the southern city-states. The treatment we received from the Persians was much more forward and honorable.

Although barbarians and invading 'masters' of the Asian nations, any time they made a deal with us they kept their part of the bargain with honor. They never lied to us nor did they try to praise for gain and then turn about face and stab our back. I wish our southern kin could do the same!

You see I am a very old man. I am about the last survivor of my King's generation while he's gone. Some of his offspring are also gone, Filippos and Alketas. Perdikkas is now our Timenid King and now I have to take leave because I am tired and because my grand son can take over and narrate to you all the events with a more clear mind, for he collected additional information from other sources and sees things from a different prism and perspective. I am sure he will not disappoint your thirst for knowledge nor your intelligent evaluation of how and why things developed the way they did.

With these words I bid you fare well. I will be happy to see you again tomorrow -if the gods allow me to live one more day. If not, remember me with kindness, judge my sincerity with open mind and pass your judgment and knowledge to your kin."

The old man stood up with some effort and one could clearly hear his old bones crackling as he did so. He slowly disappeared through the door of the sitting room to his chambers. Young Stasanor, obviously pleased by the praise of his grand father on his ability to narrate his own and expanded knowledge, offered some more wine and dry fruit before picking up. He started with a small 'recap' of the events before the last battle at Plataea.

"After the victory at Salamis, the southern city-states held festivities at the isthmus, called Isthmia, for several days. Even during these festivities though, the pride and ego of each of their leaders and each state's jealousy of who did what and who did the most, brought discontent and almost caused the ruin of their alliance. Athinians accused the Korinthians of cowardice, claiming they returned to battle after all was clear and victory was at hand. The Peloponnisians accused the Athinians of thick-headedness and ego, demanding honors they did not truly deserve. Aegina was given the honor and prize just to spite Themistoklis, although the Aeginitan navy presented itself with extra valor during the fight. Ar-gos, the Peloponnisian Argos, neutral at the time, was playing games threatening alliance with Mar-donios, to keep Spartan influence in check.

The Athinian refugees in Salamis and Aegina were demanding a return to their city eager to salvage what was left and rebuild. Themistoklis' ego was hurt, as he was denied a pan-Ellenic recognition and, even worst, the unconditional adoration of his fellow country men! He threatened negotiations with the enemy and that cost him the leadership of Athinae to his opponent Aristidis 'the Just'. Meantime, no one mentioned the subtle but crucial help Makedonia provided at Pinios and Thermo-pylae, nor the timber smuggling for ship repairs. The deeds done, Alexandros was placed at the furthest sector of Ellenic minds.

Only the Spartans honored Themistoklis, but they did so with their own interests in mind. He was accused of being a Spartan lover (a Spartan honor guard escorted him to the border after his visit there) and his 'Just' opponent saw that he was exiled from Athinae. In return, Themistoklis moved (via Makedonia!) to the court of his former deadly opponent and became Xerxis' advisor at Sousa!"

Stasanor took some wine, ate a few dried figs dipped in honey and returned to his narration, picking up from where his grand father left. "Mardonios getting tired of waiting and in hope to infiltrate or divide the Ellenic alliance at Plataea, ordered Alexandros to seek audience with the opposing leaders and convince Aristidis (he was now the Athinian general under Spartan Pafsanias' command) to remain in place on the hills. The true plan of Mardonios was to keep the allied army away from another water source and starving (he had intercept the Ellenic supplies from Pelopon-nisos), while he would per-form a circling move and then attack in force. And, who else would be more appropriate to propose such action/inaction to the Athinians but a Persian's in-law, an Athin-ian benefactor and a King whose kingdom was open to Persian wrath if he wouldn't perform what was asked of him? I am sure you guessed right! Alexandros then was sent to meet Aristidis.

The King could not refuse but he asked to go alone, ostensibly because he did not want Aristidis to be alarmed if he would see movement coming from the Persian camp. Mardonios misjudging Alexan-dros' determination to be helpful to his own countrymen, agreed. The King, a lone rider in the dark of the night, approached the Athinian wing and asked to talk to Aristidis and Pafsanias alone. He did not want other witnesses present, for he knew from experience of the Persian network of spies. He revealed his identity only when he was left alone with the two leaders at Aristidis' tent and after he made sure no ear was close to them when doing the talking.

Alexandros revealed Mardonios' plan in every detail. He asked of no favors except to be remember-ed for his services when the war was over and the country free of invaders. He then returned to his 'master' to report a 'successful' mission. When Mardonios made his move of encirclement, all posts on the Ellenic side were reported alert and the move was cancelled, causing confusion in the Persian lines. New line-up orders had to be issued.

Pafsanias had to move nonetheless, because of thirst and famine in the army. The heights occupied until then had become unattainable. He called for council and it was decided to move during the night to a new location a little east of Plataea, a location by the river Iroi named Nisos, the island, as the river formed two branches there. It was a ridge-like location which would still give them the advantage of being on a higher ground, plus adequate water for the troops. The move would also free the new food supply contingent which was stranded at Dryoskefalae because of Persian cavalry activities until then.

The night march to the new location started with the center contingents of allied city-states, which promptly got lost in the unfamiliar territory. Eventually they formed their line by the sanctuary of goddess Ira, in front of Plataea itself. Pafsanias realizing that, ordered the Athinian contingent to close the gap between his troops and them and move along when he did. By the predawn light, Lakedaemonians and Tegeans started to move south also. The Spartan officer Amomfateros held the rear in support of the move to the shrine of Dimitra. Some say he refused to move out of tradition holding that no Spartan retreats before the enemy. That is partially true. I had the honor to meet him and discuss the maneuver in person. He refused to move his troop, unless he was given the honor to be the last to withdraw, thus protecting the whole army move to its new camp.

With the light of dawn now, Mardonios was informed of the Ellenic army's move and, seeing only the Lakedaemonian part of it, made the fatal mistake of thinking the Ellines were in full retreat and abandoned the field. The Athinians could not be seen, as they were covered by a hill. He ordered then a cavalry attack, sending the Thessalian heavy horse under Thorax of Larissa to encircle the Spart-ans. The other Persian units followed on a head-on attack, not wanting to be thought as cowards but that led to an attack without cohesiveness. Mardonios' own contingent followed in order, because he was leading them in person.

Now, when the first Thessalian and heavy Persian cavalry met his Lakedaemonians, Pafsanias sent a message to the hidden Athinian contingent to come forth and strike, sending the archers first. As Aristidis complied, he met the horse contingents from Thivae and other Viottian cavalry, mixed-up with the Illyrians of Alexandros and got engaged there by necessity, leaving the Spartans and Tege-ans to face Mardonios' heavy troops alone. Initially, the Persian archers and javeliners caused some casualty on the Lakedaemonian lines but Spartan training and discipline proved itself once more. When oncoming Persian infantry closed-in preventing any room for redeployment of the archers and horse, Pafsanias ordered full attack. As at Marathonas and Thermopylae, no Persian armor was a match to heavily-armored oplites, especially when they were Spartans. Slaughter ensued and Pafsanias pressed on. The troops stationed by the Nisos since the night march, now seeing the Thivan horse encircling the Athinians, came to the rescue. Athinian propaganda of course is looking at that with contempt, saying that such help did not exist once the Thivans routed their 'saviors'. They conveniently forget -as it's customary to them- that the Thivan horse chasing the rescuers stopped pressuring the Athinian contingent, giving Aristidis the needed breathing space!

Meantime the Korinthian and Megarian contingents came to fill-in the split center of the Ellenic lines and hold. I do not know how Aristidis would have hold if not for them, regardless what the Athinians claim now! Alexandros held his Illyrian horse back, letting them scatter and loot from the dead. He could use the excuse now that them being Illyrians, he had hard time disciplining them. The Persian general Artavazos (Ahrtabardiyia) being against any attack from the beginning, now in place to have full view of the battle, was bringing his own troops in a leisurely manner.

The battle between Lakedaemonians with the Tegeans on their side against the heavy Persian infan-try mixed with the light archers (who could not now use their bows) had turned against the invader for good. Mardonios tried to give his troops a boost in morale conspicuous on his Nissaean horse, was doing what a good fighter and leader can, by example. But Mardonios fell from a stone crushing his head, as -ostensibly- was foretold by the oracle. The Spartans credited the deed to Aimnistos (you know what the name means: one who will never be forgotten) very aptly applied.

Seeing that, Artavazos, still approaching leisurely and having an overall view of the battle, turned his troops the opposite direction and abandoned the scene in haste. King Alexandros joined him at once, as did the Thessalian horse and they all traveled northward. Artavazos let the Thessalian rulers think that he was on a special mission, while the Thessalian horse had all the interest to keep their run-away secret and Alexandros pretended he was escorting the Persian general to provide accom-modation during his 10,000 strong army's cross of Makedonia to Thraki.

The ones who put up some further strong resistance against all odds, were the Thivan cavalry which had turned back after chasing the troops from the Nisos location, and the still strong but now des-parate troops of dead Mardonios. But the tide had already turned. All the Thivans could do was to have an orderly retreat into their city, with Plataeans and Athinians in hot pursuit. What saved them from further Athinian wrath was that Pafsanias sent message to Aristidis, asking for help to dislodge the remaining Persians who now had barricaded behind the palisades of the original camp Mardon-ios had built.

When the Ellenic forces finally, following the heroic example of the Tegeans, got inside the Persian camp, a general slaughter ensued. Of the almost 10,000 Persians enclosed, only two to three thousand managed to stay alive and they were sold at the slave markets.

Artavazos finally made it across the Ellispontos with his troop decimated from illness and attacks from marauding Thrakians. In spite his cowardice while he still could have made the difference albeit Mardonios' death, a practical Xerxis praised him for bringing back most of his division. In finalizing my narration, I don't need to remind you (because you are well versed in southern city-sta-te history) that it is said the very same day of the victory at Plataea, the other Spartan king, Leotyhi-dis, was also victorious at Mykali (that Asian-by-the-Aegean promontory), decimating the Persian fleet with the help of Athinian triiris led by Xanthipos. Now, don't get mixed-up. One Spartan king, the young son of Leonidas did remain in Sparti as being too young for war and Pafsanias being only a regent, not a true king. Spartan law of one king remaining in the city was not then broken.

From the Persian spoils of the battle a magnificent spiral stand depicting three entwined snakes having a cauldron placed on their heads, burns eternal thanks to Apollon as it's dedicated and set in the sanctuary at Delfi. On the bodies of these snakes, all the names of the victorious city-states are etched. Needless to say no mention was officially issued on King Alexandros' actions…"

Younger Stasanor stopped his narration there. We had some more drinks and food before we called for the night. The next morning I said my good-byes to both Stasanors and headed back home to Am-filohia, after I promised transfer of my knowledge to my own son Aristomnimos, who's also a good scribe…

Back at that time in Makedonia, Alexandros had now the opportunity to consolidate his hold of Am-faxitis ordaining his firstborn son Filippos as regent in that region. His second son Alketas was given the easternmost areas of the kingdom, ruling over Mygdonia and the new gain, Vissaltia. From the silver mines of Dysoron, Alexandros was able to issue for the first time ever true silver Makedonian coins. He also dedicated to Delfi a gold-leafed statue of himself. He had been just renamed by the Athinians a city benefactor and a true protector of Ellas, retaining the diminutive Φιλελλην, meaning the Athinians had the need of more timber to build their empire…

Now middle aged, Alexandros became a grandfather. By Filippos he got Amyntas and Agirros. Al-ketas brought to life a new Alexandros (grandfather was really pleased), Agelaos and Yefyros. Per-dikkas, the third son of Alexandros, married a bit later three brides. The first a Vrygian, Ladjike/La-odiki, gave him Aeropos and Pafsanias. His second bride was the Lynkestian Kleopatra, giving birth to Iraklis and the third wife, the Kristonian Simihi, rewarded Perdikkas with yet another son, Arhe-laos. Perdikkas then, was awarded the regions of Almopia, Pieria and Vottiaea. The remaining two younger sons of Alexandros were still too young and remaining under tutelage at Aegae.

Most of Persian presence had withdrawn at the eastern ends of Thraki, trying to recover their pres-tige after such loss of face against the Ellenic city-states. Makedonia was -for the time being- the pet child of the south and its northern neighbors were quiet and contended with what the short lived Per-sian control had achieved in terms of peace and relative prosperity through unimpeded commerce.

Still, Makedonia needed peaceful times in order to assimilate its gains and the people. For some years, this held true. Alexandros could see clouds gathering at the horizon though. Athinae was succeeding in gaining the alliance (albeit a forced one at times) of the city-states in Halkidiki, as well as at the colonies established long time ago in Idonia and coastal Thraki. Slowly but surely, Attiki was reaping the produce (be it mineral or otherwise) of vital for the Makedonian kingdom areas, becoming more demanding and autarchic. Before long, all Persian presence in the neighboring Thra-ki was pushed out by strong Athinian activities and confined its presence in the interior of Asia-by-the-Aegean and at the shores of southern Efxinos Pontos.

Alexandros could clearly see the Athinian plan: take all seaports under Athinian control and force all interior states (including Makedonia) to deal with Athinian consent or denial on all import/export matters! Such move had only one goal: chock the ability of independent dealing and economy. He was not as strong as he would like, to answer by building his own naval power in order to counteract.

Makedonians could be fishermen but were not sailors and, most important, his sea bordering cantons were not as yet completely assimilated to the idea of a common kingdom, common goals.

He made arrangements for a union in wedding his younger sons to daughters of influential families of the coastal city-states, in hope of forestalling Athinian plans and secure sea venues for his king-dom. Menelaos was married to Anthi of Krousis and Amyntas to Kleopatra from Rahelous, instruct-ed to make sure they were keeping good relations with local dignitaries -as well as with Athinian pol-icy makers. Sparti, with its inward political structure, needed not his concern.

Alexandros felt it was now time to deal with old scores, Elimiotis and Orestis. Both kingdoms had offended his predecessors and himself and tried to take advantage of circumstances, regaining his lost authority. He prepared and army and, with help from Lynkestis, Derriopia and the Vryges, he attacked Derdas. Before departure to the front, he consulted with his land lords and clan heads and left Perdikkas on the interior state affairs at Aegae. Alketas and Filippos were to remain in charge of their given dominions, but Perdikkas from Aegae was to give the final word on domestic issues. He, Alexandros, would wage his war and deal with the out of state affairs.

Alexandros made one major mistake by using the Vrygians though. Evdikos' son Vardylis was now in charge of the Vrygian tribe and he -initially- kept his father's word of honor to Alexandros on the campaign. The Orestians though had very close ties with the Ipirote Molossians and Haones and, as those were in close alliance with Elimiotis, they all turned pressure on Vardylis to change sides. Not wanting to go against his father's word of honor, Vardylis just withdrew his troops and retired. Next, pressure was thrown on Derriopia, which did the same. Lynkestis fearing eventual invasion withdrew most of its supporting troops and left Alexandros mainly on his own.

This war lasted for some years with varying result. Finally a chance was given to Alexandros. He was informed of a move of Derdas to meet with Argeas of Orestis at Keletron. From there, they were to attack Lynkestis and force either its alliance or its occupation. Alexandros decided to strike first and strike unexpectedly. He moved his army up the river Aliakmon toward Aeani, the capital of Elimiotis. He was confident he would surprise his enemy and be able to bring this war to a successful end. Unfortunately his plan backfired. The 'informants' were but Derdas' agents. As Alexandros moved up-river and before the slopes of Askion and Kamvounia open-up to widen the river valley, Derdas' trap closed in on him. The Timenid Makedonian army panicked and took off, deserting the King with only a few supporters! Alexandros fell in battle and with him the houses of Olganos, Klitos and Ptolemeos ceased to exist...

The news of that loss traveled very fast back at Aegae. The houses, land lords and clan heads along with the remnants of the army called for an immediate general assembly. Perdikkas was proclaimed the next King, although Filippos was Alexandros' firstborn. A delegation of some most important heads of the remaining houses were sent to Derdas and Argeas, working out a very unfavorable peace for Timenid Makedonia. Filippos, feeling cheated, sent a message that he would keep his holds on Amfaxitis and Kristonia, declaring himself King! His action cut Alketas off his province of Vissal-tia, which promptly fell under the influence of Athinae and caused the loss of the silver mines. Alketas settled in Mygdonia and waited. The second King named Perdikkas on the Timenid Makedonian throne, started his reign under bad auspices...

"I, Stasanor son of Tilefos and grand son of Stasanor, have now become the secretary of King Perd-ikkas and what you are about to learn of his time comes from me, as I have witness it. Following my grand father's example, I pass all that I know verbally. Only my official documents are recorded on parchments or papyros leafs and stored in the King's vaults for safekeeping. I will start this narrat-ion a little before King Perdikkas took over so I can refresh your memory on events which took place here and elsewhere. You will then have a most accurate knowledge of what transpired when and why! Make yourselves comfortable then honorable visitors and scholars, enjoy your food and drinks and listen to my accounting of events."

"While King Alexandros was still alive, many events took place which, directly or not, forced Make-donia to adjust policies accordingly. Most of those events happened outside our kingdom. Their im-pact, nonetheless, had its role played in Makedonian lives and future course as a state. I am sure that most of you -if not all- have knowledge of all the major events which took place in Ellas until now, but I am also sure you do not know some of the particular details which brought Makedonia in the state the kingdom is at present! I am glad to see that among you, most honored guests, is Aristomni-mos son of Glafkippos from Militos. Although we have just met -like with most of you- seems to me it is important to know that -his esteemed by all father- was my acquaintance, as well as my own father's. This simple fact -if I may boast about it- gives me the added credence on the impartiality of my narration and the truthfulness of my words, as he can attest if needed.

With the victory at Plataea and withdrawal of all Persian forces, all refugees returned to their homes. The Plataeans rebuilt their city, Aegina breathed in content not having to support Athinian refugees any longer and inheriting riches from the spoils of war. Sparti returned her troops home and, basking in glory, tightened her grip on the Peloponnisian city-states. Thivae was seething in fury, defeated at Plataea and losing control of that city to Athinae, but unable to do anything about it and thankful the allies did not pursue her demise as a Medizing state.

Athinae started rebuilding her homes but, mostly, rebuilding her fortifications and 'alliances' among the needy island states, as these were looking for protection from the still strong Persian navy.

Themistoklis gone and Aristidis being on his way out of dictating Athinian policy, a new leader emerged alongside of Kimon, son of Miltiadis, the hero of Marathonas. This new leader was none other but Periklis, son of Xanthipos, the Athinian admiral at Mykali. He and Kimon ostracized Themistoklis for good and forced Aristidis into oblivion. Soon, both Kimon and Periklis saw that an Athinian empire was developing under the Dilian Treaty of alliance. You remember Dilos the island of god Apollon was burned some twenty years before Plataea by Datis and Artafernis? Well, the same island was rebuilded and rededicated to god, served for a while as the safe keeper of all revenue coming from the Athinian 'alliance' with island and sea-bordering city-states.

Athinae used that revenue for a continuous capaign against Persia on one hand, showing her naval force on the other, to convince, guide or force (mainly the coastal city-states) to enlist and contribute either by placing their fleet under Athinian leadership on the war effort, or, preferably, pay the service in silver or gold and let Athinae do the job. The contributors in kind (navy) were usually the bigger city-states of the coast and, for that they more or less had the status of a full-fledged ally. The other, smaller city-states were soon turned client states with obligatory payments and diminished status in the 'alliance'.

Makedonia did not fit anywhere. There was no naval power worth of any mention as most of the Makedonian ports of some value were under Athinian domination anyway and, further, the kingdom did not even have more than a hodge-podge cavalry (difficult to transport) and barely adequate to defend its own integrity. A! But Makedonia had the most and best timber for ship building therefore Perdikkas had the 'status' of an allied King -at the beginning.

Kimon then supported an Egyptian uprising against Persia, while at about the same time Thasos revolted against the Athinian dominance of the Dilian Alliance. Meantime Xerxis got murdered and Artaxerxis became the new High King. He took over vigorously the affairs of his empireand his first act -after securing his throne- was to put down the Egyptian rebellion. Athinians mourned many a dead on that but recovered by defeating Thasos, confiscating its fleet and bringing the island back to the 'Alliance' under reduced status and with heavy penalties to pay in silver and gold.

As the Athinian adventure in Egyptos ended in a disaster, Periklis had Kimon ostracized and Efial-tis (his other Athinian ex-colleague and now opponent) put to death, thus becoming the sole leader in Athinae. At about the same time a great earthquake occurred in Lakedaemonia, giving the opportun-ity for an apprising of the slaves. Sparti put down this uprising with a most inhumane way but, that engagement gave the opportunity to Periklis to attack Thivae and wrest Viottia from Thivan domin-ance. The event caused a war between Athinae and Sparti but both sides needed recovery from the previous wars and they came to a difficult understanding.

Periklis ordered the building of the so-called long walls, a defense system of enclosing within two sets of walls all the way from Athinae to her new and more protected port, Pireas. He moved also at the same time the treasure of the "Alliance" from Dilos to Athinae, ostensibly for better protection. The negotiations with Sparti produced a thirty year truce between these two city-states and their perspective coalitions. That also happened to be the year King Alexandros died in battle. Kimon was 'pardoned' and returned to Athinae but Periklis sent him out of the city's political arena, giving him the task to continue war against Persia. Kimon fought at and around the island of Kypros but just after a naval victory followed by one on land, he died in action.

King Perdikkas continued the supply of timber to Athinae, trying to keep her interest away from Makedonia. His brother Filippos, still vexed, conspired from Amfaxitis and Kristonia, securing a secret support from Periklis. Alketas, to his credit, remained faithful to the Assembly's decision keeping his lands in service of Perdikkas. Periklis playing a double role on Makedonian affairs, named (free of any charge as it was) Perdikkas a 'friend and ally' while he allied Athinae with Derdas and Filippos. Athinae next sent a body of oplites to occupy Therma on Anthemous and Pydna on the very Pierian coast!

Perdikkas then had only one option: he negotiated with the city-states of Halkidiki, convincing them to revolt against the Dilian (Athinian now) League. In order to be freed from multiple fronts, Periklis sent Kallias to negotiate a truce with Persia and attacked the Halkidiki confederation of city-states en force, abandoning at the same time (his mistake) his plans for Filippos and Derdas. Derdas then sued for peace and Perdikkas (wisely) agreed. That found Filippos isolated but he continued harassing Perdikkas' borders. Perdikkas had no choice but to take steps against his own brother. Members from the houses of Agis, Filotas and Antiohos offered to take care of the problem and Filippos got assassinated in a few months later. Halkidiki is still fighting the Athinian contingents supported by her navy but Perdikkas is in no shape to assist. Makedonia is in dire need of reorganization and consolidation of fragmented loyalties!

Athinian colonists supported by a strong force of oplites and navy took the small junction city of Ennea Odi (nine ways/routes), located on the mainland by river Strymon, a Thasian post until then. The city now, renamed Amfipolis, as it straddles both banks of the river, is walled. The road to any future consolidation of what the makedonian Kings consider Makedonian lands is closed for now.

Periklis then formed an alliance with Shytalchi, an Odryssian king in Thraki, called Sytalkis by both Makedon and Athinae. Periklis moved to save any harassment on a new colony, by diverting all the ambitions of Sytalkis against Makedonia. Periklis' move was brilliant and Perdikkas had hard times as he tried to keep the Thrakian king in check. With more Athinian support from the navy, perhaps Sytalkis' offence could succeed.

Thivae was the 'savior' of Makedonia unwittingly, as the city-state declared war against Athinae (with undercover moral support from Sparti), trying to reclaim her holdings in Viottia. At the battle by the town of Koronia, Thivae achieved just that, defeating the Athinian forces led by Periklis. An- other revolt occured in the island of Evia, the city of Halkis being the leader. There, Periklis was more successful in putting it down but remained lenient, as Evia was sorely needed and being almost attached to Attiki. He now had hard time back home sustaining his political hold and abandoned Syt-alkis, who had to withdraw back to his kingdom in Thraki.

Letting a sigh of relief, the Makedonian King sent his brother Alketas (as second in command of the kingdom), his own son Arhelaos and several of the most important heads of the clans and land lords, to negotiate new terms of a peace which would hopefully last and give him time to reconstruct his kingdom, healing all wounds! Among these negotiators was Stasanor, his trusted secretary. A new deal was closed. Makedonia was to be left to care of its own but shipments of timber would have to double through tariff rights from the occupied Therma and Methoni. On the other hand, Athinae would support Perdikkas on any future attack from Sytalkis.

No sweat for Periklis! He holds Makedonia hostage, albeit he would like to occupy the whole king-dom and turn it to a new Hersonisos (the Thrakian area by Ellispontos where from most grain was and is coming to Athinae). But he cannot do that, for more problems diverted his attention: A revolt of the island of Samos on the eastern side of the Aegean and the colonization of Thurii on the Italian peninsula and expansion of Athinian influence in that part of the Ellenic world. The Samian revolt ended in short time with most of the islanders slaughtered or sold in slavery and Athinian κλει-ρουχοι (colonists) took their possessions and land."

Here Stasanor stopped. The day was late and the guests were getting tired. They all agreed to take time for refreshing themselves and meet again at dinner, but just for that. He would continue his narration the next morning after affairs would be taken care of and have his guests full of eagerness to learn more and compare with their own knowledge from other sources.

In due time the group gathered again the next day in the same guest room. "Would someone like to remind me where I stopped yesterday?" Stasanor asked. Proving worthy of his name, Aristomnimos had the answer ready. Stasanor picked-up again, his Makedonian accent pronounced with the lack of many vowels missing, especially at the end of nouns and pronouns. But then, everybody had gotten used to that peculiar Makedonian way of pronunciation and all were at ease with his narration.

"The building and walling of Amfipolis was finishing at that time, another success for Periklis! Athinae under his leadership seemed to be the undisputed leader of whole Ellas! The shrines and temples on the Athinian acropolis, the Akropolis now, were and are the subject of admiration and jealousy by all! Money from the mines at Lavrion and -mostly- from the levies of the 'alliance' and with the sweat and blood of thousands of slaves beautified the city beyond expectations! The Athin-ians now have the time and money to devote all their bodily and (mostly) mental capabilities to arts! The City became the Center of beauty and knowledge, with promises to reach even higher! Only one big draw-back. All these were built at the cost of the 'alliance' with slave labor from other Ellenic city-states and the elevation (plunging I say is the apt name) of Athinian ego and contempt for others' abilities and freedom.

Meantime King Perdikkas was hard at work, reconstructing and appeasing. Many a wedding took place sponsored by the King between houses. Some of them loyal from the beginning, some with lost interests and on Filippos' side a while ago and some hanging on the sides, waiting to grasp the first opportunity of better placement and gains. The King opted for renewed loyalty to his person, uniting all, against future interior or exterior dangers. It seemed it was working. Athinian success or failure did not concern the King at all! Although Makedonia could ill afford commercial dominance and ex-tortionate dictations from Periklis, it was known that times do change and, when complete unity within the kingdom could be achieved, things would get much better!

Fate has other dictations stemming from higher authority. The war between Korinthos and Korky-ra for the right of calling Epidamnos on the Illyrian coast a colony of their own, brought Athinae at the side of Korkyra and at odds with Korinthos and Sparti. The thirty year peace treaty signed not long ago, became a mute point within weeks! A new war started between the southern city-states which, initially, did not concern King Perdikkas. Let Athinae and Sparti war. Less interference in Makedonian affairs! Concerns about the movements of Sytalkis and those of Orestis and Elimiotis were more than enough to keep Perdikkas preoccupied.

Soon after this war started, Potidaea of the Halkidiki peninsula revolted against Athinian dominat-ion. Athinae reacted with vigor and, to secure any flanking, returned (temporarily) Therma to Make-donia. As soon Periklis secured the submission of Potidaea, turned on Anthemous on the pretext that the Anthemountians helped the Potidaeans and occupied the area, isolating Therma. There was nothing Perdikkas could do but to join the Athinian 'alliance' in order to keep Therma.

In a couple of years after these events, another sigh of relief with another chance of better days to come came to be in sight. A strange plague befell on Athinae, as all Attiki was moved within the city walls, leaving the country at the mercy of Spartan troops. Many Athinians died and the city seemed to fall in despair. A false hope. Athinian policy did not change. More demands came for additional timber and the control on sea venues for import-export tightened with a forcible takeover of Therma.

The same year and with full Athinian blessing, Sytalkis made his move again. He had on his side Filippos' son Amyntas, who survived his father's assassination few years past and had also Athinian naval support. Sytalkis attacked and invaded Kristonia, Mygdonia and Amfaxitis, forcing Alketas to flee to Aegae and Perdikkas. Sytalkis placed Amyntas as a puppet king and took all the loot he could carry, leaving the country open to the purported Athinian occupation which was to follow...

Thanks given to the gods, Athinae was unable (or lost interest) in keeping up. King Perdikkas entered negotiations with Sytalkis' nephew who persuaded his uncle to return to Thraki. Amyntas was forced to capitulate. At the same time the Athinian strong man Periklis, died from the plague and new hope rose again -in vain. Sparti now, took advantage of the Athinian loss, invaded Attiki and set siege on its allied Viottian city of Plataea. The island of Lesvos also revolted against Athinae, with the city of Mytilini leading it. Encouraged, Perdikkas dissolved his forced alliance with Athinae and moved to Spartan side.

Sparti was happy to have one more ally but, being a land power, did nothing to relieve the blockade of Makedonian coast, nor did Sparti sent or asked her Thivan allies to send support troops to Make-don. They were both more interested to reclaim Plataea. The following year the small city-state fell to Thivae and Mytilini to Athinae. King Perdikkas was forced to change camps once more. Makedonian timber found its way to Piraeas, as more ships were to be built for an expedition to far-away Sikelia. Perdikkas was also forced by allegations -which could not be ignored as such- to order the execution of Amyntas and his son. Athinae lost its puppet but Perdikkas could not shake Makedonia free from the 'alliance'.

As you all know, Athinae invaded the next spring Peloponnisos itself, bringing small damage but great concern on the Spartan side. Continuing, Athinae took Pylos and fortified it, raising a revolt against Sparti on the area of Elis and Messinia and, after a siege and frontal attack, the Spartan defenders on the island of Sfaktiria surrendered (!) for the first time ever, to Athinian general/dema-gogue Kleon. Athinian power rode high but a setback at Dilion in Sikelia and a peace arrangement by the city of Gela brought an armistice between Athinae and Sparti. About the same time news from Persia announced the death of Artaxerxis and the rise of yet another Darios on the throne.

In spite of the agreed armistice, Sparti and Athinae continued warring local wars trying to better their positions, one against the other. This led to new battle on the Makedonian and Thrakian fronts.

Amfipolis was the main target and trophy. Sparti, faithful to operating close to home grounds, sent a half Spartan, Vrasidas, in charge of a few thousand freed (as long as they would fight) slaves and metikous (the non-Spartan Lakonians) via forced marches through Thessalia (the region being strongly pro-Athinian) and Makedonian guides, to Makedonia.

The deal was to rid of Perdikkas' Illyrian foes and recover Lynkestis first, but Vrasidas' main aim was the taking of Amfipolis. Meantime Athinae sent Kleon as an answer to Vrasidas, by ship. Spar-tan interests being first in Vrasidas' mind, abandoned (on a pretext) Perdikkas in the middle of the operations in upper Lynkestis. Perdikkas retaliated by cutting the food supplies off Vrasidas.

Vrasidas answered with looting and slaughter villages and people on his way to Amfipolis where he got in first, before hurrying Kleon. We all know that King Perdikkas stayed within the Spartan 'alliance' as long as the siege of Amfipolis lasted and Vrasidas with Kleon got both killed at that.

The loss of these two opponents, the fact that both Sparti and Athinae needed a bit of recovering time, allowed the Athinian Nikias to negotiate another truce, having as arbitrator none other but the High King of Persia! Again, while this 'peace' lasted the two sides waged a race as to who would bet-ter the other on holding a more advantaged position. Perdikkas was compelled to rejoin the Athinian 'alliance' and more timber went to the docks of Piraeas and Faliron.

The Peloponnisian Argos having to settle a very old score with Sparti was persuaded to follow the Athinian lines of policy. Two years later, the combined armies of these two states met the Spartans and their allies by the city-state of Mantinia. After an inglorious loss, Argos sued for peace of thirty years with Sparti and Athinae lost its foothold in Peloponnisos. With that, Milos revolted but Athi-nae recovered the island and sold its inhabitants to slavery, while replacing them with colonists from Attiki.

Alkiviadis, the nephew of the deceased leader Periklis, was next the rising star of Athinian ambit-ions and politics. A pupil of the philosopher Sokratis and keen observant of his late uncle, knew how to debate and gain support. Alkiviadis convinced the Athinians of the need to extend the war in a new frontier, ostensibly to gain the resources of Sikelia by bringing Syrakousae (the leading Sikelian city-state) to her knees. Within months and with added help from Makedonian timber, a huge Athinian fleet left the harbor of Piraeas heading west. Just before leaving the port and the city, parts of the heralding news to Athinians and holy statues of the-so-called Ermis stylae were found desecrated. Accusations against Alkiviadis (true or false is unknown to us) followed him and his immediate friends. He was let to start the expedition and lead, only to be recalled to stand trial a few weeks later. He escaped and turned himself in the service of Sparti!"

Here Stasanor stopped his narration again, feeling tired as he was under the influenza for a number of days lately. This was the last time we all saw and spoke with that gentle soul, since he was found dead the next morning by his chamberlain.

> "...Because the love of honor is
> the only thing untouched by
> time and, when idle times
> come with age, the 'gains' are

not (as some say) what gives
us greater satisfaction, but
that honor by itself!"
Periklis, Athinian leader - Ellinas.

IX

"I dedicate this book to Stasanor's memory, may the gods have him rest at the Ilyssian Fields, one among the just. You all know my works in record keeping on the last war which brought Ellas to ruin and loss of our Ionian city-states of Asia-by-the-Aegean back under Persian rule. I, Aristom-nimos the son of Glafkippos from Militos, although faced with public problems -as well as personal ones- since the last re-occupation of our lands by the barbarian, feel the need to honor Stasanor son of Tilefos, the Makedonian from Evropos of Almopia and secretary of King Perdikkas House of Ti-menos. I do this because I found his narration accurate and mainly impartial. In spite of being now far from Makedon (as I returned to Militos after his death), I have the need to honor him (by writing this time) what I happen to hear and know for sure following what investigation I am capable of, so you the readers can now have it in writing and not just through narration. May the Musae guide my mind and hand to be worthy of Stasanor's integrity as I record the years after him.

Nikias' peace now wasted, Sparti renewed the war invading Attiki and occupying Dekelia. By the end of that same year the Athinian army met with disaster in Sikelia and was defeated by the Syra-kousians, led by another half-Spartan named Gylippos. As this disaster became known, Athinian 'allies' revolted en mass! The Athinian Empire seemed to be falling apart. The Persian High King Darios entered the fray, supporting with gold and silver the Spartan efforts. He also retook Ionia and most of the other city-states in Asia-by-the Aegean.

Perdikkas saw the opportunity to disengage from Athinian dominance and tried to save what he could. He recovered most of Anthemous but not Therma and he couldn't expel the Athinian guard from Pydna and Methoni. The King went to meet his ancestors with a broken heart. He wasn't able to truly consolidate what his father left, nor to free parts of Makedonia under other states' influence.

His name became synonymous of one shifting alliances in the politics of the southern city-states. It was not his own fault; adverse circumstances dictated his moves, internal problems let his efforts fail as goddess Tyhi played hard-to-get during his reign.

The houses and the general Assembly of clan heads and the army selected the next King. Alketas as the younger brother and still faithful to Perdikkas was by-passed for Arhelaos, Perdikkas' son. Al-ketas had once more to bow before the wish of the Assembly. Alketas' sons, Alexandros, Agelaos and Yefyros took things more seriously. They tried to woo the favors of Sefthys (Sephty) who succeeded Sytalkis as the Odryssian king in Thraki. Arhelaos was informed about it and Alketas with his sons were put to death. Just as a precautionary measure (because rumor was abundant), Arhelaos order-ed the death of his own half-brother Amyntas. The latter was acused of a conspiracy with Athinae and Elimiotis. Athinian interests and propaganda acused Arhelaos in the words of philosopher Platon, as a savage barbarian and a villain King. I think that if Athinae had not tried to seduce Alketas' sons, Arhelaos would have no reason to turn against members of his own family. Besides, what Athinae could say of her slaughtering the Samians or the Thasians and Dilians? On one hand we had persons who would gladly depose and kill the King out of personal ego and ambitions and, on the other, whole generations of killed or sold to slavery, just for want of independent policy of their state. Who truly was the barbarian? One who defends his own life and country or the ones who conspire against others?

The death of King Perdikkas was hailed by both Athinians and Spartans as the death of a person with no scruples. Both city-states avoided to take under account their own opportunistic alliances aiming toward the expansion of their own power in Ellas! For most Makedonians, the loss of their King was somewhat mellowed by the prospect of Arhelaos' ability to govern. The young monarch had a good start. Freed early from any domestic challenge, he could (given the right opportunities) bring his kingdom back to its former extend and unification or even surpass that.

For the time being Makedonia was still entangled with the war of the city-states and allied (as present needs dictated) with the Spartans. Arhelaos did what he could to keep his distance from act-ively getting involved in the war. He needed the time to consolidate and appease his subjects.

There were many who disliked the death of members of the royal family and many who approved that. The houses of Agis, Filotas and Antiohos were divided in their loyalties to the new King. House Agis of course was on the side of the King, faithful to their motto since the times of their progenitor Alketas. For the rest, the official word was support for the King but Arhelaos could sense the inner struggles. He had to prove that their official line of choice in supporting him was not a mistake.

Necessity and the best interests of the kingdom had forced him to act against family, like his father had done when there was hardly any other choice. Arhelaos was ready and willing to give it all for the state. No more killing -if that could be helped- and no more active participation in a war which was bringing nothing but ruin to his country. He could not dismiss his alliance with Sparti as yet though and that was keeping Athinae out of meddling with Makedonia -as Sparti had gotten the upper hand with help from Persian money. On top of it, the Persian High King was still nominal ally as well as powerful, in spite of set-backs.

Among other things, Arhelaos saw the needs of the state would be served best if his capital city was in a more central location and with access to the sea rather, than what Aegae had to offer. Obviously Aegae would remain a royal city, as being the cradle of Timenid power but it would serve heretofore as a largely ceremonial one. He searched his domain and his eyes fell on Pella, the small fishing town by the center of the lagoon and at its north shores. Yes, it was located in a lagoon who's access was controlled by both Methoni at the lagoon's entrance from the south and by Therma on the gulf's east shore, but it was of easy access to the open sea, especially on a moonless night with small ships which could bring in and out contraband goods undetected -as they'd have the mast down and row-in in silence.

Having a capital in such a central location the King would have an easy access to the vital plains of Vottiaea, Almopia and Amfaxitis, within striking distance from his eastern borders and Axios' north-ern parts, Paeonia and Pelagonia. Eordea and Pieria were comfortably secured after all these years, as was Imathia. All he had to do is build the place-up, to make it worthy of its potentials.

So he did. He invited architects from all known fellowships from the city-states, promising lands to ones that available money could not buy and removing local village families into the new city for ad-ded work and trade hands. He hired the best builder his treasury could afford for the royal palace on the highest hill of the town and walled the area. The most famous painter of Ellas, Zefxis, was com-missioned to decorate the walls of the new palace with frescoes depicting mythical scenes of heroic deeds from the past. The entrance of the King into his new capital city was celebrated for two whole weeks. Many a dignified citizens from all Ellas were invited and many did come to attend, some led by curiosity, some from envy and some because they truly enjoyed the event.

While Arhelaos was building his new capital, the war of Athinae and her allies against Sparti and her confederate city-states continued. Many revolted from the new Athinian alliance but either were brought back by force or convinced to rejoin. Arhelaos stayed his course, a nominal ally of Sparti but open in his relations with Athinae. On internal matters, he faced one or two revolts from Lynkestis and Pelagonia but he was successful in dealing with both. The royal Lynkestian House of Arravaeos was brought to recognize Arhelaos as King of Makedon once more. Illyrian and Dardanian raids were rare, as both tribes were preoccupied in warring each-other. Things were also quiet on the Thrakian front as Odrysses and Trivalli were consolidating their holds on Aftariates, Sintikes and Odomantes.

Makedonia entered the Pythian games at Delfi and Arhelaos won the first place with his four-horse chariot. He also invited the great Athinian philosopher Sokratis, but he was turned down by the sage who preferred to stay at home. Arhelaos took one more step by engaging another Athinian, a port-master to revamp the tolls on the harbor taxes, which -in turn- generated some extra income. He also sold timber now at regular prices to Athinae. Athinae was still holding the access to the open seas but now was not strong enough to take on multi-fronts and was desperate on having ships built for her war effort against Sparti. Additionally, Sparti (with money from the High King) was also building a naval power and that brought even more money to the royal treasury of Makedonia.

The Athinian poet and theatrical genius Evripidis being shied away by his fellow citizens, asked for and received hospitality at Pella. He wrote a few of his last plays there and was rewarded by receiv-ing the revenues from the town of Ihnae. The poet had a very tragic death after a few years of his stay; he fell victim to wild dogs, as he wondered one night in the country-side. He was buried with honors outside the city of Pella, on a hill overlooking the lagoon.

Alkiviadis, the Athinian general who took sides with Sparti after the expedition to Syrakousae was under way a few years back, returned now in Attiki as general of all war effort against Sparti. Athi-nae was truly in need of some success and was looking for a savior. He managed that initially, forcing Makedonia to rejoin the 'alliance' once more. But Arhelaos, as with Sparti before, did not engage his troops in the war. He just paid a sort of a tax, sending timber to Athinae on a largely reduced price.

Sparti did not let this go unnoticed. She sent her allies the Thessalian city-states (Thessalia had turn-ed its back on Athinae now) and Thivae to persuade Arhelaos to change sides by raiding in Pieria. Arhelaos could do nothing but oblige.

Within the year two disasters forced finally Athinae to capitulate. First, they lost a naval battle at Notion. That was somewhat balanced by a victory at Arginousae but, then, Athinae lost her whole fleet at the Aegos Potami location in Hersonisos and Athinae was put under siege. By the end of the year Athinae was brought to her knees. Spartan troops entered the city and placed a government in line with their interests. The war finally ended. Makedonia had no other option but to join the new confederation of states under Spartan tutelage. It brought some gain as Therma, Methoni and Pydna were annexed to Makedon.

At about the same time the High King Darios died, succeeded by his son, Artaxerxis (the second under this name). Athinae now had as rulers a group of thirty ultra conservative men, faithful serv-ants of Spartan dictates. Within a year though, Athinae mastered their expulsion and reinstated her old system of Dimokratia/democracy. They even managed to rebuild their defensive long walls to the port of Piraeas.

Spartan interest on Ellenic affairs limited itself mainly up to Thivae and Viottia, leaving Thessalia and Makedonia on their own. Never being interested in far-off ventures, Sparti went to war against Persia for a short time ostensibly to liberate Ionia but, then, made an alliance with the High King and the city-states of Asia-by-the-Aegean stayed under Persian rule. Arhelaos continued his policy of ap-peacement within, as well as without. His family had grown, having seven children by now. The old-est, a daughter named Myrsini, became the bride of Yfestias' house, married to its youngest off-spring, Leonidas. Next, Amyntas and Argeos were born to Arhelaos, followed by Pafsanias and Anth-iklia. A sixth child was given to him by the last of his wives, Kleopatra, cousin of patriarch Alketas' house of Agis. Their boy was named Orestis. Arhelaos was now feeling secured. The King even gain-ed the admiration of the Athinian Thukididis, who took the pain of recording the latest struggle between Athinae and Sparti, which left Ellas at the mercy of the High King's whim and money.

Arhelaos also tried to improve on communications between his kingdom's remote areas by building new roads and maintaining them. Feeling the time was right, he introduced some reorganization in his (until then) rag-tag army of 'volunteering' land lords and clan heads, by securing their almost permanent presence in his service. Makedonian cavalry became almost equal to the Thessalian horse.

The Orestian king Sirras incited by Derdas from Elimiotis, moved again into Lynkestis and made its king, Arravaeos, seek alliance with him. Arhelaos could not afford a three-way war. He worked through diplomacy and neutralized Derdas by giving him the hand of Anthiklia while forcing the Lynkestian Arravaeos return to the fold. In order to isolate both Sirras and Derdas from any further grandiose plans, Arhelaos got involved in Thessalian affairs, trying to favor Larissa's family of the Alevades. Farsalos and Ferrae the other two strong Thessalian city-states reacted forcibly and a war broke out. The combined armies of Farsalos and Ferrae got the upper hand and refugees from Larissa found their way to Pella, bringing the efforts of Arhelaos to an end. Arhelaos had to be satis-fied with the appeasement of Elimiotis and Orestis for the time being and the Timenid Kind did so.

Goddess Tyhi happened to have one of her foul moods again! Barely eight months after Orestis'

birth, Arhelaos was victim of a hunting accident. An inattentive page from the house Antiohos named Krataeos (and cause of this accident) was put to death -as was his whole immediate family. For many, this accident brought back memories of King Filippos' on another hunting 'accident' and there was strong rumor of Thivaean, Thessalian and Elimiote connection with this latest one. They looked upon connection with Ellinokratis from Larissa and Dekamnihos, another Makedonian clan head. But no proof was ever found for that and the houses with the clan heads and the army had to make their choice for a new King. Argeos and Pafsanias were by-passed as half-Makedonians on their mother's side -Kallisti being a princess from Parorvylia. The Assembly chose Orestis (son of Arhelaos and Kle-opatra) although still an infant but Makedonian on both sides of parenthood. Aeropos, half-brother of Arhelaos was the designated regent until Orestis' coming of age.

Within three years Aeropos took over the kingship amidst protest from the house of Agis, which brought that house to disaffection and (almost) cost its existence. Most of the other houses and clan heads excused their support of Aeropos as being the strong man to keep the country out of trouble while Orestis was still just an infant. Nonetheless, Aeropos did not live long enough to prove or disprove his value to the state. He died out of a sudden illness two summers after he was named King and was unable to stop a strong contingent of Spartans under Agisilaos to move freely through and as they were pleased.

The Assembly now named Aeropos' son Pafsanias as the next King. As soon as that occurred, the state came under internal division. In spite the majority vote from the Assembly, Pafsanias lacked the backing of many major land lords and, mostly, army leaders. House Agis now favored Amyntas, the son of Arrideos who -in turn- was grand son of Perdikkas's half-brother Amyntas. Orestis by now was set completely aside, his mother preferring to wed again to a distant cousin of hers and remove the child from Pella and the line of succession. Other houses went on the side of the other Amyntas, the so-called 'the Little' who was also great grand son of Alexandros and son of Arhelaos.

Amyntas 'the Little' did not waist time in asserting himself and -for a while- Pafsanias had to share the throne and name as the Makedonian King. Their joined kingship did not last more than a year. The Elimiote king Derdas as in-law of Alexandros, felt he had a say in the state affairs. Being in favor of Amyntas, son of Arrideos, he fooled Amyntas 'the Little' into a private meeting at Aeani and killed him. In turn, Amyntas son of Arrideos murdered Pafsanias, thus becoming the sole ruler of Timenid and Argead Makedonia. There was a distinction until then of the words Timenid and Argead. The direct line of the first Perdikkas as descendant of Timenos inherited that name. The other branches of the same family as coming from Peloponnisian Argos but still 'in line' as royal family were called Argeades. With Amyntas of Arrideos now, both names got fused in identity.

Amyntas eager to calm passions and internal strife, having on his side the support of his in-law Der-das, moved to secure the Lynkestian vote of confidence. The Lynkestian king Arravaeos had a son from the time of Arhelaos, named Sirras. Sirras became Lynkos' king when Aeropos ruled and had a daughter by a Haonian Ipirote/Illyrian princess, called Avdata or Evridiki, depending on who was the one addressing her. Amyntas asked and received Evridiki from Sirras, bringing closer ties with Lynkos once more.

This union was not to Illyrian interest and ambition toward Ipiros and Makedonia though. Since Arhelaos' times but careful not to cause undue alarm, Illyrian kings fromed a union between Parthines and Tavlantes and started forming a powerful Illyrian state. Its latest king was Bardyla (in Makedonian-Dorian dialect he was and is known as Vardylis) felt now strong enough to challenge.

Ruling the area around lake Lyhnitis and beyond to north and west, he disliked the idea of Lynkos being under the immediate influence of Pella. Finding the kingdom now in a rather weak condition due to recent disunity, he attacked.

On his attack he was supported by the Orestian king Argeos and the two were too much for Amyn-tas. The King was forced to abandon his kingdom and seek refuge in Thessalia, after he 'secured' his eastern provinces by lending the area to the powerful confederation of Halkidiki city-states under the leadership of Olynthos which is located on the north end of the gulf of Toroni and ruling over Akti, Sythonia, Pallini, Krousis and Vottiki. Now Olynthos came to rule over Anthemous, Ramelous, Mygdonia and Amfaxitis also, provided that Olynthos would support Amyntas now and in the future.

Amyntas was thankful of Thessalian hospitality provided by the leading Larissaean family of the Alevades, while preparing to return to his kingdom with their support and that of his in-law Derdas.

Vardilis took what loot he could from Makedonia, but having inadequate forces to keep the whole area occupied, he left Argeos as nominal king, letting the Orestian to deal with the situation.

Amyntas now supported by Derdas and the Alevades, returned to Makedonia and negotiated a treaty with Olynthos (too weak yet to ask for his lands back) to provide the Halkidiki confederation with white fir logs for ship-building, under payment of duty fees. To balance that, Amyntas formed a friendship with Amfipolis, Akanthos (which -although located in Akti- was independent of Olynthos) and the city-state of Mendi. The Olynthians returned Amfaxitis to Amyntas but retained their hold on the other eastern provinces of Makedon. The King needed time to recover his entire kingdom and did not argue. He turned against Argeos and Vardylis, forcing the Orestian king to return to his former borders but not totally securing Lynkestis again. Lynkos remained semi independent but a friendly buffer kingdom to Pella. Just as an added good measure for balance on his eastern front, A-myntas befriended the Thrakian (mostly Ellenized by now) king Kotys (Kot in Thrakian lingo) by adopting the latter's son-in-law and mercenary Athinian, Ifikratis.

A few years later the King felt secure enough to demand from the Olynthians his eastern provinces back. The Halkidiki confederation reacted forcibly, claiming that those provinces were given as a gift for their support to him. They attacked and, having superior armament and discipline, marched into Pella, forcing Amyntas to take refuge at the old capital of Aegae. Amyntas sent for help from Sparti, the only power in Ellas to intervene at the time, supported by delegations from members of the Halk-idiki confederation itself (Akanthos and Apollonia) complaining of excess domination from Olynthos, which had 'agreed' with Athinae and Thivae to dominate the area against Spartan interests.

Sparti listened and responded. A force under Evdamidas came to Potidaea and occupied the city, aided by forces from Amyntas and Derdas. Later, Olynthos itself was under siege and, eventually, the Spartans took that city also, forcing her to dissolve of its confederation. Sparti's high-handed treat-ment of subordinate Ellenic city-states though did not help the overall cause nor did help Amyntas to recover all his provinces. The whole area had just a change of rulers. Nonetheless Amyntas was able to receive Anthemous back.

A new coalition of Ellenic city-states with Athinae and Thivae as leaders was now formed, against Spartan domination. Athinae managed to form part of her old 'alliance' and Thivae came to domin-ate most of Thessalia and all of Viottia. At the same time, a second but much smaller confederation of Halkidiki city-states was re-formed, under Olynthos again. Most of the north and the Thrakian city-states re-joined the Athinian 'alliance' and Amyntas -although not formally- recognized the interests of his kingdom to side with Athinae and supply again the much needed timber for her fleet and let-ting Athinae know she could reclaim her dominion over Amfipolis.

On a parallel development, Iason the ruler of Thessalian Ferrae became the strong man in Thessalia causing the Athinian dreamer of a united Ellenic confederation of states Isokratis, to send a letter asking Iason to lead Ellas. Iason had the upper hand in Thessalia for some time and Amyntas saw it was his interest to become a friend. So much so that when a border dispute came along between Elimiotis and Perrevia, both Derdas and Iason trusted Amyntas' judgment to solve that dispute.

During the King's last year in life, serious events took place which changed the fates of many a city-state in Ellas and directly affected

Makedonian affairs. First, Iason died and that gave the King a chance to interfere in Thessalian affairs. He favored the return of the Alevades in charge of Larissa, blocking any further ambitions from Alexandros who was now ruling Ferrae replacing his father. A-myntas felt strong enough to place Makedonian garrisons at Larissa and Krannon.

While enterprising in Thessalia, Amyntas' opponents in Makedonia staged a rebellion and named Ptolemeos of Aloros as their king. This Ptolemeos was related to the Argeades by marriage to the sister of Alexandros, Evrynoi and was an experienced administrator and general from the Olynthian campaigns. Amyntas was again in trouble.

Sparti was eyeing the progress Thivae was making in Viottia and her hold on Thessalian and Makedonian affairs with envy, for Sparti was the supposedly undisputed power (with the blessing of the High King and disunity of the city-states). As Spartan high-handed dictations turned most Ellenic favor toward Athinae and Thivae, the latter was the one which gained more prominent name. The city-states were still reluctant and/or afraid to abandon Lakedaemonian leadership in favor of the Athinian, as memory of her first attempt was not yet forgotten or forgiven. Thivae on the other hand took her time to re-establish full control of Viottia and subtly check the power of Ferrae, now that Iason was gone and his son Alexandros was not as energetic and aggressive as his father. Under the leadership of two prominent men, Pelopidas and Epaminondas, Thivae became a very strong city-state.

Sparti would have none of this. She campaigned against Thivae and the two armies met by the Viot-tian city of Lefktra. To their utter surprise and shame, the Spartans were completely defeated and had to pull out of Viottia giving a free hand to Thivaean advances. Now Pelopidas, as Alexandros, son of Amyntas succeded in Makedon, took a strong Thivaean army and marched into Thessalia. He took over the places where Makedonian garrisons were established not so long ago and dictated his terms to both Thessalia and Makedonia. Alexandros of Ferrae had to give-up any further ambitions and Alexandros of Makedon had to hand over thirty prominent Makedonians as hostages to Pelop-idas. Among those hostages was the King's youngest brother, Filippos.

Pelopidas' arbitration of the Makedonian throne's issue confirmed Alexandros but allowed Ptole-meos to hold his gains. Ptolemeos took advantage and managed to order and execute Alexandros' murder. The kingdom needed Thivaean arbitration once more. Pelopidas directed that Ptolemeos would remain regent-protector of the (still minor in age) two brothers of Alexandros, Perdikkas and Filippos. For a measure of good behavior though, Pelopidas now demanded and got twenty addition-al hostages from Ptolemeos' side, including his own son, Filoxenos. Not long after this settlement, a new pretender to the Makedonian throne appeared in the face of another Pafsanias who claimed re-lationship to Pafsanias son of Aeropos, therefore to almost forgotten (by now) Orestis.

All the efforts of Amyntas for longed stability seemed to be wasted and gone for good. Makedonia was on the verge of total dismantling! Internal differences and strife could not be settled without external involvement. Aside from Thivae, the situation awakened the interest of Athinae, the new Olynthian confederation in Halkidiki, Illyrian intentions and even subtle designs from the aged-by-now Thrakian king, Kotys!

To make things more fluid, Pelopidas -who mainly had Thivae show interest to the north- died. The other Thivan strong man, Epaminondas, had his eye side set on the south affairs of the city-states. He campaigned against Lakedaemon itself and forced Sparti to set Messinia free. To protect that invest-ment, he settled a city -Megalopolis. He soon died also at another battle against the Spartans by the city of Mantinia. Thivan power remained but greatly reduced.

The older of Amyntas' two remaining sons, Perdikkas plotted against Ptolemeos of Aloros and had him killed, with help from the house of Agis, a house still closely attached to the most direct line of Timenid House. The Athinians seeing the indifference of Epaminondas in Makedonian affairs moved in to fill the void to their benefit, with -potentially- greater danger for the Timenid/Argeades royalty. They needed to recapture Amfipolis and re-establish their former influence in Halkidiki. Initially and with time needed for Perdikkas to secure his throne, he campaigned in support of Athinian troops under Timotheos, against Amfipolis and Potidea.

When that happened, Perdikkas entered Amfipolis after a mutual understanding and held the city with a Makedonian garrison to support its own body of citizen-oplites against Athinae. Perdikkas was defeated though by the Athinian general Kallisthenis and, later, Timotheos retaliated stronger by retaking Methoni and Pydna from Perdikkas. And we all know that defense against Athinian ad-vances was not the only concern of Perdikkas. He managed to bring his teenaged brother Filippos back from Thivae and gave him a post toward the north-eastern borders, to hold old Kotys at bay, while Perdikkas got ready to resist Illyrian penetration by another old but still strong foe, Vardylis!

Meantime, the king of Orestis had moved under the Haonian Ipirote leadership, friendly to Var-dylis out of fear. That move, left all north-western front of Makedonia open to Illyrian fancy of the moment. Perdikkas had no other choice but to forget Athinae and Kotys and face-off Vardylis. He gathered most of the available Makedonian force of four thousand strong cavalry and light armed footmen and moved. He asked the support of the Haono-Orestian coalition but, king Arryvas of Haonia did not move on time out of fear of Vardylis. Perdikkas marched alone to a total disaster! Makedonia lost three Kings in a very short time and, along with Perdikkas as the latest one, almost all of the four thousand men who had followed him!

The kingdom once more was in peril of total decomposition! And most of you dear colleagues and students of record keeping, worshipers of the divine Muse of History are more than familiar with, as the events are most recent! It is now up to you -as I in turn am getting old- to continue the impartial recording of events as they occur, not as your particular state and politicians dictate! I know, this entails some danger of disaffection, exile or -even- death penalty, depending who you work under but the truth has to prevail albeit under pressure and -at times- subdued and secretive and in disguise!

I have felt this kind of pressure many a time and, as you see, I live now mostly thanks to your own charity and good will by donating tuition for your training. But you knew all these things before you came here and had your mind made already! Stay the course my friends and colleagues, for the temptations are plenty! I know one of you; you Evmenis from Kardia, barely a teenager, are almost ready to serve King Filippos as apprentice record-keeper of his aging Epokillos. Serve your King fairly but do not overindulge his ego nor give-in to the silver of his enemies! This is the only way you can honor me, all of you, if you are of the opinion that I served my teachers fairly and honored them in return proving thus that I have honored them in return."

With these words, Aristomnimos son of Glafkippos from Militos ended his dictation to copiers and apprentices under his tutelage. This was to be his last class for he was now to retire for good. The students picked-up their tools and, one by one handed their teacher his due money and a present for an added 'thank you'. The total amount wasn't much, but enough to pay off the small plot of land he had arranged for himself and one servant (freed slave actually who wanted to stay with him). That would be adequate, as it could support them thanks to its small garden and few olive trees. He finally would retire away from political pressures, away from recording events for unworthy men who had his services because of his need to make a living. His students now had his own version of truth, the only one he knew from the beginning but couldn't present publicly for obvious reasons. With some luck and lots of hope for better times, this truth would reach future generations…

SECTION THREE

UNIFICATION AND EXPANSION

From 5th Century BCE to 4th Century BCE

"As it's been said, if it there was no Filippos, there
would be no Alexandros the Great or Dimosthenis'
venom! Because of Filippos the World (and Alexandros)
benefited. Because of Dimosthenis and
Rome the World misjudged and Ellas suffers…"
Apostolos Grigoriadis, Makedonian Ellinas.

"Ellas, rather the whole of Evropi, never produced
such a man after all as Filippos, son of Amyntas!"
Theopompos of Hios, Ellinas.

X

A little recap of past time events is deemed necessary, to give the man his due respect for what he only achieved!

The youngster was playing splashing in the pools of water and mud, down the road from the royal palace with his friends, now chasing each-other, now wrestling and trying various grips according to their understanding of the Olympic rules of the famed games. He did not hear his mother's call for clean-up and dinner. Queen Evridiki was furious, standing and calling Filippos from the top of the walled Pella acropolis where the palace was enclosed. She turned to her other sons below and both Alexandros and Perdikkas made sure the sly smiles were erased off their faces. She waved her hand to them in a motion of "go and get him!" and the two youngsters nodded in return their agreement and run out of her sight.

Filippos had just stood-up above Parmenion, covered in mud but elated because he had just prove to his friend that neither height nor hours of training could best a strong determination of wanting to win the contest—any contest! Parmenion was known to spend lots of time in wrestling, imitating the style(s) of the famous Olympian or Pythic games winners. He was also the tallest of the gang of royal friends spending their days escorting the prince and looking after him, without any undue disrespect on his part because of his rank. Filippos just happened to be the first among equals.

The youngest of the royal princes, Filippos was shorter and stocky for his age—his body not as well formed as his friend's. He was rather dark haired when compared to his companions, his deep blue eyes giving a contrast the court ladies were envying in secret. His naturally curled hair added to his handsomeness as they fell on his young shoulders. Although stocky, there was not one fat part on his body and the muscles were rather well defined. He would grow to be a very handsome man—if wars and bad luck befalling Makedonia so often lately would allow it . . .

The galloping horses made Filippos turn his head and take an instant stance of defense. Too late! The two horsemen with Illyrian helmets on their heads were too close. They scattered Filippos' friends as they came barreling down, scarcely missing the still laying in the mud Parmenion. The first rider welded his sword above head to keep the prince's companions at a distance the other grabbed Filippos by the mudded hair and lifted him up to his horse not even slowing down. With a horrific war cry, they continued galloping having the prince straddled face down on the neck of the horse and turned around the corner of the acropolis' wall and out of sight.

After they turned at the walls' end and away of any detection, the horsemen brought their mounts to a stop. The one who had Filippos face-down on the mount, grabbed him by the hair again and turned his face, only to discover that Filippos had a grin on his face and was winking at him! "I know you Alexandros! I would recognize your voice even with plugs in my ears! That war cry of yours is no-thing new to me. I recognized you also Perdikkas! Besides, you're both too young to pass as ferocious Illyrians. And, just in case both of you have any doubt, Perdikkas now look what's touching our brother's belly—in case I was wrong!" Perdikkas came closer and Alexandros looked down. A shining short knife was on the hand of Filippos ready to strike Alexandros under his sternum!

The three brothers burst in laughter. "Mother's been calling you, rat!" Alexandros said when the laughter stopped. "We thought we would give you a scare and have you mind time, place and ears toned when a call comes." Perdikkas added. "Come-on now, let's go wash and be presentable for dinner. We have a delegation from Thivae to entertain and Father says it's serious." "Look!" Alexandros complained. "You got me dirty now!" "Then, you should not have me taken on your horse!" Filippos answer was, which caused a flat hand on his but by Alexandros who guided his horse to a new gallop, Filippos tangling and re-bent over the horse's neck, his companion friends just ap-proaching in haste and armed, only to see their prince fly with his brothers laughing and teasing.

The Thivaean delegation was entertained that night at the banquet hall of the palace with all due respect to a rising power. King Amyntas made sure plenty of undiluted Makedonian wine would be served to his guests, because he thought this was the only way to get the real cause of their visit in Pella by getting them drunk. The three princes were instructed to attend and learn as much as pos-sible, until their time to retire as they were all still under age to stay—let alone drink—with their elders. The youth followed their Father's instructions to their best of abilities. Alexandros, as the older, was all attention at the beginning—until he got tired and started fooling with Perdikkas in secrecy. He was just turning ten plus four in a month and Perdikkas was two years younger. As for Filippos, if it wasn't for Father's wish, Alexandros would not allow the kid to even present himself, let alone partake! Filippos was to turn ten in three whole months from now. But that was the wish of the King and Amyntas and his wishes had to be obeyed.

Filippos kept his eyes low while sitting among the elders at the right of his Father and in line of age after his two brothers, listening intensely and absorbing. Thivae wanted the full support of Makedo-nia in her Thessalian plans, regardless the ties with Iason of Ferrae. The Thivaean delegates were also espousing Athinian demands for more timber, as it seemed inevitable to have, soon, a war against the Spartan domination. It would be to Makedonia's interest to side with them, or they could come to an understanding with Illyria or Thraki—or both! Clearly, Amyntas should weigh his options before staying allied with Sparti!

Obviously, due to etiquette, the words did not come out of the delegates' mouths like that, but Filip-pos could clearly read their meaning. He was not born yet to live the hard times Father had just few years ago running on the mountains for dear life and depending on the good will of 'uncle' Derdas of Elimiotis and Thessalia, but he had full knowledge of it from his brothers and Mother's stories at bed-time when she wanted him frightened. Filippos could not stay to find what his father's answer would be, as he and his brothers had soon to leave but he knew Amyntas would play for time and see what would develop without risking any more than he could. And he was right.

"Why do we have to answer to so many and why we have to supply without any true gain the city-states?" he asked his brothers many a time as he was growing and learning. They were elder, closer to Father's affairs and more experienced than a kid of ten plus three by now. Father was not looking good lately. All the years of fighting, running and recovering lost grounds had taken their toll. Alex-andros was more and more involved in state affairs and he was the usual responding person to Filip-pos' questions. "We are not strong enough to withstand any external pressure yet! After all the bad luck and fighting against enemies from within—as well as outsiders—we have to be careful how we act!" "All I hear is about Athinae wants this or Sparti needs that! We had the chance to show some-thing in Thessalia and now Father's again in trouble! What Thivae is asking from us now?" "Our ally, Iason of Ferrae died and his son Alexandros is not of his father's caliber. Thivae wants us to obey their interests." Alexandros finalized and took off.

Filippos returned to his thoughts. "When I grow-up and be able to negotiate terms along with my Father and brothers, Makedonia's interest will be first! I will force Sparti to become more isolated in far off Peloponnisos. I will make Athinae the mistress of my whim and Thivae will have to bow her ugly head before the House of Timenos! I swear it in the name of Father Zefs and all the Olympian gods!". Those were the unuttered thoughts of the young prince before following his brothers . . .

Amyntas died unexpectedly before Alexandros turned ten plus eight. In one more year he would be-come adult; for now he was still a minor according to Makedonian tradition. If that was not enough, Ptolemeos came forth to claim the throne and the Thivan Pelopidas was invited by the somberly thinking clan heads, to avoid another war for succession and further weakening of the state.

Pelopidas flatly placed his demands: Makedon was to remain united but Ptolemeos would supervise King Alexandros until the latter would become of age or on further Thivan notice. Makedon was to hand three times ten hostages of the highest rank, to ostensibly keep peace but in actuality to allow Thivae a stronger say in Makedonian internal matters— or else!

Alexandros still in mourning, had no choice. Among the hostages was his youngest brother Filippos. The Mother Queen Evridiki never forgave Alexandros for that. Perdikkas tried to reason with her to no avail. Besides, he had to go to Illyria, also as a hostage. Alexandros married Evrynoi but Evridiki did not attend. A year later Alexandros was found murdered in his sleeping quarters! Suspicion ob-viously fell on 'uncle' Ptolemeos who gained the most by becoming the caretaker of the two remain-ing royal princes (one still hostage in Thivae) until Perdikkas would come of age, but there was no proof, in addition to the fact that Ptolemeos had kept King Amyntas' sons from Gygea (another wife) isolated and 'behaving'.

Filippos was the 'guest' of the Thivaean strong men Pelopidas and Epaminondas and he hated every minute of it! He had the mind (well versed out of Makedonian needs during the—mostly hard times of existence) to keep it all to himself and observe. He liked the way Thivan infantry contacted itself in exercise mimicking battle conditions. He saw Pelopidas and Epaminondas drill their troops time and time again to perfection and he thought of the Makedonian lack of discipline in battle. He was curious of the special relation between men of the so-called Sacred Company (Ιερος Λοχος) of three hundred Thivaean oplites, inseparable in all ways of life—especially during battle. He wanted to learn more of it and one of the noble Thivans and host named Pammenis, was more than happy to show 'the back-water' brat what it all meant. Filippos never forgot the lesson. It would come back to him like a nightmare which needed an outlet every time he'd drink excessively.

The death of Alexandros filled Filippos with dread. He made a promise not to allow a thing like that happen again, as long as he lived! Pelopidas was called back in Makedonia to calm things down again and dictate new Thivan terms. He brought back with him another twenty hostages, confirming Per-dikkas' right to the throne and bringing Ptolemeos' son Filoxenos as additional hostage, while an-other 'uncle', Pafsanias this time, placed his claim on the Timenid throne! In one surprise move, A-thinae came to the rescue of House Timenos, primarily because Athinae could not allow a total control of Makedonia by Thivae. On a move by Pafsanias (with help from Olynthos) to take the throne, Athinae sent Ifikratis who stopped him and sent him back to Halkidiki.

Pelopidas got killed soon after his return to Thivae and Epaminondas loosened-up the care of Ma-kedonian hostages as his concern was the Thivan superiority in the south against both Sparti and Athinae. Filippos made sure Filoxenos was found dead at the stadium where youth (captive or other-wise) was exercising daily, thus avenging Alexandros. In a short time after that, he was happy to learn that Perdikkas got rid of Ptolemeos (while Olynthos held Pafsanias as a refugee) and arranged for the return of the Makedonians kept hostage in Thivae, to the Motherland.

Filippos was now a young strong man of about twenty years of age. His return to Pella was celeb-rated for days and many a children came to be born as a result of his drunken nightly 'outings' to the houses where the palace guests were still preoccupied celebrating his return. He found the time though to make sure that he and Perdikkas saw the end of Ptolemeos' kin. They were found dead, like Filoxenos had been one morning, struck by unknown assailants. Argeades of House Timenos were in control of their destiny once more.

The state though was in dire need of salvation. North Peonians were raiding now in southern Pae-onia and Amfaxitis, the old Tharkian king Kotys had his eyes on Kristonia and the Illyres were knocking at Derriopian and Lynkestian doors, making progress! Perdikkas assigned to Filippos the care of the eastern borders and he started preparations for facing the Illyres first.

Perdikkas now as King of Makedon installed his brother as general of the eastern provinces in the kingdom and Filippos started hard work at once. Both brothers were in agreement that the inno-vations of Arhelaos on military roads and the need to bring closer to central control of not only the clan heads and land lords but also the rest of Makedonian kings was a paramount concern, got them moving. Perdikkas wanted to rid the country from any further Illyrian raids and penetration once and for all first. That would force the permanent incorporation of Lynkos, Orestis, Dassaretis and Derriopia into the fold. He had to move against old but always dangerous Vardilis. Athinae convinc-ed Perdikkas to join her in trying to recapture Amfipolis and the King, feeling indebted, agreed at the beginning. Seeing the resistance of the Amfipolitans and realizing he would damage his own chances of future cooperation with Amfipolis, Perdikkas ordered Filippos to withdraw the Makedo—nian troops which supported the Athinian effort. This angered of course the Athinians who sent ships with Timotheos in charge and who, in turn, retook the coastal cities of Methoni and Pydna from King Perdikkas.

Still, King Perdikkas could not try to counter this Athinian move first. His priority was always the danger from the north, namely Vardilis. He started his preparations, leaving the Athinians in charge of his sea routes again. Filippos was furious with the developments, especially seeing that Thivae had freely give the go-ahead to Athinae by her inaction and indifference. He asked for and got permis-sion from Perdikkas to experiment with the army under his command, the army of the eastern prov-inces. Impressed by the Thivan ways of exercises as he was, he put his contingents of about 2,000 strong—but totally untrained men—to hard work.

There was not a day during which one would not find Filippos and his army 'sweating it away' from the drill fields by the banks of Ehedoros or (after hard marches) the foothills of Vertiskos. So much so, that the Thrakian kings beyond Vissaltia took notice and passed it on to Olynthos. The Olynth-ians kept Pafsanias on their side, looking for a chance to intervene, while the Athinians found a candidate in the person of Argeos, son of Amyntas and Gygea, who was in exile there and under their protection. Perdikkas was trying to mobilize a substantial army in order to oppose the multitudes of Vardilis. At the same time, he tried his hand in a form of alliance with the Molossian Ipirote king, Arivvas. The Molossian king was reluctant to come to an alliance, feeling the Illyrians would contend themselves in Makedonia and leave his kingdom in peace. Having the Orestians now also under his power, he was ill advised by them against Perdikkas.

The King had to do what he could, alone. He counted on Filippos to be keeping 'an eye' on their half brothers from Amyntas' union with Gygea and any other external dangers. Whenever his state af-fairs and preparations for the Illyrian campaign would allow, Perdikkas was at his brother's side ob-serving the innovations Filippos was introducing during that vigorous training. Perdikkas admired the new formations of the falanx but, most of all, the long pike each oplitis now had to carry using both hands. He regretted the state affairs wouldn't let him observe and understand better Filippos' drills but he totally approved of his brother's innovations. He wished to take the new taxis/corps of these oplites with him against the Illyrians but Filippos assured him they were not ready yet.

Perdikkas summoned then what army he could from Vottiaea, Imathia, Pieria and Eordea and marched against Vardilis. It was right after the one hundred plus four Ellenic games had taken place in Olympia when Perdikkas moved against Vardilis. His army consisting of most of the King's Eteri/

Companions in eight hundred-strong cavalry and close to four thousand infantry, moved into Lyn-kestis and on to Derriopia. Vardilis waited in ambush at the north-west slopes of Varnous and the Makedonians were decimated! Perdikkas fell fighting among his men and Lynkestis with Pelagonia, Dassaretis and Derriopis were now at the mercy of the invaders.

Filippos had to return to Pella at once. He left in charge a small contingent to safeguard his allotted lands Antipatros, son of Iollas, a bright and trustworthy officer who was showing daring initiative and took off with the rest, to see what he could save from the kingdom. Perdikkas had his son, Amyn-tas just born. But this wasn't the time for the regency to debate as to who the next Makedonian King would be. As he headed toward Pella, Filippos recruited whomever he could find from Amfaxitis, Vottiaea and Imathia. Arriving in Pella, the army under him from the units he was training for so long, was the main and only army Makedonia now possessed. The remaining of clan heads and land lords had no choice but to follow-up the acclamation.

Antipatros sent him the message that his small force was now facing intrusions from Peonia and there was strong evidence that Pafsanias now exiled in Thraki, persuaded king Kotys to invade and that was imminent, having also the support of the Olynthians. If that wasn't enough, Athinae sup-porting the other pretender, Argeos, was preparing a fleet with about 2,000 mercenaries to send to Methoni, aiming to take Aegae! Filippos sent the messenger back, giving full power to Antipatros in negotiating terms with the Peonians, king Kotys and the Olynthians promising free trades, gifts and future cooperation. He also instructed him to withdraw the Makedonian forces stationed by Amfi-polis, as Perdikkas had them, in order to re-enforce his own small contingent of troops. Antipatros moved fast and achieved what his King asked of him. Now Filippos had some time to deal with Vardilis and the Athinian expedition. Vardilis came first.

Filippos tried to negotiate with the Illyrian king also, but got refused. He took then his army and marched against Vardilis. The Illyrian made the mistake to take this move lightly. His unexpected victory against Perdikkas just few months ago, made him think that Filippos would fall under the same category. He did not know his opponent. The well trained Makedonians of Filippos annihilated the Illyrian forces and Vardilis sued for peace. Filippos accepted readily, as time was of essence—if he wanted to save Aegae from Argeos and the Athinians. In order to 'cement' the deal and have Vardilis in the best of behavior, he took the Illyrian king's great-granddaughter, Avdata, as his wife.

Now Filippos had some time on his hands to deal with Argeos, the Athinians and Methoni. As things developed, Argeos with the Athinian mercenaries, moved on to Aegae as soon as they had landed in Methoni, in hope that the people would accept him as their king and give more prestige on his claim. That did not happen. As Argeos was preparing for a siege, news of Filippos' approaching came and he marched back toward Methoni, to secure himself and his Athinians behind its walls. King Filip-pos' Makedonians fresh out of their success on the Illyrians, fell on Argeos' mercenaries and forced them to run for dear life! Argeos was captured and promptly put to death. Athinae was approached and a tentative deal was arranged for alliance, Filippos reminding them he had abandoned Amfipolis to itself, (ostensibly) giving Athinae a free hand there.

Filippos returned to Pella for celebrations, a well deserved rest of few weeks for his army and some personal relaxation with his wife. The King was pleased to announce soon that the queen was now an expectant mother. He did not rest for too long though. The army was still something of a novice and, unless the success thus far was to be considered as luck rather than well deserved result, needed a lot more training. That was done again on a daily basis and the new recruits arriving from Lynkestis and Pelagonia had to work twice as hard to reach the caliber of the eastern lands 'veterans'.

Now Filippos saw the time was right to take some more steps toward the permanent security of his kingdom. First, he appointed the Lynkestian king, Alexandros, as the King's own Eteros with equal rights—as if he was part of the elite since the beginning—and promising to have Alexandros' sons at Pella's Court as pages until their manhood year, with full education and privileges! Next, Filippos approached the Elimiote king Derdas and his brother Mahatas, making a deal of non aggression between the two kingdoms. That isolated Orestis to having only the option of Molossis and its king Arivvas as ally.

Filippos sent Antipatros to keep an eye on the eastern front and Parmenion was sent to recruit and guard the western approaches in addition to putting Orestis under pressure with his presence at the border with Eordea. At the same time Filippos continued the training of his army forcing them to drill for hours on end, rewarding the ones who excelled, encouraging the ones who needed prodding.

By the year's end, the King welcomed his first child as Avdata gave birth to a daughter. They named her Kynnani (nicknaming her Kynna). Filippos now was ready to relieve Antipatros from the pressure of the northern Peones. He moved his army with the speed of lightning and met the enemy at Stenae, by River Axios. Victory was complete. Paeonia and Parorvylia became part of the Timenid/Argead House, the long-ago Damasias' dream becoming a reality . . .

King Filippos returned back to Pella and pursued diplomacy. He got closer to Derdas and Mahatas of Elimiotis, arranging to have the hand of Fila (niece and sister). The wedding took place in the old capital of Aegae making King Filippos an in-law and placing Derdas so much closer to Timenid will and policy . . .

Dimosthenis was in deep thoughts lately, mostly absent-minded and neglecting his business Athinae had trusted him to pursue. His wife of two years was about to give birth and she truly had difficult time finishing the job. She was at the house surrounded by doctors and mid-wives for two whole days! The kid coming was making sure he/she would kill her and Dimosthenis was very upset. He truly loved his wife, that fragile Skythian daughter of Ghylo (Gylon in Attik dialect) and Khava (Ka-valli). He wedded her in spite of objections from his family back at Peania in Attiki. The Pandionis clan was up in arms when he informed them and did all they could to prevent his wedding. But the city (a rather enlarged commercial station in the chersonese by Tanais' mouth) of Nymfaeon was too far and Athinae's entrusted role to Dimosthenis too important. He was the one who secured the city's much needed grain imports, dealing with the barbarians at minimum prices. He had married Gchle-ovla (Kleovouli in Attik) but now their kid seemed to be doing what relatives threatened some time ago but were unable to! It was right after the ninety plus eighth games in Olympia and the time for the small Pan-Athinian procession back in Athinae. Dimosthenis, son of Pandion, worried about his wife and, at the same time, very seriously homesick. He hated that kid, whoever might be, whatever its gender.

One of the mid-wives came out in the peristylion where Dimosthenis was brooding, smile and tears mixed on her face. His heart leaped with anxiety. Was Kleovouli all right? Well, in a way yes, but very weak and in need of a long time care. A sigh of relief. "You're a father now, Master!" the mid-wife informed him. "Wha . . .? Oh! What is it?" "A boy, Sir, albeit a very small one and very . . . for-give me, Master, should I say . . . frail?" "Frail?! He just about managed to kill his mother! You say frail? My son?" "Don't punish me Master! The kid's really very small for a boy of a father like you, you'll see . . ." Dimosthenis did not wait for her to finish. He rushed to his bed-chamber forgetting A-thinae and duty, forgetting to show restriction and self-discipline among these barbarians as he headed to see his wife . . .

Seven years had passed since that early morning at the north shores of Pontos in Nymfaeon. Dimos-thenis found himself in turmoil again, losing his beloved wife who had never recovered since giving birth. He was now standing before her freshly dug-out grave—the styli with her name on was not ready yet—with his son whimpering next to him. Dimosthenis' fondness for his son, also named Dimo-sthenis, had not grown in him through the years.

He had brought Kleovouli to the fine weather of Attiki, in hope of recovery. He had abandoned all profitable business in the north, taking over the sword-making family industry, all for nothing! The gods had not blessed him with another child nor did they improve Kleovouli's health. On the con-trary, she melted away like the bee's wax when put under heat, consumed like the oil in the night lamp. Now he was left with a seven year old son he disliked. Observing the kid like it was for the first time ever, he noticed that young Dimosthenis had grown somewhat. He would become an average size man by the looks of it, but he would for ever remain skinny and weak looking.

The father averted his eyes from his son. The continuous whimpering of the youngster was getting unbearable. His own immense pain for the loss of his beloved wife was more than enough! Dimosthe-nis felt like whacking the kid to silence but held back. This specimen, this son of his (the face likeness would not allow any doubt) was all what was left of his union and love with his wife. Reasons of decency—and continuous disregard to the Pandionis' clan resentment about the marriage—dictated he would continue to care of the child until his coming of age. For now, he was too tired, too emotionally drenched to think further. He called the child to follow for their way back home. Dimosthenis was in big surprise to hear his son's voice answering with a very pronounced stutter. He thought it was the trial of one losing one's mother, the shock in a time of stress. He nodded and led the way home . . .

Parmenion sent an urgent message to Filippos as the summer was giving way to fall that the dread-ed Illyrians were preparing for a new move in the spring, this time under the leadership of the Tav-lantian king, Gravos (Ghrabosh). That could not be allowed, not after the recent victory over Vardi-lis who was still leaking his wounds after the loss of close to seven thousand warriors. Filippos order-ed Parmenion to strike at once and strike hard. He sent Asandros, Parmenion's brother (they were both sons of Filotas from house Pallas and house Klitos—on their mother's side) with some reinforce-ments and the faithful general did what was asked of him. Gravos never expected such a late in the season offense move nor the speed by which it was delivered. The Tavlantians sued for peace and ac-cepted Filippos' supremacy and dictations on policy. Antipatros used this latest Makedonian victory to the King's advantage, as he made sure to keep the Thrakian king Verisadis (Behrishad) informed through 'leaking information' and under close surveillance, keeping the eastern borders of Makedon peaceful for the time being.

This welcomed freedom of worries now gave Filippos the opportunity to ensure political close ties with Thessalia, feeling he still needed a buffer zone against Thivae. He approached the strong city of Ferrae first, which— as being closer to the gulf of Pagassae—could be of some use against future Athi-nian pressure and achieved an understanding cementing the deal with yet another wedding to Nike-sepolis, daughter of the leading family from the line of Iason. Next came the city of Larissa, old and faithful ally from earlier days. The Alevades had no quarrel in offering the hand of Filina to him . . .

Two new wives within the span of a year kept the King busy in Pella but not idle in military matters. Filippos continued training his army and new recruits on a daily basis. He paid extra attention to details and organized the close cooperation of the falanx (all armed now with the long sarissa pikes) and the cavalry. He kept the sections and divisions of both the footmen (now called Pezeteri) and the Eteri of his cavalry under regional divisions, in order to install stronger competition among them, realizing that the pride of the former small regional kingdoms now under his lead were not some-thing easily forgotten by their members and leading houses. Thankfully, Athinae and Thivae were preoccupied with their own problems and had left him free to do what it took.

Orestis' leading houses and clan heads made now their move to enter in alliance and Filippos took the opportunity to demonstrate that there was only one way for such union: his absolute leadership as the King. The Molossian Ipirote king Arivvas did not like the idea, but Filippos kept him calm by promises of a much closer relation and profitable future. He sent to Arivvas' wedding with Troas a very expensive wedding gift and moved to the region of Orestis the head of house Agis and close friend, Orestis son of (the long dead now) Attalos. House Agis finally returned to the ancestral region and was put in charge there.

King Filippos did not have only the Agis house relocate; he sometimes asked, sometimes ordered other houses and small clans to move from one place to another, preferably taking clan heads and land lords from the borderline areas down to the Vottiaean or Amfaxitan plains or toward the works of reclaiming fields around his new city of Filippi, which until then was surrounded by swamps. This new acquisition came about the time when Athinae, after pressuring Amfipolis to rejoin the Athinian Empire. Amfipolis refused and Filippos thought this was his time to retake the city which he had abandoned a little while ago.

The Amfipolites were rightfully feeling rejected then and now felt they were a pawn of expansion-istic policies from both sides, therefore refused Filippos' overtures also. He moved and placed the city under siege, aided by the expert work of some Thessalian siege masters who had studied the develop-ments of the trade in Sikelia. To keep the Halkidian confederation off his back and break the Athini-an efforts to form an alliance against him, offered Potidaea to Olynthos after expelling an Athinian garrison stationed there (taking first under his protection and relocating the descendants of house Ptolemeos and Haridimos of Krousis) and paid off the Illyrian Gravos, whom the Athinians tried to ally. Athinae declared war on Makedon but could do nothing because Filippos acted when the Aegean winds were unfavorable for the Athinian fleet . . .

King Arivvas was arguing with his wife Troas on the behavior of her sister Olympias. "I don't un-derstand it!" the king was saying. "It's like two different sets of parents gave birth to the two of you.

That sister of yours is driving all of us crazy with her antics! To be bringing snakes here in the palace is something I will not be tolerating. I do not care if she wants to devote herself to any kind of mystic ceremonics, I don't care that she acts more like a man when her mood switches, nor do I care if she gets herself killed in her frenzy at her Dionysiac revelries with her maenads. But snakes! Snakes? I will not allow any of these serpents in my House. Tell her it's my will, or she has to move out! I tried to get her a decent man among my leading clan heads and you know that. But show me one who wouldn't come after me and accuse me for misleading him, even revolt against me, when he finds out what kind of a woman I betrothed him to. Why can't she be a little like you?"

Troas kept her head down listening, not only because of respect toward her husband and king of Molossis, not because he was right being angry for Olympias' behavior, but mainly because she knew if this situation would continue, she would also be in a very bad predicament. She was thinking all these times her husband would storm-in and complain or threaten all kinds of threats, how to either convince her sister to restrain herself or find a way to divert Olympias' activities to other, less public-ly observed venues. She knew that Olympias had her own mind and nothing in the world would make her change. Her sister was a very difficult character—to say the least. Once she'd put something in her mind, there was no power on earth to make her change. On the contrary, she'd continue with more passion when she'd find that others were against her wishes.

Olympias had shown some interest at a young Makedonian prince a few years back when attending the Kavirian Mysteries in Samothraki—at least that's what she said upon returning—but that came to nothing, since the introduction was a very brief one and the two got lost in the crowd within minutes.

Olympias had return to Ipiros dreaming of deep blue eyes and dark, curly hair but, as the time went by, that dream faded and other interests (not family oriented ones) had taken her fancy. In contrast to Troas' own complexion of a regal but modest demeanor of a young woman with blond-reddish hair and soft brown eyes, Olympias was red haired, taller by almost a head, her eyes of that chestnut color capable of changing from unreadable hue to outright darkness of a deep, raging sea! Troas was sure her sister was a person of absolute extremes and the deepest sense of ancient prej-udices, mysticism and ego. She knew Olympias to be also a very jealous person . . .

They were from ancient royal bloodline, going all the way back to the misty times of hero kings and the famous war in Tria. Her own name, Troas, was a constant reminiscence of that era. They were direct descendants of Ahilleas, through his son Neoptolemos who left the land of Fthia after his re-turn from war, to settle in Ipiros and take the Molossians under his leadership. So was her own hus-band and distant uncle, Arivvas. But if for the two of them this was something to simply be proud of and tell stories to grand children, for Olympias it was a constant challenge of proof, the very air she was breathing!

There were three children from the house of Neoptolemos (namesake of the first Neoptolemos) and uncle of Arivvas the two girls and Alexandros. When Neoptolemos died, Arivvas took over the throne until Alexandros would come of age. To secure his status even further, he married Troas. By neces-sity and decency in family matters, the other two became his charges but Olympias proved to be too much for the conservative and image-conscious Arivvas . . .

Dimosthenis, son of Dimosthenis, was pacing to and fro on the rocky beach of the eastern side of cape Sounion, stuttering his words of a well arranged speech he would have to deliver at Arios Pagos in a few days against his so-called guardians, Afovos (he would teach the miser what Fovos meant!) and Dimofon. He had lost his father some years ago now and these two 'guardians' from the clan of Pandionis from Peania had the distinct privilege to care of his becoming a man, a well educated one—according to his status.

They educated him alright, but they also squandered his inheritance! His character would never al-low that go unpunished. Dimosthenis was not a person to develop doubt and distrust for someone and then forget about it. Even if they were proven not guilty, he would find a way of punishing them!

Because of this suspicion he had asked (and they were stupid enough to give-in) to have him study under the famous orator Kallistratis, even under Isokratis and Isaeos. Now his studying would pay—back, except . . . except this damned stuttering of his! If he hated his two ex-guardians with a passion, he hated even more the nickname he was given because of it (in addition to being half-barbarian) as Vatalos, meaning both—a stammerer and an asshole!

He had very short time to present before the Athinian citizenry his claim and he should better be successful. He had to bring an end to laughter behind his back, just because he was the son of a 'barbarian mother', because his guardians had cheated him, because he could not say a full sentence without this cursed stutters. He had the Athinians admire his speech writing abilities with his latest demonstration on the case of Formion against Apollodoros. Truth to be told, many accused him of selling the information of his writings to the latter for some silver, but that did not bother him. One had to make a living, didn't he?

Dimosthenis was feeling agitated and thirsty. He tried to calm down. Agitation was making his stut-tering more pronounced. The hot day didn't help either. He drunk some of the water in his flask and, in doing so, an old wife's tale came to mind. When perspiration occurs, body salt is wasted and needs replacement. He thought of drinking some sea water, but that would be too much. Instead, he picked-up a rounded pebble and put it in his mouth. While sucking it, he continued reading out loud his written accusatory speech (no reason to waste precious time along with body salt) and he stopped in mid sentence. Trying to utter the words with the pebble in his mouth gave him less stuttering! He tried again and the result was the same. Triumph! Was his hour was finally approaching? Dimos-thenis returned to his loud reading of the speech with renewed vigor. He would have to devise something for his mouth when speaking at Arios Pagos before the Ekklisia and the judges, something he could conceal and, at the same time, something helpful . . .

Athinae was in a difficult position. Her renewed Empire, albeit much smaller and more independent in its parts than the old one, still found Athinian control too much for any measure of comfort. Many city-states, members of this new 'alliance' made up their minds to secede. It happened the fall of the year before the hundredth plus fifth Olympiad, when Filippos was turning his eyes toward Amfipolis and his east frontiers. Athinae could not let the Empire fall to samples. She could not afford it. She sent her fleet loaded with oplites (Athinians and mercenaries) to quell the revolt. That was against the interests of the Persian High King, Artaxerxis/Artaxshasha (the second under that name) who promoted with money this revolt.

At the Athinian Ekklisia of citizens, Dimosthenis (having secured some of his inheritance from Afo-vos and Dimofon and serving a year as triirarhos—caretaker of a navy vessel—and full of confidence in himself, proposed restrain in navy expenditures, against the line of his ally and mentor Efvolos who was asking for better equipped and more numerous navy. When among the revolting city-states the island of Rodos with a powerful navy of its own joined by proclaiming its own independence, Di-mosthenis changed his mind again, asking the Athinians to use money from the Theater budget to build a fleet, whereas Efvolos (seeing the impossibility of success) recommended now restrain. That brought one against the other, especially when Aeshinis (another well known Athinian) took Efvolos' side. Dimosthenis lost in both occasions and that created a rift which would not be bridged until the very end of their lives . . .

King Filippos seeing that Athinae was not able to open-up two fronts and, (for good measure) oper-ating in times of prohibiting winds he enveloped Amfipolis and took it. To Athinian demands and declaration of war which could not happen until the city-states' revolt was over, he answered that it was possible to have Amfipolis given to Athinae, if Athinae was prepared to move out of Pydna, free-ing the south-west entrance of Thermaikos gulf. Meanwhile, he celebrated the birth of his first son, Arideos, by the Larissaean wife Filina and invested his expansion in the area of Krenides (after the city had asked for help against the Odrysian king Verisadis who controlled Idonia among other areas of Thraki). Filippos made sure the control of Mount Pangaeon and its gold mines would come under his rule as most of Idonia. He promised Krenides a speedy response. Athinae made a pact with the successor of Vardilis, Klitos (Khlecht). To counter that, Filippos asked for closer relation with the Molossian kingdom.

Arivvas jumped-in. Taking the opportunity, he offered the hand of his own niece Olympias. Seeing the beauty of the young woman and realizing she was the one he briefly met at Samothraki, Filippos accepted. Olympias had finally what she was looking for. The young prince (now King) and a crown on her head!

The wedding took place in Pella and Filippos 'convinced' Arivvas to let him have young Alexandros (heir-apparent to Molossian throne) as a guest at the Makedonian court until becoming of age. That gave Arivvas a free hand in the Ipirote affairs and obliged to Filippos for that. Klitos had to keep quiet in his lands and the Athinian plot came to nothing.

Next, as Filippos moved toward Krenides, Verisadis died. Other Odryssian kings such as Amadokos (Amudokh), ruling from beyond Nestos river up to Maronia and Evros (northern borders), Kersov-leptis (Kcher-Soblepht) ruler of the eastern most Thraki Beyond Evros to the Efxinos Pontos, were too busy with their own affairs to bother with the small area between Strymon and Nestos. King Fil-ippos took Krenides and, moving-in mountaineers from Orestis, Lynkos and Pelagonia, renamed the city Filippi and gave it special status. He also ordered the draining of the swamps surrounding the area, giving the new land to the newcomers. King Filippos then returned to Pella and sent his troops to take Pydna, as the Athinians did not bother to answer his proposals.

There were few months past when Olympias, shining with pride, had come to the King announcing her pregnancy. Filippos was ecstatic. He loved his new Queen and, in spite of her difficult character, he thought the world of her. Olympias was not exactly happy with her husband though. Oh, she did love him but the 'dream' of her youth was not what she thought. First, Filippos had other wives to care for and, one of them, had given him an heir! What if hers would be a son? Didn't she have a dream of a great fire descending into her womb at the night of her wedding? It was before Filippos had finally come to the chamber (the drinking bouts between the men celebrating took many hours after she retired and got ready), before he took her—after she had fallen asleep waiting for him.

She had sent to Dodona for an omen and the Oracle told her of the coming of a son who would rule, invincible, the earth . . . But Filippos already had a son, Arrideos, from Filina! Olympias was sure her baby would be a son! But what then? She looked upon Filina and infant Arrideos as intruders. To have both of them taken out was too risky. She could not count on the devotion of her Makedonian servants, not yet. She was the newcomer, the Ipirote outsider and she knew she would remain as such, unless . . .

She found it was easier to dispose of the infant. Filina was not Makedonian either but her Thessalian roots were closer to Makedonian feelings than Ipirotic ones. The child was also the King's son, no doubt about that! The same deep blue eyes, the same stocky little body. Filina though had given the child to nurses for a proper Makedonian upbringing and those fools were not particularly careful as the security of the inner palace yard was giving them time to attend their own. Olympias knew she would find an opportunity. She only had to be very careful and bide her time.

Filippos was—as usual—far from Pella, putting Amfipolis and Krenides/Filippi to order when the op-portunity presented itself to Olympias. The infant Arrideos was left to play in his oversized crib alone (as his nurses were washing clothes in the near-by covered wash area across the court yard) with the little (still a puppy) dog which was laying outside the crib, looking expectantly at its young master for a pull of its tail or a sharp—but always welcomed—grabbing of an ear. The oversized crib was placed by the palace wall in that inner yard, half covered by the building's shade. The prince had the choice to crawl on either side (shade or sun) within his confinement. At the moment, the young prince was preoccupied with few of his wooden toys, a lion, a chariot and a cart with the team of oxen attached to it.

Olympias looked carefully around. No one wandered in the yard and the most to be seen were the legs of the nurses washing clothes at the far end, under the shade of the covered wash area. She went through the sleeping chambers of the palace, stopping at the doors of each royal wife's room. All of them were preoccupied with their house duties and their maidens. Olympias had hers sent to do some shopping in town and was not worried of an early return. Guards were posted only at the main en-trance of the palace and in front of the King's bedchamber. The back entrance to the palace was part of the wall of its acropolis and locked. It would be used only in case of extreme emergency. She climb-ed the staircase next to it and found her way to the battlement. The sloppy roof of the back end of the palace was almost touching it. She balanced herself for a moment and took the step . . .

Elaniki found her Queen standing at the parapet of the battlement at the back end of the palace and watching the beautiful sunset on top of the silhouette of mount Paikon, the last sunrays gleaming on the lucid waters of Lydias and the lagoon to its south-east. "No wonder you've not come to th'calls m' Lady! The young prince got almost kill'd by a faulty rooftop tile! Thank the gods, the tile hit his crib wall first and lost some of its velocity. The kid is in bad shape though and the doctors have big doubt if he's gonna make it or not . . .."

Olympias' brows almost met at the crown of her nose and her eyes took that deep sea coloring which no one who did not live with her for years knew what it meant. "Poor Lady, she is very upset!" Elaniki thought to herself and, seeing Olympias raising her hands to the sky and uttering unfamiliar Ipirote words, found best she should retire and leave the Queen alone in her sorrow . . .

Hearing the bad news, Filippos returned from Krenides/Filippi riding his horse alone, within two days! The King went straight to Filina's chamber to see what happened of his son. He found all the doctors around the infant's bed, changing the bandages. There were some good and some bad news. Arrideos would survive, thank the gods, but they doubted if the kid would have all his faculties in order! Filina had made a ball of herself in a corner and no power on earth ever made her stop her crying since, especially when—in later days—Arrideos would sneak in to see his mother and wonder why the lady was always in tears . . .

Filippos could do nothing but hope Olympias was with a male child now! He went to her chamber for solace and the Queen was very happy to oblige. In the process of love-making and her pathos, she made the mistake to utter words of possession and succession of a son much better than Arideos. Fil-ippos was taken aback and thought of unnecessary cruelty on her part. He stormed out and spent the night drinking with Parmenion and Antipatros, who—by that time—had come to Pella also and offer-ed their King whatever solace a man could offer to another. The next night he returned to her ready to make-up, only to find that—in her pique—she had the bed covered with her pet snakes, sheltered until then at a specially made sanctuary of goddess Ekati at the west end of the acropolis. The King left the next morning in a very bad mood from Pella to Pydna and the war. This was the first of their legendary fights which were to make them look at each-other like strangers in years to come . . .

Athinae meantime had arranged alliance with the Olynthian confederacy of Halkidiki, the Illyrian Gravos, the Peonian king Lyppeos (Lyppech) and the Thrakian successor of Verisadis, Ketriporis (Khetripur). Filippos was forced to summon the best of his political charms and deal separately with each of them, leaving Athinae and her declaration of war isolated once more. To the Olynthians he offered the most attractive price of Anthemous and Potidea, the others he bought with the newfound gold from the Pangeon mines and continued the siege of Pydna, which fell shortly—after some Make-donians from within the city decided the rule of Filippos was preferable to Athinian domination.

As the city fell, wonderful news reached the King. Olympias had given birth to a healthy son, his horses had won at the Pythian Games and Parmenion—with a show of force—had sent Gravos to his domain, accepting Filippos' overlodship. The lucky day was the 12th of the month Loios (15 of June to 15 of July), in our terms the 26th-27th of June. The King returned to Pella to celebrate the birth of his new son and Olympias was conscious enough not to have her snakes in the bed-chamber this time. Of their past fight nothing was said and each accepted the other's happiness of a son like nothing had happened. They named their newborn son Alexandros.

The Thivan 'host' of Filippos' youth years Pammenis sent to check Athinian influence in east Thra-ki, was denied passage through Ketriporis' lands, although his overlord Odryssian king Kersovleptis had already agreed to it. Filippos marched against Ketriporis (he wanted to rid himself of Pammenis and youth memories fast) and Amadokos, and they both were forced to accept his sovereignty over them as his client-kings. Athinae still involved in her coalition war against her subject states stood by watching.

King Filippos now had some time to reorganize and tend to domestic affairs. Further south, Thivae got involved in a 'domestic' dispute and ruined the subject city of Orhomenos, raising it to the ground. Also, realizing excess control in her immediate area, Thivae caused the protest of Fokis which soon turned to a full scale war. The small mountainous Fokis resisted successfully the Thivan advances but it was soon apparent they could not hold for ever. They asked for help from Athinae and Sparti but all they got were promises of support. Desperate for money and in need of hiring mercenaries to augment their numbers, the Fokians borrowed money from Delfi, with the under-standing of returning the amount in due time and continued their resistance.

The Makedonian King saw the advantage of the situation and immediately besieged Methoni. Being a brave man and giving the example, he was constantly in the front lines. This eagerness cost him his right eye as an arrow from the defenders found the opening on the King's helmet. Filippos let the siege continue and returned to Pella to recover.

Thivae, finding hard time to subdue the Fokians, now turned the whole affair to a propaganda war and accused the Fokian leader Onomahos of stealing the money from Delfi. The truth to be told, the Fokians under Onomahos had all the will to eventually pay back but, as the war dragged, more money was needed and, soon, they found that they had borrowed much more than they could ever pay back. In a short time, the whole Ellas was split in two groups. Some thought the Thivans were right (propaganda lessons from Athinae were well taken), others were on the Fokian side.

In Thessalia Larissa and Ferrae found now a new reason to compete against each-other. According to tradition, Larissa had the option of choosing the Leader of the Thessalian confederation of city-states in the region. Fokis, in hope that Ferrae (due to its recent power) would be of help against Thivae supported that city-state and Ferrae took the opportunity to force the appointment of her own choice as Leader (Ταγος/Tagos) in Thessalia, named Iason.

Meantime, although recovering, Filippos did not remain idle. He saw to continuous reorganization of his units and their rigorous training, venturing again toward east and securing further his borders with Thraki, encircling the Halkidian confederation of Olynthos. Now the King received a call for help from Larissa. As past relations with Larissa and its leading family of Alevades were always in good terms, Filippos saw the opportunity to place Thessalia on his side solving their problem. The Ferraean Iason was in the meantime killed and Filippos moved in easily, placing a garrison in Laris-sa, to protect the interests of the city against Ferrae and Fokis . . .

In far-off Sikelia, the Τυρανος/Tyrant-leader of Syrakousae, Dion, (uncle of Dionysios) controlled much of the island, trying (unsuccessfully) to prove Plato's theory on governing a state. In Ellas proper King Filippos found that he would have to move against Fokis, as his interests were laying on the good faith and support of the Thessalians. Being a pragmatist he could see that Thessalia as a very close ally of Makedonia (a subject state— if it was to come to that) would serve as a buffer zone on any expansionistic ideas from Thivae, Athinae or Sparti from the land approaches, much as now (he hoped) Molossis was doing. Having the Ipirote Alexandros growing in his court served his plans much better than he originally thought. The kid was almost eight years older than the younger prince of Makedonia but the two Alexandri were already like brothers. When the Ipirote Alexandros' time would come to rule Molossis, Filippos was sure he would see Makedonian interests as his own. That was exactly what Filippos wanted to happen with Thessalia also.

For the time being, Thessalian interests had to be looked-after first. He gathered his victorious (thus far) army and marched in Thessalia, heading against the 'impious' Fokians. Thessalian city-states and cantons gathered around him, isolating Ferrae and forcing the city to join. Filippos continued his march confident. The Fokians held a big surprise for him, as their general Fayllos was sent by Ono-mahos and beat the Makedonians soundly. This first ever defeat of Filippos awakened him from his dream of being successful with the training of his Makedonians. He immediately saw where his falt-ed moves were and what was needed to avoid future embarrassments like this one.

Filippos returned to Pella and got back to work with the army. First, he separated the 'old' hands from the newer recruits, for the simple reason that the former were not as keen to learn and use his new tactics and would panic with the first adversity—as they were used to the old oplites ways in full armor and regular length spear. He also saw the need of scouting the approaches before he met with any foe. Had he done that, he could avoid defeat. By doing so, separating the old from the new, gave him another headache. His veteran troops thought he wanted them out of the army altogether.

The King was very aggravated returning from the exercise fields outside Pella. He did not know how to solve the problem of his veterans and that smelled trouble. At first he heard some voices of complains and doubt of their worth. Now he was hearing loud voices of concern about their future and demands, of being treated unequally and without gratitude on their past service. This was get-ting very close to mutiny and he would have none of that!

He went straight to the baths, followed by Parmenion and Antipatros. While bathing and rubbed-down to shake the day's labor off, they drunk and discussed various ways of solution to the problem. They remained there until very late and ate nothing, while they solved nothing! The wine had finally gotten to them by the time they split and each went his way.

Filippos had especially hard time in find-ing his way to the royal chambers, on account of his blinded right eye and the blurring of his left be-cause of that wine drinking.

He saw young Vrison and Dimitrios standing guard at the double doors by the entrance to the royal chambers and he nodded for assistance. Vrison moved to help his King and Filippos placed a heavy arm over the youngster's shoulder. They headed for Filippos' own bedroom when the King changed his mind. He would go and seek some relief in the company of his Queen. Maybe she could come-up with an idea how to solve the impasse with his troops.

What happened next could only come out of the twisted humor of Aristofanis at the Athinian thea-ter. Only the actors and the scene were real and their own thoughts got unfolded by their own twisted misconception, not humorous at all. Filippos scratched the Queen's door (or he thought he did) to let her know he was coming in with company. The heavy door was hard to open and Vrison switched hand on the hold of his shield, to help open, forgetting the instability of his drunken King. The door opened and Filippos saw the Queen sitting on her bed, covered with snakes and, gods have mercy, five years old Alexandros in the midst, playing with them! Filippos' mind went back to the night he first saw her with snakes, after Arideos' accident and freaked out again. As he yelled at her and moved forth, he stumbled and tried to hold onto Vrison, bringing him down also and on top of him-self. Olympias was then turning her head toward the sudden outburst and saw her husband in her bedroom, drunk and with a guard on a very strange placement above his King and, further, faced red out of embarrassment.

"Cursed be you! You . . . boy lover! You bring your Thivan ways in this room before your Queen and your child?!" She snarled her words at him, eyes wide and dark, carrying the typhoon of a bottomless abyss of pain, hidden behind her anger getting caught with the snakes, hurt by her own miscon— sept (too late!), the young prince wide-eyed and puzzled of the sudden outburst and left to fall back to the bed—the snakes rushing out of the way.

Filippos was getting up with difficulty, shoving away the now fearful Vrison, when her words stop- ped him half way, sinking in his mind with most painful clearance of thoughts best forgotten, of hateful years and, to top it, the impudence of Olympias when she was the one who needed a lesson!

"You! You barbarian specimen of 'royal blood'! Are you capable of accusing me? Your King and Master? What are you doing with MY SON? What dark lessons are you teaching him?" He took a step toward her, ready to cast a blow with his hand on her face. He had to teach the backwater Ipirote 'queen' a lesson never to be forgotten! He stroke her face sending her reeling on her back and, with the other hand, grabbed the Queen by the neck and started squeezing cutting the air from her. Olympias brought one knee up hitting Filippos square on his private parts, making him let go mo-mentarily. Alexandros, over his shock by now, placed his body between his parents. "Stop it!" The command voice of the hardly five year old boy was like it came from the mouth of a veteran. Olym-pias looked at her son in awe, as did Filippos. The King was still hurting, both bodily and mentally. He wanted to really strike and strike hard! But the boy was now standing before him covering as much as his small body could that of his mother's. What made Filippos hold himself back though was not the youngster's fragile body but Alexandros' eyes. The blue hue had left them, replaced by the darkest (almost black) color the King had ever seen!

Filippos brought his raised hand down, looking from his son to his wife and back. Olympias raised herself to her knees and pulled Alexandros closer, before her. The prince twisted his body free and, without looking at her, asked Vrison "Will you see that the King is safely escorted to his chamber?"

Vrison looked in astonishment at the Prince, then the Queen and at his King. Filippos nodded to him his consent and turned his back toward the door. The two of them started out of the room, heads down. Olympias, wanting to have the last of it all, picked-up a heavy amphora and hurled it against her husband. Vrison seeing the projectile heading against his King rose his shield yelling: "Ypo tin aspida Sire! Under my shield!" At the same time he pulled Filippos and the shield stopped the am-phora shattering it to pieces. Filippos turned with renewed anger but this time Vrison was ready and pulled him out.

Alexandros' body was now shaking and all the blood was like it had drained from his face. Olympi-as tried to bring her son back to her in her arms, to offer warmth and comfort but Alexandros push-ed her away and—without a word—he crossed the room and went out the open door to his quarters not looking back. As he was going to his room, he passed the King's chambers and he could distinctly hear items thrown against the wall and breaking, Filippos' voice totally somber now cursing and threatening.

Alexandros stood there momentarily, face still pale, eyes still wild. Another violent body shake took place and the young Prince's knees almost buckled under him. Vrison jumped toward Alexandros, fearing the young boy had had it, feeling for the Prince's pain and ready to provide any assistance he could. Alexandros raised his hand to stop him and turned his face giving the guard a look which said "Thanks, but no!" Then, finding—only the gods knew what—stamina he walked into his room and closed the door behind him.

The next day Filippos left Pella for the exercise fields, leaving specific orders behind him. The young Prince was to be taken to the far wing of the palace under the care of Elaniki, Klitos' older sister and daughter of Dropidas. Under no circumstances was the Queen to see her son, unless the order was coming directly from him! Further, she was to be kept in her own chambers with only the assistance of two servants, adequate for all her personal needs. On the other hand, the Prince was free to go wherever he pleased, excepting the Queen's quarters.

On the field that day, Filippos called for a review of his discontented veterans and, when they got in order for inspection he addressed them in warm and praising words for their past services while he assigned them to a new, most important one: They were to be named Ypaspistes, guarding their King's life in battle 'under their shields' forming now this special army unit! The stasis/mutiny was thus thwarted, Olympias being unwittingly the solution of the problem with her last act the night before. Vrison was also rewarded as he was placed in charge of a section/lohos in the new order.

The royal split lasted for almost one whole month. The arrival of delegates and the festivities at Dion in honor of Zefs closed the gap—in a way—as the royal family had to appear publicly, but did not ease the overall resentments for a long time after that. Alexandros was kept under Elaniki's care and was allowed to visit now his mother for sharing the mid-day meal but never during the evenings. Filippos was spending his nights in the company of one of his other wives or in the company of village youth -depending on how drunk he was at the time. As for Olympias, she spent her days accusing her husband in any way she could to whatever ears she had listening, while -at night- she'd offer to Ekavi or to Dionysos and utter words her two assistant maids would rather not listen to.

All this time Alexandros would spend his time mostly in absentminded plays with youth in the pal-ace yard and cool words when visiting Olympias, warming only somewhat in the presence of Elaniki (he called her Laniki), who seemed to have gotten the youngster's attention and need for comfort with her kind and understanding personality and caring for his feeble half-brother Arrideos.

Filippos saw his son only during state appearances and those were rare and cool. Filippos wanted to have his son closer to him but did not know how to approach, while Alexandros was taking the awkwardness as a message of isolation. To further isolate Alexandros from Olympias, Filippos started looking for a full time teacher for the prince, for a paedagogos of some renown.

He soon had a visit from Arivvas who, alerted by Olympias' letters of complain, came to mend what things he could. Filippos being still very much in love with Olympias and not wanting to lose what advantages he had from the alliance with Molossis, agreed to reconcile and accepted Leonidas, an uncle of the Molossian royal family, as the paedagogos of Alexandros. The deal was sealed with a night at Olympias' bedchamber and things went back to normal, the otherThessalian wife of Filip-pos, Nikesipolis, was left in a secondary position. That night Olympias became pregnant again.

Meantime Sistos and some other towns of the Athinian confederation in Thrakian Hersonisos had revolted and Athinae answered by massacring all adult males of that city and sold the rest to slavery. The same spring, Filippos taking advantage of the start of the Etesian winds which prevented Athi-nian ships to sail north, moved in Thessalia again, his army ready now to face once more the Fokian sinners of the Oracle and their allies. At a field where the crocus was in full bloom, between the towns of Eretria and Anhialos, the Makedonian forces won a resounding victory. Athinae and her allies responded by closing the pass of Thermopylae with an army but Filippos' plans were not to face them but to secure Thessalia on his side, as he had done with Ipirote Molossis. He went to Laris-sa where he called for a pan-Thessalian conference and he was duly named Tagos/Leader of the city-states of all Thessalia! Receiving the news of Nikesipolis having had a baby daughter, he named her Thessaloniki (Thessalon= of Thessalia + niki=victory).

Filippos returned to Pella, stopping first at Dion for the annual festivities in honor of Zefs and then at Aegae, where his mother's tomb was ready and her body was lain in it with due honors. There, he discovered that Olympias was also pregnant because of their last consolation among them when Ar-ivvas had come to mend things up. Upon his return to

Pella Filippos ordered to have parts of Mag-nisia and Perrevia of Thessalia under his immediate control, in order to have easy access to the passes from Makedonia to Thessalia. He re-enforced this by bringing settlers from the Pierian town of Valla to Pythion by the Petra pass and placed the area under the direct administration of the Eli-miotian house.

Hearing that there was some move on his eastern front from Thrakian tribes, he marched his army speedily to the Mygdonian lands, demonstrating the power of his army to move fast at any direction -a thing which settled matters there and then, as he marched all the way to the Propontis and back. Feeling secure and having the need to rest his troops, he returned to Pella attending to festivities and internal affairs, leaving the southern city-states (in particular Athinae) to wonder about his next move. The birth of a new daughter from Olympias, gave him reason to celebrate time with family and further warming-up to his Queen and son. The newborn girl was named Kleopatra.

"I, Evmenis of Kardia, was employed by King Filippos to keep his correspondence and public laws and journals for him, that same year. Henceforth I am the one who kept an account of events -as they developed- in a private collection of memories and put to books for posterity. The time was right after the 106th meeting in Olympia of Elis for the pan-Ellenic athletic competitions. In Thraki, that same year, the kings Amadokos and Kersovleptis were at odds, the latter being under Athinian pres-sure to enter alliance. King Filippos could not allow that, hence his move to Propontis. As Tyhi had it the King and I met in person, though I was already employed by him for some time and we had an immediate rapport resulting in my promotion as head secretary. I remained faithful to him (Filippos also befriended me, shown by his actions in bestowing me honors and riches) as I did to his son Alex-andros -after Filippos' untimely death. I see that I am well ahead of events though. You can receive full knowledge of what transpired since I was first employed, by reading my books and then form your own opinion."

Olympias was preoccupied with the needs of her son Alexandros and her brother Alexandros. For the first, nothing was good enough and every convenience to make his life easier was her demand to everyone she could muster, with the exception of her uncle Leonidas. The paedagogos of the young prince could not be bought or threatened. Leonidas was an admirer of everything Spartan and he was sure to administer his own understanding of discipline to Alexandros. The prince was not al-lowed to sleep with adequate covers during cold winter nights, nor was allowed to dress in soft, im-ported clothes. His food was measured by Leonidas himself, so as to be just enough for the prince in keeping him out of starvation! Olympias was furious but she could do nothing, except of sneaking now and then some items of comfort -and having constant fights as she would invariably get caught in doing so! She thought of poisoning her uncle but she knew the suspicion would fall squarely on her and she did not dare.

Alexandros -by his character- would absorb all punishments and hardship from Leonidas in silence and with a goal to withstand all to the very end, just to prove that he was above everything. To be sure, the stories he would hear from his mother, when visiting, about the progenitor Ahilleas and the deeds of the hero, made the kid wanting to surpass that fame any which way possible and, if hardship was the way to do it, so be it!

Filippos was getting tired having to play the role of mediator. He understood Olympias' love for her child (although he thought was overprotecting and close to a sick passion of a mother for her child, as Olympias would hardly show love for their daughter Kleopatra), as he understood the harshness of the teacher (we wouldn't want to raise anything but a strong heir to the throne), albeit that harshness was -at times- more of a retaliatory nature (to the youngster's mother) than instructive measures. He started thinking of finding a new paedagogos, of a more renowned caliber, without offending irrepar-ably Leonidas, Olympias, or Arivvas. As things were, he had no choice but 'wait and see' -for now.

Olympias' second concern about her brother Alexandros was not in any better terms. She could see clearly the young man's admiration for all things Filippos did or say, the hours he spent at the King's side learning, absorbing, imitating. Her mind would go to Filippos' past at Thivae and the rumors of Thivan habits with children and youth. Oh, she had no reason or proof but her mind wouldn't let go of it. The idea was the cause for further fights with both her brother and her husband, especially when Filippos would return half drunk from the men's drinking hall supported by Antipatros and Alexandros on each side. For Antipatros, she did not care any more than she did when Filippos would lay with a lesser woman. She was better off when the King would take his drunken passion on another than her. But her brother? What was between her brother and Filippos? She would confront each when suspicions raged in her mind and she would find herself running against a wall of cool re-ception to begin, turning to outright fury from both. Her brother became a stranger, meeting her only when there was no other way and her husband would avoid her for days on end after each con-frontation. She knew she had just about lost her brother's affection, she knew she was losing her husband's and she was afraid she would lose her son's love -a thing she would never be able to live with. She turned more and more into her devotion on the Mysteries and Ipirote superstition...

King Filippos was at a loss with Olympias' tempers and (mostly) false accusations. Further, he was able to see what those tantrums were doing to his son and that was driving him more to the extremes in his relation with the Queen. He could ill afford to have Alexandros taken away from his mother al-together, simply because he knew he would lose more of a son. On the other hand, he could ill afford to have her manipulate the kid with her imagined wrongs done to her. When he was near her, he wasn't enough and when he had to campaign, he was unfaithful and he didn't care, especially when he had to leave Antipatros in charge of the internal affairs. Filippos knew of the antipathy Olympias held for his friend and the reasons why and he felt trapped. Couldn't the woman understand that male bonding was something totally different from a man-to-a-woman attraction? Besides, whom he would leave in charge of the state when at war? Olympias, with her impulsive personality and tit for tat disposition? In any case, this was Makedonia, not an Ipirote quasi state and women were free to any initiative within the proper running of the household or the religious affairs, even consultation, as long as they knew their boundaries, a thing totally strange to his wife, who would not hold back once she thought she had some rights. No, Antipatros would have to be the regent, until the boy would come of age. As a matter of fact, he started to enjoy Antipatros' stern refusal to give-in to Olympias.

The woman had found her match! As for Alexandros, Filippos needed to have him come closer. It was time to have him admitted to certain state meetings and learn. Olympias could not possibly bitch about it and, in combination with the paedagogical time and exercises with the local youth, it would keep Alexandros as much away from the influence of his mother as possible. Win-win situation!

The King made up his mind to start having Alexandros attend some of the royal audiences, the ones he would not be too uncomfortable with. The kid was turning almost six. In a couple of months it was his birth anniversary. It would give Alexandros pleasure to know he was considered old enough to attend and that would bring him closer to his Father. Filippos knew already that his son was showing exceptional cleverness and tendency to never quit until proven better than anybody else in the circle of his friends. With some care he could become a truly fine leader.

Filippos had his chance. Emissaries from the High King were to arrive in Pella in few days. The war of Athinae against the island of Rodos was coming to a turning point. Persia did not want Makedonia to assist the Athinians with timber; besides, on paper, Makedonia and Athinae were still at war, in spite of some overtures made by Efvolos the Athinian ruling party's leader -now that Athinae needed all the timber she could get for the war effort- but it came to nothing. The Athinian was trying now the back door, approaching the Olynthian confederacy which responded in favor.

The King had to be out of Pella, to the eastern frontier because of this disturbing move by the Olyn-thian confederation in Halkidiki. He did not think that war with them was eminent but he had to ride up-close and demonstrate his readiness. If the Persian delegation was to arrive when he was still pre-occupied around Anthemous, this would be one opportunity for Alexandros to receive them as the King's heir -with Antipatros standing at his side (in case of need).

He called for his son. Alexandros came to the study of his Father, still red from the exercise court with his hair damp from the quick wash, but clean and properly dressed. He stood before the desk of his Father with respect (but distant), looking at the King and at the two generals flanking him, Par-menion and Antipatros, with curiosity but holding his head up. Filippos observed his son for a long time. The youth was rather small of frame for his age but very well built. His face was beautiful, one could take it as a girl's from a distance but the rest looked very much of what it was. A young boy who spent time in the exercise court, knees and elbows scared from wrestling and weapons practices.

"How are you doing with your classes and Leonidas?" Filippos asked -to start the conversation. For some reason, the King was feeling uncomfortable when addressing his son, still not knowing how to bring the youngster closer. "I am sure my King has his daily reports from Leonidas himself." Alex-andros replied (was that the only reason his father asked for him?) still with respect but obviously more distant now. "I cannot judge myself Father, but, having not being disciplined for several months lately, I think I am doing well." (A little more warmth in his voice now). "Is this the reason my King has asked for me?" Filippos had raised his brow with Alexandros' first sentence. (A 'smart' remark, like one Olympias could have come-up with. Had the woman seen the boy before presenting himself here?) The King held his temper. This was no time for arguments and mannerism lessons.

The boy's follow-up warmed the King's disposition and he stood up to show he had something very important in mind to say. "I am to go to Anthemous with Parmenion here, tomorrow. We are expect-ing few emissaries from the High King and they should arrive in a few days. If I am not back until then, I would like you to represent me..." The King could not finish his sentence. Alexandros' face lit-up and the boy rushed and jumped onto his Father's arms. "Father! I will not fail you! I will see to it that you and Makedonia are well represented! What should I know about them? What's their purpose of coming to us?" Filippos held his son tenderly at the beginning, embarrassed -for he did not expect such reaction- and looking now at Parmenion, now at Antipatros who were both smiling. He realized the spontaneity and delight of his son for such an honor and held the youngster tight now.

Finally the ice was broken! Filippos was delighted with the result. He held now his son at an arm's length, looking at Alexandros' face with a broad smile. "Wait! Wait! Don't you get over excited on me now! Yes, you will be in my stead receiving them and I will inform you of the reason for their visit in a while. First I want you to know that Antipatros will be at your side at all times while they are here, in case you need his service. Now, now, don't you lose your smile! He has done this several times in the past and his experience is to your advantage. It's like if you would be stand-Ing at my side -a thing which might happen if I return on time. Now, let us sit down and all three of us will be giving you what advise we know you will need and feel free to be asking questions"

The four of them stayed at Filippos' study for hours informing, asking and answering questions, planning. Their dinner was served to them there and, finally exhausting all possibilities, father and son kissed goodnight and each headed toward his chambers...

The Persian envoys arrived at Pella the beginning of the month of Daesios. Filippos was still in An-thenountian lands, playing cat-and-mouse with the Olynthians who were supposed to be his allies but kept open relations with Athinae, supporting Efvolos' designs. Olympias had her maids work over-time helping her get a new hiton for her son, of much softer material than what Leonidas was allow-ing the young prince to be dressed with, convincing Alexandros that a Makedonian prince had to be equally well dressed in receiving foreign dignitaries and she knew the Persians would be dressed! Her son accepted his mother's insisting advice with reluctance, feeling he did not have to show equally barbaric custom being overdressed. He was pleased to find out that his new hiton was not what he feared. It was done with taste, a medium blue color accentuating his eyes and color of hair, with gold- trimmed hem and silver embroidering of the Makedonian star-burst on the chest level. A soft leather belt out of deer hide was nicely fitting on his waist, with special attachment for his dagger.

Antipatros gave his look of approval when the young prince met him on their way to the audience hall and that made Alexandros feel more at ease. As they entered the hall, the Persian envoys rose from their seats perplexed and on guard. They knew Filippos was away and they expected his deputy (Antipatros or someone else -it didn't matter) to receive them, but a child? They knew Filippos had a son -reports were easy to reach Susa from every corner of the earth- yet, a child?...

The Makedonian heir was reported of being about six years old but this child (obviously in higher order than the escorting middle aged general following at a distance of respect) wasn't even looking of being over five. Were they fooled? Was Filippos playing against the High King a game this upstart country and old vassal state could ill afford? A closer look at the youth's face dissolved their thoughts of protesting or (worst) leaving without an audience amid threats which they would certainly have used under any other circumstances. The youth seemed to be reading them like an open book! The color of his eyes turned to dark, unfathomed color at their hesitation in accepting him as his father's representative. They changed attitude immediately and let a sigh of relief seeing the color returning to normal (or was it the light playing with their vision?).

Alexandros returned to being in a pleasant disposition and gave them a warm smile, nodding his permission for them to sit, as he took his place on his Father's throne. Antipatros waved at a servant to bring a stool for the kid's feet were way off the floor, but Alexandros dismissed the offer showing not a bit of discomfort. Antipatros remained one step behind and on the side of the throne, a discreet smile on his face, showing his amused but proud acceptance of the prince's decision.

The young prince ordered a servant to offer refreshments to the honored guests and opened-up the conversation. "My Father asked me to entertain you and apologizes for his absence. State affairs he could not avoid but attend to in person, keep him away for a short time -I am sure- and he will see you as soon as he returns to Pella. I hear you are visiting us bringing pardon from you King to two of our guests here -one being a compatriot of yours- which is a good thing. Memnon and Artavazos are good men. I am sure High King Artaxerxis Ochos will use their services wisely."

The senior Persian envoy smiled politely nodding his head in agreement, while the other two of his escort stole a perplexed, questioning look with each-other. Such a young boy offering an opinion to adults for their High King's practices? Was Filippos playing games with them? They kept their heads low, unless they'd have to face the darkened eyes again. To their astonishment, Alexandros had detected their subtle exchange as he showed by coolness in his voice and a steady stare on their faces -but he continued addressing the senior envoy. "I also hear you have arrived to ask us for assist ance in delaying or stopping altogether our timber sales to Athinae. Why is it that the High King needs us to do that? If Athinae are to be kept weak on the war against their former allies, the High King can provide navy and troops against them -now that Mentor has helped him quell the satrapal revolt in Egyptos. Memnon's brother is also a good soldier and he would serve equally well in this!"

Now there was a general reaction of all present, guests and Antipatros. The kid was proving to being much more 'in the know' of affairs than expected from a youngster his age! Anticipating Anti-patros' possible interference, Alexandros raised his hand and continued. "The High King must have the recourses in such a large state and from so many nations under him. Not so? How many does he lead under arms?"

By the time Alexandros finished his sentence, there was a settlement of feelings and opinions among the listeners. Antipatros' chest seemed to be swelling with pride for his young prince (albeit some jealousy pinched his heart -couldn't his own son show some of the prince's cleverness and insight? But Kassandros' interests were just play and reluctant schooling yet -and Kassandros was by two whole years older than Alexandros!), while the Persian envoys decided that their temporary host was at least as clever as his father. So be it then. They would give the child a lesson of the High King's might!

"The power of our High King" the senior envoy took over the conversation with a slight bow of the head in acknowledgment of the youngster's aptitude "has untold numbers of troops and recourses! At any given time we can field tenths of thousands of troops. As for our navy, our Finikian subjects can put under oars over three hundred vessels of war! But that is not the point my young prince. The High King needs to know His friends -as well as he knows His enemies! Makedon, since the times of your great grandfather, has been a faithful ally of the High King and your father has received thus far a 'free hand' and the blessings of our Lord and Master of all Nations in all his endeavors. It would be a waste of Persian recourses and materiel if He had to spend His time on Athenians trying to rebuilt their long past power so close to our Asia-by-the-Aegean holdings. Let their former allies face the Athinians as they are; unaided by your father Athinae gets what it deserves. They do not aid your efforts when you need them -do they? Your country is in undeclared war with Athinae and they have aided your opponents every chance they had thus far!"

Alexandros tilted his head the side he favored when in thought and looked like he was ready to say something in response. Changing his mind, he smiled nodding in agreement and offered some more wine and sweets. He then offered his opinion on their request and asked his next question. "I am sure my Father will have his response to your request when he meets you. Now please tell me about the roads in your kingdom. How long does it take for one to travel from the coast of the Aegean to Su-sa?"

One more way to impress the kid now they thought... "Oh, young lord! The High King's mes-sengers can cover the distance within three weeks -when regular travel would take two months! The Royal Road is at the service of our Lord and Master at all times of the year and his heralds and troops can move through, faster than anything else!" "Does the High King lead his men in person? Is he a brave soldier in war?" "Yes, young master. He is the bravest and most just Lord!"

Alexandros' head tilted again in consideration of the answer and got ready for the next question, when the trumpeter's sound outside heralded the arrival of King Filippos. Alexandros stood-up and made the announcement to the Persian guests, who also stood-up from their seats, heads looking down in added respect.

Filippos entered the hall in short time after that, not bothering to change first his dusty from the road cuirass and hlamis. He was anxious to find out how his son handled the audience. As the envoys bent deeper their heads and bodies, the King eyed his deputy with a quick questioning look. Antipat-ros winked at his King with a broad smile which made the face of Filippos to light-up with pride and pleasure. He greeted his son with the expected formality though and Alexandros responded in the same manner. Filippos asked his guests to return to their seats and resume with their wine and sweets while he told Alexandros to be ready for the official dinner later in the evening. The young prince's face lit-up, understanding the pleasure and pride of his Father but kept the etiquette by responding formally and then, returning to the envoys, thanked them for their respect and attent-ivness to him and promised to see them again at dinner. Passing by Antipatros, he made sure the man received a 'thank-you' nod for just being there...

> "Parental sins bring nothing
> but hardship on their own
> children!"
> Ellenic Proverb

> "Through my work, I've been in two countries
> thus I know that the Chinese and you Greeks
> have many good proverbs. The trouble is that
> yours you have 'em apply to all -'xept you!
> Now that you 've come to stay in my country
> I give you this advise: stay away from making
> the same mistake an' you 'll get ahead! Aya!"
> Lester A. Bill, American from Vermont.

XI

The company of the prince's friends were sitting in the shade of the horse stables after finishing their chores of cleaning and grooming, having some watered-down wine and their Spartan-like lunch. The subject of their conversation in hushed voices was the events of the previous day and evening. They were a close-knit bunch of various ages, which (under other circumstances) would not have them being so close. Klitos Melas for one and, then, Ptolemeos, were a few years older and, normally, closely connected to grown-ups.

405

But this was anything but a normal situation. Alexandros had their love and devotion not only because he was the heir to the Makedonian throne alone. To be just, the majority of these young men were close to Alexandros because they believed in him. There were one or two who were there because they could not afford being absent either because of personal desire to be with the few and selected like Filotas son of Parmenion, or, forced by their father(s), like Kassandros son of Antipatros and Alexandros of Lynkos, son of Aeropos and grandson of the last 'independent' Lynkestian king nam-ed Alexandros also.

Either Klitos son of Dropidas and brother of Ellaniki, or Ptolemeos son of Lagos, were the small gang's leaders and advisors (when prince Alexandros was not present). "I have to truly admire our prince for his character after what happened last night." Klitos concluded following-up a remark made by Ptolemeos on the new fight between the King and his Queen. "I was there" Evmenis jumped-in "because I was following the King after the Persians retired for the afternoon rest and both of us were to seek Alexandros (we knew him to have gone to see his Mother) and the King want-ed to have all the details from the prince's meeting with the Persian envoys from his son's own mouth. As we approached the Queen's chambers, we could hear the commotion. Olympias was chastising her son for being too enthusiastic with his Father's acknowledgement of Alexandros' handling the reception.

She was complaining of being the last to be acknowledged and respected by her own husband and son, because Filippos went straight to meet the Persians instead of seeing her first. She was then chastising the prince of being supportive of his Father's behavior, speaking with such enthusiasm of our King's trust in his son's abilities to handle the guests."

"My Father was there too!" Kassandros interrupted with desire to lessen Alexandros' claim to fame. "He helped Alexandros with the envoys' reception!" "I am sorry to inform you lad that your father did nothing more but introduce the prince to the guests and I know that from your own father as he was reporting to King Filippos and mine own father, while I was standing by and waiting to greet my Father upon his return with the King." Filotas interrupted with a smirk on his face. Kassandros' face reddened but put his head down and said nothing.

Perdikkas, son of Orontis from Orestis' house of Agis let a soft disapproving sound from his mouth and made a statement. "It's one thing to be competitive Kassandros but an altogether different thing when you cannot control jealousy! Better be careful my friend and drop-off such ideas!"

"We better stop bickering and let us find out what exactly happened, from the ones who know. This is the only way to keep abreast of developments and help ourselves by helping Alexandros. Like it or not by being attached to him either because of love or by necessity, we are part of his life with its problems or their solution -if there's any! He goes up, we follow. He goes down, we're damned! There's no other path for us to follow and we better realize it now!" Ptolemeos ended his brief speech and looked around at each face of his companions, to make sure his words were understood.

Aside from Klitos Melas (the Black and Elanikis' brother), Ptolemeos, Kassandros and Filotas, there were also in that company 'old hands' like Arpalos son of Mahatas from Elimiotis, Perdikkas and Alketas sons of Orontis -house Agis of Orestis, Pithon, son of Kratevas of Eordea and 'new-comers' as Klitos Lefkos (the White) from Paeonia -house Iraklonas- his family residing now (after orders of the King) in Filippi/Krenides, as was the Lynkestian Alexandros and his brother Arra-vaeos, sons of Aeropos, Nearhos son of Androtimos from Lato in Kriti (emigrated to Makedonia few years back) and Evmenis from Kardia, the recently employed scribe of the King (not on duty at this time).

"What I heard from my cousin Krateros, who was with the King's pages when Filippos came from Olynthos to see the Persian delegation, is that Alexandros lingered outside the Hall waiting for his father to finish and receive the King's own opinion on his performance with the guests, thus delaying his visit with the Queen who was anxiously waiting to hear from her son and that was the spark for Olympias' anger." Perdikkas informed the group.

"Yeah! I had a talk with Laomedon son of Larihos from this Pellea Hora (Pella's environ), who was the guard on duty outside the Queen's chambers when Alexandros went there and her screams could be heard even through the heavy double doors!" Arpalos jumped-in. "She 'dressed' Alexandros up and down with his 'indifference' to his mother's feelings and anxiety to be informed of the outcome of his interview of the Persians and the King's 'misbehavior'. They should both come and see her first -instead of being so absorbed with their 'manly' affairs- she hollered. Instead, her son lingered about, to discuss state affairs which could wait for later and her husband gave the barbarians the honor of seeing them first after his return and then sended a 'minion' (that was a slap in the face for Alexandros) to tell her he (Filippos) would be there shortly, further delaying, further setting her in the background!"

"I was with the King as he prais'd Alexandros for 'is handling the 'guests' and 'is desire to hear more of it from Antipatros, while sending the prince to 'is mother with the instruction that the King had not forgotten 'is duty and that Filippos would be going to see Olympias shortly." Klitos Melas took over the conversation in his thick Makedonian dialect. "The King ask'd for and was inform'd in detail of 'is son's commendable performance. He was very happy and said so to both Parmenion an' Antipatros. I was just a few steps away from 'em -'s my duty called for- being in 'is escort. Then the King gave the necessary orders for the preparation of the evening's reception an' official dinner an' he headed for the Queen's quarters in good spirits. At that, I was dismiss'd to go and see after my own an' I don't know what actually happen'd next."

"My Father said that the King's parting words to him and Antipatros were: 'I see that my seed has produced a good future for our country!' before he headed toward the royal quarters." Filotas added thoughtfully.

"And who can blame the King for being so proud of his son? Too bad the elation did not last longer than it took Filippos to get to his Queen's chambers..." Arpalos picked-up again. "Laomedon was stiff with fear hearing Olympias' tirades and seeing the King approaching the chambers. There was nothing he could do to prevent the King from hearing. Filippos burst into the room almost bringing the heavy double doors down in his fury! He shoved the Queen to the floor yelling that Makedonian interests and his son's learning to handle diplomacy were much greater than the whims and desires of a semi-barbarian Ipirotan brat! While Alexandros was standing there ashen and immobile from dread as to what might happen, Olympias stood-up yelling the credentials of her ancestry and accusing the King's own background of being insignificant and worthless! The King, in his fury, shoved Alexandros aside and slapped Olympias sending her back down on the mosaic floor. Alexandros left the room running..."

"I am sure he went straight to his new 'beloved friend' Yfestion son of Amyntor from Pellea Hora!"

Kassandros let the words fly before thinking. "You could be more of just a pest in our midst if you have had any interest in friendship instead of looking for self-gratification of your jealousy and big ego!" Arpalos hissed at him. Kassandros jumped-up in fury but the looks from Klitos Melas and

Pto-lemeos forced him to sit down again eyes cast to the ground. Perdikkas stood-up and went to sit next to him in threatening mood, moving his hands in a forbidding fashion on any further remarks out of taste.

"Just for anybody's curiosity and second thoughts, I know where Alexandros went after the fight. He went to see and spent the night with Lysimahos, his old Teacher on the epics of Omiros, the one he calls Finix. I was detailed to guard the entrance to his rooms and I saw him going by and entering Lysimahos' one. My duty ended past the middle of the night and he was still there. He returned to his quarters in the morning and, later, he went to visit his half-brother Arrideos. And, as I know, he's still there." Nearhos informed the group.

Ptolemeos went on to say: "As for the King, I know he went to spend some consolation time with his new favorite, that kid Pafsanias from the Orestian house of Antiohos and son of Kerastos, before ap-pearing at the banquet for the Persian envoys that evening. He was already half-drunk when he came to entertain them."

"In a way, I cannot blame 'im" Klitos Melas said and stood-up. "I got t' get goin'. My own duty time's comin'. I've to take the new recruits on to teach 'em some ridin'." He left, leaving the rest in their thoughts on the events of the previous day and they returned back to the conversation.

"I wonder if there is anything we can do…" Nearhos started saying. "We can do what Arpalos is doing" Kassandros intervened, still fuming from the recent word exchange and wanting to hurt in return. "Absolutely nothing!" And, turning to face his opponent, he continued: "How come you're more closely related to Arrideos yet Alexandros is the one who spends more time looking after that nincompoop's needs for company and attention? Arrideos being nuts and you being crippled, the two of you should be constant companions!"

Ptolemeos and Perdikkas rose to place the insolent Kassandros in his place, but they were too late.

Alexandros had approached the group undetected -as they were absorbed in their conversation- and was there in time to hear Kassandros' remarks. His hands fell heavy on the offender's head and the young prince pulled Kassandros by the hair, lifting him up and throwing him flat against the pile of horse manure, piled to be taken out of the stables. "There is where you belong!" Alexandros' eyes were emphasizing his words, deadly as two daggers thrown at an altar offering. "I suggest you stay there for the rest of your life!" Perdikkas and Ptolemeos placed their bodies between

Alexandros and the dumb-founded and horrified Kassandros, holding with difficulty the prince away from his in-tended victim. Evmenis, with the assistance of Nearhos and White Klitos, lifted Kassandros up and send him running away but not before Klitos made sure his fist fell square on the arrogant kid's face braking his nose.

Alexandros' friends gathered around their prince offering excuses and promising a better day ahead, if only they could go and train alongside the recruits of Black Klitos, by the banks of Lydias.

"First, we go and fetch Yfestion from his father's estates!" the prince gave-in to the proposal. On their way they met the Molossian Alexandros and the group sped toward their goal, out of the palace gates and through the city, following the westward contour of the lagoon's shore.

Antipatros appeared before Olympias that morning with orders from the King, telling the Queen that she was to remain in her chambers until further notice. Olympias crashed a few vases and small chairs as her husband's messenger left and, when she calmed down a bit, she wrote a long letter of complaints, accusations, curses and destitute to her sister Troas, demanding the intervention of Ariv-vas. She then proceeded in taking her pet snakes to her Altar of Kyveli and offering her sorcery chants and burned incenses.

Alexandros sought the company of his friends (especially Yfestion's) and Finix, finding solace in the wisdom of the latter and a willing listener in the person of the former. He avoided his Father and refused the calls of his Mother for the next two weeks. Both Filippos and Olympias were devastated but none would admit fault and take the first step for reconciliation. As for Kassandros, Antipatros saw that his son had his hide turned blue and (after recovery) was sent to Alexandros apologizing and asking for forgiveness…

King Filippos was furious for many reasons. First, he hardly had his son by his side and the damned wife of his was the cause of losing the kid once more. Second, Olynthos was playing games with him, making overtures to Athinae (now involved in a new war on account of Fokian against Thivan dom-ination in Viottia and Delfi) disregarding oaths of friendship with Makedonia. Thirdly, he had inter-septed Arivvas' answer to Olympias, saying that the Molossian king would come to her aid when visiting Pella soon -on account of her upcoming anniversary as Queen.

Time to get rid of Arivvas for sure and, if need be, his niece too! He was the King of Makedon! No Ipirotan bitch would insult him any further, taking family problems to her relatives and throwing his name in the mud. And, who in hell did Arivvas think he was? Filippos did him a great favor back when he wed that insolent niece of his. The young Alexandros of Molossis was the best candidate for the change of guard in the Ipirote throne. Time to take his son out of Olympias' reach, time to teach a lesson to all concerned...

Filippos started looking for a new teacher for his son in a place away from Pella and getting his troops ready for a final show-down with Olynthos and to show Athinae that when the city-state was listening to a certain Dimosthenis, it was against its interests when dealing with Makedon (especially when he was called more dangerous to Ellas than the Persian High King). He soon found the right teacher for Alexandros. This was the well known Aristotelis, pupil of Platon and recent resident of Atarneas, on the southern area of Tria and across from Lesvos, under Ermias. Aristotelis was the son of Amyntas' (Filippos' own Father) physician Nikomahos, from Stagiros/Stagira of Halkidiki.

Aristotelis had left Athinae after Platon's death, bitter for not inheriting the lead of the Platonian school at the Akadimos' estates, as Spefsipos had taken over it -being Platon's own nephew and the sentiment in Athinae being anti-Makedonian (although Stagira was not part of Filippos' kingdom at that time). So, Aristotelis moved to Atarneas and soon got married to Ermias' daughter. Seeing that Atarneas was receiving the suspicion of the High King, Aristotelis had just moved to Lesvos, at the invitation by his friend Theofrastos, a botanist. He answered that he would accept Filippos' offer and he would come to Pella as soon as his engagement with Theofrastos would come to conclusion.

The King knew he had to wait -if he really wanted the best as his son's teacher. Meantime Filippos played his cards wisely. Letting Olympias suspect nothing, Filippos received the visit of Arivvas on her anniversary along with other dignitaries and there were festivities for several days. Arivvas went back to his kingdom satisfied, Olympias was left with the impression that she had won and her brother Alexandros escorted their uncle back to Molossis and the palace at Vouthriton.

Within weeks there was unrest in Molossis and Arivvas was deposed and was never heard of again. Filippos sent Parmenion to the Molossian borders, ensuring the succession of young Alexandros to the throne and getting parts of Paravea as a 'thank-you'. Olympias took her anger on her maids and devoted her time on mysticism and Dionysiac revelries. Of course, each time her son Alexandros was visiting with her, she found ways to poison his thoughts against his Father. Her favorite claim now was that she didn't conceive because of her earthly husband but because of a god's visit the night before her nuptials.

Young Alexandros was disturbed witnessing the rift between his parents and most of the time he was torn by indecision. He loved his Mother, as every male child feels more attached to a mother. He respected his Father as his King but he feared Filippos' wrath when dealing with Olympias' stub-bornness and ego. Adding the character of Filippos in handling youth, Father and son were drifting apart again.

Alexandros found himself spending more time with Finix, conversing about the heroes such Ahil-leas and, with Yfestion, on matters of training and hunting concerns. He also started paying more attention to his teacher of music, as he found out that the sound of the kithara was soothing his tormented soul. As for Leonidas the paedagogue, Alexandros never really liked his Mother's kins-man, especially his stinginess. One day when offering to Iraklis, Leonidas scolded him for spending so much incense for the hero-demigod. Alexandros told the old man to mind his personal affairs and leave his own to him. That cost him a week of less food and lighter covers in the middle of the winter. He took it without a word of complain.

King Filippos had had it with Olynthos. This city-state negotiated now with Athinae, against all their oaths taken for alliance and mutual assistance with Makedonia. They obviously had to be dealt with and severely. Filippos moved in Halkidiki and started operations against the Olynthian alliance.

Dimosthenis delivered a strong speech in Athinae before its Dimos of citizens but the mood was to negotiate. Athinae was in a mess with her involvement in the war for the control of Delfi and just out of the war against Rodos. The Dimos assembly asked for an emissary to travel to Pella and get the best terms possible for peace with Makedonia, as soon as weather would favor the trip. Dimosthenis observed carefully before raising his hand for permission to add himself to the delegation. There was Aristodimos, a minion of Filippos' silver for sure, Filokratis the instigator of peace negotiations with the arrogant King of the semi-barbarian northern tribe and Aeshinis the pet dog of Efvolos, there-fore also a possible traitor to Athinian interests and supporter of Midias nonetheless. He would show them all what he could do in negotiations against usurpers! Wasn't

Amyntas, son of Perdikkas, the rightful King? The youth although not killed, Dimosthenis was sure he was kept in a dungeon some-where in the north, half-starved to death. He raised his hand.

The citizens of Athinae had one more surprise for Dimosthenis. Before any delegation would ready for Makedonia, before any possible help was to travel north to Olynthos, there were matters closer to home to be taken care of. The island of Evia with Halkis out of all allies was showing tendencies of dropping out of the alliance. An expeditionary force was voted to go there and secure the place.

Dimosthenis asked for recognition, to try and persuade the Dimos to forget Halkis for the present and send aid to Olynthos. He was denied a second chance and the voting took place. When the result was announced by the herald, he was horrified with the decision and angered further more by look-ing at Midias' face smiling toward his direction but not looking him in the eye…

By the time Athinae ended its military affairs in Evia, Olynthos had fallen to King Filippos and the few Athinian oplites caught in the city were captured. The Olynthians were sold to slave markets, adding silver to Filippos' treasury and the city was torn from the face of the earth. One by one, the rest of the confederate to Olynthos cities fell or surrendered and Filippos treated them accordingly.

Dimosthenis saw now the need of an armistice. Athinae was spent and needed time to recover. First Rodos and theFokian war for Delfi, next Evia and (minimal) support of Olynthos, now the war in Fokis and Viottia still in full swing, Filippos had to be asked for peace. What with the weather, what with the wars and, mostly, with procrastination, the delegation started north with one more person added. Iatroklis had been captured during the fall of Olynthos but Filippos was persuaded by Aristo-dimos to set him free without ransom. Dimosthenis welcomed both, the gesture and the addition. The first was indication of Filippos' readiness to negotiate; the second, good will in doing so.

The delegation departed from the port of Pireas at the end of the Makedonian month of Xanthikos, just before the beginning of Artemisios, to avoid the coming of the northern winds which would make the trip very difficult -if not impossible- as it was known to blow from late spring though the whole summer. It did not help at all, as they run onto foul weather and were delayed first by the promon-tory of Magnisia across from Evia's Artemision and, then, as they approached Pydna. They finally entered the protected waters of the Pella lagoon to the west of Therma at the end of Artemisios and with constant rain.

Filippos heard of the delegation being on its way, as soon as the Athinian ship carrying them entered the lagoon and he was prepared. The King went to the Queen's chambers asking to see his son, as he was notified Alexandros was visiting his Mother. Having in mind to introduce Alexandros to an Athinian delegation (as he had done with the Persians) and not to get into an unforeseen argument with Olympias, Filippos took his time, sending the announcement ahead with Elaniki.

He entered the room finding the Queen sharing a bowl of fruits with Alexandros, looking innocent but for the shade of a wicked smile at the corner of her lips which Filippos was fast to see. The King held his temper. No time now to start something. Whatever the witch was saying to his son, he would offer something better! He smiled to both and then ignored her. "We are to have the Athinian delegation arriving late tonight." He told his son. "They will be offered quarters and we will receive them tomorrow for lunch first, then I will offer them an audience with you on my side."

Alexandros jumped with anxiety and gratification for the invitation. "I shall be ready for them and by your side Father!" Filippos' smile broadened. Here we go kid, me and you once more! He stole a side look toward the Queen. Olympias' smile was gone. Good! The young prince had also noticed his Mother's sudden sullenness. "What is the matter Mother?" he questioned, concerned. Olympias had to think fast. "Oh, nothing, just a Mother's jealousy of missing her son. I had in mind to have you escort me in offering to Dionysos and then to Iraklis and spend the day -since you are free from schooling, (Leonidas being ill) then have dinner in the garden, if the weather would permit it." Alexandros looked at his Mother. He did not believe what she said. He was old and experienced enough now to be able to tell of her mood changing. He looked at his father. Filippos seemed to be preoccupied with adjusting his royal cape. Alexandros' face lost some of its color. "We can do that the day after tomorrow Mother." He offered coolly, and asked for permission to withdraw. He received a hearty one from Filippos and a dismissal move of the hand from Olympias. He ran out to find Yfestion…

The Athinians arrived in Pella's small harbor late that evening, as their ship had to move slowly under oar, in order to avoid sandbars created from the rivers' silt and changing locations and shape constantly -according to nature's whims. There was a delegation of Makedonians waiting their arrival at the docks, with Antipatros being the high dignitary of the visitors' escort to the city. The Ma-kedonian spring was of the winter quality by Athinian standards. The evening mist prevailing, gave an extra chill to the bone for the unaccustomed visitors and Dimosthenis felt it more than anybody else -but did not dare show it. He looked at his fellow delegates with envy. Aeshinis with his athletic posture (and his years of actor's training) had not even bothered to throw a cape over his broad shoulders, riding, clad only in his hiton. Filokratis being the elder was excused to wear a hlamis over his travel clothes and, Aristodimos being accustomed to Makedonian climate, rode with comfort. As for the rest of the delegation, each one looked rather at ease in the chill of the evening breeze.

Dimosthenis kicked his horse with his heel to move in with the rest. His preoccupation had slowed him a bit and made him look out of place, as the closing riders of the Makedonian honor escort had to wait for him. The added wind as he did so, gave him an unwanted shiver and he cursed the country and its climate but he caught-up with the delegates. Aeshinis turned his head and looked at him smiling. Was the curse said out loud? Did it show to the rest that he, Dimosthenis, was the weakling?

Dimosthenis returned the look defiantly. "To Adis with you, failed actor!" he thought and he looked indifferent at the rest of his companions. None of them seemed to have noticed anything and that calmed him down some. He didn't like the chill and, now, the horses feeling the proximity of their ride's end, picked-up their pace on their own, making him even more uncomfortable, to outright cold. He gave a loud sneeze and Antipatros wished him the gods' blessing. He nodded an embar-rassed 'thank-you' and continued, head up, straight ahead. A snickering sound from the side of Aes-hinis and Filokratis turned his face red and he was thankful of the darkness -the night was fast ap-proaching- escorted by one more unwanted and louder sneeze. Antipatros held his horse, bringing their pace to a slow trot and asked if all was all right with the distinguished guest. To Dimosthenis' positive (but rather forced) answer, he politely informed them that a hot supper and good wine was prepared and waited their arrival, to ease the fatigue and discomfort of a long trip. They continued on the remainder of their ride under torchligh and, soon, the gates of the city were in sight.

The visitors and their escort crossed the city streets at a north-east direction, amidst almost indif-ferent looks from the inhabitants going about their last business of the day, closing shops and last teasing minutes among friends heading for a night's supper and a home rest. Pelleans were used to visiting delegations from all quarters by now and the Athinians were no novelty.

At the entrance of the palace gates in the acropolis, there were some youth milling and waiting for their arrival. Dimosthenis felt the inquisitive eyes of them on his group and, particularly, the eyes of one medium sized kid, no more than twelve years of age, next to another, a head taller and (obvious-ly) older. Surely servants—judging from their homespun dress—who did not look sharp enough or ready to help the delegates dismount. 'Ah, naturally background country fellows who are not trained the proper ways! What one could expect from a country like this one?' He curled his lips in con-tempt, making an impatient gesture to these two particularly, to help him dismount. The rest of the group was already met by servants coming out of the gate and tending them. The two Makedon-ian youths looked at each-other, obviously not understanding his status and need of service which made him more intolerant of peasant manners and upbringing. Not wanting to make a scene (Aeshinis should not be aware of this Makedonian affront and have grounds of future embarrassment to Dimosthenis' reputation back home), he gestured emphatically without a word. He saw the taller youth stiffening (was defiance tolerated in this forsaken country?). The shorter though held his co—servant in check by raising his hand and approached the visitor. "Sir?" He obviously did not know who he was dealing with. "Dimosthenis is the name, brat! Help me now dismount before I have them skin your hide!" The eyes of the youth grew too large and his nostrils flared in anger.

Dimosthenis hesitated involuntarily. He never in his life felt so threatened, so vulnerable! One more proof one had to tread one's way carefully in these parts. He regretted for being so presuming and not wait for proper assistance like the rest of his group (they were all now being helped and preoc-cupied with their dismounting, so no one was paying attention to him), but what was done, was done. Besides, the youth seemed to be holding his ill manners in check and got a hold of the horse's rains. The other one, at the sorter's nod, came to give him a step for dismounting, by joining his palms under Dimosthenis' sole.

The Athinian took a better look at the shorter youth. The eyes had been kept low now (the kid must have realized his offensive manners), but his fists remained clenched tight (need for further disci-pline!). "See that I get a good rub-down after our meal. Your weather doesn't seem to agree with what I am accustomed to." (There! This ought to give him the time to teach a thing or two to this un-kept but—torchlight permitting to observe the youth's handsomeness—pretty boy servant and, sure to get the desired result, a pleasant night after all). He turned to join the delegates as they were now following Antipatros into the palace, without waiting for a response. An order is an order, regardless of the low, contemptuous training of servants. He thought he heard the youth talking in their rough Makedonian dialect, saying something like: "I'll see tha"e gets what'e's askin' for!" but he did not turn to slap the mouth uttering those words, for he was in a hurry now to join the others and get away from the humid cold, his nose full of sinus' mucus by now and a severe headache coming! He needed his warm food, the strong wine and the rub-down (with its trimmings)! The audience with Filippos the following day had to find him in full strength and fitness.

The night passed with Dimosthenis waiting in vain after supper in his room for the servant boy or boys to come and give him his rub-down and comfort. He called several times down the hallway but all he got was the indifferent looks of sentries posted at the end of the hallway (becoming frowns by the third time he inquired). He gave-up and covered himself with the blanket he was given, keeping all his traveling clothes on him—and still not finding comfort. He discovered he was given a north side room, its wall cold to the touch with no brazier in sight to take the chill off. He resolved to pace up and down rehearsing his speech until he would either get warm or dead-tired and fall asleep then. To his utter disappointment, neither of the two happened. He spent his night pacing and rehearsing.

The next morning found him in a bad mood but the breakfast and luncheon given in the delegates' honor were ample and of good quality, so he felt more at ease by the time he had to get ready for the evening banquet and the King's audience. Some color had returned to his cheeks after the good food and a short rest after morning meal time. He even managed to get a brazier going in his room (request placed through Antipatros) and, now, dressed in his finest dinner clothes (care was taken to have under dress also) he was ready to face the King and lay down the Athinian grievances with the flair only he could possess.

He had his mind on keeping notes of what Filokratis and Aeshinis would speak of, for he suspected either one was in Filippos' payroll (didn't he, himself, apply for some financial aid from the High King? Why others would not have the same frame of mind—but for the opposite side?)! It would be a new triumph for him after the recent success he had against Midias—although the charges were not deliveredas political pressure had achieved the desired result.

It was then announced the audience would be held by the King right after mid-day's meal, allowing ample time for the speeches before the evening reception and banquet. Dimosthenis followed his fel-low delegates, speech in mind now and wondering what his Athinian political opponents would present—their speeches preceding his. He dreamed full power of Athinian polity once (he was sure) he could accuse either or both Aeshinis and Filokratis for 'Filippising' and succeed in exiling them . . .

They were led to the audience hall of the palace and sat across a marble throne which was decorat- ed with ivory, gold and silver covered scenes, taken from the deeds of Iraklis and keeping in line with the proclaimed ancestry of the King. Behind it and between the two side doors leading in and out the room, a painting done during the days of King Arhelaos depicted the fight among the champions of the Tria war, Ahilleas and Ektoras. About half way between their seats and the throne, there was a marble altar dedicated (as its sculpted words proclaimed) to Zefs and Iraklis. It would serve to open the negotiations with an offering, thus ensuring the good intentions of the King to listen and judge unbiased. But, aside the burning coal on the altar, there were no braziers in the vast room. Dimos-thenis was glad he had the mind to wear undergarments.

They were served some sweets and watered-down local wine while waiting for the King's entrance, a thing Dimosthenis determined was taking a rather long time to happen. Was Filippos trying to put them at a disadvantage? The King had changed the audience time a few times already! He looked at his fellow delegates. Both Aeshinis and Filokratis seemed to be at ease and had engaged Aristodimos in some small talk. Iatroklis was talking to an elder Makedonian who claimed to be the prince's teacher on classics. He felt isolated but that did not bother him. Let them talk. When he would be done with his speech, they would have more to talk about and it would all be about him.

At long last, Parmenion and Antipatros walked-in announcing the King's entrance and nodding to them to rise. Filippos entered the hall followed by a youth (presumably the apparent heir, Alexan-dros), his chief body guard and another youth holding the bowl with the aromatic incense for the altar offering and the oath to be taken. Dimosthenis recognized this youth immediately. He was the taller of last night's insolent servants. He made a mental note to complain—after all was done—to Filippos and demand their punishment.

The King was now greeting them in perfect Attik dialect, starting with Filokratis and a broad smile on his face. Next came Aeshinis (did the smile broaden more?), Aristodimos and Iatroklis. Then, the King turned to Dimosthenis. His smile now showed a worn but still full set of teeth and the good eye shined (in mockery?), but the tone of voice remained polite and proper. Dimosthenis was taken aback but showed no trace of it. The upstart was soon to find he was no match to his better.

Now Filippos took a handful of the incenses from the bowl the youth was holding and threw it on the altar, uttering the proper invocations. He was followed by his heir apparent (the blond youth had kept his head casting toward the floor (Makedonian custom or shyness and timidity?) andthen, both the deputies, Antipatros and Parmenion. That done, the other youth went out of the door and returned with a small chair also decorated with ivory, gold and silver, placing it on the right of the throne. The King took his seat, motioning the others to do the same. Alexandros (it had to be him) followed the gesture but kept his eyes downcast as he sat on the small chair. Parmenion and Antipatros remained standing and flanking the King on each side, the chief body guard taking his place behind the throne and the two royalties. The Athinian delegates resumed their sitting.

Filippos was served a cup of wine took a hearty sip and addressed the delegates. "I assume you have prearranged the order of who's speaking first? Good! Let us then attend to business!" Filokratis stood up and delivered his speech with eloquence and ease, although it was obvious he did not press hard and left room for Filippos to maneuver. Dimosthenis took note of it. The King thanked the speaker and reserved his right to answer after the hearing of all delegates. Next to rise, Aristodimos.

He was obviously too anxious to make his point which resulted in being insufficient, thus giving Fil-ippos more ground to maneuver. As he finished embarrassed, the King thanked him and took some more wine, ready to hear from the next delegate. Iatroklis was next in line, opening his speech with a warm 'thank you' to the King for sparing him from the disgrace of slavery at the end of the war against Olynthos. The King was polite in accepting and regarding his magnanimity as nothing more than a gesture from a civilized opponent to another. Iatroklis' speech left much to be desired. The man was obviously taken by Filippos' gesture and counted for nothing further than paying back his debt. He would pay more in time when back in Athinae. Aeshinis now stood up. Dimosthenis honed his attention, ready to take note of the political grave-digging, upon return to Athinae, of his hated opponent.

To his utter surprise, Dimosthenis heard Aeshinis' speech hitting all points of Athinian interest—and strongly! His well trained voice spelled all grievances Dimosthenis himself had in mind (and counted-on) to highlight his own performance! He looked at the King. Filippos was attending in all seriousness, obviously impressed and leaning to whisper to Alexandros at each strong point of Aeshinis' speech. The prince would then nod but he kept his head low and eyes cast on the floor. Obedient brat, taking lessons! Dimosthenis hoped the heir apparent would not be of his father's caliber when fully grown. Damned!

He had been sidetracked and now Aeshinis was coming to conclusion. No chance of accusing him of planning treacherous deals upon their return to Athinae. The King thanked the speaker warmly (would that be an indication?) and turned his attention expectantly to the next speaker, Dimosthenis.

The orator stood-up and cleared his throat. Now his time had come! Never mind what points Aeshi-nis has covered. It was he who would run the beast ragged and force the acceptance of Athinian in-terests. Filippos smiled again, showing his teeth and his eye sparked once more. No, that will not do! No upstart would make the great Dimosthenis bow!. "The Athinian position in these negotiations King, is . . ." The princeling raised his head and the pair of blues faced the orator like deadly daggers ready to be thrown at their intended victim. Dimosthenis froze. The face was unmistakably recog-nized. This was the second youth of last evening's meeting. Now cleaned, dressed appropriately and combed, but no mistake about the identity. Did Filippos know about the incident? Was that the reason why the show of teeth and the spark of the eye? If so, what was the risk for Dimosthenis?

Filippos waited politely, apparently unaware of the orator's reason of discomfort and loss of plan-ned etiquette attention and mannerism (now the mouth of Dimosthenis pointedly dropped open). Seeing no recovery, Filippos cleared his throat to get the needed attention and, keeping polite, he in-quired: "If you need time dear fellow, please do take a breath, sip some wine, recollect your lost thoughts and start from the beginning!" He gave the example by picking-up his cup and taking a mouthful.

Dimosthenis was living his worst nightmare. He sensed not only the two blue daggers kept on him unblinking, but also the amusement of Filippos and (worst) the smile from Aeshinis and Filo-kratis (were they in the scheme notified beforehand?) and the open smile from the other youth, with a triumphal spark in his eyes! Parmenion and Antipatros were having their eyes averted, one scratching his beard, the other pretending to adjusting his sword belt. Aristodimos' face had turned red with embarrassment and kept his head down and Iatroklis was facing him questioning with his eyes.

Dimosthenis gave it a go starting again. "The Athinian posit . . ." Alexandros' face smiled at him an equally deadly smile full of mockery and contempt—the 'dagger' eyes of his still unblinking. The orator felt his knees unable to hold his frame up. He sunk back on his seat, cold sweat running over his whole body. "I . . . didn't . . ." he muttered. Filippos rose from his throne. "It is perfectly acceptable to feel somewhat discombobulated, dear fellow (unmistakably a patronizing tone now escorted with the full toothed smile), although I fail to see the reason why. Nonetheless, it seems to me that all points of your proclaimed grievances have been covered by your fellow delegates and now I would like to state my points of view . . . Is there something we can do to comfort you? Guard! Take the poor fellow to his quarters and see that a physician goes to tend him. He really looks sick!"

The great Dimosthenis was escorted back to his room. He refused a physician's attendance and stayed there until departure time. He took a corner on the ship sailing back to Athinae, not uttering a word during the trip. His hatred for anything Makedonian grew to the point of suffocation! His vengeance would be coming swift, starting with Filokratis and Aeshinis. He would . . . He dreaded his obligatory return to Makedonia for the agreements' ratification and the knowledge that the Athini-ans would approve the peace as was proposed. He made a promise not to forget the insult, never to give-up, until the time he would see the demise of both Makedonian upstarts.

Yfestion told the event as it happened many a time to the rest of Alexandros' friends who were not there to witness it. "The King wanted to take the head of that 'mighty' insolent rat!" he repeated time after time. "But Alexandros asked his Father to go along with his plan! I think Dimosthenis will have his tongue tied-up for years to come after this fiasco!" Yfestion was wrong about Dimosthenis' tongue but it didn't matter to the group of the prince's friends. They all left for Mieza and Aristo-telis' teaching, within a week after the Athinian delegation got on its way back to Attiki.

The group of Alexandros' friends, many of whom were few years older than him, got right to work under the tutelage of Aristotelis. The man proved to be a person who loved detailed analysis of every subject he had in mind any given day. They studied reasoning, first as was taught by the great Sok-ratis and his best student Platon (Aristotelis' own teacher while he was studying in Athinae), then re-versed the order and tried to really reason those views as logically acceptable or reject them.

They studied mathematics and the course of nature on living things, Aristotelis having several help-ers in his employment, kept records of any and all results and conclusions. Then, they would switch to plants and trees. Then back to human thoughts and on to medicine, a thing Aristotelis felt obligat-ed to teach, experimenting with remedies of alleviating pain and healing wounds—if not for any other reason but because his father was the court physician of Alexandros' grandfather, Amyntas.

Days in Mieza were going by fast, everybody being busy under the instructions and keen eye of their Teacher. Visits to Pella or to Aegae were rare and during only State holidays and rituals at which the whole royal family was needed to be present. In those days the young men would go to their families, while Aristotelis was left behind (most of the times because he wanted to) to supervise his helpers cat- aloguing his findings, to finish his anatomical observations on animals and classify old and new herbs and plants. He also undertook the issue of a much more accurate reproduction of Omiros' Iliad, as he found the copy Alexandros had from his—fondly called Finix—old classics teacher (when still under Leonidas' tutelage), very rudely inaccurate.

As for Alexandros himself, these side events in Pella or Aegae were very rarely pleasant breaks from his schooling, because of the (almost constant) bickering and counter accusations of his parents. Not so much from Filippos who (as King and man) held himself above explanations (let alone rap-prochement by his wife), as much from Olympias. She would see treason and bestial behavior in her marital relations (some true, most imaginary) and never failed to accuse the King to her son.

Alexandros dreaded these visits, but loved his Mother and felt obligated to listen. Each time a visit came to its end, he would return in Mieza mentally and physically drained. So much so, Aristotelis had to send finally a message to the King inquiring and begging for a stop to whatever made the prince being so absentminded and indifferent for days upon each return.

This led to a big fight between Filippos and Olympias, bringing—as a result—the end of any sort of normal husband and wife relations among the two. Filippos turned to chasing younger girls and she got more involved in her mystery rituals, curse issuing spells and 'friendly ears'—wherever she could find ones. She made sure she would secretly send letters lining all her grievances to Alexandros. Of them, some were intercepted by the King and burned; many found their recipient, poisoning further the relation between Father and son.

In one of these compulsory 'family' reunions (this time at Dion for the festivities of the Olympian gods), Olympias almost caused the death of Alexandros. Filippos had just found a very pretty girl, daughter of a local land lord in Pieria and, soon, this was a common secret. During the festivities and with the pretext of observing the Dionysiac rituals of women, Olympias had the poor girl find an 'ac-cidental' death, excused as the cause of the ritual's frenzy but imprudently letting its real cause to reach Alexandros' ears.

He was so devastated, he took off on to the slopes of Olympos, riding his horse and determined not to ever return home. His heart could not accept any more of his Father's infidelities (no matter what the excuse), nor could it stand knowing his Mother of being a common murderer! Yfestion, being his ever closest confidant, learned of it when all was over and—in a day of carelessness—confided the story to Evmenis (regretting later and threatening with death—if this would come to Alexandros' ears).

Alexandros took off—as said—in the middle of the night, up the ravines and slopes of Olympos on his horse and armed only with his dagger, a thing ritualistically worn concealed by any and all members of the Makedonian royal family's men. He was gone for days, driving everybody crazy back at Dion as they searched for him. Eventually, Perdikkas son of

Orontis and Krateros son of the Orestian Al-exandros and both from the house of Agis, found him lying half-dead in a ravine. They were led by the sight of vultures circling lower and lower. A mountain lion was dead on top of him with the prince's dagger firmly embedded on the animal's heart. The prince had suffered several wounds (few of them quite serious) from the lion's claws and teeth.

It took weeks for Alexandros' recovery. Officially the event was excused as a childish venture and the prince's desire to do a man's deed. He was awarded his manhood, presented with a fine sword and gilded scabbard, a man's hlamis trimmed with purple hem (Olympias' present of regret?) and was sent back to Mieza. No private apologies were given nor there were any asked. Getting back at Mieza, Aristotelis called Alexandros and handed him the specially prepared edition of the Iliad, with written notes here and there by the Teacher's own hand. The book became the focal point in Alexan-dros' life and a welcomed distraction from the gloom of his private affairs with his parents.

Meantime King Filippos had his hands full with military expeditions. The Thivans were in great need of support against the Fokians as the latter were defeating them during a religious-caused war.

The whole of Viottia was up in arms siding with the Fokians against Thivan opprecion. Thivae had no place where to turn to. Athinae was her bitter enemy for generations. Sparti, a former ally against Athinae, was the oppressing enemy only recently beaten by the Thivan great generals Pelopidas and Epaminondas. There was no way of mending this wound now. Thivae turned to Filippos.

He gladly accepted the challenge. It would give him the opportunity to show what Makedonia now was to his (not that long ago) 'generously hospitable' hosts of his youth. Besides, it would keep his army trained and fit, his land lords and vassal ex kings more attached and dependent, further unified under a common cause. But first, he had some business to finish in Thraki. Filippos had fought against Thrakian kings in the past; first with Kotys and then with Berisade (Verisadis in Ellenic), then with Amadukh (Amadokos), now he had to face the last two and Kersobulpta (Kersovleptis).

It was aimed to cut some strength out of possible Athinian allies, bring some revenue in from looting, secure in a more permanent basis the east-north/east Makedonian frontier and keep the coming Athinian delegation waiting, speculating if he would accept the finalization of the peace deal.

With Amfipolis finally fallen and secured, Pydna was given as appeasement to Athinae.

Dimosthenis, on his way to ratify the Athinian will for peace with Makedon, sent a messenger back to have the people convinced in sending a contingent of re-enforcements to Thermopylae in aid of the small Thivan force holding the pass (to hell with past enmity) before the threat of Makedonian ad- vance, in vain. The Athinian delegates came and stayed in Pella, waiting for the return of the King for weeks on end. Dimosthenis tried to convince the fellow delegates to going and meet Filippos where he was campaigning but they outvoted his proposal. Finally they got a message that the King would meet them at Ferrae in Thessalia.

Filippos met the delegates as he was marching into Thessalia, the pretext being he was about to mend his affairs there. The bulk of his army under Parmenion marched through another pass into Viottia, bypassing Thermopylae and forcing its garrison to return to Thivae. The deed done, Make-donian forces were now active in the affairs of the southern city-states! Filokratis, Dimosthenis, Aes-hinis, Aristodimos and Iatroklis had no choice but to place their names in the peace treaty and re-turned to Athinae to have it displayed publicly on stones. Years later, when Dimosthenis felt strong enough with the favor of his fellow citizens, he accused the rest of the delegates as being in the pay of Filippos (but that is an internal Athinian story and I will skip its details).

As customary by now, Antipatros was left in Makedonia to care about the state and keep an eye on the peripheral enemies. Alexandros and his friends were elated to find out that the ones of younger age would be training with the homeland forces (the older ones were in service under the King in Viottia, or on border patrols under the orders of Antipatros), each attached to a cavalry or foot unit and interchanging positions (in order to familiarize with all tactics). They left again the 'old man' Aristotelis at Mieza to continue with his studies on nature and the cataloguing of species.

The war against Fokis lasted several months but, eventually, the Makedonian forces were victorious giving the final battle of that war at Pagassae, luring the Fokians down from their mountainous country and Filippos was hailed as the savior of Ellas, the man of the hour, respecting (and respected by) the gods and the rights of Delfic sanctity. The King had in mind additional accomplishments aside his military victory and achieved his goals with phenomenal political maneuvering and tact.

First, not wanting to alienate completely any of the southern city-states (for now he had greater goals in his mind), he imposed a yearly payment-fee on the Fokians without bringing the impover-ished state to its knees. He only ordered the exile of its leader Onomahos and dispersed the populous few towns to the country side, demolishing all fortifications. No slavery, no slaughter, no ransom demand—as customary by all previous winners of any wars. Second, he asked (and the Amfiktiony, the pan-Ellenic Council, could not possibly refuse after showering him with such accolades) and received the two seats of Fokis in the Council of Amfiktiones, while securing under his name those seats which belonged until then exclusively to the Thessalian states—but now he was Thessalias'

Tagos/Leader. Now the Makedonian King had his voice heard with a clear sound over the whole country of the Ellenic city-states! He returned to Pella happy with his accomplishments.

Filippos returned home to find Antipatros waiting with anxiety to report the domestic affairs. No family members were present. Olympias was keeping her nose up since their last fight. Arrideos was obviously not in a condition to present himself and was not expected. But what of Alexandros?

Antipatros was quick to report to his King. The boy (actually, a true man—by his deeds—now) was at the frontier in Lynkestis, returning victorious from a battle against Illyrian invaders who (knowing the King's absence south) had raided the country side. Alexandros and his Eteri-friends serving under Klitos' contingent in training, were sent to repulse the invaders. The prince refused to remain in Pella and Antipatros was unable to hold him back. Klitos Melas was seriously wounded (but now recovering in Iraklia) and the prince took upon himself to bring the campaign to a successful con-clusion.

He gave battle and reported through a messenger the full dependence of Derriopia to Makedonia. The prince was speeding to return to Pella, after leaving a strong part of the army to secure Der-riopian compliance to agreed terms. The King had simply arrived sooner than expected, as his son was to be in Pella some time late the next day. Filippos' heart leaped with joy and asked for further details—if any. Now the face of Antipatros grew a bit concerned, not knowing how his King would receive these details.

The King's brows came close together, as Filippos braced against hearing something terrible. He gestured Antipatros to go on. The trusted 'second in command' took a deep breath and informed his King. The prince, taking over the contingent after Klitos' injury at the first skirmish with the invad-ers, achieved his victory (according to the messenger's report) introducing his own first-time-tried innovations of arraying the falanx and attack, a reckless move (once presented to the officers with more war experience) but which proved to be a well thought and calculated move when implemented in battle. Because of that innovation, Alkimon, the Pallinian and leader of the mercenaries in the contingent, was fired on the spot by the prince for reluctance of obeying the orders of battle.

In his place Alexandros had appointed Theoharis son of Dimitrios, house Menelaos of Imathia—and the mercenaries had accepted and loved it! Now, after the result in battle and always according to the messenger's report, Alexandros' name was constantly in the mouth of every trooper with admiration and praise. The word was spread and the home stationed troops were also in love with the abilities of the prince.

As Antipatros' report progressed, the King's eyebrows eased their connection above his eyes and a broad smile ended up lighting his face. "Now that proves I did a good job having this kid, ahmm . . . I mean man, brought to this world! If his innovations proved to be the right thing to do, if his personal judgment of men's capability to follow or not orders is sound, then, why were you so concerned and reluctant to tell me? You should be more concerned if the opposite had happen! He proved confident in himself taking action when needed by placing himself in charge, won us a battle, reinforced Derri-opian dependence on Makedonian hands—as you just said. By the name of all gods I'm proud of him! I only hope his mother would stop turning his mind with her venom! Ah, my friend, you gave me the best news I expected to receive! I grade this higher than what I just achieved in my campaign south! Let us go and have a drink in my study, while you report to me of all the other events which took place here in my absence." Antipatros, his concerns eased, followed his King to his study, making sure to order wine and assortments on their way to it.

Alexandros arrived late after mid-day's meal, escorted by but few of his Eteri-friends, the ones whose horses were able to keep-up with him. Mindful of having past quarrels repeated, he sent a message to his Mother that, he would visit soon after he would clean himself and change. Instead, he hurried to his Father's study, after checking with the sentry in charge as to the King's whereabouts.

Alexandros knew that if his Mother would find out, he would have a big fight in store. His duty to the King and Father though had to come first and quick, regardless of personal differences and feelings. He was by now almost ten plus five years of age. Young kid by all accounts but proved to be a man!

He had his manhood earned in recent past and his leadership in battle just few weeks ago. Most of all, the men had accepted it and adored him! He was anxious to see his Father's reaction on that! He nodded hello to Pafsanias, the man on duty and the King's purported new favorite youth, scratched on the study room's door and entered.

Filippos almost toppled the study table as he rushed to stand with Alexandros' entrance. His face enlivened more with the wine consumed and a good mid-day meal digesting—along with, thus far, excellent domestic affairs running smoothly—at the sight of his son. Past quarrels put aside, the King embraced his son warmly and received an equally warm embrace and kiss from Alexandros. "Son, I am really proud of your performance! I promote you to squadron leadership in our cavalry. You did earn the distinction. Sit down and give me all the details of your campaign and have some of the wine here. It will ease your body pains after such a hurried ride back home. You didn't have to kill horses to make it back here as fast did you?"

"No, Father, I didn't; you've seen to it for us to have the best cavalry in whole of Ellas. True, the animals are exhausted and some could not keep-up with my pace but none perished and, even better, except of the misfortune of having Klitos wounded seriously, none of the men was lost either. I am here to report to you, my King and Father, we returned with only one hundred men wounded, only twenty of them somewhat seriously. Klitos is recuperating in Iraklia Lynkestis comfortably and he should be back with us in a month or so. The rest of the wounded men are on their way here, trans-ported in wagons I ordered made especially for their needs. They should also be arriving within the week ahead. Now, here are the details as to how I operated . . ."

Filippos' face beamed with pride and pleasure. He looked at his old friend and subordinate as like saying: "Didn't I tell you?" Antipatros returned the smile as best as he could, proud of the heir's accomplishments, envying because Kassandros (his own son) would never have done such a deed. He politely asked to be excused, leaving Father and Son in their new-found happy relationship . . .

After Alexandros' report, Klitos the Black was promoted for his valor and wound to the rank of Illarhos, leader of two cavalry squadrons. Yfestion,

Ptolemeos, Filotas, Nearhos, received honors for their valor beyond the call of duty—as did Perdikkas son of Orontis, house of Agis and Polyperhon son of Simias, both Orestians. Olympias was furious learning through her spies of Alexandros' meet-ing with Filippos before the former giving her honors visiting first upon his return. A look at her son—as he entered (finally!) her rooms—convinced her that he was a kid no more and decided to keep her revenge for a more convenient time—perhaps it would find its target easier and hit harder then! She accepted her son all smiles and asked to hear first-hand of his deeds. She later took on Kleopatra with all her anger and fury . . .

Alexandros and his men spent a whole week in Pella enjoying the adoration and entertainment of-fered by the people—now all privy to the prince's accomplishments—before ordered to return back to their studies in Mieza and Aristotelis.

Filippos sent Antipatros (he needed some action to come out of boredom from staying in Pella) against the Thrakian Kersovleptis (in secret—but known to Filippos—alliance with Athinae) who acted with his brothers against Makedonian interests in the region. The capable general successfully con-cluded this campaign, inviting the King to receive in person the strong points of Sirris, Serreon Tihos, Doriskos and Ieron Oros. The Serreon Tihos and Ieron Oros had Athinian garrisons which were expelled, as foreign forces allied to Makedon, on an enemy land.

Kersovleptis retained his king-ship for some more years, contrary to Athinian general Haris' accusations that he was deposed. The next step for Filippos was to secure his new holdings. He moved into the lands of the Laei, Vissae and Agrianes, making sure they understood who they had to deal with from now-on. He returned to Pella bringing hostages, among which the Agrianian king's son—a youth about Alexandros' age.

The King did not have much time for rest in Pella. Reports came from the north-west borders that Vardilis had amassed new Illyrian troops and headed south/east. Filippos made up his mind to put the old fox out—this time for good. He assembled his forces and moved toward the Haonian lands which were in immediate danger. He met Vardilis' forces striking like a lightning and forcing the old foe to sue for peace one more time. Filippos agreed again, making sure this time Vardilis was suc-ceeded by his son and the whole tribe was placed under a severe restriction in movements and having to pay the war expenses, plus an annual tribute.

The following year the Illyrians united under the leadership of Plevr (Plevratos, according to Ellenic appellation) and Filippos was once more warring against them. He completed this campaign soon and with success (to Alexandros' disappointment that his Father had not call upon him to partici-pate) and Plevratos was confined with his tribe of Aridaei above lake Skodra. Filippos returned to Pella with a severe wound on his left leg which kept him permanently limping. Some indication on a brewing attack from Kersovleptis, forced the King to demonstrate one more time his Makedonian supremacy sending Parmenion and Attalos to the job there. The King took a light expedition to the country of Vissae and Sartrae, building a stronghold city at the banks of river Evros, named Filip-poupolis—a constant reminder to theThrakian tribes as to whom the real boss of the area was.

Alexandros and his friends received the news at Mieza and celebrated the event but escorted the letter of well-wishes with the usual, by now, complain of being left behind. Filippos answered that he considered his son's education more important for the time being. There were future wars to come and the King had in mind to allow his son portion of the glory. The prince had to obey.

Lambarh, the young Agrianian prince/hostage was assigned to cleaning the royal stables in Pella, although his status was obviously higher than that of the real stable hands. He did not mind it, for he had the same duties back home, when not on the move because of wars, famine and the like, a stable condition of any tribe between the great mount range of Aemos (Ehmu in his language) and the Rodopi (Rhodpe) range. True to be told, some of these stable hands were initially intimidating bas-tards. Some Ellines, some Thrakians, others Illyrians who had long forgotten their roots and acted like they were the lords and victors—instead of being the vanquished.

Worst of them all were the Ellines who, left to their fate for lack of ransom by their city-states (or purposely kept in bondage by the King—as a lesson and reminder to the ones back home), acted in contempt and tried their best to break his own spirits. After a series of fist-fights and the events being reported to Filippos, the King made it clear that Lambarh (known now as Lamparos) was to be total-ly undisturbed and above any insults to his tribe or to his person. The Makedonian overseer a much decent fellow by the name Kallas (a veteran of many a war and disabled during one), was ordered by the King to see that all would be as Filippos wished.

Kallas thought of transferring Lamparos to the domestic help but the young Agrianian (he could converse in broken Makedonian dialect by now) insisted in remaining at his post as a horse groom. Kallas took the initiative of making him then head of a crew at the stables, a move which was hap-pily approved by the King himself—in spite of the young age of this royal hostage.

Lamparos loved horses. Why, every true Thrakian had the horse on a pedestal so-to-speak. Their very life depended on their horses back home. He took his new task to heart and, soon, he was the living example of horse caring and grooming, his team soon to take equal pride and win numerous favors because of their devotion to their job of keeping at the royal stables the best kept, best trained stock of horses. Before long, Lamparos was trusted to choose the very horse the King himself was to ride on, be it on a war campaign or to the exercise field.

It was a fine spring day, late into the final days of the month Artemisios when Alexandros received the order from his King and Father to return to Pella with his friends for good. Filippos deemed the educational courses being adequate now and, knowing his son's character and eagerness of being in-volved in state affairs, didn't want to push too far. Filippos wanted an all around experienced heir to his throne, not a philosopher/ruler like the Syrakousan pupil of Platon, Dion. Besides, Alexandros was not the person who would want something like that. The young man was open to learning, curi—ocity and want to discover being a major part of his nature, but delving for long on the same sub-jects was not a fruit he liked either. Aristotelis' job was done and rather well. The Teacher received a handsome stipend, enough to get him start his own school (as he desired) in Athinae—and then some. Teacher and pupil parted fondly, with present given to each-other and the promise to keep in touch . . .

Olympias received her son with open arms loading him with presents she personally had made or chose, while she re-established her long held series of tirades and complaints on Filippos' treatment or, in her mind, lack of respect on proper royal status and bloodlines. Before long, family affairs had returned to 'normal', meaning mistrust, hurting one-another and driving Alexandros to moods of extreme changes.

Yfestion had the honor and, to his understanding of a true friend's devotion, the duty to hear the problems and lighten the burden as best he could. He came to hate the Queen and avoided Olympias' presence at all cost! As a member of the elite class of the King's pages and the prince's Eteri squad, he was forced to serve guard's duty at the royal quarters quite often and that was a very difficult task. On those occasions, he was hurting to know he had to stay at his post while Alexandros was storming out of his Mother's rooms, blood drained completely out of his face and eyes turned to that darkest of colors. Some times, if he was lucky, Perdikkas would happen to go by and the young Agis' house descendant (loving Alexandros as much but also knowing he wasn't Yfestion in the prince's mind) would gladly take-on the duty, letting Yfestion go after Alexandros and offer what meager consolation was to be offered. On these occasions (and they were becoming more frequent as the time went by) Yfestion knew the gossip of those who saw him running after the prince would run rampant but he didn't care. His duty, his fidelity and devotion was solely Alexandros' well being and stability of mind. Besides, no one dared to be fool enough in letting his thoughts be heard. Once or twice—at the beginning—fools like Kassandros or Filotas received a good lesson from his fists or those of Per-dikkas and Ptolemeos and they learned . . .

News from the eastern front brought the army in full readiness. Kersovleptis, enticed by secret Ath-inian promises, was moving again in Thraki. The King had to teach one more lesson. Filippos needed a large number of horses to be purchased, as a stock for training and replacement of the ones that would be lost or put-in for pairing the mares for next spring's newborn foals. Daesios, the month of country fairs and local festivities was in its midst. Horse dealers from all parts of Ellas (even from the Persian held Asia-by-the Aegean) were invited to array their stocks to be judged and (hopefully) bought by the King.

It was an outing event for most of Pella's inhabitants, a show-off for most of them and a chance to see and to be seen. The open fields east of the Lydias' mouth to the lagoon were festively decorated and honor wooden benches were placed behind the pedestal and thrones for the King and Queens. The horses would be paraded and tried before Filippos' eyes, to be accepted or rejected. What the King would pass, others of lesser demands could and would buy.

The dealers responded eagerly to any such invitation of the King. Filippos was known as a no non-sense buyer who was willing (and able) to pay good money for the right stuff. Lesser dealers, eager to gain fame either because they happened to have good stock at that time or in hope they could pass what they thought as good, paid hefty commissions to the known ones and let be the first to present their horses to the King. Filippos knew it but didn't mind. Besides, there was always a chance for something unexpectedly good.

The crowd gathered early at the open field and some, eager to bet on the value of the animals, visit-ed the stockades judging and placing their bets on preferred horses. It was a nice sunny day. The remnants of early mist by the shore of the lagoon were lifting, promising an equally warm as festive spring day. Most of the palace help who had no pressing duties to perform, made sure to be a part of it and, among them I, the King's scribe, Evmenis from the city-state of Kardia.

The King's arrival was announced by the call of bugles and the cheer of the long line of onlookers who (not coming early enough) had no choice but to line-up on the road. He was preceded by these very buglers, a small number of his personal guard (to make sure the road would remain open and unobstructed), the ceremonial shield bearer and the King was holding his Queen's hand (public appearances demanded such care). The rest of the royal family was trailing (the heir to the throne, lesser wives/queens and children) and flanked by the rest of the guards (just in case). Every-so-often the King, clad in his festive cuirass, would stop to greed someone either because he liked him or because he deemed it necessary, shaking hands and exchanging few words. He would also motion to the guard to let in few petitioners, taking their written requests and passing them to the secretary on duty for further consideration later.

Filippos arrived at the pedestal with his and Olympias' thrones, waved to the cheering crowds and sat down. The Queen sat on her throne to his left and Alexandros stood on his right, his left hand rested on the King's throne upright back frame. The rest of the royals and nobility took their seats on the benches behind them. The prince had the face of a disturbed youth (another family fight that morning?) but, dressed in his best and the sun shining on him (more so on him than the rest?) he looked like a minor god revealing himself to his faithful.

A designated bugler sounded his trumpet. The show was to begin. Filippos beckoned with a move of his hand. A well-kept youth moved from the back and sat by the foot of the King's throne. Alexan-dros seemed to be taking notice of that face for the first time. He bent to his father and whispered a question. Filippos answered with a smile, pointing at the youth. Alexandros nodded in understanding and smiled back. The youth was none other than Lamparos, the King's own horse groom.

The dealers started presenting their horses. They paraded each one before the King's stand, led by each horse's groom while the dealer numbered loudly the reasons why the King or any of the Make-donians should invest the money for the purchase. As a last proof of the animal's value, the assigned groom would mount the horse and lead it to a trot, a charge or any maneuver was deemed worth the attention and (hopefully) the purchase. That failing, the horse was led out of sight and back to its pen for the next exhibit, at a less demanding court or for a not so-well-to-do Makedonian, provided some small profit would materialize.

As the heat of the day progressed along with the time and show of better horses, servants and small vendors were offering refreshments and sweets or food to King, Queen and nobility, while selling the same stuff to lesser spectators, outside the seats of honor. Several horses were purchased already. Some outright, some after a consultation between Filippos, Kallas who had hobbled at the fair and taken his place on the other side of the royal platform with the throne and Iason, the official royal trainer of horses. Now and then Filippos turned to Alexandros, making or receiving a comment on a certain horse. Father and son seemed to have eased their tension as the show progressed. Olympias sat at her throne seemingly undisturbed, except that her eyes were darting to and fro (hurt when looking at her son, hateful when they were directed at her husband).

Once or twice Iason was ordered by Kallas to mount a certain horse for better evaluation of the ani-mal. Once or twice, Lamparos was asked a question—a thing which never failed Alexandros' notice. Each time it happened, the prince seemed to pay attention to the royal hostage's response and each time he lifted his head with a smile, obviously concurring with the youth's answer—whatever that was.

The most valued chargers started now to parade before the King. The bid for a great purchase was now in full swing, the best dealers bringing forth their pride and choice. Few went by and even fewer were purchased by the nobility, after the King's rejection. The well known Thessalian vendor, Filoni-kos the Farsalian—a very successful horse dealer—presented himself and made the announcement that he possessed the best horse the

King could dream of was about to be presented. Filippos smiled happily because he had previous deals with Filonikos and had never been cheated.

They all waited for the groom who would bring the horse in. Some sort of commotion was already heard from the far pen and the anticipation grew. Instead of the horse with its groom, the commotion coming from the stockade intensified to some alarming degree. Filonikos' face darkened and he started pacing, all concern. Not willing to lose the King's attention and favor, he barked a sharp order to his assistant who hurried running toward the pen. Filonikos excused the delay as being the cause of inept help and drummed his looped whip impatiently against his thigh.

The entrance of a magnificent, all black charger pulled and pronged by several grooms made the entrance to the reviewing ring. All heads turned in admiration toward the spirited horse which, despite the handling of so many hands, seemed unwilling to calm and allow proper presentation. He had a sweat, but (obviously) not because he was ridden; rather the charger was sweating because of his fight against being brought-in, his eyes rolling wildly and his head rearing each time the grooms mistakenly were letting the bridle a bit lose.

Embarrassed, Filonikos made light of it by saying that the horse had obvious high spirits, befitting to its future owner. Filippos, Alexandros, the royal trainer and grooms had been standing up now admiring the horse but skeptical about its willingness to obey. Filippos had his right hand on his face stroking his beard, eyebrows almost connected, in thought. "Are you trying to have me killed by that horse?" he half-joked to Filonikos. "Sire! I wouldn't ever have dared such thought! Let me show you!" Red-faced from anger, he let his whip unfold. The horse reared its head in spite of the hold by so many grooms and one of its forelegs sent one to the dust in untold pain. Filonikos backed a pace in fear. "Well, there you have it!" Filippos said, his good intentions gone. "Better luck with your choices my friend, next time around." He motioned for the horse taken away and another dealer's entrance.

"That would be a total waste!" Alexandros' voice sounded next, full of excitement. Filippos turned to his son obviously disturbed. Was the kid presenting himself a better judge than the King—and in front of all people to see? What kind of folly was this? Had Alexandros forgotten his place or was it a new trick enticed by his mother? He looked at Olympias. The

Queen met his eyes with her usual an-tagonistic expression but nothing more. He looked at his son. Alexandros seemed genuinely concern-ed and truthful in his belief.

"Let me humor the kid" Filippos thought. "No need for a confrontation here in public, unless I find out there's something more behind this outburst of his King's judgment on horses." Turning to his son, Filippos asked him what he meant by stating such opinion. Alexandros replied excitedly but with due respect. "Father, the horse is an excellent one! Obviously they have not treated him properly. He is . . . he is scared of them!" The King looked at his trainer Iason, his stables' overseer Kallas with dis-belief and questioning. The men looked back at him undecided, feeling they were about to tread in hot water. "Sire? May I?" Lamparos' voice soft-spoken and his Agrianian accent more pronounced in his effort not to offend, made Filippos turn. "What!" The King was now truly disturbed. "Sire, I believe prince Alexandros is right . . ."

King Filippos stood there for a moment, his good eye jumping from Lamparos to Alexandros, then to Iason and Kallas. Iason thought the moment had come to diffuse whatever was possibly brewing. "Let me try the horse, Sire. Alexandros may have a point there . . ." There! It was said, he would take his chances. If he failed, well, he would be the one to be blamed, for listening to minors but, the main thing, the goal to avert any public showdown between Alexandros and the King would be avoided.

Filippos gave it a brief thought and nodded his approval. Iason moved slowly toward the animal which now was restless but not offensive. He took the bridle from the hands of the groom and spoke softly to the horse. It seemed to be calming down more and the experienced trainer saw the oppor-tunity. He placed himself rapidly by the horse's side and jumped onto its back. The charger stood for a long moment still. Alexandros and Lamparos started saying excited something like: "No!" At the same time Iason thought, with relief, that his job was done. Then, in no time, the charger reared, came down with force and lifted his hind legs kicking and twisting. Iason found himself kissing the dust!

Iason's face was the prime picture of disbelief as to what happened. So much so, the King had but to laugh and, turning to his son, he asked if that was proof enough for a young one to pay more attent-ion to the elders' knowledge and judgment. "But I am right Father. So much so, I am willing to pay his price myself!" "You will . . . what?! Your allowance—as it is now—will have this horse paid when you will be twenty! And, let me tell you, as your judgment proves to me, I don't think I will be allowing you more money soon!" Now that's a lesson to be learned by imprudent meddling with grown-up affairs. The King dismissed with his hand the Thessalian dealer. "Father! I am willing to have it a try myself!" Alexandros' voice came loud and clear, in his particular sound of absolute faith and determination of knowing what he was doing.

So be it. If the young fool wanted to break his neck, Filippos was now angry enough to allow it to happen. He turned to his son in a challenging manner. "It is a deal then. You tame it, I pay. You fail, you will have to!" Alexandros took the challenge unflinching. He took the pin off his dress cape and let it fall off his shoulders. Yfestion and Ptolemeos with Perdikkas standing right behind him could do nothing but pick it up from the ground. Alexandros moved carefully toward the horse having a look exchanged with Lamparos first. Finding full understanding, the prince smiled at him and pro-ceeded.

Filonikos had lost all the blood from his face. He cursed inward the bad stars letting him fall in such a trap and moved to stop Alexandros. What if the stupid kid would break his neck? He dreaded the thought of it. A look from Alexandros' eyes kept him in place, immobile. He only nodded to his grooms to let the damned horse free. The charger stood undecided in his newfound freedom. Alexan-dros stood before it at some distance and started talking to it, smoothly, for some time. When he observed that the horse now was paying attention only to him, he moved slowly to the side. The horse raised its head and followed, turning his eyes first then his neck, then his whole body, following the movement of the human, beating the ground with his hoofs, uncertain.

Alexandros continued his slow move and sweet talk and then stopped. The late morning sun was hot and casting the youth's shadow to his right and the horse's out of the animal's view. Alexandros rais- ed his hand slowly, keeping the smooth talking. The horse stood still. The young prince edged his way always talking some obviously reassuring words. He came close to the horse's head, placing his forehead against the animal's nose. In the deafening silence, one could hear the distant sound of the limpid waves touching the shore of the lagoon or the occasional fly passing in search of exposed sweets at the vendors' site. All were quiet and in suspense.

Alexandros placed his right hand under the horse's head, where the jaw stops and the neck starts, soothing words continuing. His fingers worked something between caress and tickle and his left hand took the rope hanging from the bridle, without pulling it. The charger raised his head and his ears went back, the eyes alarmed and rolling downward, toward the young man. The voice was soothing though and, feeling no pain or other threat, its head lowered to normal. His hoofs stopped digging the ground. Alexandros kept talking to the horse in a whisper. The charger neighed like in complain and lowered his neck more. Alexandros right hand moved from under the neck to the horse's mane, still caressing. Then, the prince's fist held that part of the mane firmly and, before anyone was able to think what would come next Alexandros was on the horse's back.

The charger stood still, apparently taken by surprise. The prince bent forward whispering still, now his left hand under the horse's head, caressing and rubbing reassuringly. They both stood there for a very long moment. Then, at Alexandros' touch of heels on the charger's sides and a strong voice of encouragement to move forward, both horse and young man on top of it, turned toward the sun and sped out of the fair grounds galloping. A heartfelt cheer came out of the crowd! Filippos was jumping and laughing, clapping his hands in delight. Olympias stood up from her throne, one hand shading her eyes toward the direction her son and the horse had gone. All there was to see was the dust lingering behind them and getting more distant—until that was gone also—toward the plain at the north-east, far off from the lagoon.

Filonikos let a sigh of relief come out of his mouth. Then, his eyebrows creased again. What if the damned horse would throw his rider off out there? He swept the sweat off his face with his hiton. "Oh gods! Let me have a peaceful return to Farsalos!" He looked anxiously, along with the others who started having similar thoughts now, toward the east. After some time (it seemed a very long one) the spec of dust became the outline of a rider on a horse followed by the dust and—to everyone's relief—Alexandros came finally trotting back. Both rider and horse were sweating but (was that pos-sible?) both seemed to be beaming with satisfaction.

The crowd roared in welcoming the young conqueror of horses. Filippos had come down from the royal platform, hands wide open, tears of happiness running down his cheeks wetting his beard. Oly-mpias had also stood-up from her throne, one hand on her breast above her heart, eyes beaming and teary. The royal couple seemed to be in total coincidence of emotions and pride this once.

Alexandros drove the horse to a stop just a few paces before the King and dismounted a perfect dis-mount, by the book of instructions by Xenofon. As the youth's leg went above the horse's neck in doing so the shadow of it run before the animal. The charger's eyes rolled momentarily but he stood still and only snorted. Alexandros nodded to Lamparos who came fast but calmly and took the bridle ropes from the prince's hands. "We were both right, weren't we?" Alexandros said. Lamparos bow-ed his head in agreement. King Filippos looked at both young men questioning. "Take him away now Lamparos, he's still afraid of humans and this crowd here is gone wild!" Alexandros ordered.

Alexandros turned then into the still open arms of his Father. "My King, as you see, there was no-thing wrong with the horse. He's only a spirited one who had the misfortune to be handled by brutes—until now." Filippos held his son tight on his chest, tears of joy and pride still running down his beard. "My son, today you proved yourself once more. This kingdom of mine seems rather small for your inheritance." He kissed Alexandros and had his son's kiss in return. Filippos turned to the crowd lifting his son's hand up. They went crazy. Nobles and common moved forward, each trying to shake hands with Alexandros and Filippos or—at least—come have a close look on both.

Father and son basked in the newfound happiness and closeness. After a while they pushed their way back on the royal platform. Olympias was gone. She had left Kleopatra behind to excuse her. "The Queen had too much of excitement and concern for her son's well being and the emotions run high on her. She had to retire but she'd be waiting to receive her son's visit as soon as all this hoopla was over and done." Filippos and Alexandros lost some of their beaming from their faces, each on his own thoughts for what was to come. The crowd's adorations and cheer brought them back to the happiness of sharing common ground. The presentation of other horses resumed. Filippos paid the agreed amount to Nikomahos (nowhere near to what eventually has come to be believed) and the dealer hurried out, thanking the gods for his good luck. "I did notice that the horse had been abused and that he also was scared by his own shadow. Lamparos noticed that too." Alexandros said to his Father. "Did you see the white mark he has on his forehead Father? Looks like a bull's horns. I know now his name. I will be calling him Voukefalas!"

The King hugged his son over the shoulders with one hand and placed another kiss on Alexandros' head. He motioned to him to sit on the

Queen's empty throne next to him. Lamparos now returned and asked for permission to speak. That given, he reported to Alexandros that the horse had been rubbed-down and given fodder and fresh stall. Alexandros thanked him and said on a matter of fact tone that henceforth only the two of them were to be the charger's caretakers. Turning to the King, he expressed his desire to have Lamparos moved to his own quarters as a royal guest of Alexandros himself. Filippos thought it was too much for a barbarian's son (royal or not) but, not wanting to spoil the happiness of the day, readily agreed.

Olympias turned all the fury of her hate to the first made she ran to, on the fact that her son looked so happy in the arms of the King and Father. Then, on Alexandros when he (finally) came to her quarters for the usual and established visit. "You think I pained for your birth and raised you to become one with that woman chaser that drunkard fondler of young men? The gods should have burned me alive before blinding me to accepting his marriage in my line of family. He allows you to go and break your neck riding such a horse and then pretends to be proud of your folly. What does he care? He claims to be capable of producing more sons and what he comes up with? An idiot and baby girls out of inferior blood lines, leaving me, the true Queen and taking away my own son!"

Alexandros was conciliatory at the beginning of her tirade. "Mother, he is my Father and King! I know he didn't think I was going to succeed and wanted to teach me a lesson. Like most, he had not pay true attention to that horse and he didn't mind me showing him he was wrong! . . ." "Your Father?! Ha! He's nothing! I had my dream the night before our so-called wedding. The God Father i s your Father! And let me tell you . . ." Alexandros didn't let her finish. The blood drained (as al-ways was during their fights) from his face. He stormed out of the room and was gone. He didn't visit her again for several days.

The war against the Thrakians was in full swing. Filippos was forced to advance further north-east, to the banks of the river Istros, coming to blows with Skythian tribes who crossed the river in allian-ce with some Thrakians. So much so, that he overextended his lines and was forced by necessity to retreat. On his way back he met with a near disaster. Skythians and Thrakes set an ambush and he had several of his army killed. In the middle of winter (his campaign had lasted longer than anticipated) he retired in the lands of the Vissae, above Rodopi and by the valley of river Evros. His troops almost revolted because of the hardship they encountered and their loss of all the booty collected thus far.

Filippos managed to bring things back to order, with the help of the trusted Parmenion and his new son-in-law Attalos. The King rewarded both handsomely. He ordered the building of another city-stronghold in the midst of the Trivallian lands which he named Kavyli, so he could have a start point—in case of future campaigning there. He returned to Pella after a long and arduous campaign married to yet another woman, the daughter of Kottel (Kothelas) a Sarmatian king who had aided Filippos, from the area of the Ellenic colony (and now free city-state) of Odissos—the one by the river Tyras/Danastris (either name is in use). Her name was Medh, Ellenized to Meda.

Alexandros tried in vain to convince his Mother that the new bride was nothing more than a wedding of political convenience. She accused him of siding with the King, simply because he was also a man. He saw there was nothing but more fighting in store and he gave-up. Not knowing where to direct his frustration and anger, he devoted his time exercising. He spent more time among the training fields of the falanx, the cavalry and, discovering an old chariot, he had it refitted, teamed with horses and—as it would be driven either by Yfestion or Lamparos—he ran after it and would jump-on or jump off it in full speed!

Filippos observed all these and kept his anger to himself. Olympias was just by name only his Queen now. He thought many a time to send her back to Ipiros but he needed her brother (the king of Mol- ossians now) his ally and flank protector against the Illyrians. Alexandros of Molossis and brother of Olympias was proven a very good friend and admirer of Filippos, to the point that his sister had many a time accused him of being in love with the King (something that simply was not true). Now that he was the king of the Molossians and had (with Filippos' help) the Haonian tribe of Ipirotes accepted him as overlord, he felt more obligated in following the Makedonian chariot and leadership. Certainly, Filippos was not about to disturb this relationship.

Filippos took time to go to Thessalia and settle things there his way, as the proclaimed Tagos/leader of all Thessalian states. Rivalry between Farsalos, Larissa and Ferrae was not to be allowed or toler- ated any longer. His affairs there held him for several months. Upon his return to Pella, he faced a double jeopardy.

His favorite (in recent years) Pafsanias, the Orestian in the body guard of the King, being off duty at the time Filippos was in Thessalia, came to odds with one of Attalos' men who—in turn—was seek-ing Filippos' favors. Attalos invited then Pafsanias to a dinner ostensibly to bridge the difference and have the by-gones be by-gone. Instead, he made sure Pafsanias was intoxicated to the highest and had his servants molest him and throw him out on the street!

Pafsanias asked for an audience and could not be turned down. Filippos heard his just complains but he could do nothing, for two reasons. One, Attalos was Parmenion's son-in-law and any move against him would bring the King at odds with his best general and, second, Attalos had shown such a bravery during the last campaign in Thraki, Filippos had promoted him to generalship and the man was liked by his troops! It took Filippos' politician manners and persuasion to calm Pafsanias down a bit and named him leader of the King's bodyguards.

Filippos knew that Attalos should not have done what he did. But he had little option—if any—on taking any action against him. Instead, gave his word that his further relation with Attalos' friend as the King's favorite had—as proof of faith and sympathy—ceased existing. Pafsanias accepted the judg-ment with reluctance.

Olympias was first to know of the incident through her numerous spies who she favored and they had hopes on return favors and promotions, as she was still the Queen, and tried to inform to Alex-andros her version of the event. I happened to be talking to Antigonos son of the Elimiote Filippos who—at the time—was assigned guard duty at the entrance of her quarters and could not help but hear their argument. Alexandros, the moment his Mother started her usual tirades and before she got to the 'meat' of her venom and ire for Filippos, cut his Mother courteously but firmly off, telling her that he was not interested at all on the King's personal troubles. Curiously, she did not insist and the start of a quarrel remained just a start. The rest of their conversation was switched to mother and son type of visit, as she asked and was sent for sweets and wine. I saw Alexandros later and he was very calm and collected.

The King, having the solution to this problem pronounced, turned his attention to state matters.

He discovered that his son had engaged an ili/squadron of Eteri cavalry exercising with a shorter type of sarissa, the pike his foot Eteri/companions were using with such a success. The King curious and somewhat bothered why his son had taken the initiative without consulting him first, called Alex andros to a hearing. The prince presented himself before his Father rather irritated, as he knew the reason of being summoned.

Father and son had few words before proper explanations were exchanged. Alexandros pointed out that these lighter but well equipped cavalry could and should work as prodromi/scouts, along with even lighter equipped psili troopers, as a necessary force of guarding the flanks and scouting ahead.

Had that been the case, no hardship would have occurred on the latest Tharkian campaign.

Filippos thought of his days of innovation while his brother was the King, and agreed. Some damage in his relation with his son had occurred again though. The King in an effort to recover lost ground asked for a large scale of mock battle, arraying the foot falanx with the cavalry and allotting to Alex-andros the leadership of the newly formed divisions of scouts. The result was beyond expectation and Filippos made sure to pronounce that loud and clear before everyone. Alexandros thanked his Father and politely but coolly asked for permission to withdraw. It was time, he said, to go and exercise Vou-kefalas (the horse was not used—unless necessary) with Lamparos and Yfestion. Filippos nodded dismissal (now peeved but keeping his temper).

"Ptolemeos, Yfestion, Perdikkas and Krateros had a few cups of wine with me and told me the story. For you who -in reality- has no true idea as to how the Makedonian army since King Filippos took over the kingdom and brought it to such a prominence now operates, I have to open here a paren thesis and let you know how it all worked and I will show (I hope) why we love being Makedonians even if some of us were not born here."

"Le sort d'une bataille est le resultat d'un instant, d'une pensee. On s'approche avec des combinaisons diverses, on se mele, on se bat un certain temps; le moment decicif se presente; une etincelle morale prononce, et la plus petite reserve accomplit."
Napoleon Bonaparte.

XII

King Filippos—as we all know by now—took over a very poorly equipped and undisciplined army (excepting his own trained taxis/battalions) at the death of his brother and a kingdom ready to fold. Through his experience from his captivity in Thivae as a hostage and his improvements and inno-vations, he brought Makedonia in a state of eminence, a power most of the city-states (as well as the barbarian neighbors) now feared and respected!

He, firstly, equipped the foot soldiers (the rag-tag of the past) with the extra long pikes from cornel-wood and about twenty two feet long, with a leaf-like blade in front and an extra heavy (for balance) blade aft. In case this new pike (called sarissa) would break, the footman could use the other part as a shorter spear, even as a javelin. Also, in cases of an enemy cavalry attack, this aft blade served as anchor on the ground, steadying the sarissas as they pointed at the oncoming riders and horses.

Secondly, he installed discipline in his falanx of footmen and demanded vigorous training, a thing unheard of prior to his taking over. During exercises he had the foot soldiers carry sarissas of two extra feet in length and full protective gear with thorax, shield, sword and greaves. He also had them carry at least three day's worth of provisions and reduced the burden carriers to just one per ten men. Thus, most of the equipment was to be carried by the soldier himself, making him strong and able to withstand all kinds of hardship.

Thirdly, he never stopped the training or the campaigning, regardless of weather conditions. That was an extra advantage against the enemy who, usually, campaigned in good weather only. The horse Eteri/companions, being of rank and file of the nobility, were also forced to train alongside the foot, thus receiving a good knowledge of combined maneuvers and delivering a decisive blow on the enemy when and where it counted most.

The foot falanx was divided in semi-independent sections (for added freedom to take advantage when called for) but in close enough unity with the rest, so to present a unified and easy to guide front. Each small unit of the falanx was the lohos of sixteen men, each bearing the sarissa, a smaller than usual shield hung from the left shoulder, a sword for thrusting and cutting (with a curve on the cutting edge for blows over the opponent's shield) when needed and was led by its Lohagos (usually the grad-uate from the last page class serving the King) and his assistant, the Ouragos.

Four lohos units (lohi) made a tetrarhia led by the Tetrarhis. Two of these tetrarhies made a taxis led by its Taxiarhos. In turn, two taxis combined made a syntagma which was led by a Xenagos or Syntagmatarhis. Four of these make a hiliarhia (also called taxis) and is led by the Hiliarhos and, four hiliarhies constitute a simple falanx which had approximately four thousand and ninety six men, counting heralds, trump-eters, standard bearers and adjutants.

Since the King got a permanent hold of the Pangaeon mountain area with its gold mines and having under his control the silver mines of Paeonia and Parorvilia regions, he has the luxury of the best hired oplites from the rest of Ellas, men who, not having enough land to sustain them at their indi-vidual city-states, have taken the role of the professional soldier and went to the service of the highest paymaster. They are not as reliable as the home troops but Filippos has a very strong will, he is as fair as one can be and keeps them in strict discipline. They provide their own equipment, as they are used to it and fight according to their standard—but dare not deviate from the King's well explained battle array as it's outlined to them before each battle starts.

The contingents of the peltastes, these rather light equipped oplites are the King's support troops and his defeated enemy chasers. Armed with small shields and carrying a spear and sword, they help the 'psili' who are slingers and archers to open the hostilities, then, upon victory, they chase the enemy away, bringing his casualties even higher. They have as vigorous a training as the rest of the troops.

Since the King became the Tagos of all Thessalian states, the army has been augmented by the excellent Thessalian cavalry units, for many years the best in all Ellas—except that now the Makedon-ian cavalry iles/squadrons are better even than those from Farsalos. These Thessalian iles are divided and operate the same way and have the same armor and equipment as the Makedonian ones. In bat-tle, they attack in rows of four abreast and the King has seen to it that they can turn on any direction upon a given signal, so they can form a new line of attack thus changing their direction to where is most needed. Prince Alexandros is training his ili of Makedonian horse to a new form, him being on the lead and then the rest progressively forming a wider line. They create this way a kind of wedge, capable of penetrating the enemy lines and splitting them apart!

I know, I sound too proud for a non Makedonian but, most of us have developed this pride because of King Filippos' abilities to install in all of us pride for belonging to a state which is just to its citi-zens, with no constant strife, or political changes and—through them—exiles or property confiscations and (in no few occasions) murder. Obviously here we have one man ruling us all, the King. But the King—if only out of tradition and Makedonian decency—has to listen to his people and, if their comp-laints are just, he has to respond immediately! We have among us now Mytilinians, Kritans, Thrak-ians and a whole bunch of other Ellines who gladly accepted a Makedonian identity and citizenship on their own accord. As long as one abides with the laws and traditions of Makedon and serves the King within the limits of common decency without being a burden to anyone, gets the King's approv-al and is accepted by the rest of the citizens.

I know, I was telling you of the army . . . Ah, yes! The King has also invested in hiring several of the most known engineers, be they Makedonians, Thessalians or from other parts. He has them build siege machines, bridges and other war equipment, such as katapeltes and vallistes. The former are huge wooden bows on platforms on (or without) wheels for their transport. Their have a twisted cord of animal guts attached to the ends of the bows and these are mechanically tensed to give the pro-pelling power to the heavy and long arrows they are to send toward the enemy. These arrows cover treble the distance the best regular bow can, and pierce several rows of opponent oplites! The latter are supposed to have been invented by the Finikians and work in sending heavy stones or metal balls on the walls of a besieged city or fort, eventually tearing the walls down and allowing entrance to our troops.

The engineers also instruct their work force to build siege towers on wheels which are brought be-fore the walls and, either use the battering ram (covered in them for safety) to tear a wall down or (made taller than the walls) throw a bridge on them and our troops get on those walls with less risk than using simple ladders. These machines are protected from fire by having fresh animal skins laid in such a way as to cover against every possible ignition coming from the defenders. There are open-ings through which javeliners and archers can keep on firing, depriving the defense any real chance of getting the upper hand. Obviously, ladders and other older-invented equipment are in use too. The Thessalian Polyidios, his right-hand Diadis and many others contributed to creating these new machines—as well as improving the old ones.

Sappers are also an integral part of the King's forces. They are entrusted the mining under the walls of any besieged city or fort, forcing part(s) to collapse and giving an entrance to our troops. They are also to detect and stop the countermining from the defenders and help fill the moats in parts for the final assault. Last—but by no means least—come the contingents of cooks, supply experts, wagoners and onager drivers who are responsible of the well being of the army on the move.

What is most important in such a structure is the fact (and everybody is made to understand this) that all are subject to their merit! There are no promotions, no favors because of who knows whom!

Several times (and I know this first-hand) the Queen has put pressure to either the King or to Alex-andros for better placement of one of her favorites. The King has flatly refused any such favor (an-other reason for their constant fights). Alexandros, having such love for his Mother, doesn't openly refuse (unless it's of utter importance) but never has given room to such convenience unless it is based on true merit.

Filippos is recognized by almost everyone as the King with a 'fair hand' although (I am sure) there are many who don't see it that way. These people are mostly the declared enemies of Makedonia, the undeserving favorites of the Queen or some lord's or clan head's minions and the ones on Athinian, Thivan or (even) Persian pay. From Sparti there isn't much we hear lately, as the Spartans are still licking the wounds Thivae had given them few years ago.

Granted there have been set-backs on many an occasion but, as the King is fond of saying, he just takes a 'breather' or withdraws a bit, in order to charge even harder the next time, like a ram does! And, recently, he gave (in my presence) a sample of his good humor too! Having Parmenion and An-tipatros present for a serious state matter (I was keeping notes) and to save time, he had his barber come in for a hair and beard trimming. When the man asked the King how he'd like that done, Fil-ippos said: "In silence!" In most occasions he tries to show reason to his opponents and, in many instances, has just proved that. Many cities have come to realize their alignment with Makedonia is much more profitable that fighting against and that is due to King Filippos' reasoning and his open arms. He is very proud of his ability to save lives when it comes to that. But he also knows how to strike hard and without mercy. In general, Filippos pays what is due when it is due.

Most of the newer territories of our Makedonian state (some incorporated during the Persian in-vasion and becoming independent at the difficult times during the reign of King Amyntas) have already assimilated themselves and all their citizens consider the fact that Filippos is their natural King. They/we all love the freedom of approach we have at any given time, for praise or complaint. We have the right to call him by his name and discuss matters with him as equals. The Thivan and Athinian slurring of his name is (to us) nothing but an indication of true envy. Unable to defeat him in war—as well as in politics and reason—they do nothing else but call him (and us) names, because Dimosthenis would love to have the Athinian leadership revived at the expense of Makedonia. Yet, as democratic as Thivae or Athinae like to present their states, one (anyone) of their citizens needs to make an appointment to discuss his problems with the Arhon of the year or the ruling Arhons, unless the problem is brought before the general assembly at given dates.

But I think you understood—by now—my meaning of all these things and it's time to return to the unfolding of the events as I have recorded them.

Filippos received word that Thraki was on the rise again, its tribes and kings ready to believe the A-thinian propaganda of Dimosthenis. Filippos had to act fast, his belief being that attack is the best form of defense. The independent city-states of Perinthos and Vyzantion being Athinian allies have had a heavy role on the Thrakian unrest. The King made-up his mind in teaching yet another lesson. Before marching against them, he sent envoys asking those city-states to surrender (according to the last treaty with Athinae they were to have been allies to us) with the promise of a fair treatment.

They refused. Filippos marched then into Thraki delivering a good blow on the Idonians and Odo-mantes, bringing both regions under Makedonian rule by forcing their kings to abdicate. He sent a good number of notables (along with these two kings) to Pella to serve as hostages and incorporated the two regions into the Makedonian kingdom, having now the river Nestos as its eastern frontier.

Before marching further against Perinthos, he sent the Agrianian prince/hostage (guest, according to Alexandros) back to his country, the youth promising to convince his father to aid the Makedonian forces by pressuring the Thrakian tribes of Trivalli and Vissae, while the King would march through the lands of the Satrae, Sappaei and Vistones, quelling the unrest. To tell the truth, Filippos wasn't so sure that Lamparos would fulfill such a promise. Alexandros though was very convincing and sure of his trust on the barbarian 'friend' of his.

As it happened, the Agrianes proved faithful allies bringing the Vissae and Trivalli to reason and the King crossed from the southern approaches unopposed, as the Thrakians changed their minds and sided once more with him. The only concern was from the Odrysses, but they withdrew their forces further north-east and Filippos arrived at Perinthos without any loss and set-up his siege of the city.

Athinae was up in arms with this development but could do nothing as they were unprepared for war. Dimosthenis convinced the Athinians to send an embassy to the Persian court asking for help. The High King of Persia Artaxerxis (Artaxsaca), the third Persian High King by that name, feared that Filippos was ready to cross into Asia after Perinthos and Vyzantion and declared war. He sent the brother of Memnon, the Rodian mercenary Mentor to aid Perinthos with money and his advice in withstanding the siege. Mentor brought with him several ships with supplies and a few good miners who took over the building of a counter-mining force from the city, their aim being to force the col-lapse of the King's tunnels when tried undermining the city walls.

Soon the siege was turning into a long time consuming proposition, costing lives and money. The Persians also started transporting troops on the Thrakian peninsula (with obvious permission from Athinae and Vyzantion) causing the King to withdraw some of his troops before the city walls and send them to guard his flank. Worst, Vyzantion knowing the King's navy being inadequate for a sea-side guarding of Perinthos, they were sending troops and provisions by sea.

Filippos had to ask for reinforcements from home. He had prince Alexandros stay in Pella as the regent, with the experience of Antipatros at his disposal. When the messenger arrived asking for additional troops, Alexandros took the opportunity presented. He ordered Antipatros to remain in charge of the state's affairs in Pella and took the falanxes and cavalry he was training with for so many months toward the east and in support of his Father and King.

They arrived before the siege army's camp grounds at Perinthos within few days' time but not be-fore meeting and receiving reinforcement from Lamparos and his Agrianians, giving a decisive battle on their way against a mixed army of Vissae and Odrysses who, unwisely, tried to block the way. Ale-xandros ordered the building of a station/city within the lands of the Satrae, by the springs of river Ardos, as a forward starting point for the Makedonian forces—in case the Thrakian tribes needed a strong reminder as to who's the boss! He, naturally, named this city Alexandropolis.

Filippos was happy to receive his son with the new troops and, when he was told about the battle on the way to meet him and the city/station, he gave his son a questioning look escorted with a smile. Al-exandros gave details of the battle (to the King's delight) and excused his naming of the city as a pre-caution to his Father's achievements stating that, as things were going with his Father's success and city building, unless acting now, there would be no chance for him to build a city or a glory to rest upon.

Filippos embraced his son laughing and pointing him to Parmenion, Attalos and Klitos Melas, who happened to be present. Klitos laughed along heartily. Parmenion looked at his King, then at Alex-andros and shook the latter's hand expressing wishes for a more glorious future. Attalos offered his wishes for future success to both—the King and Alexandros—rather absentminded, his excuse at Fil-ippos' questioning eye being that he was preoccupied with the urgent problems of the siege. The King dismissed him off handedly, saying that the city was going nowhere and the plans to press harder the very next morning were in order. He gave Alexandros another hug and ordered for their meal.

The pages on duty (among them Meleagros son of Neoptolemos—house Apellas), Menandros from Sythonia (house Asteropeos), Iraklidis of Antinoos (house of Pallas from Vottiaea) at the order of the somatofylax/ guard of the King (Pantordanos son of Kleandros—house Pelegon from Pelagonia) run to place the order passing by the head of the guard Pafsanias who (never again in the same room with Attalos) was stationed outside the royal hut (built for the siege and serving the needs of the King).

As the next morning came, there was a general assembly of officers and a conference took place for the next attack on the city walls set to start the day after at first light. Every possible way of achiev-ing a quick victory was studied thoroughly and all kinds of measures were proposed and taken. The siege was already taking a long time and, the longer it took for a final resolution, the more restless the neighboring tribes could become (aided by Athinian promises and Persian gold). The assault went as was scheduled. Alexandros' troops, eager to show their recent upgraded value before the

King were more than commendable, followed by the rest of the troops' willingness not to be outdone.

Antigenis from house Damasias from Paeonia lost his eye there. Yet, this assault had no better end than the many previous ones. The Perinthians put up a very solid defense, aided by arrivals from Vyzantion—via sea transports. Filippos was forced to call the attack off.

At the meeting after this failed attempt, the King was very irritated and no one could blame him, as he could not blame anyone else among his generals and troops either. He decided he should simoulta—neously attack Vyzantion. The move, he proposed, would prevent any further aid to Perinthos from that Athinian ally and give the opportunity sought for the take of the city.

He split his grand army in three parts. He left Parmenion with all the mercenary troops and the engineers to continue the siege of Perinthos. He appointed Alexandros to take his own and sweep the coastal areas of recently 'allied' city-states in southwestern Thraki, as they were reported to start staging yet another revolt against him. He took the rest of the Makedonian troops for his unheralded attack on Vyzantion.

Alexandros did not have much trouble in his campaign on the Thrakian shores and the eastern Hal-kidian peninsula. He reduced the ones who resisted with a speed that left them wonder at the youth who was fighting like a veteran of many wars and, received renewed assurances of friendship from the wise ones who could see clearly who had the upper hand. He returned to Perinthos in support of Parmenion on the continuing siege of Perinthos, only to find that his King and Father had also return from Vyzantion, failing to take the city by surprise.

The King had arrived before Vyzantion undetected. He chose a cloudy night for the surprise attack—wooden siege towers ready beforehand and rolled in silence against the walls. From that moment on, nothing went right! The clouds parted before a full moon, the city dogs started barking and every citizen-soldier was alerted up at the ramparts. Not having with him enough troops for a sustained as-sault or properly staged siege, he was forced to withdraw fast. "That damned, unpredictable Propon-tis weather!" Filippos was mad because of this failure. He set his plans before Perinthos one more time and wished the damned city would finally fall.

Father and son worked diligently with Parmenion and Attalos and the rest of the officers for solut-ions. As they were conferring one day, a big commotion was heard from the camp. They all got out of the hut to see what this was all about. It was reported to the King that some of the mercenary troops had gotten to fighting with some of the Makedonians from Orestis, on some spoils they had interest on, taken from the countryside and the little quarrel had taken unforeseen proportions as the officers in charge unable to restore order.

Filippos became very angry. Without a word, he motioned the man reporting the squabble to give him a leg for mounting the horse he'd come up with. Alexandros asked him to arm himself first before going down to the troops but the King dismissed the idea as making too much out of nothing he couldn't handle as was and kicked the horse forward. The prince noticed the horse was restless with an unknown rider on its back and, worried, he asked for his own to be brought with speed. He also asked Pafsanias to assemble the guards and be ready for action. He went into the hut and armed putting his sword belt on and grabbing a javelin. Voukefalas was waiting for him and he mounted, following the direction his Father had gone. Pafsanias meantime was assembling the guards and Yfestion had summoned the pages, to follow in support, hopping he wouldn't be late.

Filippos had arrive by the quarreling troops, now numbering several hundred. He raised his voice and the outliners made room for him to pass toward the center of it all, while closing in behind him.

His horse became more frightened by the noise and reared. The King unprepared for such a move fell off and under it. A big shout rose from the quarreling troops: Teasing and insulting calls from the mercenaries, a horrified one from the Makedonians. Alexandros kicked his horse to a gallop, calling for support "The King is down! The King is down!" Pafsanias and Yfestion with the guards and pages in tow, rushed forward wishing to be on time to help.

Alexandros, urging Voukefalas and uncaring on who got stampeded, arrived in time to see that one of the mercenaries had killed the King's horse, causing it to fall on top of Filippos and immobilizing the King under it! He threw the javelin against the offender, piercing him trough. The crowd pulled back momentarily, stunned. The prince dismounted and, keeping Voukefalas as shield on his back, drew his sword and cut the throat of the next mercenary who—imprudently—had raised his, ready to deliver a blow. This speedy action forced a wider circle to open and gave room for Alexandros. He noticed the eyes of the mutineers turned on their purported leader and the man was marked.

Anxious voices were heard approaching from behind him and, as Alexandros turned he had time to see Pafsanias dispatching another mercenary who had his spear raised to strike from behind and Yfestion covering with his shield his friend and prince from yet another blow. He sent them both a thank-you look and redirected his attention on the fallen King. Filippos looked stunned but unhurt and unable to move under the dead horse. With the guards and pages now in place and more Makedonians on hand, the mutiny was over. The leader of the mercenaries marked, was put in chains and later executed before the whole army, along with several of his accomplice. Filippos put all his mercenary forces under the leadership of Makedonian officers, instructing them to keep a keen eye on them and report any and all minor incidents to him immediately. But the lesson was received and understood already. No further incident ever occurred after that and the siege continued.

Now Alexandros was ordered to return to Pella. Filippos did not want to keep more than the neces-sarily needed troops before Perinthos, in case Athinae would entice the Illyrians again in undertaking another raid against Makedonia.

Alexandros returned and took over the regency from Antipatros who, as we know, was left to guard the Makedonian interests back home. Queen Olympias informed by her spies of the incident before the walls of Perinthos, wanted to know from her son its details first-hand. Alexandros fell for it and, with the innocence of a man assisting his Father and King in time of danger, let her know everything. That led to a stormy fight. She wanted to know how Alexandros didn't take advantage of the situ-ation and let the old 'unfaithful, pederast, polygamist bastard' find an end he rightly deserved and proclaim himself King! Alexandros looked at her like one would see a viper ready to strike and said so. The shouts could be heard through the hall outside the Queen's chambers and a horrified Antigo-nos son of Filippos of house Agathon from Pieria came later to my room to tell me—after oaths of secrecy and several cups of unaltered wine.

The prince brought forth the duty of a son to his Father and King, chastising the Queen for her im-moral thoughts and wishes. She had answered laughing to his face that Filippos was anything else but his father and it was she who had conceived him through divine intervention and will. Alexan-dros asked her then to prove it to him and her answer was she'd do it in due time. After that, the prince had left her room slamming the heavy door behind him, all blood absent from his face. It has been over two weeks now since the fight without him even sending a word to her—let alone visiting as in the past.

We, Alexandros' friends gathered last night to see if there was anything we could do to ease his pain especially now that we received the news of the King forced to lift the siege and battling against Triv-allian intruders aided by Skythians under king Atthea (Atheas) from above the river Istros and Athinian promises for a free hand in looting—if they were successful in killing the 'tyrant'. The King was forced to move against them, his troops tired from such a long siege and set-backs, with disast-rous result. He was defeated, wounded on the same lame leg once more and forced to withdraw to Filippoupolis for recovery and restructure of his army. Parmenion was assigned to be in charge of rebuilding its moral while the King was fighting for his life from the wound.

After a long time of debate as to how we could do anything, it came to conclude that we should stay out of it and keep as low a profile as possible. Many feared Olympias' wrath, others of the King (no business of ours to get involved in his family's business) but most of us thinking of the damage such involvement would do to Alexandros. We decided to be as accommodating to him as we could, with-out any hints of our knowledge regarding his latest show-down with the Queen. This was a recom-mendation of Filotas and Yfestion with which Ptolemeos agreed (a rare phenomenon) with him.

Alexandros continued to govern with the help of Antipatros, keeping away from his Mother. When time would allow him the luxury, he was exercising with us or used the chariot to mount or dis-mount it while in full run. On rare occasion he would join us for a drink and the subject invariably would come to state that he regretted he had not continue his campaign on the way to Perinthos further north, renting the Trivallians incapable of any ability to act against the King. He swore, next time he would go all the way to Istros and put the Skythians to the place they belonged. But now we had to wait for the King's recovery and pray he'd have it soon.

News from the south city-states were coming urgently to the court in Pella now. The Delfian League was accusing Athinae (via Thivae) of dedicating their new treasury at Delfi to god Apollon without first consecrating it (the true offence being their dedication inscription: these <dedicated> shields were taken from the invading Persians and Thivans fighting against Ellas). Athinae had sent a dele-gation of three to answer the accusation. Among them, Aeshinis. He handled his assignment with success, accusing instead the Amfissians (Thivan allies) of impiously cultivating fields dedicated to god Apollon and gaining the Amfiktionic vote against them. The Amfiktiones then convened at Ther-mopylae, to pass judgment on Amfissa.

They formed a sort of a league against them, opting to create an army to ensure obeisance—with force if necessary. They knew though that this would be an almost mute proposition, because no city-state was adequately prepared to field such a force. All show would be a token one, unless the Makedonian King, the one who marched against the impious Fokians not long ago, would consent to intervine.

Alexandros, to Antipatros' relief, decided to wait the return of his Father for an official policy on this subject. Reports were now coming from Filippoupolis that the King was recovering, the fever was gone and he should be coming back soon. At the same time Alexandros was happy to have Aes-hinis score a per-sonal triumph against Dimosthenis. He liked the former actor since he had first met him years ago and was happy he had narrowly escaped Dimosthenis' accusations of complicity to Makedonian interests and on the payroll of Filippos.

Now Dimosthenis was in a bind, not wishing to antagonize the Thivans, as the Amfissians were their allies. He was dreaming of an alliance of Athinae and Thivae against Makedon, in spite of all the past enmity between the two city-states. He would love to have an alliance with them but he feared the Athinian public had not forgotten the Medizing of Thivae against Ellas when Xerxis invaded. Make-donia was a Persian ally then too, but it was because Makedon had no choice at that time. Thivae had volunteered her services to the invader. In later years Athinae declared openly against Thivaean in-terests of dominating Viottia. Filippos had accepted that dominance, and Thivae as his nominal ally. Dimosthenis was a declared enemy of Filippos but was not a fool. He had to wait.

His last fight with his Mother being an old incident by now and half-forgotten, Alexandros resumed his visitations to the Queen's chambers and—to her questioning—was open with the state affairs. He caught her a few times being at the statue of Ekavi and chanting strange prayers and his mind went to the unlucky barks of the dogs at Vyzantion and the King's almost fatal wound. Seeing no guilt in the eyes of her blank face and finding no reason to suspect further after discreetly interrogating the maids attending her and his sister Kleopatra, he dismissed the idea.

His free time continued to be devoted to his personal exercise, the home troops and, now and then attending to his half brother Arrideos and the seven-year old half sister Thessaloniki, born to Filip-pos by his third wife Nikesipolis from Ferrae, Thessalia. Kleopatra was more fond of the other sister, Kynnani (fondly called Kynna), a matured girl now, fathered by the union of the King with the Illyr-ian Avdata many years after the nuptials and during one of Filippos' great fights with Olympias, during which the King had remembered the grand-daughter of his former enemy Vardilis existence in the royal household. Kynna was now betrothed to cousin Amyntas, son of Perdikkas.

Kleopatra (it was whispered in Pella) was in love with Perdikkas son of Orontis, house Agis, and the young man was equally fond of her but did not dare to go and ask for her hand. He was a close friend of Alexandros, that could not be denied and the family, the clan, had been supporting the Timenides royal house for generations since the times of first King Perdikkas and the Orestian Alketas. But still young Perdikkas and Kleopatra felt they could love one-another from a distance. She was too timid a girl (Makedonian custom on women's contact not being helpful), she feared her Mother (Olympias would take on her whatever frustrations she had— or thought she did) and her relation with her King and Father was almost nonexistent. Perdikkas, on the other hand, respected his King and valued his friendship with Alexandros so much, he never dared to even hint on his affection for Kleopatra.

Letters to and from Thraki were a daily exchange and (as the bad winter weather) the King's recov-ery was slow coming to an end. The King instructed Alexandros to remain as regent in Pella but to send Antipatros to Delfi as the Makedonian delegate in the name of the King. There, Antipatros was to support covertly the move of the city-states to chastise the Amfissians for their impiety, gauging the stance Thivae and Athinae would take. The leadership of the Delfic league, the Amfiktiones, had fallen on the shoulders of Kottyfos from Thessalia and, Filippos being Thessalia's designated Leader /Tagos, Antipatros' job shouldn't be too difficult.

The talk of Alexandros with his friends shifted from the teachings of Aristotelis and their applicat-ion to the everyday's life. He missed his favored dog Perittas (the animal had recently die) and his Queen-Mother's persistence that he should start looking for a suitable bride irked him. The possibil-ity of an upcoming war in the south irked him more. Alexandros had many hours of talk with his most trusted friend Yfestion about his personal problems with the Queen and the King. Their friend-ship had grown to a point of no return, to a point which bad-mouthing people made suggestions about (they both knew it but, since no one would dare come about in the open, they had to ignore it). Yfestio felt as the most privileged person in the world with this open trust of Alexandros and was more than willing to stake his life on the line for his friend. That, and his fear and hate for the Queen.

Yfestion knew Olympias hated him (thinking he was the reason her son was not so interested in girls)and he returned the feeling tenfold! Only thing, he couldn't nor would admit it or let it show—from fear of losing Alexandros' trust and friendship. On that (but not in many other issues) he had the support and sympathy of Ptolemeos son of Lagos and Perdikkas son of Orontis.

Winter now was coming to an end and the news from Filippos was that he could now walk (albeit with great difficulty and a very pronounced limp). From the south, report came that Kottyfos had won a small victory with his combined city-states army on the Amfissians and they'd agree to recall the exiled leadership of yore and expel the ones who guided the city to offending Delfi and god Apol-lon.

Alexandros sent a courier to his Father with this latest news. The answer came from the King with-in few days. Filippos knew that Kottyfos' victory was not a decisive one and, therefore, the Amfissi-ans would not keep their word after achieving a truce. Athinae had not send a delegation to Delfi at the synod of Amfiktiones earlier in the winter, playing the role of deaf-mute and Thivae was still an ally of Makedon—but a very suspect one. Peace was not about to come that easily and Makedonia should be ready. Filippos praised his son for his ability to govern thus far and now wanted him to prepare the army, without raising any suspicions in the south and only Antipatros should know of this.

Alexandros got into action immediately. The preparations were let to be known as preventive measures for an uprising reported in Illyria and messengers were also sent to Ipiros, ostensibly to coordinate with king Alexandros of Molossis. Olympias, seeing that her son's visits took longer now to materialize and were much shorter than they used to be, called him urgently and demanded to know what was keeping him so far from her. Didn't he love her any more? Was the meager assign-ment of the regency gone to his head? Did he think Filippos had given him the world? He was noth-ing more to the King but a measure of convenience, he should have known that! Wasn't Antipatros standing always next to him, always sending—the gods know what—reports secretly to the King? And, how come he had time with his friends—especially that Yfestion—but no time at all for his Mother?

Alexandros let her finish with her tirade and, finding that she eventually had nothing more to say, he gave her in cool tones the explanation the public knew about the Illyrian campaign. As for Antip-atros, Yfestion and the rest of the Eteri, they were with him because each one was working alongside him preparing the army and he had to let them know his plans in full so they'd understand what kind of action they had to take, when action was needed! She looked at him right in the eye and he knew she didn't believe a word he said but he didn't care now. Her knife had found its target, she had wounded him once more and now she was calmer but not yet finished.

Olympias changed the subject and now wanted to know why her son wasn't actively looking for a suitable girl to wed, or even be spending his free time with. He was about seven plus ten years old and she wanted to start having grand sons. He asked her if she thought him of being a girl and want-ed him wed in such early age. He wanted also to tell her that Kleopatra was, ought to be, her prime concern, the girl being in love with Perdikkas, as he wasn't as blind and knew his sister's secret love.

But he thought better and kept his mouth shot. Kleopatra was the target of his Mother's ire when she couldn't vent on him. The girl did not deserve any further hardship.

He embraced his Mother and placed a kiss on her head (he'd grown taller than her for some time now) and bid her farewell. He had to attend to his duties. He heard pots and small tables turned and breaking after he closed the doors going out. He nodded hello to young Nikanor guarding the hallway and turned around the corner smiling. His dagger had also found its target. They were even . . .

With spring well under way, the home army left Pella heading north. Antipatros was left behind to exercise the duty of the regent now that Alexandros was on his way to Illyria. The prince had taken under him most of the foot and horse companions available, heading for Orestis and Dassaretis, to meet with Alexandros of Molossis and his army and, combined, fight the Illyrians. Arriving in Ima-thia, Alexandros divided the army. He took with him only the Agima, the horse ili assigned to him in person as the heir to the throne and two taxis of sarissa bearing falanx. Attached to those were five hundred light horse the prodromi/Ypaspistes for reconnaissance. The rest of the force was dispersed and housed in the towns of Edessa and Veria, with orders to speed in support of Antipatros— if there was ever a need. As for the Illyrians, the Molossian army under uncle Alexandros and his own Agima and the two taxis with the prodromi would be sufficient to face any Illyrian force.

Meantime, they were to proceed to their true destination and true business. A big wedding had been planned. Hrysogonos from Krousis, house Haridimos and Klitos Lefkos (White—to differentiate from the other Klitos) from house Iraklonas from Paeonia, were to get married to old royal house of Lyn-kos. One sister and a first cousin of its last king Aeropos' sons were the brides.

Aeropos was dead some years ago and King Filippos still in Thraki, recovering from his wound. Alexandros was to represent the King and Aeropos' sons would stand for their house. The eldest was named also Alexandros and he had assumed the local leadership of the clan. His two brothers were Eromenis and Arravaeos. In actuality they were cousins of prince Alexandros, as his own grand Mother (Filippos' Mother) was born to their royal house of Lynkos.

The three Lynkestian brothers received the heir to the Makedonian throne, a short distance from the Orestian town of Keletron and escorted Alexandros and the two bridegrooms to Iraklia, the cap-ital city of Lynkestis. They were curious to see what truth was held behind distant rumors from Pella on the dashing character of their future King. The son of the Ipirotan witch did not impress them at first sight. Where was his manly beard? Smaller in stature than they but just about in their years, he had his face clean and his armor (times were not so peaceful to exclude its use) was too fancy for the highlanders of Lynkos.

A better look at his retinue told them that they all followed his fashion and had their faces clean-shaven. Yet his scars indicated war hardship and experience. Was it true then that he was so clever and daring in battle? They didn't exactly believe it. Any heir to the throne is bound to have myths spanned around his person. Their rare visits in Pella or Dion during festivities when they were young never brought them close enough to their cousin for a real evaluation.

The weddings went on schedule with lots of merriment. The troops were billeted in houses with families, sharing all the food and wine there was to share. The Lynkestian brothers were surprised to see that no matter what the festivities were, there was always time for a three hour exercise outside the city. They were obliged to follow the example. Alexandros explained to them that, just in case the Illyrians had something in mind (he was sure several merchants visiting Pella and in the pay of the Athinians had passed information of the rumor and preparations via the ports of Epidamnos and Apollonia). The Lynkestian Alexandros started changing his mind and respected the prince more as the days went by, as he had some time spent in early years at court and remembered few things. The other two were still skeptical.

On the tenth day of the wedding festivities, word came from the Molossian king Alexandros that he had caught the tribe of Atintanes by surprise, while they were preparing to receive re-enforcements from Dexares, Tavlantes, Gravaei and Parthines, under the leadership of Kossos (Khosha). The Mo-lossian king took hostages and the Atintanes had agreed to let the invaders pass unaware of the fact that their moves had been detected. Their guides would lead Kossos via the passes of Pindos to the land between the lakes Lyhnitis and the great Vrygiis. He would close-in behind them and, when A-lexandros would attack at his place of choice, he would bring in his Molossians to finish the job.

Alexandros then called the officers to a war council and explained the situation, telling everybody what his task would be and how to proceed. They would start toward the lakes in three days, under total secrecy. The people of the city were to continue the festivities and the grooms would be excused from the campaign, along with their families. Their army should reach the valley between Vrygiis and Lyhnitis within a day and a half, marching with a bit extra speed and be in place for the trap be-fore the arrival of the Illyrians, the terrain being only too well known. That agreed and understood, he sent word back to the Molossian king with instructions for action.

The trap worked in a perfect way. The Illyrians caught between the two armies had no other way to go but to the shores of either one of the two lakes. There they had their last stand and many were kil-led. Many more were captured and—under orders from Alexandros—were not put to death. Their leader Kossos was also captured alive and brought before the prince. There, with what little know-ledge of the Makedonian dialect he had, confirmed that the Illyrian campaign against Makedon was encouraged by Athinian agents and he had made his move to strike first.

Alexandros had him promise peace in the future and less dependence on Athinian urging and false promises of an imminent fall of Makedonian power. Receiving such promise, the prince asked for several leading men from the invading tribes as hostages and let Kossos return to Illyria with the remnants of his army free, to the astonishment of both the Molossian king and the Lynkestian brothers. When questioned, he told them that he wasn't looking for the extermination of people or for the creation of new feuds. He was just making sure Makedonia was not to be bothered for a long time after this battle and free to deal with the south any way the King wanted.

He saw to it that the war booty was fairly divided between the Molossian troops and his Makedoni-ans (including the Lynkestian home guard) and praised all for their valor in battle. The Lynkestian Alexandros was impressed. He asked to enroll himself to the ili of Eteri cavalry attached to the prince and was accepted readily. He left behind his second brother, Eromenis, in charge of the Lynkestian home affairs—aided by the third brother, Arravaeos. The troops returned quietly to Pella and, within three weeks after their return, King Filippos finally made it back from Thraki.

For most of the way Filippos was carried laying in on a cart pulled by two pairs of oxen, propped in a thick layer of hay and stopping at frequent intervals—as he was still hurting and unable to walk or ride. Just outside Pella, the King ordered for his horse. He had to be seen by the people that he was still the man they knew, capable and as ready as ever! He was helped to mount and arrived at the palace traversing the main Pella streets under the cheers of thousands gathered to welcome him and his troops.

Alexandros, with his Mother on his right and Antipatros on his left (and two steps behind) was wait-ing at the gate—as etiquette required. Seeing the King having difficulty in dismounting, he rushed forth to offer his hand. Olympias' face was lit observing Filippos in such a condition but clouded im-mediately, the minute she saw her son taking such care of his Father. She bit her lips to bleeding but said nothing nor did she move. No place here for a fight.

Filippos observed her and smiled under his mustache with contempt but uttered only the proper words of a husband returning to his wife after a long absence. She answered the like. When Filippos turned to enter the palace waiving a last acknowledgment to the gathered people, supported by Alexandros and escorted by Parmenion, Antipatros and Attalos, she gave a look of pity to Pafsanias who—as leader of the guard—was placing his men to their posts before letting the rest disperse and turned leaving to her

461

chambers. Pafsanias watched her until she turned in past the entrance, his eye-brows connected in thought. He then resumed his duties.

She expected her son to come to her soon after and give her his report on the King's condition, crav-ing to hear how weak he was and what a damage he'd receive from such a wound, to rejoice and quench her thirst of revenge. When that did not happen, Kleopatra and the maids in attendance had their fill of terror and beating . . .

While the King was recovering (the leg now was truly lame and his walking never expected to improve) the Athinians guided by the fierce speeches of Dimosthenis, had broken the marble stili of their former alliance with Makedonia to pieces. Formal declaration of war was duly pronounced. The Athinians were convinced that Filippos was looking upon them as a new source of slaves and income, forgetting (how convenient for Dimosthenis!) his treatment toward Athinae just few years ago at the end of the war against the Fokians. He could've marched then against Athinae and bring the city to its knees but didn't. That did not matter to Dimosthenis or to his supporters. What mat-tered was the search for a chance to bring the Makedonian upstart down!

Filippos sent a message for a compromise, the finding of some new common ground and an end to mistrust. The Athinian general Fokion, the one who proved the only capable Athinian to inflict some damage to Makedon in the previous conflicts, declared his belief of Filippos' good intentions. He was almost put to death! What saved him was his impeccable record of the past and his reputed fame as a man of justice, second only to the long gone Aristidis the Just . . .

Persian gold now was passing through the hands of Dimosthenis and the power of money had him riding very high. Still, Fokion was too Athinian, too well known a hero. Dimosthenis diverted the flow of money to different channels. He bought citizen votes to have the Athinians approve the creation of a large fleet. Wasn't the navy the reason Perinthos and Vyzantion were still under Athinian influence? Was not the lack of navy vessels what forced Filippos to release the convoy of ships loaded with grain headed for Athinae, which he had captured with treachery? Never mind the need for training special crews to man such a fleet. Numbers would do the talking here and now! Look what had happened to Olynthos when the Athinians had no adequate ships to send for relief (he had no mind in mentioning that the real reason for the fleet not arriving in Olynthos was not its numbers but the season and the opposing winds). He convinced them and by that, new taxes were imposed on them, leaving him with more than enough Darics to stop any work for living and devote his time in making speeches against the 'tyrant' of Ellas . . .

Dimosthenis turned next in building an alliance with the Athinian oldest foe, Thivae! He sent agent upon agent to talk with Thivan notables and convince them of the futility of their alliance to Make-don. Athinian navy was the key to keeping Filippos in check but he still had a way of coming south! He could and would enforce the passing through Viottia, through Thivan territory of influence. Then, what of Thivae? Where the old glory of mastering the whole Ellas (including Sparti!) would go? Humbled, they'd be forced to follow the "semi-barbarian's" chariot in subjugating Ellas for ever under the Makedonian yoke!

The fact that these 'semi-barbarians' had loved Evripidis and followed his tragedies with equal—if not surpassing—enthusiasm as the Athinian public (before they exiled him) and his last breath was given in Makedonian soil outside Pella and buried there with honors the very Athinian public had denied him, meant nothing to Dimosthenis. The fact that he had (along with other Athinian dele-gates) marveled at Pella's splendor, achieved only at the times of Periklis in Athinae, the Makedo-nian court being so superb and providing such magnificent array of educators, builders, artists that made her the envy of Ellas when Athinae (after the death of Platon) had lost much of its lumines-cence and was now led by men of speech rather than men of mind, did not bother him. He had one goal in mind: ruin Filippos any which way possible and elevate Dimosthenis to the pedestal of the Aritodimos and Aristogiton (who's statues were long taken away by the Persians).

He kept making contact with Thivan exiles and merchants, seeking their understanding and com-pliance. Thivae was reluctant. Makedonia was the force they were allied to. Filippos was the one who confirmed their rule over the towns and cities in Viottia. He had lived among them (albeit as a host-age) and knew them. Athinae was the old foe of yore, the oppressor who wanted Thivae pay tribute—until the day she got defeated by Sparti, with the help of Thivae. Athinae was the one bringing forth so recently the old shame of Medizing. What if now Filippos wanted to reduce her to a vassal state? They would wait and see . . .

Meantime in Makedonia the King was recovering. He could ride now and be at the exercise fields with his army for most of the day. There were new tactics introduced, two royal squadrons of horse, and Father with son were exchanging views and battle formations were tried and readjusted with improvements. Olympias was fretful and taking any excuse to lay her frustrations on her son. Filip-pos could clearly see that and one day he went to face her himself. She had no choice but to accept him at her chambers. As was predicted a big fight ensued, none giving ground to accommodate the other. It caused him Alexandros' distance (she suffered the same but she was happy to see the Father and son rift renewed).

Filippos became busier as he had to follow the events developing in Delfi with the Amfiktiones (no Athinian delegates appeared). Kottyfos reported that the Amfissians were not keeping up with their obligations to exile their impious leaders and he was unable to enforce the will of the Amfiktiones with his sample of army. Antipatros was sent once more to represent the King. Kottyfos then pro-posed that Makedon, who warred against the Fokians in the past defending the rights of god Apol-lon, was to be asked to do so again. Antipatros agreed on behalf of the King, offering Filippos' sug-gestion to shoulder all the expenses of the Holy war. The Amfiktiones accepted the offer with votes of thank-yous and the drafting of a very flattering letter sent to the King. Preparations in Pella for the coming war intensified and that brought Father and son close once more . . .

The King's army marched toward Thessalia and, crossing the Tempi valley, met with the Amficti-onic forces of Kottyfos and picked-up the Thessalian heavy cavalry—as appropriate for the Tagos of all Thessalia when heading for war. They headed south to southwest, toward Amfissa and Delfi and were joined by some small, token forces from the states of the Amfiktiony. Filippos thanked each leader of these forces and placed him (with swift, no nonsense briefing) to his place, under Makedonian command. Still, no Athinian forces showed—as it would have been proper under the Amfiktionic obligations to join. Dimosthenis had the Athinians persuaded to remain out of it. Any connection with the decision to wage war against Amfissa would antagonize his efforts to befriend Thivae and he couldn't allow that to happen.

The army arrived in Thermopylae and Alexandros made sure to lay a wreath on the plate by the grave-mount of king Leonidas and his Spartan and Thespian heroes of the Persian invasion. He read the epigram: "Stranger passing-by, herald to Sparti that we lay here faithful to her Law!". To his friends present, he commented that while Leonidas was undoubtedly a very brave man, he was not a true tactician. Had he been one, he would have made sure the Fokian troops guarding his rear would not have allowed the Persians pass trough the mountain pass and encircle him.

Meantime King Filippos went to the fort by the narrows which (you recall) was held now by Thivae as her forces had expelled the Makedonian guard after the war against the Fokians few years ago with the excuse of needing it for better hold on the Viottian vassal states. Filippos, with his dry humor but obviously intent on doing business, thanked them for taking good care of it but, now that he was here and as their principal ally, he would take over. They had no choice but to obey. Filippos left a strong guard to keep the fort and the army moved to camp in the town of Elatia, taken years back from the war against the Fokians.

The King's engineers got right to work, rebuilding the town's fortifications. This would be a perma-nent stepping stone for Filippos' business in southern Ellas. He had grown tired of the dishonest deals and treaties with the city-states. He wanted them to know that, from now-on, he would be the one dictating and they would have to either follow or face the consequences!

For that reason he sent a delegation to Thivae the minute the army camped at Elatia and before crossing into Viottia proper. He asked them to declare if their purported treaty of alliance with him still stood, numbering the injustices done to him by the Athinians, whether they had declared war or (as done many times in the past) covertly, putting others to do their job. At the same time, he sent Pa-rmenion with a strong contingent to occupy the town of Kytinion, securing the road to Amfissa and in place to move for the completion of his task for the Holy war and avenge god Apollon. His message though—with the bulk of the army remained in Elatia—to Thivae was more than clear. Would they re-main his allies and give him right of passage or he would have to move against them and, obviously, against Athinae also?

In private, discussing the possibilities with Alexandros and the other officers, he stated that this should settle the affairs with the city-states once and for all. "If Thivae knows what's best, they will declare for me and that ought to wake-up the Athinians and throw Dimosthenis and his party out, bringing Fokion in charge. Then, we can all work toward a permanent peace and a campaign against the true offender to Ellas, Persia!"

Alexandros could see his Father's desire to have Athinae embrace him as a friend, not seeing him as the worst opponent. He personally had his doubts. Dimosthenis was preaching for years now that Makedon was the declared enemy of that state and Filippos was marching south to enslave them. The faint move against Illyria just a while ago had been believed, with the known result. Now, the Maked-onians were at the doorstep of the city-states. Wouldn't the Athinians believe Filippos was coming to ruin them? How would be possible for Fokion to gain the leadership of Attiki?

The King saw the reasoning and concluded that the whole situation was on the hands of Thivae and the result of Thivan vote. "If they vote for keeping the alliance with us, Dimosthenis can do nothing! But if Thivae votes to side with Athinae, then we have to war against them both. I am not so worried of the Athinians. Their time is past, irrevocably. We do have to worry about the Thivan Sacred Band though . . . They still bask in the glory of Pelopidas and Epaminondas' time! Their ancient vows still standing, from the times of our ancestor Iraklis with Iolaos and their victories to none more famous than Sparti are not of a past long gone."

The following was told to me much later, when I met and had a conversation with the Athinian Arhon, Dimadis.

While this conversation was taking place in Elatia, Athinae received the news of the town's occu-pation by King Filippos and the city went crazy. Everyone went up and down in the Agora, asking for more recent news, discussing the possibility of Filippos' march against the city itself, about ask-ing of assistance from other city-states or just wait for the inevitable to happen. No one slept that night. Dimosthenis closed himself in his study and worked preparing his next day's speech before the Athinian Dimos. His time had finally come. He would show them he was the man of the hour! They gathered at the usual place of the city's council at times of urgency, the hill of Pnyx, just across and a bit below the venerated Akropolis—he goddess Athina's statue with its gold spearhead casting its shadow on them while it shone in the first rays of the sun rising from beyond. It was very early morning. The crowd was noisy and the Arhons had hard time putting it in order. The older ones could still recall the time when the news of their defeat at Aegos Potami had arrived. Was that to be repeated? The Arhon in charge raised his voice louder than he intended, sounding rather like being in panic. They all waited in silence. Who would speak? Who would offer a solution and deliverance?

Dimosthenis raised his hand for acknowledgment and stepped up at the rocky platform for the speaker. The silence was deafening. He looked around at their faces satisfied his prophesies had come true. His eyes stood a while longer looking at his opponents gathered on one side of the hill. They still had the audacity to look straight at his face. He would deal with them shortly! He took a deep breath and started talking . . .

The Thivan citizens' Assembly gathered at their Agora, below the Kadmia acropolis. The Maked-onian delegates were invited to speak first, being formal allies. Once Antipatros was acting again as a regent in Makedonia, Parmenion was the main representative of the King. Alexandros had come with the delegation but preferred to remain an observer rather than speaking. He reserved that right only in case of need. He didn't see the necessity, for Parmenion spoke eloquently and to the point. He reminded the Thivans of the good relations between the King and their city, his help during the war against the Fokians and his consent on their city's supremacy in Viottia.

He noted to them that the King was not asking them to war against Athinae on his side. He simply wanted to know for sure they would not side with Athinae against him! "Just give him the right of passage" he said "and stay neutral—if you so wish." They questioned the King's move to rebuild the fort at Elatia; why hadn't he consulted them— being allies? He answered the fort was essential station for supplies and refitting, if the war against Amfissa would take time, like did the one against the Fokians. The King did not want to burden his ally the Thivan citizens with additional expenses nor with the risk of severing their ties and warring against Amfissa, a formal ally of Thivae. The city had suffered enough loss from the last war. Filippos did not want to ask for more!

They saw he was right. The King had Thessalia under him but the Thessalians were taken good care-no complaints were heard. Thivae had his blessing over Viottia. Athinae was an old foe who recently had placed offensive epigrams against them in Delfi. They voiced their satisfaction and Parmenion sat down, finished.

The Thivan Arhon in charge invited then the Athinian delegation to come forth and speak. Dimos-thenis rose from his seat (all this time he had kept his head down, not looking at the direction of Ale-xandros and the Makedonians) and stepped-up on the elevated podium of the speaker.

467

He started to speak of their common interests and saw immediately that he was about to lose them altogether.

There was hardly a house in Thivae without some gripe against Athinae stemming from the distant, as well as the recent past. He hurried to proceed. He uttered his party's will to recognize Thivan in-terests in Viottia, unconditionally. That would include the old contested city of Plataea, the one and only solid Athinian ally in Marathon against the Persians and during the war against Sparti (and Thivae)! Never mind the old Athinian decree granting every Plataean the Athinian citizenship for ever! In addition, in case of war against Filippos, Athinae was ready to follow Thivan leadership to commanding all forces. Inward, he counted the money spent to buy Thivan votes and wondered . . .

The Thivan citizens were listening in doubt, looking at each-other for possible insight, unwilling to accept readily such an Athinian turnaround. He stepped up gesturing, hardly capable of hiding his desperation. He turned to remind them of the glorious days of Pelopidas and Epaminondas, the A-thinaean alliance with them to bring Sparti down, the heroic deeds of their Sacred Band. He smiled ironically to their faces, challenging them. If they had lost their courage of old, then, the only thing he would ask for would be the right of way through, for Athinae would face the invader alone, as in Ma—rathon! He could see now he had hit the right cord. For the first time, he looked toward the Make-donian delegation. Alexandros met his look unflinching. That witches' son! Didn't he know to dif-ferenciate defiance from defeat? He turned his attention back to the Thivan citizenry.

The speakers from the two opposing camps done, the Thivans called for the vote. One wicker basket would hold the yes for war, the other the nay. One by one, the citizens cast their individual pebble.

The two delegations were called to wait (far apart from each-other) at host houses for the result of the voting. Back at the Agora the pebbles were tallied painstakingly and slowly, under strict super-vision by the Arhons of the city.

Alexandros with Parmenion brought the news to the King by the next morning. As they arrived and went to his tent, Filippos asked to be alone with just his immediate council of officers and, of course, the delegation with his son and his trusted second-in-command. Aside from hearing their report, he read the letter the Thivans had sent. Filippos read it loud as was still the custom of older generations not trained to read to themselves in silence. He read the declaration of war calmly with only a small sigh giving away his disappointment on a lost hope. "Well, if that is what they want, they shall have it then!" Alexandros felt his father's inner ache more so than the others. "I am sorry Father! Dimosthe-nis will pay dearly for his folly. That, I can promise to you." Filippos looked at his son. "He is not worth the trouble my son. Forget him. The Athinians will, when they come to their senses."

The King was not willing to see that Athinae would hate Makedon to no end, just because she could not lead. He was still hopping things would change, even if it took a major defeat in the field of war. "We will play the game of cat and mouse with them for a while now." he declared. "We put to test a doubtful ally and we saw where he stands. Let us prepare to march in punishment of the offenders of holy Delfi. Ellas is looking upon us as the sword of justice! We do not want to disappoint." "Are we not to march against the combined enemy now?" Parmenion and Attalos wanted to know.

Alexandros looked at his father, winked at him and replied in his stead. "The city-states have the citizen army to bring before us. They cannot afford keeping it under arms for ever as we do with ours. Further, the Athinians cannot afford the pay of their mercenaries they recently hired to match our number. We are the only ones in Ellas having a standing army, thanks to our resources. Let them bleed out of money and when they do, then we deal with them."

Filippos put his arm on his son's shoulder in full agreement with the assessment. "Let them simmer for a while. Who knows? There may be still time to wise-up and come to an understanding with no blood of Ellas shed unnecessarily! Meantime, we liberate Delfi from its offenders . . ."

The Makedonians moved westward, leaving the hastily armed new allies to wait in vain for a show-down. Fokion arrived back in Athinae from a futile mission arranged by Dimosthenis' party too late to change anything. Urging the city to get the Oracle's opinion, he was told by Dimosthenis that it was only well known the Pythia was on Filippos' payroll and was dismissed. Athinian oplites march-ed to Thivae and were received with carefulness and suspicion. Old differences were hard to die.

They moved to block the passes to Amfissa. Filippos ignored them. He took his time in Fokis, re-building the torn-down old fortresses, skirmishing now and then to keep them on their toes and pul-ling away each time.

Dimosthenis hailed these as victories against the 'tyrant of Ellas' and his country bled financially and so did Thivae. Winter was in and any action was suspended for months. Dimosthenis was forced to send the mercenary troops, ten thousand of them, to Amfissa's defense. The Athinians were not willing to pay idle troops.

Filippos faked a retreat, claiming disturbing news and possible revolt from Amfipolis, just before the spring thaw and before rivers would become impassable, he crossed the passes (unmanned be-cause of winter) and appeared before Amfissa. The mercenaries put a good fight but, as such, they knew when to ask for terms. Some returned to their homes, most enlisted to Filippos' army with better pay. The Amfissians surrendered unconditionally. The leaders were exiled and the holy plain was left uncultivated and fell fallow for the god.

At the first warm days of spring, Delfi celebrated its deliverance, crowning Filippos with golden lau-rel crown. Father and son posed to artists for the sculpturing of their images, their statues dedicated to god Apollon. The Amfiktiones hailed the King with long speeches full of flattery. Alexandros' friends urged him to consult the Oracle and get any doubts out of his mind in what pertained to his Mother's claims on his birth. He admitted to Yfestion that he did want to know for sure but this was not the time to ask. "Pythia would give me now what she things is the proper answer. She's best to be taken by surprise!" Instead he went to the theater to applaud the performance of his favored actor, Thettalos.

The King moved his army further south taking Nafpaktos on the gulf of Korinthos, a strategic point commanding the entrance of it. He returned to the west side of mount Parnassos, setting forts at the passes and river crossings for future use, manning them with his mercenaries, under trusted Make-donian command. Now and then he feinted marching to the east putting Thivans and Athinians on an edge and then withdraw, having maneuvers and games held to keep his army in shape.

Dimosthenis was in his glory back in the city of Athinae, proclaiming their new alliance's superior-ity against the 'barbarian' since he was repulsed several times now! "Don't you see?" he kept on say-ing. "It's full summer now and time for war activities and, yet, he has his army withdrawn back to his base at Elatia. He is worried I tell you, we put the fear in him! We will proceed to hold the route at Viottia, close to Kifisos river before Lake Kopais and deny him passage once and for all. Now is the time to put an end to his ambitions!" He moved the Athinian army again toward Thivae volun-teering to serve as a common oplitis and convinced the Thivans to join at the southern banks of the river, denying access to the road south.

Filippos got his army ready. He held a war council before marching south and entrusted his left wing with the Thessalian cavalry and the second royal horse Agima to Alexandros. He explained his plan to all, making sure they completely understood it. He addressed Alexandros in private, after dismissing the rest. "Son, I know you were looking for this appointment for a long time now. This is the time you got it and I trust you will prove worthy of it!" "Father" Alexandros replied with fervor "I will not be alive to have you regret your decision and have you tell it to my face!" So, they march-ed south to face their destiny . . .

They entered the valley of Kifisos and, as they headed toward the river they could see the opposing army having bivouacked on the south bank, tents and huts erected according to city-state affiliate ties. On the right as Filippos could see, were the Athinians camped and had in charge (according to Viottian informers) of their troops the general Haris, who chose the slopes of Parnassos to lean-on. "Our luck!" said the King. "He's very predictable." At the center there was a motley of various city-states of lesser power, the ones which had no choice but to follow the Athinians and/ or Thivans to battle. On the left, the opponent's right, were the Thivans anchored by mount Akontion and the river and led by Theagenis, a veteran of the Pelopidas/Epaminondas school and a though nut to crack. He was the designated leader of the allied army.

Filippos looked long and hard at the Thivan camp site, old memories of his hostage years coming full force to mind. He turned at length to his son and, smiling, he said "I have not given you a lesser assignment, have I? Look at the end of their line next to the river's bank and the hills; there's their Sacred Band holding the place of honor. I present you this gift, my son! Make sure you respond to my signal!" Alexandros was too moved to speak. He held his father's left hand firmly for a while, a reassurance that he understood completely. I was standing just a few steps behind them, ready to take dictation of the King's orders, when called. The Makedonian camp was ready within the hour and forward posts were assigned to keep an eye on the opponent. The rest settled for the evening meal and the fires were lit on both opposing sides, for the night was fast approaching.

The King received delegates from the various Viottian city-states under Thivan power, who had smuggled through the lines to voice their grievances on Thivan oppression. He promised them all justice. Having had their dinner, Father and son bid each-other good night and each retired to his post. Filippos on the right wing in charge of the Makedonian cavalry and the royal guards Alexan-dros on the left, with his horse iles from Thessalia and his own Agima. Parmenion with Attalos were in charge of the center with the sarissa holding falanxes.

The sun rose from the east, filling with light the upper slopes of mount Parnassos across the river. The small town of Heronia—still under the shade—was up already, its inhabitants vying to get the best possible view of the oncoming battle, holding lit torches on hand. The fine summer mist lifted from the river revealing the opponents had placed themselves battle ready.

Filippos looked to his left. His son, following orders, had his horse concealed behind a forest of sar-issas and the small hill leading to the river's edge in front of the Thivans. He made the proper offers to the gods, sure that Alexandros would be doing the same and adding his own to Iraklis the progen—itor of their royal house. The King wished mentally his son luck, patience for the signal and prompt-ness on delivering the blow. He then turned to the trumpeters to have them sound the advance. The sun shone fully now all over the valley giving an added brightness on the green of the olive trees, the yellow of the ripen wheat and the red of the poppies. The paean songs were echoing on the slopes of the mountains as each contingent of the allied army sang its own giving the cacophony a peculiar hue of sound. The Makedonians descended the hills in utter silence, attention paid to the trumpet signals.

Dimosthenis was placed in the seventh line (out of eight total) of the Athinian falanx. He regretted his rush to volunteer and his full gear was already giving him great discomfort. It was to be a very hot day. At the sound of attack, he moved forward with the rest. He couldn't tarry; there was one more line of veterans behind him pushing forward. He took solace on the fact that the front lines were manned by young, vigorous warriors 'full of piss and vinegar' eager to prove themselves on the field of honor. The paean sung loud, gave him more courage and he started thinking of victory . . .

The royal Agima of Eteri cavalry opened the attack from the right wing of the Makedonians, follow-ed by the falanx of Pezeteri the foot soldiers carrying their long sarissas. They crossed the river easily for the rushing high waters of the spring thaw was an event of the past already. The clash of arms was severe. The Athinian line backed before the onslaught of the forest of long sarissas and impetus of the charging horse but was able to hold, albeit with many falling before the battle even started.

The rest of the Makedonian falanx followed suit and the center now faced the allied city-states of Ahaia, Korinthos and some Aetolians who managed to get to Heronia on time. Most of them were enemies a while ago, fighting each-other for small border disputes. Now they were competing against the professional Makedonians, vying to show individual (as well as collective) valor to prove their worth to former rivals. Their line also held the first push, but Attalos kept the pressure on them.

Further left on the Makedonian line, Parmenion received the staunch and calculated resistance from the equally professional force of Thivans, spearheaded by their famous Sacred Band, num-bering a total of a thousand warriors—if one included the support troops of the Band. Based on pairs of lovers with oaths of supporting one-another in all turns of life until death, they were formidable. Their armor shining and their shields locked they presented a front impenetrable to any attack. The experienced Makedonian general knew he would have a tough time against them. He prayed the King was right in entrusting his son with such a tusk and for Alexandros to act with the proper force and on time.

Both armies seemed to be trying and develop the oblique offence, introduced with such a success by the two legendary Thivan generals, Pelopidas and Epaminondas. The Thivans because they had matured in performing it, the Makedonians because the King had studied and improved on it as he was held hostage in his youth and, later, as the leader of his own professionally trained army. A whole hour had passed already and the wings alongside the center were moving back and forth, un-able to break through on either side.

Makedonian trumpets sounded a call. The King could be seen on top of his horse at the summit of the hill moving his horse left to right and back, gesturing and urging. With the sound of the trumpets his royal Agima reformed and led one more attack on the Athinians. Many more fell but the line held again. Then, a miracle seemed to be at work. Slowly but surely, the Makedonian sarissa falanx seem-ed to be pushed back!

Invigorated, the Athinian youth (the ones that were still standing) with the shoving help of the more seniors in the back, picked-up pace and pushed forth more! A triumphant roar was heard from the Athinian wing. Young and old pushed forward, reinvigorated. Dimosthenis' chest swelled under the hot breastplate and started yelling with the rest: "On to Makedonia! Take Filippos alive!" He raised his head up and he could see through the waves of sarissas the top of the hill where Filippos was. The King was gesturing to an apparent messenger. "Oh, gods!" he thought "Athina, protector maiden, daughter of Zefs and patron of my city, give me the satisfaction! . . ." He imagined standing before the Dimos, golden laurel crown on his head, posing for the sculpturer's sketch. His statue would be plac-ed before the Parthenon, for future generations to admire! He doubled his effort and pushed and shoved forward, drenched in sweat . . .

The King's messenger arrived and gave to Alexandros the verbal message: "Be ready for the trum-pet's sound!" Alexandros turned to his companions of the Agima. He raised his longer than usual javelin, the lance he instituted for his cavalry. They formed behind him like a flock of geese, narrow edge in front, then widening in the rear. Yfestion and Ptolemeos right behind him, then Nearhos,

Perdikkas and Alexandros' cousin Amyntas son of Perdikkas the dead brother of King Filippos, then Alexandros the Lynkestian, Klitos Lefkos, Krateros and Kassandros son of Antipatros (Alexandros had to include him not wanting to offend the father) and so on, followed by the Thessalian horse. They moved slowly behind the hill, placing their horse to the right of the Sacred Band of Thivae, unobserved.

The Thivan general had push Parmenion's falanx from the river front, keeping in mind not to lose contact with his left, where the Aheans and Korinthians were fighting when, suddenly, he saw them pulling to their left. He sent a spotter to see what the cause of it was. He returned to report that the Athinians had pushed the Makedonians and, therefore, the line had moved to keep the connection. "Pushed Filippos back? Were the Makedonians retreating in order or had dropped their gear and run?" the spotter replied they were retreating with commendable order. Theagenis cursed his luck to have amateurs leading his left wing. He ordered the last two lines from his Thivans to move and cover the gap between him and the center and sent the spotter to tell the Athinian idiot, Haris, to hold and not push further. He then thought of the King's son. Where was Alexandros?

The Maked-onian cavalry by Filippos' side was not all that the King could field. Theagenis felt the hair on the base of his neck stand up and a chill run up his spine…

Filippos gave the order. The trumpets sounded the prearranged signal. Alexandros raised his lance again and the cavalry galloped forward, appearing from the side of the concealing them hill to the exposed side of the Sacred Band of Thivae. They faced about, forming a double front. Parmenion ordered his falanx to press harder. In the center, Attalos held the line keeping the lesser allied city-sates busy and Filippos on the right signaled the all out attack. Now the Makedonians took on their paean and pressed hard forward. The King trotted from right to center to the left. The whole valley was covered with a thick cloud of dust, making difficult the assessment of the turn of the battle.

Finally, another great sound arose from the Makedonian left. The Athinian line was breaking and so was the center of the opposing force, too thin in the effort to have a solid line. The King was anxious to hear news from his left. Had Alexandros succeed? Was he alive? He thought he could detect Parmenion's falanx move also forward but the dust and the distance didn't let him be sure.

Dimosthenis froze in his place. The push forward had stoped and he felt the opposite push coming from ahead. He raised his head above the shield and his mouth gaped open. There were only three lines left ahead of him, the Makedonian sarissas penetrating through in a dangerous proximity! Of the young ones from the front lines most were dead! Between him and the murderous sarissas were the middle aged citizens and behind him the very old, the ones who had come to add to the numbers. His joints felt incapable of supporting his moves. He slipped on the blood of a dead citizen and fell to his knees. A shove from the enemy sent the Athinian before him tumble over him with a curse.

Grasping for support from each-other, they stood up again. Dimosthenis looked around him in panic. What had happened to the dream? Few more fell down in the front and the first enemy sarissa came forth and retracted passing by him on his right. He looked for the protection of the shield of his companion to his right and found an empty space. He dropped his own shield and lance and turned around running away…

Alexandros fought until there was no opponent left to fight against. He had three lances broken and replaced and then fought with his sword. He knew of killing at least three Thivans at the very begin-ning of the attack but, then, he was lost. Piercing and hacking he moved forward opening the way. The Agima was following in unison undeterred of the staunch defense the Sacred Band put against them. The Thivans fell to the last man faithful to their vows, mixing their blood with the lipped waters of Kifisos. The shining armor and shields of the Thivan lovers had turned to the rusty colors of dried blood as they all lay on the ground, facing outward their mortal wounds on the front of theirbodies…

Father and son inspected the field after seeing the Makedonian wounded were taken care of. Filip-pos wanted to see where the Thivans fell and seeing the hip of dead bodies, stood there in deep thought for a long time. Their glory, as he knew it during his young years returned to him and didn't want to leave. "They all fought with distinction Father!" Alexandros' voice brought him back to real-ity. He let a deep sigh and ordered me to have the fallen be counted. I asked Pafsanias to help and he detailed some of the royal guard to assist. It took me some time and had all of them counted. They had fallen to the last man where they were standing. Later, Perdikkas told me that Alexandros talk-ing to him and Yfestion and Ptolemeos of their valor, had tears in his eyes.

There were over a thousand Athinians dead and as many captured and wounded. The Thivan loss was similar and for the rest of their allies, one only could tell that they had suffered greatly -the dead bodies of their comrades covering the whole center of the battlefield. Our loss was also significant, considering the ones who died later from their wounds -but nowhere near the numbers of the oppo-sition.

It was now long past the mid of the day. There was not enough light time left to collect our dead. They would have to wait (under guard for fear of scavengers -human as well as animals). The dead of the opponents would remain on the field until such time the King would grant their collection or refuse it. Meantime the prisoners were rounded-up and placed under guard also. The King, Alexand-ros and the officers proceeded to offer thanks to the gods for the victory. Alexandros made sure to offer to Iraklis also. Then, he went to wash -it was his personal peculiarity to be keeping himself clean at all times- and joined his Father and King later for supper and wine to commemorate the vic-tory.

As the flow of wine became steady and most became rather intoxicated, Attalos proposed to have a comos danced and sang and Filippos took-up on that and ordered the flutists to play. He took the lead and started dancing and singing, his lame foot dragging on the ground. Passing by the stockade of the Athinians, a captured eupatrid named Dimadis called on to the King the words of the well known tragedian: "When Tyhi has given you the scepter of Agamemnon o King, are you not asham-ed to act the part of Thersitis?"

The King was not drunk enough not to feel the admonition. He stopped the comos immediately and ordered the release of Dimadis. He asked him to be among the petitioners for the recovery of the Athinian dead. As for the prince, Alexandros cast his eyes to the ground and left the victory festiv-ities going to his tend and staying there till the next morning.

Dimadis was sent to Athinae with the King's message: Athinae was to abolish her so-called empire (although that was mostly wishful Athinian thinking, once the few who followed her were not like the old dependent city-states paying tribute), the people were to vote for immediate alliance with Make-don and bring the party of Fokion in charge of the city affairs. In return, the King would release the prisoners without asking any ransom, he would not march into Attiki and he would return the dead for proper burial! The stunned Athinians had no other choice but to accept, thinking the terms so much more lenient than what Dimosthenis had preached or what a victorious Sparti had imposed on them in the past.

On the other hand, Thivae was given no choice but to surrender unconditionally. They had been a faithless ally and had to be punished accordingly. The King ordered the Kadmia to be garrisoned by a good number of Makedonian troops, the citizens to kill or exile the anti-Makedonian leadership among them and give-up their rule over the Viottian city-states for ever! The only exception was the honorable burial of the Sacred Band. They were cleaned, placed on a pyre and had their remains in a common grave mount, where they had fall. A sculptured statue of a lion was ordered to mark the place.

When Dimadis returned with the rest of the envoys with the Athinian acceptance of terms, the King let his Athinian prisoners know they were free now to go. Many of the Makedonian officers demand-ed the King should have marched to Athinae instead of letting his prisoners free. He looked at them smiling. "One never knows what kind of reception we would have had doing so . . . The Akropolis fell only once through all the years of the city's existence while undermanned and to Xerxis! I will not be the one to complete such an infamous act!" Alexandros wanted to know why the King had not demanded at least the handing over of Dimosthenis. "They will have him pay for his folly sooner rather than later. Do you think I would want to make a hero out of him?" was Filippos' answer.

He told Dimadis that the Athinian dead were soon to follow the road to their city for proper burial.

Filippos ordered next the care of the remains and their skeletons were put individually in wooden boxes and loaded on carts to be driven to Attiki and Athinae. He called Antipatros from Pella and, when he came, he assigned Alexandros and him to head a formal delegation for the official draft of peace according to his terms. "Don't you want to go to Athinae Father?" Alexandros asked.

The prince, like most Makedonians could not understand the King not going to Athinae as a benevol-ent victor making his point with a glorious entrance.

Filippos let a sigh and told his son that sending the heir to the Makedonian throne had nothing offensive in nature. The coming of the man who brought the Athinian quasi empire to its end on the other hand, would certainly be to them as a slap in the face, salt added to an open wound. Maybe at another, more appropriate time . . .

Alexandros rode toward Attiki with Antipatros, his second son Alexarhos, the son of Parmenion Filotas, his own cousin Amyntas and me, escorted by the Agima minus many of our friends who were to return home for various reasons. I was ordered by the King to write down in full detail the peace agreement with Athinae and oversee they placed it in all crossroads of the city for public view. The King with the bulk of the army took the road back and stopped at Dion for thanksgiving to the gods with athletic competitions and festivities. He was to be the honored guest at the estate purchased near-by by Attalos. Perdikkas told me much later that he observed that Pafsanias never entered the house—as his rank of leader of the guard would allow him—nor did he ate any of the food served to all at the estate. He slept out of the bounds, at a near-by hamlet and he kept sullen and unapproachable.

Meantime, when we approached Dekelia, the small town at the border of Attiki, Dimadis was there to receive us along with a number of notable

Athinians known for their trust in the King's policy. We entered the city the next morning from the side of Keramikos, where the tombs of old and recent notables are mostly located. We noted a newly cleaned place and we were told that it was assigned to receive the remains of the fallen in Heronia. We stopped there to see that the unloading of the carts would proceed with due order and respect.

That done, we continued following the wide road through the Agora. The affairs of the city had to be looked through, regardless of hard times and the specter of defeat still so raw. There, we were met in civil but guarded manner by Aeshinis and Fokion, while Yperidis made a monkey of himself as he purposely spat on the ground seeing us entering. He was completely ignored. As for the 'great' Dimo-sthenis, he was nowhere to be seen (we were told no one had seen him since the day he came back running away from the battle).

We were lodged at the houses of Dimadis and his fellow delegates who had come to Heronia with the Athinian acceptance of peace. The next day they took us to see the Akropolis and visit the Parthenon, the temple dedicated to goddess Athina. Next to her statue we were shown the olive tree, the one burned by Xerxis and reinvigorated itself as soon as the Persians withdrew. Alexandros asked to visit the Akadimia, where his tutor Aristotelis had walked alongside Platon and had a private conversation with its current director, Xenokratis.

On our way back to Dimadis' house, I left the party under the escort of an Athinian in our service to go and see the progress of the peace treaty draft done by specially assigned Athinian secretaries. Up-on my return, Antipatros told, flashed with anger still hanging about him, of an affront to our prince's person. An Athinian member of the peace party had approached Alexandros and offered him the love services of a bought youngster. Alexandros listened in horror the offer and, hardly keeping his temper, ordered the offender to never show himself before him again, saying that he did not do anything to deserve such proposal! Dimadis swore he had no idea beforehand of such an insult and things were let as were but the enjoyment was gone. The next day we received and approved the peace treaty as written, affixed our names on it next to the Athinian ones and departed.

On our way back to Makedonia, we received the news that the Persian High King Artaxerxis (the third one under that name had died) and his son Artaxerxis the fourth the one also called Ochos now was on the throne.

King Filippos wanted us to return to Pella with no delays. Arriving there and after paying a short visit to his Mother and hearing once more her complaints, Alexandros reported to the council his father had ordered to convine. The King wanted to speed up the unification of Ellas under Makedonian guidance and have the combined Ellenic armies move now against Persia. He knew by past studies and experience that this was the right time, since each new High King lately had hard times securing his throne in the empire. Soon enough after the council and proposed stages of readiness, we received the news of Egyptos revolting and Ochos campaigning to recover the lost province of his empire.

Filippos made his move. He marched south again, crossed the narrow neck of land connecting Peloponnisos with the rest of Ellas to Korinthos and toward Lakedaemon and Sparti. He enforced his will upon the city-states to accept Makedonia as their leader against Persia and avenge the wrong doings of Xerxis. He knew he had to, because Ellas could not afford any more wars between city-states. The ideas of Isokratis' letters to him for a unified Ellas had been understood, found attractive and now had to be put to work. Since one could only impose this union from a point of power, the King had no alternative. Most of the city-states (especially the small ones which could do nothing more—until now that is—but place themselves as satellites to Sparti, Thivae or Athinae and pay tribute on top of it) found the idea also attractive and joined voluntarily. Few had to be persuaded by a simple show of force. Sparti rejected any and all offers giving a high handed reply, as if she still was at the peak of her power and not the third rated state of present reality.

We did not enter Lakedaemon, finding it a waste of time and respecting Sparti's past glory. The city-states understood and sent delegations in Korinthos to seal the deal and draft the rules of partic-ipation for the new campaign. The King just sent a warning to them not to force his hand and went to Korinthos where delegates from the rest of Ellas were waiting to start working on the details of the proclaimed Κοινη Ειρηνη, the Common Peace.

At the same time in Athinae, the tombs had been readied to receive the remains of the fallen in He-ronia. As customary, someone had to give a speech for their valor both at everyday life and during the battle. Their sacrifice for the city and state could not go unnoticed much more so because of the grief their loss brought to most houses.

The peace party, the so-called Filippizers by Dimosthenis, the ones he constantly accused of being in the pay of Makedon, would not be the right ones. What they were supposed to say? We told you so? Besides, many -if not most- of them had fought at Heronia and with valor and distinction, like Dima-dis. Respected persons like Fokion or Aeshinis were not suitable, for the reason that when offered their services they were denied the honor and/or sent to other, unimportant missions to chase ghosts!

There was only one person in whole Attiki who should eulogize the heroes. The one who sent them there to die, the one who run first in terror, the one who had been hiding since (one would hope out of shame)! That one was Dimosthenis. They sought him and told him. He had to accept and he did...

Alexandros spent several weeks with his Father and other notable Makedonian delegates and friends in Korinthos working out the Common Peace. The King was very lenient in his demands. With his suggestion and prodding, a Council was created from representatives from all city-states, each with equal power as any other -regardless the size of the state. They were to meet four times annually, making sure no state would infringe on another, none would war against any other any-more!

They were to keep their own recognized political establishments with no changes on their systems what-so-ever, in order to preserve the current peace. The King asked them to join Makedonia in waging war against Persia to avenge the past wrong doings of the old invader, to liberate the Ellenic city-states in Asia by the Aegean and force the High King to cease interfering in Ellenic affairs, sup-porting wars against one-another for his benefit. He asked to lead them united to a new era of glory and prosperity and they accepted. All, except Sparti. That state didn't even bother to send an observ-er! They were ignored and they were left to brew in Lakedaemon...

The city-states offered the King the title of Ηγεμονας, Commander-in-chief, and agreed to support the campaign against Persia with men, money and navy, according to each state's ability. The par-ticular responsibilities of each one were left to be worked out by the Council and most of the Maked-onian delegation took the road back to Pella.

While staying in Korinthos, Ptolemeos (being part of Alexandros' own Eteri) in his free (mostly stolen free) time sightseeing the city, met and fell in love with Thais, an Athinian etera who lived for a number of years in the city of the famous Lais. He was lost in her arms like never before and he con-vinced her to follow him to Makedonia. Obviously, this gave us all the opportunity to tease him a lot!

Love being love, he paid no attention. His answer was that her beauty did not prevent him from per-

forming his duties (that was true) and that we were simply very jealous of his ability to attract such rare a beauty. By the time we returned to Pella the novelty had ceased to exist and we let them be.

We returned to our homes before the King. He had accepted a new invitation from Attalos to spend few more days at his estates. After all, the King deserved peaceful time and some recuperation from his toils and hard-won recognition from Ellas! Filippos ordered Alexandros to act again as regent, keeping him (Filippos) informed through messengers. Pafsanias asked and received permission for leave of absence to visit his wife and family in his estates in Orestis. Klitos Melas replaced him for a short time as Leader of the King's guard.

Returning home and going to visit his Mother, Alexandros found Olympias enraged. Through her spies, she knew the reason Filippos had accepted Attalos' invitation. During the King's last stay at the estates of his officer, Attalos had introduced his niece, a girl named Kleopatra, daughter of Ippostratos and the King fell in love once more!

Alexandros tried to calm her, stating that the King of Makedon had the right to marry several times, thus forming alliances and securing further his position internally and externally. He had already been married to four wives before and after his marriage with Olympias, hadn't he? She should keep her dignity! She was the officially recognized Queen and the rest shouldn't matter. In any event, she had not accepted the King to her bed for years now! Was it better when the King had the attention of young men?

Naturally, she accused him of siding with his 'so-called father' (because men were men!) against the only one who truly loved him and cared for him, namely, his one and only Mother!

Alexandros left her rooms the usual way after a fight, exhausted and in a wild state of mind. He stayed away from her for days, until the King returned with the announcement for his forthcoming marriage to Kleopatra (he bestowed on her the additional name Evridiki, for reasons unknown to any -except the two of them). In his preparation to move against Persia, he considered important to open an additional door and made public his intentions to wed his first-born son to the daughter of the Satrap of Karia in Asia by the Aegean, Pixodaros (Pihsodaryiush).

Alexandros in a very taxed state of mind because of the recent fight and his Mother's continuous ideas of plots by the King against her, knowing also that poor Arrideos was far from being consider-ed a normal minded person, took the whole thing as an affront to him personally from his own King and Father. Instead of talking it over with Filippos, he chose to voice his concerns and complained to his immediate friends.

Aside of talking to Yfestion, he brought the problem and discussed it before the brothers and companions Erygios and Laomedon, sons of Larihos from Mytilini, Lesvos. Also with Ptolemeos son of Lagos, who looked upon Alexandros as an older brother (many insinuated he was a real half-brother knowing the King's ventures in his youth), with Arpalos son of Mahatas and Filotas, son of Parmenion. Yfestion and Filotas advised caution, as no one knew the true plans of the King. The others sided wholeheartedly with his notion to take immediate action and null the effect of this 'affront'.

Olympias did not help either but -seeing a serious drift between Father and son- sided by Alexan-dros' motives and urged swift action. The prince took the opportunity and sent Arpalos to be his intermediary agent to Pixodaros and enlisted himself as the primary groom of the bride! Arpalos left Pella accompanied by Nearhos on the pretext he was following a troupe of actors on tour, among which was Alexandros' favored one, Thettalos.

When King Filippos found out about this crossing of his plans almost had a stroke! He ordered the immediate arrest of Arpalos, Erygios, Laomedon, Ptolemeos and Nearhos and had them escorted out of the kingdom in exile. Next, he ordered Alexandros to his study and, when the prince presented himself before the King, Filippos let him have it!

"Do you think that I am doing all this work so you can spoil everything? Don't even dare to utter a word! Just listen and listen carefully! If you ever counteract to my wishes and plans, I will have you send in exile -or worst! Did you know how old Pixodaros' daughter is and you were so anxious to ask for her hand? Let me tell you! Only an infant! I presented your half brother as a groom, because of his condition and in hope that -by the time all would be in the open- we would be well past Karia with no concern of Pixodaros or his feelings. But, meantime, he could have been our best supporter and ally, with me sending Parmenion and Attalos with troops to pave a road for us late next year! I don't know what is with your Mother -and now with you always trying to second guess me! Now: promise me solemnly you will not act in anything, unless you consult me first! Because, I swear to gods and Iraklis, I will have you put away! Is that clear to you...boy?"

Alexandros had nothing to do or say. For the first time in his life, was talked by his father and King in such a manner! What was worst, he knew he was wrong, acting out of impulse and falsely hurt pride. He gazed at the floor until he was sure the King was waiting for his required oath of keeping out of schemes in the future. His face like a freshly whitewashed wall, he called upon the gods and Iraklis to be the witness of his promise. Then, he turned around and started going. "I don't recall having you being excused!" Filippos could not let his anger diminish. He wasn't perfectly sure Alex-andros would not go and do something crazy. The boy/man was at times worst than his Mother!

The prince turned to face his Father and King, head still down, without a word. "Look at me!" The eyes facing Filippos were darker than the deep sea and void. The King felt he had to clear his throat. "You are dismissed now!" Alexandros left almost running out of the King's study leaving the door open behind him. Pafsanias, being outside to change the guard at the entrance of the King's quarters, looked at Filippos who had busied himself to reclaim his calm as best he could and, with a wicked smile, he closed the door softly.

A few months passed-by with father and son seeing one-another rarely and on need-to-do basis. Publicly, there was no admonishment, no demotion nor an acknowledgment that something had gone wrong. When at the exercise fields, each took care of his own sector of troops to maneuvers and the King would inspect only during established dates. In politics and every day affairs of the Kingdom Alexandros was called to participate only when absolutely necessary, because of delegates from other states. He spent the ample free time he had now by working on personal exercise running behind the old chariot at full speed, mounting and dismounting. He missed his close friends in exile and his talks with Yfestion, Perdikkas, Iraklidis, Pefkestas and Filotas, the subject was sure to come up all the time.

Olympias tried to console her son in her way, but, being of what her nature was, she managed to alienate him even further. Because of his love toward her, he did not stop visiting or try to accuse her for the ill advice she had given him on the Pixodaros affair. But his visits were rather short in duration and further apart from the former three-four time a week visits. In fact he turned down several invitations to dinner at her quarters, with various excuses. She knew the truth and she would twist the knife of guilt whenever she thought she wouldn't face his total rejection. That hurt him most and -in times of solace- being alone with Yfestion, he opened his heart to the only person he now could trust with absolute certainty.

The only other person who had some sort of parental influence and closeness was the old tutor of youth, his favored Finix. They would spend hours reading together the epics of Omiros Aristotelis had copied painstakingly for Alexandros, or read the works of Xenofon, the famous Athinian general who managed to extract the whole Ellenic mercenary army from the (now dead) High King Artaxer-xis' armies and brought them back to Ellenic-held lands with very few losses.

Alexandros knew that in a relatively short time the King, in charge of all Ellenic forces would cross to Asia against the Persian foe and that he would also be there. That was his consolation. He did hope that his exiled friends would rejoin the expeditionary force either because the King would need their valuable assistance, or, because (he prayed) Filippos' heart would soften by then and grand them clemency. But his Mother's blood in him would not let him go to his Father and ask for it!

Summer went by and the preparations for the campaign were in good order. The advance army under Parmenion and Attalos had some initial success but now was on the defensive. The new Artax-erxis had thrown on them all his might and they barely were holding some key cities across the Ellispontos sea channel as a foothold for the ones to follow them. At the beginning of the month of Dios, the King announced his wedding plans with the niece of Attalos against advice (from Hrysogo-nos son of Filippos from Krousis house Haridimos) to leave it for another time when conditions in the King's immediate family would change for the better.

The King had found himself being in true love (the only other time was with Olympias -how long ago really?) and, besides, the girl had become pregnant! He did not want to leave behind him an unsettled affair at the hands of Olympias and her scheming mind while he was fighting in Asia. At-talos was called to return for the preparation of the nuptials at Pella, which would take place right after the festivities at the town of Dion in honor of Zefs and the Olympian gods.

The wedding itself was a rather low-keyed affair, for it had no great political significance outside Makedonia itself. The girl was just the niece of a noble Makedonian -to be sure- but that was that. Nonetheless, representatives from the other city-states came to attend feeling it was their duty to the proclaimed leader of Ellas and, Filippos being raised with true Makedonian hospitality and eager to bond the Ellines any which way, put his best up front to accommodate. Pella was décorated for the event in a hurry.

Olympias was, again, furious! She called Alexandros to her chambers to forbid him attending such a 'treacherous' affair! Alexandros saw things from a different perspective. He pointed that the wed-ding was not a big deal and, as the recognized heir to the throne, his duty to the King was to comply and attend. He also had in mind (when the King would announce he would grand wishes to his guests) to ask for the return of his friends from exile. Olympias couldn't believe "how callous" he was! "What if she gives him a son?" Alexandros' answer was "What to make of it? By the time he grows to be of any threat to me, the King will be over sixty years of age and, by that time, I will make sure he knows my worth of being his heir!"

The men for the wedding party assembled at a big banquet hall of Attalos' house dressed their best, crowns of vine on their heads in honor of Dionysos and the rites of the Ymenas, the wedding ritual itself. The act had taken place earlier and the bride, like any every well mannered and proper Make-donian bride, had gone to her chambers with some of her closest girlfriends to prepare for the late night 'reception' at the house of her husband. Following the Makedonian tradition of course, fest-ivities in Pella had started about seven days ago and were to continue for as many.

Filippos was sitting at his royal couch (laying on it would be much later) already under the influ-ence of the strong Makedonian wine served. To his right, the new in-law Attalos, was consuming even more, in total happiness. His relation to the King now elevated him much higher than he ever hoped to be! He was already dreaming of future greatness and fame. To the King's left was Antipatros, much more somber and engaged in a conversation with the Korinthian Dimaratos, who had brought with him the exiled from Syrakousae ex Tyranos, Dionysios the Younger.

Alexandros, as the heir to the throne, was seated across from the King surrounded by Yfestion, the Athinian host (now a guest) of his stay in that city Dimadis, Kinos (he was soon to marry Parmeni-on's daughter),

Agathon son of Tyrimmas from Eordea, Pefkestas son of Alexandros from Mieza, Fi-lotas, Perdikkas and his cousin Krateros both of house Agis from Orestis and some others.

In the space in between these two seated companies, leaving a big empty space for the wedding show performers, were the places of all the other guests, forming a rough rectangular parallel to the walls.

They were the delegates from the other city-states of the south, Thessalians, Viottians, Peloponnis-ians, islanders and few of the subjected and friendly Illyrian and Thrakian chiefs. Alexandros of Mo-lossis had send an envoy with the king's best wishes and a golden vine crown which Filippos wore with pleasure, showing in public that -whatever the rumors- he was in favorable relations with Olym-pias' own brother. Of course, among all these guests were the relatives and members of Attalos' clan.

There were many short speeches and good fortune wishes coming every-so-often from various guests, speaking either as individuals or on behalf of their states and the wine started flowing faster than the -intended to escort it- food. Just about everybody started getting under the influence, first the southern guests as they were accustomed to drink it mixed with water and not Makedonian style.

Being of Thrakian stock and equally good (if not better) in holding it, I passed time observing the level of sobriety or lack of it among the guests. As I was recently promoted at the head of the King's scribes, I was invited to attend and seated between Hrysogonos and Selefkos son of Antiohos the Or-estian who, coming to the banquette rather late, had not find room close to Alexandros.

Hrysogonos was already past his tolerance in wine and leaning half-asleep on his couch and Selefkos had started a deep conversation with a bigwig from Trikka (I've forgotten his name) so I was free to look around and amuse myself observing. I noticed that the King had rather a lot to drink already, and, as I caught up now and then some of his words, they sounded (to me) blurred. Hey! The man was in love, he had just wed his bride and had all these admirers (true or pretending ones) at his fingertips! Attalos was also very much under, with a very good cause. His station in life had quad-rupled within few months; he had become the in-law of the strongest person on earth (this way of the Aegean any way) and the future was open to him for all to see!

I took a look toward Alexandros and his friends. Seated as he was between Yfestion and Dimadis, he was engrossed in some serious conversation with them, paying little -if any- attention to speeches and praises of the various guests. He was hardly drinking. All the time through my observation, he may have had two or three sips from his cup. On the other hand, his friends around him were having a real good time emptying their cups and getting louder all the time.

Alexandros not being able to hear what Dimadis was saying in all this noise turned disturbed and called at his friends for a softer tone of voice. At that same time, Attalos rose wavering and calling out loudly for silence. He was about to toast the groom. All faces turned to him. In a stentorian voice full of self importance and in order to cover the soft talk of those who didn't care about what he was to say, he turned and addressed the King. "I wish you, Filippos, a happy life with your young Queen and one with many children! I hope one of them will grow to be a true Makedonian heir to your throne!"

Adis, the abode of the underworld god Pluton cannot be as gloomy as the banquet hall became as soon as Attalos' words were heard and started to sink-in. Most heads turned toward Alexandros, cup by his mouth ready to sip a drink but suspended in air the -motion unfinished. Some of the heads were turned to Attalos not willing to believe what was heard and some to King Filippos, waiting for reaction.

I had a vantage of placement and I could see all three with no effort or need to turn my head from side to side. First, I saw the familiar drainage of face color in Alexandros, while -at the same time- I could see the King struggling to make sense in his clouded mind of what caused the sudden silence. I could also see the vanity still engraved on the face of Attalos, indifferent to the insult he just threw on the face of the prince.

At that instance, I saw a shiny object flying and hitting Attalos square on the face breaking his nose! It was the cup Alexandros used to drink his wine. Simultaneously, we all heard the distinct voice of the prince bellowing "And what are you, worm, calling me? A bastard?"

The King stood up not totally balanced and raised his hands to impose his will and have the fight come to its end before it would spread. He turned to Attalos who, meeting Filippos' glance, lowered his head in shame now of his folly. Next the King turned to his son. The face he saw was the spitting image of Olympias in her youth and at her times of rage. His mind clouded from the drinking, he thought it proper to have her put in her place at once. Addressing Alexandros/Olympias he ordered an apology. The eyes of his son's face turned that deep dark sea color and the blood disappeared from the cheeks, leaving a white expression void of any life and crowned by a (misplaced now) wreath of vines on a ruffled set of golden hair.

The King waited for the apology and saw it wasn't coming. Alexandros was standing erect, hands rested on each side by his waist, eyes looking straight and challenging. The King's face turned from red to purple. "Ah! Her character! Have I got no son? If the kid had at least put his head down…" the thought was clear on his face. He glanced with his good eye around the hall. The south states' guests were looking at him expectantly. Could their leader put an order in his house? How was he to lead them in Persia if he couldn't set things in order here? Cursed be the moment he ever loved her…

"Now! Boy, do as I said! Apologize to me!" "Not before he kneels and apologizes first, before me!" was the answer. Filippos had it. He would teach a hard lesson now. Placing a hand on his ceremonial sword (he was the only one with a weapon allowed in the hall), he moved from his couch toward Ale-xandros. Being seated for a long time, already drunk and with his lame leg, he lost his balance and fell. "I warned you not to cross me ever again in your life!" he yelled hitting the floor. A laugh and a sneer hit his ears harder than the public disobedience. "Look at your leader men of Ellas! He pro-poses to cross with you to Asia and he's not even capable of crossing from one couch to another!"

Alexandros' friends were finally coming out of their lethargy and, fearing of worst to come, they pushed and shoved him out of the house, while Antipatros, Klitos Melas, Hrysogonos and others were helping the King up and tried to calm him down a bit with words of understanding and tisk-tisks on youth impulses and lack of judgment.

Alexandros and his friends jumped up on their horses and galloped heading toward the palace. On their way there, he gave them his orders. "Any one of you who fears reprisals from the King toward his family and/ or himself, ought to stay here! I am taking my Mother and heading toward her broth-er's domain in Ipiros. Who wants to come with me, take your arms and what you can carry, take spare horses and meet me at the bridge of Lydias." They all dispersed to their houses to do what they were told, leaving him alone as he entered the palace's gate. The guards there didn't even have time to realize it was him passing but he had given them the right recognition word, so they let him pass.

He got to the palace and run to his Mother's rooms. As he approached, he saw Pafsanias who looked at him in a strange way. But, then, Pafsanias was always a bit strange and, lately, more so because of Attalos' climbing up the ladder of success. Alexandros didn't give it a second thought. Pafsanias' mood was not his concern at this moment. He just gave him a look of recognition and continued his run. Without scratching on the doors, he pushed them open and entered while he ordered Polemon of Tymfea who was guarding at that time to make sure no one was to come in her room under penalty of death. He woke her up and ordered her to get ready fast, taking only what was necessary for a journey on a horse lasting three to four days of fast ride. "Don't ask any ques-tions; don't wake-up anybody, just do what I tell you! We will talk on the way out like nothing is out of place!" He turned and hurried to his chambers.

She was ready in no time and went to the court, to find Alexandros with four horses ready. They met his friends waiting at the bridge of Lydias and ready. Just before leaving, Alexandros told Filo-tas he would have to stay behind. Filotas tried to protest but he cut him sort. "You have a lot more to lose coming with me than the others. Your Father is in Asia and you are now in charge of your fami-ly and clan. Stay here! I will remember you and find a way to keep in touch!" With that, he turned and they galloped heading west to south-west.

They rode through the night crossing into Imathia and by-passing Veria toward the Eordean moun-tains of Askion and the borders of Orestis. On the way Alexandros told Olympias of the fight. She started saying how right she was not wanting him to be at that place to begin with, but he cut her sort telling her this wasn't the time to argue who's right or wrong! They still had to cross Eordea and hide somewhere before Orestis and daylight.

Her answer was they only needed to cross into the Orestian lands by morning. There, she knew of a safe place to stay, get fed, change clothes and get some sleep before continuing through the Pindos heights and the ford of river Aoos into her brother's kingdom. He looked at her puzzled but she just smiled and motioned him to have patience. The rest of his friends followed in silence and some distance, showing respect.

They entered Orestis in record time, avoiding towns and by-passing villages. They crossed the river Aliakmon at the pass (unknown now to them, it was close to the tributary river where Levaea used to be), stopping only to change riding horses and using the spare ones, so none would die of exhaustion under them. The sun had not come on top of the eastern peaks of Askion left behind them yet, just the daylight being enough now to see clearly the narrow path she had taken leading them to… where?

They came on top of a hill and, before them, the opening of a small fertile valley. Across, at the other end they could see a mediocre, rather fortified complex of few houses, a small river serving as its moat on the open side, the outcrop of low but seer rock defending its other sides forming some-thing like the shape of the last quarter of the moon. She just said "We're just about there" and kicked her horse leading the way. The others followed. They were exhausted and in dire need of a bed and some sleep. And so were their horses too...

Getting closer to the complex they could see two guards armed in old style with spears which probably belonged to their fathers at one time and breast plates made out of animal skins with some metal scales attached on them. They were seated on either side of the gate to the complex, past the small bridge and the 'moat'. When they saw the riders coming, they got up and grabbed their spears while one called on a third guard not visible until he appeared from under the bridge. That one run past the gate to probably call the alarm worried by the sudden and totally unexpected approach of riders.

"Let me do the talking" Olympias said guiding her horse ahead. She crossed the bridge ahead of the others. Arriving before the two guards who didn't know what to make of it all, she ordered:

"Tell your mistress that her Pellean Mistress has arrived and is seeking shelter. Now!" They looked at her suspiciously for a moment. Deciding the newcomers presented no immediate danger, one nod-ded the other to obey. As he turned to go through the gate, the guard who run in before reappeared escorted by a woman in her mid twenties and an infant in her arms. Seeing Olympias and recogniz-ing her, she bowed and told the guard to hurry and have the people prepare rooms for her guests. She then motioned for all to follow her and they entered the inner court of the complex.

Alexandros thought the face of the 'mistress' was somewhat familiar but couldn't place it. He lean-ed more toward Yfestion as they were now dismounting in front of the apparent stables building and looked at him questioning. "If I am not wrong, Alexandros, she's the wife of the King's chief body guard, Pafsanias!"

Alexandros was surprised. He turned to his Mother. "I told you I knew of a safe place for us" she said with a wicked smile and held her hands forward to be helped down. Alexandros remained perplexed but decided

491

not to push the issue. Had his Mother have an affair with Pafsanias? Is that why he had looked at him so strangely last night found so close to her quarters? Was Polemon also cognizant of such an affair—if it truly existed? He wanted to know! By the time the 'house mistress' showed them to their rooms, Olympias turned and, dismissing any ideas of interrogation, kissed him and entered hers closing the door firmly behind her.

The prince felt like busting in and demand answers but he was tired and he did not want to have another fight before witnesses. What had happen the night before was enough hurt and exhaustion cause. There was always time later. He entered his room, made sure he washed thoroughly and dropped in his bed. By the time he pulled a thin cover over his body, he had fallen asleep.

They found their horses rested, fed and watered the next morning. Alexandros was in a hurry to get moving. He wanted to cross in to Ipiros before the King's men could find them tracking down their trail but the 'mistress of the house' told him to relax. She had taken care of things while they were sleeping. She told him Pafsanias' instructions were—in case this or something similar would ever happen—to send the men to destroy all signs of their passing and create tracks leading to Lynkestis. Then, using the flow of Aliakmon coming down from its springs on mount Vernon thus covering their tracks, to cross over the passes of Voion and return to her keep from north. Nobody after that would be able to connect the two . . .

Alexandros looked at his Mother astonished. "You knew of all these? You knew it could happen and planned with him everything?" She, as usually, did not give him a straight answer. "Let us have our morning meal; we are going to need all the sustenance we can get! The trek from here-on is much more difficult. We still have to cross the peaks of Pindos and river Aoos before we meet my brother and safety!" "We will then, Mother, but under one condition: as soon as we finish and get going, I want to know everything! Do not put in your mind to hide something or try to trick me with lies! I will know and, by Iraklis, I will lead you back to the King and surrender myself to him! Don't try to test me!" She saw he was dead serious with his threat and, letting a deep sigh, she agreed.

On their way through the passes and mountain peaks of Pindos, she told him. She had seen the anguish and desperation of Pafsanias when the King promoted Attalos and, later, his desire to somehow get even by taking a small revenge. So, she befriended him and foreseeing what could pos-sibly happen when Filippos announced his new wedding that her son so foolishly had agreed to attend, she asked for Pafsanias' help, which was gladly given. As for the preplanned coverage of their tracks, he had told her his instruction to his wife were given long ago, in case he had to run for his life from Attalos' hands.

Alexandros listened and knew she told him most, but not all. She told him part of the truth but not the total truth! He figured his chances of returning to Pella and saw they were slim to none. The complete truth did not matter so much after that. He let her in the company of Perdikkas and slowed down to ride with Yfestion. He needed a venue to vent his anguish, someone who would hear him and hear him true. Yfestion was always the one to do so when needed . . .

They arrived in Ipiros the next morning, after they spent one more night at a summer lodging of an Orestian shepherd—long abandoned now since the summer days were gone. It was the first day of the Makedonian month of Avdiaeos and the snow on the Pindos range was deep in most of the passes, making their progress very slow. They were lucky no one had fallen in a ravine no horse was incapacitated. Now they started descending toward the Molossian lake following the narrow paths leading to Dodona and the winder palace of Olympias' brother Alexandros.

The king of Molossis received an early warning of strangers approaching and came out of the town escorted with his company of horsemen to investigate. Seeing his sister and nephew leading the small group of weary travelers, he was truly taken by surprise. He urged his horse forward, waving his men to wait at some distance. He had this premonition that such a sudden unannounced visit was of no good omens. Approaching, he greeted his relatives warmly—as was his duty— and formally offered hospitality. Finishing with the proper greetings, he wanted to know the reason of their sudden com-ing to his kingdom. Asking, he was addressing his nephew and namesake, for he knew the character of his sister when coming to tell the truth but leaving her personal interest out of context.

As they headed toward town and warmth and somewhat ahead of the others and the king's escort, Alexandros told his uncle the whole story. The king fell silent for some time digesting what he was told by his nephew. He could see Alexandros' point as the young man (known to him since almost the time of birth) was famous of his strict adherence to the Omeric meaning of the word αρετη meaning excellence in all and—especially—in matters of honor. He also knew more than well his own sister's ways of making herself unpopular to even her closest relations.

Adding to that was his own sense of owing big to his mentor, the King of Makedon, Filippos. His duty as the brother of the injured party on the other hand, obliged him to accept the visitors with open arms, provide shelter and protection and, ask from King Filippos some sort of an explanation (very remote possibility here and, probably, with good reason). He cursed (inward) his sister . . .

At the palace he offered all available accommodations his poorer treasury (compared to the Maked-onian) could provide and let them recover until the next day. Then, he would have a man to man talk with his nephew, trying to see what he can do to be fair to all, yet keep himself and his kingdom out of either the Father's or the son's wrath.

The next morning after breakfast the two men had time to be alone. With the excuse of inspecting his home troops and check their readiness, the king let his sister 'have a women's talk' with his own mother and his aunt. As they arrived at the 'inspection' site the king asked Alexandros' friends to busy themselves with the act and report any and all shortcomings of his cavalry, compared to—by now famous—Makedonian one. He and prince Alexandros walked away with their private conversa-tion.

"I know I am a burden to you uncle" the young prince started, to the king's relief—as he had it difficult to finding proper words and bring the subject up. "I know King Filippos knows by now that we are here, I don't care how well our tracks were covered. He has his pathfinders and scouts to rely upon—and they're very good at their work!" A short pause and he continued. "I ask nothing for me and my followers. I would not impose on you such a burden. I am only asking you to see that my Mother is safe with you, as it is your duty to your sister!"

"I will keep her here with me for as long as it takes, safe and well attended. You don't need to wor-ry on that, I know my obligations. But, where are you going? Which place in Ellas will give you shelter? Stay here and I will do my best to convince the King that it's not to his advantage to have you wandering and giving reason to his enemies in accusing Makedon as an unstable and divided kingdom which doesn't deserve the leadership of Ellas!"

"No, uncle, it is best I go. Just make sure you supply us with fresh horses and few days worth of provisions. I will never forget your offer and your guardianship of my Mother's honor! That, I swear in the name of

Iraklis and the Olympian gods! Do not try to persuade the King to have us back be-cause he won't listen. His pride was hurt almost as much as mine. He will reconsider in due time when I will prove to him beyond any doubt his mistake. Trying now will get you nothing but trouble and I don't want to be the cause. I have, we have been close since we met so many years ago and I know you love me—as I do you. You need Filippos' tolerance—if not outright friendship! I will go north to Illyria. Some chiefs there owe me their very lives. It's time for them to pay me back."

Within three more days of preparation and supply gathering, the small band of riders headed north toward Illyria. There was no good-by really between Mother and son. Alexandros visited Olympias the night before his departure and she only asked him if all was ready. He answered positively and tried to tell her his arrangement with the Ipirote king on her safety. She cut him short, showing him she knew all about it and it didn't matter to her. That irked him very much. What the woman finally wanted? Return to Makedon and starting a civil conflict? Marching against his own Father? No mat-ter what she had told him about the divine visit to her upon his conception, he believed little of it. He had to wait for the right time and ask the Oracle when not expected. He coolly placed a kiss on her forehead, said goodnight and the next morning he was gone.

The going further north into Illyria was tough and the snow storms they encountered severe. But king Kossos had his arms open when they finally arrived at his township, a poor example of a king's stronghold. But Illyria was famous about its poverty and tendency of its people to roam rather than settle, work and create. Gatherers rather than farmers, takers (when convenient) of ready-made than creators, they survived in their mountainous country deprived from the few fertile coastal plains which were taken centuries ago by settlers from the southern city-states. Makedonia had to pay the price of it in years past—until King Filippos' reign. Kossos had met the power of Makedon and received his defeat from the hands of his now guest and had not forgotten the lesson.

The grayed now king offered what best he could to his guests. One thing one could count on was the ever true Illyrian hospitality, especially when offered to settle a heavy debt. Kossos owed his life, in-deed his kingship, to the magnanimity of Alexandros. He had to pay back and—if this was the time—so be it! One thing was in the mind of Alexandros though knowing the Illyrian custom on debts. How long would Kossos

495

have them under his roof paying that debt off? He resolved to do what he could to extend that sense of debt in the eyes of the Illyrian king. So, when in the course of talk and acquaint-ing again Kossos referred to his troubles with the neighboring Parthines and Aftariates, Alexandros offered his services in subduing these troublesome neighbors . . .

> "Division is the curse of Ellas and
> we seem to be divided always at the
> most inappropriate times!"
> Andreas G. Rados, Makedonian Ellinas, Freedom Fighter-W.W. II

XIII

Back in Pella King Filippos was upset with himself, angry at his son and completely enraged with Olympias. As soon as she left, he ordered an edict to be published which—in effect—divorced him from Olympias for good. He let Alexandros' status remain up in the air, for he knew the worth of his son and the love every Makedonian trooper held for the young prince. Being upset of himself for not taking proper care to contain the ambitions of Attalos before things turned so ugly, he ordered the fool back to Asia to rejoin Parmenion.

He learned of Pafsanias' assistance to the fugitives but did not bother to mention his knowledge to his leader of the guard—let alone to admonish or punish him. The man had truly suffered from the insult of Attalos few years back. He, Filippos, had promise justice. Well let this be part of the promise and leave things be. In any event, the sullenness of Pafsanias had faded somewhat since Attalos was sent back to Asia. Let things now settle-down.

Basically, Filippos blamed everything on Olympias and, when he received a letter from the Ipirote Alexandros mildly questioning of his sister's honor, Filippos didn't bother to even answer. Let her stay where she belonged. She'd be someone else's headache now! The Ipirote king was indebted to him in any case. He would let him be, as long as Olympias was to stay there under his 'protection'! He forbade any discussion in public or in private of his family affairs.

Only Hrysogonos—and that only at times of utter loneliness and half drunk—would dare to mention the problem to his King and try to somehow bring some sense back, looking at the overall benefit to the state by reuniting Father and son. For the moment, things were to remain as were; nothing more, nothing less. The new Queen Kleopatra/Evridiki gave birth to a daughter soon after Alexandros left. Filippos welcomed his new offspring with his usual celebrations but did not recall Attalos to Pella.

Pafsanias was noted to be more sociable. He was even granted a short leave to see his wife and he returned with a faint smile on his face. Things were mending. Filippos counted on time to solve eventually all the problems. Patience had served him well before. Mean time, he was preparing for the expedition to Asia . . .

Alexandros started getting uncomfortable under the 'care and hospitality' of Kossos. To be sure, the Illyrian king was all politeness and friendliness toward his 'guests'. But, with the war against the Aftariates and Parthines concluded with absolute success, he could see the power and respect by neighboring tribes to his host had risen to a very high level. Plus, the Illyrian now had a good know-ledge of Makedonian execution of tactics in battle. How long would it take him to feel absolutely powerful to try his luck again at the expense of Makedon? And where would Alexandros and his friends stand in case this ever happened?

He discussed this at length with Yfestion and the rest when alone and, preferably, far away from Kossos' town, during their (well established now) hunting ventures. "We are going to be accused—and rightfully so—if things will ever lead to a new confrontation between Makedon and the Illyrians! We caused Kossos' new strength and time will come soon we will have to leave this place, perhaps in a hurry!" By now, Arpalos, Laomedon, Erygios, Ptolemeos and Nearhos had come and joined their prince and the rest of their common friends, sharing their imposed or self-afflicted exile in equal misery.

Yfestion and Perdikkas volunteered to travel back to Makedonia and present themselves before the King asking for leniency. Arpalos asked to be added to the group. Ptolemeos and Nearhos voiced their doubt on this proposition and Alexandros sided with their opinion. "The King is going to arrest you all and even put you to death! I cannot afford losing you, not now, not ever! There has to be an other way. I know now that our absence from Makedonia doesn't produce the desired effects and it's divisive by its nature. On the other hand, my Mother's honor cannot go unsatisfied for ever. I care not of my own status—the King can decide for himself. My Mother was injured by Attalos' remarks and that needs to be addressed—if I am ever to return home!"

The name of the proper mediator came suddenly to Ptolemeos' mind. "I still keep contact with my love in Korinthos, my beautiful Thais! Now you know why I have no money left out of our spoils from the last war helping Kossos. I pay well the runner to send my letters to her and receive her re-plies! I can ask her to approach our host when we were in Korinthos, Dimaratos. The King was truly taken by this clever Korinthian politician. Dimaratos was also taken by you Alexandros and he said so—and did show it—many times in many ways! I am certain all of you remember that! Well, maybe he is our man. What do you say?"

They all agreed that Dimaratos had left the best impressions with his contact and civility and clever-ness during their stay in Korinthos. Filippos had him high in esteem and they knew he had kept cor-respondence with the Korinthian. They all put their money together and sent Ptolemeos' runner to Thais.

King Filippos was surprised to see Dimaratos coming to Pella. "You should've let me know before-hand my friend of your intention to visit. As it is, I have a heavy schedule going all the way to Prop-ontis inspecting the stations I have set for their readiness to have our forces supplied on our way to Asia next summer." Dimaratos smiled his well known dignified way and told the King that Filippos' schedule suited him well. With permission, he would escort the King and have time to discuss urgent matters with him away from Pella's court and 'big listening ears'! So, they traveled together with the sole company of the King's secretaries and body guards.

"You have to set your house in order before you venture in Asia my friend!" Dimaratos had asked for permission to be up-front and totally candid—and got it. "The House Timenos cannot afford division while heading in charge of all united Ellas against Persia! Your son and his mother and friends have to be—at least for the eyes of all—at your side!" Filippos looked at his friend long, his good eye betraying a trace of mist. "I know I shouldn't have allowed wine and anger come over my best judgment at that cursed hour! But the kid insulted me! He was warned before not to cross me in front of others, nor to take matters on his own without consulting me first! And that idiot, Attalos! I will have him stay in Asia for good. Yes, I want my son back, but his mother . . . Olympias is another thorn in my side, embedded in my ribs! I should have sent her away when the kid was still young! No, I will not have her return!"

The inspection lasted almost a month and the conversation continued among the two, every time they were out of ear dropping. The only reason I know about it is because Dimaratos is also my good friend and told me everything when I asked, some time later. Eventually, with give and take, the King agreed to have Alexandros and his friends back. Olympias would have to wait and simmer in Ipiros, until such time Filippos would see fit. He needed time to mend things with his son, without the venom of Olympias poisoning their new relation and understanding . . .

Alexandros received the message the month of Loios, just days after his date of birth. Originally he did not want to discuss anything further, unless his return would mean the return of his Mother and with all her honor restored as the Queen of Makedon! Yfestion, Ptolemeos and Perdikkas sought to mellow him in accepting the King's terms. It would be a new start! Things would and could be work-ed out when the two, Father and son, would get together and opened up. He agreed reluctantly.

He sent message to his Mother promising speedy return to her past status and another to the Ipirote Alexandros thanking him for all his good will and informing he would continue getting the good at-tention of the King—as in past. He did not forget Dimaratos to whom (along with a thank-you letter) sent a golden bridle he had taken from an Illyrian dead chief, in indication of his lasting friendship and indebtness. Alexandros' original intention was to have that bridle for Voukefalas (he had really miss his horse left back in Pella). They packed their few belongings, bade farewell to Kossos and took the return road to Pella . . .

"Since I was not there and have no personal experience and knowledge of the exact sequence of events and verbal exchanges as those took place, I learned about all these from Ptolemeos—after the return of the group to Pella and I write these with the reservation of one being informed 'second hand', plus my own possible errors in understanding or hearing. I am trained to scribe though—as you know by now—and I am confident I have informed you properly of what I was told."

The return of Alexandros to Pella was received by the majority of Makedonians with a sigh of relief. Passing through towns and villages, people were lined-up to welcome him back and wishing him good fortune. They were blessing the King and his son for the wise decision to put the past quarrel aside. Especially when the group arrived at the outskirts of Pella where the King and the home guard of the army were stationed to receive them, the reconciliation which took place brought tears to the eyes of most.

The King was on his horse, surrounded by his body guards and, lined on the side, were Alexandros' former Agima of cavalry and the lohi and taxis of the Pezeteri who had commanded in the past, or had as secondary officers in their ranks his exiled friends. Arriving before the King, the group dis-mounted and stood before him in attendance. Filippos obviously moved, but holding his place, ex-tended his hand. The prince walked up to his Father and, taking the extended hand, placed a kiss. The King then moved to dismount from his horse and, as Alexandros offered his shoulder, army and civilians gathered to watch the event, bursted into shouts of joy.

The King dismounted and put his arm on his son's shoulder, facing troops and people. There was a pandemonium! Tall sarissas were vibrating in the air as they were shaken by the Pezeteri; swords were clanging against shields emblazoned with the star-burst of the Argead emblem, people were now openly crying of joy and, then, the Makedonian war cry rose from the innermost of all in unison!

The attending priests crowned with wreaths of vine and twigs full of green oak leaves with acorns, led a sacrificial bull to a makeshift altar placed there for the occasion. Father and son followed their steps. An invocation was given and the sacrificial knife was presented. The King took it and motioned to Alexandros. They both held it together and, at the given sign, they plunged it into the animal's lowered neck for the kill.

When all was finished, they rode back into town and went straight to the Palace. Filippos turned to Alexandros and told him he wanted to have a serious talk with him in the presence of only one other person, the royal scribe on duty. It so happened that the person to listen and record such an intimate conversation was I, the Thrakian-become-Makedonian. We all headed toward the King's study room. Pafsanias, as head of the guards, followed close-by, ready to take orders. Alexandros only looked at him nodding with a smile (I later figured it out it was to say thanks for the unexpected hospitality given in Orestis as the self-exiled ones were heading to Ipiros).

Making sure the study room doors were closed and Pafsanias charged to keep all out of sight by standing guard himself, the King ordered me to be ready and start recording his deal with his son. I was to place my name as a witness at the end, under their individual signets. I thought I should protest, for this was strictly a matter between Father and son. They both read my mind. Filippos just pointed me to sit at my desk and Alexandros gave me his special smile indicating he was comfortable with this.

"I have a special reason having a witness to our conversation" the King opened-up. "You and I have had our misunderstandings in the past and I don't want that repeated anymore than you do! For in that case, both of us will come to regret it much more than we did during the last . . . ehm . . . misandven-ture! Evmenis here will serve as a reminder to both of us! Now, I will ask you to listen without any interruption until I am finished. You will say what you have to, after I am done. Well then! I know I did not handle the incident at my wedding the way I should, but neither did you! I know that your pride was hurt—as it was mine mind you—and I know, better than you think, of your sense of honor! I was drunk, I admit it. You weren't! You should have kept your mind together better! I am the King and you are my heir to the throne, my son! I have no quarrels with you except that you have taken your mother's side once too often, without considering my feelings! That idiot, Attalos, realized his mistake and—in spite of being as drunk as was I—and obeyed my order and put his head down. Why didn't you? Don't answer that, I know! Look! I cannot deny you your love and devotion toward your mother. Zefs only knows how many nights she spent twisting your mind with her imaginary plots of mine against her. Keep your love for her, but consider me from now-on! I wish things were different,

I wish I could still feel something for her for the shake of all of us but I can't! I do love my new wife and present Queen and that is not going to change! She is pregnant again and this time she may give me another son. That should not change one thing, provided you prove to me that my choice of pardoning you and your friends was not a mistake. You are a true Vasiliskos, a King to be—as they fondly call you—by your own right and not only by my blood. You have proved that to all, many a time! What you need to prove now is that all I have invested in you so you could be who you truly are, were not investments thrown in the wind! Answer this question now: Have you understood all I said?"

Alexandros nodded with his head, fists clenched, body erect but not in defiance. "Good! Then, I will continue. This . . . escapade of yours put the whole plan and preparations to almost a halt. It brought the name of our House in the mouths of many who delighted to see we were divided.

Don't let this happen again, ever! I won't and I swear it to you in the name of all Olympians, but I have to have your word on it too! I gave you—and your friends—your former ranks and duties back. Don't fail me!

As for your mother, you have to wait. I have to let her simmer in her own devices of self-inflicted misery! Your namesake, her brother, proved himself a very wise man. He protested on behalf of his sister's honor in good measure and taste. I will have to reward him for that, soon . . . So! Back to your mother. I will not have her come here now. She never managed to make herself liked by the people.

I promise you this though: Provided you conduct yourself with dignity and respect to my wishes, I will see that she returns in some proper time before our march to Asia. Depending to how pleased I will be, she may even return as a Queen. Meantime, we have to reacquaint ourselves, you and me!

The son has to realize that his Father is not what his mother claimed him of being! One last thing: As I said, I cannot stop you from loving her. But for your own sanity and peace of mind, stay away from her as much as you can! Remember these words of mine, especially when I am gone to meet with our ancestors! She may love you, she may even still feel something for me, but she is a des-tructive woman! She will ruin you, she will burn you; she will eat you alive! Love her—if you must—but from afar. I don't expect you will take my word easily; I then ask you to go and visit your sister Kleopatra and your half sisters and brother. Take a good look at them and see how much better they are now, her being away and leaving them be unhindered from her accusations, punishments and threats!"

The King stopped talking. He took a sip from his wine cup and looked at his son questioning. Alex-andros let a deep sigh out of his mouth. Without a word, he pressed his signet at the end of my writings. He then looked at his Father in absolute calmness and said "My King, your will is my com-mand! I will obey and I will prove to you, you weren't wrong in calling me back. As for my Mother, I can promise you also that she will return as a Queen, in time proper!" He then asked for permission to go, so he would be ready next morning to take command of his Agima. If they were to perform their duties as expected, he had to start the training at once . . .

Filippos looked at his son a long while. He really loved his mother! Should there be a wall between him and his son because of it? He also let a deep sigh come out of his mouth, then, in a clear sign of reconciliation, he opened his arms. Alexandros stood reluctant facing his father. Then walked to him and the two embraced. It wasn't the deep, loving embracement of father with son but the wounds were very fresh and this was a new beginning. Alexandros went to the door and opened it, then walk-ed out. A sullen Pafsanias leaned over and closed it again. I couldn't help but notice that face. Did he hear the conversation? If so, was his face so more sullen than ever because he didn't like what he heard? I looked at the King. Filippos was busy cleaning his good eye. I kept my thought to myself.

Delegations from Makedon and the—allied now—southern city-states, as well as Illyrian and Thraki-an subjected or allied kingdoms were constantly coming and going to and from Pella. There was more of a response to the call from the latter than from the former. Alexandros, finding that his constant exposure at the King's side was a big factor in warming-up their relation, asked for a talk with his Father (he was still addressing Filippos the formal way, my King, but in a more familiar manner). The two met at the King's study, as usual and, as it was ordered by the King, I was present to write down what their conversation would bring, bearing witness.

"My King, I have observed the reluctance of our Ellenic allies to fulfill their promises in providing troops and supplies—that includes Athinian ships for transport through the Ellispontos. Do you see that we will have to demonstrate our strength by marching south once more?" Alexandros opened the conversation with this question, using no introduction to his concern—as is his character to come forward to the point and expecting an equally forward answer.

The King gave him a knowledgeable smile, shook his head negatively and answered. "I understand your concern and I would say you are right. But marching south again and imposing our will—no matter how right—will enforce the declaration of our old past and still powerful enemies of us being the tyrants of Ellas! It will go directly against our preaching in Korinthos of free will among the El-lenic states. Why do you think I did not march against Sparti when they refused to acknowledge the fact that they are not capable of leading any longer? I could have erased them from the face of this earth easily. There is no way they could in recent past, cannot now, nor will they match our strength or tactics at war in the future! Yet, I let them be living and existing with their faded dream.

I did that to emphasize our guidance on Ellas under the free will of the states to participate! As long as they are giving me a token of support, no, let me say it differently; as long as none of them moves against us, I have to hold on to my preaching: United under each one's free will to avenge past wrong doings, with Makedonia leading and no more warring against each-other!

The wounds against their pride as past leaders are still fresh. That will fade with time and time is on our side. We just have to make sure we take advantage of what they offer us and win our battles against the High King. With our success established and properly presented, Ellas will follow more willingly. This same reason held me from going to Athinae when I sent you!"

Alexandros thought of these words carefully, a line between his eyebrows indicating his deep and serious engagement in evaluating his Father's reasoning. He nodded his acceptance of the King's evaluation with respect. He then told Filippos that a strong detachment of Paeonians had arrived and were at the parade grounds ready for inspection. Darron from house Damasias was their leading man and, according to Alexandros' own observations, the detachment needed some time of arduous work alongside the light cavalry in order to be coordinated with the Makedonian ways of war tactics.

"He also informed me my King that a distant cousin of his from the northern Peonians is heading toward us with some five hundred archers and javeliners on horse. The name of this Peonian is Dar-ka son of Krasha and is escorted by a soothsayer of renown, a fellow named Gribas who sent word he asks you to grand him an audience as soon as he gets here."

Filippos looked at his son questioning but Alexandros could only shake his head and shift his shoul-ders indicating his ignorance of further details. The King nodded and his son continued. "Seems to me proper to attach Darron's detachment to the ili of Valakros son of Nikanor from Akti, the one who had just married to Antipatros' daughter. He is a rather ambitious and daring, a good match with the temperament of the Paeonians. As for the northern Peonians, I recommend they train under Plevrias, the Pelagonian. He speaks their language and he is good in following orders. I think they will get used to our ways easier under his command."

The King contemplated his son's suggestions for a while and found no fault to anything Alexandros had recommended. He gave him a condescending smile and was rewarded with one himself. He then put on his sword and parade helmet and, escorted by Alexandros, walked out calling for his horse and body guard for the parade grounds and inspection of the new arrivals.

I noticed Pafsanias give a nod of salutation as they both marched through the door. Was it directed to both or to Alexandros only? My eyes couldn't tell for sure. Filippos passed him with a motion of his hand to follow and Alexandros (ever polite and acknowledging others) gave Pafsanias one of his 'I noticed you!' smiles and followed the steps of his Father. Pafsanias stood for a moment looking at both as they turned around the corner and, then, suddenly conscious of my presence, closed the door with a growl (an almost daily affair of his in the presence of others) and I heard his steps hurrying to follow our King and his son.

I am glad that recently the conduct between Father and son has improved and that has been noticed by all, servants or family, soldiers or visitors. There is more ease in the presence of both and smiles do come more often on their faces. I double checked it with Yfestion (that young man really loves our prince!) and Ptolemeos as discreetly as possible. They both had the same opinion as I. My hope is that when Olympias returns she will not be the cause of a new rift between the Father and his son!"

"All the preparation for the expedition to Asia and against the Persians is almost completed. It is spring coming now in Pella and the trees are full of leaves while still holding on to their flowers which will soon turn to unripened fruits, along with a plethora of wild flowers of all hues and colors all over the fields with predominant the green grass and the red poppies. In the cultivated fields the wheat stocks have grown distinctly and their color is turning toward the eventual golden hue of ripening.

There was a feast and games already at Dion during which the King announced the return of his Queen from Ipiros shortly after this month of Artemisian winds would close and Daesios would begin. While at Dion for the festivities and surrounded by delegates of all the participating city-states of Ellas allied to Makedon, Filippos sent for a word from the Oracle of Delfi and a messenger to Ale-xandros of Molossia to prepare his sister for her return trip to Makedonia.

'By the way, King Filippos thought it proper to also give the hand of his daughter Kleopatra to the king of Molossia and all Ipiros, as a thank-you for the good care provided to the Queen of Makedon and the aptly demonstrated friendship all these years between the two kingdoms. If king Alexandros would accept, he then could escort his own sister back to Makedonia and have the wedding take place at Aegae during the farewell festivities and offerings to the Olympian gods before the march to Asia.' the King's message to the Ipirote Alexandros read.

While waiting for the answers from both places, we all returned to Pella and resumed the every day tasks. The King having in mind that my parents were getting too old and, having to follow him to war in Asia, he said I should go home and visit them—perhaps for the last time. As it happened, Filippos was right. I barely had time to arrive at my home town of Kardia and my Father fell ill with the local doctors unable to cure him. He died with my Mother and my siblings (I have six of them; two bro-thers and four sisters, me being the middle born one, twin to my sister Elpiniki) by his side, three days after my arrival. Mother's heart failed her from her sorrow and died two days later. I stayed with my siblings as long as it took me to arrange my share of inheritance be properly divided among my sisters, as they are not married yet. I want nothing for myself, as I plan to follow the King and stay in Makedon upon our return from Asia.

I returned to Pella and found it full of activities. Word had come from Pythia the High Priestess of Apollon at Delfi, as well as from king Alexandros of Molossis. The King offered me his sympathy for my loss and gave me few days away from my duties to recover. Prince Alexandros came to my house along with Filotas, Perdikkas, Yfestion, Krateros and Arpalos to offer some diversion and their sym-pathy. The rest of our friends were out of Pella, on maneuvers with their units.

Alexandros could not keep his excitement on the upcoming march. He told me of the Oracle's an-swer to the King's question: 'Garlanded is the sacrificial bull and its slayer's hand steady and ready to slaughter the victim' (or something very close to that, as I do not remember the exact words after all the downpour of the events preceding and following). I got excited too, as the omen was obviously very favorable to our cause. Persia had the bull as a revered symbol and Filippos had to be the slayer with the steady hand in readiness to slaughter!

I spent the days I had to myself walking around and keeping my account of events in order, as I had always in mind to pass it on to my descendants if the Olympians would grant me some or to trusted hands—if childless—when death would come to take me too. As I already said, Pella was a very busy place now. Aside from the final rush for needy things on the advent of our march, there were orders placed by the King to prepare all necessary things for king Alexandros' wedding to Kleopatra (she is inconsolable—as is Perdikkas—seeing her love totally lost to her)! She is a Timenid girl though and a proper Makedonian daughter. In her veins rushes also the noble blood of Ahilleas' descendants. She will marry her uncle keeping faith on her Father's judgment. As long as her Mother will stay away from her, Kleopatra can have some happiness in her life!

Another set of activities was the commissioning by the King of several Makedonian and other Ellin-es, all of them renowned sculpturers, in making the likeness of the twelve Olympian gods seated on their thrones, from clay but painted and prepared to look like being alive, among us mortals! I went to observe their work, to take my mind away from my personal grief. I noticed there were thirteen of them working with their helpers, on thirteen statues—one of which was kept away from the rest and behind a draped section of their workshop. When I tried to be nosy, I got kicked out.

That moved my curiosity to further investigation and asked around, even bothering the prince. Ale-xandros knew nothing of it and, when he tried, he was told politely but firmly that it was the King's will to keep it a secret. It made me more curious. When I returned to duty and found the King in a very good mood, I dared to ask the question. He made me swear on the souls of my dead parents I would keep the secret. After I took the oath, he smiled and, with obvious pleasure he told me the thirteenth statue was of his image! My mouth dropped open. I pointed to him the seriousness of placing himself on the same level with the Immortals. He laughed and assured me that he did pay respect to the Olympians. His statue was much smaller and it would come at the end of the present-ation, in some distance from the rest. "Where these statues were to be placed or presented?" I asked pushing.

He looked at me again and said: "Once you took an oath, I can tell you. They will be brought to the theater at Aegae, after Kleopatra's wedding and before my entrance to it, before all the delegates and guests of Ellas to see! I will enter after they are placed in a circle facing my image in their midst and see what impression that will bring on the faces of our allies. I want them all to know the Oracle gave me the favor of Apollon and the Olympians for our march in Asia. I know the High King will have his observers there to report to him. I want them to tell him what I need him to know!" He looked at me all serious and finalized: "Now you know. Until it happens, not a word to anyone!" I had but to repeat my oath and he let me go.

I did not like the idea but there was nothing I could do. Filippos had his reason to act like he did and he seldom was wrong in his doing! . . .

"M' name's Evripidis. No, not the one who wrote plays for the theater in Athinae and died far in cursed Makedonia! I'm the son of Patroklos, a Megarian who resides in Athinae, having m' tavern just on the far side of the harbor in Piraeas, right 'cross from the island of Salamis. I want yous to know that I'm just a tavern owner with no proper schoolin' and no interest in anythin' else but money makin' so I can leave this miserable place sooner than later and return to me home city in comfort! That said, I hope you understand why I write happenin's which happen'd just a while ago. Either way things go, me writin's will bring money to me, provided I find the right person(s) to sell and will save (perhaps) me own skin, in case things go wrong an' Filippos comes askin'.

Well, here's how things an' events took place in me humble place of work: One late afternoon I was surpris'd to see a very known Athinian politician, the one who has the lead of the whole Dimos the last few years, though in some disgrace lately, cause of the lost battle in Heronia. My surprise was justified because in me tavern I mostly get harbor craftsmen, sailors and seldom some passing-by persons of some status who are on their way to an' from me home town an' beyond. Now, no need for names, not yet. I'm sure yous all know who I'm talkin' about!

He came like a man hidin' from the gods themselves lookin' all 'round him to make sure none was makin' who he was! I knew, cause I happen'd to be present in one of his long tirades, at the foot of the rock where th'Athinians gather to talk their state business and though that was some time ago, I recogniz'd 'im immediately!

Any way, he made sure me last customer had gone b'fore he came to me and ask'd to rent me place for a whole day! He wanted no one else to be there, 'xept himself and three to four other 'ssociates of him—as he call'd 'em. I remember th' exact date 'cause I knew it then 't was for somethin' big! 'T was the last day of the month 'Nthestirion when he first came to me that late evenin' an' he wanted my tavern for the mid of the following month, the 'Lafevolion. He offer'd two gold Dariki coins for me place an' me silence!

I got to say, me being greedy, I asked for more. You can imagine my surprise by having that accept-ed, though he protested strongly! I knew then and there that 'e was really cookin' some'ng and kept my eyes and ears open. He had me swear oaths of secrecy and told me if I was t' fail 'my side of the bargain he would send his people t' break everythin' in me place, plus me own body! Well, it takes to be very stupid not to figure out he had somethin' dangerous in mind. I took the money and made the deal. Haven't told nobody of this 'xept writin' it in this tetraptiho in me own hand for its future use.

On the fifteenth day of 'Lafevolion, he came—actually I found 'im waitin' for me to come—to me place just 'fore the sun rose 'bove the distant cape Sounion. Before long, four other men arrived, each on his own an'—in spite of the good weather of a nice early spring day—they all had their hats pull'd down to their ears, not wantin' to be seen by people who shouldn't see 'em. One was from Ma- kedonia, I could tell by 'is hat, the petassos. As for the others, one obviously was from the lands of the High King, as he was bejeweled with all kinds o' rings and chains 'round 'is neck an' he spoke the language worst than me. The other two I couldn't make out their whereabouts, hard as I tried but don't matter. He who's in charge 'as a name an' that's enough for me!

They chose a table at the far end of my empty tavern, though they knew nobody was 'bout to come in. I got their orders for wine and food an' I had to go to the kitchen to prepare it, so I miss'd much of their early talk but that don't matter. From what I heard I have 'nough to know they was makin' arrangements for the killin' of Filippos!

They didn't want me 'round 'em an' I had no work t'excuse meself bein' near. So, I went back in the kitchen and pretended I was doin' some work in there but I had my ears open for every and any word I could make from them plannin'. Then, I thought of my cellar and made it known I was going there by callin' them loud 'fore I did. Th' Athinian gave me permission to go 'bout my business, reliev'd I wasn't gonna be 'round them. I headed straight to the small cellar and out its side door to th' attach'd stable by its 'hind side. There, there's an old window out o' use for years now and boarded-up with small stones fitted loosely which serv'd in the past to bring light and some air in the tavern (I now have the air and light comin' in from the enclos'd yard). From that old window I could hear 'em talk an' also see 'em faces, as now—thinkin' me absent—took off their head covers and spoke louder.

The Makedonian was sayin' they'd secur'd the man who'd do the killin', as he was as close as one could be to the King. But, he said, their man was needin' some money for his escape helpers who'd do it only if they'd get paid enough for their riskin' it. After that, he had the protection of a very high person (I was made to figure it had to be someone from the royals) and needed no assistance.

The obviously Asian then, look'd at the Athinian 'xpectin' him to give the money. The Athinian said nothing, only returned the look at the Asian and waited. The Asian then let a deep sigh of resentment but pull'd his bag of money from inside his fine robes and handed the Makedonian three silver pieces and one gold Darikos. The Athinian complained it was too much but the Makedonian took it ignor-ing that comment.

The other two were observing without a word. When the money passed hands they voiced their thoughts an' questions as to how the city-states would move to rid 'emselves from Makedonia once an' for all. Th' Athinian and Asian both vouched the support of the High King with money and, if necessary, with troops crossin' from Asia to Thraki.

Noticin' I was absent for some time now and not knowing what I was doin', th'Athinian rose from his seat and started callin' me. I run from my spyin' place to the kitchen, makin' sure I took with me a big sack full of onions to clean and chop as if I had in mind to do cookin' for the next day.

Th' Athinian told me to bring 'em some more wine and I noticed they'd placed their hats an' hoods back on and speakin' in low voices again. I did what I was told, knoing I had heard enough and act-ually needin' t' hear no more to know what the meetin' was all about. Only thing I was curious of was when they were planning' to act an' how. But that didn't matter t' me either. Time would show soon enough 'nd I wasn't in a hurry t' know more . . .

I made good my presence in the kitchen by cleaning the damned onions and cryin' like a baby doin' it. At about the mid of the day, they ask'd for a full meal which they ate in silence or talk'd nonsense. When they finish'd the Asian left (with another sigh) payin' the money for their meal and drinks. I brought 'em their horses from the stable and, one-by-one, they left using diff'rent roads and at times when no travelers were about me place.

I wrote this to safeguard me interests an' see if it'll bring me some extra money. If I'm to find hard times—one never knows the will of gods and Tyhi—my son knows where I keep it until it can serve. He can use it to get me out of trouble and make some profit too."

"This documented story fell onto my hands much later, in Korinthos and during the pan-Ellenic meet to reconfirm Makedonian leadership under King Alexandros. I paid a good sum of money for it and, in time, I will use it to show the Athenian treachery to all!"

"Daesios has always been the spring month of festivities in Makedonia, as the good weather settles in the country for good and only the highest peaks—like those of Olympos or Tymfi or Varnous—still keep their snow covers, having thus an even more majestic presence through the clear spring air. The people are eager to take part in festivities and come out from their long winter confinement indoors. A more than usual attractive reason has them buzzing around this spring: Word came that king Ale- xandros of Molossis has accepted the hand of princess Kleopatra and the wedding will take place at our capital city of Pella. The downside of it is that he's bringing back his sister, Queen Olympias, mother of our beloved prince Alexandros and Kleopatra, the future wife of a king. But her presence is a necessity and people hope she will keep her nose out of scheming—after the lesson she got from the King with her lengthy exile. Because of our love to our prince Alexandros we all show pleasure (in his presence) about the return of the Queen even if it is Olympias.

In a way, I believe the King has made the right move as the time approaches fast for the march on to Persia. Stability is needed and, with Antipatros as regent, she will not be able to do what she wants. News from the small expeditionary force sent some time ago to liberate and receive the assist-ance from the Ellenic city-states in Asia by the Aegean, are not so encouraging now. Parmenion reports the Satraps of the region have amassed some serious numbers of warriors and their heavy cavalry outnumbers ours ten to one! Some of the city-states were forced to return to their former status under Persian rule and our forces had to retreat leaving a big part of Ionia to the enemy.

Meantime the Peonian forces arrived and yesterday I witnessed a strange meeting of the King and the soothsayer Gribas who insisted on having an audience with Filippos for weeks now until the King finally gave-in and accepted him. Gribas insisted seeing the King alone but Filippos made it clear that—if the soothsayer had something to say—the King had nothing to hide from his regent (Antipat-ros was present) nor from his personal scribe. The Peonian gave us both a long interrogating look and, being obviously satisfied, he warned the King of an imminent danger. We all wanted to know what he meant but he could not tell anything else except that his god had appeared in his dreams and urged him to warn the crowned King.

Filippos smiled and thanked him for his concern but, as he well pointed out, he was the King for sure but not a crowned one, since the only distinction of his Kingship was the diadima/diadem every Makedonian King was known to wear—and that only during festivities! Antipatros and I agreed and the soothsayer left telling us that his mission then was accomplished as the god perhaps had meant the dream to be for another, a crowned King. As for us, we got back to business forgetting the warning within a short time.

Olympias arrived in Pella escorted by her brother the king of Molossis and his personal retinue two or three days after our meeting with the Peonian. Prince Alexandros was beaming with happiness and, to our delight both Olympias and King Filippos managed to present themselves amicable—at least in public. The wedding took place with all the trimmings of a royal affair. There were festivities held in just about every Makedonian town, village and hamlet. Even Kleopatra seemed to be calm and she was observed smiling at the guests when she was going around giving them small favors in return of their honoring her with their presence and their wedding gifts. As for poor Perdikkas, he was on mandatory leave back in Orestis, per orders given—wisely—by prince Alexandros.

Word came to us that the contingents from our allied city-states of the south were now on the move and the last of them should be camping at our assembly area just across from Axios and by the Am-faxitian town of Ihnae within the next three weeks. Filippos then decided to have the last festivities performed at Aegae instead of Pella. He declared that an expedition as big as this ought to start from where Makedonia started its glorious existence, adding that Aegae was the ceremonial capital of our kingdom and at the foothills of Olympos. All the statues of the gods—finished by now—were covered and transported to Aegae. The numerous embassies from the city-states, the subjected and allied kingdoms and Makedonian land lords and clan heads, moved ahead to Aegae, vying ho would get there first and secure better accommodations. By now, early fall had come.

The royal household moved three days later and arrived at Aegae in one day, in spite of torrential rain which surprised all of us as it came totally unexpected. Filippos' mood was a bit down because of that at the banquet given that night, fearing the festivities would be spoiled. The next days' sunshine brought the smile back on his face and the festivities started with the proper sacrifices to the gods with poetry and musical competitions at the theater. In the evening there was another banquet in honor of the victorious poet and musician. During that, delegates of the allied city-states presented the King golden crowns depicting entwined laurel branches or those of oak, decorated with acorns.

The King accepted all these with grace and a good word to each and every delegate. The only one approaching the King with no crown was the Athinian delegate, the advocate Yperidis, close associ-ate of none else but Dimosthenis. He asked Filippos to think in favor of his Athinian allies and forgive the delay of presenting him their golden crown. Somehow, he said, their runner got detained and the arrival was expected in a very short time. Filippos accepted the excuse in good spirit and remarked that he was sure of the Athinian good wishes and that he would accept their token to the leader of all Ellas when it would arrive, with equal delight. When every delegate was done, Filippos asked me to see that the crowns would be placed one on each statue of each god ready to be presented at the theater before the public the next day and, what was left, to be sent to Delfi and Dodona as votives. I left the banquet and took care of my King's request.

The next day a bright sun hit the slopes of divine Olympos and the crowds started early toward the theater. Town people and visitors from the country side lined early at the sides of the route the King and his family would take from the old palace to the theater itself. Actually, the distance is minimal and, under ordinary circumstances, the royal family could enter it from the gate connecting it to the palace grounds. In fact, that short route was taken by the Queen and the royal wives, their assistants and the rest of royal family members, including Arrideos, Kynna, Kleopatra, Fila, Nikesi-polis with Thessaloniki, Filina, Meda and Kleopatra/Evridiki with her infants, two girls by now but still not officially named.

They took their places in especially arranged seats before the προσκηνιον, the area before the actors' stage. In the center and in front of their seats was a throne where the King was to seat, facing (like them) the guests and the crowd with the two Alexandros' standing on each side of him. The gods were to be placed at the ορχηστρα, the actual performing space, in a semi-circle facing them. The delegates and guests with Makedonian nobility would seat at the lower παροδος/sector of the κοιλον/ tier rows, whereas some of the common people would take the upper. Most commoners though had to stay outside due to lack of space.

Filippos with prince Alexandros and king Alexandros of Molossis by his side, would take the round about road, so they could be seen and cheered by the gathered people and so they did. First, the statues of the gods, all painted life-like and crowned by the crowns given the night before, were car-ried on special platforms by the royal pages. Zefs and Ira were leading the immortal images and Posidonas, Pluton, Athina, Apollon, Artemis, Afroditi, Aris, Yfestos, Dionyssos and Ermis followed in order. Behind those were the priests and priestesses in their service, chanting hymns. Three heralds, one in white holding his staff and two by his sides followed, sounding their trumpets at every turn of the road. Last and smaller was the statue of the King which was to be placed facing the ones of the gods.

There was some space left and there was the King on his war horse but unarmed, wearing his dia-dem and holding the Leader's staff given to him in Korinthos. To his right and a step behind was prince Alexandros riding Voukefalas, also dressed in white hiton and having only his dagger belt on.

On the King's left and in line with the prince, was king Alexandros of Molossis in his dual role as brother and son-in-law at the same time. He was holding the King's ceremonial shield with the ivory statuettes and the Makedonian star-burst emblazoned on its highly polished face. They were met with wild cheers from the crowd all the way. Behind them was the royal bodyguards led by an in-animate Pafsanias—but then, what was different? Pafsanias was always just like that!

I followed the retinue with some other scribes a little further behind. We were all instructed to keep records of the whole festivities, as the King's dream of leading Ellas to avenge the wrong doings of Persia was coming to its fulfillment. Naturally, all of us would have to follow the campaign too.

The last turn of the road brought the entourage at the open space before the main public gate to the theater, on its east side with the old palace as a backdrop up on the hill. Everybody stopped. The King and his son with king Alexandros, dismounted and their horses were taken away. The heralds sounded their trumpets thrice to let the people in the theater know the ceremony was to begin. One unblemished bull was brought and the King made the sacrifice (a cover was introduced so he would not stain his hiton) at the altar placed for the occasion just that day.

Before the priests could examine its entrails, the Athinian delegate Yperidis came running with his currier holding the delayed Athinian golden crown. He excused himself again and begged the King to accept it as sincere indication of Athinae's friendship. Filippos happily accepted and, turning, he handed it to standing by his side Pafsanias. The leader of the body guard seemed reluctant but he obeyed. Yperidis protested that the King ought to have the crown put on his head and Filippos, anxious to proceed now, did not object. Time had passed and the crowd inside the theater was getting loud in anticipation.

Filippos motioned for the process to continue without delay. Yperidis run past the statues of the gods and disappeared in the shade of the covered dromos/way leading from the gate to the enclosure of the open air amphitheater. The priests passed the slaughtered bull to their assistants and followed the entering statues of the gods and that of Filippos followed by the admiring shouts of the crowd.

The two Alexandros, son and son/brother-in-law looked at each-other puzzled. Filippos smiled happily and explained. Then, he asked them both to proceed following the heralds, who were about to cross the gate and enter the covered dromos. Alexandros of Molossis started to go but had to stop as prince Alexandros had some objection to the matter. I heard him say that the King ought not to be left without his two sons. Filippos seemed to listen for a moment. Then he turned to Pafsanias and told him to send the guards ahead, to be placed at the edge of the two πάροδοι/actors' entrances to all ορχηστρα/acting space, facing the people.

Pafsanias, standing still at the side, seemed of being in a dream of his own but obeyed the order. The King seeing his son and son-in-law still waiting, he asked again of them to get going. Prince Alexan-dros put his hand on his dagger belt and started unfastening it, telling the King that he shouldn't remain unarmed and alone. Now Filippos' face darkened. He reminded prince Alexandros—rather harshly—of his promise to obey his King at all times since his return from exile. Alexandros stood rigid for one more moment and then, bowing his head before his Father and King, took the arm of his uncle and both of them hurried through the covered theater entrance.

I asked the King if his scribes should also go in before him. He said that it was all right to wait for his own entrance and then come, as he expected the awed crowd to continue its shouts and cheers long after his entrance, which would give us plenty of time to scribe everything down. I returned to my fellow scribes while Pafsanias came to him and whispered something to Filippos' ear. The King seemed annoyed as he limped ahead of his chief body-guard and he grabbed the crown on his head and placed it more firmly. By that time, they both got lost in the shade of the entrance.

We stood there in the empty space until we heard the crowd's exclamations rising, more than they did before. Thinking this was their salute to the King, we run to enter worried not to miss a thing. As we approached the covered entrance, Pafsanias run out passing among us and throwing several to the ground, yelling that the King was down! I could have stopped him but I thought he was running for help . . .

I run into the theater and the view sickened me, although I have had my share of blood, turning my stomach. The King was down covered in blood, a sword (the guard's sword!) right under his sternum and pushed-in up to its hilt! Prince Alexandros was just lifting the King's head in his arms, tears run-ning down his face. Alexandros of Molossis was calling the men to arms and I saw Perdikkas (when did he return from Orestis?) running along with Leonnatos and few others after Pafsanias.

I tried to get close to the prince and my King but it was impossible. The rest of the royal guard had already formed a circle around the body of Filippos and the prince while king Alexandros of Molos-sis had gone to the royal seats determined not to let his bride come near the horrible site. He had her already covered in his arms holding her tight and her face was buried against his chest, shoulders moving rapidly as I could hear her muffled wailing.

I looked at the other faces of the royal family. Olympias was standing erect but not moving, fists clenched and eyes darting from the spot where her son was still holding his Father to Kleopatra/Ev-ridiki who, in turn, had her little daughters held against her bosom, collapsed on her seat—head down. I thought 'that is how a true maenad looks like'—as I observed Olympias eyeing her rival! I felt sorry for Attalos' niece and her lot but I knew her fate was sealed already.

Filina and Nikesipolis were taking their children, half-witted Arrideos and young Thessaloniki away, using the other parodos of the theater. Avdata with her daughter Kynnani (Kynna) had clustered together with Meda and Fila, sobbing and not knowing what to do or where to go until Amyntas came to aide. Now other land lords and clan heads along with army officers and soldiers seemed to come out of their stupor and came closer to the cordon the body guards had formed with Alexandros holding the dead Filippos in the middle. I saw Yfestion, Ptolemeos, Parmenion's sons, the Lynkestian Alexandros, Krateros, Antipatros and Antigonos the one-eyed, running to the spot and they took me pushing along.

Prince Alexandros had just covered his Father with his own hlamis/ cloak and stood up, tears run-ning freely on his face while his white hiton and hands were covered with the King's blood, now turned to deep crimson as it dried-up. The guards then let us through their circle. I took off my cloak and approached Alexandros, having in mind to try and clean some of the blood when I heard a loud forceful voice, the voice of Lynkestian Alexandros hailing the prince as our next King! Instead of using my hlamis to clean him, I placed it on his shoulders voicing at the top of my lungs the same words, joined by the hundred voices of the rest present . . ."

> "Success comes not only with daring. It also takes a cool mind to calculate all aspects and possibilities. No bridge ought to be burned as one moves ahead!..."
> Stavros Katakalos, Makedonian Ellinas.

XIV

The body of the assassin Pafsanias was brought-up almost torn to pieces as his chasers fell upon him with their swords. Ptolemeos expressed his disappointment because Alexandros had ordered to have Pafsanias interrogated so we could find out who else was behind this horrible deed. Being too late for that, he asked Perdikas and Leonnatos to keep themselves available for questioning when our new King would be calmer and ready. He then turned to go to the council held at the study room where we all conferred to see what the next step should be to secure Alexandros' rights as our King.

The body of King Filippos was placed in the old palace's reception hall where experts were now cleaning it and preparing it for temporary burial until the royal grave King Alexandros had ordered to be prepared with all possible speed, was ready to accept the body permanently after it was ritually burned.

Men were sent meantime to get the family of Pafsanias, as the Makedonian law demanded. While they did that, they discovered letters addressed to him by the Lynkestian Alexandros' brothers, suggesting they would agree to assume the throne as scions of the royal family through the line of King Perdikkas, one of the sons of King Alexandros who reigned during the Persian invasions! This evidence put blame also on the shoulders of their brother Alexandros, the one who first hailed our prince as King of Makedonia! It was necessary they would all be tried by our military court for high treason and men were dispatched to bring them to Pella and their brother was placed under guard.

There was also the case of prince Amyntas, son of King Perdikkas the brother of Filippos, who was killed during an Illyrian campaign. The prince (now King) Alexandros did not want to take steps against his cousin and husband of Kynna though, as prince Amyntas was obviously not interested on claiming the throne and was also a close personal friend. On the other hand, it was important to get rid of Attalos who was already reported of trying to have the troops under him in Asia-by-the Aeg-ean mutiny and men loyal to Parmenion were sent to see to it.

King Alexandros did not want to have any harm come to Attalos' niece Kleopatra/Evridiki nor to her little daughter and her newborn son. That did not set well with Queen Olympias and everybody knew she would find eventually an excuse to have them all killed.

Reports started coming from the south that the (until now allied) city-states were ready to denounce their alliance with Makedon and Thessalia already was in preparation to distance itself from being a Makedonian protectorate. King Alexandros sent Antipatros as the seasoned negotiator, to see that the Thessalian confederation would remain as was under King Filippos. The old hand returned to Pella to report that the Pinios pass was closed by mount Ossa and he was told to return to Makedonia as the Thessalians had made up their minds to secede.

By now we had entered the month of Panamos (the equivalent of the Athinian Skiroforion) and the tomb to accept King Filippos' body was almost ready at the royal burying grounds at Aegae. King Alexandros ordered the army to prepare for a march in Thessalia and, upon its return, the burial of King Filippos would take place with all honors due . . .

The hill of Pnyx across from the Athinian acropolis was covered with citizens eager to listen to the great Dimosthenis. The 'Filipizer' Fokion talked to them earlier suggesting they keep their calmness and caution. The Makedonian King was dead, that was true enough but Makedonia was still intact. Dimosthenis had the word on sent to him back in the month of Dios by Yperidis, via horse relayed couriers and the news had arrived in Athinae only three days after the death of Filippos.

The orator had found his sound of magic again after the long silence following Heronia. He had come to the Agora jubilant spreading the news and calling the people to rejoice. Now he was calling them to arms once more to restore Athinian power to its former glory! He had runners sent already to Thivae calling for alliance once more and did the same to Lakedaemon though he really didn't expect the Spartans to answer his call.

He came out from among the cluster of his supporters, slowly, methodically climbing the rocky outcrop of the speaker. Silence fell among the murmuring crowd and its divided opinion exchanges.

He stood proud and spoke of the favors goddess Tyhi had bestowed on Athinian men. He almost spat when mentioning Alexandros by name, depicting him as a spoiled little man who—due to his age and lack of experience and support—would be an easy to defeat opponent. He did not tell them that the dark angry eyes of a fourteen year old boy were still haunting him, because he was sure that the twenty years old young man could not now meet the triumphant look of the avenger of the Athinian glory and might . . . They listened to him spellbound and made the decision to prepare for war . . .

Alexandros and his army arrived at the entrance of the pass to Thessalia and found it occupied by a strong force of Thessalian foot and cavalry. Antipatros was left at Pella to keep an eye to the north. The King sent Parmenion this time to achieve some sort of an agreement but he failed just like Anti-patros earlier. They camped and Alexandros called for council. Ptolemeos, Yfestion and Perdikkas suggested immediate attack. Parmenion, Klitos Melas and Kinos wanted to give the Thessalians time to think. Krateros with Nearhos suggested taking the bulk of the army in secrecy and come to Thes-salia via the pass King Filippos had used years ago, from the Elimiean side of the border.

The King listened to all and then spoke. It was not to their advantage, he said, to alienate the Thes-salians by spilling blood nor did he want any Makedonians killed. To use the pass from Elimiotis would take much time, more than he could afford. Yet, Thessalia had to be forced to come to an understanding that, even if the King's name had changed, the King was still the King!

He ordered the taxis of psili, the light infantry, to work under the instructions of the engineers and cut steps on the far side of the mount Ossa slopes, undetected by the Thessalian force which he would keep occupied by remaining at the entrance of the pass. As soon that would be ready, the taxis of Kinos would climb the steps, followed by one taxis of prodromi and two iles of light cavalry and one taxis of archers. When behind the Thessalian positions, they should sound the trumpets and he would then march to enter the pass placing the Thessalians in a very disadvantaged position.

They worked day and night and finished their job within days and the stratagem worked! Thessalia had no choice but to ask for negotiations. Alexandros agreed to accept their delegation provided they would adhere to all his demands. They did. Alexandros was recognized as the Tagos of all Thessalia like his Father before him and—to make sure there would be no further misunderstandings—he plac-ed guards at the acropolis of Larissa and that of Farsalos.

Having received news of Athinian preparations for war and possible alliance again with Thivae, he continued southward. Thivae sent delegates to meet us at Thermopylae, still occupied by our gar-rison left there by King Filippos and submitted their agreement to follow as was arranged after Heronia. The King placed a garrison at the Kadmia acropolis just in case. At the border of Attiki, Athinian delegates came running to us asking forgiveness for their rush decisions. Alexandros accepted that also but now he could see that his presence was necessary at the Council of all Ellenic states in Korinthos and continued his march south.

The King and his army arrived in Korinthos at the end of Loos (mid of the Athinian month of Eka-tomvion) and Alexandros addressed the Council, emphasizing the need to stay in alliance and contin-ue the interrupted preparations for the campaign against Persia. News, he said, arrived from Asia telling that High King Artaxerxis Arsis was dead before the assassination of King Filippos. A distant relative had come to the throne under the name Darios, from the house Kodomanos. The new High King would surely have his hands full trying to establish himself as he was not fully legitimate. The time to move against Persia then, was now!

The Council accepted the King's right to lead readily and bestowed him the title of Στρατηγος Αυ-τοκρατωρ (Absolute General in charge) of all Ellenic forces, as they had done with Filippos not too long ago. Alexandros now was satisfied. No more Ellenic blood spilled and his hold on the alliance of city-states secured! Sparti was again the only absent state claiming they were born to lead only and never to fol-low. Alexandros didn't even bother for an answer. He sent the bulk of the army back to Makedonia via the main route and he crossed the gulf to the town of Itea and on he went to Delfi. He wanted to receive the omens for the campaign when the priestess was not expecting him. He said so when asked by Yfestion why such a sudden decision to see the Pythia. "When prepared, she will tell me what I want to hear either because of fear or of any interest in future favors. Unprepared, she will have to tell me the truth!"

We arrived at Delfi mid morning, to be told that the day was not proper for Pythia to be consulted.

Alexandros smiled at the apprentice priests who had come to receive us and politely asked to be shown to Pythia's abode so he could place a gift at her doorstep. That done, the King stormed through the door and came out dragging the Priestess forcefully, not listening to her protests and leading her toward the god's Tholos temple where she was to give her divination. Everybody stood motionless observing such an unexpected event, caught by surprise! Finally the Pythia gave-up her protests telling the King she would obey his wish as she found him invincible. Alexandros let her go at once after that, telling her that she had then given him the true answer and no further divination was needed.

We returned to Aegae for the proper burial of King Filippos. Arriving there, Alexandros had yet another fight with his Mother as he found out that Olympias had seen to killing Kleopatra/Evridiki and her two children, disobeying his orders to let them be. The deed was done though and he could do nothing to correct the wrong. It was decided to have the young victim buried in the anteroom of the King's grave, her kids buried elsewhere. The body of Pafsanias was also brought and burned at the entrance of the grave and his ashes thrown to the wind.

The body of Filippos was exhumed, cleaned, placed on a pyre and cremated. His bones were later cleaned and dressed and placed in a gold rectangular box, the golden crown offered by Yperidis the last few minutes of the King's life in it. His arms and various vessels found their place in the King's chamber along with a couch for afterlife needs and the marble double doors were closed.

Outside the grave the trials of the Lynkestian brothers of Alexandros son of Aeropos were held and the assembly found them guilty. They were executed and their corpses along with the horses held to accommodate Pafsanias' escape were burned and placed in the prodromos way to the grave.

Alexandros ordered the work to continue on the grave until everything was done properly inside and out and he prepared to campaign to move up north as reports came from Thraki for an uprising of the Trivallians aided by Skythian tribes further north. By the time all was ready, we started the march at the beginning of the month Artemisios.

Lamparos the king of the friendly Agrianes sent message he would support with some of his forces. The army moved out of Pella and took the east road to cross Axios at its lowest fording, as the thawing of the mountain snows had not reach the lower lands yet and the river was wider therefore its waters less rushing. Then we took the road cross Amfaxitis to the town of Amydon and moved eastward picking up local contingents. A small fleet sailing from Vyzantion (now our ally) was to enter Istros and cut the retreat of the Trivallians beyond the river.

Reaching Vragila in Kristonia, we crossed Ehedoros who, in spite of the snow thaw was still a semidry river since the coming of Xerxis' multitudes which had completely drained it and it never recovered since. Some five hundred light cavalry met us there from the parts of Mygdonia and Vot-tiki. We continued past lake Prasias and took the road by the river Strymon, moving now north toward our subjected lands of the Maydi (or Maidi) against who the Trivallians had inflict heavy los-ses. We passed the first narrow pass between the mountains of Vrontous and Dysoron uneventfully, picking up some of the Maidi forces scattered here and there and restoring order in the country side.

In spite all of these, the army was moving on a double speed, as the King made it clear he wanted to get within the Trivallian lands as soon as was possible. We came to the hills leading to the pass by mount Dynax and we stopped to organize the array of the army, as Alexandros had word from our prodromi riders that the enemy was holding the pass and the high ground around it. Their king, a man of the repute of a brave but reckless individual named Syrmis (Shyrms) was there too.

Alexandros presented the reports from the prodromi to the officers' assembly and after listening to each one's suggestions he outlined the way he wanted the battle to develop. The taxis of the sarissa falanxes would form across the mouth of the pass, on the most suitably leveled ground and in lose order. He guessed that all the loaded wagons the enemy had amassed by the entrance of the pass were to be released downhill to fall onto our advancing army. If that was the case, the lose falanx would be able to move away from the oncoming wagons open corridors on their path and let them Pass through doing us no harm.

The Ypaspistes were to flank the sarissa bearing taxis and move to get the high ground from the enemy and the cavalry was to follow close and chase the enemy after the break through the pass. He instructed the leaders of the Ypaspistes that the men should –in case wagons were send against them ordered the leaders of the Ypaspistes that their men should—in case the wagons were set lose against them also—to act like when they had to lock shields storming a wall defended by archers but, this time, to lay down with the shields locked above their bodies and let the wagons roll past above them, the men protected by each shield's hollow. Then, the wagons past, they were to attack vigorously the heights and he with the sarissa taxis and the cavalry would press the enemy head-on at the pass.

I watched the whole thing develop as Alexandros predicted (scribes are not fighting unless the enemy breaks into the camp) from a safe distance, but close enough to see all the details of the battle. We hardly had any casualties as the wagons rolled over the shields and through the corridors of our men. A scrape here and there a broken arm or leg and that was that! The Ypaspistes stormed the heights and dislodged the enemy (who was astonished by our feat) supported by a lohos of Kritan archers at our service. Meanwhile, the King led a head-on attack at the main enemy body and the forest of sarissas was too much for anyone to stand against it.

They took off as they could and we chased them until nightfall. The army returned to camp for the night and Alexandros ordered early departure for the next morning, as he did not want to give the enemy time to regroup. We followed their tracks for three days of quick march, crossed mount Aemos range and found out that they had taken refuge in the forest by the river Lynginos, which in turn empties its water in the great river Istros. Lamparos' men had by now joined us and served as guides and pathfinders alongside our own Prodromi.

As soon as Alexandros found the whereabouts of the enemy, ordered the sarissa bearing taxis to move through the tall grass stooping and holding the long sarissas horizontally, like during attack, so they would not be easily detected on their approach. He told the cavalry, which he split in two, one group on the left, the other on the right, to dismount and lead the horses in place and wait for his signal of attack. The taxis of our archers and the Prodromi with the Agrianes were to move openly against the enemy, engage and lure the Trivallians out of the forest.

It happened as he had planned. The Trivallians seeing it easy to push back our light troops came out of the forest and set to close battle with the Prodromi and archers. This gave the opportunity to Alexandros to order Filotas to attack from the right with his cavalry and Iraklidis with Sopolis and their cavalry units from the left. The King led in person the taxis of Pezeteri with the sarissas, bring-ing the enemy to an unwanted situation. Many Trivallians fell during that battle in spite of their bravery and, before long, they run for their lives across the river and took shelter on an island in the middle of the flow of mighty Istros, where they had their women and children secured beforehand.

They thought they were safe there, as they had support from the Getae, a strong Skythian tribe beyond Istros. We camped this side of the mighty river and tended to our wounded and buried our dead, fifty archers, Prodromi and Agrianes—all told. The enemy dead were about one thousand and we let them at the discretion of the locals, as we had done at the pass few days ago.

The king ordered a council meeting to see how we would cross the river and give a final lesson to the Trivallians and their allies, thus securing once and for all our northern allies and client kingdoms. During the meeting we received word that our fleet from Vyzantion had just arrived and anchored around the river bend, unseen by the enemy.

We could see the fires of the Getae camp across Istros and could hear their calls to and answers from the Trivallians trapped on the island of Pefki. Alexandros knew the Getae were about to try and cross the river with boats and attack us along with their Trivallian allies. He said that our attack upon them should come first, unexpected by the enemy. Receiving the officers' reports, the estimated strength of the Getae was about triple the number of our horse but half the number of our foot.

Alexandros sent word to our ships to approach during the night in silence, guided by our camp fires and load (upon arrival) four iles of cavalry, which were transported across, past the Getae camp. The ships returned and by making our men to fill animal hides with straw and other floating materials, he ordered as many as possible to go on the ships and the rest to cross the river down-stream on these floating devices or on any small fishing boats we had confiscated from the locality.

The night passed mostly by these activities and in utter silence. By sunrise the King had across the river a taxis of sarissa bearers under Nikanor, the second son of Parmenion, plus some archers. The King was in charge of the cavalry's royal Agima, while Filotas led the rest of our horse. They were assembled by a vast field of high corn, thus hidden from the enemy who had not bothered to place outposts judging the river wide and fast enough for their safety.

Our men moved up the bank with the foot and archers having the river on their left and the cavalry further inland guarding their right. When they cleared the field and came out in full view, the enemy was completely taken by surprise, as they did not expect us to have achieved such a feat in a single night! Utter confusion reigned in their camp as they tried to prepare for battle and the King ordered our men to advance rapidly in a tight form of the falanx called synaspismos, the archers raining ar-rows overhead on the enemy and the cavalry charging from the left side of the Getae spreading more havoc and causing heavy casualties.

The Getae had no choice but to flee toward their 'city', located a few stadia distance up river. The falanx pushed forward still hugging the river bank and the cavalry pursued rapidly the retreating enemy. Their 'city' having no walls for defense was abandoned by the Getae who took with them as many of their women and children as they could and retreated far into the open country hiding in its tall grass vastness.

Alexandros did not try to pursue them any further. He put his troops to collect what booty there was under the supervision of Filippos son of Mahatas and Meleagros son of Neoptolemos and order-ed the 'city' destroyed as a lesson to the Getae. Then, all the army was transported back to our side with the ships. The King was now confident the enemy had had enough and the river would be the frontier line of our parts of influence for a long time.

Upon return to our side, mindful of the gods as he always was, he sacrificed to Zefs and Iraklis, as well as to the river Istros, thanking them for favoring us. He praised the captains of our ships for a job well done, as he did with all the ones who distinguished themselves in battle and waited for the Trivallian delegation to come and ask for leniency. He did not bother to try a landing on the island of Pefki as he knew they had no other choice and, thinking along the lines his Father would act, wanted to have the Trivallians tamed under us but strong enough to protect this side of Istros in case of future raids from other tribes.

He was right. King Syrmis came in person asking for pardon and with promises to be our ally for ever. Oaths were taken and exchanges were made, us taking several Trivallian nobles as hostages to secure long term good will. At the same time, several other tribes sent delegates to assure Alexandros of their good intend to remain our allies. Among them were chiefs from the tribe of Keltes, which expands all the way to the sea of Adriatiki, skirting the Illyrian lands. They also assured the King that they want peace and alliance.

While we were dealing with the tribes of the north-east, runners came from Antipatros reporting to the King that the Illyrians were preparing once more for war. Did Alexandros want his regent to campaign against them or should he wait the King's return to Makedon? Alexandros' answer was to have the home troops in readiness but Antipatros should stay in Pella like nothing was happening.

Next, Alexandros sent message to his friend Lamparos to have his Agrianians on the ready for peace keeping in the region and he with our army, moved south-west on the double, in spite of our troops being without any true rest after this campaign. But everybody understood that speed again was our best ally in facing the new danger, so we marched. According to the requirements established by King Filippos some years back and reinforced by Alexandros, there were no extra camp followers or women and nagging peddlers to slow us down. Provisions were made ready for our needs well ahead by special agents in the service of the King, to keep our delays at a minimum.

We arrived at the border of Derriopis with Dassaretis by the river Lihnidos which empties in Lake Lyhnitis, a little to the north-west of the Vrygiis lakes in record time. Behind us we had left the friendly Agrianians and the Peones in charge of our security. Of the attacking Illyrian armies of Par-thines, Tavlantes and Gravaei under the leadership of Glabka (Glafkias) and Glydo (Klitos), none knew we had them where Alexandros wanted them!

They had invested the town of Pelion before our arrival and—as we got in the area—they had taken it and felt secure behind its walls, reorganizing to further penetrate in Makedonia—for they thought us of still being in Thraki. At the same time though, we received news from friendly Vryges that the tribe of Aftariates was coming south through the land of Penestei and our situation would perhaps be in jeopardy. Our only approach to Pelion was through the pass between the lakes Lyhnitis to north-west and Vrygiis to south-east. If the Aftariates found out of our position, we could be cut off!

If that wasn't enough, a runner came with the news that the Ellenic city-states and in particular Thivae and Athinae were talking of renewing hostilities with us, as rumor had it that Alexandros had been killed in Thraki. Filotas son of Menis, the Tymfean, who had been sent to the Makedonian gar-rison in Kadmia acropolis of Thivae right after the battle with the Getae, was reported to have been isolated there by the new Thivan administration of Arhons. The King had to act fast and hard.

Alexandros sent word to Lamparos asking the Agrianian king to see that the Aftariates were taken care of by Agrianian forces. Lamparos answered immediately sending back the same runner with the message that he was on the move against the Aftariates, which secured our back. Then, we marched through the pass, toward Pelion which was held by Klitos and waiting the arrival of Glafkias, so they could move further south-east.

Now here I feel I need to give an explanation to the ones who have no knowledge of these parts and it is possible there will be some confusion with the locations and their toponyms. You need to thank Perdikkas son of Orontis who, reading what I recorded, made me aware of this little problem. There are two towns named Pelion, the one I have mentioned above which we passed through coming down the pass between the lakes and the one held by the Illyrians which is further south-west, between the rivers Apsos and Eordaikos, very close to the borders of three tribes: the Atintanes, the Dassaretes and the Haones (the latter being under the kingship of the Molossian Alcxandros).

This is then the town we were after and its approach was also through a very narrow pass. At some places of the pass we could hardly have four men marching abreast. The higher ground of this pass was held also by the men of Klitos, which made our job so much more difficult. There was no help from the Molossian king Alexandros, since he was campaigning at the south side of his kingdom against the Aetolians who had allied with Thivae and Athinae.

Our Alexandros ordered the Prodromi and a few lohi of slingers and archers to take the heights from the men of Klitos and that was accomplished with some effort but with very light casualties and we were able to pass through, having the river Apsos to our left and, as soon as we got in the open valley out of the pass and before the town, we formed and attacked to storm it. Unfortunately, the retreating from the heights barbarians had time to alert Klitos and he had placed strong defense at the walls of the town.

We had no siege equipment with us, because it would have slowed us on our fast march to get here. The King ordered the camp to be set and we made the necessary preparations for it along with set-ting enclosures and earth mounts around the town to keep the enemy inside and under observation. Some taxis of Psili and Prodromi were assigned to cut trees down in order to build some towers and ramming equipment for the siege. The enemy made couple of attempts to break through our lines but failed leaving behind a number of dead, as we also failed storming the town one more time chasing after their retreats.

It seemed it would take us some time there and provisions were not adequate. If that wasn't enough, Glafkias arrived with his army and his vanguard managed to take back the heights from us, now placing our army between his forces and the ones in the town. Everybody looked upon King Alexan-dros for a solution and the King had it!

Receiving word from our friend Lamparos, the Agrianian king (the barbarians would let through anyone coming to us, thinking they had us at a disadvantage and they would have more of us for the kill), that he had engaged the Aftariates so they could not add their numbers to our enemy forces. Alexandros ordered the army to assemble in battle order. All taxis of sarissa bearers lined up, with our cavalry and taxis of psili at the left and right extremities for protection and ready for battle.

Instead, Alexandros called for drill demonstrations and faint attacks at always different directions, compelling the enemy to keep on shifting forces and not knowing if the next move would be a real attack or not. This stratagem brought the Illyrian forces to confusion and disarray. They lost their coherence of battle unison and, at the proper time, the King ordered the crossing of the river at the ford, thus securing us grounds for foraging and the recapture of some key heights for guarding our camp and army better.

The enemy tried to recover after the initial surprise but our archers and the constructed from local timber vallistes and katapeltes with their superior range of throwing missiles, kept them at a distance and inflicted heavy loss on the ones who tried their luck against such rain of weapons on them. Ob-viously, we had but only few accidental injuries among ourselves during this operation and the King was cheered by the army as he run from place to place overseeing the execution of his orders.

Alexandros was everywhere during this re-crossing of the river and was exposed to danger more than the foremost posted archers and cavalry units who were covering our moves. With a timely counter attack, he even saved the lives of Filotas' ili when the later found itself under severe pressure from the men of the Illyrian Klitos. During this rescue operation, the King was wounded twice! Once by a sling stone on the head and, next, by a mace on the base of his neck—but he kept on fighting!

With our line of safe passage through the narrow pass secured and open access to provisions now, most of the officers advised the King to send for additional troops from Makedonia or to retreat after leaving enough men to keep the pass secured from further Illyrian penetrations. Alexandros would have neither. He would not give the impression to the barbarians that the Makedonians were remote-ly considering retreat and he had in mind securing the safety of the borders for many years to come.

We camped where we stood and he ordered a vigilant observation of the enemy moves. Two days passed and, at the third, reports came from our prodromi that the enemy was careless of his own vigilance and was carelessly camped before the city with its gates open, to accommodate the needs of the troops inside and out of it. To Alexandros, this was the opportunity he was waiting for. The King ordered immediate battle array with outmost quietness and kept it concealed from enemy observat-ion, while having the officers study the terrain ahead in every detail.

As night came, he gave the order of attack. He sent again the archers first to cross the river. Then, the taxis of Perdikkas and Kinos followed along with the Agrianian detachment, ordering the rest to follow-up rapidly. Without waiting to see the rest of the army crossing, the King fell upon the unsus-pecting Illyrians catching most of them in their sleep. There was nothing else the enemy could do but to stand and die or flee. Some did stand and died but most took off as fast as they could, among them Glafkias. Alexandros pursued the enemy all the way to the heights of the Tavlantian mountains while he ordered parts of our army to take Pelion from the Illyrian Klitos.

The Illyrian, seeing that he could not hold the city as he was left with few of his forces, he set it on fire and took off to meet Glafkias and the remnants of that army back at the coastlands of the sea of Adrias. He sent envoys asking for clemency and pledging his willingness to remain peaceful in the future. Alexandros accepted but made sure we took a number of chieftains as hostages, to secure the Illyrian pledge. He also ordered the rebuilt of Pelion with adequate fortification of the city and troops to keep it under our control with no fear of being overcome again.

As the negotiations with the Illyrian tribes were about to be concluded and oaths were taken, we got the message that first, the High King—hearing of our successful campaign by Istros—and fearing the Illyrians would be of no match to our forces, had send a large amount of gold Darics to Dimosthenis and the latter was distributing the fortune to everyone who was willing to take arms against us, with special target the Thivan exiles. To invigorate them, he made sure he had agents to spread the rumor that King Alexandros was fatally wounded and our army had fallen in disarray. He also abandoned the faithful Athinian allied city of Plataea to Thivan rule.

Alexandros got really angry as he considered the Athinians were double dealing and the Thivans ready to succumb to the Persian gold and Dimosthenis' lies. The King was not fearful of the Athinian politician and his schemes. He knew we could beat either or both again and Dimosthenis had no personal ambition to repeat risking his life after the fiasco at Heronia. On the other hand, the King knew that a renewed war with any of the city-states would delay us from taking of to Asia and it would create a big risk of alienating a good number of them. He ordered the immediate move of the army southward and with absolute secrecy, but first we sacrificed to Dias, to Pan and Iraklis, in recognition of their help to our victory. We skipped the customary games though and we marched south through the mountain passes as to keep our move undetected.

Meantime, Thivan exiles moved from Athinae and returned to their city in secrecy, urging and bribing the Thivan citizens to overthrow its leaders and expel the small Makedonian garrison King Filippos had placed at Kadmia acropolis after Heronia. They also promised Thivae would receive Athinian reinforcements immediately. The citizens believed these promises and, with the bribes received, revolted. They exiled their government, killed two of our troopers—as they were shopping unsuspected—and forced the rest of our garrison to barricade behind the walls of Kadmia.

With our rapid march we reached the Thessalian town of Pelina by Pinios in only seven days! We rested two days gathering some allied Thessalian forces and some of the Viottians who fled after the change of government in Thivae, out of fear for their lives. We resumed our march moving a bit slower now and arrived in Onhestos passing Thermopylae in total secrecy. The whole march took us only thirteen days!

As we arrived before Thivae, the astonished Viottians who had allied with the new regime gave up and sent embassies to ask for leniency—which was granted. All of a sudden, Dimosthenis and his Athinians became dead silent and forgot all promises to Thivae waiting for the events to develop from the safety of distance. We camped in such a way as to block the road to Attiki, cutting off Thivae from any possibility of relief coming from Athinae.

Alexandros dictated and I wrote a letter to the citizens of Thivae, promising to be lenient to all those who would surrender, asking only for the ring leaders Finix and Prothitis to be handed to us as host-ages. As we learned later, most of the citizens were in favor of the terms but the returned exiles fear-ing we wouldn't keep our word, managed to convince the Thivans to continue. They erected a stock-ade facing the trapped garrison and manned their walls.

The King tried again to negotiate and held our troops at a distance, not willing to fight Ellines—if he could help it. Few days passed and all efforts for peace were rejected. The King prepared our troops for assault but still kept his hope that the Thivans would come to their senses. Perdikkas and his taxis though, finding a favorable moment to move, attacked and broke the outer stockade erected by the defenders, using the vallistes which had just arrived. Amyntas, the cousin of our King stationed next to Perdikkas, followed with his men, fearing the taxis of Perdikkas will receive all the glory of taking Thivae and the battle started in earnest. Alexandros seeing them make progress and fearing their taxis might get isolated, ordered a general attack sending in the contingent of Agrianians and having the rest try their luck at other points of the walls, for diversion.

The wall where Perdikkas attacked fell but he found a second stockade behind it and he was severe-ly wounded. Amyntas took over the leadership and our troops drove the Thivans by the temple of Iraklis and trapped them there. The Thivans doubled their effort and, as our troops could not use effectively the long sarissas in such quarters, were pushed back. Alexandros was ready though and sent in the Agima of Ypaspistes and the Agrianians the minute the Thivans—thinking they had us—made the mistake to open a gate in order to give a full scale attack. Our garrison attacked them at the same time coming out of the Kadmia acropolis and from the side of the temple of Amfion.

It was the beginning of the end. The Thivan cavalry, comprised by the rich exiles who had the most to fear now, fled the city from the north gate which was guarded by a token of our troops and dis-persed. Our falanx formations now had an easy task of eliminating any further resistance, as most of the Thivans now were surrendering rather than persisting in fighting.

All the oppressed by Thivan dominion Viottians such as the Fokians, Orhomenians and Plataeans, took advantage and started slaughtering anyone they found on their way. Many Makedonians seeing there was no way of holding them back, joined the slaughter and the King had a very hard time get-ting the troops under control. Then, all of a sudden, calm returned amidst the ruins.

We counted our dead. Due to the street fighting and the difficulty of deploying our sarissa falanxes, we had a greater number of dead than Alexandros was prepared to accept but he now could do not a thing about it. We had about five hundred casualties in dead and close to a thousand wounded. The Thivans lost about six thousand and about thirty thousand were captured to be sold at the slave markets, upon strong demand from the Viottians who now wished to see Thivae completely ruined. Our troops were also angered by the Thivan treachery and Alexandros gave-in to their demands, a thing he soon regretted.

He insisted though to have all descendants of the poet Pindaros saved, his house to be undemolished and the shrines and temples of Iraklis, Amfion and other deities to be left standing. His wishes were obeyed albeit with difficulty—especially from the side of our Viottian allies. Thivan territory was divided among the Viottians and the city of Orhomenos took the most of it. The Kadmia acropolis, as a strongpoint, remained and was occupied by an enforced Makedonian garrison.

Athinian, Aetolian troops and from Peloponnisian Ilia had moved (rather late) to support Thivae but, hearing of her fate, sent hastily embassies asking for forgiveness. Alexandros did not want any further blood shed among Ellines. He regretted already his softness in letting the Viottians take such a revenge on Thivae and was now generous and ready to move forward letting the bygone be bygone. Still, angered by Athinian double crossing, he asked for the surrender of nine Athinians, Dimosthenis and Haridimos being among them. The city sent a new embassy appealing and Alexandros consent-ed, insisting only to have Haridimos exiled. That done, Haridimos went to the service of thePersian High King, Darios.

It took us some time to settle the affairs, as many representatives of the city-states came to our camp either renewing their alliance with us or asking for settlements of their disputes. Many were looking to have Athinae meet the same fate as Thivae (some Plataeans openly asked for it) feeling that they had been betrayed and had come close to disaster by the policies of Athinae and, especially, of those who paid attention to Dimosthenis' urging and bribery.

Some of our lords and generals were of the same opinion, notably Ptolemeos, Klitos, Antipatros and Kinos, but Alexandros felt we should not create further enmity among the city-states. He reasoned that we all had to put the past where it belonged and look forward to a glorious future, united. 'All past differences will look and feel like a bad dream from some night long past, as soon as we march and celebrate our first victory against our common enemy!' was his response and all understood that the case was closed. We made sure some reinforcements remained in the south, to augment establish-ed garrisons in case there were still anti union elements active and we marched north to prepare for the crossing to Asia. We arrived in Pella the third day of the month of Dios, the Athinian Pyanep-sios . . ."

SECTION THREE

MARCHING TO FREE AND DRIVING TO UNIFY BY CONQUEST

From 4th Century BCE to Beyond 323 BCE

"If the Former Yugoslav Republic
of 'Macedonia' needs such a lie
in order to exist, its existence is
redundant!"
Marcus A. Templar, American

I

The company of middle-aged and old veterans were served by their own sons in the small banquet room of a remote and inconspicuous farm house in the vicinity of Filippoupolis (but far enough from the city itself and the danger of running up to unwanted old 'friends' and 'acquaintances') sat or reclined in a circle around the central hearth for warmth. The north, winter-chilled, wind of Thraki outside the house promised the arrival of some additional heavy snow to follow its path soon.

They were dinning and drinking strong Thrakian wine and ale, retelling stories their sons had herd a thousand times already, agreeing and arguing, forgetting details or adding wisdom of later days to events which took place before that wisdom had made its mark in their understanding of the enor-mity of their achieved task, as well as the equal size of blunders during and after the 'great loss'—as they referred to the death of Alexandros not that many years ago.

These aged veterans were a medley of Thrakians, Makedonians, one Persian (who took every effort to pass as Ellinas when among crowds) and one Vaktrian. They were united through their love toward the King who led them undefeated in every battle, united in their misery of misunderstanding his mission and drive when they shouldn't have, united in their need to keep his memory alive, pass it on to their offspring and, finally, united in their need to remain anonymous in the vastness of land and people, for their heads were a prize making a short but important list on the accounts of the 'heirs' of Alexandros who were ever-fighting each-other for supremacy!

They were Adamas son of Antigenis house Damasias, Sytalkis the Odryssian, Aristos of house Irak-lonas, Attalos the Agrianian and cousin of Lamparos, Filippos son of Alketas house of Agis, Mithra-na (who adopted the name Dimitrios) from house Haxamanish (Ahaemenis) nephew of Darayava (Darios) the last Persian High King, Galash (renamed Kalas) house

Oxyarta the Vaktrian and Peri-das son of Menandros house Asteropeos. They were the remaining faithful to the dream of their King, albeit guilty of misunderstanding his motives and drive when they shouldn't have—and now it was too late!

Their conversation started as usually with mild difference of opinions and they were sure to end-up in shouting (good strong wine or beer had always been the catalyst of such result) but they always ended up shaking hands, hugging and kissing, tears running down their eyes and mixing with the sweat of the heat, stemming from the hearth, the wine and the individual excitement. Their sons who were ever-present to serve them and learn would hide a smile or two witnessing the repeat of such antics on a nightly basis, or, if the case would call, intervene to avert any later remorse of a deed not meant to be done. One thing was evenly accepted from all: They were friends for life and they would remain as such regardless of opinions, accusations, remorse and/or pride!

This night's theme started with the regional pride each had running in his blood. Not that each felt any less or any more 'Makedonian' than the rest. It had long been etched in their hearts what one could call as a total devotion to Makedonia, not as a region or country but primarily and mostly as an idea, a force of unification, a sense of belonging and the attached pride of accomplishment due to that fact.

"I am—along with Adamas here—the oldest among this company and my words ought to be taken under due consideration from the rest of you who were just about yearlings asking for your mother's milk when the two of us started with Alexandros and made the rest of these idiots who proclaim themselves kings, what they are today! And, what are they? Let me tell you: They are just apes, poor imitators and chasers of the glory which surpassed every other and it can never be reached or repeat-ed by anyone!" Adamas concurred, banging his wine cup on the arm of his semi-recliner and, with a mouth full of roasted stag meat, said something like: "Here! Here! Sytalkis is absolutely right! As right as it can be of course—when a Thrakian says it."

"Why! Is there something I said you object to?" Sytalkis looked up and retorted half serious half joking. "No my friend but you mustn't forget that our age difference is merely two years apart, you being the senior. That doesn't make you Alexandros' first follower nor any better than the rest of us. Paeonia—south Peonia that is—has been part of Makedonia way before you Odryssians saw the light thanks to King Filippos and attached yourselves to King Alexandros mostly out of the knowledge he would lead you to making a decent name aside of giving you the opportunity of making a fortune."

"Sytalkis is right!" The voice of Attalos came across hoarse (he had sustained an injury from a sling stone up at the Parapamissos mountains years ago and he was hoarse since). "Even Agrianians like myself were faithful to both Kings and to Makedonia way before you. I ought to know, as king Lam-paros was related to me, a second cousin! I may have been born only six years before his death but my Father gave me all the details on the relationship of my second cousin with the Great King Alexandros."

"Let's face it friends, none of us being an Agrianian, an Odryssian or Paeonian—or Asian for that matter—can truly claim of being as Makedonian as Makedonians are! Nonetheless, most of Thraki has become Ellenized since the times before Filippos and Alexandros—we all have to agree to that!

It may be that north Odryssians still use Thrakian dialects—as Agrianians do; it may so be that the northern Peonians even under Filippos' rule remained as foreign to Ellenic customs as before him.

But we all know that most of southern Thraki—as well as all of south Paeonia from Vylazora and Astivos to Parorvilia and Sintiki have become at heart (if not yet by blood) Makedonian Ellines and darn proud of it! Ask the Satrae, the Vissae or the Vistones. What do they speak? Which alphabet they use? How do they feel?

As for us Odrysses, ask anyone from Filippoupolis to the coasts of Aegeon and the Propontis, to the east shores of the Efxinos Pontos! Not only we have adopted the Elliniki language and writing, we do feel as Ellines as the most southern city-state citizens! Obviously, they still consider us all as semi-barbarians—but there's nothing new to it. Let them have that notion." Sytalkis concluded sternly.

"You are correct my friend." Filippos, son of Alketas from house Agis jumped in. "And, under King Alexandros' eyes, we were—and are—all equal, as the gods meant us to be. How I wish we had all understood his plans! A few, like us, thanks to Evmenis' foresight and Lysimahos' hospitality and friendship, were able to settle here and in other places— albeit away from all the 'action' of the fools who think they can replace a Filippos or an Alexandros. We are at least temporarily in safety and ready to support once more the only legitimate King of Makedonia, be that Filippos-Arrideos will hold the throne being King Filippos' son or, Roxana's son Alexandros, as the legitimate son of King Alexandros."

"Polyperhon is said to have Iraklis, the son of King Alexandros and Artavazos' daughter Varsini, you know, the one who was Memnon's wife to begin with? And, they say, he's hiding him (Polyper-hon does) somewhere in upper Makedonia, just in case." Mithrana/Dimitrios let the rumored 'old news' resurface. "Of course, before anybody decides to 'attack' me here, I don't say what I just said because of any special interest of Iraklis being half Persian, cause I will support any of the three who comes forth to become our legitimate King, in spite that we know Filippos-Arrideos is a bit weak in mind."

"I don't trust Polyperhon any more than I could trust Antipatros' weakling, Kassandros!" Peridas raised his voice. "King Kassandros to you old fart!" Kalas from house Oxyarta teased him, winking at the others. "King my ass!" Peridas roared. "The idiot was not even named as heir by his own father—as old Antipatros himself isn't up to trusting that worthless son of a whore! The old man is due to die any day now but he is wise enough to keep Kassandros away!" "Yeah, but that worthless 'idiot' was clever enough to marry Thessaloniki and now he's directly related to the Argeades . . ." Attalos got back to him. "Yeah, yeah, I know. She married him only to go free from Olympias, as the old lady seems to have in mind to rid from all other Argeades except the ones who come directly from her son!" Peridas frowned, not liking (as also the rest of this small company of friends) the antics of the old Queen. "What about Ptolemeos abducting the Soma? The body of the King is now in Memfis!"

"We are getting away from the subject of our conversation now." Sytalkis interrupted. "We have no power to do or alter anything as we hide here because we have to, because of our families and the future of our sons and daughters. If and when things clear and one of the legitimate Argeades is secured as our King, then we can offer him our services openly and he will take care of the ones like Kassandros or even Perdikkas who—I hear—is acting bad. 'Till then . . . Now, where were we?"

He turned to the young sons and daughters of the company and seeing some of them were smiling—as they all had witnessed the same kind of friendly but heated exchange of opinions in several occasions in the past— he admonished them with a secret smile of his own. "Now you just listen to what we have to say, even if it is said many a time—and keep it well into your minds! You have to know what we have known and experienced. Knowledge is what may come to save you when your heads get in a line because of the would-be Kings and I hope the gods will forbid that happening."

Adamas told them to hold it and asked his daughter Ismini to get the other girls first and go to the gynekonitis, the separate rooms of the ladies, to bring to the company some more food first. Attalos turned to his son and instructed the young men and boys to see that the company had their wine replenished. "That's the only way my voice can carry and be less hoarse" he claimed. "Ha! I know by now that this is only an excuse for you're your kind of bragging drunkard Agrianes!" Filippos gave his friend a nudge from his adjacent recliner. Attalos gave a growl of pretended discontent and rais-ed his hand in a mock threat of a slap on the face, while Filippos leaned over the other side pretend-ing he was scared.

All this time Aristos from house Iraklonas kept quiet, now drinking some Thrakian beer, now pick-ing some choice meats with his knife and stuffing his mouth. Then, he decided to talk. "All right! That is enough of play you . . . juvenile delinquents! Time to be serious again if not for our sake, for the sake of our children who soon will have to face greater dangers than we did. At least, we always knew who the enemy was . . ." "I wish we truly knew my friend!" Kalas retorted. "If we had, things wouldn't have turn-up the way they did." "I am afraid you are right!" Aristos answered back. "When our kids return with their tasks fulfilled, I propose they are the ones now who will narrate the whole story as we taught them and, if it takes any corrections or their memory runs short, we budge-in and remind them. We have to make sure they know every detail and they keep it for use in their future and for their children's sake . . ."

They all agreed and Sytalkis proposed to start with his son, Yeoryios being the elder of their lot and due to getting married and worrying about his own family soon. Yeoryios was born to Sytalkis some sixteen years ago, during a leave from the service under King Alexandros, a fact which kept Sytalkis away from Vavylon which—in turn—made him feel bad for not being with his King when Alexandros died. It so happened that during the birth of the child an unusually strong earthquake hit the area, causing his wife to die just after the delivery, from fear. The boy got the dual rooted name of Mother Earth Yea's and orgi/anger and was named Yeoryios.

The younger ones returned to the dining hall rekindled the hearth and passed the food and drinks around. They waited until the 'old guard' took their portions and then, they did the same for them-selves. They now all sat at their places or reclined on their couches and Yeoryios was asked to nar-rate the campaign of King Alexandros Μεγας (the Great), warned that he should not leave anything out because that was a test on his memory as

541

well as the memories of his younger friends who were told to feel free to interrupt and correct what he would possibly fail to present as it happened.

Yeoryios cleared his throat, took a good portion of wine from his cup and started in clear voice, with a feeling of respect and duty to meet the expectations of his elders and to install the same sense of duty and respect of accuracy to his younger companions, male or female.

"The army started its drive eastward from Pella with King Alexandros at the head of the long line, for he was not one who would ever order his men with the word go. Instead, his words of advance were always 'Follow me!' They passed by the north shores of the lagoon and the gulf of Therma, behind the Kissos mountain by the twin lakes near the Vottiki Apollonia, to Argilos where they camped for the night.

The next day saw them traversing via lake Kerkinitis to Amfipolis and Avdira by the Vistonian lands. The army continued its march on a daily basis until the last of the troops arrived at Sistos on the Thrakian side of the Hersonisos, by the sea of Elli—the Ellispontos—in just twenty days! Filippos' old faithful general, Parmenion, was charged with the crossing of the cavalry boarded on ships across to Asia at the location of the Avydos. The rest of the army was to follow that move in succession, by the taxis.

The King, instead, took his closest friends, the Ypaspistes and the cavalry Agima of Companions and sailed from the city of Elaeous offering first sacrifice to Protesilaos, the first Ellinas to fall during the long-ago war against Tria, to the Olympian gods and Iraklis, leaving Posidonas last, as he sacrificed for the sea god mid-channel cutting the throat of an all white bull with his own hands. He steered the royal vessel on his own and landed at the location of cape Sigaeon. As the ship plunged at the sands of that shore, Alexandros threw his spear which pinned itself on the Asian land, thus de-claring it a symbol of conquest upon the Persian High King!

He next visited the hamlet of Ilion, the capital city of ancient Tria and offered sacrifice at the tomb of his maternal ancestor Ahilleas, as Yfestion did the same at the tomb of Patroklos. At the temple of Athina, the goddess of wisdom up at Ilion's acropolis, Alexandros took the old armor said to have been Ahilleas' own and dedicated to the goddess his personal armor. He then ordered games and feast for the next day and, at the end of those, he ordered the foundations of a new city of Ilion.

King Alexandros then joined the rest of his army of about thirty and five thousand, north-east of Avydos, by Arisvi. He continued north-eastward by the shore of Efxinos Pontos, to the city of Lamp-sakos, giving orders to his army to avoid any devastation on the countryside or to injure any people. At Lampsakos the army was provisioned by its citizens who welcomed the King as their liberator.

The following day Alexandros sent Amyntas with one cavalry ili and four iles of short sarissa bearers to scout ahead, while a small body of sarissa bearers and an ili of cavalry was sent under Panigoros to invest the city of Priapos at the mouth of Granikos river to protect against any attempt by Persian vessels to approach. The scouts of Amyntas reported that a strong force of Persians had the east bank of Granikos and lined-up in order of battle.

They were reported to be approximately twenty thousand horse and about the same number of foot, the latter consisted mostly of Ellines in the pay of the High King Darios. This force was under the joint command of Spitradata/Spithidatis who was the satrapis/governor of Lydia and Ionia and of Arshata/Arsitis satrapis of Ellispontine Frygia. They were both assisted by a splendid array of high ranking princes many of who were close relatives of Darios. They were Omara/Omaris and Mitro-barzana/Mithrovarzanis with their Kapadokian horse riders, Arshama/Arsamis, Reomidra/Reomi-thras, Petitna/Petinis, Nifhata/Nifatis, Atizyah/Atizis satrap of greater Frygia and many other nobles.

In charge of the mercenaries was the Rodian Memnon who, years earlier had been offered hospital-ity in the court of King Filippos but found Makedonian rules of conduct unacceptable and left for the Persian money and married to Barshana/Varsini, daughter of the satrap Artabaza/Artavazos. We knew he had the ear of the High King but, also, that the local satraps envied his success and wouldn't listen to his plans of warring against us. Instead of retreating in the interior and putting to waste all before our advance, Spithridatis and Arsitis rushed to come and deny us any further advance.

Fearing Memnon would receive all the glory by defeating Alexandros, the lead satraps stationed him and his mercenaries some distance from the river bank, on a small hilltop and ordered him to wait there for the result. As we arrived late in the afternoon and spotted their array, Parmenion and some other senior officers—including my Father—(Sytalkis nodded in agreement at that remark) asked the King to attack right after dark, so as to bring panic and confusion on the enemy who was so much superior to our army in horse and could outmaneuver and engulf us.

Alexandros listened with due respect to his seniors in age and war experience but rejected their plan for several reasons, taking the time to explain. First of all, he said, they stationed their horsemen at the bank's edge, which rents them incapable of free movement and prevents them of charging us. Our sarissas being so much longer ought to suffice in pushing them back with high loss in dead and wounded. Then, the night is darker with just a sliver of moon and I wouldn't like any unnecessary killing of our own by none other than us. Thirdly, while I intend to keep them occupied attacking with the falanx taxis, I will lead the royal Eteri squadron of cavalry and our Amyntas from Lynkos will try to outflank their left with his cavalry unit and an ili of Ypaspistes. As for the rest of you, I see you leading in this order: from our left, cavalry units under Kalas son of Arpalos with the Thessal-ians. Next, Filippos of Menelaos, with his horse unit from our city-state allies. Then Agathon follows with his Paeonian horse units. Next to him the taxis of Krateros, the taxis of Meleagros, then Filippos son of Mahatas, my cousin Amyntas with his taxis of sarissa bearers and next, that of Kinos and Perdikkas'. All of you will be under the orders of Parmenion. From our center and toward the right, will be the taxis of Nikanor with Ypaspistes, and, covering my back and filling the gaps will be Attalos in charge of the Agrianians (Attalos remembered his uncle by the same name and nodded his head in approval) and Klearhos with the archers. I, with Filotas and Ptolemeos son of Filippos, will cover Amyntas' left, leading the royal Agima. As I foresee, the Persians will move to their left to block Amyntas' move to outflank them. That will be my time of attack, covering his left and striking their center where their leaders are. Now my friends, unless there are questions regarding your placement, let us have our supper and sleep the night in peace. Tomorrow we will gather all the glory Victory can offer to us! Those were Alexandros' words and everyone understood and complied."

Yeoryios took some wine again, ate some food while looking around for any corrections, approval or dismissal of his words. Finding nothing but nodding heads in agreement, teary rheumatic eyes lost in memories and younger eyes rested on him with desire to hear more, he continued.

The next morning the King rose and offered sacrifice to gods and Iraklis. The soothsayer, Aristan-dros from Telmesos, found the entrails favorable and the order for battle was given. The Granikos river had many fordable places to cross but also many places of steep banks. As the officers were placing their troops according to Alexandros' plan, his engineers tried their katapeltes and vallistes on the thick lines of Persian cavalry, creating an initial havoc on the enemy. Our lines crossed the river chanting 'Enialyos!'- the name of war god Aris. All went as Alexandros had foreseen, albeit with some difficulty on account of the steep banks and the valor of the Persian horse. Memnon and his mercenaries were confined on the top of the distant hill, under Omaris, weredeprived of any part-icipation.

There was a really scary moment as the King found great danger and almost lost his life—after his successful attack on the center of the Persians. While fighting, he broke his long spear, borrowed another and killed the son-in-law of Darios, Mithridatis. At the same time, Alexandros got hit on his helmet by the scimitar of Mithridatis' own brother Rhoishaca/ Roisakis, but the King killed that one too with the same borrowed spear. Then, Spithridatis came from behind and raised his scimitar in readiness to take the King's life! Thanks be given to the gods, Klitos the Melas was right there! He saw the Persian in time and took the opponent's hand off, with a great blow of his sword. Next, both Klitos and the King took the Persian's life. Klitos decapitating him with his sword, while the King had his spear going through Spithridatis' sternum.

The battle raged for a while with both armies fighting in close quarters with no-loss-no-gain of any ground. Our army presented no center by that time, as both wings were pushing with great effort to break or surround the enemy wings. Finally, thanks to the force and drive of Alexandros, our right wing cut through and, seeing the opening gap, our sarissa taxis made a wedge and split the Persian front. Their foot army took a hasty retreat with many perishing and the only enemy remaining was the Ellines mercenaries under Omaris and Memnon at that distant hill.

They knew they had the duty—as Ellines—to stand and fight, giving no quarter and asking for none. We were sure, at that time, that most of them regretted their decision to be hired to fight their countrymen for the shake of the High King but, honor being honor, they had to keep their word. So, we attacked them and they were cut to pieces where they stood. Very few of them managed to brake through and escape. Among them was Memnon.

Alexandros went to visit and provide what was possible to our wounded, praising each one for their individual valor. In spite the fact that our loses were minimal, the King was very much moved by the sight of our dead and wounded and was seen with tears running down his cheeks while inspecting the battleground. He gave total tax immunity to the families of the deceased and asked his favored sculpturer, Lyssipos, to erect statues in their memory. They were buried in full armor and games were proclaimed after their funeral pyres.

We also buried the Persian and Ellines mercenaries out of respect to their bravery and there was no looting and plundering. The few Ellines mercenaries captured though, were sent to Makedonia to work the rest of their lives at the mines, as they were considered to have betrayed the alliance of all Ellines to unite and fight the Persians. The only magnanimity shown by Alexandros was toward the very few Thivans among the mercenaries. The King, still regretting the destruction of Thivae not long ago, let them go free.

We were asked to collect three hundred of the best Persian panoplies and clean them thoroughly for shipment and dedication to the temple of goddess Athina at the Athinian acropolis. Ptolemeos son of Lagos and Filotas son of Parmenion asked the King why we should do the Athinians such an honor.

The King smiled and said that it would be a good reminder to all Ellines as to what could be achieved when we are united. Athinae, being centrally located and visited by all was the right choice. He let that radiant smile of his on his face saying that—the one who any observer could tell was full of wit but was ambivalent as to whether the King was also serious or simply playing. Yfestion let the rest of Alexandros' friends know, later, that the King was giving through that act and smile a gentle stab on Dimosthenis and his cohorts with their unceasing machinations against us! As for the Spartans and Lakedaemonians who insisted on staying 'neutral' on this pan-Ellenic campaign, he thought of escorting the gift of the three hundred panoplies with the following dedicatory note: 'From Alexan-dros son of Filippos and all the Ellines except the Lakedaemonians, we present these spoils from the foreigners inhabiting Asia'. A stab on Sparti—in memory of Thermopylae—this one!

Finishing with several urging affairs after the battle, Alexandros appointed Kalas son of Arpalos as the governor of whole Ellispontine Frygia, as he was qualified by his previous experience of the region, being among the ones who had come with the first expeditionary force under Parmenion and Attalos when Filippos was still alive. Alexandros instructed him not to alter any working customs, nor to impose any new taxes. He was to make sure he would keep the same officials who were taking care of the region, provided they were willing to cooperate. The inhabitants were to be treated with respect, thus gaining their favor—as opposed to the Persians."

Here, Yeoryios stopped. He took some wine and few choice parcels of meat and commended: "If I am not wrong, here is where most of you—and I will say that with all due respect—misunderstood the motives and plans of Alexandros, for the first but not the last time!" "Yes, we did so! Regardless of how sorry we feel ourselves now, we did think that a 'spear-won' area and its people were and ought to be our inferiors." Sytalkis admitted. "We didn't have the same attitude as when we warred against you Thrakians, nor against other city-states." Adamas added. "That was because you had a much different notion about us from the Asians and because most of you, taught by Aristotelis and taking his notions to the letter, regarded us as unworthy people, less civilized than you were!" Dimitrios said with some remnants of bitterness in his voice. "You forgot, in your recently fount glory, what the Athinians called you—and still doas your opponents. What goes around comes around!" Kalas the Vaktrian reminded them.

Aristos took care to keep the conversation out of any possible bickering, as he said: "We all know our past mistakes by now and that's the main reason why we are bonded under this friendship and not continue making the same mistakes by taking sides with the fools who call themselves 'King'."

Filippos closed the remarks with these words: "We hopefully have learned our lesson. We agreed to remain friends no-matter-what and try to teach our children right from wrong! We can argue in the process and, I know, bitterness is not an easy pill to swallow. As long as we keep our honor and friendship, I see no reason why we couldn't bring any and all errors in the open! What better way to show our children that we have overcome our follies and we now stand united for the good of our country and with devotion to its established royal family, especially now with all the danger around it and around us."

Then, turning to Yeoryios: "You are absolutely right with your observation on our past misunder-standings of King Alexandros. By bringing this up, you help the understanding of your peers, some are younger and—perhaps—less perceptive. For that, I thank you; for it seems to me they will now remember and understand easier!"

Yeoryios nodded his thanks with a move of his head and, taking a last sip of his wine, continued: "The King called a council and made his plans known to the lords and leaders of the army. He had the option to either move toward Gordion and then to Kilikia using the direct route toward Kili Syria and the heart of the Persian state, or, as he explained, follow the coast and liberate one by one the El-lenic Ionian cities for one, but also depriving the Persian fleet—which was intact and more numerous than our—of its Aegean anchorages. This way he would rent it useless and without the risk of a naval battle against superior numbers.

All lords agreed, as it was obvious that the main reason of the campaign was the liberation of our Ionian brothers. With that, Alexandros dispatched Parmenion to taking the city of Daskylion on the north-east coast of Propontis while he, with the rest of the army marched against Sardis, the old capital city of Lydia at the time of famous king Krissos. The army marched east of Mount Ida and, in a short time, Parmenion rejoined, as he reduced Daskylion easily. Sardis was guarded by a very strong acropolis and it could be easily defended by the Persian guard there.

Thankfully the gods were on our side and we did not spend time investing the city. Its leader of the Persian guard, Mitrana (Mithrinis), seeing that there would be no support from the recently defeat-ed satraps, made the wise choice to surrender everything, including the vast treasure hidden at the acropolis. He sent delegates to negotiate a peaceful transition. Alexandros instructed Amyntas son of Andromenis to take a taxis from the falanx and occupy the acropolis. That done, the King rewarded Mithrinis with the leadership of his own local troops now in our service.

It was not appreciated by the Ellines lords, Makedonians and allies, but, as it wasn't a high position reward and Mithrinis' force a small one, they accepted Alexandros' decision and explanation that we ought to show gratitude to the ones who sided with us. Asandros, brother of Parmenion, was installed as the governor of Lydia, with the same instructions as given before to Kalas, in Frygia.

As Alexandros learned that Memnon had been send to Ellispontos with a part of the Persian fleet to raise support for the High King there and isolate our army from any enforcements, he sent several detachments from the allied troops from the city-states under Kalas and Alexandros son of Aeropos from Lynkos to see that Memnon would not succeed. As an additional measure, Alexandros appoint-ed the son of Parmenion Nikanor, with second in command the son of Antipatros, Kassandros, in charge of our fleet and sent them to sail between the island of Lesvos and the coastal city of Militos.

This way we would show the Ellines that we could and did support them even in the presence of the mighty Persian fleet sailing around. The move won us the sympathy and devotion of the Lesvians, especially the Mytilinians.

Now from Sardis the army marched to Efessos, the so-called queen of all the Ionian cities. The people forced its government to open the gates for us. Alexandros entered and had the oligarchic government (government of few connected ones, in charge of the many) to withdraw, giving the power of the city to its citizenry, establishing a democratic leadership. He asked them not to go after the previous leaders for any kind of revenge but to start anew and with justice, under his leadership.

He asked them to have the taxes paid to the High King diverted to the temple of Artemis and he made sure he paid high honors at her shrine. The money from the taxes were to be helping with the rebuild of the temple, which was burned the exact day Alexandros was born in Pella some twenty one years ago. Dinokratis, the royal engineer was put in charge of its rebuilt. Here, Alexandros posed for his portrait to be done by the renown painter Apellis and that portrait was later placed in the very temple when the work finished.

While in Efessos, the King received delegates from the cities of Trallis, Smyrni and Magnisia, along with some other secondary cities of Karia. Parmenion was sent there to receive the cities, with about five thousand Pezeteri and two hundred horsemen. Antimahos, brother of Lysimahos son of Agatho-klis from Pella, was sent with equal force to invest the Aeolian Ellenic cities under Persian rule. He did so, successfully liberating twenty four of them!

Wherever Alexandros or his deputies went, past governments installed by the Persians were over-thrown without reprisals and democratic governments were installed in their place. Taxation was left as was and—sometimes—was erased altogether. Improvements were ordered for the benefit of the cities, such as the restoration of Smyrni, a new harbor mole at Klasomenae and so many other need-ed improvements elsewhere.

The army, with Alexandros' lead sacrificed to Artemis and the rest of the Olympians and readied to march toward the city of Militos, its governor Aegistratos having sent letters of surrender to Alexan-dros. As we prepared to go, the Persian fleet approached the harbor of the city and Aegistratos got scared and changed sides.

Militos, the birthplace of the sage Thalis, was of great importance to the High King, not only as a re-supply harbor for his fleet, but also as a commercial connector to his Finikian allies and their ports. It was the 'holder' of the eastern part of the Aegean and thus, had received exceptional privileges from the Persians in the past. Protected by the promontory of Mykali from the north and the Ladi islands before its port mouth and located only a few hours of sail from the island of Samos, gave it an importance of great value to the mastering of the sea and Persian naval power. Aegistratos thought he better remain faithful to the High King and closed the gates on us.

Our forces arrived shortly after and we captured the outer city and, placing our fleet (they had returned from Lesvos) at the entrance of the harbor seizing the island of Ladi first, we circumval- lated the inner city. The Persian fleet was now at anchor across from ours, at Mykali.

Many of the lords and allied leaders advised the King to attack the anchored Persian fleet, having in mind our overall capability in nautical engagements against Finikians and Persians in general. Alex-andros was reluctant to order such an engagement for a good reason. In case we would lose the battle, the Persians would then have a free hand on the Aegean and, with Dimosthenis' friends in Athinae still active, we could be in trouble of having the city-states change their mind and turn against us. The idea of a pan-Ellenic effort and unity was mainly in the minds of great men such as Filippos and Alexandros and few supporters among the city-states of Ellas. The rest, we still had in mind petty regional notions of supremacy—I daresay that we continue to do so to this day, in spite of now knowing what we do! I see there's no objection to my thinking . . . Well then, I continue . . .

It so happened that an omen was observed the next morning: An eagle had gone and rested on the top of the Persian flagship's mast. The seers were called and declared the omen to be in favor. Zefs' bird, the eagle, was on top of the Persian fleet. Victory over them was assured! Alexandros thought so too, but in another way. Yes, we would be victorious but from the land. Winning the coastal cities and having them on our side would render the Persian fleet incapable of surviving with no anchorage available. He, as descendant of Iraklis through the Argead line, had better understanding of Father Zefs' intentions.

Militos had again second thoughts. Aegistratos sent deputation to offer the use of Militos' port on equal terms between us and the Persians. That was absurd and Alexandros turned them down with scorn. Ellines ought to side with Ellines! The siege continued. Nicanor placed our ships at the nar-rowest area between the isle of Ladi to the end of Militos' harbor, preventing any communication or exchange of troops between the city and the enemy fleet. Then, Alexandros ordered a general attack on the city.

Our engineers bombarded the walls with katapeltes and vallistes while some of the ships came close to the seaside wall with ladders attached on their prows and our men climbed on them to overcome the defenders. Many of the mercenaries defending the city tried to escape either by swimming to the island or using small skiffs but very few made it. The walls were scaled and the city was taken. The King enslaved only the ones who supported Aegistratos and he sent them—with him—to work the mines back in Makedonia. He pardoned the rest of the citizens of Militos and granted them their freedom under a democratic government.

Although the Persian fleet was offering battle on a daily basis from Mykali where they were anchored, Nicanor never made a move to accept it—as per orders from the King. Alexandros observed the Persian need to forage on a nightly basis for food and water, leaving their ships with very few to guard them. He sent Filotas with an ili of cavalry and two taxis of falanx to occupy their landing area and prevent them from further foraging.

Seeing that, the Persian fleet had to sail to Samos for victuals and made the trip daily to sustain the crews. After sometime of repeating the motion and still not obtaining any battle, they made up their mind to cut through our fleet between Ladi and the harbor, thus taking us by surprise and land in the city. Our sailors had the same needs as them, namely to go and get provisions. So, they attacked at such a time when most of our crews were on land. Alexandros, seeing what was happening, assembled what crews he could master and personally led them to a counter attack, driving the enemy back and capturing one of their ships!

The Persians got discouraged by that and soon sailed to Samos for good in spite of their numerical superiority. The King now, seeing that the omen was fulfilled and the Persian fleet was useless and being also in need of re-enforcements due to loss of men placed in garrisons or killed and wounded, ordered the burning of our fleet and the sailors to serve as falanx oplites. He insisted on using the land approach to finish the Persian naval threat by denying them anchor, used our sailors to give our troops some needed boost in men and saved the treasury of much needed money—as the ships were so much more costly to sustain than the land troops!

We then marched toward the city of Alikarnassos. The cities on our way there opened their gates to us, hailing us as their liberators from the Persian yoke. Each city was granted its freedom and, when necessary, the

King replaced their governments with democracies. These cities relying on commerce mainly were assured by the King that, the sooner the Persian fleet was starved out of the way, the sooner their commerce would flourish again!

Now, as we all know, Alikarnassos was and is an excellent port. On the part of Asia-by-the Aegean Alikarnassos is the best, as it is very well protected by both nature and man-made defenses. By now the High King had made Memnon governor/satrap of the lower part of that Asia-by-the-Aegean, as well as the man in charge of the Persian fleet operating in the Aegean. Memnon sent his wife Varsini and his children to Susa on a volunteered move to show his fidelity and, at the same time, keep his family safe—in case Alexandros would try to get a hold of them.

Memnon had in his service then some of his mercenaries since Granikos, plus the local garrison and the army Hurundabata (Orontovatis) brought in support from local levies. Also, an Athinian exile who had fought at Heronia was there to advice on the most recent tactics—as he knew them—of the Makedonian sarissa falanx. Aptly, his name was Efialtis. He advised Memnon and the latter compli-ed on making a ditch exceedingly deep, which covered three sides of the already strong walls of the city. The forth side of defense was the harbor itself and was guarded by a wallcreating two harbors and the so-called royal citadel/acropolis which was/is on a small island by the entrance of these two harbors. The island's name is Akronnisos. Aside this, there was also the older acropolis at the north-west side of the walled city as well as a third one at the south-west side of the walls close to the sea, the one named Salmakis.

The trouble was that a few Makedonian traitors were also present and in the service of Memnon. They were Neoptolemos of Lynkestis and cousin of Arraveos, who was involved in the murder of King Filippos, also was Amyntas son of Antiohos who unreasonably thought Alexandros of being angry at him and fledand Thrasyvoulos from Pella and some others of lesser importance.

As we approached to invest the city from the north-east approaches of Mylasa, the garrison of Ali-karnassos made a sortie trying to get us off balance. They were driven back with not much of an effort. Alexandros sent scouts in the area to see which would be the best place of our army to have it as a starting point with the siege and, finding that to north-east there was the small city of Myndos he sent some taxis to take it. The

Myndians agreed to surrender, provided we would come at night, so they would have an excuse of getting caught unaware. Alexandros willing to provide what he could in order to save lives, agreed. As our troops came close though, they were attacked by the Myndians.

The King was furious and, in spite of not having any ladders to scale the walls or any machines to tear them down he attacked, and, with the help of sappers, we managed to have a tower crumble. It wasn't enough though and the Alikarnassians found out about our effort and sent re-enforcements.

Forced to return to our original camping ground we set all our equipment for a regular siege.

Alexandros ordered several taxis of Ypaspistes and oplites to use their shields covering above their heads in close order so as to have the defenders' slings, arrows and javelins bounce off and, slowly but surely, the army worked its way close to the walls and filled the ditch in several prearranged sectors, so we could bring in the sectioned towers, assemble them and roll them against these sectors of the walls, for a general attack.

Memnon put his engineers to work also from the city side and they erected their own towers higher than ours, so to dominate us and fire from above. They also resolved to make night attack to catch us by surprise and destroy our works. Our guards were alert though and our outposts were rapidly re-enforced, stopping their attack on its tracks. They lost many, among them Neoptolemos. Two brave Ypaspistes, Arhias son of Anaxidotos, the one who later served under Nearhos the Kritan and Klitos Lefkos from house Iraklonas, decided to attack the sortie by themselves, hoping to give the example to the rest of our troops.

The enemy of the sortie stood its ground for a while, answering the assault of these two brave ones with equal bravery. They lost quite a few men though and called for help from inside. Meantime our men also came to help Arhias and Klitos and a general melee ensued. Eventually the sortie was unsuccessful and the enemy returned inside the walls. Although a portion of the defense wall was torn down, due to the darkness and the sudden development, we were not able to take the city. Had it happen during day time, Alexandros told the troops the next day, we should have taken the city there and then.

Right after that, he ordered the towers to be moved closer to the fallen parts of the wall, so we could reach the secondary wall the defenders had rapidly erected to fill the gap. This was the sector from the roadside to Mylasa. As we came closer, the defenders now could fire at us from the sides of the gap, where the wall still stood and, of course, from the new one straight ahead. This caused the loss of one of our towers which caught fire. Filotas son of Parmenion threw his ili of cavalry against the enemy there, asking them to act as oplites and that saved the other towers. Meantime, Alexandros led in person a renewed attack, sending the enemy back with great loss.

Nonetheless, our effort to take the city failed and the King—for the first and last time through the whole campaign—asked for temporary truce so we could have our dead and wounded taken away, as did our opponents also. That was arranged but the citizens of Alikarnassos could clearly see that their days on the Persian side were numbered, unless they could succeed with an all-out sortie."

Yeoryios needed some more wine, his mouth was going dry from all the talk and took a break. All in the company agreed the hour was late already and most voiced the desire to withdraw for some sleep.

"We can pick-up from this point on, tomorrow." Dimitrios decided for the rest. "My daughter, Roxa-ni (he used the Ellenized pronunciation) can continue the narration and we can see how much she has retained . . ." "You rest assured Father, I do retain what you and the others have taught us!" she said softly but firmly, keeping her eyes cast down as was proper.

The next day Lysimahos sent a trusted servant with a message. The "kings" were ready to war again! Filippoupolis, like it or not, could be a marshaling point of armies from Makedonia (the aged beyond expectation) Antipatros was coming through with Polyperhon marching to meet the one-eyed Antigonos against Perdikkas, his brother Alketas and their ally Evmenis. They should keep in mind to be out of town for sure and keep as low as possible, in case troops would pass by their estate.

The news was not something to celebrate about. Everybody got busy gathering what could be put out of the way, to be saved from the rovers they were sure to rove about. In the middle of the winter? They were questioning. Well, they had marched in the middle of the winter with Alexandros, had they not? Oh, yes! But those were different times! No looting from peaceful bystanders was allowed then! The men brought in what horses and cattle were left in the vicinity (animals needed some fresh air now and then and the stables had to be cleaned), made sure the stables and the ship pen were covered with mounts of dirt and dried brush to look from afar as nothing but a simple mount of earth, made the necessary preparations for a hasty evacuation of the women and children (the youth had to stay alive to carry the knowledge and devotion for the future), barricaded the estate's main house and waited.

In the gloomy mood of the times, the families gathered by the hearth and the conversation was, naturally, around the unsettled issue of succession on the Makedonian throne, the waste of life as the lords and generals were fighting each-other for individual gains and the danger they were facing in case the estate would be the stomping ground of passing armies and the possibility of the old friends being recognized by old 'friends'—now enemies.

"I don't care much about my life" Sytalkis stated. "I care about our young, our wives and, natural-ly, about the chances we may have to support the rightful heir when and if opportunity comes! For the same reason, I don't want any of our young to die because of us and the truth to be lost for ever!"

"If there's any consolation Father to what I say, I want you to know that I have written down all you gentlemen have taught us and given it to my bride to be, Eleni, for safekeeping. You all know her family, they are to be trusted; they are like us!" Yeoryios informed the company.

"I also have everything written down in Persian!" Roxani added. "It's hidden and, if we need to run, I alone know the place and we can come back and retrieve it." Attalos gave a laugh shaking his head. "I see our children have learned at least one thing. They sure make provisions and take steps for the future! I also happened to have my son write everything down and I sent the papyrus rolls to my cousin Basali (Vasilios), who lives as you know—in Astivos and no one there really knows how to read, so there's no fear—even if they fall in the wrong hands."

Filippos looked at his wife Evanthia who was serving him his portion of the mid-day meal and, with a deep sigh, concluded: "I see that we are all conscious to save what can be saved for posterity. We should have let the rest of us informed of our intentions before taking any steps—I see no reason why any one would have objected—but, what's done is done, and with best intentions. So, let us live while we can, let us continue with our established traditions of telling and retelling the story and hope we will not have to face our enemies before we are ready." They all agreed with him and turned to their mid-day meal.

That night, Roxani—true to her task and promise—picked up from where Yeoryios had stopped and continued the narration. "The Persians and mercenaries at Alikarnassos made a last effort to break the siege by attacking in force during another sortie. They attacked from two sides at the same time.

One was from the place of the fallen part of the wall, the other from what was called triple gate. It so happened that the troops stationed by the place of the fallen section of the wall, our troops, were caught by surprise and the attackers led by the Athinian Efialtis started gaining some ground. The King saw the danger and, summoning Filippos son of Amyntas and his taxis of Pezeteri, brought balance but not before losing any tower to torch fire.

Alexandros had supervised personally the protection of the towers though and, due to his attention, no further damage occurred. At the same time, Efialtis got killed and the Alikarnassians were pushed back. Because of the narrow gap of the fallen wall, they could not make it easily back into the city and behind the secondary defenses. For that reason they lost too many as they stampeded and were having their backs exposed to our troops.

At the second point of their attack by the triple gate Ptolemeos from house Iraklonas was in charge of our troops and he was successful in pushing back the attackers. As the Alikarnassians rushed in retreat over a make-shift bridge they had placed across the moat, it broke under their load and they were killed. Their friends from the city seeing they were so defeated, closed the gates in fear of our troops following through, allowing our men to kill everyone who was left outside and didn't surrender.

Alexandros decided to be magnanimous and, although if he had pressed forward the city could possibly be taken then and there, he called for a truce in hope of achieving that now through negoti-ation and avoid further loss of life. Close to one thousand were killed from our opponents but only about forty of our own, among who Klearhos the leader of our archers (Kleandros replaced him) and Ptolemeos, the son of your uncle, uncle Aristos." Aristos nodded in a somber agreement.

"By that time and rejecting the truce, Memnon and his second in command Orontovatis withdrew under the cover of the night to the acropolis called Salmakis and to the one called Royal—by the harbor— after setting on fire their tower and the buildings of the city close to the walls. The fire driven by the wind spread fast and our men tried to contain it with some success. Alexandros did not want the city in ruins but had not much of a choice. He ordered the rest to be razed and, because he saw urgency in marching further, placed Ptolemeos son of Filippos in charge of his own ili of cavalry lancers and three thousand falanx oplites and sarissa bearers to keep up the siege of the places where Memnon and Orontovatis had taken shelter. As for the citizens of Alikarnassos who thus far surrendered, he had them billeted in surrounding villages until such time when rebuilding could be feasible.

Alexandros ordered the engineers to transfer our siege equipment to Trallis and he met with the former governor of Karia (due to her husband's death years back) lady Ada, who had through the siege helped with provisions sent from her personal stronghold at Alinda, her being isolated and placed under confinement by the Persians at our approach. Because of her, most Karians sided with us! She was an elderly person but with great capability and Alexandros became very fond of her. She did too and she adopted him as a son she didn't have. The King reciprocated in kindness and named her queen of the region and ruler, with Arpalos in charge only of the collection of taxes.

Now the King saw the need to consolidate his hold over most part of the Asia-by-the Aegean. To that end, he sent Parmenion with all the Thessalian horse, the Ellenic allies, the siege engineers and equipment and the wagon train to Sardis which would serve as base, in order to secure Frygia and take the city of Gordion. To many who left Makedonia as newly wedded men for this campaign, he gave leave—as winter was approaching—with orders to bring new recruits by spring time. For the same reason, he sent Kleandros to Peloponnisos to ask the League for additional support, as many of the allies were now on garrison duty stationed in various cities.

Alexandros took the rest of the troops and marched for a winter campaign to secure Lykia, Pamfy-lia and Pisidia, as most of the Persian forces had abandoned these areas now. He wanted to make sure no port would be available in the south-east parts for the Persian fleet. He would meet with Parmenion back at Gordion and wait for the return of the troops on leave at spring time. He moved to Yparna and took the city, followed by his Ypaspistes, Agrianians, the archers, some of the falanx taxis and Makedonian and Thrakian cavalry. Next, came the capture of Telmissos, Pinara, Xanthos and Patara. The only resistance came from the Lykian city of Marmara.

Alexandros admired their fighting spirit and, in spite of having their city taken, he ordered the gar-rison he left at the city's fort to be lenient to any inhabitants who would decide to return from their mountain hide-outs at a later date. Although it was winter time and the weather and road conditions did not allow large scale movements, the King pushed our advance up the river Xanthos to the city of Milyas/Milyada. He agreed all of the aforementioned cities to continue pay the rather light taxes they were previously paying to the Persians, for the whole of Lykia was a favored satrapy of the High King all those years. Thus, Alexandros sought to have them look favorably now toward us and remain on our side, depriving the Persians from their numerous ports for sheltering their navy.

At that time, some delegates came to him from the city of Fasilis which is located by mount Klimax, bringing a golden crown to him and asking him to be their friend—which he readily accepted. He asked them and the near-by cities of lower Lykia to actively side with us and he helped them take a fort placed in their area by the Pisidians who, through it, were raiding the Lykian fields and stealing from the Fasilitans their produce.

While still at Fasilis Alexandros received a message that his namesake Alexandros of Lynkos was in contact with the High king Darios thinking of assassinating our King and becoming one himself. The deal was that Darios would give him a treasure in gold and the Lynkestian Alexandros would withdraw our troops from Asia, becoming the sole master of Ellas with Persian blessing and plenty of monetary support. Although this Alexandros was the brother of the ones who were implicated in the murder of King Filippos, as he had hailed our King Alexandros as the natural and legitimate King of Makedon he was received with friendship and was appointed to lead several taxis of the falanx or iles of cavalry. When Amyntas fled to Darios' court, the Lynkestian apparently had keep in touch with him and now they were conspiring. Their messenger was captured by Parmenion though and the plot was now known.

At this particular time, the Lynkestian was leading the Thessalian portion of our cavalry and was also a member of the King's Eteri circle. The rest of the Eteri did not really like his position and the trust the King had shown to him and now they asked for his immediate execution. Alexandros though was still thankful to the Lynkestian's proclamation of the past and he only asked Parmenion to keep the Lynkestian under arrest, by sending the son of Alexandros (brother of Krateros) Amfoteros, to instruct Parmenion accordingly. Besides, the Lynkestian Alexandros was Antipatros' son in law.

The omen which had been revealed during the siege of Alikarnassos now came to be completely understood. Alexandros was resting after a hard day's work during the siege, when a swallow came to rest on top of the royal tent making a lot more noise that is usually observed to be made by swallows. The King was in need of some peace and a short rest; tired of the persistent bird waved sheepishly his hand and managed to send it away. Yet the swallow returned immediately and rested now on the head of the half-asleep Alexandros! He was forced to fully awake and chased the bird finally away. Aristandros the seer from Telmessos had been asked to explain the omen and he told Alexandros that one of his close friends may be willing to act against the King but his acts will be a clear warning and the King will be safe.

The army attached to the King now spent the rest of the winter at Fasilis and Alexandros kept them in shape by organizing games. He also placed Nearhos, his Kritan friend, as governor of the region because Nearhos happened to have many connections there. As the weather became warmer, Alexan-dros sent the Thrakian troops, led by uncle Sytalkis here, to prepare the road and secure it and, as the weather improved more, the majority of our troops moved toward the city of Pergi.

Alexandros with the royal guards, the Ypaspistes and his personal squadron of cavalry and Agrian-ians, took the sea-side trail. That way leading to Pergi is dangerous, on account of the trail being too close to the sea—the latter being usually too rough with high waves—which obscures the passage where it is really narrow and the slope of the mountain—called Klimax—too steep to climb or build another pass higher with horses and all. The only way to go through is when the wind blows from the land side and keeps the waves at a distance from the trail. The King passed the troops through with-out any loss! Many said it was the gods who helped but we know that Alexandros had only taken a well calculated risk, as he studied the problem and saw its solution before anyone else!

As he was approaching Pergi, envoys from the city of Aspendos came to him independently and asked to be among his friends. Their only request, they said, was not to camp within, for they had no adequate lodging, nor food. He accepted and asked them to just supply us with horses and money for the needs of the army. They agreed and left to bring the request to their city. Alexandros continued toward the city of Sidi, who were ostensibly descendants from settlers of the Aeolian Kimi and, through the years of their relocation had forgotten the mother tongue, now speaking a sort of a bar-baric language, difficult to understand.

Alexandros placed a small garrison there and moved toward Sillion which was guarded by a Per-sian garrison and some mercenaries. Just before getting there, word came that the citizens of Aspen-dos were not of mind keeping their end of the bargain with him. Instead, they had barricaded their city and re-enforced their acropolis defenses as it is located by the flow of river Evrymedon and it is difficult there for one to attack and come across."

Roxani felt a bit tired and asked permission to stop for some refreshment while someone else—if kind and willing enough—would take care of the narration. It was agreed and they all took a brake for food and refreshments, the young son of Peridas who was named Theoharis and wanted to prove his knowledge asking to be the narrator. Peridas said that he was too young and needed to improve in sharpening his memory before undertaking such a job but the kid insisted and he was finally granted his request.

"The lower city inhabitants seeing their defenses were inadequate" Theoharis started, "they run to the acropolis of the city. The leaders now realizing that Alexandros had come in person got scared and sent envoys asking to keep the pre-arranged agreement. The King, knowing that his siege engines were not available, that his force could be inadequate to hold a prolonged siege and not willing to waste time there, indicated his agreement, provided he would be given prominent citizens as hostages, double the money to be given and the requested horses to be delivered at once. When that was done, he placed a garrison and marched toward Pergi and further into Frygia.

Alexandros with his part of the army arrived next before Telmissos, the inhabitants there being Pisides. Telmissos is a rather well protected city, as it is placed in a high and precipitous location with only one narrow path leading in and out of its walls. That's because on both sides of that path they call 'road' is flanked by the rough mountain and the river Evrimedon runs through. It is like one has to pass through continuous gates and those 'mountain gates' were already guarded by the Telmis-sians.

Seeing the difficulty of the situation and the besieging material being away with Parmenion and wanting not to lose too much time, Alexandros ordered his men to camp before those mountainous and rocky gates knowing that the Telmissians would not stand guarding forever. True to his pre-dicament, the defenders seeing our troops camped left only few to guard the 'gates' and withdrew into their city, feeling secure. Without breaking camp, the King took the archers and the peltastes and attacked these few defenders.

The Telmissians took off in fright and the people in the city—seeing what happened—lost faith and asked for peace again. This time the King dictated harsher terms by doubling the tribute and taking hostages. Having no time and mind to subdue all the little clans of the Tavros mountains area, con-tinued rapidly toward Pergi. But the barbarians thought they could still stop him, even defeat him. Down the road to Pergi there's a defile which they threw rocks to, blocking the road and placed a strong garrison on the slopes of either side . . ."

"I can remember the event as if it took place this very morning!" Attalos jumped-in. "I had just arrived with an ili of our horsemen, bringing supplies and I can still see the smile on Alexandros' face when he was informed of this by the Prodromi." "Well, do you want to keep on babbling, or will you be a 'good boy' and behave like we do and let Theoharis continue?" Sytalkis jabbed winking at the others. "Just because this was your only close encounter with the King, you moron, we don't have to hear it from your mouth again and again!" Attalos took a stand like being very offended, though he knew his friend was only teasing and giving time to Theoharis for some drink.

Peridas was not in a mood for interruptions. "All right, the two of you can find another time to solve who was closer to the King. Now it is the time for our children to show us they have absorbed our teachings and for us to be sure we did the job. Let Theoharis do the talking then and keep quiet, unless there's some serious omission in his narration."

Attalos and Sytalkis let a cawing sound and—at the same time—cowed on their couches, pretending they were scared. It brought laughter to all, including Peridas and gave time and opportunity to have their mouths full with some more food and wine. Finally, Peridas nodded to his son it was time to pick-up and continue.

"The stratagem on the Telmissians few days before, worked again." Theoharis started anew. "The barbarians took it easy, thinking they had stopped us and didn't place guards at night. We attacked, dislodged them and the road was freed from the rocks for easy passage the next morning. Our next encounter with the Pisidians was by the city of Salgalassos, a well fortified one. There we found them waiting between rather steep slopes where we couldn't use any cavalry and reinforced by many of the Telmissians who had escaped when we took their city.

Alexandros moved aggressively. He took under his personal command the Ypaspistes, placed the archers on his right, the falanx of sarissa taxis on his left under Amyntas son of Arravaeos of Lynkos and, to Amyntas' left, the Agrianians. He attacked the barbarians and while he and his left marched forward with vigor, the Salgassians ambushed our flanks. It was an easy thing for them to do, know-ing the area and the ground being a prime one for such a thing. Our archers had to retreat, as they lost their leader Kleandros and being the less protected from our troops.

The Agrianians on our left held their positions though and here is where 'uncle' Attalos got his first kill, wound and praise from King Alexandros! Alexandros with his Ypaspistes and Amyntas with the falanx moved forward and more than five hundred barbarians got killed before they wised and took off to the mountains or shook refuge in their city.

That did not help them. We attacked the city and took it by storm, as it was—by now—so lightly defended. Five hundred (or so) barbarians were killed here also. The rest surrendered and their lives were spared. We had only twenty killed from our side and about one hundred wounded— most of them rather lightly. Alexandros placed a small but adequate guard at the city, with instructions to have the barbarians encouraged to return, provided they would remain peaceful.

Having Sagalassos as our base, Alexandros sent several taxis supported by cavalry to subdue the surrounding areas. Some towns we took by storm, many surrendered on and soon the entire Pisidia was under our control.

That achieved, Alexandros moved into the region of Frygia having the lake Askania on the left and arrived at Kelaenae in five days only. Kelaenae is located on the mountains by the springs of river Meandros and had been built by Xerxis on his return to Persia—after being defeated by our ances- tors—as a strongpoint in case the Ellines would have followed him. The city is very strongly defended and it could take time to be taken.

Alexandros sent heralds asking them to surrender. The Persian governor agreed, provided he would not receive reinforcements and help from the High King within the next moon fade. Alexandros, knowing the city would be surrounded by us as we moved toward Gordion and not willing to waste time or men, agreed. He just left a taxis and a cavalry ili under Antigonos son of Filippos to see that the deal with the city would be kept and, after few days' rest continued his march and arrived at Gordion.

As Antigonos had been in charge of the men from our allied Ellenic city- states up to that point and now had to stay in place, Alexandros designated Valakros son of Amyntas to be in charge of the allies and, resting by Kelaenae for about ten days, our King and army continued their march to Gordion.

They found Parmenion there with his portion of troops and engineers and the supply wagons. Within few days, our men who Alexandros had send to Makedonia (as they were newlyweds) returned and brought along three thousand six hundred sarissa bearers, three thousand regular falanx oplites, three hundred Makedonian horsemen and two hundred heavy Thessalian cavalry, as well as one hundred and fifty from the Peloponnisian Elians.

Alexandros found waiting for him at Gordion an Atninian delegation also. They had come to ask him to release all the Athinian mercenaries serving the Persians we had captured at Granikos. The King listened carefully at their request but, knowing already that Athinae actually was secretly looking for ways to come to a beneficial understanding with the High King behind our back, politely refused their petition, saying that Ellines who fight against Ellines have to pay the price! He gave his promise though that, as things would improve to our advantage in the future, Athinae could then re-new the petition and, perhaps, that next time could be the time for the prisoners' release . . ."

Some commotion was heard from the anteroom—the one toward the entrance of the estate—and, in no time, Spadoklos (Shpadoklaj was his given Agrianian name at his birth) the trusted servant of Lysimahos entered the room exhausted from an apparent distant run, followed by Agathon, the estate's man-in charge. Everybody knew something unpleasant was happening or was about to hap-pen. Adamas called for a chair and some wine to be given immediately to Spadoklos and Aristos stood up from his recliner and, taking firmly but gently the out of breath trusted runner, he placed him there. Roxani meantime rushed to the kylix of wine and filled a cup and handed it over to the man.

"Take a breath first, have some wine to give you some energy and then you can tell us what's in store, for we know you wouldn't come just like this in the middle of the night without a serious reason!" Sytalkis said reassuringly and looking at the rest of the company for approval. They nodded and Kalas asked Agathon to stay but be ready to act, depending on the news to be told.

Both Spadoklos and Agathon did as asked. After a few minutes of drinking and catching his breath, Spadoklos told them that, as he was ordered by Lysimahos, he kept his eyes on the road at the edge of the estate, looking toward west, for any sign of Antipatros and his troops coming. He had placed his personal gear and stuff of need at a hut six stadia away to the east and keeping his horse always at readiness.

Well, the army had shown-up earlier this afternoon and camped—at a very close distance from his hut—for the night. They didn't have the discipline the armies of Filippos or Alexandros used to have and many dispersed to the adjacent fields for looting and 'recreation'. The reason they didn't come to the hut was that Agathon had taken the precaution to have it appear like something semi-burned and abandoned. He and Agathon dared not to move though until dark and after making sure no more of the patrols were out of the camp searching. "They will be here very early in the morning! That's not just my guess, they will follow the road to Filippoupolis and beyond." he concluded.

The men looked at each-other and Filippos gave the order for each to do what had been pre-arranged for such an event. The girls had already gone to let the rest of the women know and start putting things together. The boys took off to the stable to harness the horses and cows to the wagons which were ready for sometime now for a speedy getaway. Dimitrios asked Agathon to make sure only he would remain behind with few of the servants, pretending the place was his and keeping few of the cow herd and swine to make it more believable.

"Let them take what they want." he warned Agathon. "Don't place yourself at risk, no matter what. Everything is replaceable after they're gone, except your life! We want to find you here and well when we return." With that, the men got busy making sure no sign of their residence would be apparent and went to help getting everything together for their flight to a secret cave at the mountain to the north-west of the estate.

They started within an hour and in the dark. Sytalkis was leading with Peridas. Then the wagons, slowly to reduce unwanted noise, with the women and children and all that could be carried and, behind each wagon several cows roped to them—so they wouldn't stray. Then there were the servants flanking the sheep and goats with the help of the dogs and, finally, Yeoryios, Aristos, Attalos, Dimit-rios and Theoharis, having attached behind their horses long branches and brush. As their horses followed the track and were spread unevenly, the tracks were swept clean, covering their trail.

Their group arrived at the foothills of the mountain Dynax next day, close to mid-day hour. They stopped there at a secluded place for some food and needed rest. During their way to the mountain, they kept away from the various estates and any roads, avoiding the Evros river banks which could be occasion of unwanted meetings with people. Thankfully, they had crossed that part of the Vissae country without any incident, but now they were tired, hungry and thirsty—and so were their ani-mals.

They risked approach to the banks of the river, expecting that (being so far up) they wouldn't have any unpleasant surprises—and they were right. Their chosen stop was a place in between steep banks and with many big walnut and chestnut trees at the ridge as well as some tall oaks with their roots almost touching the water's edge as they were rooted in the little space between the banks and the water.

They built a small fire, for they did not want the smoke to be detected from a distance and prepared their meal, letting the animals free to take care of themselves within the confinement and just posting few of the servants at its entrance/exit, so the animals wouldn't disperse. They estimated to arrive at their secret cave sometime just before sunset, provided they wouldn't have any delays or any further round-about way taken due to accidental detection of people.

The trees combined with some tall dried grass gave them adequate cover from any curious itinerant herder, although the place seemed to have been out of any use or visit of humans from at least last summer. Nonetheless, Adamas asked for a couple of outposts to be stationed and that was done. Atta-los took his portion of meal and some water and, escorted by his young son Lamvros and two other of the servants, took a position further up the slope.

At the other end toward their way of approach from the estate, Peridas and Theoharis did the same. The rest of the group remained at their temporary campsite. The talk among them was confined to questions and speculations as to what would—or had already—happen to Agathon and the few men and women staying with what property was left back at the estate. They were hoping for the best and fearing the worst . . .

Agathon observed the approaching detachment of horse riders cantering through the dirt road leading to the main house of the estate. A man of rather tall stature was riding a well groomed and decorated horse (a Nissaean one as Agathon rightly judged) and wearing—the man was—an equally richly decorated breastplate and a frygian-styled helmet with red and white horsehair at its crest.

Holding the hand of his wife Arsinoi tightly, Agathon walked out of the house entrance with a set smile of servitude, pretending the unwanted intruders were a welcomed sight. Some of the household's remaining hands working (two at the pig sty and three by the stables) ap-proached slowly but firmly, closer. They were casually holding their pitch-forks, just in case the place had to be defended to the end. Obviously, they would have no chance of winning but Agathon knew they were ready to put their lives down if needed—and so was he. He braced himself and sque-ezed his wife's hand trying to reassure her. Arsinoi let a soft sigh out of her lips and set a thin smile on her face in anticipation, prepared to share her husband's fate—no matter what the outcome.

The riders came to a halt, their leader stopping just before his horse would come to touch Agathon who stood his ground, smile on his face and eyes facing the ground before him. Let the bastard who led these men understand that servitude wasn't there as company of fear and intimidation! Agathon brought his right hand to his heart and then extended it to his side, indicating a sort of a welcome to someone obviously stronger and in-charge, as Arsinoi managed to hold her smile and give a slight curtsey toward the rider. They both stood still holding their posture and waiting.

The leader of the horsemen got their message. He was welcomed—by necessity—but they weren't either afraid or intimidated by his presence. He took a studying look around him. The estate hands seemed equally unimpressed by him and his riders, but that did not concern him. If need be he would have them all killed, if just by superiority in numbers. But he would try to avoid any confrontation, as per his father's orders. Regardless his age, now into his forties, Kassandros did not dare face the wrath of his old man. Antipatros had still hope of engaging Lysimahos by his side against the other generals and 'kings'. No reason to antagonize (yet) by creating incidents . . .

Kassandros took his helmet off now, wanting to address the holders of this estate. As he spoke and stated his name, Agathon raised his head to face him. He had heard of the light blue eyes in their beady sockets, the badly scratched youth acne with its left-over marks (even after all these years) and the crooked nose leaning to the face's right side. Alexandros' punch was still there then, proving the truth to the rumors!

"We need some provisions to purchase from you, my good man." Kassandros stated matter-of-fact, his tone of voice indicating clearly that he didn't consider Agathon neither good or man but rather a subject to be exploited—when convenient—and to obey his betters. "We will purchase ten cattle and all the pigs in your sty. I am willing to offer you this." He took off a pouch attached to his sword belt and threw in his open palm (so Agathon could see) about ten silver four-drachma pieces.

"I can offer you, my lord, only five of my cattle, no pigs, but a cart loaded with sacks of grain for the same money, as Lord Lysimahos purchased most of what we had here only eight days ago." Agathon lied, making sure the man got a hint of his two-time using the word lord. He actually wanted to add that the money offered by Kassandros were money issued by King Alexandros, now in someone else's hands, but thought better and kept his mouth shot.

Kassandros got the hint. No one ever thought him of being an idiot and, with the years passing at the court in Pella or (although minimal) in Vavylon just prior to Alexandros' death, his ear had sharpened in detecting subtleties such as this one. He promised inward to himself to take 'good' care of this insolent Thrakian peasant! Thinking of Thrakian, Kassandros suddenly realized that Agath-on's Thrakian accent wasn't really a Tharkian one. What reason did this peasant have to pretend?

He made a mental note to look into it. Meantime he had to conform to orders given from Antipat-ros. Father's eyes and ears and (especially) his hand were never too far away. "What is your name my good man?" persisted on asking without letting his anger show and in hope of forcing the peasant on more talk, thus giving away the man's real accent and origin.

Agathon was no one's fool either. His officers and comrades wouldn't have the trust they had in him if it was any doubt of his abilities to deal with danger. And danger was present and real before him now. "Antilaos, son of Sympodas sire. The name in Thrakian is really Andgelaod but I thought the Ellenic pronunciation of it would be more pleasing to your ears. My father's one is Sybod and this is my wife Arsinoi, who's family is Makedonian stock from the parts of Kristonia. Her father . . ."

Kassandros cut him off with a move of his hand. He was thrown off now, as the answer came seem-ingly unforced from the peasant's mouth, without any effort in improving his 'Thrakian' accent or any other detectable hesitation. Kassandros was not interested in the man's family ties. Yet, the Thrakian would have to be taught a lesson.

Kassandros was ready to turn to his men and order some sort of a lesson given but stopped as he saw another horse detachment approaching full speed. Ahead of them he could see the general Pol-yperhon, the one veteran of Alexandros' campaigns, who Antipatros was holding in high esteem. As Polyperhon and his group came to a halt, the general did not waste any time in introductions or in—quiries. "General Lysimahos is at the camp for parley and your father wants us both to be present there. Krateros is already with him." he barked, and without waiting for an answer, turned and sped away leading his men to a gallop.

Kassandros let his face saw his displeasure and anger as he looked at the speeding horsemen. Father be damned! He had more respect and consideration of Polyperhon's say than of his own son's! It was more than obvious that Alexandros' choices (even after death) were having a weight in his father's decisions and mind frame. He briskly turned to Agathon and, throwing the silver to his feet, com-manded: "Have your men deliver what was agreed by nightfall!" Then, turning his horse headed after the proceeding distant specs, followed by his men, at a gallop.

Agathon figured he had no choice but to comply. Anything to avoid confrontation and keep the estate intact was preferable, even if that had to do with dealing with Kassandros. He told his men to prepare the animals and grain and start heading them to Antiptros' camp. He went to the coop to see if there were some more fresh eggs to collect.

Sytalkis and his group took their way up the mountain after a good rest and a meal. Soon, they saw they could not pool the carts with their loads, as the road (if one could call it such) reduced itself to a goat path and they now had to follow the river to its springs where the cave was located. They un-loaded what could be carried by the beasts on their backs, sparing none and they loaded even them-selves with all kinds of necessary things. Filippos complained a bit for he thought they were carrying too much but he was reminded that their stay at the cave could be a lengthy one. Thankfully the cave was large enough to take them in, the animals and their provisions.

They reached the place as the sun was about to set behind the other peaks of the Rodopi range, to-ward Orvylos. Aristos with Kalas and Adamas went ahead to check that no wild animals had made the cave their home. Instead, they found a small family of three and their belongings, about a dozen sheep. They had to share the space but, first, they inquired about the small family already there. The husband, a giant of a man, told his name. He was Timeos, a Makedonian who's father Damon had received a plot for honorable service, at the times of King Filippos but recently had to abandon their property and come to hide on account of running afoul with Kassandros—cursed be his name! His wife's name was Ilektra and their baby boy's name Iason.

He was giving the information freely, in his thick Makedonian accent of a rather uneducated man, although one could see the frown of concern and some fear on the face of Ilektra who immediately picked up their son—a good looking toddler—and held him protectively in her arms. Inquired how he wasn't afraid on giving such information before strangers, the giant smiled broadly, letting a set of bad teeth (several were missing) in full view. "I have been observin' you comin' all afternoon from that peak o'er there!" he said and added "Men who're in the good side o' Kassandros an' Antipatros don't make an effort to erase their tracks behind'em, nor do they take refuge at caves such's this one. I also know that Antipatros an' his army have come to Thraki 'n' on their way to Asia. Now time fo' you to tell me who you are—if you find you can trust me that is!"

Worried for the delay of the men coming back from the cave to their group, Sytalkis sent Dimitrios with few of the servants armed to the teeth, to see if there was a problem. Soon everybody came back to help with the loads and the animals to the cave, including Timeos (he took the work of four of them) and his wife, who had put the toddler on her back in a basket held by ropes over her shoulders and under her armpits. She helped guiding the goats to the cave.

As soon as all animals and provisions were hoarded in, proper introductions were made with the rest and explanations were given and taken from all sides. A nice fire was already going at one end of the cave, far enough from the entrance to be safe and undetected from any distance. Timeos told them he was using the cave for almost four months now and no person had even come near it all this time. But—just in case, as Adamas put it—they drew lots on guard duty for the following nights. Next morning they would go to where the carts were left, take them apart and carry them into the cave.

They had their dinner and settled down for some talk. The women picked up their nook and the young girls saw that they were keeping the toddler Iason happy until his time to sleep. Evanthia took to Ilektra at once and with her help, the rest of the women soon became acquainted and at ease with one-another. The men congregated closer to the entrance of the cave, keeping their arms close by—in case of need and started exchanging life stories.

Peridas told Timeos a story of them running away from Antipatros and Kassandros because of taxes owed since the last war against the revolting city-states, they had lost to debt their holdings at Pella and sought refuge in Thraki after some begging with Evmenis first, then Lysimahos. The latter allowed them to work an estate of his outside of Filippoupolis and they were happy there until the ar-rival of Kassandros. They had to leave the place because Kassandros knew them personally and they were scared they would be taken to work mining and their wives to serve like slaves at some forsaken house of Kassandros' friends.

Timeos looked satisfied with that explanation (the less the man knew of the true identity, Peridas thought, the better for his safety in case of something going wrong) and told them his story, in more details of what Aristos, Kalas and Adamas had already heard. He was the son of Damon from Almo-pia, from the minor house of Arideos. His father—as well as himself—served under King Filippos at the campaign and siege of Perinthos and Vyzantion. He, Timeos, was just a young man of fourteen (had received his dagger by killing a boar at thirteen!) at his father's service as a trainee, in hope of gaining a place with the foot Eteri of the King. When the siege failed, they followed Filippos cam-paign in the interior of Thraki.

When the army was ambushed and Filippos received a very serious wound, Damon was the one who defended the King until more help arrived and Timeos was the runner to inform the King's doctor. The two, father and son, then, were the litter bearers bringing Filippos in for the operation. Later, when the King had recovered enough and wanted to return to Pella, they were the litter bearers again! Filippos never forgot that service and awarded Damon with a good plot in Sintiki, at the east of Iraklia.

As King Alexandros left for Asia after Filippos' assassination, Damon was too old to go. Timeos did serve under Meleagros' foot Eteri taxis and distinguished himself at Granikos. Then, at Tyros, he was placed under the engineer Diadis and, during the Tyrian attack on the siege towers, he got badly burned (he showed them the marks on his chest by pulling off his hiton—the women were far inside to take notice) and lost many of his teeth. He spent several weeks recovering and, before the Issos battle, he was sent back home with the gratitude of Alexandros and two silver talents to show (Here Sytal-kis' face lit as he remembered the case and secretly nodded to his friends confirming the story).

"I came back home just'n time t' see my father 'fore he died" Timeos was coming to the end of his story. "I took care of my mother an' gave my two sisters good dowries for their weddings. Mother died the year of the Gavgamila battle. Th' year King Alexandros married Roxan' I was in good order to find me a wife too. I married Ilektra but we didn't have a child right away. Iason came to us jus' two an' a half years ago . . ."

"What got you in trouble with Kassandros?" Attalos wanted to know. "That son of a whore!"

Timeos' face turned red. "Married woman, with an infant in 'er arms, came t'me at the towns market—I was helpin' cousin Polemon unload a cart full o' lumber for the construction of a stand on account o' the coming feast of Dimitra an' Kori that was comin' up—to bring me some food an' wine.

Kassandros saw 'er (he was to have come an' attend by orders o' his father) as he was ridin' by an' he—without mindin' her state—propos'd to 'er. I could 'ave kill'd 'im (I should!) right there an' then, if my cousin woulda lemme do it. The coward didn't say or do nothin' then. He sent his men later at my place an' set it on fire! Almost got burn'd in my sleep! Friends told me about it an' I got ready to go an' see Antipatros an' ask for justice. The town's tax collector is his friend though an' he got his men after me as he found out. Took then the wife an' child and took off, for I knew they'd kill us all. Pass'd on to Thraki an' found this 'ere cave by accident. It suited me an' I stayed."

It was getting rather late. The women had apparently placed the young ones to sleep and they were getting themselves ready too. Filippos took Theoharis with him to go and check on the servants who were appointed to be the lookouts. The rest of the men pulled further into the cave, closer to the fire. Nights up here were even colder than the open Thrakian plains. Good sleep was needed until the time for the next check on the lookouts. In the morning some word was expected to come from Agathon to let them know of the events at and around the estate.

Spadoklos came up to the cave with the two other look-outs as they were the last watch of the night. Daylight made it unnecessary for them to be at their posts any longer and they needed some food and water. "Agathon sent no one with news?" asked Sytalkis when Spadoklos seemed to have finished his meal. "No my friend. But it's rather early yet. There's a possibility some troops may have camped or posted at the estate you know. Antipatros is not a fool. He knows Lysimahos is Evmenis' friend, and that

571

by association makes him a friend of Perdikkas. Lysimahos' estates may have been found a good collateral in the hands of Antipatros and his son.

Of course, lord Lysimahos wouldn't move against them any way; we all know he has troubles with the Odrysses who had recently revolted. The man who King Alexandros had placed in charge of Thraki and Antipatros had not the guts to replace when the war started with the city-states upon Alexandros' death, as we all know was a very oppressive man. When Lysimahos came and ousted him, the Odryssian revolt had already started. You were here already and you know the difficulties Lysimahos had in quelling it!

But Antipatros most likely wants to play it safe. Holding on to properties and threatening Filippou-polis with possible starvation, will give him much more leverage in keeping Lysimahos out of the war. We all know there's going to be a war—don't we?"

"You are right my friend! There will be a war between the jackals who inherited such a prize. But I still would have liked to have a word from Agathon now." Sytalkis put a hand over his eyes to shade them from the rising sun and looked down slope in anticipation. "Not from here sir, you can't see all the way down from here." Timeos pointed at 'his' peak. "I will go climb up there and I will let you know when I see something." He picked up a flask and a piece of meat his wife handed him and started climbing. The rest, leaving Spadoklos and his two other night observers to stay and get some rest, moved down hill to break apart their abandoned carts and bring the pieces here.

They had made two trips already bringing up stuff and were ready to go for the final third, when Timeos' voice was heard asking them to wait. He appeared shortly, sliding between two huge boul-ders split by the water of the river coming out of its spring a way further up. He was panting and in obvious rush to come to them. "Someone's comin' my friends" said trying to catch his breath "but not alone! There seems to be a bunch and, by their pace o' walk, there has to be with women an' p'haps children." "How many? How far?" Spadoklos and Kalas asked in one voice. "No more than ten—but not sure. Didn't stay t' count 'em. They should be here in 'bout two hours."

Sytalkis with Adamas, Aristos, Attalos, Filippos, Dimitrios, Kalas and Peridas, immediately armed themselves and, forming a semi-circle, asked the rest to come closer for developing a plan. First, they had to make sure if the approaching party were only as many as Timeos thought. He said he was pos-itive of the number and looked a bit hurt when Peridas asked his son to run up the peak and make sure. As the youth started climbing, Sytalkis made a plan for their defense.

"As much older and slower, I will stay here. I need one more of you to stay with me and half of our servants—which will make a total of ten, plus Theoharis when he comes down. The women can help throwing stones—if it comes to that. The rest of you, follow Filippos and go see what you can do . . . Who's the one to stay with me?" Timeos asked to be the one, as he wanted to stay by the side of his wife and young son. Of the servants, Dimitrios counted eight and asked them to stay.

Filippos divided his men in three detachments. On his left with Adamas in charge and Aristos as second, would cross the river here and flank the right side of the on comers. Kalas would take the right with Peridas his second and his men, to come on the left of the unknown group. He, with At-talos and Dimitrios and the rest of the servants would come head-on to face the climbing group. This way, if the coming group were from the estate will be welcomed and protected from three sides –in case soldiers were after them—or, if they were the enemy, they'd be attacked from three sides.

Making sure everybody understood his plan, he turned to say good bye to Sytalkis and Timeos. At that moment, Theoharis came almost tumbling down from the observation peak. "No need to panic! It's Agathon coming up! I could make him out because of his size and way of walking. He has with him our people from the estate, men and women!" "Something went wrong!" Spadoklos said and he rushed down the slope, followed by Attalos and Filippos. The others moved to follow but Filippos stopped them. "Only my detachment of servants. The rest remain here until we return. Theoharis, did you see anyone following them?" "No! The slopes were clear from any other move." "All right then, we will help them up, you prepare for their stay!"

They met with Agathon, his wife, Spadoklos' wife and daughter and about ten other tenants of the estate close to the place the remnants of the dismantled carts and some other heavy items were left.

Filippos sent three of his men further down slope to make sure no one had followed and to erase any possible tracks left. Meantime, he gave the newly arrived refugees time to catch their breath and asked Agathon what happened and they had to leave the estate. "Give me the sum of it, you can tell the whole story when we meet with the others at the cave."

Agathon told him about his meet with Kassandros and the deal arranged for the army's victuals. He and the rest didn't thing any harm would come, as lord Lysimahos and Antipatros with Polyperhon were holding a meeting not that far away. With the persons available, Agathon could not post look-outs covering the whole perimeter of the estate. Late last night some ones came undetected and set fire at the stables and the grain storage. In the confusion which followed and during the effort to put the fire out, the same someone set fire at the main building also. By the time Agathon and the remaining help managed to save something, three men, four women and six children had perished! They run for their lives leaving most of the animals and the place to fate.

"As we took on to the slopes, we could see fires starting at the perimeter of the estate and heard the sound of the animals driven out either by panic or by guidance. We could tell which was which and the guided ones were hoaxed toward the army camp." he concluded. Filippos and Spadoklos tried to console him and the rest for the loss. "We are sorry for the loss of some of our people but, at least, not everything was lost. We will recover in time . . . If these sons of whores don't have the decency to bury the dead, when the army will go we will give them their rights and more! I see now our men returning from their task . . . Let us go then and you tell the whole story to everyone at the cave. Then, we will see what the next step will be . . ." Filippos decided as Spadoklos was checking with the return-ed trio of men to make sure the job of erasing any tracks was properly done.

Up at the cave, proper introductions were made between Timeos and Agathon and the story was retold in details. "I know they were Kassandros' men." Agathon said after all inquiries were finished and hit his fist against his open palm in frustration. "I am sure you are right, but we can do nothing; not now!" Filippos said. "We will return and rebuild and bury our dead when they are gone. Lord Lysimahos probably has his hands 'tied' right now and we do not want to create any incident, especially when we are trying to stay undetected by our old 'friends'! If we do and get caught our lives will be worth nothing and our 'friends' will have a legitimate excuse for our demise. If we get caught for other reasons, they will have to work hard for excuses—and they are not that clever." Sytalkis added.

"I think, my new found friends, it's time to tell me who 'xactly you are an' why you're hidin' fro' Kassandros and the rest! I told you who I am an' you can check it out, for I know you're connected lords with many enemies p'haps but surely many friends too!" Timeos said with some resentment in his voice. Kalas looked at his friends first, then he gave the answer. "You are right to be a bit bitter. We did not give you a full account of ourselves, not for lack of trust—we see you are an honest man . . . We thought the less you knew the better, in case you would be asked and that, would free you of any additional trouble! Once things have worked the way they did, I will tell you! We are all close friends and associates of King Alexandros. When we saw that each one of the generals could hardly wait to cut a kingdom for himself while the King's body was still warm, we deserted and went to hiding, for we knew that our lives were to be ended ingloriously if we stayed and fought for what we thing is right. Very few of these men have remained faithful to our dear King. Through them, we ended up here, trying to stay away and keeping the faith. We are ready to serve again the royal family, when all will be placed back in order—we hope! Until then, we pass our knowledge to our children so they won't make the same mistakes as us when their time comes. I will start now with my true identity: I am Galash, from house Oxyarta and I adopted the name Kalas. Served Alexandros from Aornos to the day he died and I was his cousin through his wife Roxana. You know Badsha my wife, under the name of Vasiliki and my son Garhagha by the name Koragos."

"I am the Odryssian Sytalkis, the nephew of Sytalkis who led the Thrakians under Alexandros. This is my wife Eleni from house Ermias, hailing from Akti and this young man is our son Yeoryios."

"Adamas here my friend, son of Antigenis from house Damasias; Paeonian cavalry ili leader, under King Alexandros. You of course know my wife Dimitrias, my son Faedon and daughter Doris."

"I am Ariston, now called Aristos, house Iraklonas, member of Alexandros' foot Eteri. The three young boys and four girls you see now sitting there with my wife Melpomeni are—as you met them already—Leonidas, Mahas, Pithon, Theano, Aspasia, Nikea and Lefki. I served under Filippos here . . ."

"Filippos here, house Agis son of Menelaos, Orestian. Served as Alexandros' body guard and led one ili of Thessalian horse. I lost my son at the scuffle in Vavylon by the King's body. Now that Evanthia is pregnant—as you have noticed—I hope to have another son to carry the name . . ."

"My name is Mithrana from the house Haxamanish—Ahaemenidis to you—and adopted the name Dimitrios. My wife fell ill a year ago and died. Here's my daughter Roxani. I served the Kings—both of them. I was in

Darios' body guard to the end! I escaped death by accident and then served Alexan-dros as leader of an ili of his Nissaean cavalry in India!"

"And I, my friend, am Attalos. I am a cousin, though much younger, of the Agrianian king Lampa-ros and led the Agrianian mounted archers through Sogdiana, India and the Malian lands! This is my wife Evlampia from Parorvilia and that little man is our son Lamvros."

"Last, but I hope not least, you know me as Peridas, my wife Dikea and my son Theoharis. What you don't know is that I am son of Menandros from house Asteropeos. Both my father and I served the Kings Filippos and Alexandros. My father served Filippos as a body guard and Alexandros as an officer training new recruits before we moved to Asia. I served Filippos as his cup bearer and, later, Alexandros as a page and member of the Ypaspistes! Now you met with Agathon and his family and Spadoklos with his own.

They both served with us or under others but are of the same frame of mind as we are. The same goes with the rest of our 'servants'. They are all veterans—though some are of younger age—sharing our belief in serving only the Argead family of Timenos and no one else! Filippos is the leading figure as his family is continuously connected with house Timenos from the longest time and Sytalkis is the 'general' due to age and experience. You are welcome to join us or, if you prefer, you can stay here with your family when we return to the estate."

Timeos was listening intensely and with obvious emotion to their words. Now he stood up and solemnly declared his willingness to join and serve to the best of his ability when and where needed.

"I've nothin' but gratitude toward and fond memories fro' both Kings! It would be a shame if I can do somethin' in return but refuse to. I'm with you my friends and I pledge my family too. Thank you for invitin' me t' join your group!"

Three days later and after close observation by sending constantly men to spy on the army's camp, they learned that Antipatros had secured Lysimahos' idleness and he would continue toward Asia.

Krateros had already joined him with some more thousands and they were to strike camp in a day or two. They prepared to leave the cave and reconstructed the carts and loaded their belongings again.

Spadoklos left earlier to report to Lysimahos the events and get instructions from him. The rest returned to desolated estate and started cleaning, rebuilding and re-sowing. It was early spring at the middle of

Xanthikos (the beginning of the Athinian month of Elafevolion). At nights, the narration resumed with the added attendance of Timeos' family. The 20th day of Panamos (15th of Athinian Skiroforion), Evanthia gave birth to twins. The girl was named Alkistis and the boy Alexandros . . .

"...Ελληνες δε ειναι τουτους τους απο Περδικκεω
γεγονοτας, καθαπερ αυτοι λεγουσι, αυτος τε ουτω
τυγχανω επισταμενος και δη και εν τοισι οπισθεν
λογοισι αποδειξω."

"...They'reEllines (Greeks) since the times of
Perdikkas, as they admit themselves, and as I
also came to know, with these and by the
following words I will verify (this knowledge)..."
Herodotus (referring to Makedonians)

II

"It's time to pick up again from where we left off. The younger ones have to know the whole story and, now that Timeos is added to our company with his wife, he can add here and there of his own experiences and how events were received in Makedonia while we were in Asia!" It was about two months after the passing of Antipatros' army and the encounter with Kassandros. The estate wasn't exactly back to its former shape and functions but there had been progress. Antipatros had gone to meet the other 'kings' of the divided empire and rumor had it that Krateros was killed at a battle against Evmenis and Perdikkas' brother Alketas. There was also the rumor that Perdikkas himself was assassinated by his own troops as he went to face Ptolemeos in Egyptos. Spadoklos did not know any more from Lysimahos and Filippos wanted to have their lives back to their normal schedule.

"Last we talked about -as I remember- was when King Alexandros had arrived at Gordion! I can continue the story, as I know everything by heart and you who witnessed the events can judge my accuracy..." Theoharis said bringing the last piece of fruit in his mouth as everyone else had finished with their evening meal. The veterans nodded in approval. The rest of the clan (they did consider now themselves as a special group -a clan formed out of love and necessity- and they had agree on the term) took their seats. It was a warm starry night, the first in the month Gorpaeos and they had all have their meal outside.

"At Gordion Alexandros sealed the fate of Asia. There was that wagon, you see, which belonged to a king of old who's name was Gordios and he was the father of Midas. That Gordios had tied the yoke of the wagon for its oxen with a special knot made out of the bark of young cornel tree, which had no apparent way of untying it. You see, as the years passed-by and the bark dried-up and shrunk, the ends of that knot shrunk too and they could not be seen. In any case, the wagon was placed in the yard of the old palace and was a subject of wonder, as it was prophesized that who ever could loosen the knot would become the master of all Asia! Alexandros felt he had to try his luck. Finding no ap-parent ways of untying the knot drew his sword and cut it!..."

"I was there!" Filippos jumped-in excited. "To tell the truth I did not see the event with my own eyes because there was simply not enough room for everybody in the courtyard. But I was standing right outside, as part of the royal body guard, and when all was done and the lords and officers started coming out, I saw Filotas -among the first ones- who was smiling in disbelief and was shaking his head. I asked him what was the matter for -just before they started coming out- we had heard a loud acclamation. He laughed out loud -still not believing at what he saw- and told me: 'He did it! The King unraveled the knot and, as it becomes him, he did it his way, by Zefs and Iraklis!' He, then, explained to me what transpired. I stood there in disbelief, for it was hard for me to fathom Alexand-ros' way, until I saw Yfestion coming out with a big smile on his face and, behind him, Krateros talk-ing excitedly with Perdikkas and Ptolemeos. Then, I believed!"

"Thanks for interrupting me 'uncle' Filippos!" Theoharis pretended being hurt. "Oh, I am sooo sorry I took the pleasure away from you!" was the playful answer. "Go ahead, my boy, I have not told what the actual solution to the problem was. Besides, we all know about it by now and your telling will only emphasize the fact." Filippos added with a wicked smile, taking the pleasure to tease.

"When Alexandros saw there was no way of finding the ends of the knot, he drew his sword -as I said before I was interrupted- and cut the knot saying that the prophecy had been fulfilled and he was meant to be the next master of all Asia! By doing so, the King wanted to elevate the morale of his men, indicating that -with will and faith in one's ability- even apparent insolvable tasks could be solved and one could reach one's goals by simply employing available resources! Asia could be theirs against all odds and in spite the numbers put against them by the Persians! 'Ellenic iron' could and would prove mightier than any Asiatic contraption or trick.

Meantime, Memnon received finally all the confidence of The High King Darios and was in charge of the Persian fleet, still roaming the seas and trying to invest on an Ellenic city-state uprising, in hope of forcing Alexandros to withdraw from Asia. Darios sent money to Sparti for that reason and Memnon moved his fleet at the north parts of the Aegean. His aim was to block the Ellispontos straits and recapture Lesvos and Tenedos to secure that hold. Then he would try to land in Makedonia, thus bringing the war home.

It was fortunate that Memnon fell ill and died during his campaign before the walls of Mitylini in Lesvos. Farnavazos and Aftofradatis took jointly the leadership of the Persian fleet. Mitylini was hard to take and they promised fair treatment if the Mitylinians and Tenedians were to return to the High King. Having no help coming to their rescue at this time, they both surrendered but the Per-sians violated that agreement and brought both islands under heavy taxation and killed all the pro-ponents of Alexandros' freedom grants.

Nonetheless, all Ellenic city-states liberated in Asia at that point, remained faithful to us, as they could see the benefits of self-governing as opposed to being under Persian yoke. Alexandros' treasury also improved by the gains thus far and the fact that he sent Egelohos to Ellispontos to transform all available merchant ships to a new war fleet helped our cause. Athinae tried to enter under the flag of the Persians just because few of the merchant ships taken by Egelohos happened to be hers and abandoned the alliance, arming one hundred warships.

Alexandros sent money then to Antipatros who was able to pay for a fleet of combined vessels from Evia and the Peloponnisian allies, counterbalancing the Athinian threat. Egelohos also let the few Athinian vessels taken go free and the results were soon favorable for us. Proteas, whom Antipatros put in charge of that fleet, captured several Persian vessels by the island of Sifnos and his appearance in the Aegean made the Athinians to call their revolt off. It proved though that Athinian 'double talk' remained as it ever was and her political leaders could not be trusted.

Even then, Alexandros showed magnanimity and did not take any measures against Athinae, respecting his Father's love for her.

What the political leaders of the formally great city-state powers such as Athinae, Sparti and Thivae couldn't realize was that their time was long passed and, when they were the power to recon with, they all made the same mistake: They called upon the common enemy, the Persian High King, to be their supporter and provide finances so they could stay in power! That alone, brought resentment among the rest of the Ellines and it was among the main reasons why each one failed to unite Ellas under one leader! Alexandros was determined to avoid such mistakes, yet their narrow vision pro-hibited them to understand and they preferred to keep on dreaming…"

Theoharis had the opportunity to take some wine and rest as the company -including the women- had comments to voice on the subject of the fidelity of the city-states, as well as the lack of under-standing of Filippos and Alexandros' policies. "The small city-states, the ones constantly oppressed by the Spartans, the Athinians or the Thivans, will always be on our side -and they make the major-ity!" Saphia, the wife of Spadoklos remarked.

"Possibly -if we keep the same policy as Filippos and Alexandros. By the way these idiots who are in charge now are acting, I doubt we can keep Ellas in unity. Look how Antipatros dealt with them late-ly! Almost every city, friendly or not, has a Makedonian garrison imposed on it! From allies, they have become subjects! If the Persians could have been considered -no offense intended here my friends- equal by Alexandros, how we now expect Ellas to feel under us?" Filippos remarked bitterly.

"I surely hope the legitimate king will come of age and be like his Father! That is the only salvation I can see for our future." Kalas said. "And, although I am also a relative of Roxana, I have to admit that the infant has to be taken away from her. While under the protection of Perdikkas, there was some hope. With him now rumored to be dead along with Krateros, I don't think there are any left who have loved or understood Alexandros enough to want his son become like his Father."

"Pour some libation from you wine to Adis and Ekati and bite your tongue! You bring bad fate when you talk like that!" Ilektra spit on the floor three times for good luck finishing her words. The rest of them did the same and spilled few drops from their cups also, uttering words of forgiveness to the underworld gods. Kalas did as he was told, eager to amend.

"Having secured all Asia-by-the Aegean now, Alexandros marched to the Kilikian Gates…" Theoharis picked-up his narration again. Theano, Aristos and Melpomeni's oldest daughter was busy scribing his words down and Theoharis -noticing that from the very beginning- was careful to talk clearly leaving Makedonian dialectical accent and speaking the so-called kini, so she would have it easier.

"This defile is a very treacherous one and easy to be defended by relatively small force. To avoid it, it would take making a very big circle through worse country by land and a much bigger fleet than what we had, by sea. Thankfully Arsamis, the man of Darios in charge of the area, did not take any precaution and left the pass almost unattended.

Leaving the main force under Parmenion to camp before the Gates, Alexandros took his Agrianians and detachments of Ypaspistes and Peltastes and forced his way through, sending the few defenders to flee in panic. Fearing that Arsamis would leave the city of Tarsos in ruins, Alexandros proceeded speedily and, attacking the Persian satrap with force; Arsamis took off toward Persia proper.

There is where the King fell ill as he had a bath -right after investing the city- in the river Kydnos. Hot as he was from the march and the river carrying cold spring waters, Alexandros caught almost his death having high fever and chills. Everybody thought the King was at his death bed, except the doctor Filippos, who prepared a medicine for Alexandros to take with his wine. At the same time a letter from Parmenion arrived, warning the King of a plot against his life. According to that, Filippos was paid by Darios' agents to poison Alexandros and the King's cousin Amyntas was to become the King of Makedon!

Alexandros read the letter while Filippos was pouring the medicine into the King's wine cup. Believ-ing in the doctor's ability and friendship, Alexandros took the cup and handed Filippos the letter to read, while he drunk the potion looking at the doctor straight in the eyes. Filippos read the letter shook his head in gratitude and assured the King that he would speedily recover. Sure enough, Alex-andros was well in a matter of few days and he, with his well rested army, moved toward the Syrian Gates, another pass by the Mountain Amanos range."

"I remember well our anxiety and fear then! I was stationed at the perimeter of the city and my task was to guide whoever of our Prodromi scouts was returning with news of the Persian activities by and beyond those so-called Gates. We were all praying for the King's recovery." Timeos said some-what belatedly.

"Yes, it was time for all of us to pray, as we did later on many a time. Now let us allow Theoharis to continue for the next hour or so -before we turn in to our rooms for some rest. Tomorrow we have a hard task in rebuilding the granary though there's no grain now to store in it as Kassandros took it all" Peridas reminded all without addressing Timeos especially for the interruption.

"Well, the King sent Parmenion with the Thessalian cavalry and your uncle and namesake 'uncle' Sytalkis to secure the Syrian Gates." Theoharis continued and Sytalkis nodded in agreement. "Alex-andros himself moved to Anhialos and Soli -its port. From there, he pacified the area of Rugged Ki-likia, taking with him three taxis of foot Eteri and the Agrianian contingent (Attalos here nodded in agreement) and in only a week's campaign, he rejoined the rest of the army at Soli.

At that same time news came from Alikarnassos that our troops there had finally taken the Samal-kis and Royal citadels and now the city was ours. The Karian cities of Myndos, Kavnos, Thira and Kalipolis -as well as the near by islands of Kos and Tropion- decided to join us! The news was as good as it could be expected and Alexandros ordered games and sacrifices to the gods and Asklipios, remembering his recent recovery from fever.

He returned to Tarsos and continued to Megarsos and Mallus, restoring there the ancient Ellenic customs which were but forgotten after all those years of Persian occupation. He also sent Filotas through the Aleian plains to reduce that area and take the city of Pyramos on our side. Our scouts informed Alexandros that the High King Darios had come with a huge army to face us in person and was now stationed beyond the mountain range of Amanos. Hearing that, Alexandros marched the whole army through the Syrian Gates (already secured) and sought to find Darios.

The Persian High King did not wait for us where we had last known him to be. Thinking that Alexandros (at the time ill and recovering) had decided to stay in Tarsos and against advice from the runagate Amyntas son of Antiohos, he moved the army heading north. Using the Amanos Gates further up north-east of the Syrian ones, he placed his army to our rear. Finding our camp with our sick and wounded at the city of Issos, he massacred every single one of them! It was our King's rare mistake not to scout for other passes in the area. Alexandros never repeated such a mistake again.

Learning of the Persian presence in our rear from a few survivors from Issos, Alexandros sent a small fast ship to investigate and appraise the situation. The crew reported back and verified that the huge Persian army was camped on the west side of the river Pinaros, obviously not knowing we had crossed the Syrian Gates.

The King addressed the army which -by now- had heard the news of Darios being at our rear and the massacre of the invalids and started worrying about our supply lines and our connection and contact with home. He stressed the fact that we had faced the enemy before and we were victorious in all previous engagements. He also noted that Darios had made a cardinal mistake by leaving the open space of the plain in the east and went to occupy the narrow valley of Pinaros. Then, he asked them if they would let the lives of their lost comrades to go to Adis without revenge. 'We have never slaugh-tered any incapacitated person, be it enemy soldier or civilian who minded his business!' he said. 'Are we now to let that cowardice go unpunished?'

The army's response came with one resonant response: 'Let us go now! Lead us, and we will avenge all wrong doings!' Alexandros then struck camp from Myriandros which is being renamed Alexan-dria and marched north-west to meet the enemy marching during the night. Meantime Darios had arrayed his vast army, estimated to number over three hundred times a thousand, placing all the mercenary Ellines in his service at the center of the front line, along with his heavily armed Kardakes and all his cavalry, following the contours of the west bank of the river. The line stretched from the seashore to the foothills of the mountain range, at which point it was feasible to engulf the right wing of the coming army of Alexandros.

As Alexandros leading his army came out of the narrows to the gradually opening valley of Pinaros, he started deploying the taxis of foot Eteri first. As the space opened, he ordered the cavalry to flank the foot and proceed in battle order. The sarissa falanx was at its usual sixteen men deep. On the right and next to the mountain slopes, Alexandros sent Nikanor with the royal Agima and the Ypas-pistes, the Thessalian cavalry and some of the Makedonian one, followed by the taxis under Kinos and Perdikkas. To his left and toward the seashore, Alexandros placed the Peloponnisian and the rest of the city-states allies, under Parmenion, along with the sarissa taxis of Amyntas son of Andromenis, Ptolemeos son of Selefkos and Meleagros with his cavalry ili with Krateros as second in command after Parmenion.

As Darios observed this, he recalled the cavalry he had stationed on the east side of the river, with-out having them stand for battle. He ordered them to ride behind his lines toward his right wing and the sea, across from the men of Parmenion and having in charge of them the satrap Nabardzana (Na-varzanis). Darios himself took the usual position of a Persian High King, in the middle of the line and behind his Ellines mercenaries and the Kardakians.

When Alexandros saw the Persian cavalry moving against the placement of Parmenion, he sent behind the lines of the sarissa taxis (so they could not be seen by the enemy) the Thessalian cavalry, to reinforce Parmenion's line. He kept his own Agima, the Akontistes under Protomahos, the Paeo-nian cavalry under 'uncle' Aristos here and of the infantry, the Archers under Antiohos son of Selef-kos and the Agrianians under 'uncle' Attalos. Behind his front line and to the right, he placed few taxis of Peltastes and light cavalry, to guard his right flank from the enemy on the mountain slopes.

To eliminate such a danger then, he attacked those on the slopes first. Dislodging the enemy from that location, he held it with two iles of light cavalry and a taxi of Peltastes. He then took the rest and reinforced the line of his right wing falanx taxis, placing the Anthemoundian and Lugaean (from an area of Agrianian country) iles of light cavalry ahead of the right wing, for shock troops. He did the same on the left wing, placing before the line the Kritan Archers and the Thrakian Odryssians under 'uncle' Sytalkis' uncle. Our whole line numbered about thirty three thousand men as opposed to the more than three hundred thousand of the enemy!

Being satisfied, King Alexandros gave the men some rest before ordering the advance. Darios waited, remaining idle. Then Alexandros asking Parmenion to hold against any and all odds, called for the Paean and the whole army advanced singing. They covered the distance to the banks of the river as fast as possible, to avoid exposure to Persian archery. The left Persian wing could not withstand the assault and retreated almost immediately in disarray. The King found himself now facing the Ellines mercenaries from their left side as they held the center and the protection of the High King.

On our left, the Persian cavalry under Navarzanis gave a good push forward against Parmenion but it was held by the Thessalian cavalry, the Kritan Archers and the Odryssian light cavalry, albeit with difficulty. Our center held its own against the mercenaries (now facing double exposure) and the Kardakian heavy foot army which were helped by the steep river bank at that point.

Alexandros saw a gap forming at the right of our own falanx of the center, due to courageous fight by the mercenaries of Darios and veered to cover it. During this melee, Ptolemeos son of Selefkos fell fighting bravely, along with one and twenty others! The danger though was averted and the line was back in order!

Darios, seeing that the courage and bravery of his Ellenic mercenaries and his own brother Oxatra (Oxathris) could not stop the advance of Alexandros and feeling of being in imminent danger of be-ing killed or (worst) captured, turned his chariot to flee. The descendant of Ahilleas and Iraklis was just upon him! The chariot was abandoned in favor of a horse, on account of the uneven ground and hundreds of dead impeding the way. Darios fled like a wind, not stopping but long after crossing the Efratis! Of his thirty thousand Ellines mercenaries, only four thousand managed to follow him.

About ten thousand more escaped with their leader Vianor (the other one, Aristomidis, fell in bat-tle), followed by the traitor Amyntas, Thymodis son of Mentor and nephew of Memnon, Aristodimos of Fares and some others. From the Persian cavalry which had given so much trouble to Parmenion and the Thessalians, when they heard and saw the High King deserting, fell also in disarray and dis-persed leaving thousands of dead, as many were stampeded by their own in their rush to leave!

Among other Persians of high rank falling in this battle, were Arsamis, Reomithris and Atyzis, who initially had escaped from Granikos and Tarsos alive. It's been said that the total loss of Persian lives exceeded one hundred thousand! Ptolemeos son of Lagos claimed he put his men to fill a ravine with dead Persians, in order to continue their pursuit of the enemy..."

"I don't trust Ptolemeos' word any longer! Not after he abducted the dead King's body to Memfis!"

Sytalkis cut in brooding. "As things turned out, he may have done the Soma good!" Kalas ventured.

"The Soma/Body of Alexandros ought to have been brought here and buried at Aegae, as tradition has it for all Timenid Makedonian Kings. Had that being done, neither Perdikkas nor Antipatros or Antigonos and Ptolemeos would be able to act as they are!" Filippos stated frowning. "Roxana and her young son Alexandros would be here, under the protection of all Makedonians, we would have been in Pella also -instead of hiding here in Thraki- and Olympias, as bad as she is, would have come from Ipiros leaving poor Kleopatra to rule there in peace instead of venturing to marry Perdikkas and until her son could be of age. It all started with cursed Meleagros and his cronies!..."

The friends continued debating the ifs and buts of the developments after Alexandros' death and the elevation of Arideos (now under the title King Filippos-Arideos) his wife Evridiki (daughter of Kynna, half sister of King Alexandros), Roxana with the infant son, Kleopatra's failed wedding with Perdikkas (to get away from Olympias and to renew the old flame she had for the general), the rumored son of Alexandros and Varsini Iraklis (kept in seclusion by Polyperhon) and so many other problems, until very late. Finding no solution to any of these, they went to bed feeling down and with bad forebodings. The next narrator the following night was designated to be Faedon, the son of Ada-mas…

Next morning found them up early and, after some food and fresh milk from the goats, they set to work continuing the repairs of the estate. Mid-day meal was done (by most) at work site or out in the fields. They all returned to the main house with the sundown, washed, ate their dinner and sat to con-tinue the story. Faedon started in clear voice:

"Alexandros was forced to stop chasing Darios because of nightfall. The next day he rested and took care of his own wound, after visiting the wounded soldiers first. He sent Parmenion with part of the army to go to Damaskos where the treasury of the High King and his harem and family were kept. Detachments were left behind to bury the dead (Persian and mercenary dead were left to the locals for burial) and bring the trophies from the battlefield, such as Darios' chariot, his mantle, his bow and arrows and all the treasure left in his camp.

Parmenion reported the treasure at Damaskos found intact and Darios' family taken in custody. Among the captives was Darios' mother Sisygambis and his wife Statira and his little son. With the 'guests' in the harem, the wife of dead Memnon Varsini with her two sons were also found. Hearing that the chariot, mantle and bow with arrows of the High King were in the hands of the victor, they thought Darios was dead and started mourning him. As Alexandros heard of it, he sent Leonnatos to assure the royal family that Darios had escape alive and promised them all the protection and com-fort they needed.

Next, Alexandros showed his gratitude to the troops by giving each one monetary rewards taking special care of the ones reported for their bravery. For the wounded ones who had to return home because of the severity of their wounds and for the families of the ones that got killed, he excluded them from any future taxation to the royal treasury! He held sacrifices to Olympian gods and Iraklis and, finishing that, he went to visit and reassure his royal captives about their safety.

Queen Mother Sisygambis gathered her daughter-in-law and the rest of the women and children to receive their new master who assured them he was simply their host. Alexandros was announced and went into the royal tent accompanied by Yfestion, Perdikkas, Krateros and 'uncle' Filippos. The Queen Mother seeing Yfestion being taller and more refined in his dress mistook him as the King and, according to Persian customs, she prostrated before him as Yfestion and the others stood in em-barrassment. Warned by a eunuch of the harem, she started to apologize.

The King approached her, lifted her up and said: 'This is also an Alexandros Mother! No need to feel embarrassed!' He told them once more that their status would remain royal and that he would keep them informed of Darios' health and whereabouts as he would come to know of it.

Alexandros then appointed Valakros son of Nikanor and one of the royal body guards as satrap of Kilikia, promoting Menis (short version of Menelaos) to replace Valakros and also promoted Polyp-crhon to lead the taxis of Ptolemeos son of Selefkos, as the latter had been killed. Menon son of Kerdimmas was appointed satrap of the north part of Syria, in charge of a strong force of allied cavalry from the city-states, to secure and expand our hold in all Syria.

News of Farnavazos (Parnabashyush) sailing with some remaining Persian ships and mercenaries against the island of Hios did not bother Alexandros much, as he knew now that the Persian diver-sion and cause was at its end after our victory at Issos. There were signs that the Ellines of Kypros island and most of the Finikian city-states were ready to revolt and place their fleets in our service.

There was some disturbance though, as Aftofradatis (Atophradata) the other Persian admiral in the Aegean sailed to Alikarnassos and met with the Spartan king Agis.

Agis asked and received money to continue his opposition to Alexandros in Peloponnisos, in hope that the city-states there would side with him. Receiving the money, Agis sent his brother Agisilaos to Kriti, in order to incite the Kritans to revolt. In order to countermand these events, Alexandros did not move toward the Efratis in pursuit of Darios. Instead, he took the army southward into Finiki. He would do what he had done with the coastal cities thus far, denying the Persian fleet any anchor-age and forcing them out of action.

Heading south, Alexandros was met by Strato, the son of king Gerostratos (Yierosthruto in Semitic dialects), who was with Aftofradatis. Strato saw that their interest was with Alexandros' side and volunteered all the area under his father's and his own rule to us. The cities of Marathos, Sigon and Mariani opened their gates to us -as well as the island of Arados.

Alexandros rested the army at Marathos for a few days and he received there a letter from Darios in which the High King was asking for his Mother, wife and children to be restored to him, offering his friendship and alliance. His asking though was a very insolent one, as he attributed our victory to gods' will and favor and, as the High King, he was asking (rather telling) king Alexandros to comply with his wishes.

Our King replied at once by stating the injuries Ellas had received for years from Persia, the in-volvement of Persian kings and money in keeping Ellenic city-states fighting one-another, the implic-ation of Darios himself in the murder of King Filippos and the right of Alexandros to avenge all these. He asked of Darios to be calling him now as the Lord of Asia not as a mere king. He told Darios that, if he would come and surrender, he would receive all he could ask for. If not, Alexandros would chase him, find him and bring an end to his kingship!"

"I witnessed the writing of this letter! I was on duty in the royal tent when King Alexandros dictat-ed it to the scribe and never felt any more proud of our King!" Filippos said, feeling even now a lump in his throat. "So was I!" Adamas and Aristos added in unison. "He was a very brave man, our King was!" Sytalkis added in turn, eyes moist. "But not one who would take undue risks! He already knew Darios had no heart for defending his rights but was looking for an easy way out..."

"Are you done? We all have witnessed events like this one! Let the youth continue the narration and jump-in only when there's a mistake or a serious omission!" Dimitrios/Mithrana intervened, still hurt in secrecy of his relative's poor performance. "All right, all right!" Sytalkis gave-in. "Go ahead Faedon, we're all ears!"

"At Marathos King Alexandros received some Ellines captured at Damaskos, who were sent as en-voys to Darios, from Sparti, Athinae and exiled ones from Thivae. He treated them with exceptional magnanimity! He let the Thivans go at once, kept the Spartans only for a short time and so did for the Athinians! One of the latter, being the son of general Ifikratis the originator of the Peltastes units, he kept him by his side in a position of honor!

Next, he moved the army to the city of Vyvlos where the local authorities surrendered it to him. Its king, Enylos (En-ilah) was with the Persian fleet in the Aegean at that time. The next city to open its gates to Alexandros was Sidon, ostensibly because of ancient wrong doings by the Persians but, in actuality, because of bitter differences with the next city, Tyros.

Tyros also sent ambassadors of friendly reception, headed by their king's Azelmikha (Azelmikos) son. Azelmikos was also with the Persian fleet under Aftofradatis. Alexandros received them grace-fully and asked that they would only let him sacrifice at the temple of the Tyrian Iraklis. They feared that the whole army would enter their city as it had happened at Efessos when Alexandros sacrificed at Artemis' temple and refused such a favor.

King Alexandros was well known for his respect toward the gods and his ancestors. He explained that the Tyrian Iraklis was to him like his own ancestor, as the temple at Tyros precedes the one in Ellas at Thivae where the son of Alkmini was born and even before the Tyrian Kadmos had taken the city and birthed Semeli from whom -and by the grace of Dias-Dionysos was borne. And it was well known to all how Alexandros honored both Iraklis and Dionysos. The Tyrians still denied an entrance to their city.

As events proved, the Tyrians wanted to play equally on both sides. Stay with us as long as it suited tem or feel free to supply Darios with a fleet, depending on how things would turn in the future. Alex-andros knew better than let them feel they could play us like that! He always would give freely and he always expected others to respond the same way! No double dealing was acceptable to him and he couldn't -wouldn't- have it from no one!"

"It's getting' late again and we ought t' rest for there's plenty o' work for our old bones again to-morrow!" It was Timeos who interrupted the narration this time. They agreed and he asked for a favor: could he be the narrator the following evening? It would do him good to re-live events that caused his early return home from the campaign, as he would get his anger for his misfortune 'off his chest' -as he put it. They agreed to that also.

The following evening Timeos took the floor and started his narration of events at Tyros. "The King got angry with the 'mbassadors 'n' sent 'em back to the city. He call'd general 'ssembly 'n' 'xplain'd to us the need to take Tyros. I remember his words like it happen'd today! 'Friends 'n' allies -he said- 's not right to leave this city free to do what it wants! We need to take it so no Persian fleet will use it to serve the High King 'n' I see the need to refuse 'im any 'n' all harbors all th'way to Egyptos! You all know how the Lakedaemonians try to stir trouble at home! If we let the Tyrians free, they'll sent mo' ships to Agis 'n' money 'n' men. When we go afte' Darios, they'll cut us off our country 'n' all our supplies! Takin' Tyros will give us instead all the Finikian navy plus the one of the Kypriots! Havin' that, we can go afte' Darios with no mo' worries on our back!'

That's wha' he said, 'n' I stick to it! So, we took the old city easy 'n' camped in it, takin' its people to work for us. The new city was anothe' matter. Being built on an island some three t' four stadia far fro' shore, we had to do somethin'. Our fleet wasn't enough t' face theirs. So, Alexandros ask'd us to build a mole from the shore to th' island."

"I hate to interrupt you my friend" Dimitrios said "but -as you see- our young scribes here have hard time following your thick Makedonian accent and writing your words down. I hope I do not offend you but I also have trouble, though I am used to it more than our kids who speak the kini dialect. Either you try telling us the story using the kini, or someone else -I am afraid- has to do the narration. Oh, I know, I have an accent too! But, as you can see, I speak slowly and I am using the kini -so everybody can understand me!" "Yeah, ye'r right!" Timeos admitted. "I'll let Faedon do th' honors, for it's difficult fo' me to change! I've the right to come in 'n' interrupt when I see need to it eh?" They all agreed with a sigh of relief (especially the young scribes) and Faedon took over.

"The Ellenic army camped then within the old city sector of Tyros and everybody got to work to build a mole connecting the shore with the island. The Tyrians were (and still are) very clever people. They had tall walls built all around their new city, close to the water, thus disallowing any landing and room for placing siege towers for any past, present or future enemy. They had two very good harbors for their fleet; the Sidonian harbor to the north and the Egyptian to the south, both pro-tected from any kind of bad weather and felt very secure, since they had the provision to store adequate food stuff to last them for a long time. The island itself had also adequate supply of fresh water within the walls. Our task observed, brought nothing but laughter and mockery as they were watching us from the height of their walls.

Alexandros sent several detachments of men to bring felled cedars from the vicinity of Vyvlos and Sidon and mount Livanos, plus having the inhabitants of the old Tyros demolish their sector's walls and every other unnecessary structure. Our men cut the trees at length making posts bedded in the bottom of the sea and the debris along with brush and every other available material placed between those posts, thus making a wide enough way for two siege towers and several men abreast able to march on it.

The laughter from Tyros' walls stopped as the Tyrians saw our progress and figured that we meant business. They made several sorties using their ships to land troops on our side on the shore and all met with failure, as Alexandros had warned our men to be vigilant and he was always present or near-by and ready to take charge. When our workers got closer and could be harmed by arrows and other missiles directed at them from the island, the King ordered the construction of two high siege towers protected with screens of fresh animal hides to be both missile and fire proof. He also had the army construct movable screens of the same materials to be placed between these towers, so the work would be protected at its entire width. Behind them he had the engineers under Diadis place the val-listes and the katapeltes, which constantly bombarded the city wall, denying its defenders the conven-ience of shooting at us at will. I believe that is when 'uncle' Timeos worked there for Diadis." Timeos nodded with pride and obvious emotion and Faedon continued.

"Now the Tyrians started to consider that the work had to be stopped by every means available for fear that we could soon achieve a landing to their island. They took one old transport ship of theirs and loaded it with all kind of flammable material making sure the most weight of it would be at the stern side so its bow of prow would embed itself on the mole when it would be towed and thrown against it. They also made its mast breakable to fall forward with the impact and loaded that with many baskets full of bitumen and cauldrons full of naphtha and sulphur.

All they had to do now was to wait for favorable wind. It soon came to their aid. They towed their transport ship to two of their fastest triiris and rowed against our mole. At a convenient distance, they lit the transport ship afire and let it come to land onto our mole. The damage was complete. All our woodwork caught on fire, including our protective towers and, as hard as our men tried to put it out, it kept on burning on account of the materials used by the Tyrians!

At the same time, small fast boats from the island full of armed men came to land and, in the con-fusion, managed to kill several of ours and take few prisoners also. Alexandros of course rushed to the scene at once and, with his encouragement, we managed to repulse the enemy but the damage was done.

The King then stopped the works for some time, in order to have more lumber brought from mount Livanos and asked his engineers to start construction of new engines and widen the mole twice its width so more protective towers could be placed on it along with troops and engines to repel any future attacks from Tyros. I will have to tell you about an incident now, told to me by 'uncle' Timeos this very morning as we were working side by side, restoring our well which Kassandros had the pleasure of fouling with stones and half-burned cattle before leaving...

Although I had no reason what-so-ever to doubt his words, he swore to almighty Zefs of telling it to me as it truly happened, adding or leaving out nothing! In one of the expeditions to bring more lumber for our works, Alexandros' (very old by then) childhood tutor Lysimahos of Akarnania -the one the King fondly called Finix- and who had come to see Alexandros for the last time before he died, had taken the liberty of going (in spite his age) up to the woods and got lost!

As Alexandros heard of it, without waiting for an escort, took off alone in search of his aged friend.

The only one who mastered to follow the King on time before he disappeared, was 'uncle' Timeos and, fearful of Alexandros' reprimand of leaving his assigned task without permission, followed the King at a distance.

It was late when Alexandros was able to locate his old tutor and, fearing they would get further lost in an unknown territory with bandits freely roaming the area, the King decided they would spend the night there. He gave old Finix his own mantle but the nights up in Livanos are cold and the old man was shivering. 'Uncle' Timeos then decided to present himself and Alexandros welcomed his presence, asking him to cuddle with the old man to keep him warm, while he would go and fetch some fire from the thieves he had observed stationed at the hill across their place.

'Uncle' Timeos offered to do it himself but one look from Alexandros made him obey his orders. The King approached the bandits undetected and then fell upon them with such a clamor, they thought the whole army was after them and abandoned their site in terror. Alexandros then called both 'uncle' Timeos and Finix to join him by the fire and stayed there until morning. The next day the King brought his old tutor back to camp and charged 'uncle' Timeos with Finix's safety until -in few days' time- a ship was readied to take instructions and correspondence back home along with Lysimahos/Finix."

Faedon had to stop here as everybody noticed Timeos was taken by emotion and openly tearing. They could understand that and, accustomed to Alexandros' openness -who never hesitated to cry when occasion would call for it without feeling his manliness being hurt by the act- joined Timeos and comforted him with kind words. Yes, the King would give limb and life for the ones he loved! If only they had fully understood and appreciated that when it was needed of them!...

They had some more wine served by the girls and the younger of the boys and, drying their tears and considering making the best possible out of their loss, had Faedon continue. They noted Ilektra seated closer to her husband now and holding his hand fondly and in a manner of complete under-standing. Faedon resumed...

"About the same time, the kings of Arados and Vyvlos Gerostratos and Enylos who -as we know- were with Aftofradatis, deserted him and came back to their cities bringing all their ships to our side. These ships, with the Sidonian squadron gave us approximately eighty triiris of the line. The island of Rodos also sent to us her state-ship plus nine more. Now we were able to at least repel any Tyrian of-fense from the sea, although we weren't strong enough yet to face them openly.

We were besieging Tyros now for almost five months! Diadis and his assistant Haerias were build-ing more new siege machines and lumber from Livanos was coming uninterrupted, along with local help. The mole was reconstructed wider and progress was achieved with fast pace. The Kypriot kings then joined us, sending Pnytagoras in charge of a hundred and twenty more triiris of the line! Now we had a strong navy once more!

Meantime Alexandros had not forgotten the bandits roaming the mountain passes of Livanos and Antilivanos and were a threat to the communications with Orontis valley and the city of Myriandros/ Alexandria. Taking with him the royal Agima, the Ypaspistes, the Agrianians and half the Archers, campaigned for only ten days and brought all of the mountain tribes under control.

Coming back to Tyros and finding now our navy refitted and ready, he led in person the right wing of it with the allied Finikians, while Krateros led along with Pnytagoras the Kyprian on the left. The Tyrians who, originally arrayed for a battle, saw the King's determination got second thoughts and withdrew their ships in the harbors, content to have them guard the approaches to them. The King returned to shore, mooring our ships on both sides of the mole, where they would be protected by the weather. The Kypriots under Pnytagoras and Andromahos moored across from the Sidonian harbor and our Finikian allies across from the Egyptian one. Tyros now could be ours soon!

Then, a horrible event took place. The Tyrians brought the few prisoners they had captured during their raid to our mole and towers few weeks ago and, before everybody's view, they cut their throats and hung them in front of their walls as a warning to us! That uncalled-for act enraged every one at our camp!

It was toward the end of the month of Panamos and the men were anxious to have the job done. The last act of the Tyrians toward their prisoners had brought strong hate in our camp toward the de-fenders of the city. The King had equipped several vessels with platforms now on which we placed the vallistes and/or battering rams with long necks so they could reach the wall as we brought the vessels close to them. The vallistes would keep the defenders away from the parapets of the walls so the rams could do their jobs.

But even that task was difficult as the Tyrians had the forethought of placing rounded and lose big stones where the walls were touching the water and our ships had hard time remaining in place with the constant current and the lose stones where our ship bows rested. So we sent divers to tie the stones and our ships were taking them away to the open sea but that was taking too much time! Then Alexandros thought of using heavier anchors which they should be able to keep out ships in place but the Tyrians responded by sending their own divers who cut the anchor lines, until we replaced them with chains.

Now some of our rams did some damage on the wall and we got ready to assault that area but the King thought best we should attack from all sides to keep the Tyrians guessing where the final assault would come from and catch them unprepared at one point. At this face of the battle, the Tyrians applied the cruel means of heating sand and throwing it on our men below! The hot morsels of sand were getting into the breast-plates of our men with disastrous results, as they had hard time letting the sand out of them! The ones who threw their protection off, would get darted from above. That was the time when 'uncle' Timeos got severely burned on his chest and was forced out of action!

They were getting desperate lately, the Tyrians did, for they had send to Karhidon (their 'daughter' city built on African shore to the west side of the sea) but got no response, ostensibly because Karhi-don was at a war herself. In desperation, the Tyrians assembled several vessels and waited for the right time when our sailors would be ashore for victuals and attacked where our Kypriot allies were moored.

Alexander, though at the other side of the attack and by the Finikian allies, acted with his custom-ary speed and, manning as many vessels he could manage, led in person his own ship by circumnav-igating the island. The spectators from the Tyrian walls tried to warn their comrades but, in the din of the battle, they couldn't hear or understand. He managed to damage many of their ships and capture a few, a fact which brought great despair to the enemy -as they saw that even in their ele-ment, the sea, we could defeat them! Now came the time for the all out attack to their walls!

Our mole -twice as wide as before- had almost reached the wall side and our engines now could work on it constantly and produce some results. The defenders gave an answer to that too! As part of their wall fell, they rapidly built one right behind it, forming a semi-circle, its two ends connecting with the rest of the front wall.

Alexander wouldn't give up though. He assembled again the ships with platforms, placed our engines on them and, upon other ships, placed the Ypaspistes under the hero Admitos and one taxis of the sarissa falanx under Kinos. Parts of the rest of the fleet he sent to Tyrian harbors to see if they could force an entrance there and ordered the attack anew.

Eventually, a wider part of the wall gave way the battering vessels withdrew and others came in their place with ladders and bridges which were thrown on the fallen wall to let our people move in. Admitos then led his men forward through the wall, followed by Kinos and his men and -of course- King Alexandros. We had tough time fighting the defenders but our men (enraged by the Tyrian treatment of the captured and by the hot sands) fought like daemons and we came through.

Admitos was among the first to fall but not in vain. At the same time, our vessels broke through into the harbors and now Tyros was under attack from all sides. Our men pushed and killed on sight all, except the ones who (wisely) took refuge in temples and shrines. The last defense was by the temple of Aginor and took us some time to overcome that, but we did!

All inhabitants captured were sold at slave markets in Sidon and Vyvlos, except the ones who sought asylum at the temples and especially the one of Iraklis. Our loss during the siege was four hundred of our men and few thousands were wounded either able to recover, or, like 'uncle' Timeos, were sent back home as unable to serve any longer.

The King sacrificed now at the temple of Iraklis and dedicated the Tyrian state-ship in his honor.

The hero Admitos and all the fallen were given their last rites in splendor and games followed for few days after that. The two harbors were retained for naval use but the city on the island was burned or demolished. Later, Alexandros allowed the city to be rebuilt with settlers from Ellas and many local ones from the surrounding areas.

Here Alexandros received a second letter from Darios who, this time, was more polite in his addres-sing our King and offering his daughter Statira in marriage, all the lands west of the Efratis and life-long friendship, if Alexandros would be kind and return the Queen Mother, the Queen and Darios' sons back to him.

As proper with our Makedonian custom, Alexandros presented the proposal before the assembly, to hear the opinion of our lords, generals and clan heads present. The opinion was divided with no clear majority. Parmenion advised acceptance by saying: 'I would accept, if I were Alexandros!' to which then the King responded: 'I would too, if I were Parmenion!'

Alexandros response to the High King was that the sole Lord of Asia was now the King of Makedo-nia and, if Alexandros wanted to marry Statira, he could do it without Darios' blessing or permiss-ion! With that and after resting the army for a while, Alexandros headed south toward the city of Ye-roushalem (Ierousalim in our language), for the satrap of that district, Sanbahllata (Sanballatos) had refused provisions to us all this time.

Now, before the gates of the city, the satrap came to ask for clemency, escorted by all its High Priests and most of its inhabitants. To that, Alexandros was once more magnanimous and let the city untouched, granting even immunity from taxation every seventh year! That done, he continued south toward the city of Gaza and the Sina (Sinai) peninsula, aiming for the deltas of Nilos and Egyptos. If we could take these places, the still (mal)functioning Persian fleet in the Aegean would by necessity go out of commission and be no threat to us any longer. On the way to Gaza, the city of Akka (Ak-kho) did not resist.

By now we had come to the month of Yperveretaeos, the Athinian Voedromion. Originally, word came from Gaza that its governor, a eunuch named Vatis (Bhata), was willing to open the gates. At our arrival there though, having being reinforced by Araves mercenaries, he made up his mind to resist. Gaza being the connecting point and 'guard' of the road from Syria to Egyptos had to be taken. Alexandros tried once more to negotiate a sort of arrangement but our heralds were put to death, a fact which enraged the army, foreseeing anotherTyros!

Alexandros had the siege machines and towers come forth once more. Because the walls of the city were rather high and well kept, he chose only the places he deemed weaker and more convenient for the assault. The army built in several places earthen ramps thus bringing our machines right against the walls in those places. Several sorties of the enemy were beaten. The machines now were ready to do their job. As was his daily custom, Alexandros sacrificed to the gods before any attack on the city.

An omen from heaven was observed then as a bird, a hawk, flew over the King and let a stone held by its talons fall on Alexandros' head. But then, the bird got caught in one of the machine protective nets and someone killed it.

The seer Aristandros -always by the King's side during sacrifices- provided an answer. We would take the city, he said, but the King could sustain a head wound -if he would expose himself at the final assault. Heeding to prophesy he kept his distance from the action for some time, until a strong sortie from the defenders put our engines and engineers in imminent danger.

Seeing that the men and machines were about to be overcome by the enemy, Alexandros could not hold back any longer. He armed himself and, taking the Ypaspistes went to the rescue. The sortie was checked but the King was wounded from a shaft thrown from the walls, which pierced through the King's shield and his cuirass and wounded him on his left shoulder. This wound was a serious one as it got infected and the King had several days of high fever. The physician Filippos came again to his rescue, as he operated taking part of the infected flesh off and burning the area with a red-hot iron to cauterize it!

The army now was incensed! They doubled their efforts and a large section of the wall got under-mined and battered down and other sectors of it were made ready to be breached. They made three successive attacks on the Gaza walls while the King was observing and directing them from his tent, still recovering from his wound. The Gazans managed to repulse all three, albeit with heavy loss. The final assault came few days later, as it was conducted with even greater vigor.

Neoptolemos, honoring his ancient name, was the first to enter the city after scaling the wall and opened the close-by gate to the rest of our army. The garrison of Gaza did not surrender. They all fought desperately and fell, sword in hand. The whole siege had lasted two months and the enemy lost over ten thousand killed.

The rest of the inhabitants now were sold at the slave markets and enormous amounts of spices were in our hands, as Gaza was -and still is- the central market of such commodities. Alexandros had never forgotten the stinginess of his former paedagogue Leonidas, in Pella. Having all this treasure of spices now at his disposal, remembered Leonidas' admonition as Alexandros was acused by the tutor of spending too much incense in honor of the gods while he had no hold of its resources. Now, he sent to Leonidas one hundred talents worth of myrra (myrrh) and three hundred talents worth of frank-incense, instructing him to be generous to the gods from now-on!

It was now about a year after the Issos battle, beginning of the month of Avdaeos (the Athinian Pos-idonios) when our army marched into Egyptos. Within a week's time, we reached the city of Pelous-ion where the fleet -under the command of Yfestion- met with us. Egyptos had been reconquered by the Persians -after a successful revolt when Filippos was still alive- only recently and the country had no lost love regarding its Persian overlords, as the latter were rather severe in handling the Egypt-ians.

The satrap, Mazhakha (Mazakis), knew that and saw no reason to have a double front in defending his position. Besides, he had made the mistake of attacking the force the renegade Amyntas had brought to Egyptos after he fled from Issos, as he considered them traitors by abandoning his High King in order to save their lives. By doing so then, he had now inadequate forces to offer any serious resistance -even if he wanted to. He, therefore, surrendered to Alexandros and saved his own life.

The King now set a strong garrison at Pelousion and, splitting his navy in order to cover all sides of the Nilos deltas, sailed down the Nilos up to the Egyptian capital city of Memfis, passing by the city of Iliopolis. In Memfis, the Egyptian High Priests received him with honors and proclaimed him as the country's next Farao, among celebrations and Alexandros reciprocated by offering sacrifices to the Egyptian gods, especially to Ammun (Ammon-Dias) and the sacred bull, Apis. He rested the men and had gymnastic contests and feasts for some days.

Asking the fleet to navigate further down the Nilos and bring the rest of Egyptos under our control, he took the Ypaspistes, the royal Agima and some of the Archers, he moved north-west of Memfis ar-riving at the city of Kanopis (I believe the Egyptians call it Khannubha) by the sea. He sailed the near-by lake Mareotis and, seeing that a city there could become very prosperous and important as a commercial center, he personally chose and marked the limits of this new city which was named after him.

Alexandria is where now Ptolemeos resides and has his seat of government. It has already become very important center -although still under construction and not covering the whole area the King has marked as its limits. There's serious rumor of Ptolemeos constructing a magnificent temple in view of the island which lies across the main harbor, in which he intents to house Alexandros' body, the Soma!

Going back to continuing with the events as they took place, Egelohos returned from his activities with the Aegean fleet, to report that Tenedos and Hios revolted against their Persian occupiers, that Lesvos had been liberated by him in person and that his second in command, Amfoteros, had taken the island of Kos. Kriti now was then free of any fear of uprising, as the Persian fleet (and money) had become isolated and less than any serious threat! With him, Egelohos had several prisoners from all those places. Alexandros sent them back to their cities, to be judged there by their own peers.

Now the King felt the desire, the pothos to visit the oracle of Ammon-Dias located deep in the desert south of Kyrinaiki, in the region of Livyi, like his ancestors Perseas and Iraklis did in the distant past."

"As he explained it to us at the meeting prior to his going there, he wanted to consult the oracle on his Father's assassination by Pafsanias. To find out if all -aside the High King- conspirators had been punished, plus for some personal questions he had for asking. Those who would stay behind had to go and oversee the outlining of his future city and to start having the necessary building materials coming in. He took with him Yfestion, Ptolemeos, Filotas and me, along with half his Agima, some of the Archers and Peltastes and few local guides." Sytalkis intervened for added information.

"The King and his escort" Faedon resumed "traveled by horse and camel following the shore road until they arrived at a small town called Parhetani in local dialect, known as Paretonion to us, and directly across from the desert location of the oasis where the oracle is. Then, with the help of their guides, ventured into the desert.

They traveled for several days under intense heat and camped at night with temperatures dropped way low -in proportion to the day's heat. Suddenly, a strong sandstorm blew their way, altering all natural features the guides had in mind to follow up to the oasis. Due to this unexpected sandstorm, no one now knew which way to go, but they marched in a general direction, as the guides thought the oasis would be. Few days went by and their supplies of water run out! To conserve some energy, they now rested during the day and traveled by night, fearing the worst!

Zefs would not let them become lost tough! As unexpected the storm was, so did unexpected rain fell -to their relief and delight- giving them the much needed water which they collected in their helmets and leather casks attached to their camels! It was a welcomed omen and, additional to that one, a pair of very noisy snakes (taking also as a good omen because snakes are usually very silent) found to be going ahead of the group, like leading the way."

"That is absolutely right!" Sytalkis cut in again. "What Aristovoulos let known about two ravens in place of the snakes, is his own invention! He wasn't there, I was!"

Faedon nodded (the remark was previously done in many an occasion) and continued. "Alexandros saw the snakes' appearance with favor and ordered to have them followed. Happily, the snakes led them to the oasis, which is about 40 stadia long and, approximately, 24 stadia wide. There, is the sole water springs in the wide desert around it and there are plenty of olive groves and palm trees thriv-ing within its perimeter.

The building of the oracle stands at a high point within this oasis, shaded by several palm trees. The King went straight to that, eager to find answers to his questions. The head Priest and the others came out to meet him, like they knew he had come, like they knew before hand when to expect him -a fact which impressed everyone present. Greeting the company in broken Ellenic dialect but directly addressing the King, the head Priest called him son of Dias! Now, whether this was intentional or not, Alexandros accepted it happily."

"Filotas -I remember- made some rowdy remarks back in Alexandria upon your return from the oracle. At that time we didn't think much of it, as Filotas was still beyond any suspicion of conspiring against his King..." now Filippos said with sorrow. "We laughed, because we did not understand the policy of our King and companion, regarding the perception his barbarian subjects would have toward him with -as opposed without- a title like this attached to his name!"

"Yes! He knew what we were looking for, much better than you Ellines can ever understand!" That was Dimitrios now taking the floor. "We needed to be reassured the new sovereign was equally an agent of divine intervention upon us, as our High King was the direct link of our deity Ahura-Masda and common people! The Egyptians, alike, needed the connection between Ammun and their new Farao. We had failed because both Kamvysis -earlier- and our Darios -later- made the same mistake and we lost Egyptos while you gained it, thanks to Alexandros' foresight!"

"It's easier for us to adopt your superfluous manner of 'civilized' equality, than for you to ever come close to understanding our 'barbarian' etiquette in the relation of a sovereign and his sub-jects..." Kalas added bitterly. "Look at us! Aside trace of a different accent, our appearance is as yours, with our beards sheared in likeness of his preference and yours! Our public manners, though rude -in our opinion- have changed to imitate yours and very successfully I might add! Which one of you would be able to adopt and merge in our society? You have had only two men capable and one is dead! Look at the success Pefkestas has in his satrapy of Media!"

"We have to admit that you are absolutely right my friends!" Filippos took the floor. "The high esteem a victor has on himself because of his victories is a very hard, tall wall to climb! That is why we did not understand you whereas Alexandros did! That is why Kamvysis and Darios lost! Pride with self-complacency and vanity beyond restriction is what brings a man -any man- down! That is also why I see any and all of these generals and 'kings' falling on their faces sooner rather than later!

Our Alexandros was above all these and that is why we failed him!"

"Let us hope that his heir will become of age and take a bit after his sire!" Aristos said wishfully.

"A good thing to wish for" Attalos urged banging his wine cup on the bench for emphasis "but it's gotten late again! We will have to continue tomorrow evening..." They said goodnight to each-other, the women and children helped clean the area from left-over food and they all went to sleep over their wishes and dream their dreams of returning order and unity.

After the day's chores and repairs of the buildings at the estate, the families got together again. This time Theano, Aristos' daughter picked-up from where Faedon stopped, looking every-so-often at her Father, to make sure he approved of her narration, for Theano was rather young and, as a woman, she wasn't always sure she understood some of the particulars of war actions or politics. If their situation was different, she'd probably stay in the women's quarters just making sure she learned good housekeeping from her Mother and the other ladies -as was proper for one from a good Makedonian house. But 'uncle' Filippos had insisted all the young children and adults should know the whole sequence of events and, all who could write it down should do so and keep the records in safe places. Her voice resonated clear in the calm evening, with an occasional chirping of a late bird returning to its nest. Spring had arrived in Thraki...

"The King and his escort returned to Alexandria by the same route and from there to Memfis where Alexandros received the news that Darios was active now amassing a new army in the vicinity of Vavylon. Before departing from Memfis, Alexandros received many embassies from the Ellenic city-states that had come to congratulate him for his victories. Some really believing in him, some coming because they thought they would position their city-states in a more favorable position and, some, clearly out of need to placate him -as they had acted in bad faith against him and in favor of the High King.

Alexandros welcomed each one without exception but let them understand that he was nobody's fool! He was in a position to act with magnanimity and they had better understand that! At the same time, a small reinforcement came from Ellas, sent to him by Antipatros. There were four hundred mercenary oplites with Menidas in charge, five hundred Thrakian cavalry under Asklipiodoros and three thousand sarissa bearing Eteri.

Before departing from Egyptos, Alexandros designated the ones who would be governing the area. Being a good judge -as I am told time after time by all of you who knew him- of people and taking care the local population would feel more comfortable if governed by their own, he appointed Egyptians for the civil functions of the country, empowering them to levy the required taxes and keep the customary laws functioning with no interference from the military Makedonian leaders.

The Egyptian Doloaspis (Dhol-Asbah) was named as civil Governor, while one of the Eteri, Panto-leon from Pydna was appointed military Governor in Memfis and Polemon son of Megaklis from Pella in Pelousion. He left several garrisons in key places in charge of Lykidas from Aetolia, who was to also recruit local volunteers to be trained in the Makedonian ways. Pefkestas son of Makartatos and the son of Amyntas, Valakros, were to be the generals in command of this Egyptian army which was to number about four thousand men. Polemon son of Thyramenis was also named the admiral of about thirty triiris stationed in Pelousion, until Alexandria would have the facilities for a fleet.

With these appointments, Alexandros placed several different men in charge of the taxis and iles affected. He designated Apollonios son of Harinos to govern Livyi and to Kleomenis an Ellinas hailing from the Egyptian city of Nafkratis the part of Aravia. Kalanos came to lead the city-states' auxiliaries, Omvrion from Kriti took the place of Antiohos for the Archers, combining now both the Kritan ones with the Makedonians, as Antiohos died from sustained wounds at Gaza few months prior and Leonnatos son of Anteos (because Arryvas had died in Gaza) was promoted to the body guard. For all these appointments of course, Alexandros always kept his prerogative for immediate changes, according to individual performances.

Finishing with detailing the government of Egyptos and the appointments, Alexandros returned to Tyros where his main body of vessels was anchored. He sacrificed again to Iraklis and had a few days of gymnastic and music competitions. There, representatives from Athinae arrived with the state ship Paralos, namely Diofantos and Ahilleas. They asked again -and this time it was granted to them- to have the Athinian prisoners since Granikos come back as free persons. As for the Peloponnisians who stood against Spartan pressure to revolt against him, Alexandros sent Amfoteros along with one hundred Kyprian and Finikian ships in support of those allies.

While on the move from Tyros now, the King left Kiranos from Veria to govern the area of Finiki and sent Filoxenos to govern the south-west satrapy of Asia-by-the Aegean, who was to collect the taxes and deliver them to Arpalos son of Mahatas who would serve now as the treasurer of the State.

Continuing his way toward Thapsakos by the Efratis, Alexandros replaced the governor of Syria Ar-rimas due to Arrimas' inadequacy with Asklipiodoros, son of Evnikos and, hearing the people of Samaria had killed his man in charge, Andromahos, he spent few days re-establishing his authority there by putting the guilty to death and appointed Menon as satrap/governor.

Alexandros then arrived in Thapsakos the month of Loios (Ekanomvion of Athinae, with Archon there Aristofanis) and found the river being almost ready for crossing, thanks to the engineers sent ahead for that reason. The cause of the bridges not being ready as yet was a force Darios had send under Mazaeos (Mazh Yoush) satrap of Vavylon, of five thousand cavalry and two thousand Ellines mercenaries. They were guarding the ford and impeded the progress of the engineers. Mazaeos though, as he found that Alexandros was approaching, took off as his numbers were so much inferior to ours. The fording of the river with two bridges finished then in record time and Alexandros had the army cross over.

At the place of this crossing, Alexandros founded one more city naming it Nikiforion, for the victor-ies achieved -as well as future victories. His policy of creating Ellenic centers in Asia was that these centers could serve as refuge and source of sustenance for veterans not able to fight any longer and, points of communications and supplies to the front line being always in his mind. Although being a King -and already accused as a Tyranos, a tyrant- he established in all these cities democratic gov-erning rules! As Father says, too bad we did not understand his ways then and, even worst, the high muckedy-muck generals and would-be kings don't understand now!

As Nikiforion was founded, Alexandros and the army entered Mesopotamia. Instead of marching southward in the dead heat of the summer, he took a north-east direction, having the Efratis and the Armenian mountains to the left as he went. This way, the time of extreme heat would be spent in a country side where there was plenty for the army's victuals.

Hearing from captured Persians by our scouts that Darios had amassed a huge army by the Tigris and fearing the High King intended to deny our crossing it -as the river is truly wide and fast- instead of marching toward Ninevi (Ninehvih), we crossed the river further up north, where we were sure there was no strong Persian presence and the river could be forded easier.

Nonetheless, the task was great and, in order not to lose any, Alexandros placed a line of horsemen across the width to break the flow of the water and another line further down to help with any strugglers who lost their footing. The King himself crossed on foot, making sure he was leading his men to no unnecessary trouble! After crossing the river, Alexandros rested the army again before moving south to meet Darios.

Here there was another omen from heaven! The moon lost its light and disappeared from the night sky! Many thought it to be a very bad omen but Aristandros gave the omen its right interpretation one more time! He explained that the Ellenic favored god of light was the sun-god Apollon! The sun did not leave the sky, the moon did -and that was the personification of Astarti, worshiped by the Persians and Asiatics! Alexandros let the good omen be known and the army rejoiced!

They marched on the left-side bank of the river southward, the Kardusian mountains being on their left and within four days of march, the army met the first outposts of Darios' army -a force of one thousand cavalry- which Alexandros rapidly chased away.

We found through our scouts that the High King had chosen a right place to give battle. He had the field before his army leveled so he could easily use his cavalry plus his scythed chariots and a number of elephants brought from his subjects in far India! Our back would be against the river and toward the mountains of Armenia, easy to have us isolated there and eliminated after our expected defeat! On the other hand, in case things would not work as Darios planned, he had the open space for retreat and the walls of mighty Vavylon behind him!

His army now was almost twice as big as the one he brought against us at Issos! Having trained —as it is said- many a contingents of his new army in person, he moved from Vavylon to Arvila where he established his harem and depot of supplies and, crossing the river Lykos just before its confluence with Tigris, prepared the field to accommodate his vast army the way I just described a minute ago. There he waited us with his people from all the following nations: aside from the fifteen Indian elephants, he had two hundred scythed chariots, about forty five thousand in cavalry and -like I said- almost double the number in infantry than at Issos.

There were people from Vaktria, India, Sogdiana, Sakia and Arahosia! From Aria, Parthia, Yrkania and Midia! There were the proud Persian overlords, alongside the Kadusians, Alvanians, Sakessines, Araves from the Red Sea, Susianes, Armenians, Kappadokians and Mesopotamians with Syrians from Kili Syria! The field chosen by Darios was the one called Gavgamila.

Alexandros approached in order of battle and, at about half a day's march from the enemy and with partial cover of low hills, he ordered a camp to be made and fortified with a ditch and a stock-ade. Within it he had the captive family of Darios, best to protect them in case the Persians would break through and try to repeat what had happened at Issos with the sick and wounded. Then he gave his men a rest which lasted four days but not neglecting to have scouts observe the movements of the enemy camp and the disposition of their troops and report to him.

On the fourth evening, Alexandros had a meeting with all his officers and assigned their posts and duties for the next day's battle. He had the army start long before dawn, to cover the distance out of the enemy observation and unimpeded. It was dawning of the 25th day in the month of Yperveretaeos (the Athinian Voedromion) and five years after the assassination of King Filippos. There was some delay on the march though on account of the heavy mist and the numerous low hills which prevented the early accurate observance and placement of the enemy line.

Darios had his troops already in line of battle and Mazaeos with his cavalry just retired from the last hilltops before the open plain. Alexandros called his line to a stop as he held this final high ground to observe once more the enemy's array for battle. He called his officers again for council. Many advised immediate attack, eager to have the show-down with the enemy. Parmenion advised to have the ground before them further scouted, making sure the plain now before them was a real plain with nor hidden lows or other obstacles. Alexandros accepted the general's opinion and a new stockade was build. The army laid the weapons as if in order of battle, for speedier move when called. Alexandros with some of the Agima and Peltastes spent the day reconnoitering the area thor-oughly.

At the end of the day he called again all the officers by his tent, from lohagos to taxiarhos, from the syntagmatarhes to hiliarhous, to stratigous/generals. When they assembled he delivered them some soul-stirring words. He told them how proud the whole Ellas had become of them for their proved valor and, especially, he was grateful for all their efforts thus far! He pointed to them that this coming battle was an all-out effort to bring an end to the Persian hegemony over free people, putting extra emphasis on their obedience to orders the following day. He asked not to chant the paean as it was customary while marching against the enemy! Instead, they should march in silence and with the demanded precision, aware of last minute orders for the battle. Their war cry should strike -when word was given for it- a terror to the enemy, as it would come in unison at the right time! His orders should be obeyed with extra accuracy and speed. Each one of them would be responsible for either victory or defeat out of individual bravery and obedience to orders!

They all stood cheering and asking the King to lead them at once, so they could prove here and now their courage and obedience! Alexandros told them they would have plenty of time for that the next day. For now, they ought to go and rest, first passing his words and his love to their men! He ordered them to have double ration that evening in both food and wine.

Later in the night, Parmenion went to see Alexandros and suggested a night attack on the enemy, on account of disparity in numbers and with the reasoning that the Persians would be panicking and confused in the dark. Alexandros refused to do so, first bringing up the example of what happened to the Athinians on their night attack on Syrakousae during their war in Sikelia few generations ago, then, because others were also present and wanted them to see him completely fearless against enemy numbers, he said that it was more worthy to be victorious openly instead of trying to steal a victory in the night. Alexandros was awakened late after a good night's sleep by Parmenion. Time for war!

Darios apparently had the same thought as Parmenion, only that -instead of attacking- he antici-pated a night attack from our troops at night and held his men under arms and without any sleep. As the early morning sun rose on the plain, found the Persians waiting in battle order as follows: In their left wing stood their Vaktrian cavalry with Vissos (Besh-yoush) in charge (he was cousin of Da-rios) and Arahosians and Daans. To his (Vissos') right were Persian horse and foot then Susianes and Kardakians, in deep squares of thousands.

At the right wing, Mazaeos had his horse from Kili Syria and Mesopotamia then, toward the center, there were Mides, Parthians and Sakes followed by the Tarpourians, Yrkanians, the Alvanians and the Sakessines. In the center of it all -as customary- there was the High King Darios, surrounded by his elite body guards, his 'kinsmen' all Persian guards with the 'golden apples' as butts of their spears, the Indians with the elephants, fifty scythed chariots, Karians and Mardian archers.

The Uxian men along with the men from Vavylon and the Araves from the Red Sea were stationed right behind the center, as a reserve body to the High King. Again at the center but at its left and in front, were the Skythian cavalry and next to them one hundred scythed chariots. At the front of the right wing were Armenian and Kapadokian cavalry and some fifty more chariots.

So, Vissos commanded the left wing, Mazaeos the right... Oh! I almost forgot! The Ellines mercen-aries of the High King were placed half to his left, half to his right as added protection. On Mazaeos' side toward the center and in front of him, were the rest of the scythed chariots. All these were later verified from captured tablets of Darios' orders for the night before, as well as the day of the battle.

And, if I am not mistaken, some of them were given to 'uncle' Sytalkis from 'uncle' Dimitrios' own distant cousin and Darios' main eunuch Vagoas who was also taken prisoner after the battle and died somewhere up in the Kafkasos mountains some time later."

"I remember that poor fellow! He became a eunuch because of court conspiracies just before Darios became the High King. His lot fell with King Alexandros along with the rest of the harem in Vavylon and he faithfully continued doing his duty until he froze to death at a snowed-out pass on Kafkasos…

Oh! Sorry for the interruption! I should have kept my mouth shot! Please, continue…" Dimitrios/Mithrana admitted, spilled some wine in memory on the ground, had a long gulp from his cup and looked apologetically to all around. Theano smiled in understanding and continued.

"According to these tablets, Darios also gave his troops a good speech before battle exhorting them to defend their homes, properties and families until the invader would be sent back defeated.

On our side of deployment, our right wing was held by Alexandros, his Agima of cavalry led by Klitos Melas, son of Dropidas. To its immediate left were the cavalry iles of Glafkias, my Father's one (Aristos nodded), Sopolis' son of Ermodoros, Iraklidis' son of Antiohos; then, the iles of Dimit-rios son of Althaemenos, Meleagros from Vottiki and Igelohos, son of Ippokratis. All those -aside the Agima- were under Filotas son of Parmenion. In front of these troops for screening purposes and for filling possible gaps, Alexandros placed Valakros son of Nikanor with half of the mounted Ypaspis-tes. To Valakros' left were half of the Archers under Vrison from Pisseon of Pelagonia and, next to him 'uncle' Attalos with half the Agrianians." Attalos smiled at her, indicating she had it all right thus far.

"Further to the King's left and by the center of our main line, were first the rest of the Ypaspistes led by the other son of Parmenion, Nikanor. Next came the taxis of sarissa bearers with first the one under Kinos son of Polemo (Polemokratis was his whole name), followed by the one under Perdikkas son of Orontis (we named the river which is south of Alexandria in Syria in his honor), then came Meleagros son of Neoptolemos with his taxis followed by Polyperhon son of Simmias and, then, the taxis of Amyntas son of Andromenis but under the leadership of Simmias, as Amyntas was sent to Makedonia for new recruits.

The left side of our center of foot Eteri was under the general command of Krateros who held its extreme left next to our left wing. Next to him and our actual left wing were first the iles of cavalry led by Erygios son of Laryhos composed of allied city-states' horsemen. Next to him and further left were the Thessalian cavalry iles under 'uncle' Filippos, son of Menelaos, house of Agis…"

"I do appreciate your effort to give me all recognition as a leader of this group of ours dear Theano" Filippos said with a kind smile "but I need no special treatment! We have agreed to be all equal here, with no special recognitions among ourselves! The only thing I want you young ones to know is that my placement in charge of that cavalry was my first actual charge! And, if I humbly may say so, I did not fail our King's choice!

You can continue now then my dear, but remember: no special accolades and recognition, unless it covers all of us! We all served our King with love and as much understanding as we could and, by god's will, we will serve his family in the future! None of us here was or is any better than the rest and I don't say that to you to scold you but just as something fair to all present, which will have to continue with your generations! I hope you all understand my meaning…"

"What you said my friend" Peridas noted "indicates our correctness in making you our leader! But let's not delay further this young maiden! Her narration is a song to our ears -I can tell- even if we lived the actual events and heard the story so many times already! The younger ones can learn from her as much as from us!"

"Thank you both!" Theano said, pleased. "After 'uncle' Filippos' ili, there was the special ili of Thessalians from Farsalos, led in person by Parmenion son of Filotas himself! Parmenion was -as usually- in charge of the whole left wing. Now, because of its numbers, the Persian army could overlap ours at any time in such an extended plain. For this reason, Alexandros placed a second line at our wings and then, a third -aside of the Thrakian light lancers in charge of keeping our camp safe.

The second line on the right was two iles of Ellenic mercenary cavalry under Menidas. Behind him was the rest of our Paeonian cavalry of my Father, led by 'uncle' Adamas and, behind him was the Prodromi under Aretis. At the left wing's side, the second line was two iles of allied city-states' horse under Klearhos of Kyrros, Vottiaean; right behind him, Odryssian horsemen under Agathon from Pella, followed by foot falanx of city-states' allies under Kalanos from Pieria.

Both wings of these second lines were instructed by Alexandros to turn to their sides and impede any Persian progress if the enemy would try to envelope our wings and/or fill in any gaps of the front line. That understood clearly, he then set one more reserve, the third line as 'uncle' Sytalkis here has called so many times. On the left wing and behind Kalanos was 'uncle' Sytalkis with his Odryssians and some of the city-states' allied horse under Kiranos and other Thrakian allied horse under Aga-thon son of Tyrimmas along with two iles of mercenary cavalry led by Andromahos son of Ieron.

At the right wing and behind its second line, Alexandros placed the other half of the Agrianians who were led by their able second commander 'uncle' Spadoklos -if I am not wrong." Spadoklos smiled in agreement.

"Behind him, our King stationed Kleandros from Lamia with all the veterans and allied Illyrians. He asked them all to be ready to fill in gaps, receive and eliminate any penetrations from the elephants or the scythed chariots and support where and when needed with speed. As for our camp, he placed some of the Thrakians and one ili of cavalry under our Agathon here (time for Agathon now to smile pleased), in case it needed protection. All our horse numbered about seven thousand and our foot approximately forty thousand total.

Now my narration has to stop. Not because I am tired narrating but, because I truly do not fully understand battle developments and I am afraid I will mess it up! I ask either Theoharis or Yeoryios, Leonidas, Mahas or Pithon to take over explaining what happened. I know they are good students of all you 'uncles' and Father in military training and affairs, so it would be best if anyone takes over!"

"I will try my best sister, if I am allowed to do so by my brother and my friends" said Pithon eager to prove his knowledge before his older brother and his friends. Hearing no objection, he cleared his throat and recited what he heard from his elders in the past.

"When all was ready, Alexandros gave the signal for advance against the enemy, marching slowly and with parade precision, in silence. As they approached the enemy lines and could clearly see who was to face what, a second, prearranged signal was given by the King through the bugle. Alexandros with his royal Agima paced faster going further to his right, like he wanted to get on the enemy's left. He was followed by the rest of the right wing cavalry under Filotas and the whole movement was screened -in a bit slower pace- by the Lancers and the Archers, while the foot Eteri of the royal Agi-ma thinned their lines extending also to their right.

Darios' forces against Alexandros were the Mardian archers, Indians, the Persian 'apple' jave-liners and, of course, Vissos' own cavalry. They were forced to follow Alexandros' movement, covering their left side. The High King ordered them to pick-up pace, so they could over flank our King. Our rest of line moved meantime with proportionate speed, reduced as our far left was con-cerned, forming a continuous but diagonal line.

Darios ordered his elephants and scythed chariots to attack us. Although we had some casualties in our left wing, most of these attackers passed through -our lines opened the last minute to let them pass- with no major problems. As they wheeled around to attack from the rear and, therefore, slow-ed down, our second line detachments fell upon them and all were eliminated!

Our line had now come very close to the enemy and the paean sounded in all its glory, bringing fear on the enemy, except the forces under Mazaeos. That very capable Persian attacked our left with valor and was making some progress! Our center also, thinned to keep the line with no gaps after the move of our King, had hard time keeping Darios' center from breaking through.

Meantime, Alexandros signaled Menidas to have his men deal with Vissos' Vaktrian cavalry. But, because the enemy was so numerous, Menidas had hard time and fell behind. My Father Aristos' other half of Paeonian cavalry under 'uncle' Adamas was then signaled to come to aid and the enemy was checked. Then, our King signaled Aretis to come with his force to close the gap and, thus, the second line of our right wing got into battle early. Behind them, the archers of the third line and the veteran men of Kleandros moved to cover, our Illyrian allies remaining as a reserve.

At the center Darios ordered a general advance and, as our sarissa taxis had thinned to keep contact with our right, some of his cavalry broke through and threatened our rear and the camp. When the men of Aretis helped 'uncle' Adamas to stabilize the line against Vissos, Alexandros moved toward the Persian center where a huge gap had developed -bigger than the one at our center. The taxis of Kinos and Perdikkas followed the cavalry iles of our King and Filotas forming thus two edges, one horse, one foot and hit the enemy with such vigor, with our war cry striking the Persians like Dias' own thunderbolt and bringing havoc! Darios was struck with terror once more! Seeing his own char-ioteer falling by a sarissa, he jumped on a horse and fled!

While all these events were taking place at the center of the enemy line and our right, the left wing of our troops had a very difficult time under the pressure given by Mazaeos' cavalry and foot. Hav-ing more men under his command, he flanked Parmenion and threatened to engulf the whole sector! The Thessalian cavalry did what they could to hold, veering to the left and giving their all, supported by the iles of Klearhos, the Odryssians under Agathon from Pella and the falanx of Kalanos. Still, the wing was in immediate danger of folding and Parmenion sent to Alexandros for help.

Our King had to give-up chasing Darios. Vissos seeing the High King running for life, also gave up, freeing our troops of the right wing. Alexandros picked-up who could follow and turned to help Par-menion. Krateros and his taxis were still engaged with the multitudes of the Persian center which had broken in through our own gap and many of them were pressing our camp, threatening to overcome it and take Darios' family away!

Our Illyrian and Tharkian units there had a hard time, as many of the camp prisoners attacked them from the rear. Thanks to units sent by 'uncle' Sytalkis, the situation changed soon and the enemy was send back, most losing their lives. Our left wing with the Thessalian valor, the tenacity of our sarissa taxis and help from Alexandros now, saved the day and Mazaeos was forced to pull back in a hurry and head toward Vavylon with what troops had left!

Alexandros returned to pursuing Darios after a long delay, Parmenion finished-off the remnants of the Persian right wing and seized the Persian camp at the city of Gavgamila and its treasure. The King chased Darios up to the road leading to Arvila but the High King was already far away, stop-ping only to change horses and continuing his flight.

We lost at this battle close to five hundred of our brave men! Our wounded were numerous also, among them 'uncle' Spadoklos, 'uncle' Adamas and 'uncle' Dimitrios -although he then served the other side. 'Uncle' Sytalkis, 'uncle' Filippos and Father were highly commended for their bravery by King Alexandros and 'uncle' Agathon was promoted to the position of a Hiliarhos!

We also lost over a thousand horses because of wounds or exhaustion. The next day our dead were buried with all honors due and their pyres shone until late at night. The King rested the army and visited all the wounded, thanking them and praising their bravery. After the ashes of our dead were collected and their bones cleaned, he ordered them placed in special urns and boxes and sent them back home escorted with adequate silver coins to take care of orphaned families!

From Arvila Darios fled through the mountains (he suspected Alexandros would head to Vavylon and did not want a new encounter soon) followed by few of Vissos and his Vaktrian horse, some four thousand Ellines mercenaries and some six thousand Persians. He met with satrap Ariovarzanis and put him in charge of holding the Persian Gates pass with some thirty thousand men and he continued beyond toward Ekvatana."

Pithon stopped his narration, waiting to hear any comments on his accuracy. He looked around and all he was met with, was the silence of remembrance, heads shaking up and down in recollection and a few watering eyes longing for old glories. He turned to his mother with a questioning look on his face. Her eyes were also watered but she looked back at him nodding. He had done a good job...

> "To understand who they were and what our Makedonian ancestors did, you have to become one of them! To achieve that, there is only one way: Study them, become one with their ways, think and express the thought as they would and then transfer it in our times. It may, or it may not fit in our mentality of processing given issues and solving similar problems! But, at least, you will come to know their reasoning..."
> Dimitrios Karasotos, High School Principal, Giannitsa, Makedonia - Ellas.

III

"Alexandros did not continue chasing Darios for long after this battle near Arvila." Mahas now did the narrating. "The reasons were few, which -at that time- were not looked upon and be understood completely or were ignored altogether. Those are your words respected members of this company, that is why my emphasis here! It made an impression on me when you admitted that so many times, for I know how difficult it is for ones who have lived in such a glory to admit any failure, even the slightest one! For that, I have to admire you and I promise to follow your steps when my time comes!

Having said that, I now present these reasons: For one, the army was truly fatigued -after such an effort against such numerical odds! Second, the fabulous city of Vavylon was just few days away, with all its treasures, comforts and future value as the main basis for further pursuit of Darios. Third reason, the need to make needed changes in the army structure, as observed and understood by our King! Fourth reason was the death of Darios' wife, either because of sorrow or severe illness or both. Alexandros took time to supervise her royal burial, giving support to the surviving Mother of Darios and his children for having such a loss!

Now then, Alexandros sent only a (strong) contingent under Filoxenos to reach Susa and occupy the city, securing its enormous treasures, for Susa was one of the main treasury depots of the High Kings and their main capital city. He and the rest of his army marched rather leisurely to Vavylon but in battle order -because Alexandros did not know the intentions of its satrap Mazaeos. In spite the relative abandonment of this old city by its Persian overlords, Vavylon still had its amazing walls of approximately two hundred cubits in height, a moat and the river!

When the city was approached, the army was ordered to fan-out in preparation; but the surprise of Mazaeos coming out with the city's nobles and thousands of maidens spreading flowers on the road to receive our King and soldiers with its gates open, was something unreal! Mazaeos had fought with exceptional bravery only few days ago and almost turned the battle in favor of Darios! Yet, he was not a foolish man! When his High King took off so shamefully, Mazaeos understood who the real King was!

He came then out of his city and delivered it to Alexandros and us! Ever thankful for any oppor-tunity to save lives, Alexandros rewarded the Persian by letting him continue as the region's satrap. Apollodoros from Amfipolis was appointed military commander and Asklipiodoros son of Filon for collecting the taxes. At the same time, Alexandros appointed Mithrinis who had surrendered Sardis as satrap of Armenia, Menis became Yparhos of Kilikia, Finiki and Syria, along with the responsibil-ity of keeping the roads open, as the local tribes were trying their luck with their new government and were presenting some trouble. Menis also received money to send to Antipatros who still was fighting the Spartans.

Along with a long rest truly deserved, Alexandros endowed each man in the army with rich presents and extra pay as a way of saying thank you. Banquets, gymnastic and musical competitions were the order of the day, not neglecting though some tough exercises at certain days, to keep the army fit. He also did not neglect to see to the needs of the locals and their priesthood, sacrificing to the local gods alongside the Olympians! He ordered the reconstruction of the Baal temple which was in disrepair for quite some time now, since Xerxis' days! The Haldaean priesthood, the so-called Magi, praised him and became his most discerning proponents.

Next, our King and army marched to Susa where the son of satrap Arvoulitis (Harbaluta) came to receive our King with presents. Arvoulitis was the satrap who received Filoxenos and surrendered the city without a fight and Alexandros thanked him by keeping him in place. Mindful -as he was about the general security of every place we took- he appointed one of the foot Eteri, Mazaros from Elimiotis as the commander of the city's garrison and promoted Arhelaos son of Theodoros in charge of three thousand men assigned to keep the region in peace.

Before leaving Susa in pursuit of Darios now, Alexandros sacrificed to the gods and held again some festivities, while he made few necessary changes in the structure of the cavalry. He divided every ili in two -each part a lohos- and assigned the leadership of each lohos to the most recognized for valor Eteri, as a thanks -again- for their bravery and devotion.

Then, he led the army past the confluence point of Efratis and Tigris which is called Pasitigris and entered the lands of the Uxians. The Uxian territory is divided in two regions. The one with the plains and the cities which immediately surrendered to us and the region of the mountains, inhabited by all kinds of thieves and rough clans which never paid heed to any Persian High King in the past.

These clans then, sent message to our King that -if he needed their permission to pass in pursuit of Darios- he would have to pay them the same amount of dues as the High Kings did before! Alexand-ros saw their arrogance and knew that if he would give-in, they would be asking for more. He told the messenger to let the chiefs know that he would meet them and present to them all their due reward in person.

Using Susian guides, Alexandros sent part of the army under Krateros to occupy the mountain heights around, so no Uxian could escape and, taking the Ypaspistes along with his personal guards and some peltastes, he marched during the night through different route and got to the Uxian villages unobserved. He killed any one who resisted, captured several as hostages or for the slave markets and appeared at the place the clan chieftains and their thugs were assembled for their pay.

Surprised by the speed of Alexandros and knowing now that their pay would be death, the Uxians tried to flee. Alexandros chased them and killed many. The ones who escaped him fell upon the men of Krateros with the same result, so they sent messengers declaring their surrender and obedience to the new King, offering to pay taxes. Sisygambis, the Mother of Darios who became very fond of our King, asked Alexandros to be lenient and he, equally fond of her, agreed. He set the annual tax of one hundred horses, five hundred pack animals (mules) and thirty thousand sheep for the army's needs.

He then sent Parmenion in charge of the Thessalian cavalry, the city-state allied force and the bag-gage and siege trains via the royal road which was easily passable, while he took the foot Eteri, the horse Eteri and the Prodromi scouts along with the Agrianians and Archers and went trough the mountain passes, all heading toward Persepolis.

To get there, they had to pass through the so-called Persian Gates, a passage which was held by Ari-ovarzanis -as remembered I hope- placed to stop the progress of Alexandros. Ariovarzanis had about forty thousand foot and seven hundred horse troops under his command. While they all could have gone the royal way -as Parmenion was assigned to do- Alexandros would have been very unwise to leave Ariovarzanis with such a strong force behind holding the pass.

Ariovarzanis had placed a wall to secure the pass defensively and placed his camp behind that wall. On either side, there are steep mountains, making any attempt to flank his position very difficult -if not impossible. After sending some Prodromi to reconnoiter the pass and, in spite the difficulty of approach, Alexandros tried an attack. He was met with a rain of arrows and sling stones and was forced to call a retreat.

From captured enemy soldiers, he learned of another pass, more like a goat's path, which led to the rear of Ariovarzanis' position. Alexandros left Krateros at our camp wit the taxis of Meleagros and some Archers and cavalry to keep the Persians busy and, taking the rest he followed the Lydian slave who gave us the information of the path almost on a single file up the mountain. It was winter and the march was so much more difficult than any other time of the year.

Arriving finally after a hard night's march behind the camp of Ariovarzanis, Alexandros split his army again. He sent Filotas with some cavalry and parts of Amyntas' and Kinos' taxis to continue and bridge the river Araxis for the road to Persepolis, while he took the rest and moved closer to the Persian camp. He had prearranged with Krateros to attack when Alexandros' bugler would have announced the King's own attack on the Persians. Taking every precaution he came closer and undetected.

Seeing what was ahead, he detached one taxis under Ptolemeos son of Lagos to one side, while he took by surprise a Persian outpost (it proved Ariovarzanis was a clever general) killing all the guards so the Persians could not be alarmed. He left there a strong detachment, ordering to attack also upon his signal. There were then three attack points placed on the Persian rear; any retreating Persians would have no place to go but either die fighting or surrender.

Under normal circumstances, our divided forces were no match to Ariovarzanis' man power. Alex-andros knew that but he also knew our troops' morale as well as the element of surprise. He ordered the buglers to sound the signal for the four-sided attack. With Alexandros' cavalry attack out of no-where, Ptolemeos threw his men against the main camp of the Persians while the men of Krateros of-fered a frontal attack on the wall, _ followed by our men's attack from the fallen Persian outpost.

The Persians were utterly confused and disheartened. The defeat was a matter of short time. Who-ever tried to run, was perished either by falling down the steep precipices or killed by the detachment stationed at the outpost. Ariovarzanis managed to escape with very few of his horsemen but found the way to Persepolis cut off by Filotas at the bridge on Araxis, took off.

Leaving Krateros to follow with the foot taxis, Alexandros took his cavalry, met with the one of Filotas and came to Persepolis not giving any time to any Persian to either take the treasury and run or prepare for defense. Tiridatis (Tirhadata), the local governor of Persepolis, having in mind to gain Alexandros' favor, captured Ariovarzanis and killed him while surrendering the city to us. For this service, Alexandros sent Tiridatis to Susa to govern.

At Persepolis several hundred mutilated Ellines -prisoners of war- and stationed there by the Pers-ians like beggars, came to see Alexandros asking for assistance to make a better living now that they were freed. They would not return home, for they were ashamed by their poor condition and muti-lation. Their sight caused the army to become very agitated, looking for some kind of revenge. Alex-andros gave the suffering men money and residences to live the rest of their lives in comfort.

He was now in the heart of Persia itself! He moved on to Passargadae, original seat of Kyros the Great and maker of the Persian Empire. He reviewed the tomb of that great man and, seeing it in disrepair, ordered its up-keeping. He then returned to Persepolis for some much needed rest.

There was plenty of recreation, sacrifices and games for several days. In one of the given banquets and while under the influence of wine, Alexandros let the soldiers who were still agitated by the recent sight of the mutilated fellow country men to pillage the city and he, encouraged by his party, set the palace to fire. Athinae was burned by Xerxis. Makedonia suffered Persian overlodship back in the days of the first King Alexandros. Now it was the turn of Persia to be humiliated!

In true, as it has been told to me by all of you on several occasions, Alexandros regretted this act chastised by Parmenion and, almost immediately, ordered the stop of looting the city -but it was rather late. Our King, in spite his desire to show he was above degraded acts like this one, occasion-ally fell victim to either temporary anger or the spell of flatterers and instigators at his most vulner-able times: when under the influence of strong wine.

While the bulk of the army rested in Persepolis for four months under the care of Parmenion and Krateros, Alexandros himself campaigned in the vicinity bringing all resistance to an end. First he subdued the Mardians who were much like the Uxians. These Mardians dwelt in caves, making a living by hunting and robbing. He brought them to order in one month and in the middle of the winter!

The satrap of Karmania, an adjacent region duly offered the satrapy to Alexandros and he thus remained its satrap. His name -if I am not wrong- was Aspastis (Azhapasta). Frasaortis (Prazhahor-ta), the son of Reomithris, was appointed satrap of Persis and a garrison of three thousand Ellines mercenaries was stationed there to keep the place in order. The treasure found at Persepolis and Pas-sargadae was sent to Susa but, later, moved to Ekvatana. It took ten thousand two-mule carts and wagons and five thousand camels to transfer that horde of treasure there!

The Persian High King Darios had fled to Ekvatana in the region of Midia, since the battle of Gav-gamila but seeing that Alexandros continued going after him, he took off from there too, towards Yrkania and beyond, caring only about his personal safety. He did not prepare for any resistance but he sent three hundred talents to Sparti and Athinae, trying to have them join in attacking Makedo-nia.

If Darios had the mind of staying where he was admitting defeat or coming to Alexandros as sup-pliant like so many others, perhaps things would be different now… As our King realized Darios sent money to others in order to have us perhaps return home -instead of standing his ground in person- he vouched to pursue the so-called High King to the end!

He had now -Alexandros did- all the means in materiel, human resources and the treasury to wage a war for as long as it would take. He called (always careful to have the consent of his men) a council and outlined his position, proposing a relentless pursuit of Darios who still possessed a man power to be reckoned with. Darios had Navarzanis (Nabarzanah), Atropatis (Adruphatta) the Midian, Aftof-radatis (Aghtopradhata), Fratafernis (Prhataferna), Sativarzanis (Satebarzana), Varsaentis (Bar-sand-yoush), Vissos (his cousin) and Vissos' brother Oxathris (Ogsatra)!

These satraps were still loyal to him and governing the regions of Tarpuria, Yrkania, Parthia, Aria, Arahosia, Drangiana and Vaktria, capable of raising a stronger army -at least in numbers- than ours-including the ordered (and delivered) contingents of Ionian mercenaries and Asiatic recruits Alex-andros now had in his service. And Darios still had some six thousand Ellines mercenaries with him, led by the very capable and loyal Artavazos (Ahrtabasyioush) and his sons!"

At this point both Filippos and Sytalkis interrupted Mahas to state that they distinctly remembered Alexandros' words in that council. The rest of the 'old-timers' being assigned to either scouting or other duties were not present and had obeyed the decision of the assembly as it came to them.

"The King reasoned to us all the logical arguments why we should pursuit Darios until he would either give up or be totally eliminated." Sytalkis said. "I mostly remember his closing words" said Filippos "like it happened this very morning. He said 'We have come here to avenge the wrong doing of Persia to our home land and we cannot let the job unfinished! But, by doing so, I do not want to e-liminate every Persian we defeat! Instead, I want to have every nation say that our victories did nothing but enhance their well being and brought prosperity to all! With Darios free to work his machinations behind our back, this will never happen and that is why I cannot allow it!…'

I feel we all betrayed him and his vision!"

"We have!" Peridas added -eyes moist in remorse and remembrance. "We all heard, we all pretend-ed to understand, we all did not like his plans! We were the victors! The rest should be our servants to the end! But we were still hungry for revenge and looting and dreamed of more treasure and glory so we pretended. When time came to truly show him we understood, we refused to go further!"

"We were still in love with him then but, mostly, with the success he brought us and with ourselves, proud like the ill-fated Narkissos observing his beauty in the still waters! And that pride led us to today's problems! Although too late for any corrections, I have to apologize to you brother Dimitrios and brother Kalas! Your service to him was more sincere than ours, though he was one of us!" Aristos stood and recognized the two Asiatics and their families who were sharing their common fate in hiding from the King's successors.

Both, Dimitrios and Kalas along with their family members Roxani and Vasiliki with young Ghara-gha (Koragos) rose and -with glittering eyes- embraced each of the rest in the company, renewing the vows they had taken to remain close friends and support one-another and the final Argead heir to the Makedonian throne, be it Filippos-Arideos, the infant Alexandros or the (unknown yet to most) Irak-lis. They spent some time talking and reassuring each-other or bringing up several personal events of the past.

The bonding among them renewed, none wanted to go and rest although the night had progressed to a rather late hour. Attalos proposed and all accepted to continue with the narration, while taking the next day off from work and repairs. "When Mahas is tired talking and most feel the need of some sleep, then we stop! Tomorrow we can rest and -perhaps- continue with the gods' blessing." -were the final words of Sytalkis and Mahas resumed his narration.

"Darios did not hold this position at Ekvatana either. Finding out that Alexandros held now Perse-polis and that his supposed allies from the Skythian and Kadusian tribes weren't coming to his aid alongside with the news that his money did no good to having Ellas unite against Makedonia as An-tipatros defeated the Spartan king Agis at Megalopolis, he lost heart once more and, turning tail, he run further north-east with whatever forces and treasure happened to have at hand.

Alexandros followed, reaching Midia in only twelve days, subduing the Paratakes on his way, leav-ing Oxathris son of Arvoulitis in charge. Arriving in Ekvatana, Alexandros was met by Visthanis (Bestana), son of the former High King Ochos whom -upon death by poison from his courtier Vagoas- this Darios succeeded on the Persian throne. Visthanis had just recently left the service under Darios, as he was disgusted by the latter's lack of courage and came to Alexandros, offering information as to the whereabouts of the High King and the numbers of his remaining supporters.

With the capture of Ekvatana, the occupation of Persis -the very heart of Persia- was complete. The work the Ellines had undertaken in avenging their past sufferings from the high Kings had come to an end. Before continuing the chase of Darios, Alexandros let the city-states' allied troops and the Thessalians make-up their minds. They were free to return back home or continue with us under pay. Most decided to return home but several remained willing to share both danger and riches. The ones who would return, especially the Thessalian cavalry, left their horses to us -as we needed them badly.

Alexandros loaded each and every one of them with presents and gave orders to have them trans-ported to Evia from the Finikian shores. He then sent Parmenion with adequate support troops to subdue Yrkania, while he took the rest of the army -including the reenlisted- and marched toward Parthia. Parmenion getting to be of a rather very advanced age was recalled within weeks to come and stay in Ekvatana as the regent of the whole area and Alexandros changed his direction going to Parthia through Yrkania.

He made Oxodatis, a man who suffered under Darios, second in governing Midia under Atropatis and marched with the army to the Kaspian Sea Gates -another pass- in pursuit of Darios. The army had a difficult time dealing with the dry conditions -it was summer now- and Kinos was sent ahead to secure the provisions needed because they were scarce.

Darios now feared that Alexandros would never stop pursuing him and called for a council among his left-over few supporters he had, to decide if it would be better to stand and fight once more. They were not as faithful to him as he hoped. They had lost faith on him and they almost came to open revolt, if it wasn't for Artavazos, his sons and the Ellines mercenaries who were led by Patron. They patched-up their differences but now Darios knew that he had only very few supporters left.

As Alexandros crossed the Kaspian Gates and rested the army because of urgent need to do so, the son of Mazaeos, Antivelos (Andubulyoush) came along with a Vavylonian named Vagistanis (Baghi-shtana), as suppliants to Alexandros. They had recently leave Darios who was then placed under guard by his cousin Vissos and the satraps Varsaentis and Navarzanis. Artavazos and Patron had seen that coming and had tried to warn Darios and place him under their protection but he refused.

Now, they also had taken off, heading toward the Tarpurian Mountains. Darios was now chained with golden chains and was literary Vissos' prisoner and totally disheartened and surrendered to his fate.

This event made Alexandros to move even faster. He chose the best of the horse Eteri and Prodromi along with some from the special units of the falanx, known for their endurance. They mounted the best available horses, without waiting for the return of Kinos with provisions, left Krateros in charge of the remaining army to come after them at an easier pace and they went after Darios. They run their horses all night and rested during the next day's heat, from noon until dusk. Run again all night and reached the camp from which Antivelos and Vagistanis had deserted, the next morning.

Here Alexandros found Darios' interpreter, Melon, who was left behind sick and thus he learned of the actual facts. Vissos had now the full command of what army was left of Darios' and headed back toward his own satrapy of Vaktria. Vissos knew the importance of Darios to Alexandros and planned to hand the former High King if and when it was judged to be of Vissos' advantage, namely to have Alexandros agree to let Vissos be in charge of Vaktria. If that would not be granted, then Vissos would declare himself High King and fight.

Alexandros pushed on. Traveling the whole night and half the next day, he arrived at a village where Vissos had camped only one day ago. Most of the men and horses were exhausted beyond any doubt by then. But Alexandros, finding of a way to cut through some desert (Vissos was using the regular roads) and thus catch-up with the enemy, chose five hundred of the best horses left to him and the equal number of the best Eteri and, armed as they were, set out through the desert short cut.

During the crossing of this desert and while every beast and man was thirsty to endurance's ex-tremity, some water was found and brought to Alexandros in a helmet. The King thanked the soldier who brought it but, tilting the helmet let the water spill on the ground, for it wasn't enough for every man to share!"

"That man was our 'uncle' Spadoklos! He brought water to our King!" Lamvros the son of Attalos loudly offered his knowledge, proud that he could also offer his expert knowledge in spite his young age. It cost him a friendly smack at the back of his head by his father, the laughter of the other young kids and the reddened face of a modest Spadoklos who didn't expect his -minor to him- offer to Alex-andros to have been known in a wider circle. After they all calmed-down a bit, Mahas continued.

"Nicanor with the Ypaspistes and 'uncle' Attalos with his Agrianians who managed to keep-up with the King thus far, were ordered to follow as they could while Alexandros and his five hundred sped away. They covered four hundred stadia during the late evening and through the night and came to meet Vissos' camp just before daybreak catching them by surprise.

If it wasn't for that surprise, Alexandros could be in grave danger as the enemy was so much more numerous! As it happened, the sudden appearance of our King and troops spread real panic among Vissos' men who scattered without any resistance. The very few who resisted were killed. This, no matter how fast happened, took some time and Navarzanis with Varsaentis and Vissos killed Darios and sped, each to his seat of power, having in mind to reunite at a later date under Vissos and fight.

Alexandros arrived at the carriage Darios was held and murdered, only to find the High King's corpse. It was the 21st day of our month of Loios, right before the birth date of Alexandros. Our King draped Darios' body with his own mantle and sent it back to our troop camp to be cleaned and then transported to Queen Mother Sisygambis and the rest of Darios' family for proper burial with all the honors due to a King.

Alexandros appointed Ammin Aspyoush (Amminaspis), who had joined us since the campaign in Egyptos, satrap in Parthia and Yrkania, giving him Tilepolemos from Almopia as in charge of the military affairs of the region and, taking the necessary time to rest the exhausted army, vowed to now bring Vissos to justice.

Our men didn't like the idea of any further pursuits. Darios was dead and that was all that matter-ed to them. They couldn't see that Vissos, being Darios' cousin and satrap of a country like Vaktria could (and did) proclaim himself High King, thus obliging Alexandros to take action. Because our King may have not been yet accepted as the legitimate heir to the Persian throne but he was who had taken it with his spear, while he could (and did) portray Vissos as nothing more than a traitor and a murderer, thus gaining the gratitude and love of the Persians wholesale!

This was the time when our men started betraying Alexandros' love to them! Knowing that the King was a freely giving man -so long as love was equally freely returned to him- they (we) forgot to continue being open hearted and lay down our thoughts the traditional Makedonian way. We obeyed but we did it with reservation and second thought of mind, without letting him know of it! He under-stood it later and that hurt him and caused him to mistrust us! In return, we mistrusted him even more, poisoning all what was sacred to him from the very beginning!"

These last words of Mahas brought a new round of discussion among the listeners and the narrator, which lasted until early morning hours. The blame was placed and traveled among many persons close and distant to the King, living -as well as dead ones. They finally agreed that the blame was to be shared equally by all, as they all should have been more open to each-other -but they hadn't. They went to rest with heavy heart and the knowledge that their understanding had come too late and to very few to have made any difference.

Almost everybody woke-up late the next morning. The only person up and around they found, was Timeos. He was seated under the grapevine arbor, to the far left of the inner courtyard. On its right there was the altar to goddess Estia and a small statue of Alexandros' bust about five paces away and to the altar's right. Left of the grapevine and almost hidden by another vine, a climbing red rose bush, a service door leading to the woods and the mountainside. A well was at dead center of the yard a wall built around it for safety.

Here and there, the women had planted some fruit bearing trees for added source of shade in the hot Thrakian summers which could be at times as bad as the famous winters. Directly across from Alexandros' statue was the door to the inner chambers. The kitchen and utility rooms (including a small reception room), the baths and, diametrically across at the other end of the connecting corridor of all these, was the main door leading outside to the stables, the silo and the fields of the estate.

There were two staircases leading up to the second floor bedrooms and armory, one from the reception room, the other from the kitchen. It was clear the place had sustained a recent major fire, as repair tools, lumber and cut stone were placed in key areas for reconstruction and some of the fruit trees had obvious recent scars on their trunks but remained alive. Miraculously, neither the altar of Estia was touched nor the statue of Alexandros. There was still some respect embedded in the hearts of the throne suitors...

When asked how early he got up, Timeos said he hadn't sleep at all. He spent the night thinking of errors made, of human greed and jealousy and resolved that his heart and mind had set firmly in joining his newfound friends, no matter what the outcome. As it was already close to mid-day meal time, the women went about preparing something to eat and most of the men went to tend the ani-mals at the stables and the near-by pens, the first structures rebuilt after Kassandros' departure. In the yard, Sytalkis held Timeos back and the two of them talked a little more about the past but, most-ly, about the possibilities in their future.

The food done and ready, the women sent the young ones with containers full of it and jugs with wine and water to the outposts around the estate, where some of the tenants were always stationed for an eye to unwanted visitors. With the youth's return to the main house, every one took a seat in the ample kitchen room (the heat outside was by this time unbearable) which, due to its vastness, was somewhat cool; its connecting doors to both sides of the corridor and the one to the yard left open, created a draft and helped keep the heat low and light to come in.

While eating, one of the outposts came in with jugs to be refilled and one messenger from Lysima-hos. The governor of Thraki had just gotten a full report from the war waging generals and aspired to become kings. Things were not rosy. Krateros had been killed fighting against Evmenis who was also wounded. Though Evmenis had won, he was forced to retreat because his ally Perdikkas had been killed by his own troops, most of them enrolling under Ptolemeos who now had the Soma of A-lexandros, plus the men to back him up!

With Antipatros moving now in Asia, the generals agreed to an armistice and they were meeting at Triparadisos, the area of the three huge parks which had served as hunting and vacationing grounds for past Persian High Kings. There, they would (they rather were already) decide who was to get what part of Alexandros' vast empire, thus carving his future kingdom -provided there would be no more disagreements! Within the next month or two, Antipatros should be back. As for the regency and who was to be named 'protector' of the legitimate heirs of Alexandros, word had come that it was passed to Antipatros! That was all Lysimahos knew and, because of these developments and unknown consequences in future, Lysimahos would stop being associated with this group from now on!

"That means we are to start looking for new home!" Filippos observed bitterly after Lysimahos' man left. "Lysimahos has the right to play it safe, as -apparently- Evmenis' time is numbered and Perdikkas is dead! I don't really blame him but, on the other hand, I am disappointed! We should choose another location very carefully and -this time- purchase it outright, not depending on any one's charity... We ought to, perhaps, do that under the adopted names of Dimitrios and Kalas, or Attalos can do so, as being

Agrianian. There are plenty of out-of-towners lately coming to these parts of Thraki and Makedonia."

"We could go to my cousin's village! Basali, I mean Vasilios, will have no problem finding a good estate for us there!" Attalos proposed. "Agrianian land and people don't forget friendship as easily as you Ellines -please, I don't mean any offense here- seem to! We will all be safe there and close enough to observe events and take action when and where is needed!"

"The way I see things developing, it would be wiser -although more dangerous- to leave our good friends out of any possible trouble! I have to say thank you, Attalos, but Makedonia has to be our next place of living! We have all changed enough through the years and recognition will not come easy, especially if we get an out of the way estate. Both Dimitrios and Kalas speak good Makedonian dialect and, with the influx of so many outsiders in the country, no one is going to give it a second thought! Why, you can join them in looking for a suitable place! There are plenty of Agrianians who have moved into Makedonia due to lack of working hands through these years of constant war recruitment…This is my opinion and I will stick to it!" It was Sytalkis talking, his already lined fore-head having new and deeper lines appearing with the thought.

They talked more about their options and, finally, they put it to vote. It was decided that all adults, including the women should voice their opinion. Spadokos and his family asked to be included. "I will not leave you now my friends, nor do I have in mind to do so ever! Lysimahos has gotten all the service out of me he ever needed! I own him nothing! Besides, I will not risk having my family here in danger of being threatened -if Lysimahos turns really against us- so I will be forced to give him infor-mation of your last decisions! All, of course, provided you have no reason to reject my coming with you!"

"I, for one, hate t' miss the company of 'nyone of you! Now that I found you an' my family got bonded with yours, I vote again that we all should be together -no matter what th' outcome!" Timeos stated emphatically. The rest accepted his words with cheers. The votes were cast and it was found that Attalos, Agathon and Spadoklos received equal votes as candidates to go and search for a new place to live. So the three men were assigned to the task and were given plenty of money for a good purchase.

Each was to have his family with him, portion of the animals and few of the men of the estate, so it would look more legitimate. They were to keep in touch often among themselves, informing one-an-other of the possibilities presented. Once the three had decided on the location and purchase, they should send word for the rest to follow, while the new place would get prepared and secured. The preparation for departure lasted two days and Attalos, Agathon and Spadoklos left with their fam-ilies, animals and helpers, in the direction of Filippi, through the lands of the Satrae. The rest packed once more and moved to the cave on mountain Dynax, waiting for news.

Time sand his wife took the task of sneaking once a week to Filippoupolis for news and the needed transactions of selling and buying what they couldn't have on the mountain. They found out that Ly-simahos sent men to the old estate three weeks after their departure from it. Seeing it abandoned, he did not move to find out which direction the group had taken. Instead, he leased the estate to some associates of his. For that, Filippos and Sytalkis were grateful.

Three long months of anxiety passed before word came back to them. They spent their days and nights speculating, with great hope and equal amount of dread. There were no history lessons and narrations, except of going over the written records and making sure they were kept in detail and with no omissions of events that mattered. Peridas had the idea of recording their own adventures since the death of the King and, finding the idea worth the effort, Sytalkis had the youth who kept the events recorded make the necessary insertions.

Their new estate was purchased by Spadoklos, inspected and approved by Agathon and Attalos, near the western parts of the land of the Idones, south and west of the city of Filippi by the east bank of river Strymon. It was far from the road from Filippi to Galipsos and/or Amfipolis to Argilos, its southern limits adjacent to the marshes of Lake Kerkinitis. The purchase of few flat boats was wisely recommended by Attalos and done in Amfipolis by Agathon, who brought them up with the help of his men and at night. The escape route through the lake -in case of need- then was covered.

It took the rest of the group almost three weeks to get there, as they traveled few at the time and only by night and after thorough reconnaissance of the roads to be taken. By the time everyone was there and settled, they were sure nobody could have picked up their trail and locate their new locat-ion. They were happy for it, for events had developed rapidly in those three months. Antipatros had returned from Triparadisos, bringing with him and under his 'protection' the 'Kings' Filippos-Ari-deos and his wife Evridiki and young Alexandros with his mother Roxana.

Being now too old and having his health failing him, Antipatros named Polyperhon as regent with the care of the 'kings', by-passing his own son Kassandros. That sort of good news was counterbal-lanced by the coming of Queen Mother Olympias from Ipiros. She was mad for her step- daughter's Thessaloniki wedding to Kassandros, mad at Antipatros (as always) for naming Polyperhon as the regent -instead of her- and, mad at her own daughter Kleopatra for leaving Ipiros, to get married to Perdikkas who promptly died, leaving her in the hands of the likes of Selefkos.

She came to Pella breathing fire and bent to kill any and all who she considered responsible for King Alexandros' death in Vavylon, as well as keeping old debts paid with real or imaginary oppo-nents in Pella. Kassandros took off from Makedonia in fear of her and mad at his dying Father. He then formed an alliance with Ptolemeos, Lysimahos and Antigonos the one-eyed. Everyone in Make-donia and the empire was uneasy and expecting these events to lead to a new confrontation, including our small group.

"Our nightly history telling resumed and, faithfull in alertness so no one would miss any, we picked up exactly where we had left-off in Thraki. My oldest brother Leonidas is doing the narrating and I, along with others from each family, write it down for future reference. So, if you happen to read this papyros book, think of me Pithon, the son Aristos from house Iraklonas with kindness and remember that we tried to do our duty. News from our men going to the market place in Amfipolis told us that old Antipatros had finally die and Olympias took Polyperhon 'under her wing'! We fear nothing good is to come out of it! But, enough of this. Now it is time to go back to my brother's narration."

"The satraps who murdered Darios agreed to go to their satrapies, recruit fresh armies and meet with Vissos at his satrapy of Vaktria to either wage war against Alexandros or, if he would now stay within Persis content with his gains, to proclaim one of them as the new High King and bide their time waiting for new opportunities. Vissos being Darios' cousin was almost sure to gain the title.

Instead of doing what had been agreed, each of the satraps stayed at his satrapy raising troops for his own purpose. Fratafernis went toYrkania -where he was later joined by Navarzanis, Sativarzanis to Aria and Varsaentis went to Drangiana. Their disunity did nothing more than help Alexandros subdue them one by one, although it took him time doing it. Nonetheless, the conditions were not so favorable for us either. The army was exhausted by the latter marches and divided in distances far between units and, as previously said, not so willing going after the 'traitors' after all.

Alexandros gave the men a good rest and applied his persuasion. They could ill afford leaving -he said- behind such a serious competition, for it could cost them untold labor at a later date when they would have to come back and reconquer. They would also have to think of the good number of Ellin-es mercenaries who were still under Persian pay, as they remained with Artavazos. Should they be left to their devices and become a viper ready to strike at our backs? They were seasoned and profes-sional soldiers and they could understand tactics, albeit they would prefer now an easier life. These targets had to be dealt with.

They marched toward the Kaspian mountain range, which divides Yrkania from Parthia and into the lands of the Tarpourians, with its hundreds of streams and rivers going down the slopes and into the Kaspian Sea. In-between these, were great forests -a good ground for hiding and setting ambushes. Having to forgo Vissos for the time being, Alexandros advanced the army in three columns, for easier attaining of supplies, having in mind to meet with all at Zadrakarta, the major city in Yrkania and its capital.

Krateros took his own taxis and that of Amyntas, along with half the Archers and half the cavalry. He was to subdue the Tarpurians going through the eastern way. Erygios took the public road which was easier, having under him the rest of the cavalry, the baggage train and the city-state opli-tes who had now become our own mercenaries. The King kept for himself the most difficult road with his Agima, the royal Eteri taxis of Ypaspistes, the Prodromi and the Agrianians.

When Alexandros reached the river Ziobetis, some of the Persian renegades came to him to sur-render; among them Navarzanis and Fratafernis. Alexandros rested his column there for few days and then arrived in Zadrakarta where he met with the rest of his army. Krateros had subdued the Tarpourians and Erygios had no problems coming through. At Zadrakarta, Artavazos with three of his nine sons came to give himself up and seek pardon for the Ellines mercenaries of Darios, along with Aftofradatis.

For the Ellines mercenaries, Alexandros first asked their unconditional surrender, as they were con-sidered traitors of the Ellenic campaign against a common enemy. Only when they agreed to it, he gave them his pardon and enlisted all those who wanted to stay in our army. The only ones confined, were some Spartan envoys who were found among them.

Parmenion from Ekvatana, was to have subdued the Mardians, who were the tribe by the Kaspian Sea, so we could build a navy and safeguard the area easier. Having difficulty in doing this due to age, Parmenion sent for help and Alexandros marched against the Mardians himself. Whoever tried to flee, Parmenion took care of and Mardian lands were added to the satrapy of Aftofradatis with Tarpuria. Parmenion was sent back to Ekvatana to oversee affairs as regent.

Next, Alexandros moved through Susian lands by the slopes of the Parahoatras range. Having some difficulty in moving as fast as he would have liked because of excess amount of loot the men had put on the wagons of the baggage train and the enormous number of camp followers, here the King ask-ed from his men to get rid of everything unnecessary. Seeing their reluctance to obey, he set the example by burning everything his! It put the men to shame and obliged.

This was a second incident where the men felt disobeying and created secret hard feelings, in spite of the King's example and promise for more riches to come. Greedy men -there's always a good number of them around- kept on complaining about it and let it be heard where and when possible.

The deed though was done and the army recovered its normal speed. One more thing our men did not understand in their King's behavior was his adaptation of Persian court attire at about this time.

Alexandros had seen the need to present himself before his new subjects as they were accustomed to seeing their sovereign. When not in battle therefore, the King presented himself dressed in semi-orient attires, thus gaining more respect among the barbarians -no pun intended here, my esteemed 'uncles'!"

"No offense taken, feel free to continue!" Kalas and Dimitrios said in unison.

"Makedonian soldiers took it originally lightly, as a little whim Alexandros deserved to have. There were some though among the usual complainers who, supported by the remaining troops from the city-states continuing with us as mercenaries, kindled the little talk into an almost open dissatisfact-ion! This found fertile ground among the Makedonian officers of the 'old guard', those who had serve alongside King Filippos and were now with his 'Medizing' son!

Of course, all those cowards did not dare tell their opinion and 'hurt feelings' in proper open man-ner before Alexandros. Had they done that, he would have listened, explained and found a way to satisfy and ease their fears. So, words kept on flying around, kindling the spark…

Here in Susia Nikanor -son of Parmenion and Filotas' brother- died of fever. He had been the leader of the Ypaspistes and a very able officer! He was also the 'rein' his brother Filotas needed when he couldn't stop 'bubbling' about his personal achievements. Alexandros let Filotas take Nikanor's body for proper burial to Ekvatana and have some extended leave of absence to console his father Parmenion, while he and the army continued toward Aria and Vaktria.

Sativarzanis having come to surrender himself and Susia was left in charge of his satrapy -although being one of Darios' murderers. The King thought he could keep peace this way in Susia -having the region already taken without any casualties (except Nikanor's death). Alexandros just left Anaxippos from Pelagonia, one of the Eteri, along with some Prodromi under his command, to keep a discreet presence of our authority.

But, while Alexandros and the army were some distance away from Susia, Sativarzanis thought he had scared Alexandros and would go unpunished no matter what he did. So, he declared for Vissos and taking Anaxippos and his men by surprise, he slaughtered them all! Next, Sativarzanis moved to the city of Artakoana which was strongly defended and started collecting recruits.

Alexandros could not leave such a mess behind him! Not only it would be a bad decision, it could also show Varsaentis who -as we remember was left in charge of Drangiana- that he too could do whatever he pleased and go unpunished. 'Uncle' Filippos had rejoined the army, coming from Ek-vatana with the reenlisted Thessalian cavalry along with the taxis of Andronikos' falanx. Stopping in the middle of the way to Vaktria where Vissos -hearing the news and expecting help from the Skythes also- proclaimed himself High King taking the name of Artaxerxis, Alexandros left Krateros with most of the army to keep on marching toward Vaktria and, he, took the Eteri cavalry, the Prodromi, the Agrianians and the taxis of Amyntas and Kinos, speeding to Artakoana.

Sativarzanis managed to escape with few of his followers but most of his other supporters were kill-ed in battle and even more were captured and sold at the slave markets. Alexandros appointed then a new satrap of the area the Persian Arsamis. Reunited with Krateros' part of the army, Alexandros did not follow the roads leading to Vaktria via the passes of Kafkasos, as he knew Vissos would be expecting him to do so. Instead, he led the army via the rugged Parapamissos, passing the Lake Aria where Varsaentis was stationed, ready to join (or so he thought) Sativarzanis. Hearing that Alexan-dros was coming instead, Varsaentis fled but was caught shortly after and put to death.

Securing thus all these satrapies, Alexandros founded one more Alexandria in Aria. He then march-ed toward Parapamissos -the locals call it Indou-Koush- via the city of Profthasia. He met with scant resistance except in one place where the resident tribe challenged our army by sending darts and arrows from the mountain heights and then retreating in its forest. Alexandros sent men around and set the forest on fire, causing them to come out. Many were killed, others fell off the cliffs in their panic and some surrendered."

"Let me interrupt you here, my son" Filippos said to Leonidas. "Here in Profthasia one of the worst incidents throughout our whole campaign took place and, it seems to me, it was the beginning of the end when one judges the army's behavior toward our King! I was not only there, I was among the judges of Filotas -as was Sytalkis, though he did not judge for he isn't born Makedonian. Between your 'uncle' Sytalkis and myself, we will give you the full account of how Filotas failed, was tried and executed by us and, because of him, Parmenion was next to go by necessity!"

"Yes, I also find Filotas' treachery very important and, although you have all heard its summary many a time, I agree that 'uncle' Filippos now has to present to you the story in all its detail!" Sytal-kis added in all his seriousness.

"Good!" Timeos jumped in. "All I know is hearsay, bits and pieces and, obviously, all kinds of gos-sip which usually is loaded with lies!"

"Well, then, listen carefully and, if my aged mind leaves something out, you Sytalkis can let me know! It's been said the Filotas was a boastful fellow, bragging about our victories like they were his own doing and, many a time, feeling immune because of his old childhood friendship with Alexand-ros he downed the King's achievements quite openly.

I don't know if the recent death of his brother was of any factor, but, since he returned from Ekva-tana after Nikanor's funeral, he acted more and more like the world owed him everything and quick-er to criticize. Alexandros, faithful as always to his youth companions, pretended to see or hear no-thing!

Filotas was seeing the King along with most of us officers at least once a day. Now, when some of the pages recently arrived from home and full of themselves and hearing the complaints from the 'old school' on the King's new and 'Medizing' ways, unaccustomed to such hard work -as being relatively green horns- they thought of ridding themselves of such a 'slave-driver' and conspired to kill our King! Filotas heard of it because the best friend of the main plotter Dimnos -a young kid from Der-riopia- Nikomahos, I think, was his name, got scared and spilled the whole thing to Filotas.

Now Filotas had two chances to tell the King about it and he didn't! When Alexandros heard of it from others (Nikomahos went to ask for audience to Yfestion), said nothing and, at the dinner that night, he had Filotas join him, to see if the man would now say something. As Filotas still kept the knowledge to himself, Alexandros thought it was time to act.

He called the rest of us officers later on in secrecy and Yfestion told us of the suspicion. We recom-mended the suspects should be placed under arrest and questioned -under torture if necessary to be forced and tell us the truth. Alexandros agreed with reluctance because he didn't want to believe his boyhood friend would have any part in such deed.

Arriving at their tents for the arrest, Filotas resisted and was succumbed and Dimnos committed suicide. Nikomahos was also brought in and he named -trembling in fear- all the conspirators. They were ten of them, all pages entrusted with the King's life when sleeping! They had in mind to kill him in his sleep and had already arranged to be on duty together the following night, thus giving one-another support. They were all brought in, chained.

Filotas then was asked why he did not report what he knew to Alexandros, having so many chances to do so. He answered superficially that he had thought nothing of it looking at the King as if saying 'I dare you!' and laughed! The ten pages had already broken down and were accusing one-another and Filotas, trying to get away from sure punishment. They were all taken away for further interro-gation. Filotas kept his haughtiness for some time before breaking down under torture from Leon-natos, who always seemed to like measuring one's resistance to pain. Filotas eventually confessed.

The next morning all of them were brought to trial by the assembly of the whole army, the Maked-onian part of it of course. The others were just spectators and among them Sytalkis, Kalas, Attalos and Spadoklos. My self with Adamas, Aristos, Peridas and Agathon were among the judges of this assembly. The pages were pronounced guilty and were put to death by javelins. Filotas was brought last. He stood defiant and, when Alexandros sought to receive even a word of repentance, his answer to our King was what one would expect from a high opinionated of himself Filotas! He and his Father were the reason of us being where we were, conquerors and victorious! We voted him guilty and he had the same fate as the other conspirators.

Alexandros now was in a big dilemma. Should Parmenion be left alone to die in peace of old age? The old general had lost now all his sons. He might be very bitter against his King, right or wrong. He also had a big part of the army under his command, policing from Ekvatana where all the treasure was kept! His part of the army was mostly mercenaries and men who served under him for a very long time and felt fondness for the old man! Alexandros could not risk losing his road of com-munication with home and re-supplies of his army!

At Filotas' tent and among his personal items, a letter from Parmenion to his sons (sent before Nikanor's death) was found. Parmenion was telling his sons 'Care first for your well being and your family so we all can reach our end goal!...' Obviously, these words could mean nothing more than a Father's concern but, under the circumstances, could mean a lot more! This letter was presented to Alexandros and the handwriting of the old general was verified. Alexandros now had no other choice.

He sent Polydamos son of Illos from Lynkestis, escorted by Kleandros the Tymfean, 'uncle' Sytalkis and Menidas from Rahelous to kill Parmenion. They saw the King's dilemma; they understood it and executed their task with speed and mercy."

"I wouldn't have said it any better!" Sytalkis pointed after making sure Filippos was done with his narration. "Filotas' silence and obvious accomplice brought an edge between our King and the army!

Oh, there was still a lot of love to be demonstrated but the trust had faded now!"

"At the same time" Leonidas resumed "it was reported that among the conspirators was Amyntas son of Andromenis and his brothers Polemon, Simmias and Attalos. What made this report believ-able was that, when Filotas was apprehended, Polemon took off and was declared a renegade.

The other three brothers were then apprehended and -as by our laws and custom- were brought to trial before the assembly which, by now was in a very foul mood. Amyntas was brought first and he defended himself and his brothers with such a vigor and conviction that they were declared inno-cent, to the relief of our King who liked them. As for Polemon, Amyntas proposed he would bring his brother back and he kept his promise.

As it was found, Polemon got scared because he had developed a close relation with Filotas, being the latter's guest in every banquet occasion since the burning of the palace in Persepolis, though not so intimate a friend as to have the full confidence and share of secrets -aside trivial ones about women and plans of eventual favorite retirement places.

As it was, Alexandros saw the displeasure of some of the 'old school' officers in the fate of Filotas and Parmenion, although their fate was dictated by necessity and because of Filotas' arrogance to the end. The King now could not trust the leadership of the whole Agima of cavalry under one man! He, therefore, appointed two leaders to it. His most trusted friend Yfestion son of Amyntor and the son of Dropidas, Klitos 'the Black'.

With heavy heart, Alexandros continued and came to the region of the Ariaspians, a tribe who had assisted -in the old days- Kyros the Great and also Kamvysis serving them with honesty and thus gaining the name Ευεργετες - 'Benefactors'. Alexandros met with their leaders and they promised the same service to his person. The King accepted their offer with grace and bestowed upon them favors and their freedom to govern themselves as it was their custom.

During the festivities, he sacrificed to Apollon and their local deities and -in the spirit of good fel-lowship- he spared the life of Dimitrios son of Sympotas from Elimiotis, who was in charge of the King's personal guard. Dimitrios was demoted to serve in one of the foot Eteri taxis and his rank and place was given to Ptolemeos son of Lagos, the one rumored of being Alexandros' illegitimate bro-ther, since King Filippos was known to have had several illegal affairs with women in his youth, one of which was said to have been Ptolemeos' own mother. Ptolemeos has recently encouraged this rumor to resurface, obviously because it gives him now more 'legitimacy' in his holding of Egyptos and, having also the King's Soma in his charge, is of additional value to him!

Here there was one more little change in the re-structure of the cavalry. Having received names of Parmenion-Filotas sympathizers among the cavalry men, Alexandros set them up to serve on a new special ili. They proved the accusations false, as they distinguished themselves numerous times in the future. Taking matters on their own hands, the Eteri of both divisions (cavalry and foot) now warri-ed of any further conspiracies demanded the execution of the Lynkestian Alexandros who was left under restricted terms to live in Sardis.

Alexandros gave-in in this demand. Father, here, says it was a mistake the King giving-in (and 'uncle' Filippos agrees) as this decision was counteractive to the spirit of reconciliation and good fellowship our King was aiming for and the work of several flatterers who looked for self advancement. The Lynkestian Alexandros was among the first ones to declare for our King after his Filippos was assassinated and proved faithful even under confinement at Sardis.

Now Alexandros moved up Kafkasos, which was now found of not being the same one we had known by the Efxinos Pontos, on toward Vaktria. He bestowed this region to the Persian Proexis (Prohexana), leaving in charge of some troops for policing to Niloxenos son of Satyros, Imathian from Edessa.

The King easily subdued the region of Arahosia, building there yet another Alexandria, as he found a militarily important crossroad to do so. Finishing that task, Alexandros and the army moved onto the river Kofinos by Parapamissos, under rather severe conditions, for winter had settled in and Vis-sos -in his retreat- had burned the area to deprive us from any food.

The friendly Benefactors though, true to their promise, provided us with victuals assisted by the locals who shared all they had! Here our King learned that Sativarzanis had convinced the region of Aria to revolt. Alexandros also happened to have just received from Ekvatana the seasoned troops of Parmenion, as these were replaced by recruits from Ellas under the command of Kleandros.

Having those re-enforcements, Alexandros sent Artavazos with the mercenaries enlisted after Dar-ios' death along with Erygios and Karanos and six hundred cavalry from the city-states allies, with orders to Fratafernis to assist them by all possible means against Sativarzanis. These men obeyed his orders to the letter and, in a contested battle, killed Sativarzanis bringing Aria under our control again. The -until then- satrap of Aria Arsamis found irresponsible and in secret alliance with Sativ-arzanis, was replaced by Stasanor and put to jail.

Before crossing the river Oxos, Alexandros received back the army sent with Artavazos, Erygios and Karanos, their task completed. The King sent back home all those who had aged now, along with the Thessalian horse remained, discharged with all honors. On the way, the army passed Kofinos and the city of Drapsakos where it rested for a few days. Then, leaving

Arhelaos son of Androklos to man the high post of Aornos and making Artavazos governor of the area, Alexandros continued toward Oxos.

Arriving there, he found Vissos had destroyed all available boats and wood was scarce -as the area had been burned. Alexandros employed the same method as years back crossing Istros. As the river crossing was completed, he received envoys from Spitamenis and Datafernis asking for his pardon and they would undertake to bring Vissos in chains -thus proving their obedience to our King.

Having received such a proposition, Alexandros eased the pace of the army moving forward and sent Ptolemeos son of Lagos and Filotas son of Anteas from Almopia in charge of three iles, the Pro-dromi, the javeliners and a taxis of foot Eteri, along with half the Archers and Agrianians to go speedily toward Spitamenis and Datafernis.

Ptolemeos did what had been asked of him. Within four days he covered the distance of a regular ten day march! Arriving at the camp of Spitamenis, he learned that -although the two satraps were reluctant to deliver Vissos themselves had arranged that Vissos was at a near-by village with but very few of his troops. Ptolemeos then, left the foot Eteri in charge of Filotas with instructions to pro-ceed with caution and in battle order, took the cavalry in his disposal and encircled the village where Vissos was.

The self-proclaimed High King got caught by surprise and was captured alive, while his few sup-porters dispersed like terrorized animals do before the blazing fire of a forest. Ptolemeos sent word of it to Alexandros, asking how Vissos should be brought in. Alexandros asked the traitor should be brought before him naked, tied-up and with a in collar led by a halter!

When brought finally before him, Alexandros asked Vissos to explain why he had turned against his own King and relative, putting him first under arrest then killing him! To that Vissos answered that the deed wasn't done by him only but by a group of satraps concerned about their existence and looking for a new leader who would free them from Alexandros.

The King then ordered Vissos to be flogged and sent him back to be judged by his own peers and the surviving relatives of Darios. Vissos was put to death either at Zariaspa or Susa by being cruci-fied. The other satraps, Spitamenis, Datafernis, Katanis and Oxyartis were left alone, after promis-ing to rule their regions with justice and obey every command given to them by our King."

"There, we all thought that our adventures had come to an end!" Filippos intervened.

"Yes! We did and could not, would not understand why our King insisted on moving further!" Peridas added in all his seriousness, shaking his head with sadness. "We said to ourselves, here! We have accomplished what we came here for and now is our time to collect the fruits of our hard labor, and blood and we are bound for home and everlasting glory! Just have the King do the collecting of treasures for us back home and let us live now in luxury! If any of the young ones wants his share, let him be the one to come here and do the collecting…

We didn't come out and say so, as we would have done only few years back in Makedon. Oh, no! We thought we were too big, too accomplished to let our King know our thoughts and our desires! We certainly knew of his, his pothos and pathos to exceed the deeds of his ancestor Iraklis and even surpass -if possible and permitted- the very travels of god Dionysos! The ones of us in more intimacy with his person also knew he tried to stay away from Olympias, in spite of his love and respect toward his Mother! We decided we didn't need to consider him at all!

Our cowardice to face him like he would like us to, like he had so many times set the example him-self, didn't let us be men enough though we were the conquerors so fond of bragging about it! We were surprised he asked us to follow him further; still, keeping our thought to ourselves, we set forth pretending the same enthusiasm as before and conniving behind his back, always wanting more, al-ways thinking of the return, excellent new actors in the act of deceiving the one man who never kept a single secret of his heart from us!

You, Persians and Sogdians along with other Asians came to understand him more than us who grew-up with him and shared, originally, the same ideals and ideas! I have to acknowledge your perception and applaud your sincerity! You deserve much better than what you got after his death!"

The two Asians, Dimitrios and Kalas looked at him somberly and with visible pain of the great loss to all, more aware that their fate -not only as individuals- was hanging by a thread, depending on the luck or lack of having the next Alexandros grow-up and become their High King.

"You can not realize how costly the death of Alexandros can be to all of us, Persians and Ellines alike! Your race tends to forget much easier than ours wrong doings, except when those are a result of our actions! Take no offense, but I will play the role of the devil's advocate my friends by telling you what you may not want to hear!" said Kalas and continued "You, and I mean all of your tribes, be it Iones, Dorians, Makedonians or Ipirotes, islanders or residents of far off Sikelia, tend to blame whatever befalls you on anyone else except yourselves! You don't easily recognize what's good for you and, when that happens, you turn your back to it and ruin it with your ingratitude!

First and foremost, the Athinians who have the notion that civilization belongs solely to them and the rest of the world owes them internal gratitude for having two or three consecutive generations of extraordinary men! Their cockiness has grown to consider any thing out of their vision as unworthy and look at it with contempt, even when it could ultimately benefit them the most! That is exactly what brought them down in the first place but they -and you- will never learn! They blamed us, they blamed the Spartans, the Thivans and you for their folly and they will continue blaming, until their final demise...

Then, came the Spartans. They could have lead you all when their time came -almost did- but fell into the Athinian and Thivan trap and came to the High King for support and money, placing the rest of Ellas into a fiefdom they couldn't afford, let alone that it was being done with our money! They also blamed us and you for their fall, not themselves!

As for the Thivans, there's not much to say about those flip-flops! On our side of their own choice at the beginning, then with the Spartans and, finally, with their archenemy, Athinae! Alexandros did well when he let the Orhomenians and Plataeans do what they did! It should have been done earlier by Filippos! Of course, they also blame you for their 'misfortune' when they listened to Dimosthenis!

You, now, are not falling one step behind those, when you have accused your King and creator of your greatness for falling in love with a barbarian; for forcing you to Asian customs which he adopt-ed only to have the needed unity within his State; for having you marrying Asian ladies in an effort to broaden your narrow minds through them and see his reasoning! You turned your backs on him and blamed him for your success! Now, his generals are fighting, blaming one-another for their own folly and we haven't seen the end of it yet!

Aside from this small group -and that is the sole reason I joined you- everyone else in your race is blaming everybody else for his shortcomings! You still have the potential to become great, even greater than Alexandros, if -only- you learn to accept responsibility! I had to say that and, I hope, it offends you not, for I said it with the best interest in my mind and heart! I owe that to none other than Alexandros!"

Kalas sat down -he had stood up for emphasis to his words- and all remained in silence for a very long time, contemplating and wishing to have had the power to turn things back. Slowly, they re-turned to hushed conversation in small groups nodding and gesturing in despair. Then, Filippos stood and addressed Kalas but including also Dimitrios, Sytalkis, Attalos and Spadoklos.

"I am of the opinion that we received your message loud and clear -my esteemed friend! You are absolutely right and, as hard as it is for one to face one's own mistakes with clear mind, I think I can speak for the rest of us Makedonians and say that we are sorry! This is the reason why we have banded together, although the true substance was within us subconsciously! I have to say thank you for bringing it forth and my -personal- resolution is to remain your friend seeking advice when I falter and hoping that the same goes for the rest of this group, regardless background!"

They remained in place until very late hours, explaining, asking for further understanding and seeking support and resolution from one-another, for they recognized that their road -aside of being a very insecure one- had many hurdles to jump over on its long way to...where? Only the gods knew!

They finally retired amidst renewed oaths of fidelity and understanding.

"From here-on and until I get tired and be replaced by someone else, I would like to narrate the progress of our King and his army further into Asia." It was the voice of Koragos (Korbagha) son of Kalas coming from his corner in the semi-darkness after their evening meal the next day. Fall had come earlier this year and the chill of the nights had forced them to congregate indoors. Thankfully their new place was equipped with a huge audience room -the purchase done from the son of an old local land lord who had gone to seek his fortune in Egyptos and through proxy. Hence the semi-dark conditions (Aristos being in charge of the expenses could not see the need for extra torches).

The room had allowed them to have all of the group's members present, even the ones of the helpers and their families -except whoever was on duty to look out for any unwanted visitors. Those men having their rotation on regular basis, were missing very little of the whole story and were able to get the synopsis when their turn to participate was due. Koragos hearing no objection, he started his narration.

"Alexandros, followed by his reluctant but still obedient army, continued the march by a north-east direction and arrived at Kyropolis, the furthest point Kyros the Great had reached during his con-quest few hundred years before. The city is locat-ed close to the banks of river Iaxartis which it was mistaken as the river Tanais. Here some of the Makedonians sent ahead to secure victuals were ambushed by Skythian marauders and killed to the last man.

Alexandros went to meet them and found out that they were numbering about thirty thousand strong and occupied an excellently defendable location by a pass of the mountains. With his usual determination and lack of fear, the King attacked and received an arrow wound on his leg, breaking his fibula. The troops angered by this, attacked with added vigor (the King was still their King) and captured the place killing a great number and the Skythes asked for mercy. It was granted.

As Alexandros was by necessity carried on a litter for some time, the army came upon a town which was inhabited by the infamous Vranhides. These people's ancestors had committed a sacrilege. They had given the treasure of the temple of Apollon at Militos to Xerxis. When Militos was liberated by the Athinian fleet at the end of that war, to escape the wrath of the Ellines the Vranhides flew to the Persian court at Susa and Xerxis sent them to inhabit this town and keep them safe.

They lived on their own among the barbarians for over a hundred years in this region of Sogdiana.

Now that their descendants were found, atonement to the god had to follow. My father says that the King made another mistake by letting the courtiers and flatterers cloud his judgment and ordered the killing of all these descendants. We all know the respect Alexandros had for the gods, even those of foreign to him religions! Those unworthy courtiers played on that and got their wish enabling them later to accuse him as a blood thirsty dictator, denying any wrong doing on their part!

Alexandros then placed garrisons in this town, in Kyropolis and a few other towns along with clear-ing the defiles and passes to keep his lines secured. He then sent envoys to the Skythians beyond Iax-artis, willing to keep peaceful relations, unwilling to have the same lesson Darios the Great was taught by the Skythians above Istros long time past.

Things worked differently. No sooner the army moved out of the area and the Sogdians revolted by instigation of Vissos and Spitamenis in Marakanda, securing the help of the Skythians beyond the river. Alexandros was left with no other choice but to deal with each one separately and decisiveness and severity. The position the army was holding at this particular time was in many ways a very dif-ficult one. Away from any main support centers, in a mountainous country with unfriendly natives fired-up by ungrateful traitors who thought they could manipulate not only their subjects but also the magnanimity of a King who would gladly spare lives when thinking it as a productive measure of cooperation and mutually beneficiary.

Alexandros set the engineers to work immediately. New scales were constructed and carried by the men alongside with the portable, because they could be broken-down and reassembled, engines of siege. He sent Krateros to encircle Kyropolis and not let outside help get to it, while he marched against the neighboring smaller cities and towns.

The first day he took by direct assault two of them and leveled them to the ground, ensuring they could not be used soon again as centers of revolt. Who of the women and children were captured, the army kept them as potential income source -as you remember, they had given up all their former spoils of war recently so they could function with their former speed.

The following day, while the cavalry rode around to cut off any stragglers from town to town, the King assaulted the third city and then a fourth and a fifth. Most of the rebelled troops were slaugh-tered and the rest captured for the slave markets. Alexandros then moved to meet with Krateros at Kyropolis, encircled by the latter's men.

While surveying the walls to find the best sector for attack, he noticed a small confluence of Iaxartis was passing under the walls and through the city. Seeing that its water was rather low, he returned to camp and called an officers' assembly. He assigned each one's sector of activity and asked them to be as precise as humanly possible, for -by doing so- it could save many a life! They were to keep the de-fenders busy, attacking certain sectors with apparent vigor. He stationed the Ypaspistes and the Agi-ma with the Agrianians opposite to the gate closest to the small river and he, taking few seasoned foot Eteri went unobserved into the water and under the city wall.

As the defenders got side-tracked by the offense at the pre-arranged sectors, Alexandros and his men overtook the few guards of that gate and opened it to the stationed troops across it. The Agrian-ians and Ypaspistes rushed into the city and a fierce battle took place from street to street. Alexand-ros got wounded again on the head and neck, as did Krateros, 'uncles' Attalos, Filippos, Sytalkis and Dimitrios and many other men and officers.

About eight thousand rebels lost their lives and about as many managed to close themselves in the acropolis of the city but had to surrender the next day due to lack of water. Many of the inhabitants were chained and all these cities and towns were destroyed. Alexandros sent the surviving ring lead-ers to be dispersed in far areas, preventing any further uprising in the area. Our king proved one more time that he was true to his word and expected the same from all who he dealt with! He lavish-ed the ones who kept their word of honor and punished severely the ones who didn't!

Aware of the Skythian tribes of Massagaetes, Daans and Sakes were ready to cross the river in support of the rebels and encouraged by Oxyartis, Katanis, Horienis (Khoriyiana) and Aoustanis (Khaostana), he saw he had to face them before dealing with Spitamenis. He sent therefore Andromahos, Menidimos and Karanos with one taxis and two iles of cavalry of Ellines mercenaries to see if they could keep Spitamenis busy and he moved to Iaxartis sending ahead a trusted interpreter by the name Farnoukis (Bharnug-yioush), still hoping to arrange peace with the Skythians.

He found them still at the far side of the river, taunting him and daring him to cross, the interpreter being unsuccessful -although proven of being a very capable man. Alexandros offered sacrifices before moving on, as was always his custom. Aristandros though saw the omens being unfavorable and the King had to wait for a few days. Next time he sacrificed Aristandros prophesized that any attempt that day would endanger the King's own life. To that, Alexandros said that he could risk injury in a better way than enduring the taunting of the barbarians!"

"I remember his exact words!" Dimitrios said. "I happened to be on duty, part of his Asian taxis of Guards for the initial assault across the river and lucky enough to be about ten paces away from the altar where he stood by! He said: 'There is not always a choice available in time of war! I would pre-fer better omen but I cannot afford let the Skythians go unpunished, for it would encourage the Vaktrians more! I have to attack now or we will lose if remain in defense!' and he prepared to cross!"

"He had the men prepare skins filled with dry brush -as at Istros some years ago- and rafts for the horsemen and the sarissa falanxes. The horses were to swim across, held by tethers. To protect them he ordered the vallistes to send barrages of arrows, one of which killed one of the barbarian leaders.

The Skythians surprised by the distance of the throw moved further inland in respect. Alexandros, although not fully recovered by his previous wounds, crossed first on his raft! The trumpeters were ordered to sound their trumpets as loud as possible and the Archers with the peltastes crossed ahead of the others, crying our war cry and covering the crossing of the others with arrows, javelins and stones." Dimitrios now nodded to Koragos to resume his narration.

"As our cavalry crossed, they immediately were forming their iles and Alexandros sent first the mercenary cavalry and four iles of Prodromi against the Skythians. Although these men were about one thousand strong, the Skythians gave them a hearty reception by running their horses to them, volleying their arrows and retreat as speedily as they came thus creating a good measure of injuries on our horses, putting the iles in peril of losing their battle cohesiveness.

Alexandros perceiving the danger called around him the Archers, the Agrianian horse and the Pel-tastes under Valakros and led the whole cavalry as one body, forcing the Skythes to abandon their tac-tics and face us head-on. The King had the bugler sound and a strong detachment of light cavalry of the Prodromi veered and fell on the flank of the enemy while Alexandros himself led the Agima and two other iles as a wedge. The Skythians panicked and fighting in a way totally unfamiliar, lost more than a thousand dead and retreated as fast as they could, leaving us with more than one hundred prisoners.

Because of the heat and unsuitable water in the area, our pursuit was soon to end. Added to that was the sudden illness of our King! Alexandros being weak from his recent wounds and taxied severely during this river crossing and the ensued battle made the mistake of drinking some of the available stagnant water. Thus, Aristandros' prophesy came true! Alexandros was carried back and remained seriously ill for several days. In lives, this battle cost us over one hundred killed and more than one thousand wounded but the booty eased the mood of the men, as we captured over one thousand camels and plenty of gold and silver decorations from the enemy dead bodies and prison-ers.

Our victory though caused the Skythes to ask for terms and, in few days, they sent us envoys with the Skythian king's apology, claiming that those troops we encountered were nothing but marauders who would be punished by him in due course. Meantime, he offered his allegiance to Alexandros who accepted the excuse, not willing to engage in protracted war with them in such vastness of a complet-ely unknown country. As I said, Darios' the Great case in Skythian warfare was a lesson our King remembered well. He knew now his reputation as undefeated would be his best security at that front-ier!

He returned to base and built a new Alexandria the so-called Eshati, being the furthest one beyond Kyros' own Kyropolis which was now in ruins. At this new Alexandria, the King left who of the vet-eran troops were near retirement but had no real place to go to and some volunteered locals and for-tified it well so it could be used as a deterrent to possible future uprisings or incursions.

During this time, Spitamenis -thinking he could have a free hand as we were engaged with the Sky-thes- attacked our troops stationed in Marakanda. He was bitten-off by our garrison and retired to the west mountain range when he heard that Alexandros had send reinforcements. When Androma-hos, Menidimos and Karanos arrived in Marakanda, having in mind to prove to Alexandros their bravery and -at the same time- get rid of Spitamenis, they followed him.

He retreated crossing the river and managing to obtain the help of some nomadic Skythians. The three men in charge of our expeditionary force decided to attack. Spitamenis selected a level plain near the Skythian desert and, riding around the falanx in circles, did what the Skythians tried to do when fighting against Alexandros. Andromahos did not have the quick mind of our King and was fooled to constant movements against an enemy who had plenty of fresh horses. Soon, our soldiers got tired and became easy prey. Farnoukis, who had joined our men and was a negotiator rather than a fighter, refused to accept the leadership of the expedition and so did Menidimos and Karanos.

Andromahos saw a solution by retreating to a cluster of trees observed by the near-by small river named Politimitos and headed his troops toward it, without organizing common action with the other two leaders. Karanos tried to cross the river and most of the foot soldiers followed his horse iles. The barbarians who kept a close look for an opportunity, crossed above and beyond putting our men under two fronts and, soon, they encircled us again throwing the falanx to disarray!

Some cavalry and foot made it to a small island in the midst of the stream but they were attacked there also, as Spitamenis and his Skythes could volley our men with arrows from a distance. Most were killed and, the few who were captured were tortured first and then put to death! Out of all our men, we lost close to two thousand able men, more than all our loss during this whole campaign!

Hearing of this disaster, Alexandros left Krateros to follow with the bulk of the army while he took half the Eteri cavalry, the Ypaspistes, half the Archers, the Agrianians and Peltastes and covered the distance to Marakanda in only four days! Spitamenis retreated again toward Politimitos river in hope of repeating his recent achievement but in vain. This time he was dealing with Alexandros!

The King went to the place of the unfortunate battle and buried all our dead he could find with honors. He then returned and let the army take its anger against all those Sogdians who had support-ed Spitamenis. Several thousand were put to death and all the fortified towns and cities in the vicinity were destroyed! As we have learned from my Father and 'uncle' Dimitrios -and the rest of you I might add- this was one of the few times our King let his anger get the best out of him, as many inno-cent had to pay the price of the few guilty ones!

Because Spitamenis had gone into hiding beyond the Skythian desert, Alexandros now moved his army into those parts of Vaktria that had supported the insurrection, leaving in charge of Marakan-da Pefkolaos with three thousand troops. Here the locals rushed to pro-claim their fidelity and the King became once more magnanimous toward them. Some of the leaders of the insurrection though had taken refuge in high mountainous places. For the time being though, Alexandros rested the army at Zariaspa where we received reinforcements.

Here the King added to his dress more Asiatic customs -to the detriment of most Ellines in his army.

We all now know -at least us here- the reason of his so-called change of mind and habits. He had not really change neither his mind nor his habits as Ellinas Makedonian. He just regretted his unneces-sary roughness on the Sogdians like he had on the Thivans years past. He now wanted to make amend and show his subjects that he was the legitimate successor of Darios and, as such, he had the absolute power for their fate but -also- he was one with them too! Once he could not bring the dead back, he couldn't see or find another more convincing way of showing his regret.

The reinforcements were brought to him in Zariaspa led by Nearhos who -until then- was satrap of Lykia, Asandros the satrap of Karia, Asklipiodoros the regent of Syria, his second in command Me-nis, by Epokillos from Idonia, Menidas and Ptolemeos from Sintiki who was left to govern Thraki but had personal problems with Antipatros and was now sent to Alexandros. The total number of these troops was seventeen thousand foot and two thousand six hundred cavalry.

In order to permanently secure our positions and possession of the proper Persian plateau, the full submission of Vaktria and Sogdiana had to be achieved and settled once and for ever! Alexandros had no other choice. As soon as the last betrayers of Darios, Arsamis and Varzanis were brought in by Fratafernis and Stasanor and put in chains, Alexandros got ready to move and subdue the few chieftains who had taken on to the mountains.

Just before that, he received an embassy from the new Skythian king. The previous one died and his brother now was the king and wanted Alexandros' friendship, offering his own services to Alexan-dros and also inviting him to marry one of his own daughters, so their alliance would be even more sincere. There came also another embassy from Horasmia, the land between Kaspian and Aral Seas led by their king Farasmenis (Varash-menuch), who feared that Alexandros thought of him being Spitamenis' ally. Alexandros received both delegations with due respect and had them conclude the alliances with Artavazos whom he had appointed satrap of Vaktria.

Having established garrisons in so many places, Alexandros did not have with him at this point more than ten thousand first line soldiers and hearing that the old conclusion of the Kaspian Sea be-ing part of the Okeanos (Ocean) was just a tall tale with vast regions of land and people all along, politely told Farasmenis that he had to campaign first in India and -upon a victorious return- he would gladly unite forces with the Skythian king to conquer that part of the world too. Unlike the courent suitors of the kingdom, he had knowledge of people and his own limits. He avoided unneces-sary adventures and kept the Skythian happy!

Father says -and I found that most of you are of the same opinion- that Alexandros brought India in his conversation with Farasmenis simply as an excuse. He developed the desire to conquer India for sure only later, after Klitos' death and after his own marriage to Roxana, by invitation of Indian kings themselves.

Meantime, the Sogdians decided to revolt once again and were giving Pefkolaos hard time even in keeping the vicinity of Marakanda in order! The lesson given to them by Alexandros instead of calm-ing them down had the opposite result. Many joined the small chieftains up on the mountains or at their fortified abodes and were raiding the country side and isolated caravans with supplies and commodities! Fortunately,

Spitamenis was still hiding in the lands of the Massagaetes and was not there to take advantage.

With the new reinforcements, Alexandros made up his mind to look after the problem and resolve it for good. He sent the taxis of Polyperhon, Attalos from Mygdonia, Gorgias son of Ypolikos and Mele-agros' ili of light cavalry to police some areas of Vaktria thought of being ready to revolt also and he took the rest of the army divided into six sectors under Yfestion, Ptolemeos son of Lagos, Perdikkas son of Orontis, Artavazos, Kinos and himself, to deal with the chieftains of the Sogdians who had not united but acted independently. The rest of the army was left to camp to continue reorganization and much needed rest.

Getting by the river Oxos, the King camped near a spring which sprung both water and a black substance which can be ignited and burn. Aristandros foresaw victory after this omen but one with many victims. He was right again. The Sogdians made the mistake to close themselves in forts instead of using the vastness and mountains of their region. Our men took each one and finally met at Mara-kanda. Alexandros' column went as far as the river Margos and the city of Marginia/Antiohia, build-ing on his way six forts of our own, in order to keep the tribe of Daans in check.

Here in Marakanda Alexandros let his anger get the best of himself! As it has being mentioned, few officers of the 'old guard' had given the King reason to be temperamental with their complaints of him having turned Asiatic, because he was trying to please and return the respect he was getting from his new subjects who were unaccustomed to our simple ways in relations between citizens and the King.

There was a banquet organized to celebrate the recent victories and all the officers were invited to participate. Naturally, Klitos son of Dropidas was there too. Alexandros -as was always his custom-

started his day with a sacrifice to the Olympian gods, Iraklis and the Dioskouri, accidentally omitting Dionysos. He then took care of state matters and his daily bath and went to the hall arranged for a brief audience first, followed by the banquet.

Klitos delayed his sacrifice because of some urgent matters with his cavalry ili, trying to deal with some men who had differences and were bickering and finally managed to bring them to an agree-ment, after having shared with them quite a few cups of local wine. Then, took his intended sacrifice victim (a ram) to the altar but, realizing he was already late for the banquet, he tied the ram by the altar leaving the duty to be performed by any priest or accolade who would come next and went into the hall.

Inside the hall the banquet had already started and few rounds of drinks were passed, as people were eager to celebrate and, at the same time, invoke the grace of the King upon them. They were liberal with their praises calling Alexandros greater than the Dioskouri and even greater than his ancestor Iraklis. As I had several conversations in the past with my Father who was present at that banquet and seated close to Alexandros, I can tell that the King was a bit 'under the weather' him-self and, although he most definitely knew who was trying to flatter him, he was accepting such obvious attempts with a smile and very casually. Perhaps he needed to hear it, in want of love return-ed to him by a recently restless army.

In any event, Klitos being from the 'old guard' and having served under Filippos with great dis-tinction, thought the flattery was too much to bear. Being also intimate with Alexandros since the King's infancy and having saved his life at Granikos, gave him more confidence to voice his disap-proval. On top of it, he was displeased with Alexandros' recommendation to have Klitos placed as the satrap of recently pacified Vaktria. He thought he was side-stepped by the King and destined to be left behind, away from the real action of future glory.

With that and the wine consumed prior to his arrival at the banquet, Klitos let his mouth be free of any restrain and, in the presence of all, started downgrading Alexandros' accomplishments and praising first and foremost Filippos and then the capability of the army as a whole and himself as a distinguished leader he was!

At the beginning, Alexandros listened with the smile still on his face, letting an old friend to vent his small grievances. As Klitos progressed with his insults and came to dispute the Oracle's call on Alex-andros from Ammon at Siva as the son of Dias and scolding the King for his semi-Asiatic dress he was wearing at the banquet, Alexandros let his displeasure be shown and, having had quite a few cups of wine himself, the argument soon became a loud insult exchange, in spite the efforts of many more somber mutual friends to bring it to a stop!

Alexandros then called for the Ypaspistes and Pages on duty to put Klitos under arrest. Either be-cause of being caught unexpectedly by this severe verbal fight or because they loved Klitos for his long standing record, they were reluctant to move. That made Alexandros angrier and moved against his old friend on his own but was restrained by my Father, 'uncle'

Filippos and Yfestion, while Ptole-meos with 'uncle' Sytalkis and some others forced Klitos out of the hall.

One would think that the incident had come to an end but for Klitos who reentered the hall from another door and called upon the King by saying: 'As a reminder for your achievements, oh son of Dias, I am back here to show you that thanks to this hand of mine you are still alive and bragging!'

No one was fast enough to move, as all the guests had gone back to their drinking and talking think-ing Klitos was gone and would stay away. Alexandros, infuriated by the new insult, jumped and snatching the javelin off the hands from a dumbfounded junior Page on duty, sent it flying dead cen-ter at Klitos' chest! Klitos fell on the floor instantly dead -like one stricken by Dias' own thunderbolt!

Father says there was a long silence and immobilization among all, including Alexandros. The King's eyes had almost come out of their sockets in disbelief of his own deed and all the blood was drained off his face in horror and rejection! Then, Alexandros let a dreaded cry and rushed to the body of his fallen friend. He extracted the javelin and, embracing the dead Klitos, he begged him to rise, while cursing himself for his so un-pious act and irreverence to sacred friendship!

Then, with another sudden move, Alexandros picked the same javelin up, steadied it between floor and the wall and tried to fall upon it and commit suicide! This time people were ready for anything and Yfestion with Ptolemeos and 'uncle' Filippos managed after a hard struggle to prevent the new and most serious catastrophe from happening!

They took the sobbing Alexandros to his quarters and tried to console him -to no avail. The King ordered everyone to leave, his chamberlain -the former Darios' eunuch- Vagoas to place heavy drapes over the windows looking at the inner yard and sent him also away, bolting the door behind him! Every one was afraid the King might kill himself somehow locked in there, but Yfestion and Vagoas reassured all that they had made sure no weapon or any other dangerous object was left in the King's access.

Alexandros remained in his rooms clearly heard in his pain by all who periodically would pass and try to convince him to come out! He remained without any food and water for three days! Finally, 'uncle' Filippos with Yfestion had Aristandros the seer come to the door and call upon the King by saying that it was god Dionysos' revenge for not being honored with sacrifice before the banquet and not the King's own fault!

Even then, Alexandros didn't want to listen and come out but he was finally convinced, by hearing of the verdict the whole army pronounced -after hearing all the details of the unfortunate event. The soldiers, foot and cavalry, Peltastes and Ypaspistes, allies and mercenaries sent their officers to beg the King to come out, making sure their own clamor and calls could be heard through the stone walls of the house the King was in!

Alexandros agreed to come out and it was obvious to all he had paid his dues through pain and remorse! He didn't even let them prepare his bath -an unheard thing all these years- before offering sacrifice to Dionysos and asking the god for forgiveness! He then ordered the preparation for an extravagant pyre and funeral for Klitos, while he wrote a personal letter of apology and request for forgiveness to Klitos' older sister and Alexandros' own youth nurse, Elaniki, again cursing himself for being such an unfaithful friend!" Here Koragos stopped as they reflected somberly on the past. He promised to continue the following evening tough and they all went to their rooms to rest.

The next late afternoon and after their meal, Koragos true to his promise continued. "There were two more important events which took place around the same time as winter was approaching in that area. One was the death of Spitamenis who had given more than enough trouble to our garrisons in Vaktria and Sogdiana.

His last achievements were the ravaging of the vicinity of Zariaspa and the killing of Aristonikos with about sixty other horsemen and wounding Pithon seriously and taking him prisoner. Krateros, who was sent after Spitamenis by Alexandros, moved in and forced the Persian to retreat again in the lands of the Massagaetes, after a battle in which Spitamenis lost some one hundred and fifty men.

Spitamenis refused yet to give-up. He returned with Skythian reinforcements and advanced to Vagae where Kinos was waiting for him and defeated him with a loss of over eight hundred men. The Skythians hearing that Alexandros was also approaching after a successful siege and capture of the strong fort of Sisimithris (Sihchimidra), they decided to make peace and, to save themselves from further pursuit, they killed Spitamenis and sent his head to the King. Now Sogdiana and Vaktria could be rebuilt, for the countryside had been devastated by Spitamenis' raids. The last remaining of the conspirators on Darios' death was Datafernis but even him was captured by the Daans and was sent to Alexandros.

The second major event was not a happy one. The narrow thinking of many about the King's Asian court procedures, his dress and his appointments of Persians to high positions, was the complaint of many, in subdued tones. The recent killing of Klitos although sanctioned by the army, kept the dis-tance between the men and their King as it got fueled by one other misunderstanding.

Since old times, Asiatics revered their kings by performing a sort of prostration in their presence. We Ellines, give such an honor to the images of our gods and to long dead and deified heroes, in-cluding Alexandros' late Father Filippos. The Asiatics, out of habit and Alexandros out of policy, continued this custom. The 'old guard' disliked the gesture but many flatterers -some of them even among the same 'old guard'- started advising the King to have everybody prostrate in his presence.

Alexandros thought the idea was good, in his desire to even up the status of all and make his long sought dream of equality among the citizens of his state, with him as the focal point. It is also possible that Alexandros saw the act as a true indication of love toward him and, as a well known personality of always seeking the love from the ones he was loving, he thought nothing of it. We could know for sure only if he had explained or if Yfestion, Krateros, Perdikkas and Ptolemeos had made his think-ing public.

Out of all of them, four went to meet their ancestors and Ptolemeos is not about to divulge any of the intimate secrets shared with his King (and possibly half-brother). In any event, Alexandros liked the idea and, even because of the Ammon's proclamation at Siva, he indicated he would welcome it.

Obviously, any and all flatterers jumped on the opportunity to show their 'devotion' and the others kept their thoughts from him, only to whisper their disdain in private. Their later explanation was that they feared for their lives, for they didn't want to have Filotas' and Klitos' fate. I think we all have agreed here that this is only an excuse, for the fate of the first was derived by necessity and the second's purely by an intoxicated person's anger and the imprudence of the victim.

As things developed, at another reception of tribe ambassadors, well wishers and petition holders and with the opportunity given by the Asiatic greeting by prostration, Anaxarhos from Avdira the sophist who was following our campaigns and was among the flattering ones, delivered a speech in favor of this prostration by praising the deeds of Alexandros presenting him greater than Iraklis and equal to Dionysos! Anaxarhos was also among the ones who told Alexandros (after the death of Kli-tos) that, as being the son of Ammon-Zefs, Alexandros could have done nothing wrong!

Kallisthenis, the nephew of Alexandros' teacher Aristotelis and self-appointed history writer (an equally flattering person in the past -but now on the side of the 'old guard'), retorted by chastising Anaxarhos, saying that Alexandros would definitely deserve such honors -but only after his death.

Turning to the King, Kallisthenis reminded him that he was not a Kyros or Kamvysis but the son of Filippos and that no true Ellinas should bend in prostration before a living person, regardless of that person's achievements! He added that neither the Athinians, nor the Spartans ever prostrated before Xerxis, nor did Alexandros himself bent his head before the late Darios! That deliverance sobered Alexandros and -for the time being- the request was dropped.

The Persian magnates present and all other Asians, continued their customary prostration, until Leonnatos thought that one of them failed to perform properly due to his age and laughed at him. The King became angered, not because of the failure to be properly greeted but for Leonnatos' im-prudence and lack of respect to an elderly person. He got up and punched Leonnatos, sending him sprawling on the floor. The latter was wise enough to ask for forgiveness and retired from the reception.

Spirits got agitated as word reached the rank and file again but, with the request for prostration dropped now, things seemed to return back to normal but not for long. New Pages had recently ar-rived from Makedonia, many of them with the cockiness and attitude of conquerors, like they were the ones who led the army to victories! One of them was Ermolaos son of Sopolis and his behavior had cost him to lose the right to ride as well as a demotion.

Ermolaos vexed, conspired with another like him, the son of Amyntas Sostratos. Wanting to show to his friends that he had a mind of his own and -according to old Makedonian customs- he was just about an equal free citizen as the King, he demonstrated hid defiance at a hunt, by killing a boar di-rected toward Alexandros without waiting for the King's privilege to aim and discharge first.

The offense was not a major one and that was the reason Alexandros did not react to it immediately.

The deed though was performed in the presence of others, Makedonians and Persians and the flatter-ers in the court took advantage again to remind the King that he should not tolerate such immodesty from a subject of his. Alexandros then admonished Ermolaos once more, ordering the deliverance of the customary twenty lashes on Ermolaos' back before the whole array of the Pages in a morning presentation. Because it took the King few days after the event to do so, Ermolaos then presented himself to his friends as one being maltreated with no reason.

He and his best friend Sostratos then, approached Antipatros son of Asklipiodoros and Epimenis son of Arseas, as well as Antiklis son of Theokritos and Filotas son of the Thrakian Karsidas to bring them in their conspiracy, intending to assassinate Alexandros in his sleep when their turn would come to be the guards by the royal tent.

The gods did not allow this to happen as Alexandros had been invited to the tent of 'uncle' Dimit-rios for some drinking among friends the very night the conspirators were assigned to guard. As the night progressed and the party was about to come to its end, a woman named Syra approached the King and asked the whole company to continue their revelry, for god Dionysos was in need of more respect paid to his name.

Syra being of a repute as a woman with special powers given to her by the gods was obeyed and the party continued until morning hours thus foiling the plan of the 'would be' assassins. At the same time Epimenis either because he got scared, changed his mind or was too frustrated with the failure, talked about it to his best friend Hariklis son of Menandros who -in turn- informed Epimenis' broth-er Evrylohos. Evrylohos then went to the King's tend and, finding Ptolemeos son of Lagos who was there in duty as leader of the body guards, told him everything.

The conspirators were apprehended at once and put to questioning, one talking against the others -to save himself. Among other names, the name of Kallisthenis was involved in the conspiracy, as the philosopher and writer was said to have tutored the conspirators to rid the Ellines of tyrants -like the Athinians Armodios and Aristogiton had in old times and who's statues were rescued in Persepolis and sent back to Athinae not long ago. This implicated him greatly. Did he mean that Alexandros had -in Kallisthenis' opinion- become a tyrant or were his teachings misunderstood by the conspira-tors? No one ever found out the truth.

The truth to be told, Kallisthenis was not named as an active member of the conspiracy. His com-ments though on our King's behavior toward the Persians and adaptation of partially Persian attires during audiences and ceremonies by Alexandros was not in favor of the philosopher. He was placed under surveillance and was excluded from participating in most of the King's functions, until his death few years later. Because Kallisthenis was Aristotelis' nephew, the old Alexandros' teacher, the King now became distant and correspondence between them stopped. All of the conspirators were judged by the army assembly and, found guilty, were put to death. The King now became suspicious of just about everybody, except the most trusted friends around him and the ever-present flatterers."

> "I will argue that Alexander was a kind of un-
> acknowledged protofeminist, limited multy-
> culturalist and a religious visionary who plan-
> ned to establish a world empire of the 'best'."
> Excerpt from the preface on 'Alexander – the Ambiguity of Greatness'
> A book by Guy MacLean Rogers, Ph.D. in Classics - American

IV

Here Koragos stopped his narration and the talk for a while was some exchange of opinions and questions from the ones who were writing and missed few passages here and there, for verification.

Dimitrios and Kalas supported the view which Alexandros had adopted, a thing which Peridas and Filippos found very natural as their friends were a Persian and a Sogdian. Their own opinion was that Alexandros had moved too fast, too soon and without any preparation to ease the minds and worries of his fellow countrymen. Adamas, Sytalkis and Aristos were of the opinion that the King had conveyed his thoughts and desires to his trusted subordinates who were to transmit them to the rank and file but failed him. As for Agathon, Timeos and Spadoklos, they had only one wish: The King to have been alive and well!

"We all wish that!" Filippos called after hearing their say. "That is not the point! Alexandros was sharp enough and he should have seen the division in depth! If we failed him -and we did- by not understanding him, he should have taken the time to explain, the time to gradually introduce his innovations!"

"How much time should he devote in teaching you his openness of mind?" Dimitrios protested. "He started showing the way right after the battle at Granikos and the taking of Sardis, by appointing the local dignitaries in positions of trust! From that time until his death, ten years passed! You, Filippos, was among the ones who were taught by Aristotelis and within less than three years you considered yourselves educated enough by him! Did Alexandros have to teach you for ten years prior to his undertaking the expedition? If so, you would still be here dreaming of an empire to come!"

Filippos looked at his friend with surprised sadness. "Your point would be well taken if you had considered one main element! Aristotelis was teaching us familiar subjects and, further, he consider-ed you Persians as people who should be subjected and become servants, not equal to us! We did need the time to adjust and the King did not give it to us!

You know well -and all of you do- how my family is devoted to the Timenides from time lost in the folds of memory! You know I did follow his lead just because of that devotion and, yet, I can honestly tell you I did not understand until we -you Kalas and the rest of us- bonded together because we all loved him, albeit many for different reasons and through various perspectives!

Even now, bonded as we are in the common sorrow of his death and the hope a capable heir will succeed him, is here anyone who can honestly declare he understood Alexandros completely? There could have been one, Yfestion, as Alexandros confided everything there was to his best friend! But Yfestion died before the King and, besides, you all know how high he held himself against all of us! If Alexandros did not bother or was incapable of transmitting his ideas and ideals to us, Yfestion was the man who would keep those to himself -just to be one step ahead of everybody!

We all came to accept each-other for what each one of us actually is, only after each one's personal loss of a King we all loved and admired for many but various and different reasons of our own. Can you tell me you understood Alexandros motives completely? What if he had taken the invitation of the Skythes and turned to Evropi to marry one of their princesses? What if -doing so- he would find the Skythians deserving more honors than Persians or Ellines combined? Would you still tell me I did not learn fast enough to adjust or would you be joining me listening to a Skythian telling what you just did a while ago?"

"We all have agreed we loved the King, each according to one's measure and we have bonded in a friendship because we understood him better than most, albeit partially and with a measure of self justification. We are only human and so was he! Deification (we called his request for prostration as such, not the Persians) may have been his end of means to get people unified under him and marriage between races its supplement. But we did not see the meaning of it and that's that! Do we understand now? Probably not completely, judging by our process in conversation, but surely we are better than the jackals who are in power now and hold the royal family as hostages!" Sytalkis intervened in a tone of an arbitrator who didn't want a difference among friends to lead to any confrontation of any kind.

"Will we ever understand?" he continued "Hard to tell, as the judge who could tell us is dead and the gods remain silent! My opinion is, my friends, that if we manage to fully accept one-another and keep our friendship and aims in good standing, regardless temporary deviations and minor disagree-ments, if we learn to accept -each- all the others just for who and what we are, then, rest assured the dream of our King has been understood and fulfilled -at least by us here!"

They all shook their heads in thoughtful agreement and their conversation continued softly well into the night…

Late the following afternoon and while the able women were preparing the evening meal and the younger ones were setting the chairs and tables and brought small craters full of Makedonian wine promptly filling the cups of the men, Lamvros the son of Attalos continued the narration in clear voice, keeping attention at the same time on the speed of the ones who were writing the story and stopping here and there so they could catch-up with his speech.

The working to prepare the meal women of age had already heard everything there was to be known and they were the teachers of the young ones during idle times, especially in winter, gathered around the hearth for warmth. Presently they approached the tables and gave each male his portion of meat, white goat cheese, some garlic or onion (according to individual preference) served them-selves and sat down to hear Lamvros.

"…The army quartered at Nautaka for the winter and many delegates were arriving from all the corners of the kingdom to petition, present or complain to the King. Krateros' body of the army along the one under Kinos arrived there, as did Fratafernis from Parthia and Stasanor, from his satrapy in Aria.

Alexandros ordered Fratafernis to replace and arrest Aftofradatis who was accused as neglecting a direct order of the King, governing the regions of Mardia and Tarpuria. Stasanor was sent to Dran-giana as commander,

Atropatis replaced Oxydatis in Midia and Stamenis was sent to rule the Vavy-lonian satrapy, as it was learned that Mazaeos had died. Meantime, Alexandros sent Sopolis, Epokil-los and Menidas to Makedonia to organize new recruiting.

As spring approached, Alexandros moved the army toward a high and well defended place called the Sogdian Rock. At that rock, many rebel Sogdians had gathered with supplies to last over a year a siege and among them were the wife, his sons and daughters of the Vaktrian Oxyartis. Arriving at the location Alexandros saw indeed that the rock was a very difficult place to attack. From all sides the approach was problematic, not only because of the steepness of the rock but also because of the snow fallen in such early spring.

Alexandros -as in most cases- initially tried to negotiate a honorable settlement but the Sogdians did not accept any terms. On the contrary, they laughed at our offers as they were sure their high place was providing them absolute security. Obviously, this insult was not received in good humor by our King and the challenge presented became an obsession. Among the teasing from the defenders was the dare for us to find men who could fly first before we would put any serious claim on their strong-hold!

Alexandros could not possibly pass this kind of insult without a proper answer! He asked for some volunteers raised on the high mountains of our Makedonia and promised twelve talents to the one who would manage to climb the rock first! To the second man reaching the summit, he promised the half amount and went on until the last to climb would receive three times a hundred gold Persian coins called Darics. Before long, three hundred volunteers presented themselves equipped with small iron pegs taken from the camp tents to be used as anchors during the rock climbing. They also had long lines of rope made from flax, so they could pull one-another up.

The men started that same night their climb, using the pegs and the ropes. About thirty of them fell to their death and were later found and buried with special honors. Among them was Eforos son of Menon from Orestis, cousin to our 'uncle' Filippos from house Agis and Polemon son of Igesippos from Paeonia, distant nephew of 'uncle' Adamas and member of house Damasias. Their families, as well as the families of the other fallen braves, were declared exempt of any taxation for as long as the King lived!

In any event, the next morning Alexandros called the defenders to negotiate before it was too late. They still laughed at him, sure of their security up on that rock. Then, the King asked them to look up, at the summit of the rock, behind the cave they had as their living quarters. To their amazement, our men were stationed there ready to descent upon the rebels. Truth to be told, our men were not properly equipped for battle, as most of their gear had to be left behind the night before so they could climb up. The rebels did not know that of course and their amazement was such, they sur-rendered at once!

It was then when our King first set eyes on Oxyartis' daughter Rhoksana (Roxani in our language) and fell in love with her. Alexandros had a person to person talk with Oxyartis and the terms of sur-render were sealed by setting the wedding date at the end of two weeks hence, to give time for the resettlement of the people on the rock the installation of a strong guard there (the King had safety always in mind) and local dignitaries to prepare and attend.

The sudden -to our officers and troops- decision of the King to marry and, for that matter, to marry a barbarian subject came as a shock! Many, including Yfestion, 'uncle' Filippos, Kinos and even Krateros and Ptolemeos, advised against such honor given to rebels with no word of honor! The men were afraid that Oxyartis with his new prestige as the father-in-law would persuade not only the locals but people from other provinces and satrapies to revolt again, the minute the army would move forth.

They were also puzzled by the sudden manner our King fell in love with a woman who was beautiful -no question about that- but not near as beautiful as the late wife of Darios. If Alexandros did not fall for the charms of the captive woman of an enemy and fugitive king while he had full control and access of and to her, what Roxani had done to attract Alexandros' passion? Was it her dance at the dinner after the surrender of the rebels? The eunuch Vagoas -taken along with the harem of Darios after Issos and Gavgamila- was a much better and more sensual dancer than her!

None thought of Alexandros not having any preference to other than female gender although he oc-casionally would attend eunuch performances when asked by a good friend and not wanting to hurt feelings. Nor that he respected Darios' wife for what she was: the wife of another man and he respected her. As for his occasional relation with the widow of Memnon (she was pregnant with a child that could be only the King's son or daughter) none happened to have a thought of it! Many preferred to think it was magic spells the woman cast on our King and insisted he take a leave of her on some further expedition, while the most beautiful and eligible girl from Makedonia could be summoned and introduced to him!

At the beginning, Alexandros tried to explain to his worried Eteri-Friends his feelings and reasons (he always had reasoning beyond our understanding) for such a decision -to no avail. Only few of them such as Yfestion and 'uncles' Filippos and Aristos understood. Krateros accepted it because it was his King's desire and the rest because they saw Alexandros' anger building-up. He stopped his explanations short. He told everyone that it was his life, his decision and they had to obey him! It did not settle well with most but the thought was that he would soon get tired of her and her barbaric manners.

The wedding was full of splendor but done according to local customs, a fact which fuelled further discontent among many but nobody now wanted to cross Alexandros' will and most of the common men in the army were by the side of their King, regardless of what his whims were. So, they under-stood it -or pretended to- as a whim, less harmful than the one of 'proskinisis' or genuflection.

Just as the wedding festivities were coming to a closing, word came that some other aspired rebels from the tribe of Paraetakes having as their leader a certain Horienis (Choriyena) had taken the road to war by barricading themselves on top of Horienis' own high place a rock even higher than that of Oxyartis'. This rock approached the heights of about twenty stadia with its flat summit of sixty stadia in all!

In addition to its height, the rock was protected all around with deep ravines and had only one narrow path leading to its top, also flanked by steep ravines. For any approach of an army via this path, there had to be work done to fill the ravines first, otherwise the attackers would be forced to go in a single file and be really vulnerable as missiles and stones were sure to come flying from the defenders.

Oxyartis himself had described this rock as impossible to take even if Alexandros could produce two times as many 'winged warriors'! Aside of this being a new challenge to our King bend now to brake all records of worthy deeds by all his progenitors, the fact that word came from the defenders brag-ging about their ability to defend this rock and mocking Oxyartis for his failure to hold-on his, Alex-andros could not and would not leave such an insecure area behind him on his way to India.

He ordered then trees to be cut and thrown into the ravines along with earth and stones, to fill them up and thus widen the way of approach. He split the army in two working units. One was under his own supervision during the day time and the other worked at night under the joined command of Perdikkas, Leonnatos and Ptolemeos son of Lagos. The work progressed slowly on account of the dif-ficult ground conditions and, at the beginning, the barbarians were laughing at us. When though the work reached the throw of an arrow and (because Alexandros took steps to protect the workers from enemy fire) they saw they could not stop us from filling the ravine and widen the route of our attack on them, Horienis asked for negotiations and, in particular, for Oxyartis.

The new father-in-law proved to be persuasive and explained to Horienis that there was no way the army under Alexandros could be stopped and that, eventually, the rock would be taken with many unwanted casualties for the defenders. Horienis learning how Oxyartis was defeated was convinced and agreed to surrender without a fight and swore fealty to our King. Alexandros was contend and accepted Horienis as a friend, under the nominal supervision of Oxyartis and leaving -always mind-ful of security- a strong guard to keep the place under our control.

Horienis not only kept his word true to fealty, he further proved himself by deeds as he undertook the provisioning of the whole army as heavy winter snows fell in the area making it easy for us on food and shelter, saying that it cost him less than one tenth of what the siege of his rock had! Thus the army rested and kept warm during the difficult winter months.

With the following spring coming, Alexandros moved toward Vaktra and sent Krateros leading his falanx and the taxis of Polyperhon, 'uncle' Attalos' and Alketas' ones along with two iles of Eteri cavalry to subdue the remaining rebels among the Paraetakes, one named Khatanes (Katanis), the other Afshtanes (Afstanis). Krateros defeated the rebels at a battle, killing close to sixteen times a hundred and the leader Katanis, while capturing Afstanis and brought him to Vaktra.

It took a whole two years of campaigning to reduce the areas of Sogdiana, Vaktria and Margiana to submission. Now Alexandros had among us about thirty times a thousand young men from those sat-rapies training and fighting alongside (plus serving as hostages in case of need) and the areas served as deterrent to roving Skythian tribes from north. We now realize that Alexandros' wedding to Rox-ani, albeit guided by love, was a calculated move in securing the frontier thanks to the influence of her father Oxyartis -as was proved in the case of Horienis.

Now Alexandros placed Amyntas son of Arivvas from Dassaretis in charge of all troops in these areas and the army moved to Alexandria the city which was built when Alexandros came for the first time in these satrapies, after crossing the Asiatic Kafkasos mountains within only ten days! There, Alexandros released the man in charge because of poor performance and placed one of the Eteri -the son of Pithon from Kyrros- Nikanor in charge of the citizens and many near retirement soldiers who were given land in the vicinity as additional reward and their agreement to stay and settle.

For the satrapy from the Asian Kafkasos up to river Kofinos, he placed one of the Persian faithful named Tyriaspis (Tchyriaspa) as governor of civil affairs. From there, he moved the army -now numbering close to sixty times a thousand men- to the city of Nikaea. This army -aside the new re-cruits from Makedonia, the volunteers from Agriana and Thraki, the mercenaries from Thessalia and the rest of Ellas, had contingents upon contingents of recruited and trained our way Asian youth, thus more than doubling the numbers of the initial army which crossed over into the Persian empire.

If one added the engineers, the mule drivers, the peddlers, the women and the slaves, the total of humanity following our King was then surpassing the hundred times one thousand!

Alexandros sent then a messenger to the Indian chief named Taxilis (Taksila) located right at the border of the former Persian Empire to come and meet us along with his neighboring chiefs of India.

The Indian chiefs Taxilis and Sisikotos (Sisikouta) arrived in all their splendor pronouncing their fealty and promising complete supply in victuals and in military aid, including all their available elephants to about twenty five in number. Taxilis being at war with his chief opponent, Poros, was eager to have the alliance of Alexandros and our army.

Alexandros accepted their offer with presents on his part and, then, divided the army sending Yfestion and Perdikkas toward the country of the Pefkaliotes close to river Indos, adding to their numbers the taxis of Gorgias, Klitos 'the White' and Meleagros with half of the Eteri cavalry and all the light mercenary horsemen. The King instructed them to take all the towns on their way either by force or by persuasion and, arriving at Indos, to prepare for the crossing of the river.

On their way to Indos, Yfestion and that part of the army defeated the local chief named Astis (Usta) who had fortified his force in the major city of the area, after a thirty day siege. Astis was killed and in his place

Saggaeos (Sagghua) was installed as chief, as he previously had abandoned Astis and sided with Taxilis.

As for our King, he led the Ypaspistes and the rest of the Eteri cavalry, along with the rest of the falanx taxis and the Agrianians and the Prodromi moving into the country of the Aspasians the Gourians and the Assakines, following the flow of river Hois and the mountain paths. Receiving information of an army posed to ambush us at a strong point, he took the cavalry and about eight hundred of the Ypaspistes mounted on horse also, moved with speed and caught the enemy force still in the city where they were preparing for the ambush and took it by direct assault. During that as-sault, he got wounded -but not seriously- on his shoulder. Among other wounded of our people were Leonnatos and Ptolemeos son of Lagos.

Next, was the city of Andakas which agreed to surrender without any fight. There, Alexandros left Krateros and the foot taxis of the falanx, to subdue the rest of the region. Taking with him the archers and the Agrianians under my Father, along with the taxis of Kinos and Attalos, he moved against the Aspasians and their major city by the river Evaspla. The Aspasians burned the city and took off toward the mountain heights. Alexandros was able to cut them off before they reached the narrows and, in the battle which followed, Ptolemeos received another light wound but took the leader of the enemy prisoner.

The following city was one named Arigaeon and its inhabitants had left it burning. Alexandros see-ing that the place was of importance left Krateros -who had rejoined the King- there, with orders to rebuild it and use volunteers from the ones who were to become veterans soon and any of the locals willing to return and inhabit it. As for himself, he continued eastward and received information of the enemy now congregating in a hilly region and numbering more than Alexandros' own men.

Alexandros divided once more his portion of the army, giving charge of one part to Leonnatos, let-ting Ptolemeos take one third of the Ypaspistes in addition to the taxis of 'uncle' Filippos and the other Filotas son of Mahas from Mygdonia, two thousand archers and my Father with the Agrian-ians and half the Prodromi cavalry. As for himself, Alexandros took the third portion of the army and led them where he could see from the enemy camp fires the majority of them.

By the morning, the enemy seeing Alexandros approaching and judging he had very few men, came down from their heights and arrayed in battle order on level ground. In the ensuing battle, the King managed to force the enemy to retreat and Ptolemeos intercepted them using his force not attacking in regular line but in long wedge-like formation, taking the high ground and leaving them space to retreat further. The enemy fought hard but had to continue retreating, as they were now pressured by both parts of our army. Soon though they fell upon the approaching contingents under Leonnatos and we gained that day more than forty time a thousand prisoners!

Among other things we managed to round-up, were several thousands of cattle which Alexandros admired for their obvious grace and power. He personally chose a few hundred of the best and sent them to Makedonia, to interbreed with our stocks to better future generations of cattle here. Actual-ly, some of our own cattle -the ones with the small hump at the end of their neck- are the first gener-ation descendants of those cattle the King sent here!

After few days of rest and detailing the burial of the dead, Alexandros received word that the Assa-kines were amassing large number of troops and more than thirty elephants to war against us. As Krateros returned with his part of the army and the siege engines, after finishing with building the town he was told to, Alexandros took with him the Eteri cavalry, the Prodromi and the taxis of Kinos and Polyperhon along with the Agrianians and Peltastes and archers, moved into the lands of the Gourians, following the river and having hard time crossing it, on account of the round pebbles of its bed and the force of its flow.

The enemy did not dare to face us in the open. Instead they went to various walled cities and waited for us. The first city Alexandros came up to was Massaga. Reinforced by some seven thousand Indian mercenaries, the enemy came out of the city for battle. Alexandros knowing they would retreat behind the walls the minute they'd feel the outcome not in their favor ordered a faint retreat to near-by settlement, pretending we would spend the night there.

The Assakinians thought they had the upper hand and attacked disorderly. Alexandros immediate-ly signaled the falanx taxis, the Prodromi and the Agrianians with the archers to counter attack. The enemy was caught by surprise and, leaving behind them a good number of dead, secured themselves behind the city walls. Chasing them up to the walls, the King received a light wound about his right ankle. He then ordered the siege engines to come forth and a portion of the wall came down but the attack failed on account of the bravery of the defenders.

The next day a tower was constructed and our archers manned it, so we could keep the defenders away from the ruined wall but the new attack still failed. Alexandros then ordered a bridge to con-nect the tower with the ruined part of the wall and sent the Ypaspistes charging. Because of the sud-den extra weight, the bridge fell and many were wounded; some because of the fall some because of the volleys from the defenders. Alexandros immediately sent the taxis under Alketas to bring relief and take care of the wounded.

The fourth day now, the King had another tower erected and a new stronger bridge to connect it with the walls. After some time of hard fighting, the leader of the enemy fell and a delegation from the Indian mercenaries met Alexandros asking to surrender the city with no further loss of lives and they would serve under us as part of our army. The King was happy to accept those terms and agreed, letting them come out with their full armor and camp near us.

The King being ever careful in his negotiations with the barbarians, asked some men of Oxyartis to wear Indian clothing and mix with the mercenaries, to make sure of their intent. Soon, some of these men returned to report that the Indians had in mind to leave during the night, as they did not really want to fight on our side against their kin, cutting through our sleeping troops nearest to them and their way out to the mountains.

Alexandros asked for alertness to be passed but asked our troops not to move unless the inform-ation was to be proved true. Thus, when the Indians tried to move in the middle of the night, our men were ready and fell on them killing many and chasing the rest inside the city which now fell to us as one in battle. We lost some twenty five men but the enemy was routed. The cities of Vazira and Ora were next to fall.

Many of the enemy retreated up on high rock, not unlike the rocks we had previously encounter but the difference with this one was the rumor that Iraklis himself wasn't able to take when he had come in these parts of the world! The name of this rock translated in our language means a place where even birds cannot fly at, meaning its height is unapproachable. Obviously, Alexandros set his eye on it and led the army to this Aornos rock bent to take it and be the first in doing so!

Again, Krateros was put in charge of provisions and was asked to gather these in the city of Emvoli-ma, in case the rock could not be taken by an outright attack and needed time for a siege. Some locals came volunteering to show us an easier way up the rock and lead us to a village close to its summit. The King put them in charge of my Father's Agrianians and Ptolemeos' taxis with orders to let him know the minute they would have the village taken.

As soon the village was taken, our men dug out a perimeter moat for its defense and lit a fire from a place easily detected by Alexandros and the rest of the army below. The King seeing the signal order-ed an attack at once but the path in use was narrow the uphill move very difficult. The enemy, seeing our difficulty, took courage and fell upon our men at the village, trying to break our blockade. The Agrianes and Ptolemeos' taxis held steadily and, with the falling of the night, the enemy with-drew.

Alexandros then sent a message asking Ptolemeos to attack the placement of the Indians at the same time as he (Alexandros) would attack the next day, instead of remaining at the village. Indeed, the next morning the Indians were attacked from both sides but, again, due to the difficulty on the ground and the ravines blocking our way, there was little progress. Finally around past mid day, some of our men managed to take one of the hills on the way to the top of the rock, close enough to it so we could fire our missiles at the defenders from it.

As soon as we were able to secure that hill, Alexandros ordered the men to cut wooden poles and place them on the side of the hill toward the rock and start filling the gaps with earth, so we could charge the next day from a broader place. The enemy seeing our work and perceiving our plan saw that any further defense was futile and sent herald asking for surrender terms.

They had in mind to receive permission to go but fall upon us on their way out and kill as many as they could while getting out of the trap. Their secret plan was reported though to Alexandros by an Indian of our own. The King pretended an agreement and, when they started coming out, he gave orders to leave an open path for them. Taking at the same time a strong enough part of his Ypaspis-tes and Archers, he went and took the summit of the rock as the enemy marched downhill.

When the Indians thought they had covered most of their way down and could see their exit in the open, attacked our troops according to their secret schedule, thinking they had fooled us. Alexandros then ordered a counter attack and, as we had them covered from all sides, we killed many and more fell in the between ravines out of their terror and haste to save themselves and got killed. Thus, our King did take what his progenitor Iraklis could not!

After all was over, Alexandros sacrificed in the name of Iraklis and all the Olympian gods and gave orders to fortify the rock and place a strong unit of our army there for future safety. Hearing then that some other Indians had taken a number of elephants and planned to continue the war against us by going toward the Indos river, ordered Nearhos the Kritan and Antiohos son of Selefkos to take my Father's Agrianians and the Peltastes and go after the elephants.

The task was accomplished with the loss of only two elephants. The rest were taken by us and were put back to work carrying the timber we cut and transfer it to the river to build a fleet at the place where Yfestion and Perdikkas had gone to build a bridge for our passage."

Lamvros stopped his narration as the women called all men and the young ones for the midday meal. Suddenly, they all realized they were hungry and thirsty and got up gladly for a good meal and a short break after it. As they were cleaning, they could see the hired hands from the fields heading toward the large covered section across the stables and by the plane-trees next to the brook, for their own meal.

The men started talking of the current affairs and the latest news from Amfipolis. Things were not looking good for the remaining members of the royal family and Olympias' coming back to Pella was cause for assassinations of persons she had old accounts to settle with, the 'wanna be kings' were preparing for new war and the personal safety of Roxani with young Alexandros -as well as the lives of 'King' Filippos Arideos and his wife were in question. The women took care of the meal, ate and served and, while some started cleaning after, some checked the accuracy of the narration's record keeping by the younger ones, which served one more purpose: to learn how to write properly in both meaning and spelling.

When all was finished, some of the men went to supervise and assist with the estate's needs and the older ones went to take a short nap with the small kids and some of the women. The rest of the women and the older girls continued their work around the house and finally sat down to have their own talk according to the latest gossips. Doris and Lamvros found the opportunity to sneak past Di-mitrias and Evlampia to the orchard for some of their own talk.

When everyone returned from the estate's work and they cleaned-up, the women started preparing for the evening meal and Faedon volunteered to continue with the narration because -as he put it- he was tired of constant writing. "I learn the same when I tell the story or when I hear others! When I have to write, my mind is on that task and the words I have to write don't let me pay attention to the story as a whole -if you know what I am trying to say…"

"Yes, I think we do." Agathon answered. "Most of my generation knew only two men who were ca-pable of doing more than one thing at the same time! The first was Filippos and, the second, his own son! Alexandros notably could also read the dispatches without even moving his lips, while answering various questions and made decisions for battle plans or city building!"

"hmmm…" Timeos let the sound come out as his mind traveled back in years. "I had no personal knowledge of Alexandros' capabilities on that, but I saw with my own eyes Filippos taking care of many things all at once, even as he was carried wounded on a litter from the walls of Perinthos! You know I carried him with my Father!.." Peridas jumped-in and all could see his eyes were moist out of nostalgia of something precious but lost now for ever. "Yes, my friend" he said. "We know your good services to the King! My own Father served them both and he named me after Alexandros' own dog -well, close enough! I was very upset, as a youngster I thought it was an insult, that my own Father was looked upon me as nothing more than a dog! Until -that is- I had a talk with my Father and my first ever meeting with Alexandros right after that talk!"

Everyone spent the next few minutes recollecting own memories and thoughts, sipping some wine and in deep silence. Finally, Filippos son of Menelaos broke the silence by clearing his throat and passing his hand over his eyes and face. "We know what we had and what we lost, rather late for any recovery! Time to start serious planning for what we can save! I mean both in memory and posterity, as well as the royal individuals who are -I am very serious on my statement now- in danger, consider-ing who has taken them under 'guardianship'!"

"If we are successful on achieving our goal to rescue both Filippos-Arideos and the young Alexand-ros from the generals and their guardianship, we have to understand clearly that the result may not be exactly what we wish for! Filippos-Arideos' mentality is one thing, young Alexandros' mother is another and the generals (with Olympias' plans for the future) are the third and most difficult and unpredictable obstacle we have to overcome! You, Filippos, are in charge of any viable plan to rescue who we can! We will all obey and do our best to bring it to fruition! As for Iraklis, Alexandros' son from his affair with Memnon's Varsini, Polyperhon is supposed to have him under his 'protection' and, although he's a very close ally of Olympias, he keeps the young man somewhere unknown to any except himself!" Adamas cut-in.

"For the time being, all these words serve nothing!" old Sytalkis observed, apparently concerned. "I know Filippos is working on something in that direction and he will inform all of us the plan of ac-tion -when action is due! Meantime, while we wait here for the opportunity to come, the preparations ought to be under way and these narrations and writing of the story has to continue! Go ahead now Faedon, we are listening and you...yes, you younger ones, be ready to record his saying!"

Faedon started his narration, while the women brought-in the food and drinks, took their places and Agathon (it was his turn) evoked the gods and offered the proper portion of food at the small altar...

"On its way to the bridge Yfestion and Perdikkas had build at Indos, the army arrived at the city of Nysa, said to have been built by god Dionysos untold years back. Obviously, the King wanted to visit that place and see with his own eyes the place where a god's journey had ended. As for the rest, they believed the story, on account of some vines growing up in the area, very much alike our own grape vines. By now, we know the plant is different than our own, but it's irrelevant. At the time, the King thought the vine to be the god's gift in that land and all of the army accepted it as a fact and made sure they got garlanded by its leaves during the few days they were stationed there observing athletic competitions and offerings to Dionysos.

Now Alexandros had pass the furthest point of Iraklis' ventures of the past when the hero saved Promitheas' life on mount Kafkasos and as far as god Dionysos had gone, at the line of Parapamissos Kafkasos. He was ready to go further! He marched the army to the bridge over Indos river. There, he found Yfestion and Perdikkas waiting, along with Taxilis' thirty elephants and three iles of Indian cavalry to command. The city of Taksila was placed at the King's disposal and some more days were spent with new games and the built of a number of ships, small and large.

Indos' width is said -by some accounts- to be over forty stadia, coming second only to another Indi-an river named Gaggis or Gangis. We know not if it's as long as the Egyptian Nilos but it's certainly wider and has many rivers flown to its current, such as Ydaspis, Akesinis, Ydraotis and Yfasis -to mention a few. Reports on the native population told us the Indians were not too rich but great war-riors. If it wasn't for Alexandros' desire to surpass his divine ancestors by going further than they did and Taxilis' wish to defeat his enemy king, Poros, perhaps the King wouldn't have gone further, perhaps he would have returned to Vavylon sooner, perhaps he would have still been alive!"

"Indos river had to be over forty stadia wide!" Dimitrios interrupted "We crossed it and it took us quite some time doing so! Good thing no one opposed us then, because it would have been some mess, in spite that Yfestion and Perdikkas had the bridge secured and strong cavalry and Archers guarding it across the banks!" Faedon smiled nodding and continued.

"As soon as the whole army crossed the river, Alexandros offered sacrifices, as it was his custom at all times to honor the gods. Within one day's march the army arrived at Taksila which is located between Indos and Ydaspis and the inhabitants received us as was promised by Taxilis, giving us food and quarters. There, we were met with the brother of king Avisaris who brought to us a strong contingent of fighters and presents, as well as the governor of the region, Doxaris. Then, Alexandros called for some more cavalry competitions and games and thanked the gods one more time.

Few days later he took the army further, leaving Filippos son of Mahatas (a distant cousin) with a strong force in charge and many who needed to recover from illness and the rest of the army was marched by the King in order to cross the Ydaspis and meet king Poros in battle. For that reason, Alexandros sent Kinos son of Polemokratis back to Indos to cut the existing ships in small parts and transfer them to be re-assembled at Ydaspis for the next crossing. While waiting for that to happen, Alexandros camped by the west bank of the river and we could see the army of king Poros across, camped and ready to fight us as we would try to cross.

King Poros' army was a very strong one. He brought plenty of cavalry, chariots and elephants which complimented the foot soldiers. Meantime, Alexandros sent the Prodromi and other light armed units to find all possible fords of the river above and below our camp. With Kinos' return, the cut ships for easy transfer were re-assembled and put to water, ready to bring our troops across when the order would be given. In order to keep king Poros guessing where and when we were to cross, Alexandros divided the army and sent some up-stream, some down-stream to pretend and kept a good portion of men right there, by the ships. Due to heavy rains, the river was extremely flooded and the passage seemed very difficult -if not impossible.

Alexandros let Poros figure we would have to wait for the waters to recede for a while, but then he resumed the fake tries of crossings, making sure he had the real place of his cross and preparations for it well hidden from the enemy. As parts of our army were ordered to be going up and down the river, so did parts from the army of Poros, trying to figure out which way our attack would come from. This lasted for some time and it was obvious to Alexandros that Poros started to feel secure and followed our movements with less vigor.

Our King had the right place to cross already and -with alert guard in places of importance to let all the army units know of any and all progress at all times- he waited for the right moment. The place was at a turn of the river with an island half-way from the opposite banks. On our side, as well as on the island and the banks across, there was plenty of tall foliage which would keep our movement con-ceiled from the enemy.

Alexandros gave his orders. He made believe the attack would come from our main camp site, leav-ing Krateros in charge of it with cavalry from the Arahosians and Parapamissos, the taxis of Alketas falanx, along with the one of Polyperhon and the Indian allies. He told Krateros to cross if Poros would move the bulk of his army up-river to face our King and aid by attacking the enemy on a sec-ond front, or chase the enemy by crossing -if he would see Alexandros victorious. Other wise, he was to remain in place and repulse any attempt of Poros to cross to our side, provided the enemy had such a plan. During a stormy night, Alexandros also transferred the units of Meleagros, 'uncle' At-talos and Gorgias to another island half-way from our main camp and the east banks, for additional support on the moves of Krateros.

Then, the King took the rest of the army and in charge of the royal Agima, the ili of Yfestion, the taxis of Perdikkas and 'uncle' Dimitrios, the Vaktrians, Sogdians and Skythes mounted archers, the Ypaspistes, the taxis of Klitos the White and Kinos with some of the Agrianians, moved without being seen amidst the heavy rain and managed to transfer all undetected, using the ships and any other floating device he could, using the island as a cover. Bypassing the island then, he moved across openly.

The minute Alexandros landed, got his cavalry in order and moved forward with orders to have the rest follow as fast as they could and in battle order. The foot soldiers had some difficulty on account of the water and also some of the iles of cavalry were misguided in the dark and foul weather. As they managed to come to him, Alexandros placed them in order of his battle plan. The mounted archers were in front line, the best of heavy cavalry on the right by the river bank. Behind the front line he set the Ypaspistes under Selefkos, next to him placed the royal foot Eteri and the sarissa falanxes, having at the left wing the foot archers, the Agrianians and the javeliners and Peltastes. As for him-self, he took all the iles of cavalry and moved ahead, asking the rest to follow fast and in order.

Thinking that his cavalry would most likely meet the enemy first before the other part of the army and Poros' elephants would be difficult to overcome, he asked the archers under Tavron to be attach-ed and support; he, then, moved forward to meet Poros.

The Indian king had his own scouts going up and down his side of the river banks and soon our army movement was detected. Poros, not knowing that Alexandros was leading and the strength of our troops, sent his son with a strong detachment of chariots to repulse our men. During the battle which followed, Alexandros got wounded and his beloved horse, Voukefalas, was killed. Most of Poros' chariots could not operate properly due to rain and mud and his son got killed along with most of the Indians he led. From us the casualties were also rather heavy, as we lost many from our cavalry which attacked in sequence, ili-by-ili.

King Poros was now in a difficult position. On one side, he knew Alexandros to be moving against him in person, his own son killed. On the other, Krateros and his part of the army seemed ready to cross the river also. He made up his mind to leave at his camp few of his elephants and a small part of his army and go face our King. The clash of the two armies was epic. The Indians fought with cour-age and their elephants cost us a good number of lives until our archers managed to wound many of them forcing them to run -in their pain- confused, on their own lines. Poros was also wounded and captured. Seeing that, the rest of the Indian army retreated in haste, chased by Krateros who -by that time- had crossed the river also.

Alexandros, ever admiring courage, received Poros and asked how the Indian king was to be treat-ed. He admired Poros even more, the minute he got the Indian's answer 'Royally, like you would have expected me to treat you, King, had I been the victor!' Alexandros saw that Taxilis and Poros would here-to-for become allies under his rule. He awarded both with lands and set Poros in charge of the regions east of the river. Sacrifices were made to gods, Voukefalas was buried with honors almost equal to a hero and a city was planned to be built, carrying the horse's name, in the area.

This battle lasted most of the day, the Athinian month of Mounihion (our Daesios) with Ygemon being the presiding Athinian. Poros lost two sons among the thousands of Indians dead and we lost more than two hundred horsemen, many from the Eteri iles and more than twenty five times a hun-dred foot from our falanxes, archers and Peltastes! Games and offerings to the gods were ordered by Alexandros -as was his custom- and he also ordered the city of Nikea to be built in the area of the battleground in commemoration of the victory.

Reports that Avisaris was playing games before the battle and was about to join Poros if the latter would win, made the King to call upon Avisaris threatening that if the Indian chief would neglect to obey, Alexandros would go to him with the whole army! Avisaris obeyed sending his own brother and other notables, with money and elephants as presents. At the same time, Fratafernis and his Thrakian guard arrived and messengers from Sisikotos the satrap of the Assakines, saying that Sisi-kotos was murdered and the Assakines were revolting.

Alexandros sent then 'uncle' Filippos and Tyriaspis with a strong portion of the army to bring the revolt to its end. As for himself, he marched the rest toward the river Akesinis where some numbers of our soldiers were lost on account of the force of the river and the rocks on its bed, which destroyed several of our ships. Kinos was left there to supervise for the army's victuals and Alexandros turned toward the river Ydraotis where another Indian chief was preparing an army against us.

He led the army to victories as it was by now something like common expectation, taking the city of Saggala and utterly defeating the tribes of the Kathaeans and Oxydrakes and forcing the Adraistes to surrender. In some cases where the defeated turned to treachery and tried to break through killing as many of us as they could, Alexandros answered with severity putting to sword the majority of them. But now the army was restless. Most of the men were tired and started voicing their unwilling-ness to continue further, even if the leader was none other but Alexandros!

The King summoned the leaders of the taxis, the generals and all the officers to talk them into fol-lowing him further. He first thanked them for their vigor in battle, their sacrifices their faith in his leadership. He reminded them of the rewards they received through his generosity and their con-quests, the conditions at home before they marched together for a better future. Finally, he promised them even greater rewards if they would agree to follow him further.

There was silence among them for a long time. Finally, Kinos (who had return after securing the victuals) rose from his seat and asked the King's permission to speak. Alexandros knew Kinos' un-

dying devotion and thought the general would talk the rest into obeying the will of their King. He was wrong, perhaps for the first time ever in his life! Kinos took the side of the common soldier and, with calm voice, he stated the reasons why most of the men were not willing to go further."

"We were all tired and worn-out!" Aristos said. "Even if we were to completely understand all of the King's motives and reasoning, we were not him with his personal stamina and drive!" "We simply wanted to come back home!" Sytalkis stated -his aged voice full of mixed emotions.

"We did not mind following him, we were fresh troops yet, recent arrivals to your veteran status! Your pride didn't let us do it! You knew he had your opinion counting the highest and you could give him a great gift by consenting to have us go with him, but you wanted all the glory and riches for your selves only!" It was the bitter voice of Kalas now accusing...

Filippos stood fast up from his seat, before any of the other veterans could protest, seeing that Ada-mas, Attalos and Sytalkis were ready to pick-up a fight. "What happened then is regrettable but it is in the past and not possible to change! Kinos was right as much as was Alexandros, each from his own perspective! Yes, it was a blow to our King's will, to his ego. But it wasn't as fatal as our behavior only a few years after our return! As for the Asian troops, you are right my friend Kalas, but, where were your voices then? You could have come forth and put us to shame, you could have offered him what you profess now! We simply didn't have the frame of mind, none of us, not at that time!"

"We never truly listened to his words! More so, when we all watched him dying! I never saw a man dying so lonely, yet surrounded by hundreds of so-called friends!" Kalas said, sitting back down and emptying his cup of wine, eyebrows furrowed and tears freely running down his face. Filippos felt a big lump in his throat and, looking around read the same sentiments of shame, regret and nostalgia written clearly on all of his friends' faces. Unsteadily, he went and hugged each and every one of them. "We must stay together and try to help the surviving royals, in order to make-up somewhat for past mistakes!" He sat down again and they all remained silent for a long time, lost in their thoughts.

There was no more narration that evening. Each went to his quarters with heavy heart but not be-fore renewed oaths of fidelity to each-other and to the remaining members of the royal family...

Faedon resumed his narration three days later at the usual after-dinner gathering of the group. It took all of them all this time to reflect and renew their commitment to each-other and toward the remaining members of the royal family.

"King Alexandros heard Kinos' presentation of the unwillingness by all to march further and re-tired to his tent without a word. He remained there for three whole days, giving time to everyone to think clearly and calmly before making the final decision. On the fourth day he renewed his call but the men refused him once more. Seeing that he could not change their minds, he asked for omens.

Perhaps Zefs would come to his aid.

The omens were not favorable at all! He continued his sacrifices for a few days but the results were the same. He then let the officers know he would abide with the men's will! The army was jubilant! They were the only ones who had ever defeated their King! Alexandros accepted their lack of under-standing with sadness but, like the man he was, remained faithful to them. He ordered games and the building of twelve stylae to be erected in the name of each Olympian god. That done, he offered his respect to each deity with ample sacrifices. He then prepared the fleet to follow the river southward, having army detachments follow it downstream on both sides.

Due to the so-called monsoon rains which last a long period of time in those parts, Kinos -among many others prior or after- got high fever and died within weeks. He was buried with due honors. Finally, the fleet was ready and most of the baggage, the seriously sick, horses and many others were embarked and the sailing down-river started. They were escorted for some great distances by locals who had the time of their lives witnessing such spectacular event and singing their local songs.

Yfestion and Krateros held with their portions of the army the banks of Ydaspis river, making sure there was ample protection in case of hostile tribes further down-river. The fleet was moored some times where the river banks would allow and there, Alexandros was receiving delegations of local tribes submitting to him as allies or, when necessary, direct small expeditions to subdue them. All went well up to the point where Ydaspis meets the river Akesinis and they both unite and flow to the edge of the sea. There are some serious rapids there and many a ship got damaged and men were lost.

Stationed at the most convenient place to do repairs, the King was informed of the tribe of Mallians who were coming to alliance with other neighboring tribes in order to deny us passage further down the river and within their country proper. They were feeling they had the time to organize, as from our placement to the point where they had in mind to attack us they were protected by a desert, lo-cated to our right as we were heading. Alexandros could not allow such an act. He made-up his mind to act and act unexpectedly and from where he was least expected.

First, he attacked on the right bank the tribe of Sivae, who were ready to cross the river and assist the Mallians. The Sivae reduced to submission. Krateros was asked to remain on the right bank and 'uncle' Filippos was attached to that force with his own, in order to keep that side secured and deny any crossing of the enemy in case the Mallians would try to escape that way. Yfestion and his part of the army sailed further down with the fleet, to cut the Mallian retreat from that side when the King would attck.

Those orders understood and obeyed, Alexandros took his part of the army into the desert to either defeat the Mallians and their allies together or, in case they had not form a common front, separate-ly. He came upon a body of water and, informed that it was the last water source until the desert's end he rested and had everybody fill all available vessels with it. That done, he went on and marched through the night falling upon the first Mallian city of Agallassa the next morning. It was unexpect-ed and as he had planned. The city fell rather easily -as the Mallians were unprepared- with a loss of many an enemy.

The enemy tribes had not achieve a unified front, finding it difficult to agree on who would lead them. Alexandros then moved to the next city-stronghold, while Perdikkas with his taxis and some auxiliaries took a city on his own and chased its inhabitants catching-up with them before they could hide in some marshes of Ydraotis. Meantime, Alexandros had Pithon son of Aginor attack the fort the King was against and Pithon took it within the day. All prisoners were sold as slaves at friendly Indian markets.

The next strong place the King had to move against was the city of the Vrahmanes which was taken by sapping its walls, as there weren't many available ladders to scale. The Vrahmanes retreated at their acropolis and Alexandros was first to scale it giving the example for the rest to follow. Many Vrahmanes got killed in the street to street and house to house chase and resistance. Alexandros then rested the army overnight there.

The next day it was reported that many of the Mallians had gone by the high banks of Ydraotis. They had in mind to hold Alexandros there. The King took his Agima and all other available cavalry and moved against them, ordering the foot taxis to follow with all speed. The result was the usual -by now- success with most of the Mallians being killed or captured to be sold as slaves. They remnants of Mallian resistance then gathered at a strong citadel and Alexandros pursuit them with his usual speed.

Although the army under the lead of its King managed to bring one gate down, the exhausted taxis under Perdikkas did not have the stamina to take advantage, the cavalry being no less tired after such a speedy march. Alexandros called a stop for some badly needed rest. Meantime it was found that the army rushing to keep-up with King and cavalry had not brought the ladders to scale the walls. The ones made from local timber were very few -as timber of some quality wasn't available in the area.

Alexandros got tired and worried of possible unnecessary loss of life on our part and, driven by his usual valor, grabbed one of the first ladders available and started climbing up. He was followed by Pefkestas who was in care of the shield taken from Tria a few years ago and by Leonnatos, who hap-pened to be the day's personal somatofylax (body guard) of the King. Next to them came Avreas, son of Molon from Apollonia in Mygdonia.

The rest of the somatofylakes and Ypaspistes, fearing of the King's life and ashamed of being out-performed by these few men, started climbing up on the second available ladder, the result being they were too many and the ladder broke, leaving the King and his party alone! The four of them now had to face the multitude of the enemy who easily recognized Alexandros and started throwing all kinds of missiles against him, for any who dared to come close fell instantly either by the King's sword or by the weapons of Pefkestas, Leonnatos or Avreas!

It was a very difficult moment and the Ypaspistes asked their King to leap back to safety, on their outstretched hands. Instead, Alexandros called to have every one who loved him follow his example, jumped down the wall on the inside followed by the other three companions! With their backs on against the wall itself, they dispatched a good number of enemy soldiers, including the apparent leader of those Indians.

But, Avreas fell, hit by an arrow and Alexandros was also wounded by another arrow which pierced through the protective corselet and punctured his lung! Nonetheless, the King continued fighting until, exhausted by the loss of blood, he fell while Pefkestas and Leonnatos covered his body and fought with unbelievable valor against hundreds of enemy who saw their chances to rid themselves of the menace and gain fame!

Meantime the Ypaspistes stepped -one on top of the other- up the parapets and down they came inside the wall, to aid their King and compatriots. Alexandros by then was unconscious and seemed to be dead! Enraged, the Makedonians drove the Indians back and brought their King back to the camp. Of the defenders, they killed every one, not sparing even women or children -for they thought that Alexandros was dead!

We were lucky that particular time, for -due to the physician from Kos, Kritodimos- the King was saved! Bad news -we all know- spread fast though and the rest of the army thought Alexandros was truly dead and panicked. That panic spread even among the ones around the King and things were getting out of hand. Hearing of the situation, Alexandros had the ones in his tent carry him on a litter to the banks of Ydraotis and into a ship to sail up-river for all the army to see he was alive! They still had their doubts and, realizing that, Alexandros then raised his hand and the cheers -and tears- run freely from all present! Next, the King ordered to have his horse brought to him and -with help- he mounted and the whole countryside reverberated from the sound of swords and spears hitting against shields and the paean of thousands voicing their relief and thanksgiving to gods! Upon reach-ing his tent, the King dismounted to show them he could walk and was almost mobbed, as every one tried to come and touch him or his clothes, throwing at him whatever flowers were available near-by!

While recovering then, Alexandros had his officers protesting that he should leave up to them all future exposures to danger, although they knew very well that none could even come close to his personal valor or skill of battle and arms! The King thanked them all but could not promise that his self-control would be enough to keep him away from the thick of battle, any battle! One Viottian ally, a veteran of many years who's name -unfortunately- none took the time to note, gave Alexandros the compliment the King needed most! He said quoting the tragedian Aeshylos: 'O Alexandros, it is the nature of heroes to perform great deeds!'

At this camp location then came delegations of Mallians admitting their submission as did the Oxy-drakians and the King accepted, after receiving some one thousand prominent persons as hostages and five hundred chariots with two warriors on each, as troops under our command. Alexandros appointed Filippos, son of Drakas from Pelagonia, who had shown good sense in commanding a taxis of Asian recruits, in charge of these new areas. To help him control the tribes, the King left to him all volunteered Thrakian troops and Nikodamas of Sintiki -as second in command and tax collector.

The father of Roxana came there too and he received the additional satrapy over Parapamissos, as the former satrap, Tyriaspis, was found to be unjust and cruel. The King recovered by then, embark-ed most of the army on the ships and sailed down-stream to the place where Indos receives all the waters from the five-river region and founded one more Alexandria in the country of the Ossalians, as he saw the place fitting for basis as a market for shipping and a depot for the army left there.

Going down-stream on Indos, he added the lands of Oxykanos, Sambos and Muzikanos and chastis-ed severely the Vrahmanes who instigated several revolts. Arriving at Patala, he enlarged the city and built a dockyard to accommodate future usage of fleets. Now we were at the mouths of Indos, before the vast sea of Okeanos!

The King surveyed all the deltas of Indos to the Okeanos and outfitted the fleet to be ocean worthy for the trip from Indos back to Efratis, moving by the shoreline toward the sunset. As commander of it he named his childhood friend and companion, Nearhos. As for the rest of the army, Krateros was to lead half of it escorting the invalids and baggage train through Arahosia and Drangiana back to Vavylon while the King would lead the rest through the desert of Gedrosia and subdue the tribes on the way westward supporting the fleet also by setting up provisions and dig-up wells for Nearhos.

Alexandros and his part of the army started first, ahead of Nearhos' fleet. On their way through the desert they subdued the tribes of Aravitians, Oritians and Ihthiofages, marching under the high tem-peratures of Gedrosia and losing almost all their horses, all the treasures carried by the men and a very great number of men due to thirst and famine combined! Of the close to thirty five thousand men starting the march, some ten thousand were buried in the desert!

Had Alexandros not seen to splitting his force into three divisions there could be a greater disaster. One was led by Ptolemeos, the second by Leonnatos -who stayed at the town of Ora to aid (and be aided by) Nearhos- and the third, by Alexandros. The King had also send Yfestion with another part of the army further inland with orders to bring order in the inland tribes and meet with Alexandros at the town of Paora or Paura. There, the survivors took a much deserved rest.

While recovering at Paora, Alexandros was informed that many of his appointed satraps had ruled with much less than desired justice and neglected to send provisions for the desert crossing. Being too late to save any souls, Alexandros postponed punishment until -marching through Karmania- met with Krateros and that part of the army in Persepolis. From there, Alexandros rectified a good num-ber of abuses by replacing the officers in charge who were proved of being corrupt and cruel. At the same time, he awarded the faithful ones, as well as all the distinguished men during the campaign to India. Among them was Pefkestas who was promoted to somatofylax for his valor saving the King's life at the Mallian stronghold.

He then ordered celebrations for the victories in India with games and feasts and theatrical plays. Now he waited to hear that Nearhos and the fleet had also a good ending trip sailing the ocean and, when news arrived that the fleet had reached the coastal port of Salmous, gave an added excuse for more celebrations! Nearhos reported in person his adventures and Alexandros asked his friend to continue further until he would reach the mouth of Tigris. Meantime, Nearhos and his men were to rest for a while and receive their due honors!"

Here, Faedon was interrupted by the coming of a messenger from the working the estate hands, bringing news from Pella, gathered at the near-by town's tavern/inn. The man was obviously dis-tressed and a bad feeling hung over the gathering, as they braced themselves ready to hear what the bad news could be. Before letting the man come-up with his story though, Filippos asked for wine and fruits to be given to him and (almost) ordered to have the man 'catch his breath' before saying what he had to say.

The man, Evdimos son of Protarhos -a cousin of Agathon- thanked Filippos and drunk his wine al-most non-stop, neglecting even the customary offering to the underworld gods. Embarrassed, he asked for some more, invoked good intend to Pluton and past deceased kin, spilled some on the ground and drunk the rest. He wiped off some dripping from his beard and started his report.

"We all know that Kassandros has gone to the southern city-states for assistance against Olympias and that she sent Polyperhon in Peloponnisos to deal a blow on Kassandros' plans. What has hap-pened since is this: Kassandros has the support of Athinae and money from Ptolemeos and Selefkos.

He has raised an army and keeps Polyperhon busy, as the latter can do little -at least for the time being. King Filippos-Arideos' wife, Evridiki, sent a message to Kassandros telling him he had her support and expected him to 'free them' -and Makedon- from Olympias. Olympias intercepted the messenger and made her move. Evridiki's men would not fight against Alexandros' Mother and Oly-mpias had her men from Ipiros lure Filippos-Arrideos and Evridiki to an isolated place outside Pella.

Trapping them there, Olympias had her men wall-up doors and windows and fed the couple for some time through a small opening, while she was afraid Kassandros might show-up to free the king and his wife. Seeing Kassandros had no intent to honor his duty, she closed everything up, having the couple starve to death!

Now Kassandros threatens to come to Makedon with his army and Olympias sent message to Poly-perhon to return with his, in her support. Meantime, she convinced Roxana to place young Alexand-ros -and herself-under Olympias' own 'protection' and the old Queen is planning to move everyone at the fort by Pydna, holding it until Polyperhon' arrival, since she cannot trust any Pellean now!"

The horrible news kept everyone dumbfounded for a long time. First to recover was Filippos. "We have to move, and move at once!" he declared. "Let's have everyone ready within two hours and head to Pella! I still have there one or two distant relatives who can persuade others to side with us and take both young Alexandros and his Mother away from Olympias! If we act with speed, we can bring them here and hide them until such a time when young Alexandros can safely present himself before all Makedonians and claim his throne!"

The men moved into action. Word was sent to working hands at the ends of the estate and a fresh messenger took off to Pella and Filippos' kin still surviving discriminations stemmed from their re-lation to him, to have them ready to hide and support the coming of the band of friends.

Unfortunately, Filippos and his group of rescuers were too late arriving in Pella. By the time new traveled from the Makedonian capital to the vicinity of their estate, Olympias had prepared for the departure to the fort by Pydna and she was already behind its well protecting fortifications. The men did not dare to go there, for they knew Olympias' temper and state of mind. She would never allow the removal of young Alexandros from her protection.

Instead, she would ask them -and they could not refuse the Mother of Great Alexandros- to stay with her, entrapped and at the mercy of

Polyperhon's timely (or not) arrival or the outcome of Kassandros' venture into Makedonia! And it was well known in Pella that Kassandros was on his way, having covered most of the distance and stationed already by the Pinios valley in Thessalia!

Would he dare to fight Olympias? Would he come to an 'understanding' with her? Filippos and his friends had no other choice but hide and wait for the events to unfold.

As it happened, Kassandros did not move against Olympias right away. He came to Pella and did the unexpected. He took the bodies of Filippos-Arideos and Evridiki, had them cleaned and gave them a royal burial. The people appreciated that. After all, feeble-minded or not, Filippos-Arideos was King Filippos' son and brother of Alexandros! To Olympias, he sent a delegation bringing a letter which was written by his own wife, Thessaloniki. In that, both Kassandros and Thessaloniki were asking Olympias to place herself, her grandson young King Alexandros and his mother under the protection of Kassandros, with the understanding that Olympias would stay out of the country's affairs and politics for as long as she lived.

Kassandros knew that Olympias would never accept such terms from him or anyone else. He had placed -at some distance so they would be undetected- garrisons to keep all roads and mountain passes isolated so neither Olympias nor Polyperhon could communicate and, as he received Olym-pias' negative answer, he had them come and surrounded Pydna from land and sea. As no one would raise a hand against Alexandros' mother, he would have her starve to death!

Filippos and Sytalkis had Spadoklos, Timeos and Agathon disguise as merchants and, with some of the others posing as helpers, had them go to Pydna pretending they were selling provisions to the troops. They returned after a short time to report that Pydna was unapproachable. The garrisons posted by Kassandros were alert and nothing was going in or out of the small city either by land or by sea. There was nothing else to do but send a message to Polyperhon, to find out what he intended to do. Kalas wisely suggested the use of false names in that letter and hired one of the professional messengers who wouldn't care -except that he received enough upon completion of his task. It was good they took Kalas' advice, for they found out much later that the messenger was caught by Kas-sandros' men and killed…

"We do not claim to be descendants of
Alexander the Great!"
F.Y.R.O.M.'s Ambassador Ljubica Acevshka
to U.S. Representatives in D.C. – 01/22/1999.

"We are Slavs who came in this area in
the 6th Century C.E. We are not descendants of the ancient Macedonians!..."
Kiro Gligorov, F.Y.R.O.M.'s 1st President (Foreign Information Service – Daily Report, Eastern Europe, 02/26/1992.

V

While waiting though for results since they sent their letter to
Polyperhon, the company of Filippos never stopped their 'lessons' to the
male younger generations they had taken with them and had strict orders
given for the ones who stayed back at the estate to be doing the same.
Badsha/Vasiliki, the wife of Kalas was put in charge of the lessons at home,
since she had been in attendance of Alex-andros' wife Roxana from the
day of their wedding to the day the King died and had almost first-hand
knowledge of all events.

In addition to keeping an eye at the besieged in Pydna, Sytalkis
suggested the purchase of a small estate in Pella and the task was given to
Basali/Vasilios the Agrianian cousin of Attalos. Vasilios did as was told and
brought with him his family and some of his most trusted servants, to use
them as messengers where and when was needed, to keep contact with all
of his friends. He left his elder son Padroucla (Patroklos) at home to care
about his private affairs.

The band of devotees to young King Alexandros moved then to
the newly purchased small estate making sure they stayed out of sight
and Spadoklos, Timeos and Agathon returned to the vicinity of Pydna
pretending they were selling goods to Kassandros' troops brought to them
by Vasilios' men.

At the estate by Amfipolis, Vasiliki took her task to heart and the
younger ones continued their 'les-sons'. While she was reciting, Vereniki
(Spadoklos' daughter) and Doris (Adamas' one) were the ones who put it
all in writing.

"King Alexandros ordered Yfestion and the bulk of the army to proceed toward Persis while he took some light troops and some cavalry and marched to Susa. Arriving there, he took care of those who had betrayed his trust while he was in India. Orxinis, who had replaced Frasaortis as satrap of Persia upon the latter's death but acted with cruelty, was put to death. Pefkestas was the one now to become the satrap of Persia. The man proved to be more than capable, as he could already speak the language and had the King as his role model in dealing with the people!

Bariaxis had attempted to crown himself king and was brought to King Alexandros by Atropatis (Hastrapatiou) of Midia. Bariaxis was put to death then. At the same time, Stasanor brought from Aria and Fratafernis (Prhataferna) from Parthia and Yrkania beasts of burden and camels, much needed by the army.

Arriving at Passargadae, Alexandros found the tomb of Kyros the Great broken into and its treas-ures stolen. Its guards were put to torture but nothing could be done but to place the body back in its resting place with more treasures added and better security placed than before. People welcomed the King's return and filed complaints before him on everyone who tried to take advantage of his ab-sence all this time. Granted, some of the accusations were either exaggerated or outright false. Such was the one against Sytalkis, the uncle of our 'uncle' Sytalkis and, when Alexandros finally discovered the accusations were false, he ordered the death of these accusers -but the deed was done.

Along with Sytalkis, Aspastis (Ashpashta), Ordanis (Orhdana), Varyaxis (Bahryiouxa), Oxyatra and many others had the same fate, as they were found guilty of pillage, cruelty, revolt and embez-zlement while trusted with high offices. Tlepolemos was put in charge of Karmania. What really made Alexandros despair and feel cheated, was the fact that Arpalos, his youth companion and responsible for the royal treasury, had taken a hoard of gold and taken off, on his way to Lakedae-

It's well known that Alexandros always was true to people he loved and much hurt when they did not return respect toward his devotion. The common people had a better understanding of the King than his closest friends! His obvious intention to be just, his evenhandedness, showed everyone that their King considered each and everyone equal! If he -at times- failed, did not fail because of his own incapability to judge! As with the Sytalkis affair, there were many others false accusation presented for his judgment with overwhelming 'proof' of guilt and totally inadequate defense on behalf of the accused.

Alexandros then tried to bring all enmities to an absolute end by organizing the biggest marriage ceremony ever! Along with his intention to wed Statira, the oldest daughter of Darios and Parysatis who was the youngest daughter of Ochos -in addition to having Roxana already as Queen- he en-couraged his officers-friends and all the troops to also wed Persian or any other Asian women!

Yfestion wedded Drypetis, another daughter of Darios; Krateros a niece of the past Persian High King named Amastrini; Perdikkas received the daughter of Atropata, satrap of Midia; Ptolemeos got Artakhama and Evmenis wedded Artonis. More than eighty of the other high officers of Makedon and allies agreed to marry Asian women at the same time! Any and all of the soldiers who had al-ready marry Asian women or had them follow the army as concubines, were given royal gifts on top of having their debts paid, as their weddings would jointly take place with those of their King and officers! The number of these soldiers passed the myriad! All were part of a huge wedding banquet which lasted as many days as any great Makedonian wedding which surpassed anything done before and surely will not be matched with any in the future!

Next, Alexandros ordered the army to report all debts accumulated. Many got scared that their King wanted to either tax them or to check and see if there were any ones overpaid or underpaid, with dire results in case of disparities and most of them withheld the information. Alexandros was very upset with their lack of trust in him. He sent heralds to explain his reason. He wanted to take a personal interest in everyone's debt and pay it out of his own account! To ease their fears, he had his secretaries taking the account not to ask the debtors' names! Then, all came forth and the King paid over twenty thousand talents worth!

At the same time, Alexandros presented to the most distinguished men crowns of laurel in gold and saw that many got promoted to higher offices. 'Uncle' Sytalkis received then his official leadership of the Odryssian troops, Pefkestas and Leonnatos got promoted to hiliarchs, Nearhos was named the admiral of the fleet and Onisikritos got also crowned, as the captain of royal vessel. Everyone looked happy and satisfied; most of all, Alexandros!

Then, jealousy and hard feelings returned among the men for the following two reasons: One, Alex-andros had ordered -since the very beginning of the campaign- the organization and training of the most fit

Asian youth to Makedonian ways of war and the language of the Ellines. There were more than thirty thousand strong Asian soldiers and so well trained by Selefkos, that during their demon-stration of abilities proved equal -if not better- to the Makedonian falanx!

Not that the King had not used Asian troops in the past! He did and -in many cases- they had distin-guish themselves in action. But that was during times of war and need of victory by any means, so the Ellines had not taken any offense of the use of Asians who were considered inferior and were part of a defeated enemy. But here came to demonstrate their abilities the cavalry from Vaktria, Sogdiana, Zaraggia, Arahosia and Persian Evakaes!

Their leaders included the son of Artavazos Kofin, the sons of Mazaeos Ydranis and Artivolis, Sisi-nis and Fradasmenis, sons of Fratafernis, Istanis son of Oxyartis and brother of Queen Roxana, as well as the brothers Aftovaris and Mithrovaeos. Overall leader was of this cavalry units was the Vak-trian Ystaspis. The demonstration of this new army though, changed the mood of the veterans!

The second reason was that the King felt it was time to discharge the most aged of his veterans and send them home with an added bonus in gold, which -they thought- was Alexandros' way of buying them out and replacing them with these new troops of Asians which were already called επιγονοι, the successors! This perceived 'offense' was felt with greater force among the Makedonian veterans and tempers rose high.

Alexandros did not detect these feelings at once, as he was elated by the overall appearance of these additional troops and ordered Yfestion to take all the army toward the city of Opis while he supervised the buildings of a fleet which would take the rest down the Tigris toward the sea. When the ships were ready, Alexandros came to meet Yfestion and the army at Opis. There, he met a mutiny on account of the incorporation of the Asians and the feelings his old veterans had toward this! One more reason for their disaffection was the fact that the King was using for some time now Persian garment along his Makedonian dress.

Alexandros was taken aback when he was informed by Yfestion and some other officers about the foul mood of his veterans! He could not believe that his interest in seeing them back home safe and rich beyond any comparison had so misunderstood by those who he thought were as much in fond of him as he was of them! He let go for a couple of days, waiting their displeasure to pass but keeping an eye on those who were the most vociferous instigating unrest. Finally, he had enough!

Alexandros called for a general inspection of the whole army and, escorted by armed Ypaspistes and all the officers, he called the ones in charge of the mutiny and had them placed under arrest. In some occasions, he went himself and dragged the ones who still looked defiant, fearless of any harm which could come to him! There were about a dozen arrests and those men were taken away to go through trial before the army, as was the Makedonian custom.

Then, the King stepped up on the review platform and addressed the rest with the following words (here, I have to tell you I got the translation of his words from one of the officers, friendly to my hus-band -I think it was Pefkestas...yes! That was him!). The words the King had to say found their mark, especially because he was telling them the truth! He said:

"What I have to tell you, Makedonians, is not to keep you away from home and loved ones, as it is your privilege to go whenever you feel like, but not before I show you who you truly are! Naturally, I will start with my Father, King Filippos!

My Father then was the one who found you wandering up and down the mountains, from summer pastures to winter quarters with your few sheep and goats. You weren't even able to defend those few animals you had from the raids of the Illyrians or the Trivallians and other Thrakians! Filippos was the one who gave you proper clothing to dress-up with, he was who brought you to live in secure cities by the flatlands, he was who made warriors out of you so you wouldn't have to cower behind inadequate walls of villages or hiding in caves but made you believe in yourselves and gain freedom from all those fears because he made you capable of such bravery and knowledge of arms!

Filippos called you citizens of a lawful kingdom, which he provided with cities envied by all and ruled over you with justice; whereas you used to be led by the barbarians to and fro exactly like the sheep and goats you herded, he brought you up from servitude and made you masters of your home land and leaders of Ellas! He placed in your service most of Thraki and Illyria and forced the Dar-danes to retreat! He was the one who opened the harbors to our commerce freeing them from enemy blockades!

My Father was who, becoming Tagos of Thessalia, warred against the Fokians and Onomahos. He forced Athinae and Thivae to accept our leadership and put Peloponnisos to order! Ellas then named him Leader and in charge of the expedition against Persia! Yet, what my Father did for you is min-imal compared to what I have offered! Starting from home so poor that I had to borrow eight hun-dred talents to feed, clothe and arm you, what have I given you?

Aside my personal love and care, I gave you the rule over Ionia, Lydia, Vavylon and Susa, the whole wealth of Asia itself, to the edge of the Skythian lands and to Indos River! Who made you satraps and governors, generals and captains? I, Alexandros! And what do I have to show for all this but this Persian garment under the Makedonian Hlamis and this worthless diadem? Am I appearing to be more decorated or fancy dressed than most of you do? Who among you worked harder than me? Who of you can show more wounds -none of them in the back mind you- than those I received? Let the bravest of you come forth and compare! I can match all of his and then have some more to show! No enemy weapon that was borne or hurled missed my body. All have left their marks upon me!

I have celebrated my weddings with your own, I paid your debts. The best of you have in addition golden crowns. The brave dead have been buried with more than due honors and their statues are the décor of the home temples, side by side with our gods! Their parents are held in honor and relieved of any taxes! Now, I proposed to send you back home loaded with gold and spoils for a life to be certainly envied by all and what do I get? Ingratitude and revolt!

I will have nothing to do with you anymore! Go back to your towns and tell your neighbors how you deserted your King who traversed the earth to make you powerful, to build your reputation, to make you wealthy! Tell your neighbors that Alexandros, the one whom no kingdom has been able to resist, has been deserted and about to be served by foreigners of conquered nations! This ought to be your glory and piety to the gods. You are no longer my soldiers or my comrades! Now get going!"

The King then turned and, letting no one to follow him went to the house assigned him and remain-ed in seclusion. He gave orders only to his Asian soldiers and very few of his personal friend compan-ions, leaving all other Makedonians out. The veterans were thus discharged without leadership or any guidance. Although part of their original concern could have been excused, Alexandros' rebuke and anger, as he felt betrayed, made them see their own lack of confidence at his judgment and their own wrong. The instigators of the mutiny were put to trial and were executed.

Although the discharged veterans still held their arms and were twenty thousand strong, they felt naked without the guidance and leadership of their King. Yet, Alexandros kept his silence. In the third day of his seclusion, he asked for his Asian officers only and issued preparation orders accord-ingly for a march. The veterans seeing they were totally ignored like they didn't exist, relented and, throwing their weapons at the door of the building billeted to Alexandros, sent message that they would not withdraw unless the King had them restored to his favor!

Alexandros responded with his usual magnanimity. He came out to meet them and admitted them all to their previous honors. At that point, a veteran named Kallinis who was Ipparhos in the Com-panion Cavalry before his discharge called to the King: "Alexandros! We are grieving because you have admitted as your kinsmen Mides and Persians but have not admitted us!"

The King was surprised by such a complaint and responded with some bitterness -yet with love and reassurance: "I never thought it would have to be explained to you that all of you are my kinsmen! You have been from the very beginning!" The reunion was complete and the veterans paraded one by one before their King and each received a kiss, without minding this time that, getting it from your sovereign, it was an Asiatic custom meaning the King regarded you as his kin! At the same time, this was a sort of victory for Alexandros, after the army's refusal to follow him farther than Yfasis river in India.

The veterans then got ready to return to Makedonia, with Krateros leading and having the orders to be in charge of the affairs back home while the aged Antipatros was to bring some new reinforce-ments, equal in number of the returning veterans. This way, Alexandros felt the old general would be close to his sons for as many years the gods would have him live and, away from Olympias! For the King's mother had lately become very antagonistic and she kept on sending letters to Alexandros bad-mouthing against Antipatros. Feeling the way the King did for his mother, he could not order her to mind her own business and leave to Antipatros the political and military affairs of Ellas.

Krateros the departed, having as his second in command Polyperhon, along with Klitos the 'White', Polidamas, Amadas and Gorgias. Of the veterans, each received an extra talent and their offspring from Asiatic women stayed back at the King's expense, to be trained as Makedones. Thus, there would be no possible hard feelings back home with the backward thinking family members.

Alexandros the decided to start visiting each province and set things according to his will. He went to Ekvatana, where the treasury was kept. He took care of affairs there, especially as things were laxing after the departure of Arpalos with a good amount of gold. During this stay at Ekvatana, Yfestion fell ill and, in spite of the doctor's instructions to follow a certain diet, he disobeyed and he died. Alexandros felt the loss of his friend like no one could. The two of them were -as we all know- like Patroklos was with Ahilleas.

Alexandros prepared the funeral pyre at his friend's honor upon his return to Vavylon and the games, ceremonies, gymnastic and musical contests cost close to ten thousand talents! After the mourning time (a long one for that matter) passed, Alexandros and Ptolemeos undertook an expe-dition against the Kossaeans, as it was necessary to secure the roads from Susa to Ekvatana from these robbers. After the campaign was over, Alexandros started returning to Vavylon.

On his way he was met with ambassadors from Lydia, Karhidon, the Bruttians, Lukanians and Tyrrinians from the Italian peninsula. They had come to pay him respect and ask him to settle their disputes. As Alexandros was crossing the Tigris, he was also met by some Haldaean priests who ask-ed him not to return to Vavylon because they could foresee evil coming to him if he did at this time.

Alexandros thought they were saying this because they had wasted the money he gave them to rebuild the temple of Belos, their chief deity. He refused to delay his entrance to the city but heeded their council to only enter from the east side. The time of the year though prevented him from doing so, due to creation of extended shoals and marshes from that side of the river.

In Vavylon, Nearhos was waiting with a fleet which sailed up the Efratis and was joined by some Fi-nikian ships also. Alexandros had in mind to send colonists to cities at the Persian sea and he would then move against Aravia, known of its spices. Not having received anything bad since he entered Vavylon, the King forgot all about the Haldaean warnings. He went to the estuary of the Efratis and he built there a city, stationing many of the veterans from Ellas. That city was later named Harax.

The King returned to Vavylon once more. His exposure to the marshes seemed to have caused him high fever but, as usually, Alexandros paid no attention to discomfort. Finally, after an all night party at the residence of Medios, the fever forced him to stay in bed. In spite his condition the King did his everyday duties, albeit carried in a litter. He sacrificed each morning -as proper for a Make-donian King- and he took care of each and every state affair. After some improvement, the fever returned and this time it was fatal!

Before Alexandros died, the army paraded by his bed and, since he had lost his voice, he waved at each one with his hand. I was with Queen Roxana when he died, at the women's quarters and I have no first-hand knowledge of his last words. But it was said to us by Ptolemeos and Perdikkas that the King left his kingdom 'τω κρατιστω' -to the strongest. His royal ring was given to Perdikkas.

You know the rest, as we all went through trials and tribulations until we managed to get here. We have placed our hope to the gods that the King's rightful heir will -with our help- claim the throne and all those who brought Alexandros' dream to such a disgraceful plight will pay a dear price!"

A few days later, the group got word to prepare and meet the rest at the estate by the lake Kerkini-tis. The son of Alexandros and the youth's mother, Roxani, had been ordered by Kassandros to reside outside the city of Amfipolis. Filippos and his friends were now planning to seek employment-if that could be possible- with the royal household, so they could be at the side of the future King of Makedon. The older ones, well known to the enemies of the Timenid House would stay low taking care of the estate. The younger generation would work for or near the future King. Kassandros had to provide the young Prince with educators and bring him up as a true Ellinas Makedonian. Hope that things could eventually fall into place was high again…

EPILOGUE

"We are not related to the northern
Greeks who produced leaders like
Philip and Alexander. We are a Slav
people and our language is closely
related to Bulgarian."
From an interview of FYROM's ambassador Gyordan Veselinov
to Canada's newspaper 'Ottawa Citizen' in 02/24/1999.

This history of Makedonia (Μακεδονια, Macedonia, Makedonjia -in our times) as well as the story of our little group of friends, descendants of the first ancient ones, does not stop here where this book ended. It continues for more than three thousand years, to our present time. It is a history of forced decline paid with Makedonian blood, engineered from within -as well as from without- by ambitious persons with no true leadership and (especially) morals who took hold of its fortunes, taking advan-tage of the natural faith embedded in the true Makedonian soul of obedience to a higher authority and the nostalgic dream of unifying and leading Ellas (Greece) -and the World- once more.

Christianity through the Apostle Paul, gave a fleeting hope -at least in what concerned the religious resurrection of the idea and ideals of world unification, equality and justice- with temporary renewal from men like the brothers Kyrilos (Cyril) and Methodios (Methodius). That also failed, as there was no adequate political and/or military backing of the same caliber. In the first case, Roman power was too strong and oppressing to allow anything other than Rome's Imperatorial pantheon dictations. In the second, the Eastern Roman Empire was too weak and full of pseudo-religious zealot, mixed with ethnic prejudice.

In later years of more recent history, ethnicity played a pivotal role underlined with duplicity and covered in falsified statements from individuals acting as undercover government agents in the serv-ice of impostors within the Aemos (Balkan) peninsula, or for the benefit of the so-called Great Powers from outside. Because of that and with the help of intense propaganda from all sides of the interested parties, the world came to know Macedonia as a kind of 'salad' compounded of all kinds of ethnic ingredients. Modern ideologies and ethnic aspirations -alongside political complicity for personal gains- added further misconceptions. Population movements and exchanges as modern frontiers developed and solidified, did not counterbalance the desires of expansion or the falsification of historical facts.

These developments will be narrated in consequent books following the same form of historical novel format, in hope that persons who are not particularly interested in 'cut-and-dry' history will find them suitable and, thus, introduce them to the actual Makedonian history via the pleasure of reading 'light adventure/drama' novels.

Once again, I like to thank all the people who were kind enough to put-up with me in my effort to present this work as complete and as impartial my research and logic (not my heart) dictated. Any and all errors are mine and I will always welcome any and all documented and proven additions, corrections and misunderstood statements I made.

Special thanks to my Publishers at iUniverse (Sarah Disbrow and Dianne Lee and their coworkers who took the risk of presenting this work devoid -as I believe it is- of all modern political and social 'correctness' and I promise to follow their instructions even more with the other two books of my trilogy. I thank my proof-reader Jack Isaak and Harry and Leo Sitilides -especially for the former's help with computer. Last, but not least, my family and friends who believed in me and my limited abilities as a human.

George A. Rados

ADENTUM

"…To every one of us concerned: This entire
thesis of ethnogenesis from Macedonians is
not true! (Our connection) to ancient
Macedonians until now is founded on a series of
mystification and semi-historical truths
which are emitted from (the Government)
F.Y.R.O.M. and, that, by using and abusing
the media…"
Kiro Gligorov, F.Y.R.O.M.'s 1ˢᵗ President - 06/17/2009

Throughout the human history, every personality of universal prominence has gone through critic-ism to various degrees but none has matched the extremes of the name and fame (or infamy) of Alex-ander the Great, king of Macedon!

Given the idiosyncracy of our times with the prevalaent idea of 'political correctness' and the power of 'special interests experts' and lobbies in history re-writinng, the tendency of many historians to judge by current thinking and prone to taking political sides and views of today, the controversy con-cerning Alexander's name -and, by extension, that of Macedonia as a whole- has approached new heights.

Born to Philip II of Macedon and Olympias of Epirus the year 356 B.C.E. (July 20ᵗʰ) and passing away the year 323 B.C.E. (June 10ᵗʰ), Alexander laid claim to fame through his accomplishments as the creator of one of the vastest Empires the World has known and, at the same time, as a personality attracting both great admiration and severe criticism.

The main reasons for this controversy are, firstly, a dispute of his (and his fellow Macedonians) Hel-lenic (Greek) roots and, secondly, his repute as a benevolent all inclusive ruler of nations or a tyrant and blood-thirsty eliminator of friends and foes alike, a barbarian (with regard to today's meaning of the word). Those two reasons not withstanding, his personal life-style is also under attack and criticism. According to many 'experts' he was gay, therefore prone (?!) to all kinds of irrational behavior!

Tackling the items of dispute in order, let us examine the following facts -not fiction:

1. On his paternal side, Alexander was descendant (great grand-nephew) of Alexander I the so-called Philhellene who (due to political disputes of that time) had to <u>and proved</u> his own Hellenic roots, so he could participate at the Olympic Games. That lineage led all the way to the most revered Greek hero, Hercules! The same person (again for political reasons) was named by the same political opponents (turned 'allies and admirers') and bestowed with the honorific Philhellene, meaning (then) true friend/ protector of Greek interests. On his maternal side, our Alexander was -according to accepted lineage of his times- a direct descendant of none other than Achilles, the Greek hero of the Trojan War!

2. The spoken language in Macedonia -as well as the written one-was/is idiomatic and regional -but clearly a Hellenic one! How else Euripides (the famed Athenian tragedian) would, a few generations earlier, compose and present his plays in Macedonia, if court and commoners alike had no knowledge of what he was presenting them during performances and could not comprehend his moral teachings through his plays? Besides, the same 'problem' exists today in all regions of the Greek-speaking people. There's the idiomatic Peloponnesian, Cretan, Thessalian, Attic, etc 'tongues' and it is as common as here in our country with the 'deep South' or West vernacular, as opposed to 'Bostonian' accent! Would that accent difference make the Bostonians or the Georgians 'less Americans'?

3. If the Macedonians were not Hellenes, why—after Alexander the Great's death—would they continue promoting Hellenism in their vast Empires of his successors for hundreds of years, until their demise by Rome? Should not they revert to their 'natural customs and language'? The open letter-testimony sent to President Obama by hundreds of renown Academics clearly proves that the majority

of well known and respected Worldwide insist that Macedon-Makedinia was (and is Hellenic) and its History cannot be altered because of political ends.

4. The works of Philip and Alexander's political opponent Dimosthenes, an Athenian, did call both Macedonian kings 'barbarians'. But, first, one has to consider the source. Second, what meaning the word had at that time? Certainly not what it means today! It then meant that the person in question did not speak the 'proper', to Athenian ears, Attic dialect. Further, according to Athenian ego (which still holds today), anyone not speaking 'proper' Attic dialect was/is a 'barbarian'/eparhiotis/-country folk/not educated! Pure political propaganda then, pure egocentrism today . . .

5. The advent of Rome, its expansionistic wars against Macedonia/Greece and its active propa—ganda—in its effort to divide Greek sentiments and fidelity—adopted Dimosthenes and, lasting for over a thousand years in dominating Mediterranean and European affairs, established itself and became a fact. The proverbial "Timeo Danaum et dona ferentes" (Fear the Greeks bearing gifts) is nothing else but a Roman invented catch-phrase re-enforcing perceptions and public opinion to support the wars.

6. Alexander the Great wasn't the first ruler who envisioned World dominance—ostensibly for the benefit of all humanity. The Persian Empire itself under Cyrus the Great and Darius I was built under the same scenario and goals and it is well documented by historians of that era, as well as the ones of our times (many of who are current Alexander's critics and de—tractors). Our Alexander grew-up tuted not only in Homer but also in Kyropaedia (Cyrus' upbringing) the ways of Persian mentality regarding 'rights' and 'wrongs', in medicine, in reasoning and statesmanship.

7. Alexander was well known by his contemporaries as a person who kept his word—a trend that we tend to disregard today—even if that was costly to him. He was known as a person who detested 'double talk' to the extreme. His actions then were guided by his character openly and without any false pretense to one and all of his associates and adversaries. It cannot be claimed he 'didn't play fair and with all his cards on the table'. When crossed, he had no other choice but to be severe—in self protection—but, then, when

he would detect a true regret on behalf of the wrong-doer, he was always ready to reconcile and reward beyond call! Ever wondered who of 'our world' leaders can stand-up to par with him on that?

The destruction of Thebes was mainly the doing of former Theban-victimized citizens of the City-states from the 'Boeotian League' (Orhomenos and Plataea) who then took advantage. He aptly demonstrated his regret later, until his very end. The slaughter of Tyrian citizens took place in the thick of the battle and after Tyrians had slaughtered Macedonians and had them placed hanging on the walls for general view. The slaughter of Mallians occurred when Alexander himself was wounded and (taken for dead) out of action, by his grieving troops. The burning of Persepolis was a rather ritualistic act, avenging the burn of Athens when Xerxis took that city. As a leader, Alexander had no choice but to have his opponents and conspirators against his life put to death, regardless past relationship or weak proof of their guilt. No one in his place could or would risk be lenient and forgiving (yet he did, several times with Demosthenes, A—myntas, the Lynkestian Alexander, Harpalus and others—until he could no more)! Calling him a murderer, ought to have his detractors take a good look at our 'more civilized'

Era! When he killed, it was NOT anything pre-meditated but rather a reaction, a survival move. Who is questioning the pre-meditated slaughter of the Samians, the Mytilineans just a few years before him by the Athenian Empire? What about the Roman motto "Cartago est delenta"? If he was like Hitler, why he did respect the integrity, identity, religion of the Jews, the Egyptians, the very Persians he fought against? Why did he marry and encouraged his fellow Greeks to unite with the 'conquered' locals? Wasn't that an act of proclaiming equal—lity—as peace settled—between victors and vanquished? Wasn't it a new, just, beginning of equal standing in his (and, hopefully, any future) society? Does his Gaza act deserve the same treatment as the Holocaust or the Armenian, Pontian and Assyrian genocides? The Jerusalem of the 1st or Accra of the 3rd Crusades? The 9/11 event of New York? No true logic or investigation of his actions/reactions would justify such a severe treatment of his name! Yet, we are reluctant to call it as it is and our

Era's premed—itated genocides and acts of cruelty go unpunished and half-forgotten!

8. Finally, coming to the last argument, what is the reason of his critics to detest his personal way of life and preferences—especially when such accusations are far from being proved be—yond any doubt? First and foremost, having same sex relations does nor prove or disprove a person's ability of achieving and, this comes beyond ANY doubt, he DID achieve far more than anyone else before him—or since! Second, our society's "dos and don'ts" do not neces—sarily coinside with the codes of ethics of his time. Thirdly, as there is no absolute proof of his personal preference and as he married and produced two male offspring, shouldn't that be proof enough of his 'manliness' and have the so-called issue being dropped? Besides, what if he was gay? Are gay people incapable of doing things? It is evident therefore (at least to me) that all accusations are nothing more than an attempt to 'darken' his image (and the Makedonian one), either because of pure jealousy on his per—sonal (and Macedonian overall) achievements or because of political and nationalistic inter—ests and the money/name-making association when sensationalism get involved. Let it be un—derstood though that true historical events, accomplishments and results cannot be buried -not for long, not for ever! Alexander was, is and will remain Alexander, a Hellene king of Hellene Macedonians, a character to be judged by his achievements with impartiality and no current wishful thinking or political prejudice!

George A. Rados

MAPS

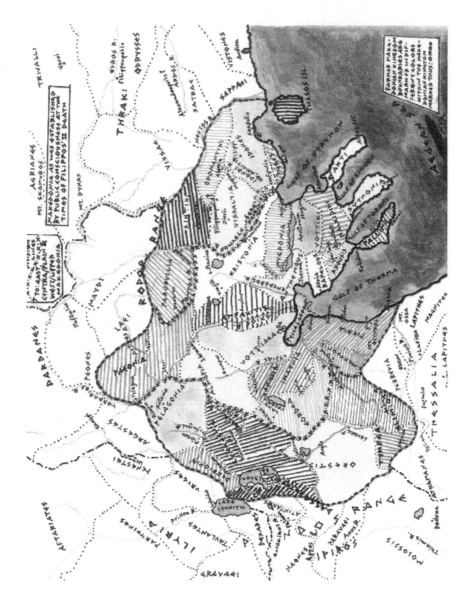

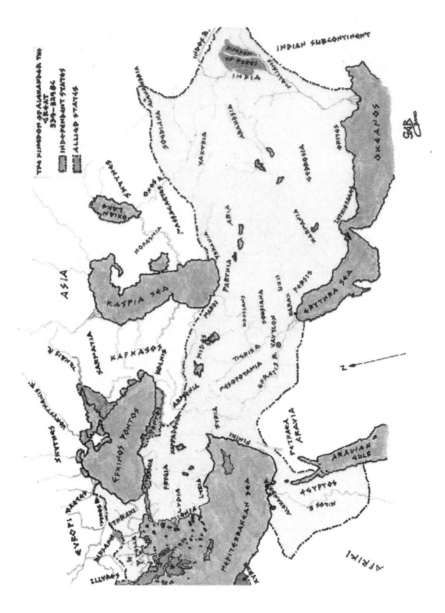

INDEX

A

Adamas: Gk. male name -also Gk. word for diamond

Adea: Macedonian-Derriopian female name

Adeos: Gk. male name

Adis: deity of the underworld - Haron (Haros) its agent (Death)

Admitos: Gk. male name

Adraistes: clan

Adrias (Sea of): possibly Etrurian name (Adriatic Sea)

Adruphata: Medean male name - Atropatis (Atropates)

Aeani: town in Makedonia

Aegeas/ Aegefs: Aegeus, father of Theseus/ Thiseus/ Thisseus

Aegean Sea: the sea of Aegeas (Aegeus) father of Thisseus

Aegina: Island and city-state - Aeginitan(s)

Aegistratos: Gk. male name (Aegistratus)

Aegos Potami: location

Aemos: (Lat.: Aemus) Mountain range, name of the south-east European
    peninsula (modern Balkan)

Aeolis/ Aeolia: region - Aeolian(s)

Aeolos: deity of the winds (Aeolus)

Aeropos: Gk. male name (Aeropus)

Aeshinis: Gk. male name (Aeschenes) - well known tragedy writer

Aesopos: archaic Gk. male name (Aesop)

Afovos: Gk. male name (Aphobus). Also, afovos (a-phobus) means not
    scared-by.

Afroditi: deity of love and Gk. female name (Aphrodite-Venus)

Afshtanes: Paraetakian male name (Afstanis)

Aftariates: Dardanian tribe (Autariatae)

Agallassa: city

Agamemnon: archaic Gk. male name

Agathoklis: Gk. male name (Agathocles)

Agathon: Gk. male name

Agelaos: Gk. male name

Agerros/ Agirros: Gk. male name

Agima: Royal Guard of Makedonias (also Agema)

Agis: Gk. male name

Agisilaos: Gk. male name (Lat.: Agesilaus)

agora/ Agora: Market place/ Place where political debates took place

Agrianes: tribe - Agrianian

Ahaeans/Ahians/Aheans: Hellenic clan (Ahaea/Ahaia the region)

Ahaemenides: Persian Royal dynasty name (also Ahemenides) -Ahaemenids

Ahaemenis: Persian male name (Haxamanish)

Ahilleas:Gk. male name (Achilles)

Ahura-Masda: Principal Persian deity

Akanthos: town in Makedonia (Lat.: Acanthus)

Akarnania: region - Akarnan(es)

Akesinis: Persian name (Acesines)

Akkho/ Akka: city

Akontion: name of mountain. Also javelin - acondistes/ Akontistes: javeliners

Akronnisos: isle (Acronnisus)

Akrovolistes: special mountaineers (Acrobolistae) -also Prodromi

Aktion/Akteon: Gk. male name -also a location

Akti: region of Makedonia -Aktean(s)/Aktian(s) also a female name

Alalkomenae: city in Makedonia

Aleian Plains: plains at the south part of Asia Minor toward Syria/ Lebanon

Alektor: rooster. Also, Gk. male name

Alevas: Gk. male and dynasty/family name - Alevades (the clan of)

Alexandros: Gk. male name (Alexander)

Alexarhos: Gk. male name (Alexarchus)

Aliakmon: Makedonian river (Aliacmon)

Aliaksej: Peonian/ Paeonian male name, akin to Alexandros

Alikarnassos: city-state (Alicarnassus)

Alitas: archaic Gk. male name

Alkamas: Gk. male name (Alcamas)

Alketas: Gk. male name (Alcetas)

Alkistis: Gk. female name

Alkiviadis: Gk. male name (Alcibiades)

Almopia: region -Almops (male name), Almopes/Almopian(s)/Almopean(s)

Aloros: town

Althaemenos: archaic Gk. male name

Altis: religious park-like enclosure, adjascent to a temple

Alvania: region by Caucasus and Caspian Sea - Alvanians (Albania - Albanians)

Amadokos: Hellenized Tharcian male name (Amadocus)

Amanos: mountain range in south Asia Minor

Amastrini: Hellenized Persian female name (Amastrine)

Amazones: women warriors - Amazon (singular)

Amfaxitis: region (Amphaxitis) -Amfaxitan/Amfaxites

Amfilohos: Gk. male name (Amphilochus)

Amfilohia: region, town

Amfipator: Gk. male name (Amphipator)

Amfipolis: city (Amphipolis)

Amfisa: city-state (Amphisa)

Amfoteros: Gk. male name (Amphoterus)

Ammin-Aspyoush: Persian male name (Amminaspis)

Ammun: Egyptian deity

Amudokh: Odryssian male name (Amadokos/ Amadocus)

Amydon: town -Amydonian(s)

Amyntas: Gk. male name

Amyntor: Gk. male name

anaklindron: recliner, couch at dinners

Anax: ancient Greek word, meaning king

Anaxarhidis: Gk. male name

Anaxarhos: Gk. male name (Anaxarchus)

Anaxidotos: Gk. male name (Anaxidotus)

Anaxippos: Gk. male name (Anaxippus)

Andakas: Indian city

Andgelaod: Vissaean Thracian male name Hellenized to Antilaos

Andri: Dexarian male name

Andrias: Gk. male name

Andriskos: Gk. male name (Andriscus)

Androklis: male Gk. name

Andromahi: Gk. female name (Andromache)

Andromahos: Gk. male name (Andromachus)

Andronas: Gk. male name

Androtimos: Gk. male name (Androtimus)

Andubulyoush: Persian male name (Antivelos - Andibelus)

Anhialos: town (Anchialus)

Ankyra: town (Angara)

Anta: Illyrian female name

Antania: town

Anteas/ Anteos: Gk. mythical giant's name (Anteus)

Anthemous: region -Anthemountian(s)

Anthi: Gk. female name (Anthe)

Anthiklia: Gk. female name (Anthiclea)

Antigenis: Gk. male name

Antigoni: Gk. female name (Antigone)

Antigonos: Gk. male name (Antigonus)

Antiklis: Gk. male name (Anticles)

Antilivanos: the Anti-Lebanon mountain range

Antilohos: Gk. male name

Antimahidis: Gk. male name (Antimachides)

Antimahos: Gk. male name (Antimachus)

Antiohos: Gk. male name (Antiochus)

Antipatros: Gk. male name (Antipater)

Antipatria: Gk. female name, name of town

Antypas: Gk. male name

Aoos: river (Aous)

Aornos: location (Aornus)

Apellas: Gk. male name -Apellis in Ionic dialect

Apis: Egyptian deity

Apollodoros: Gk. male name (Apollodorus)

Apollon: deity of light, sun, music, hunting (Apollo)

Apollonia: town

Apollonios: Gk. male name

Apsos: river

Arados: city in Finiki (Phoenice)

Arahosia: region (Arachosia)

Aratos: Gk. male name (Aratus)

Aravia: region south-east of Palestine - Araves (Arabia/ Arabs)

Aravitians: Indian clan

Araxis: river

Argilos: city-state

Arideos: Gk. male name

Arigaeon: Indian city

Ariobarzahna: Persian male name (Ariovarzanis/ Ariobarzanes)

Arravaeos: Greco-Illyrian male name

Areas: Gk. male name

Areti: deity of honor and good behavior, female name (Arete), abstract for
    excellence

Aretis: Gk. male name (Aretes)

Argeos: Gk. male name

Argestei: tribe

Arginousae: a group of small islands, place of a naval battle

Argolis: region (Argolid) also Argolida

Argos: city-state, region, male name (animals), -Argos Orestikon: city -Argian
    (Argean), also pet's
name(dog)

Argiades/Argeades: Royal Makedonian dynasty, also known as Timenides
    (Timenids) - Argeathes

Arhelaos: Gk. male name (Archelaus)

Arhias: Gk. male name

Arhon: leader of people (Archon) - Arhontes: its plural (Arhi: ruling power/
    law/ lawful)

Aria: race name - Arian(s) and regional name in Asia

Arideos/ Arrideos: Gk. male name

Arios Pagos: Athinian Law body of elders

Ariovarzanis: Persian name (Ariovarzanes)

Aris: Gk. god of war (Ares)

Aristandros: Gk. male name (Aristander)

Aristidis: Gk. male name (Aristides)

Aristo/Ariston/Aristos: Gk. male name(s)

Aristodamas: Gk. male name

Aristodimos: Gk. male name (Aristodemus)

Aristogiton: Gk. male name

Aristomenis: Gk. male name (Aristomenes)

Aristomidis: Gk.male name (Aristomedes)

Aristomnimos: Gk. male name (Aristomnimus)

Aristotelis: Gk. male name (Aristotle)

Arivvas: Gk. male name

Arkadia: region -Arkadian(s), Arkades (Arcadia)

Armenia: region/ kingdom - Armenian(s)

Armodios: Gk. male name (Armodius)

Armogh-Yioush: Old Armenian name in Persian version (Armoyiessos)

Arpal: Peonian male name

Arpalos: Gk. male name (Harpalus)

Arraveos: Gk. male name (Arrabeus)

Arrimas: Gk. male name

Arseas: Gk. male name

Arshama: Persian male name (Arsamis/ Arsames)

Arshata: Persian male name (Arsitis/ Arsites)

Arsinoi: Gk. female name (Arsinoe)

Artafernis: Persian male name (Artaferna)

Artakhama: Persian female name

Artakoana: location, region (Artacoana)

Artavazos: Persian male name - Artavasda (Artabazus)

Artaxerxis: Persian male name

Artemis: deity of forests, hunting (Diana)

Artonis: Hellenized Persian female name

Arvila: city (Arbela)

Asia-by-the Aegean: today's Asia Minor

Ashpashta: Asian male name (Aspastis/ Aspastes)

Askania: lake (Ascania)

Askios: mountain - also: Askion

Asklipios: Gk. male name - famous medical personality (Aesculapius)

Asklipiodoros: Gk. male name (Asklipiodorus)

Asopos: river

Aspasia: Gk. female name

Aspasians: Indian clan

Aspendos: town (Aspendus)

aspis: Greek word for shield

Assakines: Indian clan

Astarti: Asian deity (Astarte)

Asteropeos: Gk. male name (Asteropeus)

Astivos: town and river name (Astivo in Peonian)

Assyria: ancient state (Assyrian)

Atalanti: female Gk. name, also a town

Atarneas: town

Athamas: Gk. male name

Athina: deity of wisdom (Athena - Minerva)

Athinae: city-state, capital of Attiki (Attica) region (Athens) –Athinian(s)

Athos: mountain

Atintanes: clan name (Illyrian origin) - Atintania: the region

Atizyah: Persian male name (Atizis/ Atizes)

Atophradata: Persian male name - Aftofradatis

Attal: Dexarian male name

Attalos: Gk. male name

Atthea: Scythian (Skythian) male name (Attheas in Gk. - Attheus in Lat.)

Avdata: Illyrian female name

Avisaris: Persian male name - Avi-shareh (Abisares)

Avdira: city-state

Avreas: Gk. male name

Avydos: city-state

Axios: river

Ayoupa- Osh:Old Armenian male name (Ayiapos)

Azelmikha: Finikian (Phoenician) male name - Azelmikos (Azelmicus)

Azhapasta: Persian male name - Aspastis

B

Baal: Assyro-Babylonian deity

Baghishtana: Persian male name (Vagistanis/ Bagistanes)

Bahryiouxa: Indian male name (Variaxis/ Bariaxes)

Bardjil: Vrygian male name Hellenized to Vardilis (Bardilis/ Bardylis)

Bardyla: Tavlanto-Parthinian Illyrian male name (Vardylis/Vardilis) see above

Basali: Agrianian male name Hellenized to Vasilios

Barsand-yoush: Persian male name (Varasaentis)

Belos: Babylonian deity

Bestana: Persian male name (Vistanis)

Bharnug-yioush: Babylonian male name (Farnoukis)

Bhata: Persian male name - Vatis (Bates)

Brugha: Dardanian male name

Brutians: Italian tribe

C

Choriyena: Asian (Sogdian?) male name - Horienis/ Chorienes

D

Daans: tribe

Damon: Gk. male name

Damasias: Hellenized Thracian (Peonian/ Paeonian) male name - Damasj

Damaskos: city (Damascus)

Damoklidas: Gk. male name

Danaan(s): Greek tribal name -Danaos (Danaus) its progenitor

Daric: Persian coin (gold or silver) with international recognition

Darios: Persian male name (Darius) - Darayava

Dardania: region/state -Dardanes (Dardanians):tribe - Dardanos: male name
     (Dardanus)

Darron: Gk. male name

Daskylion: city (Dascylium)

Dassaretis: region/state -Hellenized/incorporated under Makedonian rule -
     Dassaretes: tribe

Datis: Persian male name (Datyish)

Defkalion: Gk. male name (Deucalion): survivor of the flood (see Noah/
     Gilgamesh myth), progenitor of the Greeks -before Ellinas

Deianyra: female Gk. name -wife of Hercules

Dekelia: location/fort (Decelia)

Delfi: town, site of the most famous Oracle (Delphi)

Dentheleis: Dardano-Thracian tribe

Derdas: Gk. male name

Derriopia: region/state

Derriopes: tribe -Derriopian(s) - Derriopia/Derriopos/Derriopis: the region

Dexares: Illyrian tribe - Dexarian(s)

Diadis: Gk. male name (Diades)

Dias/Zefs: principal male Olympian deity of the Greek pantheon (Zeus)

diavlos: competitive running distance

Dilian Treaty/ Delian Treaty: Treaty between Athens and Greek city-states
     (Athinian League/Empire)

Dilos: holy island (Delos/us) -Dilian/Delian - Holy island of Apollo

Dimadis: Gk. male name

Dimaratos: Gk. male name (Demaratus)

Dimash: Dexarian male name

Dimitra: deity of the agriculture (Demeter) -Ceres -female Gk. name

Dimitrias: Gk. female name

Dimitrios: Gk. male name (Demetrius)

Dimofon: Gk. male name (Dimophon)

Dimokratia: political arrangement, the ruling of the citizens (Democracy)

Dimos: citizenry (Demos) - dimokrates: democrats

Dimosthenis: Athinian orator, anti-Makedonian (Demosthenes)

Diofantos:Gk. male name (Diophantus)

Diogenis: Gk. sage (Diogenes)

Diomidis: Gk. male name (Diomedes)

Dion: town, religious center in Macedonia in honor of Dias

Dioni: Gk.female name (Dione)

Dionysos: deity of wine, merriment -but also wrath (Dionysus/Bacchus)

Dioskouri: literally meaning the sons of Zeus (Castor and Polux)

Diskos: discus)

Dodona: town, site of famous Oracle

Dohl-Asbah: Asiatic male name - Doloaspis (Doloaspes)

Dolihi: name of a village

Dorr: Illyrian male name

Dori: javelin

Dorian: Gk. tribal name -Doros (Dorus) its progenitor -Dorians

Doris: region and Gk. female name

Dorothea: Gk. female name

Doveros: town

Doxaris: Hellenized Indian male name (Doxares)

Drakas: Gk. male name

Drakon: Gk. male name (Dracon) -Drakonian/draconian rules

Drangiana: region/satrapy -Drangianes

Drapsakos: city (Drapsacus)

Drilon: river

Dropidas: Gk. male name

Dryos Kefalae/ Dryioskefalae: location

Drypetis: Hellenized Persian female name

Dynax: mountain

Dysoron: mountain

E

Edessa: town

Efesos: city-state (Ephesus), also Efessos

Efialtis: Gk. male name associated with nightmares (Ephialtes)

Efkrator: Gk. male name (Eucrator)

Eforos: Gk. male name (Euphorus)

Efratis: river (Euphrates)

Efstratos: Gk. male name (Eustratus)

Efvouli: Gk. female name

Efvolos: Gk. male name

Efxinos Pontos: euphemism for the Black Sea, meaning the 'accepting' sea

Egelohos: Gk. male name (Egelochus)

Egyptos: state, country (Egypt) -Egyptian

Ehedoros: river in Makedonia (Echedorus)

Eidjik/ Evdikos: Vrygian male name and its Hellenik equivalent

Ekati: Gk. female name associated with the underworld

Ekatompylos: location (Hecatompylus)

ekklisia: the gathering of citizens for political issues

Ekvatana: city (Ecbatana)

Elaeous: city-state

Elaniki: Gk. female name

Elatia: town

Elefsis: city-state (Eleusis) - Eleusinian Mysteries

Elimia? Elimiotis / Elimiea(n)/ Elimiaea: same region, different spelling -
    Elimiotan(s)/ Elimiotes

Elis/Ilia: region

Ellanikos: Gk. male name (Ellanicus/ Hellanicus)

Ellas: country (Greece)

Ellanodikes: committee of reps from Gk. city-states judging disputes

Eleni: Gk. female name (Hellen)

Elli: Gk. female name

Ellin/Ellinas: Progenitor of the Greeks -Ellines/ Hellenes, Ellenic/Hellenic

Ellispontine: of Ellispontos

Ellispontos: waterway (Hellespont/Dardanelles) derivatory of: Elli's pontos (sea
    of Elli)

Elpiniki: Gk. female name

En-Ilah: locality (Enylos), Asiatic name

Enialyos!: war chanting

Ennea Odi: Literally, nine ways/roads. City-state of Thasos, taken by Athens and renamed Amfipolis

Enghileis: Illyrian clan

Eordaikos: river

Eordea: region -Eordean(s)

Epaminondas/ Epaminontas: Gk. male name

Epidamnos: city-state (Epidamnus)

Epimahos: Gk. male name

Epimenidis: Gk. male name (Epimenides)

Epimenis: Gk. male name (Epimenes)

Epistrofos: Gk. male name

Epokillos: Gk. male name

Eretria: city-state - Eretrian(s)

Erigon: river

Ermias: Gk. male name

Ermioni: Gk. female name (Ermione)

Ermis: deity of commerce, messenger of the gods (Hermes/ Mercury)

Ermodoros: Gk. male name (Ermodorus)

Ermolaos: Gk. male name (Hermolaus)

Erodikea: Gk. female name

Eromenis: Gk. male name (Eromenes)

Eros: deity of love (son of Aphrodite and Ares)

Erygios: Gk. male name

Erynies: demi-god creatures, chasing through consciousness evil doers (from the Gk. pantheon)

Esperides: nymphs of the west and evening stellar constellation

Estia: deity of the household (Vesta)

Eteri: military companions, cavlry and/or foot (Hetairoi)

Evakaes: honorary title for the Persian elite troops of Alexander (Eubaces/ Eubacais/ Eubakes)

Evanthia: Gk. female name

Evaspla: Indian river name

Evdamidas: Gk. male name

Evdimos: Gk. male name (Eudimus)

Evia: island (Eboea)

Evlampia: Gk. female name

Evmenia: Gk. female name

Evmenides: upon a catharsis, Erynies could become Evmenides, soothing the
    penitent(s)

Evmenis: Gk. male name (Eumenes)

Evnikos: Gk. male name (Eunicus)

Evridiki; Gk. female name (Euridice)

Evripidis: Gk. male name (Euripides)

Evristheas: Gk. male name (Euristheus)

Evropi: Gk. female name (Europa) - also referring to the continent of Europe

Evropos: town's name

Evros: river

Evryklia/ Evriklia: Gk. female name

Evrylohos: Gk. male name (Eurylochus)

Evrymedon: river (Eurimedon)

Evryopos: Gk. male name (Euryopus/ Euriopus)

Exarhos: title and (later) male name

F

Faedon: Gk. male name (Phaedon)

Falanx: name of a military unit and/or array (Phalanx) - Falangitis: soldier of
    the Falanx

Faliron: a bay in Attica, near Athens (Phaliron)

Farao: the Egyptian king in Greek (Faraoh)

Fares: town (Phares)

Farnakis: Persian male name (Pharnaces)

Farnavazos: Persian male name (Pharnabazus) - Farnavakhoa

Farsalos/Farsala: name of Thessalian city (Pharsalus)

Fasilis: city - Fasilitan (Phasilis)

Ferrae: city in Thessaly (Pherae) - Ferraean(s)

Fila: Gk. female name

Fidias: Gk. male name (Phidias/ Phydias), great artist of sculpture

Fidipidis: Gk. male name (Phidipides)

Fidon: Gk. male name (Phidon) - sometimes found as Faedon (Phaedon)

fil-Ellin/ filellin/ fillelinas: honorific for one who cares/loves Ellas (Philhellene)

Filina: Gk. female name (Philina)

Filippos: Gk. male name (Philip)

Filippoupolis: city (Philippoupolis) - today's Plovdiv

Filokratis: Gk. male name (Philocrates)

Filon: Gk. male name
Filonokos: Gk. male name (Philonicus)
Filotas: Gk. male name (Philotas)
Filoxenos: Gk. male name (Philoxenus)
Finiki: region (Phoenicia) - Finikes (Phoenicians)
Finix: Gk. male name (Phoenix)
Fivi: Gk. female name (Phoebe)
Fokea: region and city-state (Phocea/Phocaea) - Fokians/Fokeans (Phoceans)
Fokion: Gk. male name (Phokion/Phocion)
Fokis: region - Fokian(s)
Formion: Gk. male name (Phormio)
Fovos: deity/personification of fear
Fratafernis: Persian male name (Phrataphernis)
Frygia: region (Phrygia)

G

Gabash: Vaktrian (Bactrian) male name
Galipsos: city-state (Galipsus)
Gangis/ Gaggis: river in India (Ganges)
Gavgamila: location (Gaugamela)
Gea: personification of the earth as a goddess (pronounced:Yea)
Gela: city-state
Gavanis: Gk. male name
Gavrantj/Gavrantis: Illyrian male name
Gaza: city-state - Gazan(s)
Gchleova: Scythian female name
Gedrosia: name of an Asian desert
Gerak: Dexarian male name
Gerostratos: Gk. male name (Gerostratus)
Ghylo: Scythian male name, Hellenized to Gylon
Gigonos: name of a town
Gjyr: Vrygian town
Glabka: Tavlantian (Illyrian) version of the male name Glafkias (Glaucias)
Glafkias: Hellenization of an Illyrian male name (Glakiaj) – Glaucias
Glafkippos: Gk. male name (Glaucippus)
Glydo: Parthinian (Illyrian) male name translated in Gk. to Klitos
Gordion: city (Gordium)

Gordios: Phrygian name (male), hellenized - Gordian

Gorgias: Gk. male name

Gourians: Indian clan

Grabsh: Vrygian male name, Hellenized to Gravos

Grabo: Illyrian male name - see above

Granikos: name of a river (Granicus)

Great Mysteries: mysteries performed in Eleusis. Any uninitiated participant
was put to death

Griba: Peonian male name

Gruba: Peonian male name, variation of Griba

Gygea: Gk. female name

Gygones: tribe (pronounced: Yigones) - also Gigones/ Gigonian

Gylippos: Gk. male name (Gylippus)

Gythion: town

H

Habraluta: Persian male name (Avroulitis/ Aurulites)

Hadrupata: Persian male name (Atropatis/ Atropates)

Haftufradata: Persian male name (Aftofradatis/ Autophradates)

Haldaea/ Haldea: Asiatic region - Haldean(s) (Chaldaeans)

Halkidiki: region - Halkidian(s) (Chalkidice - Chalkidians)

Halkis: city-state - Halkians/ Halkeans/ Halkidian(s)

Haonia: region - Haones/Haonian (Chaonea/Chaoneans/Chaonean)

Harax: city

Haridimos: Gk. male name (Charidemus)

Hariklia: Gk. female name (Chareclea/Chariclea)

Harilaos: Gk. male name (Charilaus)

Harinos: Gk. male name (Charinus)

Haris: Gk. male name (Chares)

Haron/ Haros: personification of death (Charon)

Heronia/Haeronia/Haeronea: town (Chaeronea/Chaeronia/Cheronaea)

Hersonisos: Literally means promontory. The name of the long promontory by
Ellispontos/ Thrakian

Hersonisos. (Another) Hersonisos is the one by Chimerian Bosporus (Crimean
Peninsula)

Hibrou: the sound of the word Hebrew in Gk. ears, Hellenized as: Evreos

Hilon: Gk. male name

Hios: island (Chios)

Hois: river

Holomon/Holomontas: mountain (Cholomon)

Horasmia: region (Chorasmia)

Hrysogonos: Gk. male name (Chrysogonus)

Hurundabata: Persian male name (Orontovatis/ Orontobates)

I

Iakynthi: Gk. female name (Iacynthe)

Iakynthos: flower name (Iacynth), also male Gk.name

Ialyssos: town (Ialyssus)

Iason: Gk. male name (Jason)

Iatroklis: Gk. male name (Iatrocles)

Iaxartis: river (Jaxartes)

Idipos: archaic Gk. male name (Oedipus)

Idomenae: town

Idomenefs: male Gk. name (Idomeneus), also Idomeneas, Meneas (nickname)

Idonia: region (Edonia) - Idones/Idonian(s)

Iera Odos: Holy Street/ Venue - The road taken for the procession of the Pan-Athinaea

Ierax: name of preying bird (falcon) and also Gk. male name

Ieron: Gk. male name

Ifanor: Gk. male name

Ifikratis: Gk. male name (Iphicrates)

Igelohos: Gk. male name (Hegelochus)

Ihnae: town

Ihthiofages: Indian clan (Ichthiophages) meaning (in Greek) the ones who feed on fish

Ilaos: Gk. male name

Ilarhos: leader of cavalry unit

Ilektra: Gk. female name (Electra)

Ili (plur.: iles): cavalry unit(s)

Ilion: city (capital of Troy)

Iliopolis/ Ilioupolis: city in Egypt (Heliopolis)

Ilios: sun

Ilisia (Pedia): place of just and rightful after death - Elysian (Fields)

Illos: Gk. male name

Illyres: Illyrians - Illyria: region - Illyrian

Imathia: region (Emathea/Emathia) - Imathian/ Imathiotan(s) - Imathiotes

India: the Asiatic subcontinent - Indos/ Indi: Hindu/ Hindu plural - Indian(s)

Io: morning deity (Eos)

Iolas/Iolaos: Gk. male name

Iolkos: city (Iolcus)

Ion: Gk. male name

Ionia: region - Iones/Ionian (Ionean) - Ionian Sea, below the Adriatic one

Ippalkimos: Gk. male name

Ipiros: region (Epirus) - Ipirotes/Ipirotan(s)

Ippias: Gk. male name (Hippias)

Ippokratis: Gk. male name (Hippocrates) later associated with medical practice/
   terms

Ira: principal deity of Olympus, wife of Dias/Zefs (Hera - Juno)

Iraeon: town

Iraklia: city (Heraclea)

Iraklis: Gk. male name (all Gk. hero of legend) - Hercules

Iraklides: descendants of Hercules, also Iraklithes

Iraklonas: Hellenized Peonian name

Iris: Gk. female name - deity

Irineos: Gk. male name

Isaeos: Gk. male name

Isokratis: Gk. male name (Isocrates)

Israyel: Israel, as sounded in Gk. ears

Issos: city (Issus) - place of a great battle

Istros: river (Istrus) Today's Danube

Itamos: mountain

K

Kadmia: the name of Theban (Thivaean) acropolis

Kadmos: legendary king of Thebes (Thivae) - (Cadmus)

Kadusians: tribe (Caducians)

Kafkasos: mountain range (Caucasus) - Kafkasian(s)

Kalanos: Hellenized male name unknown origin

Kalas/Kallas: Gk. male name

Kalhidon: city-state

Kalipolis: city (Calipolis)

Kallirdomon/ Kallidromos: mountain

Kallimahos: Gk. male name (Callimachus)

Kallinis: Gk. male name (Callines)

Kallinoos: Gk. male name (Callinous)

Kalliopi: Gk. female name (Calliope) and one of the nine Muse (daughters of Zeus or Pieros and

Mnimosyni)

Kalisthenis: Gk. male name (Calisthenes)

Kallistratis: Gk. male name

Kamvounia: mountain

Kamvysis: Persian male name (Cambyses) - Kambujyia

Kanastreans: tribe

Kappadokia: region (Cappadocia) - Kappadokian(s)

Karanos: male Gk. name (Caranus)

Kardakes: tribe (Cardaces)

Kardia: city-state (Cardia)

Kardusian(s): tribe [Carducian(s)]

Karhidon: Carthage

Karia: region - Kares (Caria) - (Carians)

Karmania: region (Carmania)

Kaspian Sea: inland sea (Caspia)

Kassandros: Gk. male name (Cassander)

Katapeltis: war machine (Catapult) plural: katapeltes

Kathaeans: clan (Cathaeans)

Kavnos: city (Caunus)

Kavyres: Thracian-Peonian deities (Kavyrej) later adopted by Macedon (first) and Hellas

Kcher-Soblepht: Thracian (Vissaean) male name (Kersovleptis/ Cersobleptes)

Kelaenae/Kelenae: town (Celaene)

Kellae: town

Keletron: city (Celetron) and lake with same name

Kentavri: Tribe (famed of being half men-half horses) - Singular: Kentavros (centaur)

Keramiae: town

Keramikos: cemetery area outside Athens (Ceramicus)

Keranos or Koranos: Gk. male name (Coeranus)

Kerastos: Gk. male name (Cerastus)

Keravnia: mountain

Kerdimmas: Gk. male name

Kerkinion: mountain

Kerkinitis: name of a lake (Cercinitis)

Kerkyra/ Kerkira/ Korkyra: city-state, the island of Corfu

Kersej: Peonian male name

Kersobulpta: Thraco-Dardanian male name (Kersovleptis in Gk. - Cersobleptis in Lat.)

Kerveros: name of underworld's guarding dog (Cerberus)

Kessos: Thracian male name

Ketro: Illyrian (Parthinian) male name

Khanaan: Israelite regional name as it would be heard by Gk. ears (Chanaan/ Canaan)

Khannuba: Egyptian city (Gk. Kanopis, Lat. Canupus/ Canobis)

Khaostana: Persian male name (Austanis/ Aoustanis/ Austanes)

Kharsidha: Thracian male name (Karsidas/ Charsida)

Khatanes: Paraetacian male name (Katanis/ Catanes)

Khetripur: Odryssian male name (Ketriporis)

Khlecht: Illyrian male name (Klitos/ Clitus/ Kletus)

Khoriyiama: Persian male name (Horienis/ Chorienes)

Khosha: Illyrian male name (Kossos in Gk. - Cossus in Lat.)

Kifisos/ Kifissos: river (Ciphisus/ Kiphisus)

Kikkones: Thracian tribe - also Kikones

Kilaetes: tribe

Kili Syria: region (Coele Syria)

Kilikia: region (Cilicia) - Kilikian(s) - Kilikian Gates: narrow pass in the region

Kimi: city

Kimon: Gk. male name

kini: common (language)

Kinos: Gk. male name (Coenus)

Kiranos: Gk. male name

Kissios: archaic Gk. male name

Kissos: mountain

Klasomenae: city-state (Clazomenae/Clasomenae)

Kleandros: Gk. male name (Cleander)

Kleanthis: Gk. male name (Cleanthes)

Klearhos: Gk. male name (Clearchus)

Kleodeos: Gk. male name

Kleodotos: Gk. male name (Cleodotus)

Kleomenis: Gk. male name (Cleomenes)

Kleomvrotos: Gk. male name (Cleombrotus)

Kleon: Gk. male name (Cleon)

Kleonidis: Gk. male name (Cleonides)

Kleopatra: Gk. female name (Cleopatra)

Kleovouli: Gk. female name

Kleovoulos: male Gk. name (Cleobulus)

Kleovouli: female Gk. name

Klimax: mountain

Klisthenis: Gk. male name (Clisthenes)

Klitos: Gk. male name (Cleitos/Cleitus/Clitus)

Kloppas: Gk. male name (Cloppas)

Kofinos: river (Cophinus)

Kokyges: tribe

Kolhis: region (Colchis) - today's Georgia - Kolhian(s)

Kopais: lake (Copais)

Koragos: Hellenized Sogdian male name

Korjed: Peonian male name Hellenized to Korednos

Korinthos: city-state (Corinth) - Korinthian (Corinthean)

Koronia: town (Coronea) and also a lake's name

Kos: Island

Kossians/Kossaeans: tribe (Cossaeans)

Kot: Thracian male name (Kotys)

kota: chicken

Kottel: Sarmatian male name (Kothelas in Gk. - Cottelus in Lat.)

Kottyfos: Gk. male name (Cottyphus)

Krannon: town

Krateos: Gk. male name (Crateus)

Krateros: Gk. male name (Craterus)

Kratevas: Gk. male name

Krenides: town, renamed Filippi (Crenides-Philippi)

Krissos: Helenized Lydian male name (Croessus)

Kristonia: region (Crestonia) - Kristones (Crestonians)

Kriti: Gk. island (Ctete/Creta) - Krites (Cretans/ Kritans)

Kriton: Gk. male name

Kronos: archaic Gk. deity, replaced by Dias (Cronus/ Kronus)

Krousis: region - Krousian(s)

Krush: Vrygian male name

Krysos/ Krisos: Vrygian/ Phrygian male name (Croesus)

Kunaxa/ Kounaxa: town (Cunaxa)

Kynnani: Gk. female name (Cynnane) - nickname: Kynna (Cynna)

Kynetas: Gk. male name

Kypros: island (Cyprus) - Kypriots/ Kypriotes: Cyprians

Kypseli: Gk. female name (Cypsele)

Kypselos: Gk. male name (Cypselus)

Kyropolis: city (Cyropolis)

Kyrros: town

Kyros: Persian male name - the first Persian High King had that name (Cyrus)

Kytinion: town (Cytinium)

Kytion: town

Kyveli: Gk. female underworld deity and (later) female name (Cybele)

L

Ladi: town

Ladjike: Vrygian female name Hellenized to Laodiki (Laodice)

Laeii: tribe

Lagos: Gk. male name (Lagus)

Lahon: Gk. male name

Lais: Gk. female name (the Corinthian courtesan of the same name was very
famous)

Lakedaemon/ Lakonia: region around Sparta/ Sparti. Lakedaemonian(s) -
Lakonian(s) -

Lacedaemon(ians) / Laconian(s) - reference to Spartan state in general

Lamia: city

Lambarh: Agrianian male name Hellenized to Lamparos

Lampos: Gk. male name, short version of Evlampios

Lampsakos: city-state (Lampsacus)

Lamvros: Hellenized Agrianian male name

Laodikia: Gk. female name - town (Laodicea/Laodicaea)

Laomedon: Gk. male name

Lapithes: tribe (Lapiths)

Larihos/ Laryhos: Gk. male name (Larichus)

Larissa: city

Lato: town

Lavrion: location in Attiki (mining place)

Lefki: Gk. female name

Lefktra: town (Leuctra)

Leleges: tribe

Leoharis: Gk. male name (Leochares)

Leonidas: Gk. male name

Leonnatos/Leonatos: Gk. male name (Leonnatus)

Lept-Darjag: Dardano-Peonian male name and title, Hellenized to Leptodarkis

Lepti-Varag: Dardano-Peonian male name and title, Hellenized to Kleptivaros

Lesvos: island (Lesbus)

Levaea: town (legendary first Makedonian capital)

Limnos: island

Livanos: region and mountain name (Lebanon)

Livyii: region/state (Libya)

Lotofagi: tribe of myth (Odyssey)

Lugaea: city - Lugaean(s)

Lukanians: Italian tribe (Lucanians - Lucania: the region)

Lydia: region - Lydes (Lydians)

Lydias or Loudias: river

Lyhnidos: town (Lychnidus)

Lyhnitis: lake (Lychnetes)

Lykaon: Gk. male name

Lykaonia: region

Lykia: region - Lykians (Lycians/Lycaeans)

Lykos: river in south Asia Minor (Lycus)

Lynkos or Lynkestis: region - Lynkestian(s)/ Lynkestes

Lyppeas: archaic Gk. male name

Lyppech: Peonian male name (Lyppeos)

Lysandros: Gk. male name (Lysander)

Lysimahos: Gk. male name (Lysimachus)

M

Magi: a Chaldaean cast of astrologers/ priests

Magnitas: Gk. male name - brother of Makedon

Magnites: tribe named after Magnitas

Magnisia: a region and a city-state

Mahas: Gk. male name

Mahi: Gk. female nickname

Mahaon: Gk. male name (Machaon)

Mahatas/ Mahetas: Gk. male name

Mahon: Gk. male name (Machon)

Maidi/ Maydi: Dardanian tribe

Makednos: archaic Gk. name - for Makedonian

Makedon: Gk. archaic male name - brother of Magnitas - archaic name of the region

Makedonia: region/state (Macedonia), Makedones

Makedonis: small region of Macedonia where Perdikkas started his kingdom

Malis: region, Malian(s)

Mallians: Asian tribe (Malli)

Marakanda: city (later Samarcand)

Marathon: location

Mardians: tribe

Mardonios: Persian male name - Mardahna or Mardanyioush (Mardonius)

Mareotis: lake in north Egypt

Marginia/ Antiohia: city

Margos: river

Marillos: city-state

Marmara: town

Maronia: town/ location

Massaga: city

Massagaetes: tribe

Mazaeos: Persian male name (Mazaeus)

Mazaros: local Gk. male name (from Elimiotis)

Mazhakha: Persian male name (Mazakis/ Mazaces)

Meandros: river name and Gk. male name (Meander)

Mega Emvolon: promontory/ cape name

Megas: Gk. word for Great (Megali: female version) Latin: Magnus and Magna

Megavazos: Persian male name (Megabazus) - Magabuxsha

Megara: city-state, Megarian(s)

Melanippos or Melanipos: Gk. male name (Melanippus) - Melanipi: female version

Meleagros: Gk. male name (Meleager)

Melon: Gk. male name

Melpomeni: Gk. female name (Melpomene) - Melpo: nickname

Medh: Sarmatian female name Hellenized to Meda/ Mida

Memfis: Egyptian capital city (Memphis)

Memnon: Gk. male name

Menandros: Gk. male name (Menander)

Menelaos: Gk. male name (Menelaus)

Menidas: Gk. male name

Menis: Gk. male name

Mentor: Gk. male name

Meropi: Gk. female name (Merope)

Merops: archaic male Gk. name

Mesopotamia: region between the rivers Tigris and
     Euphrates - Mesopotamian(s)

Messapion: mountain - Peonians called it Mezap

Messinia: region - Messinian(s)

Methoni: city-state (Methone) - absorbed by Macedonia

Midas: legendary king (Vrygian / Frygian) - Midas' gardens

Mides: Asian tribe (Medes) - Midia: the region (Media)

Mieza: village/location where Aristotle lectured Alexander and his friends
     (thought of being Midas'

Gardens of old)

Mikynae: archaic city-state (Micynae) - Mikynian/Mikynaeans(s)

Militos: city-state (Miletus)

Milos: island (Milo)

Miltiadis: Gk. male name (Miltiades)

Minos: Gk. archaic male name - Minoan(s)

Mirsyni/ Myrsini: Gk. female name (Mirsyne)

Mithrana: Persian male name (Mithrinis/ Mithrines/ Mithranes)

Mitrobarzana: Persian male name (Mithrovarzanis/ Mitrobarzanes)

Mitylini/ Mytilini: city-state (Mitylene)

Mnimosyni: deity (Mnimosyne) memory

Molossis: region - Molossian(s) (Molossaeans)

Moshe: Moses, as per Gk. hearing. Hellenized to: Moysis

Musae: nymphs, thought of being the daughters of Zeus and Mnimosyni or of
     Pieros and Mnimosyni

Muzikanos: Indian sophist (Muzicanus)

Mygdonia: region - Mygdonian(s), Mygdones

Mykali: city-state - naval battle location

Mylasa: city - Myndian(s)

Myndos: town

myriad: numerical = 10,000

Myriandros: town (Myriandrus)
Myrmidon: archaic region - Myrmidones/nian

N

Nabardzana: Persian male name (Navarzanis/ Nabarzanes)
Nafkratis: city open to foreign commerce in north Egypt (Naucratis)
Nafpaktos: city-state (Naupactus)
Narkisos/ Narkissos: Gk. male name (Narcisus/ Narcissus)
Nataniyel: Hebrew male name as heard by Gk. ears (Nathaniel), Hellenised to:
    Nathanail
Navarzanis: Persian male name (Nabarzanes)
Naxos: island (Naxus) - Naxian(s)
Neagenis: Gk. male name (Neagenes)
Neapolis: city-state (today's Kavala)
Nearhos: Gk. male name (Nearchus)
Nemea/ Nemaea: city-state
Neoptolemos: Gk. male name (Neoptolemus)
Nessos: archaic Gk. male name (Nessus)
Nestor: Gk. male name
Nestos: river and archaic Gk. male name (Nestus)
Nessouna: fictitious Egyptian female name
Nifhata: Persian male name (Nifatis/ Niphates)
Nikaea: city (Nicaea)
Nikanor: Gk. male name (Nicanor)
Nikesipolis: Gk. female name (Nicesipolis)
Nikias: Gk. male name (Nicias)
Niki: Gk. female name and deity (Nike)
Nikiforion: city (Niciphorium)
Nikodamas: Gk. male name
Nikodimos: Gk. male name (Nikodemus/ Nicodemus)
Nikolaos: Gk. male name (Nicolaus/ Nicholaus)
Nikomahos: Gk. male name (Nicomachus)
Nilos: river (Nile)
Niloxenos: Gk. male name (Niloxenus)
Ninevi: city (Nineveh) old Assyrian capital
Nireas: sea deity (Nireus)

Nissa: region in upper Messopotamia (modern Iraq) famed for its horses (Nissaean)

Nister: Dexarian male name

Nymfaeon: town (Nymphaeum)

O

Odissefs/Odisseas: Gk. male name (Odisseus/Ulysses)

Odomantiki: region - Odomantes: tribe - Odomantian(s) (Odomantean)

Odrysses: Thracian tribe (Odryssae) - Odryssian(s)

Ogsadata: Persian male name (Oxodatis/ Oxodates)

Ogsatra: Persian male name (Oxathris/ Oxathres)

Okeanos: personification of the Ocean(s) - Ocean

Okse Darjag: Peonian male name, hellenized to Oxydarkis

Olganos: archaic male Gk. name

Olooson: city-state in Thessaly (Elasson/Elasona)

Olympia: Gk. female name

Olympias: Gk. female name (name of Alexander's mother)

Olympiada(es): all Hellenic festival with competitive events (poetry, theater, athletics, etc) - Olympics

Olympian: of Olympos, above human

Olympionikis: the victor of any Olympian event - olympionikes: plural

Olympos: mountain name, highest in Greece, abode of the gods

Olynthos: city-state (Olynthus) - Olynthian(s)

Omara: Persian male name (Omaris/ Omares)

Omfalos: literally, belly button. Figuratively, center of Earth. Located in Delfi

Omiros: Gk. male name (Homer)

Omvrion: Gk. male name (Ombrion)

Onhestos: town

Onisikritos: Gk. male name (Onisicritus)

Onomahos: Gk. male name (Onomachus)

Opis: town, location

Orei: town

Ordak: Dexarian river name - the Greek Eordaikos

Orhdana: Asiatic male name (Ordanis/ Ordanes)

Orhomenos: city-state (Orchomenus) - Orhomenian(s)/ Orhomenis

Orestis: region (accent goes at the end= OreSTIS) - Orestian(s) - Orestids

Orestis: Gk. male name (the accent goes: oREstis)

Orestikon (Argos): town

Oritians: Indian clan

Orontis: Gk. male name (Orontes) - also a river named after Orontis & located by Antioch in Syria

Orovatis: Persian male name (Orobates)

Ormylia: town

Orvylos: mountain (Orbelus) - Orvyles: the tribe about the mountain

Orxinis: Hellenized Persian male name (Orxines)

Ossa: mountain below Olympus

Ostrakismos: the act of voting one into exile (Ostracism)

Oxatra: Persian male name (Oxathris/ Oxathres)

Oxodatis: Persian male name (Oxodates)

Oxos: river

Oxyartis: Sogdian male name (Oxyarta/ Oxyartes)

Oxydrakians: tribe (Oxydraceans) - also Oxydrakes

Oxykanos: Hellenized Indian male name (Oxycanus)

P

Paean: military music and song

Paeonia: region - Paeones/ Paeonian: the tribe

Pafos: island (Paphus) - Pafian(s)

Pafsanias: Gk. male name (Pausanias)

Pagassae: town

Paikos: mountain (Paikon/ Paico)

Pallas/Palas: Gk. male name

Pallini: region - also female Gk. name

Pamfilia: region (Pamphilia)

Pandionis: clan name

Pangeon: mountain (Pangaeon/Pangaeon)

Pan: forest Greek deity with affinity to interfearing in battle - see panikos

pan: meaning all inclusive (i.e. pan-Athinaean, pan-Ellenic, etc)

Pandordanos: Gk. male name (Pandordanus)

Panigoros: Gk. male name (Panigorus)

panikos: panic

Pankratos: Gk. male name (from pankration, a boxing event)

Pantoleon: Gk. male name

Paora/ Paura: town

Paradisos: Persian name for hunting and recreation area

Paraetakes: tribe - Paraetakian(s)

Paralos: Athenian state ship carrying messages

Parapamissos: mountain range (Parapamissus)

Paravaei: Gk. Ipirotan tribe - Paraevia the region - Paraevaean(s) its people

Parmenion: Gk. male name (Parmenio)

Parnassos: mountain (Parnassus)

Parnabashyush: Persian/Babylonian male name (Farnavazos/ Pharnabazus)

Parthia: Asiatic region - Parthian(s)

Parthynes: Illyrian tribe - also Parth in Illyrian

Parorvylia: region meaning next to Orvylos - Parorvyles: the tribe of Parorvylia

Parysatis: Hellenized Persian female name (Pharshata?)

Passargadae: Persian city

Patala/ Pattala: city

Patara: town

Patroklos: Gk. male name (Patroclus)

Patron: Gk. male name

Pavmenis: Gk. male name (some times: Pammenis) - Paumenes/Pamenes

Pefkaliotes: Indian clan (Peucaliotes)

Pefkestas: Gk. male name (Peucestas)

Pefki: small island of river Istros

Pefkias: Gk. male name

Pefkolaos: Gk. male name (Peucolaus)

Pelagia: Gk. female name

Pelagonia: region - Pelagones/Pelagonian: the tribe

Pelasgi: tribe - Pelasgia: the region - Pelasgian(s)

Pelina: town

Pelion: town

Pella: the third and most famous Macedonian capital city

Pellea Hora: Pella's environ - Pellean: of Pella

Pelegon: Gk. male name (sometimes Pelagon)

Pelopidas: Gk. male name

Peloponnisos: region (Peloponnesus) - Peloponnisian(s)

Pelops: archaic Gk. male name

Pelta / Pelti: small round shield (Pelte)

Peltastes: light-armed troops (Peltasts)

Pelousion: town (Pelusium) in Egypt

Penestei / Penestes / Penesti: Illyrian tribe

Penteli: Attic hill famous for its marble (Pentelic)

Peonia: region north of Paeonia - Peones, Peonian(s)

Perdikkas: Gk. male name (Perdiccas)

Pergi: town

Periandros: Gk. male name (Periandrus)

Peridas: Gk. male name

Periklis: Gk. male name (Pericles)

Perintheas: Gk. male name (Perintheus)

Perinthos: city-state - Perinthian(s) (Perinthus)

Perrevaea: region in Ipiros above Molossis – Perrevaei: the tribe

Perrevia: region in north Thessaly – Perrevians

Perseas: Gk. male name (Perseus)

Persefoni: Gk. female name and deity (Proserpina/Persephone)

Persepolis: city (one of the Persian capital cities)

Perses: tribe - Persis:the region (also Persia) - Persian(s)

Petitna: Persian male name (Petinis/ Petines)

Petra: a mountain pass between Macedonia and Thessaly

Petrion: mountain

Pezeteri/ Pezetairi: infantry (honorary name)

Phrataferna: Persian male name (Fratafernis/ Phrataphernes)

Pieria: region and mountains (Pierian nymphs)

Pieros: Gk. male name - Pieres: tribe

Pilion: mountain (Pilium)

Pinara: town

Pinaros: river by Issus

Pindos: mountain range (Pindus)

Pinios: river (Peneus)

Piraeas/ Piraeefs: main harbor of Athens (Piraeus)

Pisidia: region - Pisidian(s)/ Pisides

Pisistratos: Gk. male name (Pisistratus) - Pisistratidae (des): the clan of
    Pisistratos

Pissaeon/ Pisseon: town

Pithon: Gk. male name (Peithon)

Pixodaros: Hellenized Phrygo-Carian male name (Pihsodayioush)

Plataea/ Plateae/ Plataeae: city-state

Platon: Gk. male name (Plato)

Plevr: Illyrian male name (Plevratos in Gk. - Pleuratus in Lat.)

Plevrias: Gk. and Pelagonian male name (Pleurias)

Plexarhos: Gk. male name

Plouton: underworld deity (Pluto)

Pnytagoras: Gk. male name

Pnyx: Athinian hill

Podarilos: Gk. male name

Polemokratis: Gk. male name (Polemocrates)

Polemon: Gk. male name

Polimahos: Gk. male name (Polimachus)

Politimitos: river (Politimitus)

Polykratis: Gk. male name (Polycrates)

Polydamos: Gk. male name

Polydoros: Gk. male name (Polydorus)

Polymahos: Gk. male name (Polymachus)

Polyperhon: Gk. male name (Polysperchon?)

Polyxeni: Gk. female name (Polyxena)

Pontos: meaning sea (Pontus) but also the name of a river

Poros: Hellenized Indian male name (Porus)

Posidonas: sea deity (Poseidon/ Neptune)

Potidaea: city-state - Potidaean(s)

Prasias: lake

Prazhahorta: Persian male name (Frasaortis/ Phrasaortes)

Priapos: city-state (Priapus)

Prodromi: special mounted units (Scouts)

Profthasia: city in the Hindu Kush area (Prophtasia)

Prohexana: Persian male name (Proexis)

Proklidis: Gk. male name (Proclides)

Promitheas: Gk. male name (Promitheus)

Propontis: name of a body of sea, as one enters from the Aegean to Black Sea

Protarhos: Gk. male name (Protarchus)

Protefs/ Proteas: Gk. male name (Protaeus)

Protesilaos: Gk. male name (Protesilaus)

Prothitis: Gk. male name (Prothites)

Protomahos: Gk. male name (Protomachus)

Proxenos: Gk. male name and title, meaning: in favor of the stranger(s)

Psamitihos: Egyptian name Hellenized (Psamitichus)

Psili: light armed military units

Pteleos strait: body of sea between Evia and Pagassae

Ptolemeos: Gk. male name (Ptolemy)

Pydna: city-state (absorbed by Macedonia)

Pylos: city-state

Pyramos: city (Pyramus)

Pythia: Female Oracle of Apollo - Pythian games

Pythic (Games): Pythian

Pythion: town (Pythium)

Python: type of snake, favorite of Apollo

Pyramides: Pyramids

Pyrra: Gk. female name - wife of Defkalion

R

Rahelous/ Rahelus: region (Rhachelus) - Rahelian(s)

Reomitra: Persian male name (Reomithris/ Rheomithres)

Rhub: fictitious Vrygian male name

Rodopi: mountain range (Rhodope)

Rodos: island city-state (Rhodes)

Reomidra: Persian male name (Reomithras/ Reomithris/ Rheomithres)

Risakis: Persian male name (Rhoesaces)

Roxani/ Roxana: Sogdian female name (Roxane)

S

Sagalassos: city

Saggala: city

Sagghua: Indian male name (Saggaeos/ Saggaeus)

Sakes: tribe (Sacae/ Saccae)

Sakessines: tribe

Sakia: region (Sacia)

Salamis: island (naval battle of)

Sambos: Hellenized Indian male name

Samos: island - Samian(s)

Samothraki: island (Samothrace)

Sapfo: Gk. female name (Sappho) - a famous poet

Sappaei/ Sappaes: Thracian tribe

Saphia: Agrianian female name (Sofia/ Sophia)

Sardis: city

Saronikos: name of a gulf by Athens

Sartrae/ Sartres: Thracian tribe

Satebarzana: Persian male name (Sativarzanis/ Satibarzanes)

Satyros: Gk. male name and of a demi-god (Satyr)

Selefkos: Gk. male name (Seleucus)

Selini: moon goddess (Selene)

Sephty: Odryssian (Thracian) male name - Sefthys (Sephthes)

Sfaktiria: island

Sfinx: mythical animal, enigmatic person (Sphinx)

Sfyra: hammer, thrown at athletic competitions

Shkoupi: Dardanian town. Also Shkopi - Skopi in Greek

Shtobi: Peonian town changed to Stovi when became Paeonian

Shyrms: Trivallian male name (Syrmos/ Syrmus)

Sidon: city-state in Phoenicia (Finiki)

Siggos: town

Silichimidra: Asian male name (Sisimithris/ Sisimithres)

Sikelia: island (Sicily) - Sikeli/ Sikelian(s)

Sikinos: location

Simihi: Greco-Thracian female name

Simitis: Semite

Simmias: Gk. male name

Sina: the Sinai peninsula

Sintiki/ Sindiki: region - Sintikes (Sindikes):Thraco-Macedonian tribe

Sirras: Gk. male name

Sisikouta: Indian male name (Sisikotos/ Sisicotus)

Sistos: city-state

Sisygamvis: Persian female name (Sisygambis)

Sitalkis/ Sytalkis/ Shytalchi: Thracian (Odryssian) male name (Sitalces/ Sytalces)

Sivae: Indian tribe

Skiathos: island (Sciathos)

Skirtones: Thracian tribe

Skodra: name of lake in Illyrian (see Lyhnidos)

Skopelos: island (Scopelus)

Skotro: Illyrian male name

Skythes: tribe above Istros/ Danube (Scyths) - Skythia: the region

Smyrni: Ionian city-state (Smyrna/ Ismir)

Sofia: Gk. female name meaning wisdom (Sophia)

Sogdiana: region - Sogdian(s)

Sokratis: Gk. male name (Socrates)

Soli: port town

Solon: Gk. male name

Soma: town - There's also used as reference to Alexander's corpse becoming The Soma

somatofylax: special guardian for the safety of a king (somatophylax)

Sopolis: Gk. male name

Sossos: Gk. male name

Sostratos: Gk. male name (Sostratus)

Sounion: the south promontory of Attiki (Cape Sounion)

Spadoklos: Helenized Agrianian male name (Spadoklaj)

Spartolos: Thracian, hellenized male name (SPArtolos/ SPArtolus). Also, river name (SpartoLOS)

Sparti: city-state (Sparta) - Spartan(s) - also Lakedaemon(es)

Spitamenis: Persian male name (Spitamenes)

Spitradata: Persian male name (Spithridatis/ Spithridates)

Stagira: city-state. Also, Stagiros - Stagirites, Stagiritan(s)

Stasanor: Gk. male name

Statira: Persian female name

Stenae: town

Stenor: Gk. male name

Strymon: river

Susa: city

Susianes: tribe (Susians)

Sybod: Vissaean (Thracian) male name - Sympodas

Sykion: city-state (Sycion)

Sympotas: Gk. male name

Syrakousae: city-state (Syracusae)

Syria: region - Syrian(s)

Sytalkis/ Sitalkis: Hellenazed Ordyssian (Thracian) male name

Sython: archaic Gk. male name

Sythonia: region

Sythones: tribe - Sythonian(s)

T

Tagos: title in Thessaly for the overall leader (Tagus)

Taksila/ Taxila: city

Tanais: river

Tarpuria/ Tarpouria: region - Tarpurian(s)/ Tarpourian(s): tribe

Tarsos: city (Tarsus)

Tartaros: place for condemned souls (Tartarus)

Tavlantes: Illyrian tribe - Tavlantia: region - Tavlantian(s)

Tavron: Gk. male name (Tauron)

Taxilis: Indian male name (Taxiles)

Tegea: city-state

Telmessos/ Telmissos: city (possible two different ones)

Tempi: location (Tempe)

Temvros: Gk. male name

Tenedos: island (Tenedus)

Teos: island, city-state of

Terpsino: Gk. female name

Thais: Gk. female name

Thalis: one of the Seven Sages - Gk. male name

Thasos: island - Thasian(s)

Theagenis: Gk. male name (Theagenes)

Theano: Gk. female name

Themis: Gk. female deity and name

Themistoklis: Male Gk. name

Theodoros: Gk. male name (Theodorus/ Theodore/ Theo)

Theofrastos: Gk. male name (Theophrastus)

Theoharis: Gk. male name

Theoklimenos: Gk. male name

Theokritos: Gk. male name (Theocritus)

Therma: town

Thermaikos: name of a gulf

Thermopylae: location famed for the battle which took place there against
     Persian invasion

Thespiaea/ Thespiia: region

Thespiae: city-state - Thespiaean(s)/ Thesspian(s)

Thessalia: region (Thessaly) - Thessalian(s)

Thessaloniki: Gk. female name and (later) name of a city (Thessalonica) -
     Saloniki/ Salonica

Thessalos/ Thettalos: Gk. male name (brother of Magnitas and Makednos)

Thestios: male Gk. name

Thira: Aegean island and a city in Asia Minor

Thiseas/ Thisefs: Gk. male name (Theseus)

Thivae: city-state - Thivan(s) - Thivean(s) (Thebes)

Thraki: region (Thrace) - Thrakian(s) (Thracean) - Thrakes

Thrasivoulos: Gk. male name (Thrasibulus)

Thukididis: Gk. male name (Thucidides)

Thurii: city-state

Thymodis: Gk. male name (Thymodes)

Tigris: river

Tilefos: Gk. male name

Tilepolemos: Gk. male name (Tilepolemus)

Timenos: male Gk. name (Timenus) - Timenidae/ Timenides: descendants of
     Timenos

Timeos: Gk. male name

Timoklia: Female Gk. name (Timoclea)

Timoklis: male Gk. name (Timocles)

Timotheos: Gk. male name (Timothy)

Tiraj: Peonian male name

Tirhadata: Persian male name (Tiridatis/ Tiridates)

Tirymmas: male Gk. name

Tissafernis: Persian male name (Tissaphernes)

Titanes: Titans

Tlepolemos: Gk. male name (Tlepolemus)

Toroneos: archaic Gk. male name

Toroni: town (Torone) and name of a gulf

Trallis: city-state of Ionia

Tria: region (Troy) - Trian (Trojan)

Trikka: city

Tristl: Peonian town changed to Tristolos when became Paeonian

Trivalli: Thracian tribe (Triballi) - Trivallian(s) (Triballians)

Troas: Gk. female name

Tropion: a small Aegean island

Tyhi: deity of good luck (Tyche)

Tymfea: region (Tymphea) - Tymfean(s)/ Tymfes

Tymfi: mountain range

Tyranos: tyrant (original meaning: sole ruler for life)

Tyras: river name (also Damastis/ Don)

Tyriaspis: Asian male name (Tyriaspes)

Tyrimmas: Gk. male name

Tyrrinians: Italian tribe (Etrurians)

Tyrins: Micynaean city-state. Also Tyrintha
Tyrissa: town
Tyros: Finikian (Phoenician) city-state

U

Usta: Indian male name (Astis/ Astes)
Uxians: tribe - Uxian(s) - Uxia: the region

V

Vagoas: Assyro-Persian male name (Bagoas)
Vaktra: city (Bactra)
Vaktria: region (Bactria) - Vaktrian(s)
Valakros: Gk. male name (Valacrus/ Balacrus)
Valla: town (also Vella)
Vallista: war machine (Ballista) - vallistes(plural)
Varash-menush: Asian male name (Farsamenis/ Pharsamenes)
Vardarj: Peonian river. Hellenized to Vardarios (Vardarius/ Bardar)
Vargal: Peonian city, hellenized to: Vargala (Bargala)
Varnous: mountain
Varsini: Persian female name (Barsine)
Vasilefs: Gk. word for king (Basileus)
Vasiliki: Gk. female name
Vasilios: Gk. male name
Vasiliskos: nickname (Sometimes called fondly, some not so. Also, pet's name)
     meaning: Little king
Vattina: town
Vavylon: city and state name (Babylon) - Vavylonia: region - Vavylonii: its
     people
Vegoritis: lake
Vereniki: Gk. female name (Berenice)
Veria/ Verria: city and Gk. female name (Boeria)
Verinno: Gk. female name
Verisadis: Illyrian male name (Berishad)
Vermion: mountain
Vernon: mountain
Vertiskos: mountain

Vianor: Gk. male name (Bianor/ Beanor)

Viottia/ Viotia: region (Boetia) - Viottian(s)/ Viotian(s)

Vissae: Thracian tribe

Vissaltia: region - Vissaltes - Vissaltian(s)

Vissos: Persian male name (Bissus/ Bessus)

Vistones: Thracian tribe - Vistonia(n / ns)

Voion: mountain

Vokeria: town

Volvi: lake

Voras: mountain

Vorreas: personification of the north wind

Vosporos: the channel connecting Propontis with the Black Sea (Bosporus)

Vottiaea: region - Vottiaean(s)

Vottiki: region

Voukefalas/ Voukefalos: name of Alexander's horse (Bucephala/ Bucephalus)

Vouthriton: town

Vragala: town (Bragala)

Vragila: city (Bragila)

Vrahmanes: Indian cast (Brachmans)

Vranhides: clan, cast (Branhides/ Branghides) later Brachmans?

Vrasidas: Gk. male name (Brasidas)

Vrison: Gk. male name

Vrontous: mountain

Vryges: Illyrian tribe - Vrygian(s) also, Fryges (in Asia) - Frygian(s)

Vrygiis: two lakes, the Major and the Minor (today's Prespes)

Voukefalas/ Voukefalos: name of Alexander's horse (Bucephalas/ Boucephalas)

Vouvaris: male Persian name (Bubares) - Buhvahrau

Vylazora: town (close to today's Velessa/ Veles)

Vyvlos: city-state in Phoenicia (Byblos/ Byblus)

Vyzantion: city-state (Byzantium)

X, Y, Z

Xanthipi: Gk. female name (Xanthepe)

Xanthipos/ Xanthippos: Gk. male name (Xanthipus)

Xanthos: river

Xenios (Ksenios): one offering hospitality to a Xenos (foreigner)

Xenofon: Gk. male name (Xenophon)

Xenokratis: Gk. male name (Xenocrates/ Zenocrates)

Xeni: female nickname (Polyxeni/ Polyxene)

Xenos: Gk. word for foreigner - also Ksenos

Xerxis: Persian male name

Yakinthi: Gk. female name (Yacinthe)

Ydaspis: river (Hydaspes)

Ydraotis: river (Hydraotes)

Yefyros: Gk. male name (Gephyrus)

Yeorgios: Gk. male name (George)

Yeroushalim: Hebrew city (Ierousalim/ Jerusalem)

Yerlho(s): city (Jericho)

Yete/ Yietes: tribe (Gaites/ Gaete/ Gaetes/ Gauls)

Yfasis: river (Hyphasis)

Yfestias: Gk. male name (Hephaestias)

Yfestion: Gk. male name (Hephaestion)

Ygemon: Gk. male name (Hygaemon)

Yiahve: Hebrew appellation of God as heard by Gk. ears firstly (Jehovah)

Yiunis: Persian pronunciation of Iones (Ionians)

Ymeneos: wedding - Ymenean: of the wedding

Ymitos: name of a hill in Athens famed for honey production

Yiousef: Hebrew name as heard by Gk. ears (Joseph)

Ypalkmos: Gk. male name (Ypalcmus)

Yparhos: Gk. male name, title for a cavalry leader - also: Ipparhos

Yparhidis: Gk. male name (Yparchides)

Yparna: town

Ypaspistes: special military unit/ body guards

Yperidis: Gk. male name (Hyperides)

Ypnos: personification of sleep

Ypsizon: mountain

Yrkania: region (Hyrcania)

Zadrakarta: city

Zaparja: Peonian town - Zaparia: its Hellenized name

Zaraggia: region

Zariaspa:city

Zefs: same deity as Dias (Zeus)

Zinon: Gk. male name (Zeno)

Zinovia: Gk. female name (Zenobia)

Ziobetis: river

MONTH NAMES*

Makedonian Athinian Present correspondence

Makedonian	Athinian	Present correspondence
Peritios	Posidonios	January
Dystros	Gamilion	February
Xanthikos	Anthestirion	March
Artemisios	Elafevolion	April
Daesios/ Daisios	Munihion	May
Panamos	Thargelion	June
Loios	Skiroforion	July
Gorpaeos/ Gorpeos	Ekatomvion	August
Yperveretaeos	Metagitnion	September
Dios	Voedromion	October
Apelaeos/ Apeleos	Pyanepsios	November
Avdiaeos	Maemaktirion	December

* Correspondence to present month(s) is approximate

SELECT BIBLIOGRAPHY

MY ANCIENT SOURCES:

- Anabasis: by Arrian - Transl. in modern Greek by Lazarus Gazepis – Thessaloniki, 1975
- The History of Alexander: by Q. C. Rufus, transl. by John Yardley – Penguin, 2001
- Histories: by Herodotus, transl. by George Rawlings – Alfred A. Knopf Inc. 1997
- The Anabasis: by Xenophon, in modern Greek – Academy of Athens 1972
- The Anabasis: by Xenophon, transl. by C.L. Brownson – Harvard University Press 1998
- Cyropaedia: by Xenophon, in modern Greek – Academy of Athens 1974
- The Lives (Alexander): by Plutarch, in modern Greek – Academy of Athens 1982
- The Iliad: by Homer, transl. by Samuel Buttler, edited by Louise R. Loomis – W.J. Black Inc. 1942
- The Peloponnesian War: by Thucydides, transl. by Rex Warner in 1954 – Penguin Classics 1982
- Pausanias: Transl. by P. Levi (2 Vols.) Harmondsworth 1971

MY MODERN SOURCES – History

- Alexander: by Theodore Ayrault Dodge - Da Capo Press unabridged republication of 1890
- Alexander the Great at War: edited by Ruth Sheppard - Osprey Pub., Midland House 2008

- Alexander, the Ambiguity of Greatness: by Guy MacLean Rogers - Random House 2004
- Hellenic History: by Botsford and Robinson, Macmillan Pub. Co., Inc. (Greek transl.) 1969
- The Nature of Alexander: by Mary Renault, Pantheon Books, N.Y. 1975
- In the Shadow of Olympus, the Emergence of Macedon: by E.N. Borza, Princeton 1990
- The Genius of Alexander the Great: by N.G.L. Hammond, G. Duckworth & Co. 1997
- History of Greece to 322: by N.G.L. Hammond, Oxford 1967 - sec. ed.
- Philip of Macedon: by George Cawkwell, Faber & Faber 1978
- Alexander of Macedon, a Historical Biography: by Peter Green, University of California 1991
- Greco-Persian Wars: by Peter Green, University of California Press 1998
- The Ancient Mediterranean: by Michael Grant, Bookspan 2002
- The Rise of the Greeks: by Michael Grant, Macmillan Pub. Co. 1988
- The Founders of the Western World (A History of Greece and Rome): by Michael Grant, Charles Scribner's Sons 1991
- Historic Greek Regions -Macedonia: by M.V. Sakellarios, Ekdotiki Athinon 1992
- Macedonia, Its People and History: by Stoyan Pribichevich, The Penn. State University Press 1990
- Alexander the Great: by Paul Cartledge, Vintage 2004
- A History of Macedonia: by R. Malcolm Errington, Univ. of California Press 1990
- Alexander the Philhellene and Persia: by R. Malcolm Errington, Thessaloniki 1981
- Philip II and Macedonian Imperialism: by C.F. Edson, London 1976
- Koine Eirene: by T.T.G. Ryder, Oxford 1965
- Who Are the Macedonians?: by Hough Poulton, Indiana Univ. Press 1995
- The Falsification of Macedonian History: by Nicolaos K. Martis, Academy of Athens 1985
- Ancient Greece: by William Harlan Hale, ibooks 2001
- The Origin of War from the Stone Age to Alexander the Great: by A. Ferrill, London 1985
- The Greek Achievement: by Ch. Freedman, Viking 1999

- Warfare in the Ancient World: by B.T. Carey, J.B. Allfree, J. Cairns –Pen & Sword 2005
- In the Footsteps of Alexander the Great: by Michael Wood, California 1997
- Greek Religion: by Walter Burkert, transl. by Basil Blackwell, Harvard Univ. Press 1985
- Persian Fire (The First World Empire and the Battle for the West): Tom Holland, Doubleplay 2005
- Herodotus and Bisitun (Problems in the Ancient Persian Historiography): by J.M. Balcer, Stuttgart 1987
- The Persian Wars Against Greece (A Reassessment): by J.M. Balcer, Historia 32 -1983
- From Cyrus to Alexander (A History of the Persian Empire): Transl. by P.T. Daniels, Winona Lake 2002
- Athenian Identity and Civic Ideology: by A.L. Boegehold and A.C. Scafuro, Baltimore 1994
- The Greek and Persian Wars (499-386 BC): by Philip De Souza, Oxford 2003
- Hybris, A Study in the Values of Honor and Shame in Ancient Greece: by N.R.E. Fisher, Warminster 1992
- Persia from the Origins to Alexander: by R. Ghirshman, transl. by S. Gilbert & J. Emmons, pub. by London 1964
- The Mask of Command: by J. Keegan, New York 1987
- Alexander the Great and Hellenism: by A. Daskalakis, Institute for Balkan Studies, Thessaloniki, 1966
- Alexander the Great in Fact and Fiction: edited by A.B. Bosworth & E.J. Baynham, Oxford 2000
- History of Ancient Greece: Supervised by the U.S.S.R. History Institute and Academy of Sciences, transl. in Greek and published by G. Papakonstantinou in Athens in 1978
- The Greeks: by A. Andrewes, London 1967
- A Handbook of Greek Mythology: by H.J. Rose, London 1958
- The Mycenaeans in History: by A.E. Samuel, Englewood Cliffs N.J. 1966
- Documents in Mycenaean Greek: by M. Ventris & J. Chadwick, Cambridge 1973
- The Greek Dark Ages: by V.R. d' A. Desborough, London 1972
- Herodotus: by C.W. Fornara, Oxford 1971

- Alexander the Great: by R. Lane Fox, London 1973
- Philip of Macedon: by M.B. Hatzopoulos & L.D. Loukopoulos, Athens 1980
- Strepsa; A Reconsideration, or New Evidence on the Road System of Lower Macedonia: by M.B. Hatzopoulos, (Two Studies in Ancient Macedonian Topography) Athens 1987
- Sources of Greek History Between the Persian and Peloponnesian Wars: by G.F. Hills, R. Meiggs and A. Andrewes, Oxford 1962
- Macedonian Relations with Athens to 413 B.C.: by L.C. Hodlofski, (Thesis), the Penn. State U. 1979
- Persia; from its Origins to the Achaemenids: by Jean-Louis Huot (tr. by H.S.B. Harrison), London 1967
- The Origins & Destiny of the Illyrian Kingdoms: by F. Papazoglou (transl. & publisher unknown - Paperback, front pages missing)
- Alexander; the Greatest of Greeks: by Velopoulos, Historiognosia Publications 1998

MY MODERN SOURCES – Archaeology/ Anthropology

- Lefkadia, the Ancient Mieza: by K. Rhomiopoulou, Athens 1997
- Latries ke Iera tou Diou Pierias (Worship and Temples in Dion of Pieria): by D. Pantermanlis 1977
- Vergina: by M. Andronikos, Athens (Ekdotiki) 1972
- To Anaktoro tis Verginas (The Palace of Vergina): by M. Andronikos, Ch. Makaronas, N. Moutso-poulos, G. Bakalakis. Athens 1961
- Archaeology and the Rise of the Greek State: by A.M. Snodgrass, Cambridge 1977
- Anthropology and the Greeks: by S.C. Humphreys, London 1978
- Balkan Studies: by Ph. Petsas, Pella 1963

MY MODERN SOURCES – Historical Novels and Theory

- Fire from Heaven: by Mary Renault, Vintage Books 2002
- The Persian Boy: by Mary Renault, Vintage Books 1998
- Funeral Games: by Mary Renault, Vintage Books 2002
- The Death of Alexander the Great: by Paul Doherty, Carroll & Graf 2004

- Alexandros, Il Figlio del Sogno: by Valerio M. Manfredi – Arnoldo Moudadori editor 1998
- Alexandros, Le Sabie di Amon: by Valerio M. Manfredi – Arnoldo Moudadori editor 1998
- The Virtues of War: by Steven Pressfield, Doubleday 2004

INTERVIEWS:

Last -but not least- I have interviewed in person approximately one thousand individuals of all walks in life and from all four contemporary sovereign countries holding (each) a piece of the old Makedonian kingdom (as was recognized before "Ethnic interests" created the disputes of actual or imaginary ethnic roots). Again, I wish to thank all of them, for they gave me freely what they know about and what they believe in, their arguments and agreements to my thesis, their doubt and their hope -and I kept my word to those who did not want their names mentioned. I knowingly repeat this last statement, in order to emphasise how grateful I am to them and to have them trust me again when there will be a need!

I had to cross their opinions and information -one against the other- 'read between the lines', double check everything through established, well documented and proven historical material and dates and, finally, I wrote what I found to be closer to the truth.

Special thanks have to be addressed to my Teachers during my early school years: D. T. Delfino-poulos, D. Karasotos, E. Valsamidis, N. Sidiropoulos for they were responsible for my interest in history when it counted the most! I also would like to thank the following Professors in my Archaeo-logy and History classes at C.C.S.U. in New Britain, Connecticut, for they wittingly (or not) have an-swered my questions, filled-in gaps and commented my work(s): Dr. W. Perry, Dr. G.F. Sawyer, Dr.

D. Kideckel (Archaeology/Anthropology). Dr. A. Scopino, Dr. E. Kapetanopoulos, Dr. C. Stedman, Dr. G. Emeagwali (History).

For the help at Archaeological sites in Greece, my thanks to Dr. M. Akamati, Dr. D. Pantermanlis,

Dr. P. Nigdelis, Professor K. Papanthimou, Professor M. Triantafyllidou, the Mayors of Giannitsa Mr. St. Vamvinis (past) and Mr. N. Papanikolaou (present), Professor G. Petridis, the Pan-Macedon-ian Society's veteran Mr. Steve Gagas and his wife Niki, the World-wide Supreme President of the Pan-Macedonian Society Dr. Nina Gatzoulis, the past S.P. Dr. Nina Peropoulou, my friend and fellow Historian Marcus Templar, Dr. Guy

MacLean Rogers, my 'connecting' agent to F.Y.R.O.M. Mr. D. Grigoriadis, my 'insiders' in Albania P. N, O. I. and I. V., the Bulgarian friends P. S. and C. P., local leaders of the World-wide Pan-Pontian Society and members of the Pan-Macedonian. Also Mr. Ch. Christopoulos for allowing me to study some antiquated books in his possession, my childhood friends V. Faitas and Hari Delfinopoulos, my cousins N. Nikiforou and K. Kavounis for their early help and encouragement, my A.H.E.P.A. past District Governors Mr. G. Scarveles for his appointing me in charge of the District's historical sector, Mr. N. Nikas for keeping me as Chair of Hellenic Affairs and Mr. K. Kyprianou for his documentary presentations (irrelevant to Macedonia but very relevant to persons-in-charge attitude regardless the ages) along with his arguments, my children and, last -but most important- my wife and inspiration, Donna!

I do expect that many will disagree with my presentation, especially because it is written as a novel and the main argument will probably be that I simply present a myth. There will also be some dis-agreement for my using 'unfamiliar' appellations. My answer is that: If we have no trouble pro-nouncing unfamiliar names given to us by Science Fiction authors, there should be none with names based on originality! I did that to address the multitude of the casual readers, the ones who want to enrich their knowledge (but away from the 'cut-and-dry' venues of History class at school).

I will like to emphasise though that the <u>original and grammatically correct</u> meaning of the word 'myth' derives from ancient Greek and defines the act of <u>transmitting an event, a story, via the word of mouth but not something which is a simple creation of one's active imagination!</u> It simply may have been embellished as transmitted but, nonetheless, contains the truth.

Finally, my apology to anyone I forgot to mention! It wasn't intended!

George A. Rados

CPSIA information can be obtained at www.ICGtesting.com
Printed in the USA
BVOW08s2014290316

442219BV00001B/32/P